YORKSHIRE

Other books by this author

<u>Historical fiction by Margaret Muir</u>
The Condor's Feather

<u>Nautical fiction by M.C. Muir</u>
Under Admiralty Orders – The Oliver Quintrell Series
Book 1 - Floating Gold
Book 2 - The Tainted Prize
Book 3 - Admiralty Orders
Book 4 - The Unfortunate Isles

<u>Books for YA and Children by Margaret Muir</u>
King Richard and the Mountain Goat
The Bear that had no Fur
Grandma's Windmills
<u>also</u>
Words on a Crumpled Page (poetry)
Uncanny (short stories)
Goats (non-fiction)

(Available as e-books and paperbacks from Amazon)

YORKSHIRE GRIT

A trilogy of tales

Sea Dust
Through Glass Eyes
The Black Thread

Margaret Muir

Copyright © Margaret Muir
January 2016
All rights reserved

ISBN – ISBN-13:978-1523431090
ISBN-10:1523431091

for *Marion Dunn*

SEA DUST

Book 1 in the Trilogy of Yorkshire Tales

Chapter 1

Whitby, North Yorkshire – February 1856

Emma shivered. The cold spell had been cruel. Very cruel. Yet the picture, framed by the window, had a stark beauty about it.

The fishing port, nestled in the valley below, was shrouded in white. Snow covered the docks and wharves, the sand flat – Belle Island, and the hills and open moors beyond. Across the valley, the ruins of the old Benedictine abbey wore a vestal veil. Only the treacherous face of the crumbling East Cliff had escaped the winter mantle.

From the attic, Emma gazed down on the rooftops to the chimney stacks poking up from the snow like bare stumps awaiting spring, to the icicles hanging from the clay tiles like a line of glass organ pipes and to the street below. White. Untrodden.

To the north, the sea was strangely still. There were no white caps on the water. No waves breaking along The Scaur. The grey sky and sea melded in a haze of mauve. There was no horizon.

Near the old lighthouse, half hidden by the pier wall, Emma could see the masts of a ship. It was moving slowly towards the fishing harbour but it carried no sails.

A bird fluttered moth-like against the window distracting her. It landed on the sill settling its claws into the mat of tangled snowflakes. She watched as it hopped to the end of the ledge and started pecking at the crack in the corner of the glass. She listened to it tap-tapping on the window as if wanting to be invited in. Then she remembered the other sounds she had listened to in that room: the cough, the wheeze, the crackled breath. Now those sounds were gone and the room was silent save for the bird's beak tapping on the pane.

Suddenly the bird stopped for a while and regarded her, or appeared to, cocking its head from side to side. She wondered if it could see her. She thought not. Her dress was dark. Her shawl, spun from the fleece of a black sheep, was even darker. And there was no lamp in the room.

She shivered. It seemed so long since the sun had warmed the town.

The bird fluffed out its rust-red chest feathers and stretched one of its wings.

Hearing the faint sound of stockinged feet padding up the staircase, Emma waited for the distinctive creak of the three steps outside the attic door. The latch clicked as it was lifted. The bird cocked its head and, when the door rasped on its hinges, it flew away.

She knew it was Joshua.

He moved close beside her at the window and waited for a few moments before speaking. 'Are you all right, Mama?'

Emma nodded.

'What are you looking at?'

'A ship,' she said quietly.

Joshua pressed his forehead against the glass and scanned the harbour. He could see the masts of the fishing fleet moored against the wharves and counted several others tall ships anchored in deeper water their sails hanging lankly in the still air. Further up the harbour, three flat bottomed Whitby cats sat almost upright on the snowy sand waiting for the tide to refloat them. He knew there would be other ships hidden by the houses but he could see no movement on the harbour.

'Where, Mama?'

'By the West Pier. See, the masts are moving very slowly.'

Joshua looked to the left. 'I see it. A brig, I think, or a ketch, maybe. Hard to tell from this distance.' He slipped his hand into his mother's. 'You are cold, Mama,' he said. 'You must come downstairs. The kitchen is warm.'

'Seems strange to see a ship moving without sails,' Emma murmured.

Joshua looked at his mother. 'The seamen are warping her in.'

'Yes,' she whispered.

'Please, Mama, come down. Father is getting angry.' He rubbed her hand. 'Your fingers are frozen.'

'Look,' she said. 'Do you see it? On the roof near the chimneystack. A robin.'

Joshua glanced across as the bird fluttered from one sooty stack to another.

'I see him.'

They watched for a moment.

'Mama,' he said softly, 'there is nothing more you can do here.'

'I know.' Emma turned to her son and smiled. Something of her own pain was reflected in his hazel eyes. 'I will come down in a minute. It will be dark soon. I must light a candle.'

'Let me do it.'

She watched her son as he lit the stump of tallow. Watched his every move, his easy gait, the gentle movement of his wrist and hand. She considered his profile. How well he stood, she thought. How tall he had grown. Almost thirteen years old and grown almost to a man.

He handed the holder to her.

The voice, which bellowed up the stairwell, startled them. 'Get down here, woman!'

'Mama, you must go down.'

'One last moment,' she said.

Lifting her skirt, she held the candle towards the cradle nestled in the recess beside the fireplace. The flickering light wavered across the wooden headboard. The gossamer wings of the hand-painted fairies glimmered in the yellow light.

In the cot, the child lay swaddled in fresh linen. A bonnet, trimmed with white lace, framed the infant's ashen cheeks. Two bright new pennies rested on the tiny eyelids.

Leaning down, Emma loosened the ribbon under the baby's chin then retied it neatly in a bow. She touched the lips. They were cold. Alabaster cold.

'Bessie! My lovely Bess!' she whispered.

'Come down at once!' the voice demanded. 'Don't make me come up there to get you!'

Emma stiffened.

'I hate him!' Joshua cried.

'You must not speak like that.'

His eyes were level with hers. 'But I hate him for what he does to you. It isn't right.'

'Enough, Josh! Now is not the time.'

'But he doesn't care for you!'

Emma turned towards the empty hearth and wrapped her arms across her chest. 'This house is cold, isn't it?'

'Please, Mama, go downstairs. Please do what he says.'

Emma sighed. 'You go. I promise I will follow.'

The boy turned.

The top stairs groaned as Joshua stepped slowly down. Emma listened. She heard him stop for a while on the first-floor landing. Then heard his feet thumping down the bottom flight and the stairwell door close behind him.

Hot wax trickled over her fingers. The wick was almost spent. Carefully she placed the holder on the mantelshelf. The flame spluttered.

At the door, Emma stopped and looked back. Across the room the mouth of the fireplace gaped open – black and cold. Pockmarked grey cinders littered the grate and particles of white ash dotted the rug like flakes of newly fallen snow.

Emma knew it was time to leave. Time to leave the cradle shrouded in the shadow. To leave the child she had failed to raise. To leave behind another splintered fragment of her life. So short. So precious.

She lifted her skirt and stepped down into the gloom. Within the stairwell the musty smell of lingering mould exuded from the faded roses peeling from the walls. Soon it would be mingled with the scent of death.

Sweet. Sour. Unforgettable.

'What have you been doing up there? Wasting time again, no doubt!'

Emma closed the door quietly.

'Now the child is dead you have no reason to go up there. You're like a rat in a barn, up and down the steps. I am sick and tired of it.'

Slipping the shawl from her shoulders, Emma folded it over the back of the chair and took an apron from the dresser drawer. The crease running down the bib and skirt was quite sharp. She must have folded it when it was still hot from the iron. As she smoothed the line with the palm of her hand she could feel his eyes on her.

'I am waiting for my tea! I am going out!'

She knew his routine well enough and knew where he went every day at this time.

'The snow is getting quite deep,' she said, not needing to look at his face to gauge his expression. 'There is a pot of broth on the stove. Sit at the table and I will get some for you.'

George shuffled from the fire where he had been toasting the back of his legs. He mumbled to himself as Emma lifted the vase of dried catkins from the table and slid the velvet cloth from under his elbows.

'Joshua! Put your book away and come to the table.'

From the pot, Emma ladled the broth into a china bowl. A few drops spilled and sizzled on the coals.

'Mutton,' she said, placing it on the table.

He sniffed, splayed his knees to accommodate his paunch and rested his forearms on the table.

'At least I will not need to waste any more money on medicines,' he announced, flicking the linen napkin and tucking it inside his collar. 'Dr Throstle will get nothing more from my pocket.'

''Twas only once I called the doctor.'

'Then why does he keep sending his bill!' He tore a chunk of bread from the cob and dipped it in the fluid.

'Perhaps if you would pay him—' she whispered.

George Quinlan glared as Emma tipped the contents of her bowl back into the pot. Her appetite was gone.

'You should eat something, Mama,' Joshua said.

'Later, perhaps.'

When she lifted the kettle, she could sense her husband watching her, waiting for her to turn and look at him, but she kept her gaze to the fireplace, hiding her face, her frustrations, pain and her resentment. After placing it back on the hob and moving the soup-pot away from the heat, Emma added another lump of coal to the fire.

'Didn't I tell you, that child would never thrive?' he said. 'Weakling from the start. I knew it all along.'

She knew he was goading her.

Joshua looked up at his mother. 'Are you all right, Mama?'

She nodded, as she poked the fire.

'A waste of good money!' he announced.

Emma knew better than to be drawn into an argument. She dare not chance upsetting him. She could speak with Joshua when he had gone. She wanted to reassure her son, tell him she was all right. She knew he was concerned.

George mopped his dish with the remaining bread. Broke the cheese into two large chunks and swilled them down with a pot of ale. After polishing the grease from his whiskers with the back of his hand, he dusted his chest, turned his chair from the table, stretched out his legs and belched loudly.

Joshua turned his face away. His cheeks were sallow. Thinner than she had ever seen them. His eyes were red. The spark of youth was no longer there.

Emma fetched her husband's boots from the hall, knelt down on the mat beside the hearth and forced them over his swollen ankles. His face spoke of pain.

With the boots laced, George Quinlan raised himself and stomped his feet on the floor.

Without a word, Emma fetched his coat and helped him into it, though her fingers struggled to squeeze the buttons through their matching holes.

'Have you sponged this again?'

'Only to wipe away some stains.'

'Haven't I told you before? Do not touch it! Don't you ever listen to me, woman? Can't you see you've shrunk it?'

Emma wound the knitted muffler firmly round his neck and tucked the ends under his coat lapels. She watched as he considered his figure in the hallstand mirror and slapped his hands onto his belly, signifying, as he did every morning, that he was satisfied with his reflection.

Emma opened the door and waited on the doorstep. The air was icy cold. In one hand she held his hat and gloves, in the other his walking cane.

'Do you think it wise to go out in this weather?' she asked quietly.

He looked at her scornfully but did not answer.

Snowflakes floating over the threshold melted into spots of wetness on the floor. Across the street, the gas lamp, lit earlier than usual, glowed through a halo of misty air. Seal Street's surface of grey cobbles had been replaced by a carpet of white almost six inches deep.

From the parlour, the clock chimed the half-hour.

'And I hope you don't expect me to pay for a funeral,' Quinlan added, as he stepped down the stone steps onto the street. 'Paid enough for the infant while it was alive. I'm not paying any more now that it's dead.'

Joshua's chair scraped noisily on the kitchen floor.

'Be careful not to slip,' Emma called, not expecting a reply. She got none.

As he walked awkwardly down the street, snowflakes settled on his hat and shoulders. A hungry dog sniffing at his boots received a stinging stroke of the cane for its trouble. It ran off, yelping.

Emma closed the door on the cold.

'I hate him,' Joshua said.

Chapter 2

The rain fell straight and constant. Drenching rain which bounced down to the cobblestones and oozed up from the hillside at the same time.

The wooden wheels of the handcart splattered through puddles as it rumbled up Church Street. Racing along the gutter in the opposite direction, a stream of clear water headed downhill. On reaching the stone steps, Reginald Beckwith eased his hand-cart into the soft verge and waited. The newly painted sign hanging from its side read: MASTER CRAFTSMAN – CARPENTER – WOODTURNER and beneath those words in fine copperplate scroll, the name, *Reginald G. Beckwith*. Whilst his cart was a familiar sight on the Whitby streets carrying wood, fish, or turnips as the demand required, to the townsfolk of Whitby, Mr R. G. Beckwith was best known as the grave-digger.

Straightening his back, he glanced up the steep hillside rising to St Mary's, but the old stone church, together with most of the East Cliff, had been swallowed in thick cloud. Pulling the cape of felted wool close around his neck, he lifted the wooden box from the cart, leaned it against his stubbled cheek and settled it onto the wet wadding on his shoulder. When he was satisfied the box was seated properly, he signalled to the parson with a nod of the head.

The few mourners, standing in a silent huddle, did not see his gesture. Their faces were hidden beneath black umbrellas.

'Ready, ladies?' Parson Wakeley asked, one foot poised on the first slab of the 199 steps which wound up the hillside.

His wife, close behind him, sighed loudly as they began the trek to the top of the cliff. 'Dreadful weather,' she said.

'Yes,' Emma replied without thinking.

Joshua held the umbrella over his mother, as she gathered several folds of her skirt into one hand. In the other, she carried a bunch of snowdrops which she had picked earlier that morning.

It must have been raining when she went out. It hadn't stopped since the previous day though she couldn't remember. Her mind was occupied with thoughts of other things – her little Bess, her family, her home. Not the tall house in Seal Street or her life in Whitby, but of the place where she had grown up, of her parents and sister.

'Dreadful weather,' the portly lady muttered again, flicking at the raindrops as they ran down the front of her black satin skirt.

Dreadful weather. Emma repeated the words in her head. No, she thought, on the contrary, there was something comforting about the rain. Since it had started, the biting cold had gone. Almost all of the snow and ice of the previous few days had been washed to the sea and the streets and yards had been sluiced clean. Grass growing in the ditches looked green and fresh and the water running down the hill was clear as glass. In a strange way, she envied the water's flow. It ran so freely and always knew which way to go. No, she thought, she didn't mind the rain.

Mrs Wakeley continued grumbling. 'Why on earth they built the church at the top of a cliff, I will never know.' Her cheeks resembled two ripe pomegranates both in colour and in size. Emma wasn't sure if the deepening hue was the result of her frustration or if the lady was just running out of puff.

'Would you care to rest for a while?' she asked.

'No, must keep going!' the parson's wife replied stoically.

Ahead, the stone steps curved around the hillside, disappearing halfway up into a slowly swirling cloud which showed no signs of shifting. Emma considered the parson's wife would have made it easier for herself had she saved her breath and conversation until they reached the top.

But the remonstrations continued, one following the other and all quite unrelated: the number of new taverns in the town, the children who had not attended Sunday School, the cost of importing tea, and the pain she suffered from her bunion. When she stopped at every resting place, the mourners halted and waited patiently, the water slowly seeping through boot-seams and saturating the ladies' already sopping hemlines.

When she regained her composure, the party moved on and Parson Wakeley strode ahead, stamping his feet on each step as if in an attempt to stem the cascading stream. But his efforts were in vain and succeeded only in jetting water at his portly wife, his practice providing her with yet another reason to complain.

Whether he chose to ignore her protestations or simply didn't hear them, Emma wasn't sure, but when the next resting place was reached, he strode on, seemingly unaware that he was leaving his wife and the rest of the party behind.

It was a small group. The parson and his wife, Emma and her son, Joshua, and two matronly ladies who walked arm in arm about a dozen steps behind.

Mr Beckwith, the grave-digger, followed at a respectable distance, occasionally tutting at the slow progress. But he neither tried to pass on the steps nor take the donkey track running alongside it, instead he mumbled to himself and waited. It was a routine he was familiar with. Sliding the wooden box across his back, he balanced it onto his other shoulder as it was becoming increasingly heavy.

George Quinlan was not amongst the mourners.

The furthest corner of the graveyard was swathed in the canopy of cloud and, though the land leaned into the valley, nothing could be seen of the harbour below.

Holding hands, Emma and her son stood side-by-side by the tiny grave. The freshly-dug earth, piled around it was soft and slippery and the clay stuck to their boots.

Familiar with the burial service, the parson did not need to use his spectacles and delivered the service quickly but respectfully. Emma was not conscious of the words he spoke, only of the dreadful emptiness she felt inside. As she gazed ahead, raindrops added to the tears trickling down her face.

Mr Beckwith lowered the remains of Elizabeth May Quinlan with care. But the rain, which had collected in the hole, was trapped in its clay. For a few moments the wooden box floated like a small wooden craft on a becalmed sea but as the water seeped in, it gently settled on the bottom.

When the formalities were over, Parson Wakeley excused himself to speak with Mr Beckwith. Emma turned to the two ladies standing behind her. She had been surprised at their presence, not expecting anyone to attend the burial besides herself and Joshua. She recognized their faces but knew them only vaguely.

'Thank you for coming,' she said.

Mrs Cooper and Mrs Bradshaw had been neighbours since the Quinlans moved to Whitby more than three years ago. Mrs Bradshaw, the older of the two, lived directly across Seal Street. Mrs Cooper lived further up the hill although Emma was not sure which house she occupied. She felt abashed that in the past she had spoken very little with both women. A brief *Good Day* or *It looks like rain*, was the extent of their previous conversations. George had always discouraged any dealings with the, "riffraff over the way", and had forbidden Joshua from associating with the local children.

But a funeral was different. The ladies had come to pay their respects and Emma welcomed their support.

'Would you care to join my son and me for some refreshments at the house?' she asked.

The response was unashamedly enthusiastic. It was the first time either lady had been invited to step over the Quinlans' threshold. It was an opportunity they would not miss.

'That would be very nice,' Mrs Cooper said. 'You can't beat a bite to eat and a nice chat after a funeral, that's what I always say. Don't you agree Mrs Bradshaw?'

'Couldn't have put it better myself. Be pleased to come and join you and your boy.'

Emma had earlier extended the invitation to the parson and his wife, but Mrs Wakeley had tendered her apology explaining that her husband had urgent work to attend to. Emma considered that as a result of the freezing conditions of the past week, both the parson and Mr Beckwith would have plenty of work to do, and Mrs Wakeley would have more than her fill of funeral teas. She felt sorry for the lady. Such a depressing pursuit. It was no wonder the poor woman suffered from frustration.

'You'll excuse us if we get along now, Mrs Quinlan,' the Parson said. 'Another bereavement to attend to, I'm afraid.'

Emma thanked him for conducting the service and his kind words.

'You mind you look after your mother, young man,' he said patting Joshua on the back.

'Yes, sir.'

'Goodbye, my dear,' Mrs Wakeley said, hesitating for a moment as if she had more to say. Then she smiled sympathetically at Emma and took her husband's arm for the long walk back down to the town.

The heavy clay clung to Mr Beckwith's spade as he struggled to shovel it back into the hole. Emma and Joshua stood in silence as the oak coffin disappeared beneath the dirt and a plain wooden cross was hammered into the ground at the head of the mound. It sank in easily. Emma laid the posy of snowdrops beneath it. She could think of little, save for the fact the funeral was over.

The two ladies waited for her by the church wall.

Through the lifting cloud, the outline of the old abbey appeared dark and hazy yet on a clear day its stark features dominated the cliff top. From the mist-shrouded harbour, the clang of the Whitby bell sounded its plaintive toll, warning of a sea-fret that had moved in from the North Sea. They were familiar sights and sounds to the folks of the fishing port.

Returning to the village, the group of four walked down the 199 steps together. Down Church Street and through the older part of town. Along Bridge Street to the drawbridge which joined the east and west sides of Whitby and divided the busy fishing harbour into two parts. The bridge provided the only way to cross the River Esk. After crossing, they made their way past Flowergate to Spencer's Ghaut which led them up to Seal Street. The Quinlans lived at number twenty-nine.

'Please come in,' Emma said, as she opened the door.

The mud which had caked their boots in the churchyard had washed away but the ladies' skirts and petticoats were sopping. Despite their efforts to shake off the excess water, it was impossible to prevent the trail of drops which followed them into the house. Both ladies apologized. Emma assured them that they should not concern themselves. A wet floor would soon dry.

With heavy velvet drawn across the windows, not a chink of light spilled in. The kitchen was dark save for the glow from the coals. But the fire had kept the room warm. The company would add to that.

'Please light a lamp, Joshua.' Emma said.

Mrs Bradshaw surveyed the living-room, good furniture all polished, brass shining and linen crisp. It was clean and fresh though somewhat austere. Her attention was attracted to a picture on the wall. A pen and ink drawing. She stood in front of it.

'Your parents?' she asked.

Emma didn't need to look to know which picture she was referring to. 'Yes,' she said quietly, before inviting the ladies to sit down.

Mrs Cooper gave an involuntary shudder. 'Nice and cosy in 'ere,' she said. 'If you don't mind, luv, I'll drop me cloak near the fire to dry. It's a mite wet I'm afraid.'

'Of course,' said Emma, 'Let me help you.' She drew a chair closer to the fireplace. Mrs Cooper draped her cloak over it. Mrs Bradshaw removed hers and did the same.

Emma was aware of Joshua hovering near the stairs.

'May I go upstairs, Mama?'

She nodded. 'Leave your wet jacket. Change into some dry clothes then come down and talk with the ladies.'

'Let the boy go,' Mrs Cooper said. 'He don't want to be talking with us old fuddy-duddies.'

Joshua looked across to his mother.

She smiled. The woman was quite right.

Relieved, Joshua took off his boots, rested them against the fender and ran upstairs.

'A good lad, you've got there,' Mrs Bradshaw said.

'Thank you,' Emma said, sliding the smoke-blackened kettle over the flames. In no time, the lid was rattling. From the glass-fronted cabinet, she took a china teapot, with matching cups, saucers and plates, and arranged them neatly on the red velvet cloth. After warming the pot she made the tea.

'My, this is pretty,' Mrs Cooper said, lifting an empty cup and turning it in her hand.

Her friend gave a disapproving look.

'The china was my mother's,' Emma said.

'That's nice.'

'Thank you. I don't have much occasion to use it.' As she spoke, she realized it was the first time she had used it since the family moved to Whitby four years earlier. It was the second time that day she had thought about her mother and her life before she came to the fishing village.

Emma removed the doilies covering the plates on the table. 'A biscuit, Mrs Cooper, or a scone?'

'Thank you. Don't mind if I do,' Mrs Bradshaw said. 'Nice words, the parson spoke, don't you think?'

The other woman agreed. 'Indeed they were. You know, I always enjoy a good funeral. I ain't much for church and Sunday service, but I do like a nice funeral,' she said. 'Likes to show me respect, you know what I mean?'

'I thank you both for coming today.'

'Shame the father couldn't be here. Mr Quinlan away on business, is he?'

Emma felt the colour drain from her cheeks.

Mrs Bradshaw didn't wait for a reply. 'Seems to me, it always comes down to us women. We bring the bairns into this world and we have to see 'em out of it.'

'Sugar, Mrs Cooper?'

'Thank you, my dear.' The woman stirred her tea and helped herself to a biscuit.

'Bad business that funeral last week,' she continued.

Mrs Cooper nodded.

Emma wasn't particularly interested in tittle-tattle. Sometimes she overheard snippets of local gossip when she went shopping but because of Bessie's death, she felt she would rather not hear about someone else's misfortune. But the ladies meant no harm and, as she did not want to appear rude, she felt obliged to ask the question, although she could see that Mrs Bradshaw was poised to relate the story anyway.

'I didn't hear about it.' Emma said.

'Bad business,' Mrs Bradshaw repeated. 'Ruth Nichols, young lass, lived down bottom of Spencer's Ghaut. Pretty girl. Not more that twenty-two years old.' She sipped her tea. 'They say she fell down the stairs, poor girl, but I got it on good authority her husband pushed her. Bad business, I tell you.'

'Bad business,' the other woman echoed.

'They say she lay there all night and most of the following day. Couldn't move. They say they might have saved her if her man had called the doctor. But he wouldn't call for help. Too tight with his money he was.'

'You can bet he always had money for his drink!' Mrs Cooper added.

Emma turned away, picked up a lump of coal and added it to the fire.

'Died there where she fell, they say. At the bottom of the steps.'

'Shame! Shame!'

'Two bairns. Orphans now. He won't look after 'em.'

No one spoke. The three ladies reached for their cups and drank. After a moment's thought Mrs Bradshaw continued, 'It strikes me, in a situation like that, a woman's got two choices.'

Emma listened knowing there was no way of changing the course of the conversation, and besides, Mrs Bradshaw was intent on providing the solution.

'She can poison him, or run away! Two choices, that's how I sees it.'

Despite the shocked look on Emma's face, the fishwife nodded and reinforced her friend's statement. 'A good dose of rat poison, that'd be my choice. That would fix a man like that.'

'Well, I have to agree,' said Mrs Cooper. 'But then how's a woman going to support herself? Unless she's got means.' She dusted the crumbs from her lap into her hand and returned them to her plate. 'Or a fancy-man?'

'Mrs Cooper!' Emma said.

'Well, I ask you, what chance has a woman these days, running off on her own, especially in a sea port like Whitby? No chance at all. Too many of them foreign sailors around. Drunken louts every one of 'em. Just waiting, they are, for the opportunity to take advantage of a poor woman. I ask you, what can she do? Where can she go? Big towns is even worse.' She paused. 'I'd have to agree with you, Sadie Bradshaw – a good dose of rat poison would do the trick just fine.'

'More tea, Mrs Cooper?' Unused to this type of conversation, Emma found it rather entertaining.

'No thank you, my dear, I enjoyed that. But tell me, what about that lad of yours? Joshua. Is he all right?' She inclined her head toward the stairwell. 'Bottle it all up inside the boys do when someone dies. Don't like anyone to see 'em bawling.'

Mrs Bradshaw agreed. 'That's right. My eldest boy was just the same. Never cried when the twins died of the pox. Not for six months that is, then one day some little thing happened – I'm darned if I can think what it was.' She stopped and scratched at her bonnet. 'I remember,' she said. 'He tripped over the cat and slopped a jug of milk on me.'

Emma covered her lips with her fingers.

'It were just an accident. Splashed the milk all down my apron and I got mad with him. You know how you do? It weren't nowt really, but he just cried and cried and cried. Six months' worth of tears came flooding out.'

'Is that so?' Mrs Cooper said. 'Well, I'll be!'

'He was all right after that. It had all been bottled up inside. Them tears had to come out sometime and spilling that jug of milk, that was what done it.'

'Joshua will be fine,' said Emma, 'but I thank you for your advice and I will mind how he is. Mrs Bradshaw, another cup?'

'Don't mind if I do, lass.'

As Emma drained the last of the tea from the china pot, the older woman squinted inquisitively at the expression on her face.

'Well, I must say! Do I detect a smile, my dear?'

Emma's cheeks flushed. 'I am sorry,' she said. 'I don't mean to appear rude, but it was what you were saying about the spilled milk, it reminded me of something that happened when I was a girl. It was just the fleeting memory which made me smile.'

'Come on, lass – spit it out – don't keep it to yourself.'

Emma protested, 'No, I couldn't. It wouldn't be fitting – not in the circumstances – the funeral, I mean.'

'Now, we'll be the judge of that, won't we, Sadie? Darn it all, lass, you've done all you can for the bairn. You've given her a proper Christian burial.'

'And very nice it was too,' Mrs Bradshaw added. 'Very nice.'

'But I'll be betting that it's a long time since that pretty face of yours had anything much to smile about.' The two women exchanged knowing glances.

'Aye, come on, luv, tell us about when you were a lass. A good yarn'll warm us up inside.'

Emma set her cup down on the table. The two ladies were kind. Good-hearted. And it was strange but she was enjoying their company. Mrs Bradshaw reminded her of the old housekeeper who had been so caring towards her mother when things had become difficult. Even her broad accent sounded similar. It was something about their openness made her feel comfortable and she welcomed the opportunity to talk.

''Twas just a childish memory, but I sometimes think back to those days. Foolish really. But they were happy times – when I was a girl,' she sighed, 'a long time ago.'

'Not that long ago, I don't think,' Mrs Cooper said, her chin resting on her plump washerwoman hands. Emma could feel her eyes examining her intently. 'I have to say, my dear, it's hard to believe that you have a lad the age of your Joshua. But I'm sorry, I was interrupting. Go on tell us your yarn.'

Emma returned her cup and saucer to the table. Her shoulders dropped forward slightly and she relaxed back into the chair.

'I was only nine,' she said. 'My sister, Anna was thirteen. Papa was commissioned to work in London and Mama was invited to go with him. They were away for almost six months and the house was closed up.' Emma gazed into the fire and didn't see the raised eyebrows exchanged between the two women.

'I remember, at the time, Anna and I were terribly upset. We had to be sent away to the country to stay with my mother's sister, Aunt Daisy. We did not know what a wonderful time we would have for, until then, we had always lived in the city.'

The two women listened intently.

'My Uncle Jack had a farm in Lincolnshire with some milking cows. I remember them well. They were big and brown and bony.' A grin spread across her face. 'One in particular, her name was Molly.'

'Molly,' Mrs Cooper echoed.

Emma nodded. 'I remember running down to the cow shed early in the morning when it was still dark and cold. Uncle would follow carrying a lantern. "Don't run girls," he would shout, and "watch where you are treading".'

The women smiled.

'Funny the things you remember, isn't it?' she said, as she watched the steam rising from the ladies cloaks drying by the fire. 'I can remember the smell of that barn. It was strong and rank, and in the mornings steam would rise from the thick piles of old hay heaped at the back of the shed.' She breathed deeply through her nose. 'Uncle Jack taught us how to milk the cows.'

Mrs Bradshaw leaned forward resting her elbows on the table.

Emma corrected herself. 'No, I should say he taught Anna, my sister. She was good. Her hands were bigger than mine and she managed the job easily. I was envious when I heard the milk squirting into her pail. It just didn't matter how much I tried, I couldn't do it properly. Uncle Jack was very patient and would say "Try Molly, Emma. You mark my words; you'll have no trouble this morning". But Anna would always have her pail full before I had a trickle in the bottom of mine.'

Glancing at the two faces framed in black bonnets, Emma wondered if she should continue.

'Don't stop,' Mrs Bradshaw said, leaning back in her chair. 'I have to admit, that's something I've never done – milked a cow. Not much call for it on the Whitby wharves.'

Mrs Cooper laughed. 'You're right. The only milk we've ever had came out of a churn. Go on, luv. Don't stop.'

Emma continued, 'I would squeeze and squeeze but nothing would happen. And I would tell Uncle that I couldn't do it. Then he would whisper a few words in Molly's ear, and the milk would flow like water from a pump.

'But as soon as Uncle went off to milk one of the other cows, Molly would start moving backwards and forwards and swaying from side to side. I would have my head pressed on her belly and I would call out, "Molly! Keep still!" but she wouldn't stop. Then I would feel the back leg of the stool sinking into the soft ground and I knew that if I let go, I would topple over and take the pail of milk with me. I would beg Uncle, "Please tell Molly to keep still", and he would stroke her nose and again whisper in her ear and she would stand as still as any statue.'

'So tell me,' Mrs Bradshaw asked, 'did you ever fill your pail?'

'Never. Uncle always finished the milking for me.' She paused and smiled. 'And when Anna and I weren't looking he would squirt milk at us. And we'd laugh and squeal, and he said we sounded like a pair of piglets. By the time we got back to the farmhouse, we had milk in our hair and down our aprons and Aunty would scold us and tell us how naughty we were.'

'Just like I scolded my boy when he spilled milk down my apron.'

'That is what reminded me,' Emma said. 'But I don't think she was really angry. She'd tell us to be more careful next time, but then she would scoop the cream off the top of the milk and give us a mug-full. It was so rich and thick and it lined our mouths and warmed our empty stomachs. I can almost taste it now.' Emma paused and took a big breath. 'As I said, it was just a childish memory.'

'And a right fine little tale. I enjoyed hearing it. How about you, Sadie?'

'Good to see a smile on your face, my dear,' Mrs Bradshaw said, then with a serious tone to her voice, added, 'strange where we end up, isn't it? Sometimes I think it's just as well we ain't like them gypsies who can gaze into a crystal ball and see what the future has in store.'

'Such talk, Sadie Bradshaw!' Mrs Cooper said, rising to her feet. 'If you'll excuse us, Mrs Quinlan, it's time we were off home. Our menfolk will be none too happy if there's no tea cooking.'

'Aye, I suppose you're right,' the older woman said. 'Though I don't feel much like shifting. Got right comfortable I have and I enjoyed listening to your story.' Gathering up her cloak, she draped it round her shoulders. 'Now you mind and come and pay us a call sometimes.'

Emma promised that she would.

As she was leaving, Mrs Bradshaw touched Emma's arm. 'Now don't you forget, if there is ever anything you want – and I mean at any time – don't you be too proud to ask.'

'And that goes for me too,' added Mrs Cooper. 'I'm only a couple of doors up the street. Your lad knows where to find me.'

'Thank you,' Emma said. 'I will remember that.'

Outside, the street was bathed in its customary shadow. Across the road, an assortment of urchins had squeezed onto Mrs Bradshaw's doorstep, their gazes fixed like faces in the pictures framed on a mantelshelf. The moment their mother appeared, the two smallest ones ran to meet her, pulling at her skirt and wailing for her attention. From the doorway, Emma watched the two women as they crossed the cobbled street so engrossed in conversation they seemed oblivious to the children's demanding cries.

Closing the door quietly, Emma was thankful for their visit. They had helped to lighten the burden of Bessie's death and their company had lifted her spirits. Even the house felt warmer. Most of all, however, she was satisfied that everything had been taken care of properly. Now, her little girl could rest in peace. Now she could relax a little.

As for her husband, George, he had hired a rig and pair to drive along the cliff tops to Robin Hood's Bay. It was a journey he made every three or four weeks sometimes not returning until the following day. She often wondered what business he had in the tiny fishing village, but she knew better than to ask. For the moment, she indulged herself in the knowledge that he would not be back until late that evening.

Glancing about the room, her eyes were drawn to the picture hanging on the wall, the one which had attracted Mrs Bradshaw's attention. The pen and ink.

How many times had she gazed at it? Been called by it. She knew it intimately. Every line. Every stroke. Every detail replicated as perfectly as if captured on a photographic plate. But the picture revealed more than the subjects' images. Far more. The artist's pen had breathed life onto the paper. More life and character than any flash of magnesium could duplicate. And in unwritten words a discourse spoke from it. Words of truth, humility and love.

Her fingers stroked the moulded frame.

From within the confines of the dark oak, the man and woman appeared at ease. This was no stiff, self-conscious tableau, powdered and posed for a portrait session. Here the subjects were relaxed. The man was seated in a worn horsehair armchair. A gentle man with a kindly face, clean-shaven save for a goatee beard gone white. His flowing hair, streaked with varying shades of grey, fell softly about his shoulders. And skillfully etched into his features were lines of joy, frustration and happiness delicately tinged with an air of grief.

But his eyes concealed the deepest mystery. Pale misty eyes that had a strange opacity. As if, when capturing his soul, the artist's pen had dried. Instead of pools of black, the pupils were empty voids, not looking anywhere but seeing all. And yet, reflected from the face, here was a man accepting all life dealt with mellowness. A smile just past.

Perhaps it was his dress that had caught her visitors' attention. With neither coat nor waistcoat, his attire was quite unbecoming for a formal sitting. His silken shirt was open at the neck, its sleeves billowing down to hide slim arms which rested on the chair's wearied upholstery. His fingers, soft and slender, resembled those of a musician.

Emma's fingers touching the frame were similar.

A walking cane leaned against his leg. Its tarnished silver handle was molded to the shape of a mallard's beak.

Standing close beside him, the woman gazed down, her left hand resting over his protectively, as if a mother's hand upon her child's. An old woman, perhaps fifty years of age or more, her dress in keeping with her years: the neckline, high beneath the chin, the dress's yoke and sleeves edged with exotic lace, the fine threads fraying at the wrist. The gown's satin, shaded the colour of a winter's sky, reflected a subtle sheen and fell in gentle folds of which no crease had escaped the artist's eye.

The woman's hair, combed loosely to a bun, showed not a trace of grey. The ringlets curling from her temples hid her ears. But, like the creases in her skirt, every hair had been accounted for. Her skin was clear, save for the lines of life around her lips and eyes. Smiling, her sad eyes were directed towards her man – her husband, lover, companion and friend.

And in her right hand, she held a rose, its stem appearing wet as if just lifted from a vase – a wild dog rose, whose petals were about to shed, one petal floating gently to the ground. A graceful movement captured in the stillness of the frame.

There was a knock on the door.

'Mrs Quinlan. I came to offer my condolences.'

Mr Albert Hepplethwaite was almost as round as he was tall. His frame filled the doorway. Doffing his hat, he lifted it only slightly from his head before settling it down again. He was breathing heavily.

The smile on Emma's face faded.

'Heard about your sad loss, my dear, and thought, as I was just passing, I would call in to pay my respects.'

Something in his words rankled. If indeed Mr Hepplethwaite was *just passing*, then where was he going? Seal Street led up the western side of the valley. At the top of the street there was nothing but wind and heather. The fact that his ruddy cheeks looked about to burst and he was quite out of puff, confirmed what Emma already knew, that he was not in the habit of taking walks up the Whitby hillsides. Furthermore, she had heard it said that Mr Albert Hepplethwaite was as much a fixture leaning across his shop counter, as the sign that swung on the street outside his establishment.

The proprietor of The Harbour Pie Shop was well regarded in the town, but in Emma's estimation, he was too familiar. The words, *my dear*, had an ingratiating ring. She did not like the man, and he was the last person she would have expected to see standing on her doorstep.

'Condolences,' he repeated. 'Just paying my respects.'

'Thank you,' Emma said flatly.

'I was speaking with your good husband last week. Discussing the future of your boy, Joshua.'

She watched the rain stream from the brim of his hat, conscious that she did not want to invite him in.

He coughed into his podgy fist. 'He told me that your son has had enough of schooling. Said it was time he had a job. An apprenticeship was what we were discussing.'

A scowl puckered Emma's forehead.

'Excuse my candour, Mr Hepplethwaite, but I do not think anyone can have enough schooling. However,' she said, 'Mr Quinlan has not spoken to me about the matter.'

She lied. She was neither prepared to discuss the issue with this unwelcome visitor, nor admit that she was keenly aware of her husband's intentions. George had made it very clear to her that Joshua should bring a wage into the house. He was not interested in what the boy wanted to do, stating that he was certainly old enough to go out to work and that was the end of the matter.

But the idea of her son working for Mr Hepplethwaite was unacceptable to Emma. She had seen Mr Hepplethwaite's *boys*, their backs bent double, struggling with handcarts laden with sacks of flour and sugar. She had seen others running along the wharfside as if the hounds of Hell were after them. If this was the job which Mr Hepplethwaite was broaching, it was not Emma's idea of an apprenticeship.

Emma believed her son at least deserved the education she had had, if not more. He was intelligent, and if he continued with his studies, he could gain a worthwhile career. She felt she owed him that. But she also knew what George was like, and if he said that boy must earn his keep then nothing would sway that decision.

'Is Mr Quinlan home?' Hepplethwaite asked, dabbing a silk handkerchief across his brow.

'No. He had business which took him out of town,' Emma said curtly. 'He was unable to attend the funeral.'

'Dear me, that is a pity.' There was no scrap of surprise in the shopkeeper's tone. Was he aware that George Quinlan had not attended the funeral? Did he know that her husband was not at home? How could he know unless someone had told him?

'Is the lad in?'

'Yes,' she said cautiously. 'If you care to wait a moment, I'll call him.'

'Kind of you, my dear,' he said. 'No need to trouble the boy. But if you don't mind the liberty, I will step inside out of the wet.'

Without waiting for an invitation Albert Hepplethwaite shook the rain from his hat, stepped over the threshold, and closed the door behind him.

Emma's agitation quickened. Was her intuition wrong? He had stated that he was just paying his respects and she wondered why she should doubt that. Had she been ungracious leaving him standing on the street? She was confused.

'It's no trouble,' she said politely. 'I am sure Joshua will be happy to speak with you. Excuse me, I will only be a moment.'

The proprietor of The Harbour Pie Shop puffed out his chest and placed his top hat on the stand. The wiry red whiskers, which flared from the sides of his face, belied the fact that the top of his head was completely bald. He was uncomfortably fat and only marginally taller than Emma.

'No need to hurry yourself,' he called, as she disappeared up the stairs.

Waiting for a moment, he listened to the sounds made by the creaking timbers as Emma hurried to the top of the house. Stepping closer to the stairwell, he tilted his head to catch the drift of muffled voices floating down from the attic. Sidling between the furniture, he crossed the room to the writing-desk and ran his hand across the polished timber. Lifting the lid, he opened the front sufficiently to peer inside at the bundles of letters tied neatly with ribbon, housed in individual compartments. He noted the bottle of ink resting on a well-used blotting pad and the black quill pen and penknife lying beside it.

At the sound of descending footsteps, he quickly closed the desk lid and shuffled back leaving a tell-tale trail of damp footprints.

'So here you are, lad,' he announced, as Joshua appeared. 'I trust you have been looking after your dear mother?'

'Yes, sir,' the boy replied, buttoning his shirt at the neck.

Emma realized that the remains of the afternoon tea were still on the table. She wished that she had cleared them away.

'Your father had words with you, boy?'

'About what, sir?' Joshua looked across to his mother.

'Very likely I have a job for you, lad. Your father and I have spoken about it. Good strong boy like you will be very useful to me. An apprenticeship with the Pie Shop.' He waited for a response. 'What say you, boy?'

'I go to school,' Joshua said hesitantly.

'Don't you worry about school, lad. You'll learn more working with me than sitting behind a desk. I'll see to that.' Reaching into his waistcoat pocket he withdrew a fob watch and flipped it open.

'I need another pair of hands this afternoon. Stores to deliver to one of the ships,' he announced. 'Your father said I should come and get you whenever I needed you.'

So this was the purpose of his call.

'Which ship is it?' Joshua asked, hiding the hint of excitement in his voice.

'Bark by the name of *Lady Cristobel*. She's due to sail in the morning.'

Joshua looked to his mother and then back to Mr Hepplethwaite.

Emma picked up his boots from the fireplace and handed them to him. They were still wet. But she was relieved that Mr Hepplethwaite would leave at last.

'Go along, Joshua, and do whatever Mr Hepplethwaite tells you.'

'Good. That's settled then,' the shopkeeper announced. 'Will Mr Quinlan be away for long?'

'I expect him home quite soon.'

'Well, it is time I took my leave.' He turned to the boy sitting on the doormat lacing his boots. 'Now you be a good lad and run along. You'll be much quicker than me. Down at the shop, Mrs Hepplethwaite will tell you what to do. The sooner you are off, the sooner you'll be finished.' He opened the door. 'On your way, boy!'

Joshua grabbed his cap, glanced back at his mother and dashed off down the street.

'And I will bid you good day, Mr Hepplethwaite,' Emma said, endeavouring to usher him out of the door.

But Hepplethwaite made no effort to move.

'A good lad,' he said, combing his fingers through his knotted whiskers. 'Now if your boy is going to work for me, perhaps we could be a little less formal. You must call me Bert.' The smile on his face was false. 'The missus and I treat all the lads we take on like family, especially when they're fresh away from their mothers. The wife, she's soft with them. Likes to give 'em a treat if they work hard. Piece of pie or a jam tart.' He sneered. 'Likes to spoil 'em a bit. Too soft, she is, in my estimation.'

Emma was hardly listening. She was considering the foolish expression on the man's face, likening it to that of a boy with nothing but holes in his pockets gazing through a sweet-shop window with mischief in his eyes.

'Of course,' he said, 'I've no time for lazy louts. No time at all. A boy's to pull his weight if he's working for me.'

'I assure you, Mr Hepplethwaite, you will have no problems with my boy.'

'Good. Then that is all settled,' he said again. 'Now let me once again offer you my condolences.'

Before Emma had time to step back, the man reached forward and grasped her hand. He placed his other hand on top of it, holding it like a waffle in an iron.

Emma tried to draw away but she was firmly secured.

'You must call into my shop one afternoon,' he said. 'I am sure I have something that will take your fancy. My special treat,' he smirked. 'You understand. Perhaps I can help you to get over this unfortunate business.' Unable to bend from the waist, the shopkeeper inclined his head towards the hand he had caught.

At that moment the door opened. George Quinlan had returned early.

'So! What do we have here?'

Albert Hepplethwaite dropped Emma's hand. 'Ah! Quinlan. Good day, sir. Yes, I was just leaving. Just paying my respects on this sad occasion.'

Quinlan's fiery gaze by-passed the baker and alighted on his wife. Bert Hepplethwaite quickly retrieved his hat from the hallstand and shuffled out sideways onto the street. The door was slammed behind him.

'He came to pay his respects. He came to fetch Joshua,' Emma cried. 'I didn't invite him in. I wanted him to go.'

George Quinlan wasn't listening. He leaned back against the door unbuttoning his coat, his eyes still fixed on his wife. He let his coat fall to the floor. The wet wool smelled of tavern smoke. The buckle of his belt cut tight into his belly but he tugged it free and slid the leather strip from round his waist.

Emma backed towards the stairwell. Afraid. He followed her, his eyes glaring. Before she reached the door, his arm shot forward, slamming it shut behind her.

'It was the rain,' she begged. 'He came in out of the rain.'

His ruddy face pulsed.

Crossing her arms over her chest, Emma dropped her chin into them. She thought of Joshua and prayed he would not come home till late.

'You slut! You common whore!' George Quinlan yelled. 'So this is what you do when I'm away!' Firelight glinted on the buckle. 'I'll show you what you get for entertaining men under my roof! This time I'll teach you a lesson you will not forget!'

Chapter 3

There was little movement on the headland, save for the solitary figure.

From a recess in the abbey wall, the seaman watched, his interest stirred by the sight of a woman walking alone. He had noticed her when she had first appeared from the direction of the church. Watched her wandering aimlessly, stumbling at times, sprigs of heather tugging at her skirt.

He wondered why she was there. Why she had not taken the path, hard-padded over the centuries by the silent feet of monks and foxes. Why, instead, she had chosen to trek across the damp untrodden ground towards the cliff edge.

High above, a lone seagull hovered. It observed the intruder approaching its colony. It cried, one long wailing cry, and gave itself up to the wind, peeled back from the land and dived.

Two hundred feet below, the North Sea gnawed at the clay cliffs, spewing its foam on the bed-rock beach in a rumble of distant thunder.

The seaman poked a stained finger into the bowl of his pipe, tapped the ash onto his leathered palm and watched as the particles danced off. For a while, he toyed with the narrow shaft. Sucked on it. Then returned the pipe to his pocket. He leaned back against the weathered wall and rubbed the itch from his shoulders.

Across the barren cliff top, the March wind combed the spiked grass in sweeping waves streaming the woman's hair across her face like tentacles of a jellyfish. He could not see her features but noticed she was wearing neither gloves nor bonnet. Though she seemed oblivious to the wind, he considered she must surely be cold.

He watched her pace slow then stop. Not wanting to be seen, the sailor dropped down to his haunches. But the woman had no interest in the land, her gaze was directed firmly to the sea.

He picked a blade of grass and chewed on its sappy fibre. Following her every step, her gait stirred in his groin the tingling urge which life at sea deprived a seamen.

Between her legs, her skirt flapped like a poorly set sail.

He spat the grass from his mouth, stood up and scanned the horizon.

To the east the leaden sea supported nothing but a billow of dark clouds. There were no ships. No sails. Nothing on the seascape save the mewing gulls, their cries muted by the offshore wind.

What was she looking for?

Was she waiting for a ship? The return of a husband, father, brother? Was she come here to mourn a vessel already lost – dashed to flotsam on some uncharted reef?

Taking a pouch from his pocket, he pinched at the dried leaves and stuffed them into his pipe. The black skeleton of the abbey towered above him, its voided windows, once decked in shards of coloured glass, now framed a cold chameleon sky. The wind sighed through the abbey's empty nave. The ruin's transept long silenced to the peel of bells was now a sanctuary for bats and passing birds.

The seaman watched as she lifted her skirt. Walked forward. Her movements slow but deliberate.

Perhaps now she would turn and retrace her steps. Or find the path, he thought, and return to the town. He decided he would follow at a distance, taking care not to be seen. He wanted to find out where she was going. Where she lived. He coveted this strange intimacy.

But she bore neither right nor left. She was heading for the cliff edge.

His uneasiness quickened. Surely she did not intend to give herself to the wind as the white bird had?

His buckled shoes caught on the tussocks as he lumbered awkwardly over ground unfamiliar to his sea legs. But he covered the distance quickly and slowed only when he was close behind her. A few yards ahead, the land ended, the remnant vegetation dangling from the edge by woody tendrils.

He touched her arm.

'*Pardonnez mois, mademoiselle.* Are you all right?'

'*Mais oui.*'

'*Vous êtes Française?*'

'*Non*,' she sighed.

'Please, *mademoiselle*, I fear something is wrong. Let me help you.'

There was no reply, but as he reached out towards her, her knees buckled and her body crumpled like a falling staysail.

He supported her, cupped her chin in his hand and lifted her face towards him. The hair layered across her face streamed back on the wind.

'*Mon Dieu!*' The colour of old blood trapped beneath skin was not what he had expected. 'What has happened to you? Your face?'

Her fingers traced the swollen contours of her cheek. She looked into the swarthy face appealing for an answer. None came.

'I don't remember,' she said. 'A fall I think.' Her head rolled against his leg. Her eyes closed.

Mon Dieu! At sea, men fall from the yards. He had seen many broken faces. And he had seen sailors when they crawled back to the ship after brawling in the taverns. He knew the difference well enough. He knew the damage a man's fist inflicted on another's face. He knew the mark a knuckle could imprinted upon a cheek. What man has done this? What coward? If he were here now he swore he would kill him.

Lifting the woman, he carried her to the shelter of the abbey. On a patch of soft green, between hewn stones, he laid her on the earth, swung the coat from his back and draped it over her.

'Can I bring someone to you, miss?' he asked, sliding his fingers under a ringlet which lay across her brow. Her skin was smooth. Warm. She smelled good.

Emma stirred and remembered the gesture. The soft touch of a hand across her forehead. The scent of spring flowers around her. The warmth of the sun. And the sound of a fountain pattering softly onto a lake. It happened a long time ago. Closing her eyes, she drifted back into the dream.

'*Mademoiselle?*'

'Thank you,' she said, forgetting what he had asked.

'Let me take you home, or bring help to you.'

'Let me just rest a while. I will be fine presently.'

For three hours Emma slept – slept as the wind whipped the clouds out to sea, as the pockets of sunshine drew grey shadows in their wake which slithered over her body like drifting veils. Emma slept on the dank ground unaware her every breath was being watched, unaware of the seaman, squatting against the wall, waiting for her to wake. She slept beneath his coat tainted with the smell of salt and tar, soothed by the rhythmic sound of a knife blade drawn against a sharpening stone.

But there was no dream in her sleep though at times her mind fought to capture some memory. Like a drowning soul struggling in the ocean, she needed something to cling on to. She thought nothing of past or future, but a single image fluttered behind her lids. A mound of earth. A bunch of withered snowdrops. A wooden cross.

When she opened her eyes, the sky above was blue. She could hear a skylark singing. It was the first she had heard this year. She moved her head and recognized the contours of the abbey. Why was she lying on the ground? What had brought her to this long abandoned place?

The seaman returned the knife to its scabbard and stood up. 'At last the princess awakes!'

Emma was confused but not afraid. The Frenchman's tone was gentle. 'What am I doing here? What has happened?'

'I thought you would be able to tell me,' he said.

'I cannot remember.'

He leaned over and offered her his tar-stained palms.

'Perhaps you can sit up?' he said. 'Let me help you.'

As she placed her hands on his and allowed him to draw her up, the coat slid from her knees.

'Yours?' she said. 'You must be cold.'

'It is much colder on the sea.'

She looked up at him.

'Sometimes it is so cold, the fingers, they almost freeze. The ropes, they cut across my feet like knives. No,' he said, 'this is not so cold.'

'Please take it anyway. I am better now.' She gathered up the coat and held it out to him.

He thanked her. 'I am pleased. I was concerned.' He donned the coat and took a step back. 'Perhaps, I should introduce myself.'

Standing almost six feet tall, the sailor bowed. 'My name is François le Fevre. At your service, *mademoiselle*.'

Emma smiled. Held out her hand. 'I am pleased to make your acquaintance, Monsieur le Fevre. I am Emma Quinlan. Mrs Emma Quinlan.'

'Ah, *madame*, I beg your pardon, but you look so young.'

She could feel the blood flush in her bruised cheeks. 'I think I should not be here.'

'And, I think I am glad that I visited this place, otherwise I would not have met the Mrs Emma Quinlan.' He inclined his head graciously then turned his face into the wind, flicked back his hair and retied the strip of rag that held it.

How becoming he was. This seaman. This miscreant. The very type of man she had been warned to be wary of. Yet this sailor provoked no fear in her. Quite the contrary: she felt safe with him.

What was it about him? His touch? The deep walnut colour of his eyes? His weathered face? Or was it the lilt of his French accent? Soft. Haunting. Lyrical.

As if reading her thoughts, he said, 'I am inquisitive, *madame*. You speak French?'

'A little. Why do you ask?'

He laughed. 'Because you spoke to me in French.'

'I do not remember.'

The seaman shook his head. 'This is very strange,' he mused. 'Here I am, alone on the top of a cliff, in the ruins of a great church, with a beautiful woman who I do not know. A beautiful woman who speaks to me in French but says she cannot remember. *Mais oui*! I think this is very strange.'

'Please, *monsieur*, do not make fun of me. I think I have been a little crazy in the head. But now I am well.'

'My dear *madame*, forgive me. I am not making fun, as you say.' He kneeled down beside her. 'I would not do that.'

'I must go home.'

'Then let me help you.' He eased her to her feet.

Emma looked about, swaying unsteadily. A sudden sickness churned inside her belly. They were alone. Alone on the cliff top. Had anyone seen them there? Seen her with the sailor? How long had she been there? What had happened there? Now she was afraid.

'Perhaps, *monsieur*, if you would help me as far as the church steps. I will manage on my own from there.'

François understood.

She leaned heavily on his arm as they walked slowly back towards the churchyard and the steps which led down the valley side.

'Will you be all right?'

She nodded.

He stood for a moment considering his farewell.

'*Au revoir, madame.*'

'*Au revoir, monsieur.*'

'My ship will be in port for a few days.'

She smiled. 'Goodbye, *monsieur*.'

He hesitated for a moment, then turned and headed back towards the abbey.

The potato soup bubbled with the smell of sweet onions. A jet of blue spurted from a piece of coal. Emma drew the curtains against the growing dusk and considered what she had achieved in the past few hours. She had scraped and polished. The brass fender gleamed. The room looked fresh. Even the household items, lined up neatly, appeared to have adopted a different appearance. Why? She did not know. Did not know what had awakened her enthusiasm and granted her renewed energy.

On returning from the abbey she had first relit the fire. Then, peeled the potatoes and boiled several pots of water. Stripping off her clothes she had stood naked by the hearth and sponged herself. The tepid water, scented with a dash of salts, had felt good as it trickled down her legs. Drying her skin, she had watched the beads of water run from her feet and settle between the knots of the rag rug. She had dipped her hair into the china bowl and washed her head. After rinsing the soap from her eyes, she had admired the porcelain bowl decorated with swirls of damask roses intertwined with curling ribbons. It was a long time since she had examined the delicate artwork.

From her wardrobe she selected the blue merino. It was soft and warm. And an apron edged with a frill of French lace. After winding strips of cloth round the wisps of hair which fell around her face, Emma sat by the fire to hasten them drying.

The smell from the pot reminded her she had an appetite. It was getting late.

From the doorway of the brick terrace, she could see to the corner where Seal Street turned down towards Flowergate and the harbour. Even at a glance it was not hard to recognize the figure of her husband, George, who was standing in the middle of the narrow street. He was going neither forward nor back. Just standing. Legs apart. Hands on hips. Swaying. As she watched, he leaned forward and projected a concoction of dark coloured fluid onto the cobbles. The best port from the Faith and Compass, several pots of rum and more than a little brown ale. It splattered back at his legs.

He straightened. Leaned back and waited but had no encore. Saliva dribbled from his bottom lip. He wiped his sleeve across his mouth, spat, and continued his perambulation to the house. Two dogs snapped at each other while lapping up the liquid treat.

Emma returned to the fire and waited. The soup bubbled. The clock in the parlour ticked loudly. But George did not arrive.

Beneath the lamp pole, across the street, he had settled himself in the gutter.

The lamplighter leaned over him. 'You 'right, squire?'

'Fine! Absolutely fine, my man!' he drawled, a cock-eyed grin contorting his face.

Working with his pole above the drunken man, the lighter opened the glass and ignited the mantle. The flame burned blue for a moment then burst into a cool white haze. Doffing his cap, the workman continued on his rounds. The sound of his pole tapped its way up the hill.

The smell of burning brought Emma back to the stove. The soup! As she pushed the pot from the heat, the lid slid towards her. She tried to catch it in her lap but it slipped from her fingers and clattered noisily on the tiles.

'You are useless, woman. I always said you were useless.' George Quinlan slammed the door, turned the key in the lock and propped himself up against the wall.

Suddenly the room seemed dark. Having grown accustomed to the firelight, Emma had forgotten to light the lamp. She hoped he would not notice. Retrieving the lid, she wiped it and returned it to the pot.

George stumbled forward, rocked against the chair and grunted. He was peering at his wife, eyes half closed, head poised at a strange angle, the corner of his mouth twitching foolishly.

'Sit down,' she said.

As if by instinct, he followed her instructions, sat in his armchair and stared – gazing first at the fire, then the kettle, the poker, the box of kindling, the coal-scuttle. He studied each one in turn, inclining his head as if questioning its function. When his eyes returned to the fire, his lids were almost shut.

Emma wondered, as she had so many times, what had become of the upstanding man she had met ten years earlier? What had reduced him to this pathetic figure? Reeking of alcohol. Fat. Unkempt. Old, though not yet fifty. She remembered the very day they were introduced. The impression he had given of a proud, if somewhat pompous man. And how he had seemed kind at first. And generous. How could she forget the visits he made to her parents' house? How the idea of a union between them was distasteful, nay, appalling at first, but how she had swallowed her own feelings and considered the situation with regard to her family. Here was a gentleman who would provide her son, Joshua, with the father he had never known. He would provide for her and give her a home. But most importantly, he would shoulder the burden that she considered she was to her dear Mama and Papa. She was grateful to him for that. And over the early years, she remembered how she had endeavoured to love him, albeit in a dutiful and respectful way.

But, the man she had married had been amiable, quick-witted and astute. A sound businessman. He had promised to care for her and her son and their prospects together had appeared good. But over the years, George had changed and Emma's situation was far from that which she, or her parents, could ever have envisaged.

'Mama! Mama!' Joshua tapped on the door. The brass handle rattled but the man snoring in the chair did not stir. 'It's me, Mama. Please open the door!'

Emma unlocked it.

'It's from Mr Hepplethwaite,' he said, thrusting a brown paper bag into her hands. 'And Mrs Cooper wants to know if you have a spare candle. She says she's down to the wick in her last one.'

Sound asleep in the chair, George's lips puffed out on every breath.

'Mama?'

'I heard you, Joshua. Wait a moment.'

From the dresser drawer she sorted through the stubs of tallow.

'Take these. Tell Mrs Cooper it's all I can spare. Then hurry back.'

George Quinlan stretched out his legs, kicked at his boots and groaned.

'I'll fetch some water. You can soak them,' she said.

As Emma eased his feet from the stained boots, he grumbled. She loosened his belt. He squinted at her from one eye as she performed the ritual. She was used to it. It was a nightly chore. She always strove to make him comfortable. She wanted him to remain in his chair. Wanted him to sleep downstairs so she could go to bed alone and fall asleep out of reach of his grappling hands.

Joshua returned quietly and placed his boots in the hearth. In the firelight, his hair was the colour of polished teak.

'Mrs Cooper said, "Thank you".'

He pointed to the paper bag on the table. 'Some jam tarts! Mr Hepplethwaite said to say that you deserved a treat. And that you must call into his shop one day.'

'Hush,' said Emma, glancing at her husband. 'Please ask Mr Hepplethwaite not to send anything more,' she whispered.

'But, Mama, they're fresh.'

'I don't doubt they are!'

Lifting her skirt, Emma stepped over George's outstretched legs. Asleep, he was just another piece of kitchen furniture.

From the cooking pot she ladled a large bowl of thick white soup for her son and a smaller serving for herself.

'Tell me about your day.'

'I went to the wharf, Joshua said. 'And a sailor, from one of the sailing ships, told me about the whales. He said some are as big as a ship. And they rise out of the water to the height of a ship's mast. They can stand upright on their tails and stare at a ship from their evil eyes before falling back. And he said the sound is like the waves crashing against the West Pier. Whoosh! Splash!'

'Tall tales!'

'But it's true, Mama. And he told me that there are flat fish the shape of a serving plate but as big as this room that glide below the surface. And snakes in the sea, bright orange, and thick as a man's leg that can kill him stone-dead if he tries to grab it.'

'Goodness, son! You mustn't spend all your day gossiping. Don't let Mr Hepplethwaite catch you or you'll be for it. You must forget about ships and sailing. You are supposed to be working. You have a job now.'

'But, Mama, I was working. I took eight cartloads of flour to the jetty. And the sailor let me carry them onto the ship. Right down the ladder and into the hold. And Mr Hepplethwaite gave me a macaroon when I got back. And he asked me if I wanted to go to sea.'

'Who did? Mr Hepplethwaite.'

'No, Mama! The seaman!'

'And what did you say, pray tell?'

'I said that was what I wanted that more than anything in the world.' His exuberant smile faded. 'But I told him that I had a job with The Pie Shop. And besides, I know Father wouldn't let me go.'

'I should think not, too. Now eat your tea.'

'But he said that if I go back tomorrow, and if the captain is not on board, he'll let me climb the rigging.'

'Enough now, Joshua! Eat your tea.'

'But it's a real sailing ship. Not like the Whitby ships. And he said they needed boys like me. And maybe one day I could be a captain and have my own ship. Oh! Mama, you know it's what I want.'

'Enough of that talk, Joshua. Finish your meal.'

'But, Mama.'

'Enough!'

Emma lay awake listening to her husband stumbling around the kitchen. When finally he mounted the stairs, she counted each footfall. She knew the distinctive sound of each creaking stair. Anticipated the moment the door handle would turn.

She moved closer to the edge, closed her eyes and feigned sleep.

The bed sagged as he dropped onto it rolling her body back to his. His coal-shovel hand flopped onto her belly. She didn't move. From beneath the bedding, his sickly odour drifted into her nose.

As was her custom, she lay still, hardly daring to breathe, praying he would fall asleep, grateful that he was usually incapable of making love to her properly any more. But his lack of manhood made him angry. She knew he blamed her for his inadequacy, reminding her that she did not tend to his needs as a good wife should, lashing out at her in the darkness with his knee or foot or elbow.

But this night, unlike any other, Emma did not close herself off to his penetrating hands. This night, she relaxed. She allowed her chest to rise and fall rhythmically. Her mind was awash with thoughts of the seaman. She could see him leaning over her. She quivered to the thoughts of his touch. Breathed deeply on the memory of his briny smell.

She revisited their conversation on the cliff top, pondering on every word, wishing there were more. She recalled his gestures. The flick of his hair as he tied it. The colour of his hands as he held them out to her. She considered every minor detail, over and over again.

She wanted it to be the Frenchman lying next to her. Wanted his hands on her. Touching her. Feeling her. Such thoughts! Yet she could not make them pass. Nor wanted to. How could she feel this way for such a man? A common sailor.

George turned over dragging the bedclothes with him.

Carefully, so as not to disturb him, Emma pulled the nightdress around her shoulders and fastened the buttons under her chin. Her breasts were cold. She folded her arms across them. Her thoughts were not of sleep, but of one thing – of being with the sailor, of what might have happened in the ruins of the abbey, but didn't. Of his concern for her and of his parting words which echoed through her head: *My ship will be in port for a few days.*

She knew it was wrong, but she knew she must see him again.

Chapter 4

It was the first time Emma had ventured along the old waterfront. A compulsion to see the Frenchman had been nagging at her for several days and, despite her conscience telling her to forget the seaman, the desire to meet him had welled up to overflowing. She had to see him and speak with him, though she had no thoughts about what she would say.

Moored against the stone wharf, ketches, sloops and barks lolled on the shallow water. Further out an old collier rested on its anchor chain its seasoned sails hanging out to dry, limp and lifeless.

On the dockside, an engine clattered, slapping the air with its leather belts and shooting angry spurts of pressured steam. Barrels, near the height of a man, were rumbled over cobblestones, along swaying gangplanks and across teak decks while up above them, wooden tackle blocks swung wildly from braced yardarms. Crates and boxes caught in webs of hemp netting disappeared into the seemingly insatiable ships' holds. A mule bellowed and kicked as it was hoisted from the ground. Ducks clacked through slats in wooden boxes. A cooper's hammer thrummed. Grubby sailors gawked. It was an uninviting place. No place for a lady.

Emma pulled the plaid tightly around her shoulders and hurried on scanning the bow of each ship for its name searching for the one the Frenchman had mentioned. The name she had forgotten. Hoping that when she saw it she would remember.

Some ships looked empty. Completely stripped of cargo. On others, men hung in the web of rigging like hungry spiders. From the decks, raucous voices gave resonance to neither country nor county accents. While across the wharf, the smell of tar and linseed, stirred in iron cauldrons, drifted at nose height.

Emma wished she had not come.

The *Amelia Day* was the last vessel. Its berth marked the end of the dock. Further along, the old pier had collapsed leaving only the splintered seaweed-skirted piles protruding from shallow pools of seawater.

Emma looked across the bay. The sun had risen sufficiently to shine on the clay tiles of the newer houses at the other side of the valley. She could see the attic window of the house in Seal Street high up on the hill. On the open water, small keels and cobles swayed idly from lines bearded in weed. The pumped chords of a music box floated across the water. But behind her, the old buildings rising up from the wharf appeared even greyer than usual.

A voice called to her in a language she did not recognize. Men laughed. Faces peered. Fingers pointed. Emma quickened her pace. If only there was a rowboat to take her to the other side. She did not want to retrace her path. How foolish she had been.

A dappled grey snorted in the shafts. A pair of piglets, destined never again to see the light of day, squealed as they were lowered snout first into a ship's dark hold. A red-hot iron, dipped in a vat of seawater sizzled, alarmed a scrawny cat which fled along the quay and found refuge under an upturned boat. Emma's breath quickened as seamen, loitering on the wharf, looked furtively at her from beneath their black felt hats.

'A shilling for your purse?' one called, as he stood and cupped his crotch in a vulgar gesture. 'Five minutes o' your time. All it'll take.'

Emma turned from the voice.

'Plenty o' life in Old Tom. You'll see.'

The narrow ghaut which ran up between the buildings was not far ahead.

'Slut!' he shouted after her.

On the street, shop doorways tinkled to the sound of small brass bells. Matronly ladies stood outside gossiping while small girls in white aprons clung to their skirts. Boys, tired of pestering and tired of being ignored, climbed the metal railings of the yard opposite. Emma stopped in front of the confectioner's shop. She had to regain her breath.

Displayed in the bay window were rows of jars. Assorted sweets: gum drops, toffees, licorice. Inside the shop, tin canisters lined the shelves. Emma stood gazing at the glass but was not looking through it.

What had been going on in her head? How embarrassing it would have been if she had found the Frenchman on the dock. Imagine what a chorus of cries would have been raised from the other men – a jeering, deriding, taunting. What if George had followed her? What could she have said to justify her reason for being there? She turned from the shop window and hurried along the street.

Waiting anxiously for the old drawbridge to open, she shuddered involuntarily at the thoughts milling around in her head. The bridge linked the old town on the east with the shops, houses and busy fish market on the western side of the valley. It divided the harbour and was the only way to cross.

Stepping from the bridge's weary timbers, Emma welcomed the stench of the Whitby fleet. Blue and white cobles floated on the shallow water or rested on their sides like sleeping seals on the wet sand. Blackened nets hung web-like from half buried oars while leaning towers of crab-pots lined the quayside. No sooner was the day's haul sorted than wicker baskets, stacked with fresh crabs and lobsters, were whisked away on hawkers' carts. Fishermen, still sorting their catch, tossed fish this way and that, while rows of tables displayed the North Sea's bounty and hundreds of dead-eyes glinted in the daylight.

A score of fishwives, their aprons daubed with oil and blood, spat and argued like common gulls. Emma regarded them wistfully. They were strong women. Not soft and foolish like she was. She envied them. Envied their courage. They were victims of a spiteful sea which provided their sustenance but often claimed their menfolk in exchange. Many were wives without husbands, mothers without sons. But they survived. Emma admired their fortitude – women whose lives were ruled by the sea – a sea which they never sailed.

'Penny for them?'

Emma smiled at the old man, his knobbed fingers weaving a length of twine through a torn fishing net.

Across the harbour, the cluster of ships cradled beneath the cliff presented a pleasing picture. The picket fence of masts supported by lines of rigging reminded her of raspberry canes on a winter's morning decked in cobwebs.

'I was thinking how pretty the sailing ships looked from here,' she said.

The fisherman shrugged as he pulled another section of netting over his knee. Releasing a dead fish tangled by its gills, he tossed it back to the sea. The noisy gulls were quick to respond to the flash of silver.

Emma had seen the old salt many times before. He always sat in the same spot, surrounded by a mound of netting, or with a box of twigs beside him, busily bending the hazel wood boughs into pots for crab and lobster.

'Pull up a pew and sit yourself down,' he said. 'I could do with a bit of company.'

Emma's feet ached. It would do no harm to sit for a moment. An upturned box made a convenient seat.

No sooner had she sat down than a female voice squawked in her ear. 'You're in me road there!' the fishwife called, the smell of the previous night's haul wafting from her blood-stained hands and apron. 'If you don't shift, you'll get a pail o' guts tipped o'er you.'

'I am sorry,' said Emma, rising to her feet.

'Find somewhere else to chuck your slops,' the old salt shouted. 'You stay where you are, lass! Don't mind our Alice. Her bark's worse than her bite.'

The woman mumbled something that Emma did not hear.

'Relax yourself, lass.' The leathery skin of his weatherworn face was crinkled and dried. Emma's complexion was pale in comparison.

'It's a fine day,' she said.

'No wind,' he answered. Disappointed.

'Are you here every day?' she asked. 'I believe I have noticed you before.'

'Aye, lass. Where else would I be?'

'You never sail with the fleet?'

'With this?' he said, thumping his fist on his thigh. His leg ended at the knee where a turned wooden peg-leg sprouted from his trousers.

'I am sorry, I did not know.'

He cut another length of string and wound it into a knot.

'Do you miss the sea?' she asked.

'What sort of darn foolish question is that?' he said. 'If the sea's in a man's blood, he'd be lying if he said he didn't. Fishermen, sailors, seamen, they're all the same. The sea, she's like your mistress. Begging your pardon, miss, but once you get the taste, she won't let you go. Keeps drawing you back.'

He sighed. 'All I got is memories. And the tales the lads tell when they find the time to stop and talk. I like to listen. Listen real good, I do.' His fingers stopped working as he stared across the water.

Emma followed his gaze. 'Perhaps then, you would have heard if a French ship is somewhere in the harbour.'

He scratched at the stubble on his chin. 'Not to my knowledge, lass. Not 'less she came in last night. What name she sail by?'

'I don't know.'

As the sun cleared the cliff top, tiny flecks of metal glittered from the distant lattice of masts and spars.

'Pretty, aren't they?' Emma said.

'I suppose,' he said, taking little notice as he lifted his stump and shifted his position on the stool.

'Sailed when I was a lad,' he said, casting his eyes toward the water. 'Whales and seals were all the go in them days. Most of Whitby chasing 'em. It stopped after the *Esk* went down on Saltscar Reef. September 1826.' He sighed. 'Not more than thirty miles from home. Sixty-five brave men lost,' he said. 'I was one of the lucky ones.'

He rested his hands on the net. 'Hard work it was, but it was all a lad ever wanted to do. Aye, but that was a long while ago. Whitby ships ain't been chasing whales now for nigh on forty years, but that don't stop the young lads from getting a hankering to sail away. Some of 'em don't want to follow the 'erring. Not exciting enough. So they sign themselves up on one of them cargo ships and away they go.'

On a strip of sand, not far from the bridge, two small boys were playing near an upturned boat. The old man watched for a moment then shook his head and returned to his work. 'Often breaks their mothers' hearts. Never see 'em again once they've gone.'

Emma thought about Joshua.

Having come to the edge of the net, the fisherman dragged the section he had repaired over his knee and started again on another strip.

'Who knows what's best?' he said, sniffing the air. 'Fishing's not easy. North Sea's as cruel as any ocean. But I'd not swap it. Like I said afore, if the sea's in a man's blood, there's no getting away from it.'

A frenzied outburst by a mob of seagulls fighting over a pot of slimy fish-guts distracted the pair. It was over quickly.

'Do the ships stay in Whitby long?' she asked.

'Some do. Some don't. Depends what they're loading and where they're bound.'

'I once sailed on a ship,' Emma said cautiously.

'Like yon square riggers?'

'Yes,' she said. 'A sailing clipper – when I was a girl.' The old man stopped and watched her as she gazed across the water. 'I sailed with my family from London to Le Havre, though I believe the ship was bound for the Orient. I remember how I enjoyed the voyage. How exciting it was. The ship seemed to fly across the water. And I remember, when it was far from land with only sea and the sky around it, I asked Papa if we could sail all the way China. I will never forget it.'

The sailor laughed, 'Don't often hear a lady talk about the sea like that.'

The fishwife was standing over the pair, her fists resting squarely on her hips.

'I'm sorry,' Emma said apologetically. 'I'll move out of your way.'

'Nay, stay as you are, lass. I haven't seen Dad's chin wag so much in weeks.'

The old man winked at Emma.

'Perhaps I can come back and talk another day?'

'Any time, lass. Glad to have your company.' With that, the woman pushed a package into Emma's hand. ''Ere. There's a couple of nice haddock. Cook 'em up for your man's tea.'

'I can't take that,' Emma said.

'There's nowt wrong with 'em!'

'But I can pay you.'

'Take 'em before I change me mind!'

Emma smiled and thanked the woman bidding them both farewell and promising the fisherman that she would return and talk another day.

Unbeknown to her, behind where she had been sitting and not more than three paces away, François was leaning against a pile of crates. Emma stopped abruptly.

The pair regarded each other, their faces showing no emotion. She wondered how long he had been there and wondered if, perhaps, he did not recognize her. But surely he must. Without wishing it, a smile curled the corner of her lips.

He acknowledged it with a twinkle from his dark eyes.

To overcome her feeling of embarrassment, she spoke first. 'Good morning *monsieur*. I was admiring the ships.'

'Ah,' he said. 'And what was it about them that took your fancy, may I ask?'

'Nothing in particular, I think.'

'I thought perhaps you may have been looking for a French ship?'

He had been listening. She lifted her skirt clear of the ground and walked along the wharf. He followed her, half a pace behind.

'If I can be of assistance, *madame*, I can tell you, there are no French ships on the water at this time.'

'But you are French, are you not, Monsieur le Fevre?'

'Ah!' he quipped, coming alongside her. 'You came looking for me?'

'No! No!' she replied guiltily, 'I came to purchase some fish.' Holding out the package wrapped in paper, she could not stop her hands from shaking.

'*Naturellement*!' he replied. 'But tell me, *madame*, are you fully recovered?' An expression of concern replaced his smile.

'I am. And I thank you for your kindness.' She stopped and turned to face him. She had to ask. 'Where is your ship? What is its name?'

He pointed. 'There,' he said. 'It is in the shipyard by the sand flat they call Belle Island. You can see it from here. It has only two masts. The mainmast, it snapped in a storm. Took a good man to the bottom with it. It would have taken the ship too had we not cut the rigging.'

'So you must wait until it is repaired?'

'Yes, or sign on another ship. Some of the men have sailed already.'

'And you?'

'I think I will wait awhile,' he said, adding with a half-smile, 'I am finding this port quite agreeable.'

With a respectable distance separating them, they stood looking across the harbour to the cluster of buildings running down to the wharves on the east bank; some of the houses almost hanging over the water. Behind the rooftops, the long stone staircase of almost two hundred steps climbed diagonally up the hillside to the top of the cliff, to the parish church of Saint Mary and, beyond that, to the ruined Benedictine Abbey, silhouetted like a paper cut-out against the sky. Memories flashed through Emma's mind.

'I have stayed too long. I must go,' she said.

'Will we meet again?'

'Perhaps,' she said, offering him her hand in a gesture of gratitude.

He inclined his head and held her fingers as he spoke. 'My ship is the *Morning Star*. It will be two weeks or more before she is ready to sail.' He paused. 'I hope I will see you on the wharf another day.'

'Perhaps,' she said. 'Goodbye, *monsieur*.'

'*Au revoir, madame*.'

François watched as she wound her way between the fish stalls, around the queue of waiting carts and wagons, and across the road. He watched till she disappeared through the door of the butcher's shop.

'Nice bit o' skirt you got there, Frenchy!'

François wheeled around.

Old Tom leered at him from behind an upturned barrow.

'You mind your business!'

'Soft and warm, and tight as me fist, I reckon. Better than them loose sluts across the bay.'

François lunged toward the cart but the sailor overturned a tray of fish sending a shoal of dead herring slithering under his feet.

A gaggle of outraged fishwives scurried around, their high-pitched voices scolding and cursing.

'You touch her and I will kill you!' François yelled.

Thomas Barstow smirked. He fancied a bit of clean young flesh. What sailor wouldn't after months at sea? But this one took his fancy. Right pretty she was. Looked classy too. But not too fine to talk to a seaman. He would bide his time, and whether the Frenchman liked it or not, he would have his way with this one. That was a promise.

Chapter 5

'Spare a minute, luv, I've got something to show you.'

Emma laid down the rug she was beating. There was some urgency in Mrs Bradshaw's voice.

'Don't want to stop you doing your chores. Just thought you might like to see something.'

Emma followed her neighbour across the street into the kitchen of number 26. The heavy damask curtains were only half drawn. A musty smell of scorched cloth, wet napkins and vinegar hung on the warm kitchen air. There was little space in the room. It was crowded with furniture, particularly chairs. High chairs, several stools and straight-backed chairs in various states of dilapidation which provided additional surfaces for the piles of washing that were heaped everywhere. A thick felt pad covered one end of the large table where a pair of men's trousers lay half hidden under a damp cloth. A ball of wool and darning needles sat on top of a pile of assorted stockings. Vests in various sizes draped two large clothes horses which skirted the fender and hid the fire.

'Come in, lass. Don't be shy. Ignore the mess.'

Emma straightened her apron and brushed the dust from her face. Her nose was beginning to itch.

The matronly lady pulled a chair aside and pointed into a recess. 'There!' she said.

The corner smelled rank. A ginger cat, its fur matted into lumps, was sprawled flat against the wall. It reminded Emma of an old fox fur seasoned by moths and silverfish. As she leaned down, the cat turned its whiskers towards her, stood, arched its back, meowed then lay down again causing a burst of squeaks and wriggles. The kittens were little bigger than a nest of newborn rats.

'Born last night,' Mrs Bradshaw announced proudly. 'Though we didn't notice until this morning.

'How many?' Emma asked.

'Five, our Fred said, but I think there may be six or eight.'

'That's nice.'

Emma glanced around her neighbour's kitchen. It was the first time she had been into the house.

'Thought you might like to take one. Keep you company,' she said. 'They'll only end up in a bucket if you don't.'

'Thank you, but Mr Quinlan is not partial to animals.'

'Aye, I noticed that. Never mind,' she said, 'seeing how you're 'ere, you'd best sit down and I'll make you a nice cup of tea.'

'But, I —'

'I won't take no for an answer,' she said, swinging one of the clothes horses back from the hearth. On the grill above the fire, a large dented kettle was already steaming. She pointed to one of the piles of laundry. 'Just pop them things onto that stool yonder and sit yourself down.'

The boiling water spurted and crackled on the coals.

Emma shuffled the laundry aside and made herself a space. As she did, a small face surrounded by a mop of near white curls poked out from beneath the table. Large blue angelic eyes studied her cautiously before grasping the security of the table leg and retreating behind it. Mrs Bradshaw appeared not to notice.

'Go on, sit down, my dear.'

'Thank you.'

The washerwoman filled two tin mugs and gave one to Emma. 'Handle's a bit hot,' she warned, as she settled herself. 'Now tell me, I ain't seen you getting out much lately. Nowt up with you, is there?'

It was obvious to Emma that Mrs Bradshaw missed little of what went on in Seal Street, especially the comings and goings directly across from her front door. 'I'll get out more when the weather warms a little,' said Emma. 'What about you, Mrs Bradshaw? Are you keeping well?'

'Can't grumble.' The little girl crept to the woman's knee and tried to climb on. 'Go play outside with the others,' she said sharply. But the child would not be prized from her skirt.

'While I think on it, Mrs Cooper asked to be remembered to you, if I saw you.'

'That's nice.'

Mrs Bradshaw folded her arms and leaned her elbows onto the table.

'That lad of yours – I saw him with a barrow the other day, coming from the yard at back of the Pie Shop. Working for Hepplethwaite, is he?' She lowered her voice and leaned forward. 'Not meaning to pry, of course!'

Emma knew that anything she said would be relayed to Mrs Cooper and possibly other neighbours in the street. But in this instance Emma saw little harm in satisfying the washerwoman's curiosity. 'He's been working there for almost two weeks.'

'Thought that must be the case,' she said, satisfied. 'Said to Mrs Cooper, I did, I reckon Mrs Quinlan's lad is working at the Pie Shop.' Looking up, she blew the steam from her tea. 'Seems a shame, though, for an intelligent lad like yours to be working the barrows. Still they've all got to start somewhere, 'aven't they?'

'Indeed,' said Emma.

'But I'd be right canny of that man,' the woman warned.

'Which man?'

'Hepplethwaite, of course. Makes out he's Mister High and Mighty. Anyone would think he owned half of Whitby the way he talks.' She mopped her brow. 'I feel real sorry for his missus. Lovely lady, Mrs Hepplethwaite. Kind-hearted body, she is, and works hard too. But him – ha! I wouldn't trust him further than I could throw him!'

Emma smiled politely.

'Haven't you ever noticed when you've been in his shop, the fuss he makes of the girls and spinster ladies? Aye, and some of the married ones too!'

'Is that so?'

'Sly, he is too. I've watched 'im squeezing the women's hands when he takes the money. Gives 'em a wry smile or a wink, or he talks to 'em real quiet like.' She leaned back. 'He wouldn't dare try that sort of palaver with me!'

'Joshua is coping just fine, and he'll learn to look out for himself. He's a bright boy but, like all boys his age, he's got a bee in his bonnet about going to sea. I find it hard to understand. No sailing blood in his veins yet he seems fixed on the idea and nothing I can say is going to change his mind.'

'Well, my dear, let me give you a bit of advice. If the lad has the bug in him to go to sea, there'll be no amount of tonic will cure 'im of it. It's something as gets into their blood like a sickness and eats away at 'em until you can do nothing but let 'em go. Don't do no good to hold 'em back. No good at all. Ain't nothing to do with their upbringing or what you've learned 'em, it's just part of 'em growing into men. It's like holding a candle in a fire, sooner or later you've got to let go. I tell you, if that's what he wants – let 'im do it!'

Emma stared at the candle watching the wick curl from the molten wax into the shape of a piglet's tail. The amber flame swayed on its blue vapour base bowing towards the draught. A teardrop of hot wax trickled down the candle's stem followed almost immediately by another. The second drop faltered, stopped and hardened before it reached the holder.

The sheet of writing paper glowed in the warm light. Emma's hand rested beside it, the pen poised in her fingers. As she rolled the quill, she watched the nib's shadow rotate on the paper. Her hand was quivering slightly. She pondered for a moment, stroked the crow's feather across her cheek then dipped the sharpened nib into the ink. The writing flowed in fine copperplate scroll:

My dearest sister, Anna,

I trust you are well and Daniel and the boys. I send you all my fondest love and think of you often. How the years have flown since we were together. How I long to see you but I know that cannot be. Perhaps one day I will see you again.

Two weeks ago, Elizabeth May was taken from me. Although she was very sickly, I had prayed that she would survive. But that was not to be. Now I tell myself her death was a blessing. She was such a bonny baby.

George is well.

I am well also, though I am concerned for Joshua. He has the making of a fine young man but I fear he is becoming increasingly unhappy. George saw fit to organize a job for him, as he is now almost thirteen. George said that we could no longer afford to pay for his schooling and that it was time for him to earn his keep.

I worry about him. He is growing so quickly into manhood and has a gentleness about him which reminds me of Papa. I fear the situation he has been placed in will teach him nothing – except perhaps bad habits. He is not suited to the work and already I see a change in him. He talks constantly of the ships which visit this port and yearns to sail away. I try to discourage him for my greatest fear is that he will run away and I will never see him again.

Sometimes I feel very lonely. But I have only myself to blame. I caused Mama and Papa so many worries and brought shame on the family. If only I could have been wise and strong like you.

My dearest Anna, how I wish to see you and talk to you. If only it were possible for me to visit you. That would be my fondest wish.

But now I must close. May God bless you and keep you forever in his care.

Your loving sister

Emma

The armchair creaked as George changed his position. Saliva gurgled and caught in his throat before he sucked loudly on the air and coughed.

Emma blew gently on the sheet of writing paper then touched it lightly. The ink was dry. Carefully, she folded her letter. From one of the compartments in the writing desk she retrieved a bundle of papers tied with a fraying ribbon. She unfastened the bow and placed her letter amongst the others.

'Scribbling again?' George said, without looking at her.

'Yes,' she replied, quickly tying the bundle and returning it to the desk.

'It'll do you no good. You mark my words!'

'It'll do you no good. You mark my words.' She only meant to repeat the words in her head but they slipped quietly off her tongue before she was able to stop them. She had mocked him verbally and within an instant he was beside her.

'What was that you said?'

'Nothing,' she said, drawing her head back. 'It was nothing.'

'Nothing!'

The pot of ink remained on the bureau but with a sweep of his forearm, it skittled across the desk and settled in her lap.

'Pah! I said it would do you no good,' he gloated, hovering, as if waiting for an argument.

Hardly daring to move, Emma gave no response but within a few seconds she could feel the cold fluid trickling between her legs. Rising carefully, holding her ink-stained skirt out in front of her, she spoke politely. 'Excuse me,' she said, 'I will have to change.'

Chapter 6

The clerk peered over the rim of his spectacles, blinked at the pair and continued writing. Joshua was about to speak but Emma nudged him to be silent.

'I'll attend to you in a minute,' the man said as he continued copying details from a large journal onto a sheet of paper. When he finished, he opened the wooden shutter beside him and whistled, beckoning to one of the men on the wharfside.

A hand reached up to the sill and grasped the paper.

'*Lady Exeter* – and quick about it!' the clerk called. 'If she don't get a move on soon she'll be wallowing on the sand like a beached whale.'

Clogs clattered across the cobbles.

The clerk closed the shutter on the sea air and turned back to the desk. After running his finger down the page, he scratched his head, closed the ledger and placed it on top of an untidy pile of papers.

'Yes,' he said, looking first at Emma and then at Joshua. 'What can I do for you?'

'My son wants to go to sea. What must he do?'

The clerk pulled a rag from his pocket, spat on it, took off his spectacles and wiped them.

'Sailed before, lad?'

'No, sir.'

'Whitby lad?'

'Yes, sir.'

'Your father a seaman?'

'No, sir but I—'

Emma interrupted. 'He is strong and intelligent.'

'How old are you, lad?'

'Thirteen.'

The man reached for a box from under his desk. Lifting the lid revealed an assortment of letters and notes. Most were flat but others crumpled or folded. A few bore only smudged words jotted on the back of hand bills or scraps of paper. One note was inscribed on a small square of sail canvas. To Emma, the writing looked illegible. One sheet of ivory-coloured writing paper, half-buried in the pile, looked out of place. It was embossed with a gold crest but was of no interest to the clerk. He quickly fingered through the top-half of the box's contents ignoring the ones at the bottom. They had obviously been there a long time.

'We ain't the Royal Navy 'ere, you know!' he said, starting again from the top. 'Now, if you was a midshipman—' he added, after re-reading one. Then he closed the box and regarded the boy over the rim of his spectacles. 'Best ask around,' he said. 'That's my advice to you, lad. But if you've got a mind to go to sea—' He looked Joshua squarely in the eye, 'and I can see you 'ave, then you'd best spend some time around the ships and the men who sails 'em.'

Gazing over his spectacles, he read the concern in Emma's eyes.

'A warning though and it'll cost you nothing. There's those you'd best be keeping well clear of.' He leaned towards Joshua across the counter. 'It helps if you know a bit about a ship. I've heard tell of many a young sailor being flogged for not following the master's call, only because he didn't know the name of a line or the position of a pin on the rails.'

As he spoke, the door to the shipping office opened. The old man who shuffled in carried his back like a turtle shell. His bare neck poked forward from the remnants of his coat which hung like tattered seaweed. Emma had never seen such a stooped or bedraggled figure nor smelled anyone so rank before.

The floorboards creaked as he waddled towards the firebox where he turned and squinted at the desk from beneath a thatch of matted hair.

'Out with you!' the clerk shouted. 'How many times do I have to tell you? There's nothing for you! Not last month, not this month, not next month! You wouldn't even get pressed into service!' He shook his head.

The old seaman sniffed and hobbled out.

'We thank you for your advice,' said Emma. 'Come along, Josh.'

As they left, she slipped her hand into her son's. The wooden steps were rickety and the handrail loose. She gripped it firmly. At the bottom of the steps a group of sailors were loitering. One touched his knuckle to his brow.

'Fine day, missus,' he said.

Emma allowed herself to give a polite smile and glanced at Joshua. 'Are you all right?'

He nodded. A disconsolate look on his face.

Emma ignored his expression but accepted his arm for both comfort and support as they hurried away from the wharf area.

'I thought it would be easy,' Joshua said.

She didn't answer. 'You must get back to the shop as quick as you can. But, not one word to Mr Hepplethwaite about where you were or what you were doing.'

'But what will happen now, Mama?'

'In all honesty, I do not know, Josh. We'll talk tonight.'

'But, Father—?'

'He's away for two nights.'

Joshua hesitated.

'Hurry now. Off with you!'

As he ran, he glanced back once and waved, but the street was busy and he was soon lost amongst the pedestrians, carts and carriages.

'Madame Emma Quinlan!'

Emma turned, flushing slightly when she recognized the voice. '*Monsieur*,' she replied.

The sailor inclined his head respectfully. 'I fear you were looking for that elusive French ship again. No?'

The glint in his eye belied the serious look on his face.

Emma could not hide her thrill of delight and smiled broadly. 'You have followed me?'

'I cannot deny it. But tell me truthfully, what were you looking for this time on the wharf?'

'My son wants to go to sea. Like all Whitby boys, he wishes to follow in the footsteps of Captain Cook.' She shook her head. 'I accompanied him to the shipping agent's office to enquire about a ship.'

'I will find him a ship if he wants one.'

'What do you mean?'

'I mean, *madame*, there are plenty of ships sailing in and out of Whitby all the time and many are in need of extra hands. In fact, I've just signed to sail this evening.'

Emma's heart sank. 'You are going already?'

'*Madame*?'

'I thought you said the *Morning Star* was being repaired and it would be two weeks before it was ready to sail.'

The Frenchman looked into her eyes. 'Ah! You have not forgotten.'

She looked away.

'What you say is correct. My ship is waiting for a new mast. One has already been floated across the harbour, but it will be a few days before it can be stepped and then it must be rigged. As this will take some time, and as I am becoming bored with doing nothing, I have signed on another vessel. It sails tonight for Rotterdam with a cargo of alum and leather.'

'Across the North Sea?'

'Of course! It is not far. If the wind is fair it will take only a week and I will be back before my ship is ready to sail.'

Though she tried, it was impossible for Emma to hide the disappointment she was feeling.

'You must understand,' he explained, 'a seaman goes crazy if he is on land too long. Besides, a man needs a little extra money for ale and – other things.'

They walked in silence towards the fishing harbour.

'Tell me, François,' she said. 'What is the cost of a passage to North America?'

'That is long voyage!'

'I know it is a long way, but what I wish to know is the cost of such a journey.'

'And, may I ask, who is hoping to make this journey?'

A wagon loaded with coal, veered towards the pair. As François pushed the horse's blinkered head away, a stream of French words, which Emma had never learned from her tutor, issued from his mouth. The driver, whipping his nag responded with a barrage of English curses. The voices were drowned in the rumble of wheels as the cart rolled past. The lumps of coal, scattered on the road, were quickly removed – secreted into shopping baskets or gathered up in the aprons of passing fishwives who quickly hurried them away.

'Do you know the cost?' she asked again.

'No, I am sorry.'

Her skirt brushed his legs as they walked.

'These days many people go to the Americas in search of gold, looking for a new life but I do not know what they pay for the passage. I have sailed around the globe three times but I only sail on ships which carry cargo. I have seen ships in the Thames fitted to carry people. Too many people at times, I fear.'

'But from Whitby – do passenger ships sail from here?'

He hesitated choosing his words carefully. 'Sometimes a merchant ship carries a few passengers.'

Emma's pace slowed. 'Do you know if there is such a ship in the harbour?'

He looked out across the water to the tall ships tied up along the quay.

'There is a ship which may take a lad, but—'

She stopped and waited. 'But, what?'

'It is not going to America.'

'But the man in the shipping office said there was nothing for my son.'

'What would he know? Every ship that sails needs men!' He paused. 'The ship I speak of will take him to Australia. From there he'll have to find another ship to take him to America. But if he is fit and strong and if he learns quickly and does what he is told, it will cost him nothing. Trust me,' he said. 'When I return, I will find your boy a ship.'

'And me?' she said cautiously. 'Will there be a ship for me?'

'You, also?'

'Yes, François. A ship for me!'

The folds of serge between them hid their hands. She felt his fingers touching hers and tingled to the pressure of his squeeze.

'When I get back,' he said. 'I will find a ship for you also, I promise.'

Dusk crept slowly down the hillside, sliding across the slate roofs to the anchorage in the valley below. The still water of the inner harbour reflected the gilt-edged clouds of evening. A ship, its dark sails hanging loosely drifted seaward on the combined flow of the outgoing tide and the River Esk's current. It swam past Scotch Head and Collier Hope, past the East Pier with its new lighthouse and the treacherous rocks of The Scaur behind it, till it nosed out beyond the West Pier wall and finally met the North Sea. There it pitched and rolled, swinging its tall masts like an inverted pendulum.

Shivering in the attic, Emma watched sailors, the size of ants, scrambling out along the yardarms releasing sails. On the deck others hauled on lines at the pin rails. She watched the sails drop, luff, flap then fill and witness the dull canvas turn gold as it caught the dying rays of day. Within moments a line of white water streaked from the ship's bow while above the deck, the yards moved around in unison then slowly, almost imperceptibly, the vessel turned its head towards the east. The ship that was carrying the Frenchman was leaving Whitby. It was heading to the Continent. To Rotterdam.

It felt like a long week although, filled with the preparations for going away, each day went quickly. Emma sorted, mended and ironed. The tub was full for three whole days and she was aware her constant excursions to the washing line would have been noted by her neighbour and the news, no doubt, relayed to Mrs Cooper up the street. She didn't mind. Her only concern was George. But he showed no interest in the increase in her daily chores.

François had said he would be back in a week. Now the week was gone and everything was ready. Joshua's clothes were stored away, all neatly pressed and folded. His bag, made from a length of heavy calico, was finished too. Stitching it had made her fingers bleed but, as he had no sea chest, it had to be strong. She hoped it would suffice.

Her own clothes were ready too. Day dresses, washed and aired and hung up in the wardrobe. Her other things folded neatly in drawers perfumed with the scent of last year's lavender. George never noticed them or the large tapestry bag she had found beneath the blankets at the bottom of the wardrobe. The mice had chewed a hole in one corner but it was easily patched. She hoped it would be big enough as the wooden case was too heavy for her to carry.

Hidden from view, her hat box had been pushed against the wall on the top of the wardrobe but she had not forgotten it. She fetched a stool from the kitchen and lifted the box down. A shower of dust particles floated down with it and as she untied the ribbon and lifted the lid, she sneezed.

Inside the round box was her apricot bonnet, rucked with cream frills and trimmed with feathers and long brown ribbons. She had forgotten how pretty it was. It had matched the dress she had worn to her sister's wedding. What a wonderful day that had been. She laid it carefully on the bed. Beneath it was a lace veil, edged with tiny pearls, each delicate bead sewn so carefully the stitching could not be seen. It was her grandmother's wedding veil, handed down to her but she had never worn it.

At the bottom of the box was a pair of dancing shoes, blue ones made from the softest suede. As she turned them over they reminded her of her first ball. They had lain in the box since she and George had moved to the house in Seal Street but now her feet had grown too broad to wear them. Feeling around the box's satin lining she found a small silk purse. It was black and heavily beaded with a drawstring cord. Though it contained something solid, she neither opened it nor held it for long, but sighed and returned it to the hatbox. She replaced the shoes and veil and carefully laid the bonnet over them. After closing the lid, Emma tied the ribbon and returned the hat box to the top of the wardrobe.

When her passage was arranged, she knew she must take only clothes that would be comfortable and practical. Most of her clothes were suited to the Yorkshire weather and were mainly smart and respectable though they were now showing signs of age. She had heard it was hot in the new colony but she was not aware of what the ladies wore in those climates.

Over the past week, apart from her attire, Emma had given no thought to life in New South Wales. For the first time she wondered what she would do. How would she live if she were alone? How would she support herself? Had she imagined that François would be with her? Supporting her? How foolish to consider that! He said he would never leave the sea. Or would he? But surely in a country rich in wool and gold, where land was cheap and plentiful, there would be ample opportunities for an intelligent woman. She could offer her services as a lady's companion, a governess or teacher. She was not afraid.

A cold dampness crept over her skin. It was apprehension. Why had she not thought of these things before? Had she been blinded by her desire to get away and by her infatuation with the Frenchman? Perhaps. But the decision was made. If she stayed with George her life was over. She would become old before her years, and she would be lonely. She visualized her name daubed on a wooden cross that Mr Reginald G. Beckwith had hammered into the wet clay on the cliff top.

François had promised when he returned from Holland he would find Joshua a ship. It would break her heart but, as her neighbour said, she must let him go and pray one day they would meet again, somewhere. After that she would bide her time. François would find a ship for her and when he did, she would be ready. For Emma, waiting was the hardest. Waiting alone without Joshua would be even worse.

It was now more than two weeks since François had sailed for Holland and there was still no word from him. If Emma had known the name of the local trading ship she could have enquired about it at the agent's office. But she didn't know. She hadn't asked him and she was angry with herself. François had said it was bound for Rotterdam, but many ships sailed to ports across the North Sea. When she overhead talk of ships being frozen in the Baltic Sea ice, she grew anxious.

She did not even know if he had sailed on an English ship. What if it was Dutch? Perchance it would not be returning to Whitby but sailing from Holland to the East Indies? It could be a year before François returned, if indeed he ever returned at all.

Despite trying to busy herself to keep her mind occupied, she could not stop the stream of questions continually flowing through her brain. François had seemed kind, caring, but could she trust him? He had promised to help her, but should she believe a sailor's promises?

Joshua's frustrations made matters worse. Every day he pestered her about the Frenchman's whereabouts asking why he had not come back. For the first time, their voices were raised against each other and Emma worried that George would overhear their conversations. Above all else, he must not find out what she was planning.

As the days went by, Emma found it hard to eat, to work or concentrate. She felt tired but could not sleep. She stayed in the house, not wanting to be drawn into conversation with anyone, especially her neighbour.

But despite the disappointment that François had not returned, Emma's resolve to leave Seal Street was still strong. If the French seaman was not back within a fortnight, she must find some other way to leave Whitby.

Chapter 7

'Get a move on, boy! I ain't paying you for gas-bagging!' Hepplethwaite yelled.

Joshua dragged another bag of flour from the stack in the corner of the cellar, hoisted it to his shoulder and lumbered up the ramp into the daylight.

Zachariah Solomon, a lanky youth, was waiting by the handcart in the alley. 'Fat, old get! Couldn't even lift one!' he said under his breath.

Though he didn't realize it, his employer was listening.

'What did you say? Don't give me any of your lip, boy! A good hiding is what you need!' But when the youth stood up, the baker, who was shorter than him by several inches, edged backwards.

'You should think yourself lucky you got a job with me. As for you, Quinlan, with your hoity-toity ideas – perhaps you'd prefer to be polishing jet in one of them workshops or spending all your day salting herrings down on the wharf. Mark my words, if it weren't for that pretty mother of yours, you'd not have a job with me.' Curling his finger through his whiskers, the proprietor smirked. 'Tell me,' he said, 'When's your father got business away again?'

Joshua dropped the sack. 'You stay away from our house!' he shouted.

Albert Hepplethwaite sniggered, but as Joshua lunged towards him the shopkeeper hastily retreated up the steps into the bakery's shop quickly shutting and locking the door behind him.

'Not worth cracking your knuckles on,' Zac said. 'Forget him!'

'I hate him and his job!' Josh said, planting the toe of his boot into the bag of flour. The impact left a powdered dent but fortunately didn't split the canvas.

The delivery they were loading consisted of ten bags of flour, five of sugar, five bags of oats, four of salt, one cheese, four pounds of butter and a large jar of gooseberry jam.

'Where do I take it?' Joshua asked when the cart was loaded.

'Across the bridge. Mr Charlton's tea shop is on Sowerby Lane. It runs up from Church Street. You'll find it. Go to the yard round the back and if you're lucky, his missus might give you a bun or something for your trouble.'

Standing between the barrow's shafts, Joshua lifted the load and pushed. The cart rolled easily down the alley, one wheel on either side of the gutter.

When he started running, he heard Zac calling, 'Don't be in rush. When you get back, tell old 'Epplethwaite the drawbridge was up and that you had to wait. He'll be no wiser.'

The rumble of the wheels echoed through the gloom between the tall buildings but, at the end of the alley, the sun was shining. Rounding the corner, Joshua was on the harbour front. Ahead of him and sailing close to the wharf was a gaff-rigged boat. With the tide flooding the inner and outer harbours, it was taking advantage of the inflow and sailing upstream.

Dodging the other traffic, Joshua kept pace with it. Ahead was the old drawbridge which divided the inner and outer harbours. The iron cogs grated noisily as the heavy bridge timbers rose slowly to let the boat pass. Joshua settled his cart at the back of the gathering crowd knowing he would have to wait. It was the only bridge across the River Esk.

Leaning against his load, Joshua regarded the crowd especially the group of chattering women, their heads moving up and down like chickens pecking at grain. In contrast, an old weathered fisherman hardly moved an inch. He stared straight ahead as if gazing across an empty sea. He also watched a girl's frustrated efforts as she attempted to make a top spin on the uneven ground, and a talkative nanny oblivious to her charge screaming in the perambulator.

An empty wagon rumbled up to the bridge clearing a track between the pedestrians. When the blinkered horse snorted, Joshua eyed it warily and moved aside, afraid the animal might kick or try to bolt.

'Whoa! Nellie. Quiet girl!' the driver called securing the brake before jumping down and placing a nosebag over the mare's head. The horse responded to the oats, shaking the contents in the bag and chomping on them greedily.

As soon as the bridge thudded down, the crowd that had congregated was eager to cross. Children ran. Mothers shouted after then. Women carrying wicker trays of fish clattered across in wooden clogs. The drivers cursed.

Joshua waited till the wagon and a rig and pair had moved off before he got behind his cart. He wasn't going to take a chance. The bridge wasn't wide enough for all of them together. But he knew he must hurry. Because of the delay caused by the bridge, he had no other excuse to offer to Mr Hepplethwaite if he was late. Head down, arms outstretched, he leaned into the cart and pushed. He remembered the tea shop. He had passed it many times. It wasn't far away.

Mr Charlton was on the pavement outside his door. A flock of pigeons, cooing on the cobbles in front of him, were pecking at the meal of crumbs he had thrown for them. When Joshua approached, a pair of seagulls dived, squawking aggressively, their necks and beaks extended, intimidating the smaller birds.

Mr Charlton lashed out at the pair with a broom, but each time he repelled one, the other bird swooped. From the safety of the rooftops the pigeons watched the battle. It continued until all the crumbs were gone.

Distracted by the birds, Joshua didn't see the pothole until one of the cart's wheels dropped into it. The barrow stopped dead, wrenching the shafts from his hands. He grabbed it and fought to hold it upright before it toppled over, but the jolt dislodged the stack and the jar, which had been nestled on the top, slid towards him. He reached for it but missed and watched it fall and break into a dozen pieces, the yellow jam splattering in a sticky mess between his feet.

'You can't go throwing good jam around like that,' the rotund man commented.

'It was an accident. It just fell off. I swear.'

Mr Charlton didn't seem too concerned by the loss. He certainly wasn't angry, though Joshua expected Mrs Charlton would be cross. Naturally, the storekeeper would refuse to pay for the jam. There would be no reward for the delivery and, because of the delay at the bridge, he was going to be late back to the Pie Shop. Then he would cop abuse from Mr Hepplethwaite for taking his time, and for breaking the jar. No doubt, he would have to pay for the breakage, and if he had no wages to take home on Friday, he would likely get a thrashing from his father.

Joshua's head was spinning. He hated the job. He hated Hepplethwaite. He hated his father. He wanted to sail away to the Indies or America and wanted to leave all this far behind.

'Damn! Damn! Damn!'

'Calm down, lad and less of your blaspheming!' Mr Charlton cried. 'A paddy will get you nowhere. Follow me around to the back and we'll get this stuff unloaded. It will only take two ticks.'

'What about the gooseberry jam?' Joshua asked.

'Don't worry about that. You go round to the yard.'

Mr Charlton was an understanding man, but he was also pitifully slow. Joshua wanted to throw off the stores by the door and be gone as quickly as possible. But the shopkeeper insisted everything be carried inside under his supervision and stacked away carefully into its rightful place.

As soon as the job was finished, Joshua was off and running. Back to the river and the bridge, hanging onto the cart as it bounced along, lurching from side to side. The main street, on the west side of Whitby, was crowded with pedestrians. Joshua tried to snake between them but his pace was slowed, at times, almost to a stop.

'Stop, boy!' A voice cried and a hand tightened on his shoulder.

Joshua stopped and spun around. The accent was foreign.

'Are you François?' he asked.

'Yes. And you are Joshua?'

'How did you know that?'

'I saw you once with you mother on the wharf. Tell me where I can find your mama. I must speak with you both. I have news of a ship.'

'She's at home,' Joshua panted. 'Number twenty-nine, Seal Street.' The sweat was running into his eyes.

'I see you are in a hurry,' François said. 'I will help you and then you will take me to your house.'

Joshua's legs dangled from the front of the barrow as the seaman ran along the street pushing with all his strength. Holding tight to the sides, Joshua bounced up and down while urging the sailor to go even faster.

François slowed as they turned into the alley and stopped at the shop's back entrance. It was quiet and empty and there were no customers in the Pie Shop. Mrs Hepplethwaite said her husband was out and that Zac had just left with the last delivery for the day. She had not missed Joshua and when François told her the boy was needed urgently on the wharf – a matter of life or death – she willingly let him go.

Despite feeling guilty, Joshua said nothing about the gooseberry jam, and when they were about to leave Mrs Hepplethwaite called him back.

'Here,' she said, handing him a scone with a wedge of butter on the top. 'And take one for the Frenchman.'

Joshua thanked her and winked at François. His sailor's charm had worked a treat.

'Mama! It's me!'

Emma looked up from her needlework. 'Josh, don't shout! What is the matter?'

'The sailor wants to speak with you.'

Emma hesitated.

He repeated, 'François, the French sailor, he's waiting outside.'

'François has come back?' she cried. But the frisson of excitement was short-lived. 'He cannot come in, Josh! Tell him to go away! Tell him I will meet him somewhere else.'

'But, Mama, there is a ship! And it is sailing on Wednesday!'

'But I dare not let him in—'

'Mama! He must speak with you urgently! Let me bring him in.'

Emma looked around the room trying to clear her thoughts. George was away. He would never know. 'All right. Just for a moment.'

Outside the window she heard a shrill whistle, then footsteps and muffled voices. She glanced at herself in the mirror and noticed the colour had drained from her cheeks. Her shaking hands reminded her that what she was doing was wrong.

François inclined his head politely, as he walked into the room.

'Please come in, *monsieur*. Joshua, close the door quickly.'

Before Emma had time to offer him a chair, François spoke, 'I did not know where to find you,' he said, shaking his head. 'I have been looking for you for three days – on the fish wharf, in the markets, even at the abbey on the cliff top. I thought perhaps you had changed your mind.'

'No, not at all. But after so long, I thought you were not coming back.' She could feel herself flushing and sat down.

Joshua was watching her keenly.

'My son tells me you have news of a ship.'

'*Madame*—,'

She interrupted him: 'My name is Emma.'

'*Madame*, my ship, the *Morning Star*, is sailing this week for the colony of New South Wales. I have spoken with the mate and it is possible your boy can sign for the voyage.'

Joshua grabbed François' hand. 'Thank you, François! Thank you!'

Emma put a finger to her lips. 'One moment, Josh.'

François had not finished. He turned to Emma. 'You must write a letter for the ship's master, stating his age and saying you permit him to join the vessel. You can write, can't you?'

Emma nodded.

François turned to Joshua. 'Wait for me by the drawbridge in the morning. I will find you and take you to the ship. The mate will speak with you and unless he finds you disagreeable, he will sign you on as one of the ship's boys. Do you understand?'

'Yes, sir.'

'Do you have a hammock?'

'No.'

'A knife?'

'No.'

François shook his head. 'You must have a knife. A good sharp knife. You cannot borrow another man's. But we will speak about that tomorrow. Now I must talk with your mother.'

Joshua's eyes glistened as he shook the Frenchman's hand. 'François, I can't thank you enough. And you, Mama,' he said, throwing his arms around her. 'Now, I must get back to the Pie Shop. I must see Zac and tell him.'

Emma stood beside the seaman as her son dashed from house. The clap of his boots on cobbles echoed down the street.

François reached out for Emma's hand. 'May I?' he said, before he laid a kiss upon her fingers.

Her smile was sad. Tomorrow Joshua would be gone. And François too.

Drawing her towards him, he slipped his arm around her waist and touched his lips to hers. It was a shy and gentle kiss and it stirred in Emma a memory of a love she had experienced once before. She smiled involuntarily and closed her eyes. How strong his arms were. Protective. Reassuring. His smell was of the sea. His body drawn close against hers was firm and warm.

'And me?' she whispered, leading him to the chair. 'Is there a place on your ship for me?'

'Emma,' he began, 'the *Morning Star* is not built for passengers. It is built to carry cargo.'

She looked away. In the hearth, the fire was dying though a few smouldering red embers still glowed in the ashes.

'Besides,' he said, 'the ship is old, Australia is a long way away, and the passage can be hard for those who do not usually sail the oceans.'

'But will you take any passengers or only crew and cargo?'

She waited for his reply.

'I cannot lie. On this voyage we will have one passenger. I only know this because his baggage arrived at the dock this morning. So many trunks and boxes for one man. More luggage than all the crew together.'

'But if there is accommodation for a passenger, why can't I also sail with the ship.'

'It would not be suitable. There will be no other ladies aboard and sailors are not to be trusted. It would not be right for you to travel alone.'

'But you and Joshua will be there. I would ask for nothing more. I require little space. And I can occupy myself during the voyage. I can take books and needlework.'

'Emma, you must hear what I am saying. I know something of the master's nature, enough to know he would not take a woman on board for fear of the trouble it may cause. Many seamen think women bring bad luck to a ship, like a Jonah. And besides, seamen do not have the best of habits and there are things a lady should not be privy to.'

She stirred the embers with a twig. It caught alight. 'Would you wish for me to sail with you, François?'

'That I would wish more than anything, but—'

'And tell me, does the captain not like women?'

'I expect he does. He is a man. A married man.'

'Then please,' she begged, 'if you have any feeling for me, speak with him and ask that he allows me to sail on his ship.' Her eyes filled with tears. 'François,' she begged, 'I cannot remain here. If I do, I fear I will die.'

He kissed her hair and held her close to him.

'Tomorrow your boy will join the ship. The following day is Wednesday. We sail on the tide, at five o'clock in the afternoon. Come to the ship at four. Can you do that?'

'Yes,' she said, her breathing shallow. 'My husband is away and not expected to return until Thursday. I will come to the shipyard by Belle Island on Wednesday afternoon at four.'

He sighed. 'No. The ship will not be there. She is leaving the yard today when the water is high. She will dock on the outer harbour wharf just beyond the drawbridge. Do you understand?'

Emma nodded.

'When you find the ship, *Morning Star*, you must ask for me, Frenchy. That is the name the men call me. I will be busy, as we will be preparing to sail. You must wait on the wharf. Do not try to come on board. Wait there until I come to you.'

She nodded again.

'One more thing. I will not be free to help you with your baggage. Can you manage alone?'

'Yes. I will manage.' She smiled, 'I cannot thank you enough for what you are doing for Joshua and me.'

But his smile had disappeared and a grave expression crossed his face.

Resting her hands on his, she felt a degree of tenseness in him. 'What is it, François? You are worried.'

'It is nothing,' he said. 'Remember – come at four o'clock on Wednesday. We sail at five.'

That evening Joshua was fired with excitement and talked non-stop. Emma had finished her meal while his plate was still full. As they sat together, they spoke of ships and ports and the Antipodes, and wondered what life would be like far from the cold of a Whitby winter.

By the light of the lamp, Emma wrote a letter. She addressed it to the *Captain of the ship, Morning Star*. It would have been more respectful if she had known his name, but in her excitement she had once again failed to ask François for that detail.

In the letter, she stated she was the mother of Joshua Quinlan and that she gave permission for her son to sail. That he was thirteen years of age and there was nothing which prohibited him from joining the crew. She thanked the Captain for providing her son with the opportunity of going to sea and assured him that he was a God-fearing boy, educated to a good standard in reading, writing, algebra and geometry and that he was willing and eager to work and learn. She added that he would follow the orders given to him.

She signed the letter *Emma Quinlan*, adding the title – *Mrs*, which she enclosed in brackets. She blotted it, folded it in half then half again and placed the letter in an envelope. She closed it with a dab of red sealing wax and handed it to her son.

'You must not forget to put it in your pocket in the morning.'

'Yes, Mama.'

From the chest of drawers in the attic bedroom, she took the items she had prepared for Joshua. His clothes, all washed, ironed and folded neatly including his trousers freshly steamed, a jacket sponged and pressed, a muffler, gloves, a spoon and fork and knife, a tin plate, mug, two slabs of soap, and a comb.

Joshua's stuffed the clothes into the calico bag Emma had sewn for him, but she was concerned. It held so little. Would he have sufficient? What else would he need? She was concerned. She'd heard tales about the types of men who came ashore from ships. Heard they were hard, crude, sometimes cruel, and often dirty. She reminded Joshua about cleanliness, manners and that she would be there if he needed her.

'Mama!' he said. 'I am not a boy. Tomorrow when I join the ship, I become one of the men. A ship's boy maybe, but one of the crew.' He took his mother's hands in his. 'And if I am to get on, I must know the ship. I must learn the names of every rope and sheet and how to furl a sail. I can only learn this from the sailors. I must work hard like them and I must talk like them. But Mama,' he said, 'I will not become like them. You have taught me everything I know. But the things I need to learn now, I can learn neither from you nor books. Trust me, Mama, now I will learn as I see fit.'

The tears flowed down Emma's cheeks. He had grown up and she had not noticed. 'I love you, Joshua,' she said.

It was cold when he left the house. The sun had not yet come up. Emma hugged him. And cried again. It was as though he was leaving forever, yet she would see him again the following day.

'Take this,' she said, pressing a cold coin into his hand. Joshua's eyes widened at the sight of a half sovereign in his palm.

'Don't let anyone see it,' she whispered. 'You must buy a hammock and knife. François says every sailor must have a sharp knife.'

Joshua looked at the gold coin. 'Mama, you will need this.'

'Take it, Joshua. Speak with François. He will help you.'

'I will,' he said, pulling the cloth cap down over his ears and tucking the muffler underneath his collar.

'God speed,' she whispered. For a moment they held each other close then she watched as he strode proudly down the street balancing the bag on his shoulder.

Emma waited hoping he would turn and wave but before he reached the corner, his step quickened and he headed down the hill towards the harbour and was lost from view.

The day was long. The evening even longer.

As Joshua had not returned that morning, Emma presumed he had joined the *Morning Star*'s crew. She thought about him constantly and thought about François too, and felt lonely.

Her clothes, sorted into neat piles covered the kitchen table. She had gone through them numerous times, choosing some, discarding others then changing her mind.

She had decided on two dresses. Pretty ones. Also the serge skirt and the blue merino. Three silk blouses, two frilled aprons, and a lace shawl. She would wear her everyday grey skirt and white linen blouse to travel in. And a bonnet of course. On her feet, the laced boots she wore for walking.

By the time everything was in the bag it was difficult to fasten. She was glad she had found the tapestry bag but even that would be heavy as it was a long walk to the ship but the wooden suitcase would have been unmanageable.

She decided to wear the plaid shawl. It kept her warm and no doubt evenings on the water would be cold. Besides, the shawl would serve as an extra blanket on the ship if she needed one.

As the fire died, she contemplated writing a letter, telling George she was going away. But what could she say except goodbye. He would discover soon enough that she was gone. And Joshua gone too. She shuddered at the thought of her husband's temper. She was fearful of his anger. But soon she would be far away and she was never coming back.

The staircase creaked as she paid her final visit to the attic. The empty cradle was still standing against the wall. From the window she looked down upon the town. The moon had not yet risen. Lights twinkled from street lamps and kitchen windows. Across the valley, the East Cliff merged with the darkness of the sky. Beyond the cliffs the North Sea looked black and uninviting. If any sailing ships were out there, she could not see their lights. As she listened she could faintly hear the Whitby bell drumming out its warning.

But the following evening everything would be different. She would be safely aboard the ship and, as it swam between the stone piers, she would hear the harbour bell plainly. Then she would feel a surge as the sails filled and the ship lifted. And she would stand on deck and watch the Whitby lighthouses till they were but specks in the distance. And she knew she would rejoice.

The parlour clock chimed three. Emma paced the floor. It was almost time to leave. Despite having damped the fire, she was feeling very warm beneath all her clothing. But there was no time to change and she still had three things to attend to.

From the top of the wardrobe she retrieved the battered hat box. Feeling beneath the bonnet and beaded veil, she found the satin purse. Her fingers closed around it. Quickly she dropped it into her skirt pocket, replaced the hat box and returned to the kitchen. With the needle she had already threaded, she sewed a line of stitches across the opening in her pocket. The small bulge it made was hidden in the folds of material.

From above the writing desk she reached for the picture framed in oak and lifted it carefully from the nail. A ghostly outline, drawn by dust and insect webs, marked its hanging place. She laid the picture face down on the table. It was not difficult to slit the brown backing paper. It tore away easily. Beneath it, a row of tiny nails secured the wooden backboard. When she lifted it, the drawing paper curled from the glass. She turned it over and looked at it. The pen and ink.

Using the brown paper to protect it, Emma rolled the picture and tied it with a piece of ribbon. Opening the tapestry bag for the final time, she eased the package beneath her clothes.

Finally, from the bureau she took several sheets of writing paper and the quill. She would not chance the ink.

Now she was ready.

The air on the dock was dank and smelled of fish. There was little movement on the harbour. The bustle of the day was over. Some seamen lazed on the dockside, others on the decks of ships, talking, smoking, playing cards.

Her arms and shoulders burned from carrying the heavy bag. She knew she must find François and his ship before it was too late. She did not feel afraid.

As she hurried along the wharf, she checked the name of each vessel hoping to see the words *Morning Star*. But the ship was not there and she had reached the end of the wharf. She turned, retraced her steps, conscious of the time.

Where was it? Still in the yard where it was repaired? Should she go there to look for it? But it was a long way and there was not enough time. The worry was tightening her throat. She was feeling exhausted. The bag slipped from her shoulder and fell to the ground. A seaman leaning against the wall in the shadows called out: 'Are you looking for a ship?'

'Yes,' she said, 'the *Morning Star*.'

'Sorry, Miss,' he answered. 'The *Morning Star*'s not here. She sailed no more than an hour ago.'

Chapter 8

It was a long walk home. The longest Emma could remember. The hill was steeper, the cobbles harder, the late afternoon chill, colder. The ship had gone. So too had François and Joshua. And with them her last chance for escape.

The bag weighed heavily on her arm.

When passing a group of women gossiping in the alleyway, Emma hid her face beneath the rim of her bonnet and hurried by. Although they were strangers to her, she felt sure their conversation was about her and sensed their eyes directed at her. Her imagination was playing tricks.

Her head was buzzing. Had Mrs Bradshaw seen her leave? Would her neighbour be watching for her return? Would she guess where she had been? If so, what juicy gossip she would be able to pass on to her friend.

Why had she allowed herself to be swept along on this irrational infatuation? A whim? A hope to step out of the hum-drum of daily life and escape to the other side of the world? A fanciful dream to live an idyllic life with a common sailor in a faraway land? Happily ever after!

Thank goodness she had told no one. How they would laugh. Deride her. Call her a fool. Thank goodness only François and Joshua knew her intentions. And now they were gone, hopefully, no one else would know.

Two bare-foot urchins ran down the hill, knocking the bag from her arm.

'Slow down!' she called.

They ignored her, laughed and ran on, their feet padding softly along on the paving.

It's getting cold, she thought. *I must get home. The kitchen will be warm.* She had damped the fire before she left but, if she was lucky, it would still be alight.

When she got home she must first unpack the tapestry bag. Put all the clothes away. Hide all signs of her misadventure.

Thank goodness George had gone away.

The steps up the ghaut from Pawson's Alley were steep but it was better to go that way than walk up the length of Seal Street. This way was quicker and she was less likely to be seen.

Her shoulders ached. Her legs were sore. She sniffed pipe tobacco swirling across the street. An old man was sitting on his doorstep.

He nodded, 'Evening.'

'Evening,' Emma replied.

The bowl of tobacco glowed as he drew on it.

She hurried along, shielding her face beneath her bonnet. Hoping her neighbours were indoors, hoping the children wouldn't tell, hoping this unfortunate venture would soon be forgotten.

She stopped dead in her tracks when she saw the house door was open. She remembered shutting it when she left. Perhaps Joshua had not sailed after all. Perhaps he had come home.

Her breathing quickened. Through the window she could see a lamp flickering. But the curtains were not drawn and Joshua always drew them before dark. And he always closed the door.

Her heart was pounding. George had returned a day early!

As she stood, framed in the doorway, he eyed her, his features exaggerated by the dark shadows cast from the lamp. He was sitting at the table – leaning forward, fists clenched, knuckles criss-crossed with streaks of dried blood. Scattered in front of him were slivers of wood – all that remained of the picture frame. The sharp fragments of broken glass glinted in the yellow light.

'I didn't expect you home this evening,' she said.

His fist thumped the table bouncing the fragments of glass like hail on frozen ground.

'I can see that!'

She put the bag down.

'Tell me, woman, where do you think you were going?' His voice was low and controlled.

She closed the door quietly, unfastened her bonnet and hung it on the hallstand.

Both fists came crashing onto the table. She jumped.

George rose. The muscles in his jaw were twitching. 'Fetch that here!' he shouted, pointing to her luggage.

''Tis only a few old things,' she said, trying to disguise the falter in her voice. 'I was taking them to the rag man. I thought I might get a few shillings for them. The extra money would be useful.'

Splinters of wood and broken glass flew from the table as he swept his forearm across it.

'Fetch it here!' he bellowed.

Emma did as she was bid but before she reached the table, he grabbed it from her tearing at its fastening.

'Old clothes,' she whispered.

George ripped the contents from the tapestry bag, tipping her dresses onto the floor. His lips were quivering. 'Old clothes!' he shouted, flinging a silk blouse across the room. 'Old clothes!'

Emma's hand was on the chair. She was shaking. 'I was going to visit my sister.'

'Your sister? Huh! A moment ago it was the rag man!' The slap of his hands on the table scared her. 'You liar! You were running away!' He grabbed her nightshirt and threw at her face. 'Where is he, this fancy man of yours?' His pitch was rising. His sneer contemptuous. 'Let you down, did he?'

Emma backed away. She was afraid because this time he was sober.

'How dare you try to leave me? Make me into a laughing stock? How dare you?'

She never saw his fist. Hardly felt it. It was the second blow which threw her backwards to the floor, thudding her head against the wall. Before she could move he was standing beside her kicking his boot into her ankles.

She curled her arms across her face, drew up her legs and waited. When he stopped, he turned and tipped the bag's remaining contents onto the table. A scroll of drawing-paper was amongst them.

Unrolling it, he held it out at arm's length, laughed sickeningly, then tore it in half. Then again, and again, tossing the tiny pieces over her. The squares of paper floated down like petals from a dying rose.

The taste of blood was in her mouth. She licked it from her lips and dragged herself against the wall.

'You will go nowhere from now on! I will make sure of that!' Gathering the scattered items, he threw them into the hearth. Emma watched. One by one, slowly and deliberately, he poked her clothing in amongst the smouldering embers. She watched the silks twist, then frizzle in a burst of light. She smelt the cottons scorch, before the rush of flames consumed them. The woollens smoked and shrivelled. They were slow to burn. Everything went in. The satin gown, the black silk dress, blouses, petticoats and gloves. Finally the envelopes and paper. The fire flared and Emma closed her eyes.

It was over. His feet brushed past her skirt. She felt one final kick. The house door slammed. She listened to his footsteps die away and lay there long into the silence before she tried to move.

Her hand relaxed, her fingers stretched and reached a scrap of paper beside her on the floor. She lifted it and held it to the light. A man's face, etched in detail. The kindly eyes most striking. The pupils empty. His eyes were sightless. It was her father.

Emma's tears were silent.

'Wake up, Mama! Please, Mama, wake up!'

Emma tried to see but it was dark. The figures hovering were hazy. Was she dreaming?

'We need some light. Where is the lamp, Joshua?' It was François' voice.

She felt a hand on hers. Stroking the hair from her face. She turned her head. Only one eye would open. She touched her cheek. It felt hot and tight. It hurt. What had happened?

'Oh, Mama! I should not have gone!'

The lamp flared. She looked around. The fire had gone cold yet she was still dressed and was seated in the chair. François was kneeling beside her.

'Emma, I will not forgive myself knowing I caused this to happen to you.'

'But your ship,' she said, 'it sailed. I went to the harbour and it was gone.'

'I will explain later. Now we must get you away from here.'

The voices sounded far away and anxious. Sleep seemed an easier escape.

'You must wake up, Mama!' said Joshua. 'You must get up and try to walk.'

She raised her head and smiled at him. Her boy had come home. What more could she wish for.

A cup was pressed against her lips. 'Some water,' François said. 'Please drink a little.'

She sipped then pushed the cup away, oblivious to their quiet conversation.

'Mama, we cannot leave you here. François and I have spoken. We will take you with us but it will not be easy. Mama, you must get up! There is little time.'

François held her hands as she struggled to her feet.

'I could not find the ship,' she said apologetically.

'Hush,' said François. 'Where is your baggage?'

Emma looked towards the fireplace. 'There,' she said. 'He burned it. Everything.'

The seaman cursed, '*Mon Dieu*! I'll kill him if I find him!'

Joshua grabbed the empty bag. 'Mama,' she heard him say. 'Don't worry, I'll find some clothes for you.' She heard his footsteps on the stairs, the creaking of the bedroom floor.

'I'm cold,' she murmured.

François retrieved her shawl which had fallen by the wall and draped it round her neck. He took her bonnet and cape from the hallstand and helped her put them on. She was unable to tie the bow.

Fastening the ribbon beneath her chin, François begged her forgiveness. 'How could I do this to you?'

'You are not to blame,' she whispered, trying hard to smile when she saw Joshua appear at the bottom of the stairs.

'We must go quickly! There is no time to lose!'

Outside Seal Street was quiet. The houses were all in darkness. The light, spilling from the street lamp, formed a pale circle on the paving beneath it.

Supporting her between them, the pair hurried from the house, down the hill to the harbour then along the wharf heading in the direction of the sea. Emma's feet barely touched the ground. She did not know what time it was, save that it was late. Whitby was quiet. No one was around.

They stopped at the end of the dock. The moon, glistening on the wet sand of Collier Hope gave some light. Beneath the harbour wall was a rowing boat but it was not a Whitby boat. It had been moored to a rusted iron ring but the tide had gone out leaving it sitting on the sand. The steps down from the wharfside were crusted in cockle shells and wore a slippery coat of damp weed.

'Tread carefully,' François called.

Emma took his arm and leaned against him heavily. As she stepped down to the harbour floor she could feel her feet sinking in the sand and water seeping into her boots. François put his arm around her waist and helped her to the boat.

'Hold onto the sides,' he said. 'Do not try to stand.'

Emma clambered in and sat down on the thwart in the middle.

The French sailor quickly unfastened the line and with Joshua's help, slid the boat back across the sand and onto the narrow channel of the out-flowing River Esk. They needed little help from the oars as the river, swelled by melt-water and rain, was full. Carried along by the strong current, the boat swam passed Scotch Head and the Bulmer Street Pier. Ahead were the high walls which sheltered the Whitby harbour from the onslaught of the treacherous North Sea. The old lighthouse, like a giant Doric column, towered almost ninety feet above them on the West Pier, its bright light penetrated far out over the sea. The new lighthouse on the east side was dwarfed against it.

As they drifted between the stone walls, the surge of the sea suddenly made itself felt. Waves slapped the bow and the small boat slowed.

'Pull hard!' shouted François.

Joshua struggled with the oar.

When they rounded the West Pier, Emma glimpsed the black outline of a ship against the dark sky.

The *Morning Star* was anchored to the north-east of the main pier and less than three hundred yards from a long sandy beach. Two lights on the ship, appearing as no more than pinpricks, swayed with the swell. The two men rowed hard towards it but, though the sea was relatively calm, their progress was slow.

'When we climb onboard, you must not say a word,' François whispered.

'But—?'

'Hush, not a word!' he said. 'Once aboard, I will take you below and hide you somewhere safe. Then Joshua and I must leave. We must return the boat for the men who have gone ashore.

'But, François—'

He put his finger to his lips. 'Hush! Your voice will carry. You must be silent. No one must know you are on board and you must remain hidden for as long as I say. I will come to you later and explain. Trust me.'

Emma looked back at Joshua. She didn't understand what was happening.

'Mama, trust François,' he whispered. 'It is all that we can do. We could not leave you. It will be for the best.'

A rope ladder was dangling from the rail of the ship. François grabbed it. Their boat bumped against the hull. A moment later a head peered down into the darkness.

'Coming aboard!' François shouted.

'Who's there?'

'Frenchy and the lad.'

There was no answer. The face disappeared.

'I will go first,' François said. 'You must stand up. When the boat lifts on a wave you must take hold of the ladder as high as you can reach. Pull yourself onto it. Then climb. Do not look down. I will be at the top to help you. Joshua will steady the ladder at the bottom. Do you understand?'

Emma nodded.

The ship heaved on the swell causing the small boat to rise and fall on the passing waves. At times, despite their efforts, the boat banged against the hull, at others it swung away from the ship and swayed perilously from side to side. François gripped the ladder and climbed.

Emma was afraid to stand. Afraid to climb. The rope ladder was sliding on the ship's hull. What if she lost her grip and fell? She could not swim.

On the next wave, she tucked her skirt between her thighs, grabbed the ropes and held. Immediately, the boat dropped back into the trough and left her hanging. She could not find a foothold. Her skirt was in the way.

'You must climb!' Joshua cried.

Her arms were stiff. She kicked and felt the rope against her toe. Her legs were sore but she found a foothold and held fast. As she neared the top François grasped her wrists and pulled her up onto the deck.

'Shh!' he whispered. 'Follow me!'

He guided her aft, to an open hatch that led below. A lantern on the lower deck lit the companionway. The steps were steep. François held Emma as she turned and climbed down backwards.

At the bottom of the stairs was an oblong room with several cabin doors on either side. They were all closed. Through a hatch in the floor was another ladder, even steeper, leading deeper into the ship. They went down. It was dark. A distant pale glow barely illuminated the passageway.

François went first, bending his back near double. 'Mind your head,' he said. Emma followed bowing her head and shoulders from the heavy beams.

The air was thick. It smelled of food and men. But there was no sound except the creak of timbers.

François stopped at a small door. It was no taller than the height of a child.

'You must hide in here,' he said. 'At least for now.'

The room was black as pitch. There was no light. 'This is the best I can provide,' he said. 'When we return I will bring you a bucket and some food. You must stay in here until the ship is clear of England.'

Little bigger than a bed, the sail locker was packed with folded canvas topped with coils of heavy rope. The pile reached halfway up the door. The vacant space above it was no greater than an arm's length. Helped by the sailor, Emma crawled in on her hands and knees.

'But François, why?'

'I could not get permission for you to sail. But I had made a promise to you which I had to keep. This is the best I can do. I am sorry.'

'But what happens when the captain finds out?'

'Let me worry about that,' he said. 'Now your son and I must return the boat to Whitby. Fasten the door from the inside,' he said, 'and do not open it for anyone!'

Before she had time to speak, he closed the door leaving her in the darkness.

Chapter 9

Emma pushed the ropes to one side so she could lie flat on the stiff canvas. She could hear something banging on the outside of the ship. It sounded like someone knocking. She listened, waiting for it to stop, counting the sounds, and soon drifted into sleep.

Loud voices startled her. Men's raucous voices with strange accents. Laughing. Cursing. And the sound of feet pattering along wooden boards. A sliver of light shone through the crack around the door.

She hardly dared to breathe. How long had she slept? Did they know she was on board? Were they looking for her? Then the footsteps faded and the voices died. She could feel her heart thumping. Her hands were wet. The light outside dimmed rapidly. The blackness returned and with it the silence broken only by the rhythmical banging.

Emma settled back on her pillow of hemp rope. It was comfortably warm in the sail locker, but the air was not good. She sniffed. Salt. Tar. The acrid smell of sulphur.

What was it that François had said? She must stay hidden until the ship was clear of England. Was that possible? How long was it since François had brought her to the ship? She had slept, but for how long she did not know. She must think clearly. Did he say when he would return? She thought about George. Where had he gone when he left her? Where did he go when he stayed away? Why was he so cruel? She tried to put all thoughts of him from her mind but they would not leave her.

There was a tap on the door. She started.

'Open the door,' a voice whispered. The voice was muffled but the accent was that of François.

Untying the cord cautiously, she let the door swing open. In the dim light of a lantern, a dark figure filled the doorway. Its back appeared hunched and reminded her of the old tramp in the agent's office. She caught her breath.

'Are you all right?'

'Yes,' she said, trying to dispel her own fears.

The glow died, as François closed the door and crawled onto the canvas beside her. He touched her hand. It was too dark for them to see each other.

'I have brought a bucket and a jug of water.' His voice was little more than a murmur. 'I am sorry there is no light. But no one must know you are here. It is terrible that I have caused this to happen to you.'

Emma reached out for him in the darkness. She touched his chest. He took her hand in his and pressed it to his lips.

'I could not come sooner. I had to wait. The captain has come back onboard. And the crew also. Most of them are drunk and will sleep for a few hours until first light. Then we sail. I will come to you when I can, but it will not be easy with the men around.'

'How is Joshua?'

'He is well. And he is concerned for you.'

She felt his arm slide across her hip.

'I cannot stay,' he sighed. 'Tomorrow, I will come to you and bring some food. Two days from now, we sail into the Channel, and hopefully, two days after that the ship will be far from the coast of England. Until then you must make no sound. If you are discovered now, the captain will put you ashore.'

'I cannot go back!' she cried.

'Trust me. In a few days all will be well.'

Though it was not cold, Emma pulled the twilled cape around herself and rested her cheek into the woollen shawl. The days would pass quicker if she could sleep. After four days, the swelling round her eye would be gone. Four days and she would be far away from Whitby.

As the ship rolled, a loose barrel on deck banged against the gunnel sending the sound reverberating through the hull.

But rocked like an infant, Emma slept till the distant clanging of a bell woke her. Was it the Whitby bell? She listened, but it stopped. The rhythmic banging she had heard before had also ceased and her tiny room no longer rolled from side to side. Fearing the ship was tied up against the wharf, she listened in the blackness for familiar harbour sounds, then she realized her canvas bed was sloping to one side. It could mean only one thing – the *Morning Star* was sailing and was heading away from Whitby.

The last of the staysails had rattled up. Topmen, lying across the forecourse yard, had unlashed the gaskets. The canvas had thundered down. On deck, men had hauled on sheets and eased the lines as crumpled canvas luffed then filled. The wind was strong. The deck a litter of tangled ropes waiting to be coiled and hung neatly along the pin rails. Flying a full complement of sail, the *Morning Star* was making almost seven knots.

'Man the braces!'

Sailors scuttled across the deck.

François took the forecourse brace on the port side and waited for the call. Another seaman came up behind him ready to assist.

When all were ready, the mate looked to the master and made the call. 'Haul away!'

Working together, the sailors on the brace hauled the forecourse yard around. The other yards, hauled by other hands, moved in unison.

'Pretty package you brought on board, Frenchy!' The voice was gravely.

François craned his head around, his eyes glaring.

'Got it well hidden, 'ave you?'

François could not release his grip or he would lose control of the yard. But he knew the voice. And the smell.

'Like to give Old Tom a taste of your property?'

François clenched his teeth.

The call continued. 'Hold the main! Haul the forecourse!'

The forecourse yard was lagging behind the other. François pulled.

'I'll not say a word to the capt'n,' the voice hissed.

'Hold the forecourse!'

As Tom Barstow wound the line around the belaying pin, François grabbed him by the throat forcing him back over the gunnel till his head was hanging out over the sea.

'I promise I will kill you one day!'

'You touch me and I'll squeal like a stuck pig!' smirked Thomas Barstow.

François released his grip.

The sailor straightened, sneered at François and spat into his face but the wind carried his saliva out to sea.

'When I came to the wharf, the ship had gone.' Emma spoke in a whisper, her mouth almost touching François' ear. Their bodies were warm. As he pushed the hair from their faces, his finger caught in the knotted tangles.

'Why did you sail early?'

'I do not know,' he sighed. 'We were to sail on the outgoing tide, but soon after three o'clock the mate ordered the gangplank brought on board and we made ready to cast off. By then it was too late to get a message to you. As we sailed out through the harbour, I knew Joshua was alarmed. I was afraid he might speak to the master or do something foolish. Lucky for him he held his tongue. Had he argued about the ship sailing it is likely he would have been tossed overboard.'

The Frenchman held her to him.

'But why did the ship stop outside the harbour? I have never seen a ship anchored there before.'

'I think because the passenger we expected had not joined the ship and the captain was prepared to wait for him. That would mean he is either a close friend of the captain or he paid good money for the voyage. Most ships will wait for no one.'

'But why did the ship put to sea instead of waiting on the wharf?'

'Perhaps the captain was eager to test the new mast and rigging. Or perhaps, like the men, he was tired of the harbour and wanted to feel the sea under him again. Or perhaps the harbour master needed space on the wharf for another vessel. I don't know. All I know is that last night there was no wind. The air was dead. So we hung off the anchor. Then the captain announced he was going ashore and allowed some of the men to go also. Three boats were lowered and the men rowed them ashore and ran them up on the beach about a mile from the harbour. Josh and I were in the last one. We knew we had a few hours of freedom so when all was clear, we took the boat, rowed it into the harbour and came for you.'

'But what if you had been seen?'

'We were not seen. And the captain did not return until early this morning. I saw him come aboard and his passenger was with him.'

'And who is this man who caused fate to look so fortuitously on me?'

'A man of some means, I would guess. A gentleman by all appearances.' François released her hand, as he slithered back towards the door. 'But now I must go.'

'Is it evening?'

'It is past midnight. One day has gone already. I will be back before sunrise with some food.' He slid down from the bed of sails and held his ear to the door. With no sounds other than the ship's own creaks and groans, he opened it. As soon as he was outside, Emma fastened the cord on the inside as he had instructed.

In the mess, François had chosen a table away from the other men. A lump of bread was all that remained on his plate. Joshua slid along the bench opposite him.

'How is, Mama?' he whispered.

François' brow furrowed. 'She is faring well. I took her cheese and an apple. This morning I gave her biscuits. She eats and sleeps. But two days stuck in that hole is a long time.' He breathed a long heaving sigh. 'She cannot sit or bathe. She cannot see. It is not right for her to be there. I think I should not have suggested that we do this. It was foolish.'

'But remember how she was when we found her, we could not leave her.'

'You are right.' He sighed as he broke his bread and ate. After finishing his drink he gazed into the bottom of the empty pot.

Joshua watched him. 'There is something more, isn't there, Frenchy?'

François eyed the other men in the mess huddled over their plates. 'I worry,' he said. 'I worry about what will happen when your Mama is discovered. I cannot say what the captain will do.'

'But you said it would be all right. You told me that once we sailed beyond the English Channel the ship would not turn back to England. You promised everything would be all right.'

'Don't talk so loud! I had to promise because we had to get your mother from that place. I had to say all would be well or you would not have helped me. I had to promise to your mother or she would not have come.'

'Then you lied to us?'

'No. Do not think that. Like you, I trust and pray all will be well. But,' he said, 'now I fear there may be danger for her on this ship.'

'What danger, François. Tell me!'

'It is better you do not know. I will take care of it!'

'What can I do to help?'

'Pray for clear skies and good wind. Pray we are not grounded on the Goodwins. Pray that your mother is given safe passage. Pray, lad! That is what you can do.' François picked up his plate. 'I will take care of the rest.'

'Be careful,' Joshua said.

The seaman nodded.

Chapter 10

Hauled like a worn sail out of her hiding place, Emma's worst fears had been realized. As the sailor, who she had never seen before, bullied her along the lower deck towards the companionway, she wanted to cry out for François but she thought better of it. Not knowing what was in store, she climbed the steps in silence. When they reached the main cabin, the sailor rapped on the door.

'What is it?' a voice replied.

'Begging your pardon, Capt'n. I've brought the woman.'

'Wait a moment!'

Emma pulled the woollen shawl higher around her shoulders. The still air of the sail locker, deep in the ship, had been stuffy but not cold, and she had warmed the confined space with the heat of her own body. But now, standing barefooted beneath the open hatch, the sea air felt cold, yet she welcomed its freshness and inhaled deeply. She felt her body shaking, partly from fear but also because her legs, weak from lack of standing, made it difficult for her to accommodate the rolling motion of the ship. The sailor regarded her suspiciously as she leaned against the bulwark.

Gazing around, the deck appeared familiar. François had brought her down this way when they came aboard. She remembered seeing the doors to the six private cabins, three on either side of the short corridor and the main one at the end, and wondered if they were in use.

'Come in, Mr Thackray!'

The seaman opened the door. 'Get inside!' he said to Emma, prodding her in the back. 'Hurry up! Capt'n ain't got all day!' Stepping into the cabin, the first mate slipped off his knitted hat and tucked it under his arm.

The stateroom was broad and bright with windows set across the ship's stern. To the right of them was the captain's desk. Poised with quill in his hand, Nathaniel Preston had his back to his visitors and did not turn or look up. Emma could hear the nib scratching across the paper.

'Begging your pardon, Capt'n,' the mate said, clearing his throat, 'the two hands that were fighting are on deck.'

'I will attend to that matter in due course. Thank you, Mr Thackray, you may go.'

'Aye, Capt'n.' Knuckling his forehead, the mate replaced his hat and left, closing the door behind him.

Not knowing how she would be received, Emma remained silent, her anxiety allayed somewhat by the view from the window. Through the glass squares, a dark grey sea stretched to the horizon. There was no land in sight and it appeared that the *Morning Star* had sailed far from the rugged Yorkshire coast.

The captain continued writing.

Adjusting her stance, she waited, feasting her eyes on the room illuminated with natural light. It was a pleasant stateroom in keeping with a ship of its age, with a comfortable feel, like that of an old shoe. The writing bureau was set against the wall with tall cupboards fixed on either side. A small library decked the shelves immediately above the desk with narrow wooden fiddles fixed in position to prevent the books from falling out when the ship heeled over. The captain's chair, upholstered on the armrests, showed signs of wear as did the other furnishings which reflected a previous drawing room setting. The panelled woodwork was scratched and would have benefited from a coat of oil.

As *Morning Star* slid from the top of the swell into a deep trough, Emma lost her balance. She grabbed the oak table in front of her, trying not to disturb the maps and charts lying on it. Despite the sound of shuffled papers, the captain appeared not to notice. Emma wondered if he had forgotten she was there.

When his entry in the log was finished, Nathaniel Preston laid the quill on the desk, blotted his entry and closed the inkpot.

'So,' he said, reading from his written record but not yet turning around. The *Morning Star* sailed from Whitby on Thursday. Today is Sunday and already I have a problem. I can tell you, I am not happy.'

Emma's toes clawed the teak boards.

'Goddamit, woman!' he yelled, forcing his chair back noisily. 'You have the audacity to stowaway on my vessel! If you were a man I would have you flogged!'

Emma's chin dropped, allowing her knotted ringlets to fall across her face.

'But mark my words the man who helped you come aboard will be punished!'

'No one helped me. It was my own doing,' she said.

Ignoring her comment, Captain Preston went over to his charts and examined one. 'We are now heading for Portsmouth. Before we enter that harbour you will be rowed ashore. Where you go from there is no concern of mine!'

'But, sir, I cannot go back.'

The captain faced her. 'Damn you, woman! You will not stay on my ship!'

Emma lifted her face.

It was the first time since she had stepped into the cabin that Captain Preston had regarded her. The bruises on her face and blood stains splattered on her bodice were a surprise to him. He had not been told she had been beaten. Also, she was much younger than he had expected.

What had he imagined? An older woman – a whore – hard and worn from servicing the men who frequented the dockside taverns? A drunkard? A thief? Perhaps, yet the woman standing before him was little older than his eldest daughter. But her hair and dress were unkempt. She appeared disreputable, and he considered that if he were standing any closer she would surely smell.

'Your face!' he said, pointing to her forehead, 'did this happen on my ship?'

'No, sir. Not on the ship. It was a fall.'

Captain Preston glared. The scowl of authority returning. 'I warn you, miss, do not take me for a fool. I have no time for liars.'

Emma stroked her cheek, as if to brush the offending bruises away. 'Captain,' she said cautiously, 'I am not seeking a free passage. I have some money, enough to pay for a cabin.' As she spoke, she tore the seam of her skirt, ripping open the hidden pocket she had sewn into it. From it she withdrew the beaded purse.

Nathaniel Preston watched.

After loosening the purse-strings, Emma took out a small bundle wrapped in a crumpled handkerchief. Carefully resting it on her hand, she lifted back the lace edges.

The yellow metal glinted. Sovereigns and half sovereigns.

'Now what do we have?' the captain scoffed cynically. 'A harlot and a thief!'

The words hurt. 'Sir,' she said, 'I assure you, I am neither.'

'Then answer me this,' he demanded. 'How does a woman like you come to be in possession of such a substantial amount of gold?'

'My father gave it to me.'

'Oh, yes?' he said cynically. 'And how did he acquire it?'

'The money was for a portrait of a Duke.'

'And that no doubt was stolen from some stately house in Yorkshire!'

'It was not stolen. My father sold the painting and gave me the money.'

'Poppycock! You expect me to believe that a woman of your sort would be carrying this amount of money in her pocket? Just look at the condition of you! I tell you, I have no respect for liars and no time for thieves.'

However, after scrutinizing her intently, he paused for a moment. There was something about her that made him hesitate. Her garb was dishevelled, her hair unkempt, her face and hands grubby, yet he detected a hint of genteel breeding. Her voice was clear. Her manner polite, and for a fleeting moment his mind strayed to his own daughters and he felt a tang of pity. But the feeling was short-lived and, as the injuries she had suffered had not been inflicted by any of his men, her condition was of no concern.

'Tell me,' he said. 'Does anyone, besides us, know about this money?'

'No one.'

'Are you certain?'

'I am sure.'

Fastening the buttons of his coat, the captain leaned back against his desk.

'That is well,' he said.

Nathaniel Preston had a reputation for running an efficient ship. François had told her so. He had no time for drunks or insubordinates and, though master of a merchant ship, he dealt with both in Royal Navy fashion. He had suffered stowaways before and even seen some become good seamen. But a young woman hiding on his ship was something Captain Preston had never been confronted with. He turned his chair and sat down facing Emma.

'You are the only female on this ship, and that, in itself, is a recipe for disaster.' He paused, choosing his words carefully. 'While it is possible you are not the type of woman I would expect one of my men to bring aboard, nevertheless I cannot allow you to stay irrespective of who or what you claim to be.'

Emma brushed the hair from her eyes.

'Madam,' he said, 'I will explain, and I suggest you listen carefully to what I have to say. If my words sound blunt, they are meant to be! Your presence here puts my ship at risk. You also put yourself in danger.' He cleared his throat. 'I doubt, as a woman, you can comprehend the appetites that come over a man when he is at sea for long periods. And the men in my charge are at sea for many months, sometimes even years. You must pardon my candour when I say a man's need for a woman is often beyond his control. Some men become desperate and forget all moral values – that is if they ever had any in the first place!'

He looked across at the coins nestled in the kerchief.

'If I were to pander to your pleas and allow you to stay on board, I could not guarantee your safety. Neither the threat of flogging nor worse would deter the insatiable appetite of a woman-hungry sailor.'

Emma rested one hand against the table to keep her balance.

The captain leaned forward. 'I am informed that your son is aboard. Is this correct?'

Emma nodded. 'But he is not a stowaway. He signed on for the voyage. And,' she added quickly, 'he is not responsible for me being here.' She held out her hand. 'Please, sir, take this. Let me pay for my passage.'

Captain Preston shook his head.

'At sea, a man must have his mind clearly set on what he is doing. If he loses concentration for only a second he is in danger of becoming food for the fishes. A woman idling about on deck would be too much of a distraction.'

'But, sir, I would not idle about. I can occupy myself.' She glanced across at the shelves of books. 'Read perhaps,' she said, 'if you would allow me to stay. I promise I will keep away from the men. I will speak with no one. If necessary I will remain below decks. I beg you, sir, please reconsider. I cannot go back to Whitby.'

'Ma'am, Mrs—?'

'My name is Emma Quinlan.'

'I have listened to what you have to say. Now listen to me. We sail for Portsmouth and there you will be put ashore.' He glanced out of the window then examined the barometer hanging on the wall. 'Unless this confounded weather breaks, it will take us a week to make that port. But if the wind freshens we could be anchored off the Isle of Wight in less than two days. Whichever is the case, I assure you, you will be leaving the ship. I suggest, therefore, you prepare yourself for that eventuality.'

There was a rap on the door.

'Begging your pardon, capt'n. We're ready for you on deck.'

The captain raised his voice. 'One moment!' Fastening the remaining button on his jacket, he continued. 'Sailors,' he explained 'are not like other men. They are a different breed. Crude. Unmannered. Often illiterate. But they have one thing in common – they know the sea and respect it. They know its fickle nature and know it will probably get the better of them in the end. They also know that if a job needs to be done, no matter how dangerous, they will do it. The men aboard this ship do not question my orders. They may be men who lack any modicum of social demeanor but, believe me, they have courage surpassing that of any landlubber. And I would not wish them to be any other way. I am the master of this ship and every man on board knows it. They must respect my command and follow my orders otherwise they will suffer the consequences.'

Nathaniel Preston turned and reached for his hat. 'As I said, I could not teach these men the delicacies of moral virtue if they sailed with me for ten lifetimes.' He paused, looking directly into Emma's eyes. 'And I include the seaman we call Frenchy, in this category. He is a man who may have impressed you with his foreign ways, but he is a sailor, no less, and a man of passion – perhaps more so than the others.'

Emma blinked.

'That matter is your concern, not mine, and that brings me back to the coins you have in your hand.'

Emma uncurled her finger.

The captain's face was grave. 'If word passes around the ship that you are carrying gold, I assure you, it will be removed from your person in an instant. Sailors also have no conscience. I have seen a man's throat cut for a pouch of tobacco.' He leaned on the table. 'For that reason, I will take the money from you, if only to prevent the same thing happening to you. And I will return it to you when you are put ashore in Portsmouth. In the meantime,' he said, 'I will consider whether or not I will hand you over to the authorities.'

'But, captain, I beg you to listen to what I say. I do not lie. What I am telling you is the truth.'

The captain was becoming impatient. 'I do not have the time or inclination to argue the point. At this moment, my presence is required on deck. I have a ship to run, madam.'

There was nothing more Emma could say. She folded the handkerchief around the money, squeezed the bundle into the purse and placed it onto the open palm of the ship's captain. In her estimation, he was a reasonable man. She could appreciate his situation and he was probably right in all that he said. At this point she had little alternative and had to trust him.

'For the remainder of your time on board you will stay in the quarters where you were found. You will be allowed on the weatherdeck each day for a period of two hours, morning and afternoon. You will not talk to any of the hands. You will behave with decorum at all times and not flaunt yourself by walking about unnecessarily. Finally, if I hear of any further incident which disrupts the running of this vessel, then madam, be warned, you will be deposited on the nearest beach. Failing that you will be secured in the hold under lock and key. Do you understand me?'

Emma nodded.

'So be it,' he said as he opened the door. 'Mr Thackray, escort Mrs Quinlan on deck!'

Emma lifted her skirt and stepped out of the cabin.

The mate led Emma up the companionway. She followed slowly. Her arms and legs lacked strength, and her skirt and petticoats made climbing difficult. From the hatch, Emma stepped onto the afterdeck and, though high cloud was covering the sun, the brightness hurt her eyes. The salt air felt fresh and brisk despite there being little wind. The few sails that were set flapped but failed to fill and large squares were furled. The *Morning Star* was wallowing on the water making no headway.

'Wait there!' Thackray shouted, as he went below.

Emma waited turning away from the gaze of the sailors who were congregated further along the deck. All eyes were on her.

The interview with the ship's captain had not been what she had expected. It had left her confused, not knowing whether she should feel relieved or anxious. It also left her with many unanswered question. She wanted desperately to speak with François, but now that would be impossible. One consolation was that the captain had not ordered the ship to return to Whitby. That had been her greatest fear. But she wondered if Captain Preston could be trusted? He had taken her money but given no real guarantee he would not leave her stranded at some isolated cove on the south coast. When they arrived in Portsmouth, would he return the money to her or would he deny she ever gave it to him? After all, no one else knew about it and it would be her word against his. Who would believe the word of a stowaway against that of a respected captain? And where would she go from there? She could not return to Whitby. No, she would make her way to Lincolnshire where he sister lived. But would she have money to pay for a coach ride? And would George be looking for her there? She tried to shake the thoughts from her head.

Captain Nathaniel Preston appeared from the hatch. Mr Thackray followed close behind. On deck the hum of conversation subsided, the men stepping aside as the ship's master went forward.

Emma had never realized there were so many men on board. Perhaps thirty in all. A rag-tag assortment. How could her son wish to belong to such company? An uneasy feeling crept over her as she senses something was about to happen. Now all eyes were on the captain.

The mate tugged on her sleeve. 'Stay put! Right here!'

Emma stopped as he walked past. Gripped in his hand was a stout plaited handle from which hung long thongs of knotted leather. The tips trailed on the bleached decking.

Suddenly she felt sick inside.

As the captain walked between the men several gestured with knuckles to their brows, others removed their hats. She could see Joshua with a group of other boys around his age, but he was the tallest by almost four inches. Emma was afraid. Was he to be punished for the part he played in helping her?

The mate moved forward while the men shuffled back. Then she saw François. Stripped to the waist, he was being bound up to the grating by two seamen. Emma's legs went weak. Across the deck, another man, dressed only in breeches, was also being secured. She immediately recognized his evil eyes. It was the sailor she had seen on the wharf.

The captain addressed the men: 'For those who have sailed with me before, you know I will allow nothing to jeopardize the running of this ship. The men before you were fighting in the galley. For that they will receive a dozen lashes each. Next time they'll find themselves in irons.' He looked towards the group of boys. 'For those of you who are new to my command, take heed.' Then he turned to the man holding the cat. 'Proceed with the punishment, Mr Thackray.'

As the mate flicked out the whip, the sailors shuffled back against the gunnels.

Emma closed her eyes. But could not close her ears.

She heard each stroke. Sensed the murmurs from the men. Counted each number on every breath. Heard the splash of water and a muffled groan of pain. Then, just when she thought it was over, the same punishment was meted out to the second man.

Emma held her breath.

'Take them below!' was the call from the captain. 'Stand the men down.'

Feet tramped close by, muffled voices whispered, and Emma opened her eyes. Her cheeks were wet. She dried them on her sleeve.

The captain's pale eyes were steady as he regarded her. 'The lesson your son has learnt today is perhaps the best lesson any boy can learn on his first voyage. He will not forget it quickly and it will stand him in good stead, you mark my words.'

'All done, capt'n,' the mate reported.

'Thank you, Mr Thackray. Please return the cat to my cabin.'

'Aye, aye, capt'n.'

'And, Mr Thackray, make ready to set some sail' Turning his face to the south-east, where a line of dark cloud was forming on the horizon, Nathaniel Preston sniffed the air. 'If I am not mistaken, we will have some wind within the half hour. A fresh breeze will do us all good.'

The deck was quiet. The wind had picked up just as the captain had predicted and was blowing from the east-south-east. For more than an hour, Emma watched the men as they climbed the rigging and spread out on the yardarms like a column of busy ants. And like ants, each man performed the same task as the man ahead of him, working in unison without a single word being spoken. She heard the calls from the deck and the sudden thunderous noise as each square sail fell then the crack, like a whip as it luffed before filling. With each new sail unfurled, she felt the ship respond, leap forward and slice harder into the oncoming waves. Emma watched till all the sails were set, watched the wind hammer the heavy canvas ironing out every single crease and turning the squares into billowing pillows of downy white.

From the stern, the ship's wake swirled into eddies, the pools spinning like tops, marking a pathway across the surface of the sea. For Emma every mile was a mile further from Whitby, but every mile was also a mile nearer Portsmouth. She watched as the trail of simmering water grew longer, stretching in a long and curving line, pushing the horizon further and further from the ship.

Emma felt safe at the stern. The small barrel she had found that morning, wedged between two larger ones, provided a sheltered seat. Above her head the sheet securing the mizzen squeaked as it strained on the wooden block, thumping at times as the ship shifted on the swell.

She thought about François wondering if he had recovered from the punishment he had received on account of her being aboard. She didn't know what would happen to him now. The only thing she was certain of was that in two days' time, depending on the wind, she would be put ashore and would never see the Frenchman again.

Running her hand across her hair, her fingers caught in the tangle of greasy knots. What must she look like? Her skirt was ripped at the knee. There were stains on the bodice of her dress. It was no wonder Captain Preston had taken her for a woman of the street. She must surely resemble one.

Joshua's voice was comforting. 'Mama, eat this. The meat is good, and there is potato.'

Emma smiled at her son fighting back the tears. She took the plate in both hands and placed it on her lap.

'Are you all right?' she asked.

'I'm fine, but I did not imagine that this would happen. François had said everything would be all right and I believed him.'

'Tell me, how is François?'

Before he had chance to answer a voice shouted her son's name.

'I must go. I will be back in fifteen minutes to take you below, but I will try to visit you later.'

'No, Joshua! The captain said I should not speak to any of the crew and that includes you. I do not want you to get into trouble on my account.'

'But Mr Thackray told me it was the captain who said I should bring the food to you. Don't worry, Mama.'

Emma watched him as he ran along the deck. He was no longer her boy from Seal Street. He looked taller, more like a man. She felt proud of him and pleased that at least Joshua had got his wish.

A seagull dived, skimmed the water and without flapping its wings, glided upwards, high above the ship. Emma watched as it hovered, wondering if it would settle on the top of one of the masts. Gazing high into the rigging, a movement caught Emma's eye. A sailor, sitting astride the topgallant yard, was watching her. She knew the evil face and looked away but not before the open mouth contorted into an evil laugh. But the only sound that reached the deck was that of the wind and the creek of timbers. When she dared to glance up again, the man had gone.

Chapter 11

Emma opened her eyes to the blackness. Sleep was impossible because the pain in her belly would not go. She changed her position, rolled over on the coils of flaked rope, banging her elbow on the timbers a few inches above her head.

In the darkness, she thought of her father. Was this the hoodwink he had worn every day for the last few years of his life? Was this the veil of pitch which shrouded even the faintest hint of a midsummer's day? Was this his world – a canvas of spilled ink blotted with chimney soot?

Then she thought of her child in the attic – her tiny daughter, Elizabeth May, whose eyes, sealed with a strip of iced tears, would never see the pallid light of another snow-cold February morning.

But the pain in her stomach was worsening and though she held her breath and curled her legs to her belly, it would not go away.

She did not know how long had she lain there, awake, waiting for the sounds of morning, waiting for permission to be taken up onto the deck. She felt around for the bucket. She must use it. But it wasn't there. Someone must have removed it. She must get up to the deck. To the heads. She could wait no longer. She felt for the door and tapped lightly on it. If the seaman posted outside her door was not asleep, he would hear her. She waited, her ear pressed against the locker door, then she knocked again but could hear nothing but the monotonous thudding that echoed through the ship like a dull heartbeat.

Cautiously Emma unfastened the door and pushed it open. It swung out wide on its hinges, creaking noisily. She looked left and right. The passage was empty.

A pale glow filtered back from the mess where the men slept swaying in their hammocks like bats from tree branches cocooned in folded wings. The sounds of the sailors sleeping carried along the deck, as did the unsavoury odours of the night. Sweat, flatulence, beer and salted meat-fat congealing in the galley's cooking pots.

She could not go through the mess, she must go back towards the stern and climb the two flights of steps closest to the captain's cabin. She prayed no one would see her.

To keep her balance, Emma slid her hands along the timbers above her head and moved stealthily on bare feet. When she reached the first ladder she straightened herself, arched her back and looked up. A light was glowing from the deck above. She hoped when she reached the deck there would be sufficient moon for her to find her way to the bowsprit and the heads.

Stuffing her skirt and petticoat between her legs, Emma climbed. Her muscles were stiff but at least the pain in her stomach was subsiding. Crawling out through the first hatch onto her hands and knees, she sat for a moment. There was no one about.

The light illuminating that deck was from the lantern hanging near the door to the main cabin. Its shadows moved with the sway of the ocean back and forth across the white doors of the small private cabins. All was quiet. Everyone was sleeping

Through the open hatch above her head she could see myriads of stars swinging rhythmically against a backdrop of night sky. It was as if the ship was standing still and the heavens were swaying from side to side. The companionway leading up to the upper deck was wider than the previous one, less like a ladder and not as steep. Rolling her skirt to one side, she climbed again. Halfway up, a length of knotted rope, dangling from above, swung against her face. She grabbed it and cautiously pulled herself out into the fresh air.

Silhouetted against the blackness, a lanky seaman rested one hand on the wheel, his only light from a pale mottled moon. Though she was only a few paces from him, he did not appear to see her,

Once on the open deck, the wind caught her hair, trailing it around her face. She should have tied it back. Overhead a sail cracked and rigging rattled. Emma knew she must tread warily as finding a path along the deck would not be easy. She knew the deck was littered like an obstacle course while above her head thick ropes, seeped with oil and tar, ran up to heavy blocks which swung pendulously across the ship.

'Go steady, miss,' a voice called from the helm.

'I will,' she replied in a whisper, as she moved cautiously towards the bow.

The ship's port side was leaning to the sea. Almost close enough to touch it. Foam whisked by the bow churned along the hull, but beyond that the ocean was ink black and uninviting. Yet Emma felt no fear. Its vastness made her feel secure. So far from land. It offered perfect protection from threats and danger. She did not know what would become of her when she was put ashore but for the first time she was glad she had run away.

The old ship's heads were fixed precariously over the bow, on either side of the bowsprit. The two square seats each bore a large round hole. Though the timbers had once been sanded smooth, the wind and salt had dried them out. They were cracked and warped. Beneath the heads the bow waves crashed spraying white spume back onto the deck. Emma hoisted herself up from the gunnels and clambered onto the seat not daring to release her hold upon the ropes. She sat, her bare legs hanging over the sea.

The bow dipped. Salt water spray damped her skin. She caught her breath and held on gazing down at the sea turning from the bow. Suddenly something in the foam attracted her. Tiny pinpricks of light sparkled in the water like distant stars or silver dust! There were hundreds of them, darting up from the deep, dancing on the surface, then disappearing. Emma watched mesmerized. It was not the moon broken into a thousand fragments, nor the reflection of the heavens. Were her eyes playing tricks on her? Was it an illusion? Or was this a sample of the sea's seductive magic she had heard so much about?

A sound alerted her. She turned her head. Almost hidden by the ropes and headsails, a sailor was perched on the tip of the bowsprit. He was tapping his pipe on the baulk of timber. The sound carried along its length. She hadn't noticed him when she had clambered out. Suddenly, she was embarrassed for her situation and felt vulnerable. If she fell overboard no one would know, and even if they did, François had told her a ship never turned back if a seaman fell overboard as they would never see a head bobbing in a vast expanse of ocean and valuable sailing time would be lost in the process. Her hand was shaking as she slid forward and stepped back onto the deck. She must get back to the sail locker with all haste.

Gripping onto one object, then another, she made her way along the deck. She was thankful the ship was sailing well. The movement was smooth and there were no calls for the men on deck. Apart for the helmsman and the sailor on the bowsprit, she had seen no others.

'Damn your eyes! Watch where you're planting your feet!'

It was a man's leg not a rope she had stepped on. His body was hidden beneath the upturned longboat. Having forgotten that some men slept on deck, Emma hurried as fast as she dare. The helmsman's stance had not changed. The companionway was only a few yards ahead. For a moment she hesitated, turned her face into the wind, tossed back her hair, opened her mouth and gulped the salty air wishing she did not have to go below – back to the sail room, back to the land, back to – she dare not consider what might await her.

Stepping back cautiously, something brushed her thigh. She swung around but it was only the rope hanging over the companionway. Grasping it tightly, she stepped down into the darkness, her toes feeling for the wooden steps. The length of her skirt made her descent awkward. Drawing the folds close around her knees, she felt the air rising from inside the ship. It warmed her bare legs. The dim glow from the lantern on the deck below was welcoming.

Suddenly a hand hooked around her ankle wrenching her down the ladder. Before she had time to cry out, her chin hit the top step, snapping her teeth closed with her tongue sandwiched between. The force of the blow threw her neck back, then forward, bouncing her forehead onto the lower steps *thump, thump, thump.*

Emma's mind reeled in a near faint. Like an observer in a strange slow dream, she had no control. She could feel herself being dragged to her knees. She wanted to get up, to fight off the invading hands, but she could do neither.

A vice-like grip clamped over her face sending a searing pain through her jaw. Blood filled her mouth. Her right arm flailed the air while her left hand hung limply by her side.

Words breathed into her ear. 'Ain't this my lucky day!'

Matted hair, like greasy rope, was draped across her face.

'Couldn't sleep, could I? Then who should come looking for me but the fancy lady.' He grabbed Emma's hair and wrenched her head back. 'Came looking for Old Tom, did you? Well, now you found me, missy. But you don't look so fancy now.'

Emma's legs burned with the weight of his body pressing down on her. She wanted to cry for help, but the words would not come out. Her mouth was hanging open. She could feel something running down her neck. A muffled moan was all she managed.

'Now listen, girl, and listen good. You and me's gunna have a little arrangement, as you might say.' He pressed his stubbly chin into her cheek, his lips squashed against her ear. 'Seems you got a boy on board, by the name o' Joshua.' He sniggered. 'Nice-mannered lad. I picked 'im out.'

Emma's heart thumped.

'Good mates now, 'im and me. Showed 'im a thing or two, I 'ave. Young Josh thinks Tom's all right,' he hissed, jerking his fingers in her hair. 'You listening to what I'm saying? You do what's right by me, and your lad'll be fine. I'll teach 'im all there is to know. You got me word on that.' He breathed into her face. 'But you make one murmur and mark my words I'll hang him from the yard and feed his innards to the fishes, piece by slimy piece.' He shook her head. 'Do you 'ear me?'

Emma could neither speak nor move.

'I said, do you 'ear me, woman? That ain't no idle jest. I done it before and, on my oath, it'll give me pleasure to do it again.'

Letting out a faint moan and struggling against his grasp, she inclined her head to a nod.

'Good. Now you and me's got an understanding.'

He releases his grip and fumbled with his breeches.

'Now you be a good girl and take what Old Tom gives you?' He poked his tar-stained fingers in her mouth, pushing open her sagging jaw.

Her cheeks burned with the pain. She wanted to think of Joshua, to pray no harm would come to him. But the pain was excruciating. A mat of wiry hair was thrust against her face. The rancid smell of greasy sweat was sickening. She could think of nothing.

'Open your mouth, you slut! Remember what I said.' Anchoring her by her hair, he pressed himself between her bloodied lips, deep into her throat.

She could not breathe. She gagged.

Her free hand grasped weakly at his wrist but her strength was gone. In vain she tried to press her nails into his arms but could not penetrate his leathery skin. Pain radiated across her cheeks, exquisite pain like she had never felt before. Frantic but helpless, she let out a soft moan. She could not have bitten down on the object invading her mouth, even if she had wanted. She retched, the bitter fluid from her stomach burning into the back of her throat. It settled there. Swallowing was impossible.

Tom Barstow threw his head back, his eyes rolling as his whole body swayed back and forth exercising his bestial urge. From the ship's deck the dull rhythmic banging echoed in her brain. She sensed herself falling backwards. Down. Down. Swaying back and forth. Back and forth.

Suddenly she was drifting, succumbing to the sanctuary of unconsciousness. Drifting to the warm barn where, as a child, she and her sister had spent many happy hours.

Molly! Keep still!

She could sense the milking-stool was slipping. She knew she would tumble. Knew the pail would tip over and the milk go to waste. And though her forehead was pressed hard against the moving flank, she knew she would fall. She could smell the barn. It was rank and warm and sickening.

Why won't she be still, Uncle? The stool is sinking. Please tell Molly to be still.

'Below!' a voice echoed.

It was a faraway cry.

Uncle, is that you? Please help me. I'm falling!

Warm milk, thick and creamy, soothed her mouth. Flowed into her throat.

And with a final thrust the milking stool collapsed throwing the small girl backwards, tumbling over and over into a swirling mire of blackness.

Jack Mahoney was doing the last round of his watch. From the deck he glanced down the ladder into the dim glow of the afterdeck.

'Below! Who's that below?'

Illuminated only by the shadowy light of the lantern, he could see the sailor hunched over what appeared to be a heap of rags. 'What's your business there? Below, I say! Speak man!'

Tom Barstow had collapsed exhausted onto Emma's crumpled body having expelled every ounce of his energy. Slowly he righted himself, his body shaking involuntarily. He staggered then lolled back against the wall, his flagging member hanging from beneath his blouse.

The pile of rags remained motionless on the floor.

'My, God! What's happened?' Mahoney muttered to himself, then, in a voice that would have carried to the royals in a roaring gale, 'Mr Piper! Call the captain!'

As he spoke, the door to the private cabin door nearest the companionway swung open.

Chapter 12

Soft pillows on either side of her head prevented Emma from lolling over. The bed was warm and comfortable. The cotton sheets crisp and fresh. Sleep had come easily but had not been restful. It had been laced with strange and troubled dreams – confusing dreams that added to her tiredness.

Something touched her lips.

'Mrs Quinlan! You must try to take a drink.'

Her eyes opened to little more than narrow slits. Waking was not easy. It was hard to see. Above her head the ceiling was painted white. It puzzled her. The timbers were not far above her face. If she could lift her hand she could surely touch them. Where was she? Whose bed was she in? Her mind was playing tricks again. The bed was rocking like a cradle. Side to side. Something about the movement had made her feel faint but try as she might, she could not remember why.

'You must drink a little. It will do you good.' It was an unfamiliar voice, a man's voice, but gentle.

A linen cloth was draped across her chest. A china dish was resting on it. Again she felt a touch upon her lips. Her mouth was parched. Her tongue dry. A little of the sweet warm liquid ran into her mouth. More spilled across her chin.

'That is good,' he said. 'Please try once more.' This time his hand slid behind her head and held her as she opened her lips and swallowed.

This man was kind. Like her father when she had been ill. She wanted to say thank you but her mouth would not respond. She wanted to ask where she was. But she was tired. And felt safe. Safe to sleep. And dream.

Emma woke to the lazy swaying. She remembered the ship. The sail locker. François. But where was she now?

She was in a wooden-framed bed attached to the side of the ship, and it was light. There was a lantern hanging by the door. It was a low doorway and it was closed. Though she could see no one, she sensed someone sitting beside her but she was unable to move her head. She tried to lift her arms but they were tucked beneath white sheets. She closed her eyes again.

This time there was a figure standing beside the bed. She saw the outline of a man's head but no features on the face because the light behind him was too bright.

'Well, I am pleased to see you are awake at last.' The man moved closer as he spoke. 'Is that better?' he said, stepping aside after realizing the light was shining in her eyes. 'Tell me, how do you feel?'

Emma opened her lips but her answer was inaudible. She tried again.

'Perhaps now is not the time for questions. However, let me introduce myself. I am Charles Witton.'

Emma's right arm was fixed by her side. She could move her left arm. She wanted to extend it to him. He helped her lift it from linen and rested it on his own soft hand. His head inclined in a respectful gesture.

'And you, I gather, are Mrs Emma Quinlan.'

Who was this man she had never met before? Was he a Doctor? The gold pin glinting in his silk cravat indicated he was a man of means, a gentleman. How old he was she could not guess. Perhaps ten years her senior. His hair was dark but greying at the temples. He was well-groomed, yet his face furrowed with lines and his cheeks sunken, resembled that of a man deprived of food and shelter. He slid his hand away.

There were so many questions Emma wanted to ask. Was this the *Morning Star*? Or was she on another ship? She wondered how long she had been there. What was wrong with her? She sighed, puffing the air across her swollen lips. She touched her chin and felt the line of bandages encircling her face from chin to crown. But why?

'I thought it necessary,' he said apologetically. 'Please do not try to talk.'

She thought of George. Had he done this? Had he discovered where she was?

'You are quite safe here. There is nothing to worry about.'

She touched her nose.

'Nothing broken,' he said. 'Nothing that will not heal with time and a little rest.' He picked up a mug from the cabinet beside the bed. 'I will ensure you get plenty of both. But,' he said, 'if you are to get well, you must take plenty of fluid. This is some of my best tea. I have sweetened it. Please drink a little then I will leave you.'

He leaned forward and fed the liquid to her. She swallowed half. Sleep was trying hard to overcome her.

'Thank you,' she whispered.

'Get well. That is all I ask.'

'Are you a doctor?'

'No,' he said apologetically, 'though I studied medicine for some years, I cannot claim to be a physician.' He suddenly looked old and tired. 'But I am the nearest thing to that on this ship.'

Emma relaxed back into the pillow and her eyes closed.

'Mama, it's me, Joshua.'

Emma was not asleep. She turned her head slightly towards her son and the man standing beside him.

'I wasn't allowed to see you before. I was so worried,' he said, taking her hand.

'I'm getting better,' she said. 'I think it is all the Chinese tea Mr Witton makes me drink.' Her bruised skin still felt taught, as she smiled. 'But what of your face? Your eye is black. You've been fighting!'

'I hit a man. He said things I did not like. So I hit him.'

'And he hit you back, I would say. Have I not told you about brawling?'

'Mama!'

'I'm sorry. Tell me about yourself and your new life on the ship.'

Joshua hesitated and looked around.

'Five minutes, lad!' Mr Witton said. 'No more or you will tire your mother. I will leave you for the present.'

'Mama, I don't know what to say – seeing you here like this – it's terrible – it's like it was in Seal Street.'

'Don't talk of that, Joshua. But tell me, are you happy? Is this what you want?'

'Mama, you do not know how good it is to be on the ship, to be away from Whitby.' He shook his head in disbelief. 'To watch the sea. The waves. The sky. The wind on the sails. It's like no feeling I've ever had before. Far better than I ever dreamed.'

'Go on,' she said.

'At first I was a little afraid. When we sailed around the Goodwin Sands I was told of ships that had gone aground and of ghost ships which sail those waters. The stories scared me. And when we sailed by and I saw the waves breaking in the middle of the sea, breaking on the shifting sands, I knew the stories must be real. But when we sailed beyond Dover, I climbed the mast and I could see the white cliffs of England and the coast of France at the same time. And while I sat there, the ship heeled over and from where I sat, I looked down as the sea was coming up to meet me and it was like I was a gull diving down from the top of the East Cliff. Oh, Mama. I felt as free as the seabird. You cannot imagine how good that feeling is.'

Emma smiled.

'But, Mama, when we get to Australia you will be free too. And I will make sure no one hurts you ever again.'

Emma's voice was soft. 'But I will not be sailing with you, son. Captain Preston intends to put me ashore at Portsmouth.'

'But, Mama—'

'Hush, I must abide by what he says.'

'But, Mama—'

'Don't worry, Josh, I will travel to Lincolnshire and stay with my sister, Anna. She will be happy to see me.'

'But Mama, haven't you heard? We sailed south of Portsmouth three days ago. We're no longer in the Channel. We're heading south!'

Emma tried to raise herself in the bunk. 'But why didn't the ship go to Portsmouth?'

'It was the fog. It was thick and damp and cold – like a Whitby sea-fret but worse. There was no wind at all and I think all the men were worried though not a word was said. There was nothing anyone could do. We just sat around all day. Then when the wind blew up it came off the land and was bitterly cold and made the sea steam. So the captain set a new course – due south towards the coast of France. I heard one sailor say it was foolhardy sailing that way and that we would likely be hit by another ship. We lit the lanterns and had them burning bright all through the day. And I was put on duty on the forward deck to toll the bell. You must have heard it ringing.'

Emma shook her head.

'It was mighty cold. But we neither saw nor heard another ship. And, on the day we sailed out of the fog, it was like someone had opened a curtain. On the other side was bright sunshine and clear skies, and the sea was bluer than I have ever seen before. And behind us you could see the fog, resting like a huge ball of cloud on the sea. And not more than five miles ahead was France. Cherbourg, I heard. When the wind picked up, we headed west following the coastline for a time.' Joshua looked reassuringly at his mother. 'Trust me, Mama,' he said. 'We are far from Portsmouth, and we are not going back.'

The thoughts tumbled so fast through Emma's brain she could not hold one long enough to grasp it. 'Tell me, Joshua, how long have I been here?'

'Five or six days.'

'And you say I will not be put ashore?'

From the doorway Charles Witton answered the question. 'No, Ma'am. What your boy says is correct. The *Morning Star* is in the North Atlantic and heading south-south-west and according to the captain, our first port of call is the island of Madeira. It may take us a week to get there but, when we arrive, we will not stay long, only sufficient time to take on water and some fresh provision.'

Relief welled in Emma's eyes. Joshua squeezed her hand and bent his face down to hers. She felt his cheek brush hers.

'I will look after you, Mama. Please don't worry.'

'Enough for now, lad. Your mother needs some rest.'

'Yes, sir.' Joshua laid his mother's hand onto the bed, leaned towards her and whispered, 'François asked me to convey his good wishes.'

'Tell him, thank you,' she said quietly. 'Now go, Josh. I believe I am in good hands.'

She watched as he bowed his head to go through the doorway. 'Thank you for allowing that visit,' she said.

'A good-looking boy,' Charles Witton replied, inclining his head as he looked into his patient's face. 'You both have the same eyes.'

'You mean we both carry bruises?'

He laughed. 'That is not what I meant, Mrs Quinlan.'

'My name is Emma,' she said smiling, as she wondered about this man who had nursed her for the past week, attending to her every need while she slept. 'May I ask your position on the ship? I do not remember hearing mention of you earlier and I cannot recall seeing you on deck when I was allowed to go there.'

'But I noticed you on more than one occasion – but I will not dwell on that. Let me explain.' He paused for a moment. 'Unfortunately the ship does not carry a surgeon, much to the chagrin of the men. This, I gather, is not unusual on small merchant vessels, quite unlike the Royal Navy ships.' He cleared his throat. 'I am sailing at the invitation of Nathaniel Preston, as a passenger. As for my profession, I study insects and, if I am fortunate, I will discover some previously unidentified species in the Antipodes.'

Looking for a response, he noted that Emma's eyes had closed. Perhaps his answer had disappointed her but he would never know.

'Sadly, my dear,' he continued. 'I cannot claim to be a physician though it was always my greatest wish.'

As he spoke, he watched Emma's eyelids flickering and continued talking softly, as if for his own benefit. 'In the last six months, I lost both my wife and daughter and there was nothing I could do to help either of them. If only they had accompanied me on my last voyage to Sydney,' he added, with a sigh. 'I begged my wife to come. I felt sure the climate would improve her health.' He paused for a moment. 'She died soon in October when the weather was beginning to turn cold. She hated the English winter and in her heart I think she knew she would not see another Christmas. My daughter died several weeks ago.'

Looking down at his charge, he knew she was asleep. 'And so, my dear, like you, I am running away. Turning my back on the past and hoping that in Australia life will be somewhat kinder to me than it has been in the past.'

Chapter 13

A strip of pale light outlined the cabin door.

Emma sat up, swung her legs over the edge of the bunk and slid her toes to the timber deck. She steadied herself waiting until she felt comfortable with the roll of the ship, aware she must learn to move with it. She lit the lantern.

The private cabin was little more than two paces long with hardly width to turn around. It was smaller than her pantry at Seal Street. Wedged between the wall and the head of the boxed bunk was a compact cabinet, comprising one drawer and a tiny cupboard below it. On it was a silver-handled brush, a slab of soap in a china dish and linen cloth. A straight-backed chair just fitted at the other end. On that sat a tin jug and bowl. The water in the jug slopped back and forth but the narrow neck prevented it from spilling over. Under the chair, covered with a piece of Hessian, was a wooden night-bucket. Next to that, her boots. Built into the front of the bed were two drawers. They squeaked as Emma opened them. The timber frames had obviously warped. Surprised at what she discovered, she examined the contents.

The clothes she had worn when she had come aboard were in the top drawer. Though old and well-worn, they were now clean and neatly folded. Seeing the line of broken threads on the skirt pocket reminded her of her conversation with the captain. As she had not been put ashore then the coins she had brought on board would pay for the voyage. She thought it unlikely any would be returned to her in Sydney. She wondered where her bag was – the tapestry bag and the clothes she had selected. Then she remembered the fire, the smell of burning and fury in George's face.

The second drawer was deeper than the first. It contained the clothes Joshua had collected for her when they left. She examined each garment in turn.

The skirt. Good quality, but with an ink stain the size of a dinner plate across the front. But it was clean and warm and the stain could be hidden beneath an apron. It would suffice. Two blouses. One clean but old and fraying at the collar. The second needed stitching and had no buttons. She would tear it into strips to use for rags.

There was little else. No dresses, hose or handkerchiefs. But she was relieved to find some underwear and a pinafore. The nightshirt she was wearing was a man's, but it belonged neither to George nor Joshua.

Hanging from the coat peg on the cabin door were her bonnet and cape while the plaid shawl covered the foot of her bed. It was a poor selection – drab but serviceable. No satin, silk or fine woollens. No dress or gloves. Certainly nothing elegant yet there was sufficient for a change of clothes while the others were being washed. Quite suitable for wearing on the ship. Joshua would understand and possibly François would never notice. She would not worry about her wardrobe until the ship arrived in Sydney.

She looked again at the nightshirt she was wearing. Mr Witton must have dressed her in it. He must have washed her too and attended to her toilet. He was the only one who had fed her and had nursed her back to health. He had been very kind and she had not thanked him properly.

Making sure the bolt was securely shot, Emma undressed. She winced to the pain in her arm as she slipped the nightshirt from her head and let it drop around her feet. Kneeling beside the chair, she poured an inch of water into the bowl. The cabin was warm, the water tepid. It slid lazily, as it had done in the jug and did not spill.

The soap was greasy and after using it she felt cleaner and more alive than she had for several days. Untangling her hair was difficult. Her arm ached when she lifted it and her hair was knotted. She brushed it out as best she could and left it hanging loose around her shoulders.

When she had completed her toilet, she dressed, and sat back pondering what would happen when she was well again. Would the captain send her back to the sail locker or allow her to remain in the cabin? The sound of bare feet on the boards outside startled her. They stopped. She listened but could hear nothing. No doors opening. No voices. The bolt on the door was secure. No one could get in. The teak boards creaked. Was someone was out there or was it her imagination?

'Take my hand. I will not let you fall.'

Emma grasped the outstretched arm and allowed herself to be helped through the hatchway and out onto the deck.

Mr Witton wrapped the cloak around her shoulders. 'We do not want you to get a chill,' he said.

'Thank you. You are very kind.'

'This way,' he said, as he guided her along the deck. 'I have found a place where you can sit. It is sheltered from the wind.'

The deck was wet and cold beneath her feet. Her cloak did not keep out the wind. But Emma was pleased to be outside. She filled her lungs with the sea air.

Two seamen standing by the braces watched her progress. One nodded sympathetically. She was conscious of them watching her. Did her face still bear the colour of the bruises? Hiding her eyes beneath her bonnet, she refrained from returning the gesture.

'Here,' the gentleman said, indicating a stool squeezed between two packing boxes. 'You can sit here.'

The wind blowing from the north-east was fresh and cold, and strong enough to ruffle the wave tips turning the caps white. But her seat was sheltered by the longboat lashed behind it. She wondered if this stool was used by the sailors or if Mr Witton had placed it there for her especially.

'Will you be all right on your own? If you prefer, I can stay with you.'

'I will be fine here. I will enjoy sitting out for a while.'

'In that case, I will leave you and come back shortly.' He lifted the end of her cloak from the deck and draped it over her lap. She thanked him and watched as he made his way back toward the stern, struggling at times, to keep his balance.

Most of the men on deck, she had not seen before. She recognized the mate, Mr Thackray and the lanky young helmsman. Three sailors were leaning against the gunnels smoking while another appeared to be asleep. Jumping down from the rigging, the boatswain unfastened a hessian tool-bag from around his waist and stored it in one of the deck lockers. He smelled of tar.

Suddenly, a big wave battered the bow, crashed across the forward deck delivering a haze of spray that carried the length of the ship. Sea-foam swilled across the teak boards before running along the gunnels and sluicing out through the scuppers. Emma wiped the dampness from her face.

It wasn't hard for her to comprehend Joshua's feelings. The sea was exhilarating. From the top of each swell the ship dipped into deep troughs, sliding as fast as a leaf down a rain-swollen gutter and as thrilling as a sledge ride after the first fall of snow.

'Emma!' It was François' voice from behind her. He was leaning over the upturned boat. 'Are you better?'

'François,' she cried, somewhat afraid to turn for fear of being seen talking with him. 'I am well. But you are the one who—'

'Do not worry about me. I got the punishment I deserved and that is not important. What is important is that I brought you here and caused this to happen. *Mon Dieu*, you could have died and for this I make a promise: I will kill the man who did this to you.' The venom in his voice was real.

'Please, François, you must not speak that way. I am getting stronger every day.'

There was no reply. Emma turned around but the Frenchman was gone. She looked up into the rigging.

From the crosstrees, a pair of eyes had been observing their conversation. Thomas Barstow leaned back against the mast. With his feet spread, his body swayed with the lilt of the ship. With one hand on the ship, he buried his other into the crotch of his breeches in an ugly gesture. A trickle of brown saliva oozed from the corner of his lips. After a while he spat out the bolus of chewed leaf and the wind carried it far out to sea.

The Bay of Biscay was predictably rough. The winds gusted into squalls whipping sheets of spray from the wave crests. Troughs opened in the sea and competed against the roll of the swell. Clouds gathered on the horizon, closed and converged releasing stabbing rain which bounced headlong across the sea's surface turning it into a boiling menace. On deck, the sound of the wind was deafening. Canvas cracked as the ship shuddered from end to end and water thundered against the bow.

For two days Emma remained below. At first she was afraid; afraid of the noises as every joint of the ship heaved and strained;

afraid of the jolts and shudders fearing the ship had hit rock or collided with another, and afraid of the motion which continually threatened to tip her from her chair or throw her from her bunk. While the storm blew, she often felt unwell, and tried to sleep on the floor. But as the sea settled, and she recovered, she found herself becoming bored and restless with her limited surroundings.

Joshua visited her each day and spent as much time as he was allowed. He told her about his duties and was proud to name the sails and tell her the locations of the running gear. He spoke of the men. He said Mr Thackray, the first mate, was hard on the boys, but fair. The boatswain, a Norwegian, spoke little English and would tolerate no one around his store, flaring into a rage at the slightest provocation. He had quickly learned most of the men did not take kindly to questions and he had learned to watch and listen. He said the other three lads did the same and in the evenings they shared what they had learned of knowledge, skills, even ribald jokes. He said there were a few men on board he had not met – some of the topmen and those on the other watch. But he also added that there were a few sailors he would cross the deck to avoid.

Emma listened and spared him her motherly concerns. She left her questions about François until last. Joshua said he had recovered quickly and rejoined his watch.

Charles Witton visited little during those two days. She wondered if it was something she had said or done that made him stay away. She had enjoyed his company and missed the opportunity to speak with him. The hours passed slowly.

On the afternoon of the third day, he knocked on her door. Emma slid back the bolt.

He looked tired, as though he was unwell. She invited him to sit but he declined insisting she use the chair. He said he had been deprived of sleep. There had been an accident; four sailors injured when the halyard on the foretopgallant yard had snapped. It had brought the yard crashing onto the heads of the sailors furling the topsail below it. Though none of the men had fallen, it had taken a deal of time to lower the two injured seamen to the deck and even longer to sort out the tangle of lines and sheets left dangling from the mast. It was fortunate, he explained, that the yard had not broken or fallen into the sea. That could have brought the top of the foremast down with it. However, three of the men had received deep cuts to their heads and the fourth suffered a mangled arm.

'It doesn't look good,' Mr Witton said. 'The arm is broken. The bone has pierced the skin. I have done all I can but that is not enough. His pain is terrible.'

Since the accident, he said he had spent much time sitting with the seaman.

'The arm is infected,' he said, 'and, as he will take neither food nor water, I fear he will not survive.'

There was a deep sadness in his pale eyes. It was the heaviness of frustration caused by his lack of ability to save the seaman. He admitted he could do no more than watch him die and would no doubt witness his body commended to the deep.

After the brief visit, he excused himself saying he must rest. Emma was disappointed to see him go and saddened by his appearance. But she had barely time to lock the door before he returned. In his hand he had a book.

'You may enjoy glancing though this,' he said. 'It is only a child's book of verse, but it is one which never ceases to delight me. Perhaps it may help you pass the time. There are some excellent illustrations in it.' Without waiting for an answer, he pressed the book into her hand and left.

The yellowed paper and worn binding told Emma the book had been well used. She turned each page with care, reading verses her mother had sung to her when she was young, admiring the lithographs which illustrated each rhyme.

Before she laid it down she turned to the words written on the first leaf:

This book is presented to Charles Aislaby Witton
On the occasion of his fifth Birthday
Your loving Mama and Papa
3rd October 1823

As she read the words a second time, she heard the patter of light footsteps outside her door. The handle turned. Emma put the book down and slid to the floor but, as her hand reached for the bolt to open it, she felt pressure being laid against it.

'Mr Witton is that you?'

There was no answer.

Emma held her breath for a moment then called, 'Who's there?' With her heart pounding, she took a deep breath only to be greeted by a sickening smell seeping through the joints in the timber. She recognized it instantly. It was the stench of Thomas Barstow.

Chapter 14

Throughout the night, Emma listened to the ship, its creaks and groans, and sounds of banging which stopped at times and then started up again. Sleep came eventually but it was a troubled, restless sleep.

A knock on the door woke her.

'Mrs Quinlan!' It was Mr Thackray's voice. 'Mrs Quinlan! Captain says he wants a word.'

'Thank you,' she said. 'I will be there in a moment.'

It was dark in the cabin. She had no idea of the time or whether it was night or day. She lit the lamp, splashed her face with cold water and dressed quickly. She had no mirror.

In the great cabin, the Captain greeted her cordially. 'Good morning. I trust you are feeling better. Charles told me you have made a good and speedy recovery.'

'Yes. He has been very considerate.'

Emma hovered at the door.

'Come in. It is time we spoke. There are some matters I need to make clear.'

Emma waited. 'Please sit,' he said, gesturing to the chair by the writing desk.

Captain Preston remained standing. 'Mrs Quinlan, I am sure you are aware of my feelings towards – stowaways. I discussed that at length the last time we spoke.'

Emma nodded but did not reply.

'And you are also aware it was my decision to have you put ashore in Portsmouth.'

'Yes.'

'Believe me, ma'am, had it not been for circumstances over which I had no control, that is the course of action I would have taken. As I said to you a week ago, the running of this ship and the welfare of the crew are my prime concerns. Do not doubt that.'

He turned and faced her. 'However, to that I will add that I am not the unfeeling man you may think, and the treatment which you received at the hands of one of my men grieved me. As master of this ship I must take responsibility for whatever transpires on board.' He sighed. 'So be it. Where was I? Yes – circumstances beyond my control. You may be aware we met with inclement weather in the Channel. Thick fog made it impossible for the ship to proceed to Portsmouth. For that reason and also for the fact that you were' – he hesitated – 'unwell, I had little alternative but to reverse the decision I had made.

His gaze turned back to the sea. 'Perhaps for your sake, the fog was fortuitous. However, that is enough on that matter. Now, as to the present. I have been kept informed of your progress. You are obviously not aware that it was Mr Witton who insisted you be moved to the cabin on this deck. He also volunteered to take care of you.' He looked at her curiously. 'He seems to have taken an interest in your welfare.'

'May I say—?'

'Please, allow me to continue. On any vessel, be it a naval or merchant ship, the captain or master must maintain discipline. Sometimes it is not a pleasant task but it has to be done.' His tone changed. 'The man who did this thing to you has been punished, and I hope that is an end to the matter.' He paused. 'But, be aware, the sailor in question, one Thomas Barstow, has returned to his watch and may still be a danger to you. I advise you to be very careful. Barstow is a man with no conscience, we are all aware of that, yet I cannot have him held below indefinitely when every able-bodied man is needed on deck. However, he has been warned that if he misbehaves again he will be put in irons.'

Emma acknowledged his words.

'Now,' he continued, 'regarding your position on this ship for the duration of the voyage. After giving the matter due consideration, I have come to the following conclusion. From this point on, you will be regarded as a passenger on *Morning Star*. But mark my words, you will receive no special treatment or privileges.'

Emma listened.

'As a passenger, I cannot deny you the right to be on deck whenever you wish or to speak to whomsoever you choose. But,' he reiterated, 'I would strongly recommend you be very wary and keep your wits about you at all times. I also advise that after dark you remain in your cabin with the door bolted.'

Emma nodded.

'And when you are on deck, be in a place where you can be seen by more than one of the crew. Finally, I insist you restrict your movements to the weatherdeck and do not venture into the mess or the hold, or any of the areas the men inhabit. That would be very foolish. Do you understand?'

'I understand.'

'I believe from what Mr Witton tells me you are an intelligent woman. He has vigorously appealed your case, at times, I must admit, against my better judgement. But I trust his judgement implicitly. I am therefore granting this compromise. I feel that my offer is exceedingly fair and trust that you will abide by my stipulations.'

'You can be assured I will,' she said. 'I thank you sincerely, Captain.'

With nothing more to add, Nathaniel Preston moved to the cabin door and held it open. 'So be it,' he said.

The smell of wood smoke and tar drifted across the deck and, despite the fact the wind was keeping the brazier's flames alight, the cooper pumped vigorously on his bellows, his forearms and face glistening with perspiration. Overhead, a poorly trimmed sail crackled. On deck the slack was taken up then the seamen wound the hessian lines into neat coils and returned them to their respective belaying pins. From the anvil came the resonance of a hammer on heated metal.

Emma stood at the rail. The *Morning Star* was sailing away from the rising sun. The sky was blue and clear and the Islands of Madeira lay somewhere in the ocean ahead. Mr Witton was also on deck taking his morning stroll.

'You are looking much better this morning,' he said, after greeting her.

Emma smiled. 'Thank you. The sea air must be doing me good.' As she spoke, she thought of the conversation she had had with Captain Preston the previous evening. It was Mr Witton who had spoken on her behalf. It was he who had arranged for her to be moved into her present quarters. And it was he alone who had nursed her. She felt the flush of blood rising in her cheeks.

For a moment, the pair stood in silence admiring the sea and also observing the day-to-day activities of the ship. On a platform, high above the deck, two men were working on either side of the main mast daubing a treacle-like mixture onto the heavy blocks and lines.

Emma cleared her throat. 'Mr Witton.'

He turned his face towards her. 'Please call me, Charles,' he said.

'Charles, I want to thank you – for the loan of your book. There are some delightful illustrations. May I keep it with me for a little while?'

'But of course. If there is anything else I can do, anything at all, please feel at liberty to ask.'

'Thank you.'

'Now, if you will excuse me, I will continue my morning's exercise.'

Emma's eyes followed him as he continued his walk, zigzagging along the deck, quite unlike the sailors whose gait accommodated the movement of the ship. Beneath her bare feet the deck was holystone-smooth, its teak timbers bleached almost white from sun and salt. Darting across the water, a slender fish flew fifty yards from one wave ridge to another ignoring several smaller wavelets in between. Its sleek silver body glistened as it left its habitat and darted bird-like through the air. Above her head the square sails stuffed with wind, hung from the yards like bed sheets on a breezy Monday washing-line. How far she was from Seal Street!

She didn't notice the tiny bird until it fell. Without opening its wings, it dropped from the yardarm, slid down the filled forecourse and landed on the deck with barely a sound. It was so small. Smaller than a robin. Sandy brown in colour but with a hint of green, like the tits that flitted through the bare branches of a hawthorn hedge before the new leaves of spring blocked their entrance.

Instinctively she squatted down and lifted it into the cup of her palm.

'It's gone, missus,' the sailor said, not lifting his eyes from the rope he was splicing.

'But why?'

'Not his place,' he said. 'Shouldn't be 'ere.'

She watched as he twisted the thick end of the hemp, forcing a hole between the coils and pushing the loose ends back upon themselves.

'But, I believe birds can fly from one country to another,' she said.

'Aye, some can and do. But there's others are meant to stay put.' He slapped the rope on his knee. 'Sometimes they follow the ship, then one day they find themselves too far from home and they can't get back. Then it's too late, so they just give up and die.'

Emma stroked the tiny head, cupped it between her hands and held it close.

'No point hanging onto something that's dead. Ship's cat could make a meal of that.' The sailor tucked the last of the fraying fibres into the thick knob.

'I think I will keep it, if you don't mind.'

He shrugged his shoulder. 'Suit yourself, missus.'

Slipping the bird into her pocket, she smiled apologetically and made her way aft.

Closing the door of the cabin, she took the bird from her pocket and placed it on the cupboard beside her bed. It was impossible to make it sit upright as its head lolled to one side. Beneath its chest, its legs poked out like two bare twigs – thin and brittle.

Running her finger over it, she felt the softness of its breast, examined its delicate feathers, soft, downy, each perfectly patterned like the edges of a snowflake, greyish-white on the inside, tinted with soft brown at the tips. It was quite beautiful. Carefully, Emma opened its wings. Its miniature quill feathers were tinged with the hue of spring – fresh green, almost yellow in the glow of the lamp. Emma sat on her bunk gazing at the bird. Poor little mite.

From the locker, the glistening dead-eye stared back at her.

Chapter 15

'Land ho!'

Emma woke to the call conveyed from aloft.

'Land! One point off starboard bow!'

She felt around for her skirt and blouse and dressed quickly in the darkness. Outside her door, the pale light spilling from the companionway indicated it was almost dawn.

From the bow, Emma watched the morning's events with interest. The deck was a hive of activity. The daily work had started early. The brasses had been stripped of their green hue and taken on a mirror-like shine. The decking had been scrubbed and was still wet in patches. Some of the squares were furled while a line of men, leaning across the foremast yards, were fisting in another and lashing gaskets. Once the morning chores had been completed, the men sat around eagerly looking forward to the opportunity to go ashore. The ship's master observed the activity from the quarterdeck.

To the south-west the fading night melded in a haze of mauve and blue. On the horizon a faint grey outline hovered like a long thin cloud above the sea. As the ship sailed closer, the image changed, slowly transforming into a line of purple mountains rising from the seabed.

'Is one of those islands, Madeira?' Emma asked one of the seamen.

'Sure is, missus.'

She turned and looked back. With the sunrise, the expanse of the eastern sky burned with an orange fire born of the Sahara. And like the shiny trail left by the early garden slug, the ship's wake glistened on the face of the sea. The breeze blowing in from the south-east was warm. Emma dropped the shawl from her shoulders.

Charles had been watching her, studying her expression. 'It blows off the African continent,' he said. 'Though it is a little unusual for this time of the year.'

Together they watched as the land drew closer and the ship skirted the island. To the north, a line of peaks, ragged like a dragon's tail, drifted into the sea while along the coast, the cliffs, folding into giant rock-wave undulations, rose up like a petrified sea. On the hillsides, deep gorges furrowing the forests captured pockets of cloud in their crevices, while above the tree line, streams, shining like silver threads, tumbled over the polished mountain rock.

'The *Morning Star* will be off Funchal in a few hours,' Charles said. 'The captain plans to stay at least one night. He has friends living in the town.'

'Will you be going on shore?'

'Yes, that is my intention. But,' he added somewhat apologetically, 'the captain feels it would be unwise for you to venture ashore.'

'But if you and the captain are going—?'

'I spoke to Nathaniel about that, and though he says the Portuguese are very hospitable, and assures me this port is safer than most, we agreed you would be safer aboard the ship – providing you remain on deck. Most of the crew will be going ashore and only a few will stay.' He paused. 'Foreign ports are no place for a—' he hesitated, '—a woman alone.'

Emma had not considered going ashore until he had mentioned the idea. But now the possibility appealed to her. How she would love to leave the ship, to feel solid ground under her feet, to smell the moist mountain air, to drink from a free flowing brook, perhaps to collect seashells on the beach. But it was obvious she could not go alone. She thanked him and agreed to the captain's conditions. She would stay on the ship.

The heavy cable thundered through the hawse hole as the anchor dropped to the seabed. Amidships, the cutter was secured to the davits, swung out over the ship's side and lowered to the sea. Several fishing boats, bearing fresh fruits and flower garlands, sailed close in, but until the cutter's mast was raised and the other boats launched, the locals were warned to keep their distance. Unperturbed by the sailors' curses, the colourful craft bobbed on the water no more than a stone's throw from *Morning Star*'s hull.

The cutter carried more than a dozen of the crew mainly seated on the thwarts with two in the bow and another man on the tiller. The second boat carried ten. When it was time for the ship's boys to board, they scrambled down the ropes and hung from the ship's side, dropping into the boat as it floated beneath them, much to the aggravation of Mr Thackray watching from the gunnel. Joshua was amongst them. For the boys it was great sport, pushing and elbowing each other for a seat in the bow. For a few there was the anticipation of stepping on foreign soil for the first time and a chance to sample the exotic tastes of a new country – its fruits, its drinks, its scenery. For the seasoned seamen, their sights were set on the island's fine Verdelho, or the fleeting satisfaction of a real bed whose movement was rocked by something other than the sea.

As the rope splashed from *Morning Star,* and an oar pushed off from the ship's side, the boat floated free. The coxswain growled at the boys, threatening to throw them overboard if they were not still. The triangle of cloth filled on the short mast, carrying the boat into the broad bay. Emma watched Joshua hoping he would turn and wave, but his back was to the ship and besides, he was more interested in the port.

François left in the same boat as Tom Barstow. The sight of the seaman she despised made Emma nervous. A few times recently when her mind had been occupied, she had forgotten about him. Other times she had jumped at the slightest sound, imagined the noises of the night were the sailor loitering outside her cabin door. At times she had sensed his eyes peering at her, though he was nowhere to be seen. Even seeing him sail away made her feel uncomfortable.

As she watched, the sailor turned. His eyes narrowed and his mouth curled in a menacing grin. Emma quickly looked away but his gaze remained clinging to her brain like a leach. Blood drained from her skin. Her flesh became cold. Despite the balmy breeze, she shivered and wished she had never looked. Thomas Barstow was evil. His threats scared her. She feared him more than she had ever feared any man, even her husband, and she had no way of escaping from him. They would be together on the ship for the remainder of the voyage.

Captain Preston and Mr Witton left on the cutter's second journey. The bosun accompanied them with the second mate on the tiller. Emma acknowledged a wave as the boat headed across the sheltered bay. The smaller boat followed half empty. They would not return until late afternoon.

Though the deck was quiet Emma was slightly ill at ease. The men she trusted had gone ashore leaving her alone with sailors she hardly knew. She looked around. A couple of older salts were on deck, the others had stayed below. She told herself there was nothing to fear and settled down to watch the day go by.

The morning sun rose rapidly and with it, the wind warmed considerably. Apart from the cries of inquisitive gulls, the deck was silent. Across the water, to the west of Funchal Bay, a huge cliff face rose from sea. Waves rolling in from the south broke all along the rocky shore trimming the island with a rim of white lace. Behind the town, nested around the bay, the hillside rose in steep ridges broken by deep valleys. Waterfalls glistened like streaks of silver. It was a lovely sight.

The cook, a Chinaman, was a tall, yellow-skinned man with a mop of black hair which, when unplaited, reached below his waist. Emma had seen him on deck before, tossing slops or scraps into the sea or scrubbing out the galley's buckets. The first time she saw him she had thought him to be a fearsome man, wielding a metal ladle over his head, chasing one of the sailors along the deck screaming in his own language. The rest of the crew had been unconcerned finding the cook's antics a source of amusement.

Whenever Emma had seen him he had always been wearing the same baggy breeches rolled up to the knees and a striped jumper with sleeves cut off at the shoulders. This morning, however, when he appeared from the galley's hatchway, he was wearing a kimono. It was the colour of crab-meat, edged with a border of emerald green and tied with a sash. The silken material reflected light like sun on water. A large stained apron wrapped around his middle spoiled his appearance.

Emma observed him from a distance as he performed his chores, scrubbing and scraping the blackened cooking pots. At times he lowered a pail over the side and drew fresh seawater. As he worked he hummed a strange disjointed melody.

'You want breakfast?' he shouted, when he finished.

Emma looked around. She was alone at the stern.

'I get you good breakfast,' he said. 'You stay there.'

Apart from the Chinaman's verbal outbreak, this was the first time she had heard the man speak English. Though his face and dress was oriental, his accent was that of an American.

When he presented Emma with the plate, he smiled and bowed several times. She was hungry as she had not been eating well.

'You like? You eat!' he said, as she glanced at her meal. Two pieces of bony pork and three eggs swimming in a greasy juice. A large chunk of bread on the side of the plate was rapidly soaking up the bronze liquid.

She smiled and thanked him, nodding her head in response every time he bowed. When he disappeared down the galley hatch she sat on the boards and rested the plate on her legs. The eggs were good and though the pork had a strange smell she ate most of it and all the bread and dip.

When satisfied, she slipped the remaining meat over the side and left her plate by the galley's companionway. After shouting the words, 'Thank you', through the open hatch, the cook emerged, reached for the plate and dropped back into the gloom below.

Jack Burns, the sailmaker was sitting not far from the hatch surrounded by folds of canvas. He was sewing a patch on a sail. Beside him was a large bag from which he had selected a piece suitable for the repair. Other pieces were scattered on the deck nearby – some were big, some small, all assorted shapes and textures, some yellowed and hardened by salt.

'May I?' said Emma, leaning down and touching the material.

'Help yourself,' he said continuing his work.

Emma watched.

'It'll be good and strong when I've done with it. Strong as the rest of the jib. Maybe stronger.'

She tested its texture. 'It is quite stiff.'

'Has to be. Wind is mighty powerful. I've seen new sails ripped to shreds like they were made of paper.'

'Could you spare a small piece?'

The man looked up. It was a strange request. 'Take what you want. I got enough in me locker to make a set of royals.' He scratched his head. 'Here!' he said pushing the bag towards her. 'Take your pick. Darned if I know what you want it for.' He pushed the needle against the leather pad on his palm, pulled it through the layers of canvas and secured it firmly at the other side.

From the sail bag, Emma selected three pieces each the size and shape of a man's handkerchief. 'Thank you,' she said.

With the canvas in one hand, she wandered along the deck to the hatch that led down to the seamen's mess and galley. The captain had given her strict instructions not to go below, but she needed to see the cook and he appeared kindly. And Tom Barstow, the sailor she feared, was ashore.

Emma descended cautiously, feeling for each step with her bare feet. The air rising from the galley fire was warm. It smelled of salt pork mixed with wood smoke and tar. Above the tables three hammocks swayed gently. Two contained the rounded outline of men's bodies. Three seamen were sitting at one of the tables. She had not realized there were so many men still on the ship.

They stared at her as she climbed down. She had interrupted a game of cards. Another man lay with his head resting on his arms. He did not stir. The cook was sitting by the stove eating from one of the large cooking pot. When he saw Emma, he stopped and rubbed his hands across his apron.

'Excuse me,' Emma said, not moving far from the bottom of the stairs. 'Do you have any charcoal?'

The cook looked at the large square stove, its chimney running up through the deck above. 'No, missy. That fire, he keep going all time. He burn low in the night but he never go out.'

Emma was disappointed but thanked him and climbed back to the fresh air. She was followed by one of the seamen. He had been watching her.

'You want some charcoal?' he said in a husky voice.

She nodded.

'Come with me!'

Emma followed the man along the deck. Today the brazier was cold and empty, but from the bucket of ash, cleaned from the previous day's fire, the cooper picked a handful of charcoal.

'Grind it fine,' he said. 'It'll stop the poison in your belly.'

Emma smiled. 'So I have heard. Thank you.'

The sun was dropping towards the mountains on the western end of the island when the first boat returned. The handful of seamen who clamoured noisily on board quickly disappeared below. Joshua was not amongst them, nor François, nor Thomas Barstow.

The early evening air was pleasant and though Emma was tired, she did not want to go below while the aft quarters were empty. She was happy to see the boats returning. The mood on deck was jovial.

Joshua and the other boys were crowded in the longboat, brimful of youthful energy. The taste of local wine no doubt contributed to their animated excitement, their voices louder and more raucous than she had ever noticed before.

'Mama,' Joshua shouted, as he scrambled back onto the deck.

Emma greeted him from the rail.

'For you, Mama,' he said, pulling a posy of white flowers from beneath his shirt. Though some of the petals were crushed, the sweet scent was strong.

Emma was delighted. 'They are beautiful,' she replied, resisting the temptation to kiss her son. 'Tell me about the island. What is it like?'

'It is a pretty place. You would like it. Sam and I followed a track up the hill. It was very steep and it led to a church. It was very old and very different from St. Mary's in Whitby. '

'Did you see François?'

Joshua's answer was hesitant. 'We passed him in the town when we were coming back.'

'Was he heading for the ship?'

'No,' he said cautiously. 'I think not.' He looked towards Funchal. 'Samuel has a bag of oranges. They were growing along the roadside. I will bring you some later.'

Emma sniffed the flowers and smiled as Joshua hurried along the deck calling for his mate, Sam, to wait for him.

The wind was failing by the time the next boat returned. In place of the small sail, four seamen pulled on oars. As the boat neared the *Morning Star*, they shipped the oars sending a trickle of seawater over the captain and his friend, sitting in the sternsheets. Before anyone climbed on deck, several items were hoisted from the boat's hull – two small barrels and several bottles of wine, a basket of fruit, several bags, and a large animal carcase wrapped in linen. The final item was a black box with brass hinges. It appeared to be fairly heavy and its handling was supervised by Mr Witton. When all the goods were off-loaded, Captain Preston and his companion were assisted from the boat.

On deck, instructions were given. The barrels were hastily despatched to the hold, the carcase to the care of the cook, the bottles of wine and the basket of fruit to the great cabin and the black box to Mr Witton's day cabin.

By the time the last boat approached, the sun was low in the western sky. The sailors' return was heralded by the sound of jocular voices which carried across the water. Just one day in port had certainly raised the men's spirits. As they stumbled onto the deck the tell-tale smells of the taverns came with them. Thomas Barstow was amongst them. Emma hid behind the rigging so he would not see her. She could hear his curses as he pushed another man aside to get down to the lower deck. Her uneasiness returned. But, as the boats were hauled dripping onto the deck, and the rope ladder hoisted from the ship's side, Emma's uneasiness turned to worry.

François had not returned.

Chapter 16

'Surely, not all the men have come aboard,' Emma enquired of Mr Thackray, as the last boat was upturned and secured to the deck.

Another seaman answered. 'Three short!' he called, unconcerned.

'But – the ship won't sail without them, will it?'

'Don't worry, miss,' the sailor said. 'He'll be back.' As he was speaking, he pointed towards the harbour. A local fishing boat similar to the one which had visited in the morning was heading towards the *Morning Star*. The metal fittings on the mast glinted in the rays of the late afternoon sun. On the boat's deck flashes of red and black swirled beneath the luffing sail.

Emma watched as the boat approached, hoping it was carrying the three seamen and praying that François was one of those onboard.

A drunken voice drawled across the water. 'Ahoy there! *Morning Star!*' As the distance between the two vessels closed, the boat dropped its sail and with it Emma's heart sank. She moved back from the rail and again slid herself behind the rigging.

François was reclining amidships, his head nestled in the bosom of a dark-haired woman. Another girl was leaning against his legs, her head on the thwart beside him. Emma took little notice of the identity of the other two seamen, but their female companions were young, swarthy and attractive, their long hair flowing loosely across shoulders tinged amber by the setting sun. The men's necks were draped in slender arms, bare save for their gaudy trinket bracelets.

Cries from the deck were rude and raucous. In comparison the women's tones were mellow and inviting, and though the language was quite foreign, their words needed little interpretation.

When the fishing boat thudded alongside, the rope ladder was rolled down again.

Emma shrank back. The sailors were obviously drunk. Her heart was thumping and a sickening feeling invaded her belly. Peering cautiously over the gunnel she could see François' hand on the ladder. He leaned back across one of the women and pressed his mouth onto hers.

As the swell heaved the small boat up the side of the *Morning Star* he was pulled from the woman's grasp. She reached out to him. He reached and grabbed her hand, not wanting to let go. The girl overbalanced, falling backwards against her companion. Arms and legs lashed the air. The men on deck jeered. The man on the tiller cursed his passengers.

'Jump, man!' a voice cried. 'Climb you fool!'

The little craft slewed out then bumped again.

With both hands on the ladder, François secured his grip and slipped his foot onto the rope.

'Climb, Frenchy!'

He climbed. High enough for the seamen to grab his jacket and pull him headlong onto the deck. His eyes were glistening with excitement – his expression that of a young sailor having just tasted his first foreign port. He rolled over onto his back and lay there grinning.

The two other men were dragged on board in similar fashion. One was forced down onto the deck when he tried to jump back into the boat. A bucket of seawater dampened the spirits of all three.

François pulled himself up to the caprail and shouted to the women. Emma heard but did not understand the words. The girls understood and waved their reply. As the fishing boat drifted away, François delivered the contents of his belly to the fishes and with a satisfied expression, dropped back to the deck and closed his eyes.

Emma slid away, back along the deck, down the companionway, to her cabin. She closed the door, slid the bolt and waited. But the tears did not flow. She was angry.

How could she have liked this man? Been so infatuated to imagine she could share a future with him? She had been warned of the nature of sailors, of men like François, by both her neighbour and the old fisherman on the wharf, but she had taken no heed of what they had said. She had fallen under his charms. She had followed him to the docks. Now she was with him on his ship. Had he enticed other women in distress and received their thanks in kind? Did this behaviour happen in every port?

But he had never tried to woo her. Nor had he taken advantage of her on the cliff top near the abbey or in the sail-locker when he had the chance. He had been kind. Sympathetic. Could he love her, perhaps? If only a little. Was it his looks, his French manner and lilting accent that had beguiled her and blinded her to the truth? Even he had tried to warn her he was a wanderer, but she had not listened.

François le Fevre was nothing more than a common sailor – a maritime itinerant, a man aligned to his mistress the sea who could not, or would not escape her clutches. He was a seaman whose life would never change. Yet he had changed her life and nothing would be the same again. Now she wished she had never met him. Wished she had never agreed to come aboard his ship. Wished the *Morning Star* had sailed away and left him in Madeira.

'Emma!' The cry was loud followed by a thump on the cabin door.

'Who is it?' she called, though she recognized the voice.

'It is François! Open the door!'

Her hands were trembling. 'Go away!'

'Open the door! I want to speak with you.'

'Go Away!'

He thumped again.

Dropping down from her bunk, Emma slid back the bolt. François was leaning against the wall, his head resting on his forearm.

She could see that the door of the main cabin was slightly open.

'Here,' he said. 'This is for you.' He pressed a bundle of folded cloth into her hand.

She stared up at him.

'Take it! It is a gift,' he said, and without waiting for a response, sniffed and turned away.

Charles Witton stepped out of his cabin. 'Is that man bothering you?'

'No,' Emma replied. 'He brought me this.' She let the folds of cloth fall open. It was a blouse on which tiny flowers worked in coloured embroidery threads decorated the yoke and cuffs. The same multi-coloured silks were plaited into a braid threaded around the neck. Surprised, she held it out and shook her head. 'It is a gift from François.'

Charles Witton stood for a moment, looking uncomfortable. 'Then I will bid you good evening.'

'Very nice indeed,' François said, swinging himself down from the rigging and walking in a full circle around Emma. She smiled unashamedly. His dark eyes responded.

'I did not thank you last night,' she said.

'Last night is a long time ago,' he said. 'Let us forget about last night. The shirt is new, in case you thought maybe it was not. The women on the island—' he cleared his throat, 'the old women, that is, sit on their doorsteps and do this fancy stitching. You suit it very well. Do you like it?'

'It is beautiful, François.' She looked across to her old blouse that she had hung on the rigging to dry. 'Now I have two blouses.'

'Then I'm pleased that my gift makes you happy. Now, I must get back aloft.'

'François,' she called.

He turned and looked down.

She shook her head 'It's nothing.'

'Your gift from the Frenchman, if I am not mistaken,' Charles observed when he joined Emma on deck. 'May I say that it is very becoming?'

'Thank you,' she sighed. 'François is thoughtful. He has been good to me.'

The gentleman looked disappointed. 'Yes,' he said. 'I see that, and I now realize that this seaman means something to you.'

Emma studied his expression and the early signs of aging that masked the sadness in his face. 'Please understand when I say I am grateful to François. I would not be here it were not for him.'

'I understand,' he said gently, pulling her aside as a pair of empty barrels was trundled along the deck. 'We will be sailing early in the morning,' he said, looking up as if to check the wind.

'So be it,' she said. The words she spoke had little meaning. They were the words the captain often used, though she was never sure what meaning was behind them. Was it acceptance? Resentment? Cynicism? Or appreciation?

For Emma, the ship was her sanctuary. Save for the presence of one man, she felt secure. The crew, both officers and men treated her with politeness, or ignored her. Either way she felt no threat. She had a bunk – something the sailors did not have – and ample rations. When she had been sick, she had been nursed back to health, and cared for as if she were a child. On the *Morning Star* she felt free, without any undue pressure.

But, once the ship reached its destination, all that would change. So far, she had given little thought to what her future would hold. She had few clothes to wear and no accommodation to go to. She knew of no one in Sydney and, despite her schooling, had no professional qualifications. Though well educated, she had not been raised to work for a living. Where would she go? What would she do? She had no money. The coins she had brought with her were now in the possession of the captain. She had no claim on François, and her relationship with him was of no consequence. As for her son, if Joshua remained at sea, once they arrived in Australia, she would have no one to lean upon.

Perhaps, after all, she should have gone to her sister's home. Perhaps she should she have remained in Whitby with George and accepted her life whatever fortune that brought with it. But she had made her choice to run away and now she must stand by it.

'So be it,' she repeated softly.

From between a pile of barrels on the deck, Emma caught sight of him. He was standing near the bowsprit, his hand buried in his breeches, thrusting at himself, relentlessly. How pathetic he was, this decrepit old sailor. The man she hated and despised.

As she watched, his shoulders slumped forward, his knees faltered. He grabbed the caprail for support. After a few moments he righted himself, rubbed his crotch and went back to his duties. He was unaware and unconcerned that anyone had been watching him.

Emma shuddered. What was it about these seamen? Did the sea make them the way they were? Was it in any way connected to the movement of the body of water swaying beneath them? All day. Every day. Teasing like the tides. In and out. Back and forth. Luring them to her but giving nothing in return. Yet in the end how many would be sucked down into her darkness. Emma thought of the mothers of men who succumbed to her clutches. Names merely entered in a log as: *Lost at Sea*.

She shook her head, knowing she should not have witnessed such a thing. Surely she should have been shocked, afraid, or alarmed at what she saw, but on this occasion she had been compelled to watch this indecent act, not out of fear or anger, but out of pity.

Chapter 17

'Mr Witton, you said I should ask if there was anything I wanted.'

He put down his book and fastened his cravat. 'Yes. What can I get for you?'

'A pen and a few sheets of paper if you can spare them.'

His face warmed with a look of satisfaction, dispelling a little of the tiredness his eyes were hiding. 'That is not a problem,' he said. 'In fact it pleases me you feel well enough to write. I will get those immediately.'

'Thank you,' said Emma. 'But there is no real urgency.'

'Perhaps you would let me be the judge,' he said. 'If this wind holds, I am told we will be arriving in Santa de la Cruz on Friday. It is a busy port and we will, no doubt, find some English ships in the harbour. I have correspondence of my own so, if you will permit me, when you have written your letters, I will seal them for you and they can be despatched with mine to a reputable ship that is heading home.'

Emma smiled acknowledging his offer, but did not pass comment.

He hesitated. 'Perhaps, on the other hand, you would prefer to seal your own letters. I will supply you with sealing wax.'

'Oh, no! That is not necessary. I would have nothing that is private. You have already been very kind and now I find myself again indulging in your generosity.'

'Then allow me to satisfy that indulgence,' he said. 'You will have your writing materials immediately.'

'Missus!'

Emma didn't recognize the voice but opened her cabin door.

'Water,' the seaman said, placing a wooden pail on the floor. The water slopped from one side to another but being only half full it did not spill over the sides.

'It's hot and it's not salt!' he announced.

'Thank you,' she said, wondering why she had been afforded this luxury.

'Cook says that you are to make sure the bucket comes back to the galley.'

'Would you please tell Mr Sung, I will, and also tell him I said thank you.'

The man nodded and shuffled away.

She lifted the pail into her cabin and closed the door. The rope-handle was coarse and slightly greasy. The wooden slats, though scrubbed clean, were black around the lip with stains of various colours engrained below the waterline. Dipping her hand, Emma was delighted to feel the hot water swirl between her fingers.

Before she had chance to undress, there was another knock on the cabin door. Charles Witton's hands were full. Sheets of paper, blotter, ink, penknife and quill.

Emma accepted the items, thanked him, but lingered only briefly. She did not want the water to go cold. As she closed the door, she noted the heaviness which had returned to his face and wondered why that was.

That evening, the lamp in her cabin remained lit until late.

'I did not see you on deck this morning. I trust you are not unwell.'

Emma was embarrassed by the gentleman's attention. 'No, on the contrary,' she said. 'The writing materials you provided for me kept me occupied for a considerable time, both last evening and this morning.'

'Then I am happy. And if there is anything else I can do, please ask.' He politely inclined his head then wandered back towards the helm where Captain Preston was standing watching them.

'Mama!' shouted Joshua. 'Are you all right?' He climbed down the ratlines and jumped onto the deck.

'I am very well,' she said, breathing deeply on the sea air. 'And I can think of nothing better than being here on this ship. I don't know what life in Sydney will bring but it can be no worse than that which we left behind.'

'But Mama, I will not be—' Their conversation was cut short.

'All hands!' the call went out. 'Make ready to wear ship. Look lively, lad! To the mainbrace! Port side!'

Joshua jumped to the order. The deck came alive as men descended from the rigging. Others appeared from the hatches. Emma knew to keep away from the lengths of line snakes out on the deck. She had heard that when a rope started to run, it could burn the skin from a man's hands if he tried to hold it. With both watches called on deck, she returned below. For the second night her lamp burned long into the silent hours.

Leaning on the rail, François watched the water curl from the bow, as the ship cut cleanly through a near smooth sea. When Emma wandered forward, he spoke, though he did not lift his gaze from the waves. 'You have been trying to ignore me, I think.'

'That is not so. I have been busy. I am sorry if you think I have been rude.'

'Perhaps you have found better company amongst the gentlemen.' His words were cutting.

'That is not true.'

'But you have the passenger attending to you now. The word amongst the men is that he has taken a liking to you.' His look was cold as stone. 'And I have seen you on deck laughing with him.'

'Mr Witton has been good to me,' Emma replied. 'He cared for me when I was sick and he still shows concern. But there is nothing between us, and I have done nothing to encourage him in any way.'

'But you spend much time below decks. I thought you disliked being in your cabin.'

'Mr Witton brought me pen and paper which has kept me occupied. And cook, he kindly sent me water. Hot water. Not sea water. And I washed my blouse and skirt.' She spoke slowly trying to control the sense of irritation she was feeling. 'I am grateful to them both. François, you have been good to me and I would not be here were it not for you.' Her voice mellowed. 'It is I who have caused you pain and it grieves me to think I would cause you more.'

He shrugged. 'Time will tell!' he said, and walked away.

Why did he make it so hard for her? Why was he jealous? He was strong, good-looking, youthful. And he had stirred in her feelings which she had feared were lost forever. Her feelings for Charles Witton were born out of gratitude. He had nursed her to health. He was gentle and soft, intelligent and kind – kind like a father. She liked both men but was committed to neither. She stared ahead, unaware of the man above her in the rigging.

A pleasured smirk snaked across Tom Barstow's face as he dropped lightly to the deck in front of her. Startled, Emma looked for François on the deck but he was nowhere to be seen. 'Please, let me pass,' she said.

'Please,' he sniggered. 'Saying please to Old Tom. I like that.'

Emma looked about. No one was watching them.

'Tonight, I'll visit you. Not a word to anyone mind. You and me's got unfinished business. Remember?' His tongue flapped like a rutting goat's.

'Get out of my way!' she shouted.

'Tonight!' he hissed.

His forced laughter rang in her ears as she hurried back below. She shot the bolt hard across, and stood in the darkness with her back to the door, her body shaking.

During the long evening she slid from her bunk several times to check that the door was still locked. Though it was black as pitch in the cabin, she was afraid to undress, afraid to sleep, afraid of every sound, especially the sound of feet and creaking boards outside her cabin door.

The men appeared from the two forward hatchways. No one hurried. No one spoke. Burials at sea were always met with uncomfortable familiarity. The cloudless sky and sun lifting over the starboard side did nothing to raise the feeling of heaviness which was hanging like a wet sail over the ship.

Captain Preston paced the deck. He was in a black mood and becoming increasing impatient by the minute. Mr Thackray suffered the brunt of his agitation.

'Let's get these proceedings over and done with,' he snarled. 'What's keeping those men?'

The second mate, Will Wortley, yelled down the stairs, 'All hands on deck! Quick smart!'

The sailors congregated slowly, shuffling around the corpse stitched into its canvas wrapping. The cabin door on which it lay was at least eighteen inches shorter than the length of the man.

'Bloody waste of a good hammock, if you ask me!' a seaman mumbled as he tapped his cold pipe against his knee. 'Bloody waste!'

Nathaniel Preston scowled at the line of faces. 'Who said that? Mr Thackray find out who said that and make sure when it's his turn to go over, his hammock is weighted with a ration of salt pork for the sharks!'

'What's got into him?' one of the young sailors whispered. 'I never seen the captain in a mood as black as this before.'

'Always like this if someone dies. Gets angry as a bull-seal at breeding time. Takes it to heart, he does. Like they died just to spite him.' The talking stopped as the captain approached.

'Get these men in order! Let's get on with it!'

'All right you lot!' Wortley shouted. 'Stand straight. You! Take your 'at off! Show a bit of respect! You 'eard the capt'n.'

The ragged crew formed into two ragged lines. Joshua and the younger boys were unwillingly pushed to the front. Emma could see François standing behind them. Because of his lack of height, Tom Barstow's face was hidden behind the other men but Emma knew exactly where he was. On the narrow deck, a margin of only a man's stride was left between the row of seamen and the body sewn in its canvas envelope.

From the bow, Emma could not hear all the captain's words. She had not known the man who had died. Yorkie, he was called. Ben Yorke from Whitby. Charles had described him as blond, nineteen years of age, long-legged and pleasant-looking, save for a cast in his left eye. He said he was a good topman. Perhaps that was the reason she had seen little of him on the deck before his accident. Even though Charles had described him in detail, she could not remember his face. That made her feel guilty and disrespectful. Somewhere in the North Yorkshire port there was a mother unaware that her son had died. A mother who might learn of his fate in six months' time – or in a year – or perhaps she may never hear what happened to her boy. One thing was certain – she would never see him again.

Standing at the front of the assembly, one of the ship's boys giggled nervously until a sharp poke in the back took the smile from his face. He cursed the man standing behind him.

Joshua did not look up.

Mr Witton appeared preoccupied. He had his back turned against the morning's proceedings. He was gazing across the water as if watching a ship sailing by but the horizon was empty.

Nathaniel Preston held a worn black book in his hands, though he never opened it. The words which commended the body of Benjamin Yorke to the deep were not read, they were recited by rote. The burial service was in accordance with the proceedings set out for Her Majesty's naval ships. As it concluded, two of the older seamen tilted the cabin door, and as the ship heeled over, the body of the boy from Whitby slipped over the side and was received by the passing sea.

Captain Preston tapped the book on his leg. Like everyman on deck, he had a hankering to get away.

'Dismiss the men, sir?' the mate asked quietly.

The ship's master was staring at the cabin door on the deck – staring at the holes where the hinges had been, staring at the blood stain on the wood. Glaring at his officer, he yelled, 'What are you waiting for, Mr Thackray? Get that cleaned up and the deck swabbed!'

'You heard the captain! Move yourselves! Get on with it!'

The lines broke. The men who were not on watch scuttled below before any further duties were handed out.

Emma ran to the side. She was the only one to look back along the ship's wake in an attempt to see the spot which marked where the seaman had been buried. But the sea bore no mark and already the small disturbance his weighted body had caused had disappeared. No evidence remained of what had taken place and young Ben Yorke would quickly be forgotten.

'I could not help him,' Charles murmured sadly. His cheeks bore the evidence of dried tears.

'His death was no fault of yours.'

'I tried,' he said. 'But I lacked the skill. His arm should have been removed. I bound it but beneath the bandages it turned bad and then it was too late. I know I should not blame myself, but if only—'

Emma sensed the depth of his grief went beyond the loss of the young seaman. 'Can I be of any help?' she asked.

'Not now, thank you. I must go below. Nathaniel may need some company at this time.'

'Is there anything wrong?' Emma asked, as he reached the companionway.

'No,' he said pensively. 'Nothing anyone can change.' He stood for a moment looking along the deck. 'I don't know what it is about a ship and a man's relationship with the sea, but when things happen on board somehow they seem to be magnified. Perhaps, because it is a confined space and for those who live on board, it is their whole world. Small. Claustrophobic. They know no better. The sea is their life. They live it, twenty-four hours every day and seven days every week. It is all they wish to live for, and when they die it is the sea they wish to return to. I find it hard to understand.'

Emma waited not knowing what to say.

He paused. 'The ship will dock on the island of Tenerife the day after tomorrow. I understand the crew will be given time to go ashore. I wondered—' He paused. 'Would you care to take a drive with me into the town? I will hire a carriage. There are several places, quite respectable, where we can enjoy a cup of coffee or tea.' He looked for Emma's response. 'Or I can ask cook to make up a picnic basket that we can take with us. Santa Cruz is an interesting port and I would be happy to show you a little of it, if you would agree to accompany me.'

Emma smiled and thanked him, but her smile quickly faded into disappointment.

'What is it?' he said. 'Have I offended you?'

'No,' she said, looking down at herself. 'How can I accompany you, a fine gentleman in a carriage, dressed the way I am? I neither look nor feel presentable and I dare say my presence with you will raise some eyebrows.'

'I am not concerned how you are dressed.'

'But I am. I would not go into town dressed like this.' She held out the front of her skirt which bore the stain of ink the size of a dinner plate. 'And the only good blouse I have—'

'—is the one François gave you?'

'Yes,' she admitted

He sighed and shook his head. 'I am a thoughtless man. My head is filled with past events. At times I think I have forgotten how to care for the present. Forgive me, Emma. Say yes. Come with me, if only for a carriage ride to enjoy the sights. It will do us both good.'

'I will think about it,' she said.

'So be it.'

She watched, as he stepped back through the hatchway and descended to the lower deck. She knew he was weary.

Suddenly a rush of cold water swirled around her feet, startling her.

'Like to tease, don't you?' Old Tom hissed, as he scrubbed the deck around her.

She turned her head from his rancid smell.

'I'm sure you ain't forgotten your promise.' The toothless mouth gaped open as he dowsed the remaining water towards her legs.

Emma turned and felt for the companionway steps beneath her feet.

'Your boy got a good fitting hammock, has he?'

Climbing backwards down the ladder, his leathery foot stamped down on her fingers tight as a rat caught in a trap. Tom Barstow lowered his head to hers and breathed in her face. 'Now I'm feeling ready for you. Mark my words, in a few days you're gunna get what's coming to you!'

Chapter 18

Content as a duck sitting on a clutch of eggs, the seagull, resting on the end of the bowsprit, looked as much a part of the *Morning Star* as the brass bell engraved with the ship's name. Though the bell swung rhythmically to the ocean's pulse, the gull showed no inclination to change its position and appeared oblivious to the sweeping motion of ship's bow – rising high like the flight of shuttlecock, then crashing back to the sea like a sack of lead shot. Perched on the forward-most tip of the ship, the seagull sat like a feathered figurehead.

'Been there since morning,' the sailmaker said.

'Is that unusual?' Emma enquired.

'They like to take a ride sometimes. But he's cunning that one. I've seen him before. He was in that same spot the day before yesterday, and the day before that.' The old man got up and took Emma's elbow. 'Look there,' he pointed, 'on his chest. You can make out a sprig of yellow. I thought it was a daub of tar or paint, at first, but I've watched him cleaning himself. It's a feather all right. And bright yellow. A bit of cross blood in him, I reckon.'

'Could you ask him to stay for a while?' Emma asked cheekily.

'He won't take no notice of me, missus,' Jack Burns answered in a serious tone.

'Never mind,' she said. 'I'll be back in a moment.'

Hurrying back along the deck, Emma leapt over the lengths of rope waiting to be coiled and returned to her cabin. After collecting several items, she returned on deck and was pleased to find that the bird had not flown away.

Though the wind occasionally fluffed its feathers, the gull did not move.

Sitting down on the deck cross-legged, resting her paper on a piece of board, Emma dipped her pen in the ink and started to sketch. Jack Burns eyed her curiously.

As the ocean heaved beneath the ship's hull, roiling and turning like a body in a restless sleep, she worked. Completely absorbed. Her mind blocked off everything but the subject posing before her. She heard nothing of the cries for sails to be trimmed. Heard nothing of the whispers from the seamen whose curiosity brought them to investigate. Never noticed them as they hovered around admiring and pointing.

The seagull was copied on the paper in fine detail, from the hook of its beak, to the distinctive tip of its tail quills, each blackened as if dipped in a pot of pitch. Even the twisted feather bursting from its chest was etched lightly. She could add a dab of colour to it later.

Throughout the sitting, the bird's eye remained half open regarding the artist inquisitively.

Occasionally she stopped to examine her work. The proportions were sound, yet in her opinion the sketch was poor. The position of the eye was correct and its gaze was life-like. She had caught the correct curvature of the beak and had shaded the subtle variations in the grey feather tones without difficulty. Yet, something about it was wrong. The legs. She drew them again in the corner of the page.

'I'll give a shilling for it,' the sailmaker said.

'Then it's yours when I've finished.'

A half circle had gathered around her. Watching.

'Stone me dead!' a voice cried. 'I ain't seen nowt like that before. Like she's got the bird and stuck it on the paper if you ask me.'

The gull had been an ideal model.

'Here you are,' she said, presenting the drawing to old sailor.

The small crowd gathered on the foredeck attracted the attention of the mate. 'Give me a look!' he said, keen to know what the fuss was about.

Jack Burns, reluctant to hand over his property, held it at arm's length. 'Here. Take a gawk!' As the wind fluttered the paper, Burns gripped it firmly, as if afraid the disturbance might cause the bird on the page to fly away.

Len Thackray studied it, running his fingers along the wing feathers. Emma was concerned that if he rubbed too hard, the ink would smudge.

'Get your dirty paws off it!' the old man yelled. 'Nobody touches it!' Elbowing his way through the small crowd, he shuffled away to deposit his possession in his sea chest.

Feeling guilty at causing a disruption, Emma picked up her materials and the crowd broke up.

'I see you have been busy this morning,' François said.

Emma wondered how long he had been there.

'A little silly sketching to pass the time.'

'You enjoy doing that, I see.'

'Yes.'

'I think you are very clever, and very good at what you do.'

Emma smiled. 'It was far from perfect. It could have been better. But it amused me.'

That evening Emma ate her meal on deck. The days were longer in these latitudes and the evening air warm. She had not forgotten the captain's advice about staying below after dark, but a big white moon was rising and with several sailors lazing around, she felt relaxed. This evening felt different and she did not want to go below.

Leaning against the rail, Emma watched the sea as it curled along the side of the ship creating its own small waves in its wake. She was pleased to see François when he stepped up on deck and joined her. He read the greeting in her eyes.

They spoke of the sunset and the sea and she asked him about his life. About Brittany and what the French countryside was like. Asked the reason he had run away from home as a boy to become a sailor. Throughout the conversation she was careful to make no mention of Madeira.

'Enough of my past,' he said with a flick of the hand as if wafting his words to the wind. 'Tell me about yourself. What you have done. Where you have been.' He inclined his head to one side and looked into Emma's eyes. 'I once overheard you telling an old fisherman you sailed to France. Tell me about that. Tell me about that adventure when you were a small girl.'

'You have a good memory,' she said.

The Frenchman smiled cheekily.

'Some things in the past one can never forget,' she mused. 'Because they are printed in the mind like words on the pages of a book. Life was wonderful, when I was a child. How can I ever forget that time?'

She could feel his eyes on her as she gazed across the water to the ripples shimmering silver in the moonlight.

'You sailed to Le Havre, if I am not mistaken?'

'Yes. From London, on a big clipper ship, with my parents. When we arrived in France we were met by a coach and driven to a château – very close to Paris.'

'A château! That sounds very grand.'

'It was grand indeed and, as I was just a girl, I thought it was a palace.'

François' dark eyes sparkled. 'Tell me about this palace you visited.'

Emma took a deep breath. 'I remember it clearly. There were lots of rooms with pictures in gilt frames hanging from every wall. And in the dining hall, there was a long table and enough chairs to seat every man on this ship. The servants wore powdered wigs and strange fashioned clothes and, at night, the candelabras shone with dozens of candles.' She smiled. 'It is funny what one remembers.'

'Was it there you learned to speak French?' François asked, with a glint in his eye.

Emma smiled coyly and nodded.

'How long did you stay?'

'For more than six months. My father had been invited to paint the portrait of a fine lady. She was a widow and very rich. Her name was Madame Delaunay. Papa was a very good artist and well respected. In the past, he had painted several English nobles but it was the first time he had been commissioned to paint in Europe.'

François pulled out his pouch of tobacco and rolled a few leaves on his palm.

'*Madame* was delighted with the portrait and, when it was finished, in celebration she arranged a big party and invited many important guests. Despite their rank or status, she insisted Papa was the only *célébrité*.'

'Your father enjoyed his popularity, no doubt?'

'Alas, no. His work was popular and admired, and his services sought after, but he never wished for that. Although he had accepted the invitation to stay in France, mama was not happy while we were there. Having been raised in a country home, she felt uncomfortable in such a grand place.'

François puffed smoke from his pipe.

'But you do not want to listen to this childish talk. I am boring you.'

'On the contrary, I can see from the expression in your eyes that you get pleasure from remembering these things. I think in the past you have seen much sadness therefore these memories are good for you. Please continue.'

'Then let me tell you about Madame Delaunay. She had a son. His name was Christian and he was four years older than I. He had a fine manner and I thought him handsome, but of course I was very young. He was tall and slender with long light brown hair.' As he spoke, she glanced at François' unruly queue tied with a strip of leather. 'Christian always wore his hair fastened with a bow of silk ribbon.' Emma paused, her thoughts flittering about in her head. 'He said he enjoyed spending time with me, as it helped him with his English and he promised to teach me French.'

'And did he?'

'I learned a little, but have forgotten most of it now.'

'Until you became confused in the head!'

'Now you are mocking me.'

The Frenchman laughed. 'I would not do that. Please go on.'

'The estate was like a great park and covered many acres. From the house, a wide path led between rows of marble statues to a lake with a fountain in the centre. The water pattered from it like heavy rain on paving slabs.' As Emma's thoughts drifted, she remembered watching Christian from her window as he sat in the garden sketching or painting.

'In the afternoons,' she said, 'My sister Anna and I would wander down to the lake and sit on the grass making daisy chains or boats from leaves that we would sail on the lake. We pretended we were sailing to China or America.' She laughed. 'I never thought that one day I would take a passage to Australia.'

As the full moon rose above the ship, the sails cast shadows that swayed across the deck.

'Tell me more about this pool of water you sailed your small boats upon.'

Emma smiled contentedly. 'One afternoon, when the air was warm and filled with fragrance from the flowers, I walked alone from the *château*, through the mosaic of flowerbeds and trimmed hedges down to the lake.' She paused for a moment as the memories engulfed her.

'Christian asked if he might sketch a portrait of me. "Where"? I asked. "Here", he said, taking my hands and sitting me cross-legged on the grass. He leaned my face to one side and cupped my hands together on my lap.' As Emma spoke her head tilted to one side and she slid her hands together and, though her gaze was set on the moonlit waters of the vast Atlantic, in her mind she visualized the ornamental lake glistening with the tiny ripples from the pattering fountain.

François studied her every expression.

'I never moved,' she said, when she resumed her tale. 'I did not even blink while Christian drew my picture. And if the breeze blew my hair he would kneel down and brush it from my cheek.'

She remembered how he had laid her in the grass, had lifted the ringlet from her cheek and kissed her – her first real kiss. Remembered how he had loved her – not as the child, but as a woman. And remembered that she had allowed him to do so and felt no fear or shame.

Standing on the ship's deck, Christian's words echoed through her head, "You are very lovely". François had used the very same words in the grounds of Whitby Abbey when he had lifted the strands of hair from her face. And he, too, had laid her in the grass. She remembered how good she had felt, how gentle Francois' touch had been and how she had wanted him to love her also.

He interrupted her dream. 'But when your father had finished his work, you had to return to England?'

'Yes, and I never saw Christian again.'

'But you have not forgotten him.'

'No, and indeed, how can I?' Emma paused to consider her next words. 'Because Joshua is Christian's son.'

In the frothy spume turned from the ship's bow tiny pinpricks of light appeared and disappeared. Emma breathed the night air, her mind filled with the fragrance of the *château*'s gardens: the scent of rose, jasmine, honeysuckle and the memories of a young man she met beside a pattering fountain.

'Forgive me,' she said, turning to the sailor. 'I do not know why I am telling you this. It is something I have never told anyone.'

'Do not be sorry,' he said. 'It is the truth. Never regret your words.'

Emma pushed the hair from her eyes. It was very late and the moon was high. 'I must go,' she said.

'No,' he begged. 'Stay a little longer. For me. Please.'

Chapter 19

'Would you step into my cabin for a moment? There are two things I want to speak with you about.'

Charles Witton's tone was out of character. Emma politely accepted his invitation but was unsure if his demeanour was masking embarrassment or hiding an underlying feeling of annoyance. She followed him into his day cabin.

'Please take a seat.'

Emma perched on the edge of the straight chair, while allowing her eyes to feast on both the cabin and its contents. It was the first time she had been into this part of the ship.

It was a small stateroom, half the size of the captain's, but still spacious enough for a narrow table and two chairs. On the built-in desk lay several large leather-bound books, their spines adorned with gold embossed characters and roman numerals. A vacant space on the shelf above the desk indicated where the volumes usually resided. The adjacent cupboards fixed to the hull, ran from ceiling to floor save for a small round window. The natural light it provided, though limited, was a great improvement on the glow from an oil lamp.

Sitting in the centre of the table was the box Emma had seen hoisted aboard in Funchal Bay. The black-stained wooden box with shiny brass corners and hinges was set on its end with the lid open like a door. Seated inside in a cushion of padding was a microscope, its brasses were also brightly polished. The eye-piece had been removed and was sitting on a pad of blue velvet.

Mr Witton closed the lid of the instrument box. 'A gift from an old friend,' he said, as he squeezed awkwardly between the table and a large cabin-trunk which was taking up most of the floor space. A scrap of white cloth was protruding from beneath the lid of the chest. Its padlock and key lay on the table.

Facing Emma, Charles appeared uncomfortable. She cupped her hands on her lap and waited.

Turning, he reached for a piece of paper from his desk. 'I must know,' he asked gravely, 'are you responsible for this?' He handed it to Emma. It was the drawing of the seagull.

'Yes,' she replied cautiously. 'I did not think you would be offended if I used your writing paper to draw on.'

'No! No! Just tell me, did you really draw this?'

'Yes,' she said, not knowing how she should respond.

He leaned towards her, looking directly into her eyes. 'This is one of the most observant drawings I have seen since my visits to the Royal Society's rooms some years ago. It reminds me of the fine work of an unfortunate young artist, Sydney Parkinson. He sailed with Cook to the South Seas. You may have heard of him.'

Emma shook her head.

'The sketch is anatomically correct and quite exquisite.'

Emma smiled and handed the paper back to him.

'I gave it to the sailmaker. I believe his name is Jack Burns.'

'Yes, yes. He showed it to me and I could not resist asking him if I might borrow it.' His face and tone relaxed. 'I must say, he was reticent at first, and I can understand why. I had to promise I would return it to him this afternoon.' He studied the picture again and shook his head. 'It seems such a waste. This quality of work should be set in a frame.'

She acknowledged his compliment with a smile.

'But tell me, where did you learn this skill? Which School did you study at? Do you have any more drawings?'

'My father taught me,' she said, allowing herself to relax against the chair back. 'Both my sister and I learned to draw at home.' She digressed. 'She is far better with oils, but I have always been more comfortable with pen and ink.'

'Do you have any more of these?' he repeated. 'Could you do some more?'

'I have four or five sketches in the cabin. They have kept me occupied lately.'

'And I thought—' he said, placing the picture beneath one of the books on his desk, '—no matter. I wish to ask a favour. Would you permit me to supply you with whatever materials you require so that you can pursue your art whenever you feel inclined?'

'That would be very kind of you, sir. It is a pastime that gives me a great deal of pleasure.' She smiled. 'It also keeps me out of harm's way.'

'But where do you draw? I have not seen you working.'

'Sometimes on the deck but mostly in the cabin.'

'But the light must be poor and you have no proper bench to work on. Oh, Emma,' he cried, 'why am I so blind and inconsiderate. You must forgive my failings. From now on, I insist you work in here.' He hesitated. 'That is if you would not object to sharing these surroundings. You may use the table and you are welcome to come here whenever you wish. It would give me great pleasure.'

'That is a very kind offer, but Captain Preston—'

'Do not concern yourself about the captain. I will speak with him, and I assure you, he will understand. But I beg your permission to show this sketch to him. I am sure he will be as impressed as I am and I guarantee he will be surprised to learn that you are the artist.

Emma blushed. 'As you wish.'

'That brings me to my second question.' He edged around the table and leaned over the cabin trunk. His voice again adopted a serious tone. 'I find this matter a little difficult to broach, as I do not want to cause you embarrassment. He lifted the hasp on the chest and opened the lid.

From where she was sitting, Emma was unable to see the contents of the trunk.

Charles looked up at her. 'I understand that due to unforeseen circumstances you boarded the ship without luggage. You told me yourself that you have few clothes apart from those you are wearing now.' He breathed deeply and cast his eyes over the contents of the chest. 'This chest contains the personal effects of my wife and daughter, God rest their souls. I have no use for them.' He sat back into the chair.

Emma was shocked. 'I am truly sorry to hear that.'

'I did not know what to do with them,' he said, gazing up through the cabin window to the sky where fine lines of parallel cloud stretched out like warp threads on a giant loom. 'But, I could not dispose of them, so I had them consigned with me on the ship.' He looked at Emma. 'If there are any items here that could be of use to you, you are welcome to them.'

Response was not easy but, before Emma could speak, he held up his hand. 'I know nothing of the fickleness of ladies' fashions but I assure you the garments are of best quality materials and workmanship and if you will excuse me for saying, they will be far more becoming than the attire you are presently wearing.'

Emma fingered the stain on her skirt.

'Please,' he said, without waiting, 'you will be doing me a favour if you will, at least, accept some of these garments. And if the dresses do not fit, when we arrive in port, I will find a dressmaker to make the necessary alterations. Please,' he said, holding out his hand and helping Emma to her feet, 'take a little time. Examine them. I will leave you alone.'

As he stood beside the door, she could see the tension had vanished from his face, while the lines around his eyes fanned into a caring smile.

'Perhaps, later this afternoon, you will show me your other drawings.'

'Yes,' she said.

'I will look forward to that.'

The cooper touched the knuckle of his index finger to his forehead. 'Enjoy your day, miss.' The sailors, rolling empty water barrels across the lashed planks, stopped and gawped at Emma as she disembarked. Nathaniel Preston watched from the deck.

With layers of fine fabric clouding her legs, Emma was unable to see her feet. She trod carefully, as the laced boots she was wearing were made from the softest suede and she was afraid of spoiling them. After padding the deck bare-foot for three weeks, she was pleased they moulded well to her feet and did not pinch her toes. With her gloved hand held firmly by Mr Witton, Emma tripped lightly across the gangplank and onto the noisy quay at Santa Cruz de Tenerife.

A carriage was waiting for them. 'Let me help you,' Charles said, taking her arm to assist her up the two small steps.

'I am sorry,' she said, swaying against him. 'I feel I am still moving with the ship.'

'That is not unusual,' he said 'It is good to go ashore whenever in port. I like to reclaim my land legs, even if only for a short time.'

From the busy wharf the rig rumbled slowly through the sprawling town. As Emma's eyes flitted about, Charles Witton regarded her closely. She scanned the streets, houses, stalls and shops, indulging herself in all Santa Cruz had to offer.

'It is place of contrasts,' she said. 'The black-sand beaches. The white houses. The pale turquoise sea. The great grey mountain sombre and bare yet caped in ermine. And the colours of the flowers – yellow, magenta, violet, indigo – all so vibrant. I had not imagined it to be like this. It is charming.'

'May I say, you are charming too?'

Emma smiled coyly.

'Let us find somewhere to sit for a while. May I suggest a short drive out of the town and into the hills? I guarantee the air there will be cool and fresh.' He turned and spoke to the driver.

Emma was surprised at his command of the Spanish language.

From the garden of a small café they looked down to the ocean, a sea of blues, greens and aquamarine dotted with flecks of white – the single sails of local fishing boats.

'It looks so smooth from here,' said Emma. 'Yet we experienced so much turbulence on the way here.'

'Yes,' he sighed. 'Life can be unkind.' He reached across the table. 'May I?' he said, taking her hand and lifting it into his. 'I think you are a remarkable woman, Emma Quinlan. And, if I may say, you look enchanting today.'

'It is the dress,' she said, looking down at the layers of frills which decorated her skirt. 'These clothes are lovely.' She unfastened the bow from under her chin and laid her bonnet on the table. 'I trust it does not bring back too many sad memories seeing me wearing it.'

'On the contrary,' he said. 'It upset me to see them locked away.'

'Please, tell me of your family, if it is not too painful.'

Gazing out along the rugged coastline, Charles smiled sadly. 'My wife died of consumption in October last year. She had been ailing for several years but her death came as a shock. I felt guilty that I had neglected her. I had just returned from Australia and had not been aware how ill she was. I had always wanted her to go overseas with me. Begged her. But she would not leave England. She loved the English countryside and I think she was afraid of the long sea voyage.'

He turned to Emma. 'After her death I did not want to stay in England and as Charlotte, our daughter, was eager to see the colonies, I booked a passage for us both. The Royal Society offered me the opportunity to join a scientific expedition, which I accepted. I thought it would be good to keep myself occupied. My intention was that, when we arrived in the colony, Charlotte could stay with friends in Sydney and she was looking forward to that.

'She was unlike her mother,' he said. 'She was afraid of nothing. She had my enthusiasm for travel and a zest and confidence not usually seen in young ladies her age. Alas, perhaps, too much. Six weeks ago she fell from her horse.' He sighed heavily. 'She clung to life for a week, but never woke once in that time. I spoke to her while she lay unconscious but I do not know if she could hear me. On the seventh night she died. She was seventeen.'

Emma waited a while before speaking, 'What will you do now when you get to Sydney?'

'I will catch up with the expedition. They will not be too far ahead. I should have been with the main party when they sailed from London three weeks ago but the funeral arrangements, which had to be made, delayed me. Then I had difficulty finding another ship and thought I would have to abort my plans.

'When Nathaniel offered me a berth on the *Morning Star*, I was pleased to accept. It was fortunate for me, he too had been delayed. You do not know him as I do, but the captain is a good man. He, too, has been confronted with considerable trauma in his life, though of a different nature.' He looked at Emma. 'Nathaniel Preston is my brother-in-law. My wife was his youngest sister.'

A girl appeared from the house carrying a jug of fresh orange juice to refill their glasses. As they drank, the conversation flowed easily. Charles spoke enthusiastically of his books – his collection of first editions that were carefully packed away in one of his trunks, and of the countries he had visited. Sitting in comfortable silence, they watched a pair of butterflies flitting between the flowers and listened to the hum of bees that swarmed past them swirling skywards like a column of drifting chimney smoke. Then Emma spoke of her sister, of her childhood, of Lincolnshire and cows and memories, sharing the patchwork snippets of her life which create a lasting picture.

'Would you care to walk a little?' he said.

The verdant grass, a product of the island's rich volcanic soil, was soft beneath their feet. Overhead, trees rustled in the light breeze. Multi-coloured flowers cascaded from white stone walls while in the fields, old twisted vines, thick and nobbled, crept along fences or stood with arms extended like drooping scarecrows. In the distance, the snow-capped peak of the sleeping mountain glistened in the sun.

'So peaceful,' Charles said. 'If only it could always be this way.'

Once the sun had slipped behind the mountain, dusk fell on the streets of Santa Cruz. The night clouds rolling in from the west looked ominous.

'Damn them!' the captain cried. He could wait no longer. 'Damn them!' he murmured.

'Cast off!'

Will Wortley and two other men slid the gangplank back onto the deck, as the *Morning Star*'s bow nudged the jetty setting timber squealing against timber. The wharf recoiled under the pressure but the boys who were fishing from its worn decking were unconcerned. With a splash, the aft line dropped into the sea and the last sailor stepped aboard before the gap between ship and jetty widened.

For a moment the ship was motionless, as if not knowing which way to head, then slowly, creating barely a ripple, it began drifting seaward on the outgoing tide, floating from the placid harbour like a piece of flotsam. Without a call, the mooring ropes were hauled on board and flaked along the deck like sleeping serpents. From the yards the square sails dropped and with the helm hard over, the headsails filled. Creating barely a sound, the *Morning Star* swam smoothly between the other ships anchored in the busy port and headed for the open sea.

'How many?' the captain asked impatiently.

'Two.'

Nathaniel Preston looked back towards Tenerife. Pinpricks of light flickered from windows in the old town. The white buildings looked black while the grey volcano which dominated the island by day had disappeared into the clouds.

'Damn them!' the captain cried. 'Damn their ungrateful souls!'

Chapter 20

Captain Preston handed the telescope to his mate. 'What do you make of that, Mr Thackray?'

The seaman scanned the sea but saw nothing. No ships, no land, not even white caps. Holding the piece to his eye, he adjusted it and searched again.

'A column of smoke?'

'That is what I thought.'

'A ship on fire?'

'I think not.' Nathaniel Preston said, rubbing his right eye gently. 'If I am not mistaken what we are seeing is coming from Fogo!'

The seaman looked again. 'But ain't we still a day's sailing from Cape Verde, Capt'n?'

'By my calculations, more than fifty nautical miles,' he answered cautiously, stepping onto the larboard gunnel and leaning back against the rigging. 'If my assumption is correct and, if what we are seeing is smoke, then what we are looking at is something mighty big. I fear that is a cloud of ash which is extremely tall and is being carried this way.'

'But doesn't our bearing take us well to the west of the Verde Islands? You had no intention of sailing in there, had you?'

'Correct, Mr Thackray. A place best to be avoided. But a volcanic eruption—! That is a worry.' The captain climbed higher in the rigging, but without the telescope the ominous cloud was not visible. 'Reduce sail, Mr Thackray. Keep the same bearing but get a good man up top with a glass. Tell him to keep a close watch on that cloud, but tell him to also give a good eye to the sea. I want to be informed of the slightest change in either.'

'Aye, Captain.'

'And get the men to look sharp about furling the sails. I want everything lashed down tight and double checked, and the main hatches battened down.'

Len Thackray called for all hands but the response was slow, the men grumbled as they filtered onto the deck and climbed slowly. As the calls went out, the two largest square sails were hauled up to their yards, folded neatly and secured. The men on the downhauls moved steadily, stepping over the tangled mess of sheets and lines.

Muttered grumbles were heard from the crew who were unaware of the reason for reducing sail. The sky showed no inclination to storm, there was no damage to the ship and there were no other vessels bearing down. Besides that, *Morning Star* had been struggling to make four knots in the light conditions. In the opinion of the men there was no justification for reducing sail further.

'Tidy those lines!' the mate shouted. 'And be quick about it! I've seen lubbers do a better job!' But the men still worked begrudgingly cursing the captain's orders which had taken them from their relaxation.

'What's happening, Nathaniel?' Charles asked, as he joined his brother-in-law near the helm.

The captain indicated the direction of the possible problem and handed him his telescope. 'Very low on the horizon. Take a look.'

'Looks like a speck of grey fluff to me.'

'If I'm not wrong, it's smoke from a volcano – Mount Fogo in the Verde group of islands. What concerns me is that we were not advised of any activity before we left Tenerife. My assumption therefore can only be that it has just exploded.'

'Does that put us in any danger?'

'I can't be sure,' he said. 'It's a mountain that erupts every few years. I remember hearing about it in '52 when I was on the *Lord Clarence*, and again in 1854. What concerns me is its size. That cloud is way beyond the horizon, yet we can see it from here. That means it is huge and it is rising to a great height. If the explosion was only recent and a big one, it could have stirred up a tidal wave that hasn't yet reached us. All I know is that since we left the Canary Islands we have not experienced any big waves.' He paused. 'What we do not know is when the explosion happened.'

'Perhaps the volcano is only grumbling. Could that be possible? I gather some smoke constantly.'

'It is possible.'

'Do you intend to sail close in?'

'No. I will chart a wide course. Unfortunately that will take us further west than I had originally planned. The only hope then is that we do not get ourselves becalmed in the process.'

'What can I do?'

'I suggest you batten down anything in your cabin that is loose or fragile. If the sea builds up it could become a little damp and lumpy.'

'You have a delightful way of understating the obvious, Nathan.'

The captain winked. 'Then, perhaps I should have said, it could be like a wall of water taller than this ship swallowing everything in its path.'

'Much better,' Charles said. 'Now I understand.'

It was a wearying afternoon. Sailing with triple reefed sails, the ship made slow headway. The men on deck, now aware of the possible danger, observed the progress of the creeping cloud that had loomed up from the horizon and was advancing across the sky, broadening and deepening with each mile that was covered. Opinions as to its origin and significance were argued by the men at the rails. From her favourite place in the bow, Emma found herself more interested in a pod of dolphins that was accompanying the ship on its slow south-westerly bearing.

'I have not seen you on deck much these days.' François' tone was cynical. 'Not since you went ashore on the arm of the gentleman. I hear you now spend your time in his cabin. Perhaps you have become too fancy to speak with a common seaman.'

'François, that is not so. I have been drawing.'

'Ah! I remember,' he said. 'The artist!'

'François, I believe you are jealous. But you have no reason to be. And I have no reason to feel guilty.'

'Of course.' The disparaging tone was still evident.

'The dresses! That is what you do not like, that he has given some things to me. Is it that which has upset you?'

'I am not upset. Why should I be?' He turned away from her, his arms folded across his chest.

'François,' she said firmly. 'I like to draw and Mr Witton has generously allowed me to use his day cabin. When I work, I am alone, yet it causes you concern.'

His voice mellowed. 'No, I am pleased for you. But I admit, when I saw you leaving the ship and going with him on the island, I was jealous. I had forgotten you were born a lady. And Mr Witton is a gentleman.'

'But François, when we get to Sydney—'

'Ah! Sydney. When we get there—' He laughed a strange laugh. 'You dare to gaze into the crystal ball? You want to know what the future holds?' He looked at her, his eyes questioning hers. 'Tell me this, what is it you want to see? What is it you wish for deep down inside your heart?'

'I do not know what I wish for.'

'Then let me guess. I suggest that you do not wish to live your life alone. That you would wish to take another husband. And, if I dare suggest, since we first met by the abbey, you may have wished that man to be me. Am I right? Was that your wish?'

Emma looked confused. 'I don't know.'

'Tell me truthfully, would you like it if I were to leave the ship in Sydney? I have some money you know. I could buy a piece of land and work each day from dawn till dusk till I was an old man.' But the smile had left his eyes. 'I can tell you that is not what I would wish. Being tied to one place would be an anchor around my neck. As I told you, I've been at sea since I was a boy. Even now, when we are in port, I hanker for the day the ship will leave. I wander the wharves looking at the water wishing for nothing better than to be back on it.' He shook his head. 'There is salt in my veins and my place is here. I would rather drown in the bosom of the ocean, than die a rich man on the streets of Sydney, and that is the truth.'

His tone relaxed. 'I made only one promise to you, Emma, and that I will keep. But I made no promise to you that I would leave the sea. When the *Morning Star* docks in Sydney, you will go ashore alone. As for me, I will sail with the ship. It is better you do not waste any of your thoughts and wishes on me.'

A cry from the mainmast brought the crew hurrying to the port side. 'Boat! Four points off the port bow!'

A small boat was bobbing on the swell. It carried no sail and the sea was in control of its rudder. The red and white clinkered hull looked empty, adrift, until a man clambered to his feet and supported himself against the bare mast. He was half naked. His skin as black as pitch. His hair as white as snow.

'What do you make of it, Capt'n?'

As the *Morning Star* sailed closer, the bodies of half a dozen other men, all black-skinned were spotted lying in the boat's hull with nothing to protect them from the glaring sun.

'Trouble,' the captain answered, shaking his head.

'Pirates?' the helmsman asked.

The captain didn't answer. 'Two skins of water,' he ordered. 'Be ready to toss them overboard and be quick about it.'

'Do we shorten sail, captain?'

'No! Mr Thackray, Make sail!'

'Aye aye, Capt'n.'

This time, the crew responded quickly to the call for all hands but from the bobbing craft, the man's cries went unheeded.

When Emma realized the *Morning Star* was about to sail past the boat, she dashed along deck. 'Captain! Captain!' she shouted, pointing to the man who was flailing his arms in desperation. 'You must stop the ship!'

The boat was no more than twenty yards away.

'Stop! Stop!' she cried.

Captain Preston turned his back on her.

Before she was half way along the deck, Charles grabbed her by the arms. She struggled against his grip. 'Those men!' she yelled. 'You must help them or they will perish out there!'

'Emma, be silent!' Charles begged.

'No!' she cried. 'You must stop him. Tell him to stop the ship. Someone must help them! Are you blind?' she cried. 'Can't you see they are dying?'

From the stern, Nathaniel Preston scowled as Charles led her by the arm to the companionway.

'It is best if you go below, Emma. At least until this incident is over.'

'But why doesn't he help them? They will die!'

'He is the master of the ship and it's a decision he alone must make. Allow me to take you below.'

'No,' she said, wrenching her arms free, 'I can manage alone, thank you.'

As the small boat drifted close to the *Morning Star*'s hull, the man held out his arms in supplication. The two goatskins, tossed overboard, splashed up against the boat but no effort was made to retrieve them. Within minutes, the man's cries were left behind. The only sound on deck was the luff of a sail and the creak of the ship's timbers. Even the crew was silent. The red and white hull was soon a speck on the sea. Another piece of drifting flotsam.

In her cabin, Emma lay back on her bed unable to dispel the memory of the scene she had witnessed. The expression on the black man's face would remain fixed in her mind forever. The look of anguish, exhaustion, desperation and despair was unforgettable. She had experienced them all.

What manner of man was Nathaniel Preston? How could he turn his back on a human being pleading for help? And the other men, already dead or close to death lying in the bottom of the boat. How could he leave them to perish adrift in an open boat under a blazing sun? How could François and Charles describe the captain as a good man? His actions were incomprehensible and unforgivable.

Outside her door, the deck-boards creaked. She sat up cradling her knees in her arms. She held her breath and listened. The doorknob rattled. She watched it turn around and back. Though she had slid the bolt across and no one could get in, her heart beat quickened. Was it Thomas Barstow? She did not move. She hardly dared to breathe. The boards creaked again. Then it was quiet.

That night an eerie yellow gloom veiled the moon and the pungent smell of sulphur seeped deep into the ship. Throughout the night, the bell rang out: *clang-clang, clang-clang, clang-clang*, and at dawn a burning sunrise heralded the day. On the deck, the tiny particles of ash that had rained down overnight lay like a carpet of grey snow, broken only by the bare footprints of the men on watch.

It had been an uneventful night. No sound had been detected from the Verde Islands and the surface of the sea had not risen. The *Morning Star* was heading south. It would change course before it reached the Doldrums.

Chapter 21

'He is cruel and without a soul!'

'Emma! Listen to me! The captain is not without feeling, and he is man with a conscience. The decision he made was hard enough without your wild outburst.'

'But his decision was unjustified. He could have turned the ship. Stopped. Provided food and shelter or offered help at least. But, no, he sailed on and condemned those men without even listening to them.'

'The captain was well aware he was sentencing those men to their deaths. But their fate was already sealed,' he sighed, 'probably even before they left their island.'

Charles pulled his chair closer. 'Nathaniel knew those men would perish. He also knew if he brought them on board they would share their fate with his own crew.' He drew a long breath. 'Cape Verde is not a good place. Those men, God rest their souls, were probably slaves trying to escape. Escape!' he mused. 'Escape from their overseers, escape from an island beset by drought and famine, and escape from a mountain that had just exploded. But sadly there was nowhere from them to escape to. And they had nothing to take with them except disease.

'This group of islands is smitten with cholera and in recent years the disease has killed hundreds if not thousands of its inhabitants. Yes,' he said. 'Captain Preston condemned those unfortunate souls and they will perish, but what he did was justified. He had no choice.'

Joshua's hands were tied. As the spikes of a pitchfork poked at his bare back he slumped forward and crawled along the deck on his hands and knees. The deriding cries, jeers and taunts from the seamen echoed across the ship. There was no escape.

But he was not alone. As he was pulled to his feet, four others were lined up beside him. Two were topmast men, Irish lads in their twenties, experienced seamen who had served time on an American route, but had only ever sailed in the North Atlantic. There was the boatswain's apprentice and a Whitby boy who had sailed north to Greenland but never been south of the Thames. The ritual they were to be submitted to was mandatory, irrespective of age. No seaman was exempt if it was the first time he had crossed the Line.

From the quarterdeck the haunting sound blown from a large conch shell echoed around the deck. The ship had hove to into the wind and was now catching the breeze on the front of the sails. *Morning Star* was rolling but holding fairly still.

'What will happen?' asked Emma, concerned for her son.

'Watch,' said Charles.

Len Thackray, the mate appeared from below deck in the role of King Neptune, escorted by his entourage. His face, arms and chest were painted blue and a length of sacking was tied around his loins to represent his tail. His helpers and his *wife* were also daubed in colour. In his hand he held a pitchfork, and on his head wore a wig of fresh seaweed, wet and shiny. A small barrel-hoop honed to the size of his head, made an adequate crown. As he paraded the deck, he was greeted with cheers and whistles, some men bowing others dropping to their knees.

Enthroned on an empty water barrel, the king listened to the charges brought against the five men and delivered his maritime judgement accordingly.

As the ceremony proceeded, Charles noted an increasing concern on Emma's face. 'It is the tradition,' he said. 'The boys must go through it. And believe me they enjoy it. Ask any of them when it is over and they will tell you they would not miss it.'

Emma looked sceptical.

'Believe me. Even I was put through the ordeal when I first crossed the equator. Although,' he added, 'I was treated kindly. But I am pleased they have excluded you from their games.'

Emma watched as Neptune's new subjects were shaved, their heads then smeared with a foul looking substance and dusted with flour. With the addition of feathers from a recently plucked chicken, the victims were placed, in turn, astride a plank balanced over a large barrel.

'What's in it?' Emma asked, sensing what was about to happen.

'It is best you do not know. The contents will not kill anyone but I imagine it is not pleasant. When I was put thought my initiation I was daubed with blue, but I was excused from being taunted over the barrel. At least there are some advantages in being a gentleman!'

With the extra ration of rum in their bellies, the crew's shrieks and yells grew steadily louder. One by one the boys were summonsed to pay the required forfeit to the king. Unable to comply with the request, they succumbed to the barrel's sloppy contents and after near drowning in it, each initiate was run headlong to the gunnels and tossed overboard to the cheers of the assembled company.

When Joshua was dragged dripping back onto the deck, relief showed on Emma's face. The white of his teeth and broad smile showed through the layer of muck and grease still sticking to his face. He waved to his mother then helped haul out the boatswain's young mate, who, being unable to swim, had almost drowned. The boy's spluttering and coughing was greeted with thunderous applause from the crew.

'Sailors are a strange breed,' Emma said.

'You think so?'

'They are fit and fearless and at times seem intelligent and kind. But at other times they seem cruel and cold-hearted.'

'No different from men anywhere, I think.'

'What are you looking at?' Charles asked.

Emma drew herself back from the ship's rail and stared back into the darkness. Waiting for the moon to rise, the sails hung like leaden clouds against the black sky.

'You have been here for over an hour and hardly moved. I thought perhaps you were sick.'

'There,' she said, pointing down to the waves curling from the ship's bow. 'I am watching the stars in the sea. See them,' she pointed. 'They sparkle like tiny diamonds. So many of them. They dance in the foam. I think they are attracted to the ship as I cannot see them where the water is calm.'

'You are observant, Emma,' Charles said, leaning against the rail beside her. 'Those diamonds, as you call them, have puzzled men for centuries. Long ago, men thought they were the sun's rays which had dived into the sea. At night, they said the fiery spirits would try to escape the water to fly back to the heavens. Some said the troubled sea created sparks like those emitted when a flint strikes steel. Some said they were small fish or insects that could glow like fireflies. Others argued that at times they came alive and swirled together in a shining mist of colour that floats across the sea turning and turning like a spinning top. Some say it is an aurora. Others – an illusion.'

'And what do you say?'

'I say the sparkling in the sea is a wonder. I say we have so much to learn and so little time to do it.' He sighed to the twinkling water cascading along the hull. 'Each flash of light,' he said, 'is from an animalcule, a minute organism which only glows when turbulence disturbs it. The wash created by the *Morning Star* is causing it to shine.' He looked at her but her eyes could not be distracted from the sea. 'Your tiny stars are no illusion, Emma. They are real. Millions upon millions of them. And perhaps, as you suggest, they lie in wait for ships to pass to come to life and dance together in the foam.'

They stood beside the rail, shoulders resting together, listening as the bow pounded the sea, watching as the churning water glittered with flecks of light.

'Quiet tonight,' Will Wortley said, as he joined them on the foredeck. The watch had changed. The evening had slipped by without them noticing.

'Nothing out there?' the seaman asked.

'Nothing,' Charles replied. 'Emma, would you care to go below?'

Her back had stiffened. She straightened. 'Thank you.'

'Good night, Will.'

'G'night.'

'Take my hand, Emma, I do not want you to fall.' His palm was soft. Secure. He supported her as they ambled slowly back along the swaying deck.

'One last look,' she said. They stopped to gaze at the sea and stars, and stayed on deck till late.

The great baulk of timber that pointed the ship's way, rose and fell like a painted horse on a merry-go-round. The sailor, whose knees gripped the bowsprit, rode it while not lifting his eyes from the sea.

Other keen eyes scanned the water from the top of the foremast. Men scoured the sea's surface from the rails, each fleck of white, curl of wave, even a landing seagull was viewed with suspicion.

'One point to starboard,' a voice cried out, several arms shot out in unison indicating the direction. The ship sailed slowly.

From the port side seamen darted across the deck to watch as they passed a tall single stake, draped in a coat of dull green, protruding from the water. They watched in silence. The sunken ship was unmoved by the swirling water. The mast standing upright was like the topmost branch of some ancient forest drowned in a flooded valley.

As the *Morning Star* glided by, not a word was spoken. Ears were pricked as the lifting waves carried the ship over more than twenty wrecks scattered haphazardly along that section of the bay. Not far beneath the surface, hemp ropes plaited with seaweed waved from the skeleton ships whose arched claws extended upwards to scratch, score or gouge the barnacled hulls of unwary vessels sailing above.

This ship's graveyard was Cape Town Bay. It was a product of the Atlantic's contrary currents and the off-shore winds which in winter blew down from the north-west and made it an unsafe anchorage for any ship.

'Damn this place,' the captain hissed.

The helmsman's eyes were on the topsails as the wind spilled from the canvas.

'I understood you to say we will be going into harbour in the morning,' Charles said.

Captain Preston's attention was on the remaining square sails as they were hauled up. After the flapping jibs were dropped, he answered the question as though no time had elapsed since Charles had spoken.

'Correct,' he said. 'I will take the boat and go ashore this evening to arrange with the pilot for us to be towed into the wharf at first light.' He glanced back at his friend and lowered his voice. 'It's a course of action I dislike but I have suffered this port before. Too much congestion on the dock. You will witness it yourself in the morning, ships jostling for position like bulls in the cattle market. Some of the foreign captains have neither patience nor manners.' He glanced down at the slowing pace of the sea. 'Let go the anchor, Mr Thackray!'

The call was echoed at the bow followed by a loud splash and the rumble of iron. Giant links of chain thundered out of the locker and spewed from the ship's port bow following the iron pick down to the seabed.

'It's about time this port had a better wharf. It gets busier every year.' Nathaniel Preston was talking to no one in particular. 'It's already difficult to navigate the maze of wrecks which block the bay. If many more ships sink it will be downright impossible to get in here.'

Charles was gazing at the flat topped mountain shrouded in its covering of cloud. He was considering if now was the appropriate time to ask a favour of his brother-in-law. 'I would like to go ashore and make a trek up into those hills,' he said. 'I have not sampled this area before.'

Captain Preston thought for a moment. 'Not wise to go alone,' he said. 'Take one of the men. A reliable fellow. And perhaps a couple of the boys.'

'How much time do I have?'

'Two days. Time for one hundred tons of water, fresh fruit, vegetables and some fresh meat to come aboard. And I will make you a promise,' he said, as he looked towards the town nestled under the mountains. 'Come back alive and when we leave here we will celebrate with a dinner of roast beef and Yorkshire pudding.'

Charles smiled. 'I will hold you to that.'

Emma watched the two men from her usual seat in the bow. She noticed the difference a smile made to the captain's visage even though it did not last long. She felt it a shame that he smiled so infrequently. Perhaps it was a luxury he did not allow himself. No doubt his position deemed that he should maintain an air of superiority and authority. Yet, she noted, how kindly his appearance was when the stern features softened and melded within the curls of his side whiskers – if only for a fleeting moment.

As Charles walked towards her along the deck, she could see by his bearing he was pleased with the outcome of his conversation.

'Will you go ashore?' she asked.

'Yes. And I will ask Joshua if he would like to accompany me. Nathaniel prefers I do not go alone.'

'Is it better I stay on the ship?'

'Indeed,' he said. 'I trust you will be safe! The captain will be going ashore and apart from the men on harbour watch, I expect most of the men will want to—' He stopped and regarded her closely. 'You know what the crew is like when they are in port. No doubt they will head straight for the taverns and relieve themselves of whatever money they have. But let me warn you, Cape Town is a place of some unrest,' he said, shaking his head. 'And poverty. There are hundreds of slaves of all colours. I would advise you to be careful who you speak to from the deck. And do not chance going ashore.' His brow furrowed, as he thought for moment. 'Perhaps I should not go.'

Emma smiled. 'Enjoy your visit and do not worry about me. I will be all right,' she said.

Chapter 22

Charles Witton and his party left soon after the ship had docked. It was still early and the wind gusting from Table Mountain was surprisingly cold. Joshua, the boy from Whitby and two of the sailors were quietly pleased to be excused from the morning chores. The idea of a two day trek into the mountains excited the boys.

From the deck, the cooper supervised the stream of barrels as they were rolled off the ship and loaded onto wagons drawn by heavy oxen. Large baskets and trays, woven from leaves, were returned on board. On them was an assortment of exotic fruits some smooth skinned, some large and angular, others small and prickly. The unfamiliar but appetizing aromas were a welcome change to the smell of bilge water that the bowels of the *Morning Star* emitted.

As the routine of taking on stores proceeded, little was said. Emma watched the activity on the wharf with interest listening to the voices speaking in Dutch, Portuguese and German, and languages she had never heard before. She studied the black faces, shiny as hot pitch with broad flattened noses and hair shrivelled into tiny tight curls. She watched ragged men, their shirts hanging like shredded sails, struggling under heavy burdens. And black women, some slovenly and indolent, almost naked, and others wrapped in vibrant hand-dyed cloths balancing yellow raffia baskets on their heads.

From the rail, she noticed babies riding cocooned on their mother's backs and admired the rows of beads decorating some of the women's slender necks. Emma smiled at them occasionally but her gesture was not returned. She wanted to transcribe their faces onto paper, capture the lines and expressions, the lips, the assortment of teeth that flashed as they chattered to each other.

The sounds that vibrated along the wharf intrigued her ears. The tame monkeys chattering and bright coloured birds screeching. The workers voices singing, humming, harmonizing yet with a doleful tone. How different, she thought, these melodies from the raucous cackling of the ship's crew. No doubt their lyrics were far removed from the shanties the sailors sang. For Emma these voices were like the mournful accompaniment to a dramatic performance, but they had neither orchestra, nor conductor and they performed to no audience but themselves.

For Emma, Cape Town provided a unique atmosphere. It throbbed with the sad heart of the people yet was more rich in colour than anywhere she had ever been before. It was a place of contrasts and she liked it.

Though she had never climbed the ship's standing rigging, never desired to and never even considered it, now she had a sudden desire to do so. She would take her drawing materials up to the platform above the forecourse yard and from there she would be able to see across the harbour, over the buildings and have a clear view of the mountains running down to the sea.

With some sharpened charcoal and several pieces of writing paper rolled into a scroll, Emma pressed them into her apron pocket and pulled herself onto the caprail. Gripping the ropes she climbed the ratlines.

To Emma, the yards had never appeared to be very high above the deck. She had witnessed the sailors running up and down the rigging without fear in wind and rain, even when the ship was lurching and threatening to throw them in the sea. The men made climbing look easy – but for Emma, it was not. Halfway up, she stopped and lay against the ratlines. The hempen ladder was swaying. In her ignorance, she had not expected any movement as the ship was close against the wharf. The rope she was standing on was cutting across the soles of her bare feet and she was afraid she would lose her grip and fall.

Yet she was determined to climb. If she didn't look down, she knew she could make it to the top. It was no higher than the attic window in Seal Street and she had stood there many times looking at the street below. Emma climbed, pulling herself up, one step at a time.

When she reached the crosstrees she pulled herself through the lubbers' hole and onto the platform and quickly sat down. Her legs and arms were shaking and her heart was beating fast. But the effort had been worth it. She remembered what Joshua had said about climbing the mast. She felt exhilarated. Her fear had gone.

To either side was the criss-crossed rigging of other ships – a cat's cradle of wood and hemp. Ahead was the mountain. Since morning, the mist had melted and slithered into the sea. Now its flat table-top was clearly visible. To the side, the other mountains rolled to the ocean like giant arms offering protection to the settlement.

From her vantage point Emma could see the town, its regular pattern of streets set out spaciously. Neat houses gleamed white. The black rushes that thatched the roofs stood out in stark contrast.

She relaxed. The charcoal she had brought with her was brittle. It broke easily littering her apron with black crumbs, but she ignored them. With her back against the ropes she sketched contentedly. As the ship swayed on the harbour water she was reminded of the swing she had swung on as a child. From the wharf below she was lulled by the rhythmic humming of the natives.

Suddenly, a hand clamped around her ankle. 'Not a word or I'll toss you over!'

Pieces of charcoal dropped to the deck like black hailstones. The sheets of paper floated down like autumn leaves.

'Ain't it a pity, all yer fancy men have gone ashore?'

Emma froze, her fingers gripping the ropes. She had no escape. She was too afraid to go higher and if she attempted to climb down he could easily peel her from the rigging. She had no option; she must stay where she was.

'I ain't never had a woman on the yard before. Not that I ain't ever imagined one laid out on it.'

Tom Barstow was too big to squeeze through the hole in the platform she was on. The only way he could get onto it was by climbing around the rigging on the outside and to do that he must release his grip on her leg. Emma sat still and said nothing. Reaching down into her apron pocket she crushed the remaining pieces of charcoal in her hand. He released his grip and poked his hand beneath her skirt. She shuffled from his reach and moved closer to the mast.

He turned and spat out towards the sea. 'Now!' he cried grabbing the rails with both hands. Emma leaned forward and as his face reached the level of the platform she shot the handful of black power at him landing a deal in his eyes and some in his throat.

His head flicked. His eyes screwed. He spat much of the dust from his throat but some lodged in his wind pipe. He coughed, spat and sneezed at the irritation.

'Bitch!' he yelled. His face resembled that of a chimney sweep. His eyes burned like fire. 'You will pay for this, you slut! You will pay!'

Emma kicked at him with her feet.

He caught her ankle. Jerked her towards him. She tried to kick, to stop herself from sliding. She was being dragged down. She knew if she fell from that height she would die. She dug her heels between the slats and held on.

Having ignored the cries from the deck, the pleadings from the handful of crew gathered below, even the threat of punishment, it was only the boom of musket fire that stopped him.

'Come down, sailor! This instant!'

Tom Barstow cursed, released Emma's leg, and holding the rigging with one hand leaned out and grabbed the nearest shroud. For a moment he hung suspended then, as agile as an ape, swung himself across the rigging, wrapped his leg around the taut stay and slid down to the deck.

Before Mr Thackray had time to have him held and shackled, the sailor jumped from the caprail down onto the wharf. The crowd of spectators ducked as the musket boomed again. From the mast, Emma could see it did not hit its target. The man she hated was running, weaving across the quayside, his red eyes flashing back at his pursuers, his blackened face bursting like a slave running from the dogs.

'I should not have gone,' Charles Witton said. 'I felt it when we were away. I was afraid something like this would happen.'

'I am all right,' Emma said, 'but I am concerned what will happen now? Has the captain returned? Has he been told?'

'Of course,' said Charles. 'And he was not impressed.'

Emma's brow tightened.

'No, you misunderstand. Nathaniel disliked that seaman – despised him with a vengeance. I gather he has had trouble with him before. But, he has to admit that Barstow is a good topman and he cannot afford to lose any more men. Tomorrow, at first light he intends to send a gang into town to search for him.'

'You mean they will bring him back to the ship?'

'Yes, if they find him and if that is the case, I guarantee he will be spending his time in the hold and not in the rigging.'

'And if they do not find him?'

'Then we sail without him and you will have nothing more to worry about again.'

'I should not have climbed the mast, should I?'

'No you should not!' Charles cocked his head inquisitively. 'Though I would have liked to have witnessed it. I have to say it was a brave thing to do – albeit foolhardy.'

'It was a wonderful view.'

'I don't doubt it.'

Emma smiled and looked at the line of small boxes on the cabin table. 'Some things you collected?' she asked.

He nodded.

'Perhaps you would show me.'

Charles studied each box in turn, examining the name he had scribbled on the label. 'You will like this one,' he said eagerly. As he lifted the lid, the closed wings of a butterfly fluttered as if a breath of breeze had blown on them.

'Is it dead?' Emma asked.

'Almost.'

She regarded it sadly.

'They have an extremely short life-span,' he said. 'And I am sure it has served its purpose on this earth. Now it will serve my purpose and be immortalized.'

Emma laughed. 'Immortalized?'

'It is true. By drawing its likeness, I will record the life that is gone. Your drawings will capture it forever. It is important to remember that.'

Emma turned her face towards his but the scientist was engrossed with the new additions to his collection.

'Will you go ashore tomorrow?'

'No!' he said. 'I have more than enough samples to keep me busy. Tomorrow I will pack most of them away and would be most grateful if you could assist me.'

Emma nodded. 'Certainly.'

'Nathaniel tells me that we will be heading south to catch the westerly wind which will carry us across the Indian Ocean to Australia. He also says the southern latitudes can have a tendency to be 'a little lumpy' at times.' He smiled. 'Believe me, Emma, when he says that, he means we could be heading into some fairly heavy seas.'

'Hard to larboard!'

The helmsman spun the wheel, hauling the rudder hard across.

'What is the matter with him? Damn Yankee fool must be blind! Hard to port, I say!'

Alas, with a laboured crack and squeal of timber on timber, the *Morning Star*'s bowsprit slid onto the deck of the larger ship. It settled for a moment resting like a sperm whale dragged up a slipway then slowly, as if the lines had broken, it started to slide back onto the water. The American clipper shuddered and slowed as the pair still tangled together turned in an arc of ninety degrees. Shouts rang out from both decks but the voices were drowned by the sound of three dozen luffing sails, flapping violently like a gaggle of angry geese.

'Starboard rudder, Mr Wortley! We must get off her back before she breaks us in half. Get the jibs down before they are shredded!'

With each passing swell the *Morning Star* rose up and crashed its bow back onto the deck of the American vessel while sails flapped uselessly.

'Braces, Mr Thackray! Get the yards around!' The calls were echoed along the deck. Seamen ran to their stations.

The ships were stuck together like two flies copulating and they were drifting with the current towards the rocky coast. As the men hauled the yards around, the wind began to fill in the square sails and with help from the waves *Morning Star* separated herself from the unwelcome union.

'Watch the forestay!' the captain yelled. Too late. It had caught the clipper's forecourse yardarm. The *Morning Star*'s bowsprit, with a girth of three-feet, heaved and creaked. Drawn tight as the string on a bow, the forestay snapped, catapulting itself loose. The topmast swayed then fell, rattling to the deck in a crackle of canvas and falling rigging.'

The two ships floated free.

'If I had a thirty-six pounder, it would give me the greatest pleasure to put a hole right through her! Damn that ship! And damn the master! He must have been drunk to sail across us like that! Or blind! Did you get her name, Mr Wortley?'

The seaman didn't answer the question. 'Up there, capt'n' he yelled, pointing into the tangle of broken rigging. 'Man down and another caught in the lines!'

More calls were coming from the deck.

'Mr Thackray, get someone up there, quick as you can. I don't want to lose another sailor!'

Another cry rang out. 'Man overboard!'

Captain Preston, unable to see what was happening from the helm ran along the deck gazing up at the tangled wreckage suspended above. As four sailors, climbed the rigging, two others scrambled down. On the deck a seaman nursed his head in his arms, another held out his hands where the brand of a running rope had burned deep into his palms. A third was helped aboard, wet, but otherwise unharmed.

'Get some help up there!' the captain shouted. 'Mr Thackray, can you see what is holding that man?'

'There's two of 'em, up there. Young Sam's got his leg hooked between the sheet and the clew line. The other is trying to cut himself free.' He shook his head. 'If he falls from there he will hit the deck.'

'Tell the men to climb warily. She's not holding by many threads.' The seamen already aloft were securing the broken topmast which was swinging perilously above the deck.

The sound of the collision brought Emma hurrying on deck but, as she had to stop well clear of the damage, she was unable to see what was happening around the foremast. Nearby, François was leaning against the rigging, his head resting on it, his foot on the bottom rung. Why wasn't he climbing?

'Get up there Frenchy, what are you waiting for?' the mate yelled.

François climbed slowly and Emma lost sight of him behind the canvas.

With a resounding thud, a body fell onto the deck. Almost instantly a pool of dark blood flowed from the sailor's head. There was no other movement from him. Harold Dodd would never climb again.

'Below!' the cry came down. 'We need more hands! We've got Samuel but he's a dead weight.'

Half an hour later, with a rope tied around his chest, the unconscious boy was lowered slowly down the rigging, passed gently from the arms of one man to another, down to the deck.'

'Mr Witton, would you take a look?'

Charles watched as the young sailor was laid on the deck. His eyes were open. Only a few yards away, the body of his dead mate was being ignored. The pool of blood had already congealed. It was almost black, like spilled pitch set hard on the teak decking.

The rope was eased from Sam's chest. He would recover.

'Mr Kaye, get up and see what the damage is!'

The carpenter knuckled his forehead and scrambled up the rigging against the struggle of men climbing down.

Captain Preston sighed. 'Let's get that mess cut down, Mr Thackray.'

'Aye, sir.'

The captain watched as his men set about the laborious task of removing the damaged ropes and timbers. The work went on throughout the afternoon. As it proceeded, little was said. Hal Dodd's body was neither moved nor covered, the men merely worked around it as though it was another piece of fallen debris.

Charles posed the question cautiously to his brother-in-law. 'Will you take the *Morning Star* back to Cape Town?'

'And chance being buried in that salty graveyard? No, thank you! I will find a sheltered cove and providing there is no major damage to the hull, we will repair at sea. Mr Kaye assures me we have enough timber onboard to rig up a new topmast. The carpenter is a good man. I trust him. He has checked the two yards which came down and they are not cracked. The sails have only suffered minor damage and can be patched. And we have lockers full of shrouds and rope. They may be old but at least they will not stretch. Once the mast is up and rigged, we can head for the forties.' He looked at Charles's concerned expression. 'It will not delay us long.'

'And the man who fell?'

'We will bury him in the morning.'

'What of the other ship?' said Charles. 'Shouldn't the accident be reported to the authorities?'

'That was hardly an accident, the fool sailed across my bow!' He calmed himself. 'But in answer to your question, officially, yes. But I doubt it will serve much purpose as I do not have the ship's name and I'm damned if I am going into that port again, even in a small boat. If I am not wrong, she is a tea clipper making for the Indies. Did you see how she headed out with all haste not even stopping to offer us assistance? She suffered less damage than us, and time for her is money.' He sighed. 'If I complained about her it would amount only to one captain's word against another. And by the time that ship sails this way again it is unlikely this incident will be remembered.

'This is a cursed place,' he added. 'I have a broken mast and have lost another good man. The sooner we are away from here the better.' He smiled wryly. 'Let's hope the American's next encounter is with *The Flying Dutchman.* That ship will give her a run for her money.'

Charles laughed. 'You believe in such legends?'

Captain Preston took a deep breath before answering. 'I have seen some strange things at sea which beggar explanation.' He paused. 'You may well smile at me for saying so. You are a man of science and you know many things. But ask any man who sails the sea, officers or common sailors alike, they will all give you the same answer and will remind you there are things at sea that are never spoken of in jest. I have witnessed strange happenings, inexplicable sights, sounds that would make your blood curdle and, I might add, with good men alongside me. As to *The Flying Dutchman* and a belief in phantom ships, I prefer to keep an open mind.' He turned abruptly. 'If you will excuse me, I have a ship to sail and I do not have the time for idle talk.'

Despite the lack of canvas, the *Morning Star* made four knots as it sailed south. The wind was favourable and the sea current assisted their passage. Leaving Cape Town Bay in their wake, they headed south rounding the southernmost tip of the African continent. Late the following afternoon, after bearing north, they found a secluded cove with a clear deep-water channel leading into it. Sheltered by a peninsula of land on the eastern side and a narrow reef to the south, the water in the bay was flat as a mill-pond and blue as any Pacific lagoon. Around its edges the sand was white and the crystal water abounded with fish. It was an ideal location to refit. The *Morning Star* sailed in and dropped anchor.

As night fell, small fires flickered on the surrounding hills. Natives perhaps? In the morning naked men carrying spears were seen running along the beach. With no knowledge of the area, Captain Preston ordered the crew to stay on board. There was a job to be done and he did not intend risking the loss of any more of his crew. The combined watches were already short of five seamen. The order to stay on board was extended to include Charles Witton. The entomologist was both disappointed and disgruntled but, after presenting his arguments, he realized it was pointless trying to sway the captain. His decision was final.

Mr Kaye and his mates worked amidships. The timber yards, resting on the rails, protruded from both sides of the ship. It took the combined strength of four men to haul the topgallant sail along the deck, and finding enough space to accommodate the folded canvas was not easy. Jack Burns, the sailmaker crawled over it, scouring every inch, checking his old patches and cutting and stitching new pieces to it. Curling smoke from the brazier ran up the rigging carrying with it the reek of tar. Ropes were cut, spliced, tarred, stretched and oiled. The clang from the blacksmith's anvil rang out across the peaceful bay. At midday the sun burned overhead and the men's eyes squinted against the reflected glare from the water.

The hands not engaged in repair work, were found jobs on deck. As there was no space to swab or holystone the teak, the ship's woodwork was varnished, brasses were polished and polished again, and yards of old rope were converted into oakum. Were it not for a large shark, which constantly circled the ship, the men would have been occupied caulking the hull or scraping the weed and barnacles from below the water-line.

Although a couple of men were prepared to chance their luck for the sake of a swim, the threat of punishment deterred them. As it was, the cook caught a small shark on a baited line. Not all the men would eat the flesh, claiming they were eating the bodies of dead sailors, but for those who did, it provided three good meals and soup for several days. Needless to say, the buckets of water hoisted from the bay served to cool the men, though the carpenter was not amused when a gallon of salt water hit him full in the face.

To escape the sun, Emma stayed below occupying herself with her drawings. She had only seen François from a distance since they left Cape Town. There was much she wanted to speak to him about but he had ignored her and appeared preoccupied. She wanted to tell him how relieved she was, knowing that Thomas Barstow had not been found in the town and was not on board. She had worried at first that he may have sneaked onto the ship and be hiding somewhere. But as the days went by, she worried less, realizing that the scratching sounds she heard at night, and the squeaking of boards outside her cabin door, were the sounds made by the ship itself.

She wanted to talk with François the way they had talked on the deck when she had told him of her past life. Now she wanted to hear more about his life and the places he had visited. She wondered if she had upset him. She knew he was jealous of the time she spent in Charles's day cabin. Then she remembered what he had said about being in harbour – that he hated it and how it made him feel confined. She told herself he would be different when they were sailing again. Once the ship was underway there would be ample time to talk with him at length.

On the afternoon of the fifth day, the jury-rig was swayed up and bolted into place, then the yards were raised and lowered several times to test the running gear.

'I will speak with Mr Kaye,' Nathaniel Preston said. 'He did a first-class job. This afternoon we will see if the sailmaker's work is equally sound. Prepare the ship, Mr Thackray! We sail out with the tide!'

Chapter 23

'Mama! Mama! Open the door. It's me, Josh! Please open the door.'

Emma put down her pen.

'Hush, Josh, don't make so much noise. What's wrong?'

'François is sick!'

'Sick? Where is he?'

'Come with me, I'll take you to him.'

The air that greeted them as they climbed down the steep ladder smelled foul. The bottom of the ship was dank and dark. Light spilling from a single lamp was unable to penetrate far into the bowels of the ship, unable to penetrate the black crevices that separated the piles of stores, cases, bails and barrels crammed into the hold. In a space, barely wide enough to fit a man's shoulders, François was curled against the ship's hull, his arms cradling his chest. He was wet and shivering like a cornered rat.

'Gracious! What has happened?'

'I don't know. I heard Samuel calling for Mr Witton not more than a few minutes ago. He said he'd found Frenchy and he thought he was dying.'

'Don't say that, Josh. Please don't say that.'

François opened his eyes but did not move. 'I am fine,' he said, looking no further than the barrel against his head.

'What is wrong, François? What are you doing down here?'

'I heard a rumour the captain had purchased some casks of Verdelho in Madeira. It is a mighty fine wine they make on the slopes of that island and I thought I might sample some.'

'François, how could you? You're drunk. Josh said you were sick. Get up! You are wet and dirty. You can't stay here.'

'Leave me!' he demanded. His eyelids drooped then closed.

'I'll get him up.' Josh leaned forward and grabbed François' arm but as he did, the sailor's body arched. He groaned and tried to rise but flopped back banging his head on the side of the ship.

Joshua leaned forward to try a second time. Taking the Frenchman's arm, he heaved it off his chest. 'Mama, look!' he cried.

The sight made Emma clasp her hand to her mouth. A brackish yellow stain had soaked the front of François' blouse and dirt encrusted the blood-streaked matter across his chest. The cotton shirt was stuck to it. The smell was putrid. It sickened her.

'Oh, God! Hurry, Josh, get Mr Witton.'

'I'm here.' Charles was standing behind her along with several other men. They had all crowded into the small area.

'We must get him out of here and quickly!' he said. 'The air is foul. You boy! Samuel! Can you get your legs behind him and lift him a little so we can get him out from there.'

'Where are you taking him?' Sam asked. 'You can't put him in his hammock! He made me promise I'd not let anyone put him in his hammock. I think he's afraid he might get sewn into it before he's dead.'

'Please help him,' Emma begged. 'You must do something.'

'To begin with, we must move him from here. The mess deck will not do. If he can be hoisted up the ladders, he needs some fresh air.'

Charles looked around for the strongest men to lift him. 'Look lively, but gentle as you can.'

From the hatchway a crowd of faces peered down into the semi-darkness, blocking out the light.

'I want warm water from the galley,' shouted Charles. 'Take it amidships on the weatherdeck. I want it in a basin and not a bucket, mind. And I will need the apothecary's chest from the captain's cabin. And some clean rags.' He touched Emma on the sleeve. 'It is best you go up top and wait there. I will take care good of François.'

Emma hesitated then nodded. The men stood aside for her to pass.

François' head rolled onto his chest as Samuel eased him away from the side of the ship.

'Gently, men!' Charles called.

Heavy as a bale of sodden wool, François was carried up to the fresh air. On deck, the afternoon sun still burned bright but had lost its heat. With no wind, the *Morning Star* was as still as a ship in dry dock.

'Set him down there. Bring something for his head to rest on. Those sacks will do. Help me to sit him up. Stand back! Let him get some air. You there! Get some drinking water!'

Emma helped rest François' head onto the cushion of sacking.

'What happened?' she whispered.

He opened his eyes.

'Did you fall? How did you get hurt?'

Charles interrupted, 'Emma, no questions, please. First I must see what I can do for him.' He looked up at the group of men. 'Does anyone know how long he has been in the hold?'

There was no response. No one had seen him go below. No one had missed him.

'Who is on his watch? Surely one of you must have known he was not on duty?'

A seaman volunteered the answer. 'Been no call for sail these past two days.' He looked up to the dead canvas. 'A man's left much to his own devices when conditions are like this.'

'Emma, when did you speak with him last?'

'I cannot think. Was it yesterday or the day before?' Her eyes were filled with tears. 'I have been busying myself below deck,' she said. 'I have seen little of him since we left Cape Town. I thought he was avoiding me. Angry with me. I never once considered he could be ill.'

'Emma!' Charles's tone was quietly stern. 'I suggest you go to your cabin while I look at this wound. It may not be pleasant.'

'I will stay.'

Perspiration filled the furrows on François' brow. He ground his teeth and groaned as Charles Witton peeled the piece of blood stained rag from the Frenchman's chest. A soft cheesy substance oozed from an open wound.

François coughed and cursed.

'This is a mess,' Charles said quietly. The measure of his fears showed unmistakably on his face. 'How on earth did you do this, Frenchy?'

François closed his eyes and turned his head away. It was indeed an ugly wound. Not a long slice, but deep and damaging. The skin around was mottled, red and blue and too dead to be stitched together.

After cleaning the wound the best he could, Charles bound François' chest with a long strip of linen sheeting. A second cut discovered on the seaman's arm was dry and crusted so he left it uncovered.

As Charles wiped his hands, Emma sat down on the deck beside him. By this time, the sun had dipped behind the gunnels and was about to sink. The interest the crew had initially shown in the injured man had dissipated. Most had left and gone below or moved to another section of the deck.

Despite Emma's efforts, François refused to eat, taking only a few sips of warm rum with sugar and a little water. His breathing was shallow and when he coughed, the sweat from his forehead dripped onto the deck. She wiped his face and neck.

Though he kept his distance, Captain Preston remained on deck throughout the proceedings and was advised of the progress by Len Thackray. As the day ended, he wandered along the deck. 'It's time we spoke,' he said quietly, addressing his brother-in-law. 'Join me in my cabin when you are free.'

Charles looked down at Emma. 'Will you stay with him?'

'Yes.'

'Then I will come back later.'

'What are you looking at?' François asked quietly.

Emma turned back from the rail, surprised he was awake. The moon was shining in his dark eyes.

'I was looking for the tiny stars which sparkle in the sea. But tonight they are not here.'

'They will come back,' he said. 'I promise you.' He tried to sit up but was unable to move and could not hide the pain burning in his chest.

'Let me help you.'

'Promise me one thing,' he said, as she leaned towards him. 'Whenever you see the stars in the sea you will think of me?'

'Why do you say that, François?' A deep sadness welled in her eyes. 'You will get well.'

'Promise me!' he said.

'I promise.'

'My knife,' he said, feeling for it on his hip. She touched his hand to the scabbard. 'Take the belt. Slide it from me. Give it to your son. A seaman needs a good knife. This is the best. I bought it in Toledo.'

'I cannot. You will need it.'

'I have another,' he said wearily. 'It is in my sea chest. Do as I say. Give this to your boy.'

Emma slid the belt from around his waist. 'François, I am afraid.'

'Of what? You have nothing to fear.'

'But this thing that has happened to you makes me afraid. Who did this to you? Was it Thomas Barstow?' she asked anxiously. 'Is he on board the ship? Is he hiding somewhere – in one of the lockers where you hid me, perhaps? Tell me he is not here. I am afraid of him. Afraid of the darkness.'

François reached up and touched her face, brushing the tears from her cheeks.

'My dear, Emma, I swear the man you fear is not on this ship. Believe me, Tom Barstow will never bother you again.' He tried to lift himself. 'Help me,' he begged. 'I want to smell the sea. I want to look at it with you. Perhaps together we can conjure up those illusive diamonds you see.'

With one hand resting on Emma's shoulder, his other pressed across his chest, François struggled to the rail. Each breath he took pained him. He coughed, leaned on the caprail and rested his head on the rigging. Across the glassy surface, the moon splayed a broad pathway of silver. It stretched from the ship to the distant horizon.

'How beautiful she is,' he said, gazing at the sea. *La mer.* So like a woman.' His body tensed. 'Look,' he said, 'how soft and flat she lies in the night. Smooth, like silk. Black. Beguiling.' His tongue touched his lips, 'I can taste her salt,' he said. 'And listen.' His voice was barely a whisper. 'Listen. Hear her breathe. Softly. Slowly.' He paused. 'She sleeps.' With his fingers gripping the rail, his body rocked back. 'It is time to go,' he whispered, placing a gentle kiss on Emma's mouth.

'No, François!'

'Remember me.'

His skin was wet as an eel's and she could not hold him. As he slid into the water, there was hardly a splash.

Emma's cry reverberated across the ship. 'François—!'

But the Frenchman did not hear her and the sea was quick to swallow him up.

Chapter 24

As the waves battered the ship's bow, the luminescent particles flickered then faded. Hundreds of them. Thousands of them. Hour upon hour. Shining and dying throughout the night.

'You must go to bed! Get some sleep! This is doing you no good!'

Emma ignored Charles's advice and remained on deck all night gazing into the water or staring down at the strips of bleached teak between her feet.

'Penny for them?' the sailmaker said, when he came up on deck at first light.

She looked up. 'It's nothing,' she whispered.

'You might call it nothing,' he said, shrugging his shoulders. 'But if you'll pardon me for saying, miss, I see a spare anchor hanging round your neck and if you're not careful it will carry you to the bottom of the sea also.'

He leaned against the rail beside her, puffing smoke as he sucked on his pipe. 'See out there! See that splash of white water.'

Emma looked in the direction he was pointing.

'Whales!' he said. 'Killer whales. Pod of them, if I'm not wrong.'

'Killer whales?'

'Don't fret about the name. Playful they are.' As he spoke, in the distance, a giant black head, streaked with white, broke the surface, raised itself to an enormous height then flopped heavily onto its side. A gush of spray shot high in the air.

'They be swimming from the Southern Ocean. Heading north to the Arctic.'

'That is a long way.'

'Aye.'

'Like all whales, they're always on the move. If they stay in one place too long the whalers get them. But I reckon you would know that coming from Whitby. Now seals,' he said, 'they're different. They just stay in one place. Never go far. Seems they're waiting to be killed. If the sealers don't get 'em, the polar bears do.' He prodded his finger into the smouldering leaf and gazed out to sea.

For quite some time, they watched the whales in silence until the last one sounded and disappeared.

'If you'll take my advice, missy, you'll not let your heart stay in one place too long. Haul up your anchor and sail even though the sky looks black. Believe me lassie, there'll be fair winds waiting for you beyond the horizon.'

Emma smiled. 'Thank you,' she said.

The sailmaker touched his cap. 'My pleasure, miss.'

Days slipped by and invariably Emma could be found standing in the same spot at the ship's rail.

Charles Witton looked into her eyes. 'You are thinking about François, are you not?'

Emma nodded.

'You have not spoken of him since his death. I do not mind if you want to talk to me about him.'

She turned her face to the wind and let it blow the hair from her eyes.

'He would have died on deck, Emma. You realize that, don't you?'

She nodded.

'And François knew it. That is why he did what he did.'

'But what had happened to him? What had caused that horrible injury? He must have fallen, yet I saw him two days before he died and he was well.'

'He may have appeared well,' Charles said. 'But, I believe François had been carrying that wound for several days before the infection got the better of him.'

'But why didn't he say something to one of the men? Why did he go away and hide in the darkness like a cat waiting to die?'

'From what I have learned of seamen, they are insular men. They are tough also. They have to be. And when you begin to understand them you realize they think they are invincible.'

'But François was hurt. Badly hurt.'

'Indeed. It was a deep wound and hard to say what caused it. When I saw it, I was afraid for him. It was obvious the poison from it was spreading through his body.'

'Was there nothing you could do to help?'

Charles clenched his fingers. 'How many times in my life have I asked myself that question? If only I had learned more when I was a young man. If only I had become a doctor, maybe I could have helped him. Maybe I could have helped my wife. My daughter. Maybe I could have helped the man who fell from the yard and many similar poor souls. Look at me now,' he said. 'I rather spend my time looking through the eyepiece of a microscope than looking at my sick neighbour. I know more about the house-fly than I know about the human body. That is no achievement to be proud of. Yet, ironically, here on the ship, I am regarded as some sort of man of science, a medical man who can perform surgery, a man who has the knowledge to administer to all manner of ailments.' He sighed. 'But that is not so. I am none of those things and, at times, it depresses me. I did all I could for François. I am sorry, Emma, there was nothing more I could do.'

She wanted to reassure him. To tell him he should not feel the way he did. She wanted to tell him she admired him for what he had done and for how kind he had been. But, though her mind fought to find the right words, they would not come, and the silence that existed between them carried with it an air of uneasiness.

Charles continued, 'Like many young men of my time, I was a fool. The idea of being famous through making great discoveries, appealed to me. I wanted to be like John Henslow, the botanist,' he laughed. 'Yet I had neither the tenacity nor the brain.'

'But you studied. You are a scientist and are well respected. How else would you be invited to join a scientific expedition?'

'I have a wild iris named after me,' he said, with some degree of pride. 'A distant relative of the saffron crocus. But one cannot measure the name of a plant against the value of a man's life.'

'You must not denigrate yourself. You did all you could for François, and I doubt any physician could have saved him. Even I could smell the badness that was eating him. I saw it oozing from his chest.' Her brow furrowed. 'And I know he would not have wished to die in a hospital bed.'

'Strange as it may seem,' Charles said, looking up as the yards were braced and the ship slowly began to wear around towards the east. 'It was those things you talk about that took me away from medicine.'

Emma listened. It was good for him to talk.

'I had planned to be a doctor, like my father. I moved to Leeds where there is a fine Infirmary. But I found the work depressing. So much infection and death. I was a young man and I could not bear to see it. I'm afraid the prospect of following that profession disillusioned me, yet I became intrigued with the various bacteria that inhabit our bodies, those tiny organisms only the microscope can see. Because I was tired of seeing people die, I chose to escape. I went overseas in search of the exotic things I had only read about. I suppose I was a selfish young man.'

Emma passed no comment and listened.

'When I returned to England three years later, I went back to the university, but it was not medicine I studied, it was insects – entomology. So now,' he sighed, 'I can tell you what insect a man crushes beneath his feet – but not what disease he is dying of.'

They stepped aside as the cooper rolled a heavy barrel along the deck towards the galley hatch.

'Now, if you will excuse me,' he said. 'I am a little tired. I was awake early and I think I will retire early.'

'Of course,' she said quietly.

He inclined his head. 'Good night, Emma.'

'Good night.'

Emma woke late feeling stiff and sore. The air in her cabin was stuffy. She wanted to get out.

'May I get something from the chest?' she asked, from the doorway of Charles's day cabin.

He looked up from his journal. 'Please help yourself,' he said, and continued writing.

With a selection of clothes draped over her arm, Emma thanked him and reached for the doorknob.

Turning in his chair, Charles spoke softly, 'I am pleased to see you, Emma. I have missed you these past few days.'

She hesitated as if wanting to say something.

'I have been watching you on deck – always gazing to the horizon. What is it you are searching for?'

She shrugged.

'You must excuse me for saying, but at times you seem lost. And very alone. Yet you have acquaintances on the ship. Many of the seamen enjoy having you on board and they respect you. And you have your son,' Charles said. 'And, for what it is worth, you have me. It saddens me to see you like this.'

Emma thought about his words and sighed. 'I sometimes think I am like the tiny diamonds in the sea. While the ship sails they live, they shine. But when the ship stops, their light is extinguished. I feel my life is the same. While we are sailing I am safe, alive, content, but when the ship docks in Sydney, what then? What will become of me? Where will I go? I do not like to think of that time. It frightens me.'

'You must not be afraid.'

'But I have never been alone before. Not completely alone. For thirteen years my son has been with me. But when we reach Sydney that will change. I know of no one in the colony. Joshua has said he will care for me, but I know his heart is set on staying with the ship. It is his wish and I would not press him to leave.'

'Then I shall stay in Sydney and not join up with the rest of the party. Then, at least, you will have someone you know.'

'How can you even consider that, Charles? The expedition is the purpose of your voyage. That is your wish, your dream. And besides, you do not know me.'

He turned and looked away.

'But thank you,' she said. 'I must consider my future. I have no money therefore I will have to find some suitable occupation. I can offer my services as a governess or a lady's companion perhaps. Even a housekeeper. I have never been in service but I am sure I know what is required.'

Mr Witton looked troubled. 'Please, Emma, before you say more, listen to what I have to say. I have friends in Sydney. Influential friends. When the ship docks I will make enquiries with them. At least allow me to do that.' He shuffled in his seat. 'What you have just said makes it easier for me to speak. I have a proposition that I find somewhat embarrassing to put to you.' He turned his chair towards her. 'You are a fine artist. Extremely talented. I have watched you draw and know how much pleasure it gives you. Would you consider following in your father's footsteps and earning some money from your talent?'

'Are you suggesting I paint your portrait?'

He laughed. 'No forgive me, I am talking in riddles. As I explained earlier, I am an entomologist. I study insects – all manner of small creatures – crawling, flying and swimming varieties. I have with me, on board the ship, hundreds of specimens that I collected in England and during my travels overseas. Amongst them I am hoping to discover some exotic species that have never been recorded. But that involves a lot of work, examining each one, weighing, measuring, dissecting and cataloguing the details. And when I make my notes I always draw a likeness of the specimen.'

'To immortalize it,' Emma said grinning.

His face was serious. 'My artwork is poor. Like a child's compared with yours.' He leaned forward. 'Emma, while we are on the ship, would you do some work for me? I have a wooden chest bursting with specimens that requires attention. I have the new microscope which I collected in Madeira. And,' he added with some embarrassment, 'I will pay you for your services.'

'But I have never drawn an insect before!'

He waited, allowing the idea to filter through her head.

She smiled. 'But tomorrow I will try.'

Above the deck of the *Morning Star* the topmen released the replacement sail. Leaning along the yardarms they looked like wooden pegs on a giant washing-line. Emma recognized some of the sailors. They belonged to François' watch. He should have been up there with them.

The square of canvas crackled and slapped as it dropped and filled. On the deck the sheets were trimmed. The *Morning Star* was making six knots, sailing tight on the strengthening wind.

Overhead, a huge flock of migrating birds clouded the rising sun. They flew in formation, the shape twisting and turning like the changing patterns of a kaleidoscope.

The smell of cooking drifted up through the galley hatch. Mr Sung's head popped up from below. 'You want breakfast?'

Emma nodded gratefully.

'You stay. I bring breakfast.'

The sailmaker bade her good morning. Another sailor nodded to her.

Emma smiled. She was feeling better.

'Please come in, Emma. I have everything ready.'

The day cabin was cluttered. A second, slightly smaller, wooden trunk had been hauled into the room. It was pressed against the chest containing clothes which already occupied much of the floor space. The trunk was open and almost empty, its contents having been placed on the oak table.

Stacked one on top of each other were numerous small boxes each bearing a neatly written label. In front of those was a pile of books and journals and beside them a flat leather case. A pair of tweezers, a small sharp bladed knife, scissors and pins lay in its blue velvet lining. A light wooden box, divided into compartments, held a quantity of circular dishes and several small bottles with glass stoppers. The coloured fluids swilled from side to side though there was little movement of the ship. With the microscope taking pride of place in the centre of the table, there appeared little spare space for Emma to work.

He anticipated her concern. 'Let me clear some of this away. Draw up a chair and sit down.'

Emma watched him as he contemplated where he could store his possessions. After realizing that his desk was also littered, he returned the piles to the chest.

'Paper,' he said. 'Paint, ink, quill, penknife, pencil, charcoal, blotting paper, water and cloth. There,' he said, pleased with the provisions, 'I think you have everything.'

Emma dusted the table top and placed the sheet of paper in the centre. After sharpening the quill she waited, poised like a scholar waiting for her instruction to commence.

'What do you want me to draw?' she asked.

He examined the labels on several boxes, reading some, opening others and examining the contents. He talked to himself in what sounded like Latin, though Emma did not recognize any of the words. After sorting through the pile, he reached for a glass dish which was covered by a white cloth.

'This,' he announced, 'is fresh. A beautiful specimen!' He picked up the insect with a pair of tweezers and placed it on the paper. The smell of ether hung in the air.

Emma recoiled.

He regarded it carefully through a magnifying glass. 'Now that is nice,' he said. 'Very nice indeed. *Periplaneta orientalis* – the common cockroach. I think you will have noticed a few of this family on the ship.' Enthralled with his specimen, he failed to notice the expression on Emma's face. 'Take a closer look. The glass enlarges it. It truly is a lovely specimen. Excellent for dissection.'

As if expecting it to crawl across the paper, Emma touched it gently with the tip of the quill feather but it did not move.

With Charles standing beside her, she pushed the lace cuffs back into her sleeve, draped the rag across her knees, dipped the pen, shook off the excess ink and sketched the first lines on the paper.

Charles Witton smiled contentedly.

'Excellent. Excellent,' he said, as the insect developed. 'Female!' he announced. 'If you look carefully you can see the joints in the antennae,' he added pointing with the tip of a pin. 'Yes,' he said excitedly, as Emma transcribed the details, the armoury of the femur's minute spines, the fine hairs covering the *cerci anales*.

Suddenly, feeling flushed, she blotted the beads of sweat from her forehead. The air felt heavy. Perhaps it was due to her nervousness at being observed so closely.

The door burst open. 'Charles!' the captain cried. When he realized his brother-in-law was not alone, he stopped abruptly.

'Do come in, Nathan. There is something I would like to show you.'

'Later, Charles,' Captain Preston said. 'I fear we are sailing into some rough weather. The barometer has dropped too quickly for my liking and I fear this is an ominous calm we are suffering. I would like you to join me on deck. But,' he said, pondering the multitude of objects scattered around, 'I would suggest that everything that is not bolted to the floor is housed securely.' He turned to Emma. 'If we strike a storm, I suggest you remain here or in your own cabin. The sea could get quite rough.'

Chapter 25

The air in the stateroom was stagnant. On returning from the deck, Charles had lit the lamp and, though eager to continue with his specimens, had heeded the captain's advice stowing everything back in the trunk. Though not wishing to, he had to satisfy himself with his reference books. Emma tried to read, but the shadows see-sawing across the page made it difficult.

The storm hit suddenly with almighty force laying the ship almost on its beam. Men were thrown to the gunnels as the sea foamed across the deck. Barrels torn from their lashings spun like tops. The pitch kettle steamed.

The helmsman was sprawled unconscious against the rail and the wheel was spinning faster than a windmill in a gale. Cries could be heard from all directions. The ship shook with each wave, while sailors, soaked to the skin, scrambled to gain a footing, to bring the ship around and haul in the remaining sails. Water flooding the deck was cascading through the open hatches to the decks below.

Charles had been standing by the bookcase when the force of the storm hit.

Emma's breath was punched from her chest as she was thrown forward from the chair and into the edge of the table. Above her head the lamp shattered, showering her in glass. Burning wick and oil floated down like tiny incendiaries. Smelling her hair singeing, she brushed the particles from her head instinctively. With fire falling into her open book, the pages ignited. For a moment the flames lit the room. Emma grabbed the book and dashed out the fire despite burning her fingers in the process. Then she fell forward. The ship having righted itself was shuddering ominously but, thankfully, they were still afloat.

From the deck came the sound of muffled cries. Their frantic tones were unmistakeable.

'Charles!' she called, in the darkness. There was no answer. She reached out along the floor. 'Charles! Where are you?'

The fiddle on the bookshelf had broken showering books and journals across the floor. Through the window, a strange rose coloured light was visible. It was the colour of the storm.

Charles was on the floor. The initial impact had thrown him across the cabin. He was motionless, his face pressed between deck and cupboard.

'Help! Someone please help!' Emma cried.

But the thunder of the sea and roar of the wind swallowed her voice.

Afraid to stand, she slid down to where Charles had fallen. As the ship listed again she rolled him onto his back.

'Charles,' she called softly stroking her hand across his face. His brow was wet and sticky. Blood. But he was breathing. 'Please wake up,' she begged. There was no response. She must go for help.

It was even darker outside the cabin. The companionway hatch leading up to the deck had been fastened down. The boards under Emma's feet were wet.

The door to the captain's cabin was swinging from side to side. She shouted again. No one answered. Every able-bodied man was on deck. She must go to the companionway leading up from the mess. Hopefully it would still be open. She knew of no other way to get help.

Emma was not afraid of the darkness. She had survived days of blackness in the sail locker. She knew all the men would be on deck. And Thomas Barstow was no longer a threat. Providing the ship stayed upright, she had nothing to fear.

She climbed down to the mess deck and let her hands guide her along the low passageway. A glow from the mess encouraged her. It was the galley stove. And the smell. Burned broth brought back memories of Seal Street.

The tables, suspended from ropes, were swinging in unison. She grabbed the ropes to support herself to the far end of the long room. As she got closer she could see the hatch above the ladder was closed. A noise, like a rat scratching in the corner, attracted her. Then a groan.

'Who's there?'

'It's me, ma'am. Samuel.' The boy pulled himself up into a sitting position. She could see his face in the pale light.

'Are you all right?'

'Not really,' he said. 'I fell through the hatch when she went over. Twisted me leg. I'm afraid I've broken it good and proper this time. Can you get Mr Witton to take a look, do you think?'

Even in the shadows Emma could see the boy's leg was folded at a strange angle.

'Mr Witton is hurt too,' she said. 'Are all the men on deck?'

'Aye, all hands were called.'

There was no one to help Charles or Sam. She must do the best she could.

'I will be back,' she said. 'Wait a while.' It was a foolish statement. The boy was going nowhere.

Charles Witton opened his eyes.

'Please do not move,' Emma said, wiping blood from around his nose. A lump the size of a large quail egg had risen on his forehead. Emma pulled a thick woollen cloak from the chest of clothing. It made a good pillow.

'Now please stay where you are,' she said. 'You will be all right, won't you?'

She got no reply. His eyes had closed again.

Amongst the books scattered on the floor were pieces of the wooden fiddle broken from the bookcase. They would make a good splint. Strips of cotton from her petticoat would serve for the binding.

Emma returned to the boy as quickly as she could and with his help applied the splint to his leg.

'I'm sure Mr Witton will fix it properly and the carpenter will make you a crutch.'

'I reckon you did a good job. See, I can move my toes.' The pain showed on his face. 'I just hope me leg will fix quick. I don't want to be put ashore.' He sighed. 'I ain't been too lucky lately, 'ave I? What with the mast breaking and now this!'

'I think you are probably very lucky!' Emma said, looking down on the boy who was Joshua's best friend. Sam was the same age but six inches shorter than her son. He was a mere slip of a boy and the soft blond curls which bubbled from his head were a refreshing change from the untended greasy mops that most sailors hid under their moth-eaten hats.

'I suggest you don't try to climb,' Emma said.

'I ain't going nowhere, while she's blowing like this!'

When she left him, Emma felt inclined to touch his hair or plant a maternal kiss on his forehead. He had not complained once about the pain. He would make a good seaman!

Emma returned through the darkness to the stateroom and her other charge. As she kneeled down beside Charles, she could feel his eyes examining her face. The pale light from the window was reflecting in his eyes. Outside, the storm clouds were finally breaking up.

'I think the worst is over,' she said.

'I hope you are right.'

Despite opening the cabin door slowly, the hinges creaked. Charles ducked his head as he stepped into his day cabin. The lump on his forehead had gone leaving only a bluish-yellow bruise.

'Shall I leave?' Emma said, the quill poised in one hand, a piece of rag in the other.

'No! Please stay. I just want to sit and rest my legs for a while. I find it tiring standing on deck for long periods. Please,' he said, 'do not let me disturb you.'

Charles flopped down into his wingback chair. It was the only comfortable chair on the ship, even the ship's master did not have such a luxury. As he closed his eyes, Emma wondered if he would fall asleep.

Working silently, her hand hardly moved and the tip of the feather waved only slightly. On a tin plate in front of her, with its wings fanned out, was a dead moth.

Charles was watching, not sleeping. At first, his eyes followed the movement of the quill, a soft heron feather that turned in a curl at the tip. The hand holding it was equally soft. Fine and delicately boned. Fine like the French lace around her wrist. He followed the line of her arm resting gracefully on the table. Her back so straight. He studied her neck, slender with soft wisps of hair falling onto it from her bun. The same curling wisps framed her face.

As Emma's eyes bounced back and forth from paper to specimen she sensed she was being watched. She turned. 'What is it?' she asked.

'Nothing,' he said. 'I was just watching you and thinking.'

'I must finish the fringes on the wings,' she said, as she continued drawing.

'Young Samuel is doing well,' he said. 'You did a splendid job on his leg. Tell me, where did you learn to fix a fracture?'

'The doctor treated my sister's leg when I was a child. It is something I will never forget. I remember the sound of the bones grating together and her screams when the doctor straightened it.' She shook her head. 'Samuel never murmured. He was very brave.'

'Very brave!' he echoed.

'It is finished, I think,' she said, smoothing the blotting paper over her work. 'I will add a wash of colour later.'

Charles stood beside her chair.

'Lovely,' he said.

'I hope it is correct.' Emma waited for his comment but he made none. Wondering if she had omitted something or not copied the specimen correctly, she looked again at the markings on the moth's wings and compared them with the zigzag lines she had etched on her paper. She studied the wings' circular spots which stared back at her like a pair of large round eyes.

But Charles's eyes were set on neither insect nor picture. He was gazing at Emma with a warmth she had not seen before.

'Lovely,' he repeated, lifting her chin and placing a kiss on her forehead.

Emma closed her eyes.

'Please forgive me,' he said 'It is a long time since I have felt this way. I did not think it was possible. Thank you.'

'It is I who should say, thank you,' Emma said. 'You have given me so much.'

'I have done nothing,' he said.

On the desk, the quill rolled round in the inkwell as the ship slid gracefully down the side of the swell. In a few more days they would be disembarking in Sydney and their journey would be over.

Chapter 26

'Mama, I want stay with the ship.'

'I hear you,' Emma said.

'Mr Thackray said I've done well, and from him that is indeed a compliment. And the captain said that because I learned geometry and algebra at school, he would teach me to use the sextant on the next voyage. Captain Preston was in the Royal Navy when he was young,' he added.

Emma was not surprised.

'He said that if I was serious about a life at sea I should think seriously about signing on a navy ship. He said if I worked hard I might become an officer one day.'

'Really! And when did he say this?'

'Some weeks ago.'

'But you did not tell me.'

'I thought you wouldn't approve.' He paused, looking enquiringly at his mother, 'I thought you disliked seamen.'

'I think perhaps I have learned to know better. My only wish is that you will be happy with the choice you make.'

'I have never been so happy.'

'So I see.'

Joshua laughed. 'I can also say I have never been so cold, so afraid and so tired all in the same day.' He looked out to sea. 'When I climb the mast, Mama, and sit up top and the horizon is one big circle around me, I can tell you, there is no feeling to equal it. Imagine, Mama, if one day I was master of my own ship. Captain Preston says it is not impossible.'

Emma smiled anxiously. The memories of the voyage had left her with mixed feelings. 'But the types of men on board,' she said. 'The dangers, the hard work and the weather. Don't they bother you?'

'Of course not. Those are the things I enjoy.'

Emma touched his hand. 'We have come a long way, you and I, and I am not speaking of miles from England. You have grown to a man, and I—well, I'm not sure, but my life has certainly changed.' She sighed. 'I have thought for some time that you would choose to stay with the ship, so what you say comes as no surprise. I love you, Joshua,' she said, 'and I wish you well. But promise me this: promise you will write and tell me about the places you visit and the things you do. And if ever you dock in Sydney, you must find me if that is possible.'

'I promise, Mama, I will.'

Nathaniel Preston looked uncomfortable as he ushered Emma into his cabin.

'Please, take a seat.'

He waited until Emma was seated but chose to remain standing. Picking up a small roll of patterned cloth from his desk, he regarded it with a concerned expression on his face.

'There are two things I must speak with you about before you leave the ship.'

Emma watched as he turned the bundle over in his hands.

'Firstly,' he said gravely, 'I will give you this. In doing so, I must add that I have considered my actions carefully and in this instance have again taken the liberty of seeking the advice of Mr Witton. This,' he said, looking down at the item resting in his palm, 'was amongst the personal possessions of the sailor, François le Fevre, the man we all knew as Frenchy.'

Emma cast her eyes down.

'I understand it was his last wish that your son, Joshua be given his knife.'

'Joshua already has François' knife.'

'So be it,' the captain said. 'However, this knife,' he said, offering the package to her, 'was found in his sea chest. Perhaps your son should have this also. But I suggest you look at it first before you decide. The rest of Frenchy's property, his clothes and sea chest, will be auctioned amongst the men as I understand there is no family to claim them. As for the pay that is owing to him, that will be donated to the seaman's fund for widows and orphans.'

Emma took the bundle and could feel the metal enclosed within it.

'Be careful when you open it. It is very sharp.'

Emma nodded.

'Now I come to the second matter,' he said, as he cleared his throat. 'It would appear I owe you an apology.'

Emma was puzzled.

'I am referring to the money you had with you when you – how shall I put it – embarked on this voyage.' He leaned back against his desk, his hands clenched behind his back. 'I am afraid I accused you of various offences, not least of being a thief. For that I offer you my apology.'

'Thank you,' she said. 'I can understand why you would question a person in possession of such a large sum.'

'I am afraid your appearance made me assume you were a vagrant. And the fact you were in the company of a sailor, made me think your morals were those of a woman of the taverns. For that I am also sorry.' He inclined his head to one side. 'You must agree, the circumstance relating to our first introduction were somewhat unusual. However,' he said, 'before I go further let me say, my opinion was influenced by Mr Witton who, I might add, has nothing but praise for the assistance you have given him with his work these last two weeks.'

He continued, 'Knowing everything is not always what it appears on the surface, I must admit I find myself intrigued with the circumstances that led to you stowing away on my ship and the fact you were carrying a bundle of gold coins. Of course, I cannot press you for an explanation if you do not wish to speak of it, but,' he said, 'it would be interesting to hear. Material for my memoirs, perhaps, or a story to tell to my grandchildren.'

Emma smiled as she imagined Nathaniel Preston surrounded by an audience of boys and girls. 'A story for your grandchildren then,' she said.

With the captain seated and leaning back in the chair, she began. 'I told you my father was a portrait artist. His work was perfect in technique, proportion and perspective. It was what the art world wanted at that time. He not only reproduced an almost identical likeness of his subject on canvas, but was able to transcribe their thoughts and feelings with his brush. It was as if he could capture their very souls on paper. Because of his special gift he was in great demand and he worked very hard.'

The captain nodded.

'And I regard myself as fortunate, not only was I his daughter, but I was also one of his pupils. He taught me from a young age.'

Emma paused. 'But I digress. You asked me about the gold coins. As I told you, my father sold one of his paintings and, I might add, was paid handsomely for it. He gave me the coins on the day I left home to be married. I remember his words well: "Take this", he said as he pressed them into my hand. "It is my gift to you. But mind it carefully". He made me promise I would tell no one about it, not my husband-to-be, my sister, or Joshua, who was only an infant at the time.

'I did not want to take the money but he insisted. "This is not for you to waste on frivolities", he said. "It is for that time in your life when you have urgent need of it". I asked him when that time would be. "You will know when that time comes", he said. I remember his words clearly – "Trust me, you will know".'

Captain Preston listened intently.

'Papa and I were very close and I could see he was troubled. He was not a well man.' There was sadness in Emma's tone. 'His sight was leaving him.' Emma sighed. 'How tragic that affliction is for anyone, but for an artist—' She shook her head. 'When I came aboard the *Morning Star*, I had few possessions but I carried the gift my father had given me. During the dark hours I spent in the sail-locker, I thought about him a lot and decided he would have wished that I used the money to pay for my passage. He would have been happy knowing that his gift provided me with the opportunity to find a new life.'

'I would like to have met your father,' the captain said.

'It would have been his pleasure, sir.'

'Then you accept my apology.'

'Of course, captain, and I thank you for not putting me ashore in Portsmouth.'

Nathaniel Preston smiled. 'It is the Almighty you must thank for that, not me.'

'I do,' said Emma. 'Every night in my prayers.'

Emma returned to her cabin, warmed by her conversation with the captain, but saddened by the reminder of François which she carried in her hands. He had told her he had another knife, but she had forgotten. It had been carefully rolled in a sleeve torn from a woman's blouse. She placed it on her bunk and unwrapped it carefully.

The knife was old and unpretentious, but its blade had been honed so many times the metal had worn extremely thin. Its tip had also been sharpened to a point like a stiletto. A rust-coloured stain ran down the length of the blade and despite the wooden hilt being ingrained with grease and sweat, the brown stain had seeped into it. A length of plaited twine was bound tightly around the cracked wood preventing it from splitting further.

Turning the knife over, Emma noted several notches and scratches pecked into the hilt. They appeared to be deliberate marks. Apart from the row of single lines, two figures had been carved into the wood. They had worn smooth over the years and were difficult to read. At first glance Emma interpreted the scratchings as the numbers, '8' and '1' but as she turned the knife around she realized what they were. The letters carved in the wood were the initials 'T B'. The knife was not François'. It had belonged to Thomas Barstow.

His knock was soft yet it startled her. Charles closed the door quietly as if entering a room where someone was sleeping.

As Emma looked back towards the door, the fine brush trickled a line of water droplets across the table. Quickly dabbing the pearl beads, she rested the sheet of blotting paper across her work deliberately hiding the drawing she was working on. 'This is your room,' she said. 'You should not knock.'

'I'm sorry to interrupt you,' Charles said, conscious of an expression on Emma's face he had not seen before.

'I was just finishing. I will put this away.'

'Will you show me what you are working on?'

Emma looked guilty.

'It is nothing in particular,' she said. The brush in her hand was dripping spots onto her apron.

Charles looked down.

Her eyes followed. 'How careless of me.'

He took the rag from her hand, kneeled down and carefully dabbed away the marks. 'There,' he said. 'It is gone.' As he returned the cloth to the table, his hand reached out towards the picture she had shielded. 'May I?' he asked.

Emma nodded and sat down.

Charles studied it. It was a portrait of a man and woman. Neither was young nor well-dressed. The man was slender of build and appeared rather frail. He was seated in an old armchair. Resting against his leg was a walking stick with a metal handle moulded into the shape of a duck's bill. Standing beside the man was a lady of similar age but more robust than the man, of proud stature and with a kindly expression, though her face was touched with an air of sadness. One of her hands rested on the man's arm while the other held a single full-blown rose. A petal had shed from it and was falling to the floor. The rose was tinted with a touch of paint – the softest pink. It was the only dab of colour on the pen and ink work and it was still wet.

Charles sighed heavily. 'Your parents?'

'Yes,' she said, looking down at her work.

'There is something about this drawing which is remarkable. Your father, I think. Yes,' he said. 'His eyes! They are so striking, so intense and so alive. I feel they are looking out at me from the page.'

Emma smiled.

'Did you copy this from a photograph?' he asked, looking around the desk expecting to find one.

'It is a picture I carry with me all the time,' she said. 'In my heart.'

He looked from her to the drawing and back again. His hand enclosed hers.

She was still holding the sable brush.

'Is there space for another in your heart?' he enquired, drawing her towards him.

Her throat was full. Her eyes welled with salty tears. 'You are so kind,' she said. 'You remind me of my father.'

He tensed.

She sensed his disappointment. He had misunderstood.

'I loved him very much,' she said.

The evening was cool.

From her favourite place in the bow Emma listened to the group of sailors huddled amidships around the blacksmith's fire. Joshua was amongst them. She could hear his voice. Heard him laughing with the others.

When a piece of wood was thrown into the embers, sparks danced into the air and Emma thought about François. She thought about the tiny stars which shone in the sea and wondered if she would forget him when she left the ship. Leaning over the rail she looked down at the water curling from the bow.

In her hand was the roll of cloth. She opened it. The blade glinted in the moonlight.

Emma gazed at the sea as she let it fall. She knew that soon she would never see the illusive stars again.

The knife sliced silently into the water and disappeared.

Chapter 27

Sydney, Australia, 3 July 1856

As the rain stopped and the sun, rising from the Pacific Ocean, breathed gold on her tired canvas, *Morning Star* eased through the mile-wide headlands and sailed into Sydney harbour. Emma stood in the bow as the ship headed slowly towards the town's quay. By the time it tied up against the wharf, the sky was clear and the chill had gone from the air.

It was a grand harbour, broad and deep and well sheltered from the open sea. So different from the sandy flats of the tidal estuary of the River Esk, she thought. The vessels moored around the semicircular quay were grand also. Tall masted clippers and schooners, far bigger than the ships that visited the Yorkshire port. But, the Whitby wharves were always congested.

Like Whitby the shops and houses around the wharf area reached almost to the waterfront and the sounds of machinery and the clatter of wheels and hoofs was the same. But unlike the north coast fishing village, the boats in this harbour lacked the bright colours of the herring fleet.

Sydney was not what Emma had expected. On the dock there was a lot of noise with raised voices and everyone appeared to be in a hurry. Waifs wearing little more than rags were the only ones loitering about. They looked like beggars. Emma asked herself, wasn't Australia a rich country like America? Wasn't Sydney supposed to be like Boston with fine houses and elegant families? Hadn't men come here recently to make their fortunes on the goldfields?

Having dressed in pink satin she felt uncomfortable. She did not belong in this foreign port. Where would she go? What would she do when *Morning Star* sailed and she was alone? How many times she had asked herself these questions and yet she still had no answer?

From the aft companionway, Charles appeared followed by another gentleman – a stranger who had come aboard earlier. As the pair approached, she heard Charles say, 'I would like to introduce you to my widowed cousin, Mrs Emma Quinlan.'

They all smiled as the introductions were made.

'Emma, this is the friend I spoke of, Sir Percival Seaton.'

The older man bowed. 'I am pleased to make your acquaintance, Mrs Quinlan.'

A tentative smile hid Emma's surprise.

'I have received good news of my expedition,' Charles announced. 'The main party was delayed on their voyage. After more than three weeks of idling in the Doldrums, they had to sail almost to South America to catch the Roaring Forties. The group is no more than a week ahead of me.'

'That is good news indeed.'

Charles turned to his friend. 'I must admit, I had not relished the idea of travelling the countryside alone. Now I shall be able to catch up with them before they get too far ahead.'

'And what of your young cousin?' Sir Percival said, as he glanced at Emma. 'Where will you be staying, Mrs Quinlan?'

Before Emma had the opportunity to say anything, Charles interrupted.

'Would you permit me to answer for you, Emma?'

She nodded, relieved.

'As you know I had originally intended to arrive in Sydney some months ago, which would have allowed time to organize accommodation for myself and my daughter. But under the circumstances—'

'Yes, I understand.'

'My predicament now,' said Charles, 'is that I am undecided about my future. The expedition will take me into the hinterland for six or maybe nine months. When I return there will be considerable work to be completed, namely cataloguing the specimens that I hope to collect.' He turned to Sir Percival. 'Emma is assisting me. She is an invaluable help. I do not know what I would do without her.'

'You are very lucky, Charles, to have such a conscientious cousin.'

'I am indeed,' Charles said. 'And Emma has graciously offered to put my work in order while I am away, a chore, I must admit, that has been eluding me for some time. But she will need somewhere to work.' He took a deep breath. 'The problem I have at the moment is that I am undecided if I am going to make Sydney my permanent home. I may seek to gain an appointment with the university but, if nothing is forthcoming, I will consider leaving the city and buying a parcel of land in the country. At present,' he said, 'I feel it is unlikely I will return to England. There is nothing there for me now, but it is a decision I must give some thought to.'

'And your position, Mrs Quinlan,' the gentleman asked. 'Will you be staying in Sydney? I do hope that the answer is yes.' He continued without giving Emma the opportunity to answer, 'If you will excuse me for saying but there is a considerable shortfall in the number of educated and well-bred young ladies in this colony.'

'I have no plans at the moment,' Emma said, 'but as Charles says, I will require somewhere to live and a place where I can continue with the work I am undertaking.'

'Emma is a talented artist,' Charles said.

'Indeed? That is very interesting,' he said. 'Tell me, Mrs Quinlan. Would you consider accepting my hospitality for a short while? I know my wife would be delighted to have an English lady for company. We have a large residence and we can make ample space available for you to pursue your work. If it is suitable, you could stay with us at least until your cousin returns and you are both able to come to a decision about your future.'

'That is very generous of you, Percy. Is it not Emma?'

'Extremely,' said Emma cautiously.

'Excellent! My wife will be thrilled.'

Despite the freshness of the winter air, Emma's hands felt clammy. She watched as the two gentlemen disembarked and talked together on the wharf. Behind them the rows of buildings were grey and daunting – bond stores, agents and shipping offices and chandlers' stores.

'And welcome to New South Wales, Mrs Quinlan,' Sir Percival called. As he climbed into his carriage a street urchin, dressed in tatters, hurtled by almost knocking Charles off his feet. Two men and a couple of stray dogs were in hot pursuit. It was not what Emma had expected.

'I hope you will forgive me for taking certain liberties,' Charles said, when he stepped back on board. 'I apologize, I did not give you the opportunity to answer for yourself.'

'I did not have any answers,' she said.

He paused. 'What I said was the truth. When I return from the expedition I must make a decision about my future and it is not easy.' He took Emma's hand. 'There is another question I wish to ask you and I find it difficult.' He led her to the boatswain's deck locker and invited her to sit with him.

'I think fate had a hand in throwing us together on the *Morning Star* and for that I will be eternally grateful.' He spoke softly. 'Sadly, when we embarked, we were both burdened with grief and for you in particular the voyage has not all been smooth.' His eyes settled on the ships bobbing on the harbour. 'I believe a ship is an artificial environment. Like a cocoon. And like a cocoon, sometimes strange and unexpected things emerge from it. On the ship you faced dangers, and life for both of us on board was foreign to any life we would have encountered had we been thrown together on the land. But, I contend we have both emerged from the voyage somewhat stronger and wiser for the experience.'

He continued, 'Sydney also is a strange place. It is a city filled with English folk but it is far different to any English town you or I have ever known. It is a town you will either love or hate. Whichever the case, you must live here for some time before you can make a decision.

'If you will take my advice, Emma, you will accept Sir Percival's generous offer of hospitality. You will be residing with genteel people in most respectable surroundings. I could think of nothing better. And, by the time I return, you will be in a position to decide what the future holds for you.' He paused for a moment. 'I want to help you, Emma, and I would like to be part of your future.'

Emma sensed his embarrassment. 'What is it, Charles?'

'With your artistic talent you are invaluable to me, but what I am thinking is of far greater consequence than that. But for the present, I have a suggestion. If you are willing, I will leave you with sufficient work to keep you occupied while I am away. As I said on the ship, I do not expect you to work for nothing, therefore I will arrange for an amount of money to be paid into a bank account for you. It will not be a great deal but it will be sufficient to provide you with some independence. And, if I might suggest, your talent as a portrait painter would be well sought after were it to be made known. A reputable lady artist would be very well received in this young country.

'Now,' he declared, 'I have spoken too long and probably said too much. Please tell me you find my suggestions agreeable?'

'I could not wish for anything better.'

Relieved, Charles sighed. 'Then before I finish, there are two more things I beg of you.'

Emma inclined her head.

'Firstly, I ask that you remain in Sydney until I return and, secondly, that while I am away you allow me to write to you. May I do that?'

'Yes, of course,' she said. 'My dear Charles, it seems to me that from the time of my accident on the ship, I have been in your debt, and I have done little to show my gratitude. Without you I would not be here and none of this would be happening.' She rested her hand on his. 'I promise I will be here when you return, and I will look forward to receiving your letters and news of how the expedition is progressing. As to my decision whether I leave this town or stay, that is a choice I will make when you return. I am sure with your help and advice I will not make the wrong decision. And,' she said, 'as for the drawings, it will give me great pleasure to continue. I will try not to disappoint you with the quality of my work.'

'Excellent. Then that is settled. I am relieved.' He stood up and filled his lungs with air. 'Mrs Quinlan, if you would care to take my arm, I will take you for your first stroll on Australian soil.'

With one hand grasping Charles's arm and the other on her skirt, Emma stepped from the gangplank onto the quay. The smells reminded her of Whitby – of seaweed, fish, and meat roasting.

'If you bought a farm in the country,' said Emma, 'would you have a house cow?'

'No!' he said grinning. 'I would have a herd of cows. And all the milk you could drink.'

'Then I will think about what you have said.'

'Now it is my turn to say, thank you.'

The ship had been Emma's home for almost four months. Leaving it was not easy.

It was midday when the carriage stopped on the wharf opposite the gangplank. It was followed by a dray wagon. The ship was quiet. Most of the men had gone ashore. Others were resting below decks.

Though Emma had boarded *Morning Star* with almost nothing she was leaving with two large trunks: one full of clothes, the other packed with Charles's exotic specimens, equipment and journals.

Beside his own trunk, Charles had an extraordinary number of boxes and cases. Joshua and two of the sailors hauled them up from the hold and loaded them onto a waiting wagon where Charles made sure everything was secured firmly.

For Emma, saying goodbye to Joshua was the hardest. She tried to joke with him and make light of the fact he would soon be sailing away, but when he hugged her for the final time the tears flowed fast and free.

'Your boy will be fine,' said Charles. 'He is in good hands.'

Joshua rubbed his cheeks on his sleeve. 'Goodbye, Mama, I will write, and I will find you when I sail to Sydney again. I have not forgotten what you asked.'

Two seamen appeared from the companionway. 'Begging your pardon, ma'am, we got something for you.'

Jack Burns had a sheepish expression on his face. Standing beside him was Mr Kaye, the ship's carpenter, the quiet man whose skill had repaired the ship several times during the voyage. '*Morning Star*', Burns said, handing Emma a model ship fully rigged in fine twine and boasting a full complement of sails neatly furled to the yards.

'Replica she is,' he said. 'A bit smaller than the real one. Kaye whittled it. I just did the sails. And she's rigged right proper, just like the *Star*!'

'Thank you, gentlemen. This is remarkable.'

'Might do to give the wood a bit of an oiling occasionally,' the carpenter said.

'I will, and I will treasure this along with my memories of my time on board.'

'Aye, well, best be off.' Jack Burns lifted his cap, turned and hurried back along the gangplank.

Mr Kaye touched his knuckles to his forehead. 'Good luck, missus,' he said. 'Aye, and to you too, governor.'

'Thank you, Mr Kaye,' Charles replied. 'And I wish you both a safe voyage home.'

Emma stood by the gangway cradling the model in her arms as the two men climbed back down the hatch.

'I believe you have won a few hearts,' Charles whispered to her. 'Let me help you. We must get started. We have a long drive ahead of us and our hosts will be expecting us before dark.' After helping Emma into the carriage, he seated himself opposite her and relaxed back into the cushioned upholstery. 'It will feel strange sleeping on beds that are not rolling but I think by tonight we will both be ready for sleep.'

'Goodbye, missus! Good luck!' a voice shouted, as the carriage started to roll. Young Samuel was balancing on the ship's rail, waving his crutch in the air.

Joshua ran along the gangplank and onto the quay. 'Goodbye, Mama!' he yelled.

Emma leaned from the window and waved her handkerchief until the carriage turned from the water and the two boys were lost from sight.

It was early the following Monday morning when Charles slid the canvas bag hard against his saddle that was loaded on the back of the same flat wagon. This time his luggage consisted of few items and he insisted that he load them himself.

'You are taking so little with you,' Emma said.

'Too much, I think. I have to be prepared to carry everything by horse or mule as the wagon will probably be unsuitable for the route we are taking. Dear Emma, I wish you were coming with me, but such a journey is no place to take a lady. But,' he said, 'it worries me to leave you.'

'I will be fine. I could not have imagined a situation more generous that I have here, and Lady Seaton is a dear kind lady – and this lovely house, and the fine people I have been introduced to during the past two days. I could not have wished for anything better.'

'Then I am pleased. When I am away, I will write, but despatching mail may not be easy.'

'I understand.'

'If all goes well, I hope to be back by Christmas. Are you sure you will be all right alone, Emma?'

'I will not be alone.'

Charles's face was serious. 'You will stay here until I come back, won't you?'

How many times had she heard those words? 'I promise,' she said.

'Good. Then I must say goodbye.' He held Emma's hands in his. When she leaned towards him, he reached his arms around her. 'I did not think it would be so difficult to leave.'

'God speed and bring you back safely.'

Charles climbed onto the bench seat next to the driver and with a flick of the whip the pair of horses snorted and the wagon slowly rolled down the long driveway. Emma stood watching it until it finally disappear from view.

Lady Seaton was standing in the doorway. 'He will be back in quick sticks, my dear, you mark my words. Come along, we have work to do. You must help me with my preparations for next week's reception. We will be entertaining over a hundred guests. Everyone who is anyone has been invited. It will be a wonderful opportunity for you to be presented and make some new acquaintances.'

Emma tried to smile, though her only thoughts were for Charles.

'Come inside, my dear, Mr Witton will be back before you know it.'

Chapter 28

Although it was still early, the large reception room was filling quickly.

Lady Seaton, descended on each group of newcomers as they arrived, flitting between guests like a nervous butterfly. Emma had feared awkward questions but against the background of voices, the clink of crystal glasses and the rustle of silk on silk, conversation flowed freely. Most of the Sydney residents wanted snippets of information about England. Anything, from the amount of snow that had fallen the previous winter, to the state of the railways, to Palmerston's power as Prime Minister and the growing legend of Florence Nightingale who had nursed the wounded during the Crimean War. Emma answered as best she could and listened to various opinions but would have preferred to sit quietly and savour the strains of the string quartet.

'Mrs Quinlan. I hardly recognized you.'

Emma spun around to the familiar voice. 'Captain Preston,' she said, holding out her hand. 'I am so pleased to see you. Lady Seaton said you might be attending. I was surprised to hear you had not sailed.'

'Unfortunately we are waiting on a consignment of wool. As soon as it arrives and is loaded we sail for London.'

A servant approached with a platter. The captain waved the food away.

'Perhaps we could get away from the noise for a moment,' he said. 'There is a small matter I must speak with you about.'

Somewhat surprised by his request, Emma accompanied him through the French doors. The courtyard, bordered by a garden, overlooked a broad apron of neatly trimmed grass which sloped to the banks of the Parramatta River. Across the water a herd of long horned cattle were grazing in the marshes.

'Is it something about my son, Joshua?' she asked anxiously. 'He has signed on for the return voyage.'

'Yes, he has signed but it is another matter I need to speak with you about. I have something for you.' Reaching in his pocket, he took out a black satin purse and placed it on Emma's palm. 'A gift from your father, if I am not mistaken.'

Emma closed her fingers around it. She could feel the coins inside. 'Thank you,' she said quietly. 'You are a kind man.'

'I'm not sure everyone would agree with you on that matter!' Captain Preston allowed himself to smile as he offered Emma his arm and escorted her back to the main reception area. 'Now, if you will excuse me, I will leave you to enjoy your evening. I plan to return to the quay early.'

'Would you tell my son you have seen me?'

Nathaniel Preston bowed. 'I will. Goodbye, Mrs Quinlan.'

Watching him walk away, Emma thought of the ship that had carried her halfway across the world, of its captain, and of her father whose gift to her was far greater than mere pieces of gold. As she clutched the purse to her chest, her eyes filled with tears.

'Now my dear,' said Lady Seaton, sweeping across the floor with obvious intent. 'I do not want to see you on your own. There are so many people to whom you must be introduced. Come with me. You must meet the Governor and Lady Denison. They arrived a few moments ago. I have just told them what a talented young lady you are.'

Emma followed dutifully as the hostess skirted the spacious reception room nodding pleasantries to everyone she passed.

Though the governor was surrounded by a group of people, Lady Seaton bustled her way through. 'Sir William, allow me to introduce Mrs Emma Quinlan?'

Emma curtsied.

'Mrs Quinlan,' the governor said. 'I am delighted to make your acquaintance. I trust you like our town.'

'Indeed. It has a beautiful harbour and the countryside around is very pleasant. I hope to see much more of Sydney in the near future.'

'And I hope we will see a lot more of you in the future.'

'That is very kind of you.'

'Tell me, how was your passage? A good one I hope?'

'It was a good journey.'

'I am pleased to hear it,' he said glancing at his wife. 'We found the passage most tedious, didn't we, my dear? The accommodation was terribly uncomfortable and the service quite abominable. However,' he sighed, 'we have to make these sacrifices at times, do we not?'

Emma was obliged to agree.

When Lady Seaton's attention was directed to another group of guests, Emma was relieved. It gave her the opportunity to escape from the noise and chatter to the peace of the small garden. Outside the sun was bright but the day cold even though there was no breath of wind. How different, she thought, from her special place in the ship's bow. How she longed to hear the sound of the sea, to feel the salt on her face, to witness the sea's illusive diamonds and to gaze in awe at the changing hues of the evening as it transformed the sky in a kaleidoscope of colours.

The area, which was provided for Emma to work in, was delightful. It was a long narrow room, on the ground floor, with French windows overlooking the river. Facing north, it allowed the winter sun to stream across its polished floor.

It took Emma quite some time before she could commence the work Charles had left for her as Lady Seaton allowed her little time to herself. She was forever interrupting, enquiring if she needed anything, offering assistance, requesting her company to visit the city or to stroll with her in the gardens. She also insisted Emma take time to read the British newspapers, despite the fact on arrival they were four months out of date and any significant news had already been printed in the *Sydney Morning Herald*. It was only when the novelty of Emma's presence had worn off, Lady Seaton allowed her time to herself.

Apart from work, Emma wanted to write to Charles, and Joshua, but she had no way of contacting either. Her correspondence would have to wait until she received letters from them.

It was with some difficulty she wrote to her sister telling her briefly about the voyage and what had happened since she left Whitby. She wrote about Lord and Lady Seaton and the fine house she was living in, and about Charles Witton explaining how kind he had been and the opportunities he had provided for her. Emma concluded by mentioning Joshua, saying he was well but not telling her that he had sailed away with the ship.

When the letter was sealed she handed it to Sir Percival. He assured her it would be despatched on the next mail-packet sailing to England.

September heralded spring in New South Wales and it was beautiful. Though the eucalyptus trees showed little evidence of the changing seasons, the wild flowers bloomed in a rainbow of colours – red spider flowers, blue leschenaultia, golden wattles, and wild orchids. At night, the fragrances of the garden drifted in through the open windows, the strong scent of daphne and boronia, and native frangipani. Emma listened to the clicking of the cicadas and hum of the beetles' wings as they buzzed frantically around the room. But as she lay on her bed and looked at the white painted ceiling, her mind wandered back to her bunk on the *Morning Star* and the man who had nursed her back to health.

With every passing day, the midday sun rose higher in the sky and the temperature grew warmer. The freezing mornings which had seen ice form on the bird-bath outside the French windows, were gone. By seven o'clock the days were warmer than she had ever known in Whitby. By midday the heat almost unbearable.

For weeks, Emma's work with the specimens kept her busy. She began early in the morning, when it was cool, but by noon found it impossible to draw as the sweat from her hands dripped onto the paper. During the afternoons she would spend her time reading or referring to Charles's journals. The study absorbed her.

Occasionally, when she was wandering in the garden, she would catch an insect and take it indoors then attempt to identify it and draw a likeness of it, carefully recording each specimen in the hope she might discover something new before Charles returned. It was three months since he had left and Christmas was still weeks away. She tried not to think about him.

But Emma's progress with the backlog of work was halted when Sir Percival requested a portrait of his wife. He described it as a commission, though Emma refused to accept payment saying it was the least she could do to repay their kindness.

Lady Seaton was not the easiest of subjects. Unable to sit still, or sit quietly, she was constantly talking and fidgeting, adjusting the folds in her skirt or tilting the angle of her head. But three sittings were all Emma needed. She could have managed with less but Lady Seaton insisted.

The long room had become both laboratory and studio for Emma. She was mostly left alone and particularly enjoyed working after supper when the household had retired and everything was quiet.

When the portrait was completed, Lady Seaton was ecstatic and immediately requested Emma paint Sir Percival, insisting she start right away. With her ladyship's wide circle of friends, word of Emma's talent was quickly relayed around the Sydney gentry and soon she was receiving requests for her services. She refused them all, but one gentleman was not easy to deter. He visited the house on three occasions expressing interest in her talent. Emma accepted his compliments politely though she felt unsure if his intentions were honourable.

As the weeks went by, Emma thought more and more about Charles and when Lady Seaton asked for help in making plans for the forthcoming Christmas festivities, Emma accepted, relieved at the distraction.

Lady Seaton mopped her brow as she wandered over to the easel by the window. A white sheet was draped over it. 'May I see what it is that you have been working on, my dear? I do so like looking at your work.'

Emma lifted the cloth from the canvas.

'My, my! It's Mr Witton. And such a perfect likeness.' Clapping her hands, she stepped back. 'How did you manage to capture his face without even a single sitting? You must carry his image in your head.'

'In my head – and here,' Emma said, resting the flat of her hand across her heart. 'I did not realize it myself until I started painting.'

'Oh, I must show Percy, he will be so impressed. And when Charles returns, I am sure he will be delighted. That won't be long now. Didn't he say he would back for Christmas?'

'If all went well.'

'Have you received word from him?'

Emma shook her head.

'Don't worry, dear. He'll be all right. You wait and see.'

Christmas came and went with all its celebrations, as did New Year. The house had a constant stream of guests passing through the door, even the governor and his wife called in one afternoon to take tea. Much to Emma's embarrassment Lady Seaton made sure Sir Percival's portrait was displayed to advantage.

But despite the hubbub of activity, Emma could not stop worrying about Charles. Even when entertaining visitors, she found herself not listening to the trivial conversation and, on more than one occasion, had to ask them to repeat their questions before she could reply.

Charles should have been back by now. There had been no word so she had no idea what could have delayed his return. She wondered if something was amiss.

As the weeks passed with still no news, Emma grew more and more anxious. She didn't discuss her concerns with Sir Percival or his wife but knew from their whispered words that they too were worried about Charles's welfare.

It was an oppressive afternoon in March. The temperature had been hovering around one hundred degrees when a violent thunderstorm struck unleashing its full force directly over the house. Standing beside the window, Emma watched as the courtyard turned white under a barrage of hailstones. Because of the noise, she didn't hear the knock or see the door open but, when she turned from the window, Sir Percival and Lady Seaton were in the room standing side-by-side at the door. Their stance was unusual, almost childlike. Sir Percival had a piece of paper in his hand; Lady Seaton a handkerchief.

'Sorry to interrupt you, my dear,' Lady Seaton said.

'Please come in.' Emma raised her voice to be heard above the thunder. 'You are not interrupting me. I was just watching the weather. The contrasts here are so extreme.'

For a moment there was silence.

'You tell her, dear,' Lady Seaton said, nudging her husband.

Sir Percival stepped forward. 'I am sorry, Emma, but we have received some bad news and felt that you would want to be informed.'

Emma's fingers covered her lips. 'It's news of Charles, isn't it?'

Lady Seaton walked over to her and took her hand. 'No, dear, it's not that. It's the ship you sailed on, the *Morning Star*. She was returning to Sydney and was lost at sea.'

'No!' Emma cried. 'Where! When!'

'In Bass Strait, off the Furneaux group of Islands. She should have docked in Sydney two weeks ago but never arrived.' Sir Percival shook his head and handed the letter to Emma. 'This news has just arrived. It includes the names of the men who survived the sinking.'

Emma took it and ran her eyes down the list. She read it again, and then again, looking for her son's name, but it was not included.

'We are so sorry, dear,' Lady Seaton said.

Emma face was pale. 'What happened?'

'It appears there was a fire on the ship that started in the stern section below deck. The men managed to put it out, but not before it had disabled the rudder. Without steerage the ship drifted. The master thought they would clear the islands as they were well to the north, but a gale blew them onto an uncharted reef.' Sir Percival shook his head. 'There are treacherous currents and winds in those waters! It appears that master stayed on board with a handful of crew while two boats were lowered. One was swamped and several of the men drowned. The other boat picked up the survivors and managed to make it to shore. When the men returned to the beach the following day they found the ship had broken into pieces and there was no sign of anyone on deck.

'But how do you know this?'

'Word was carried by the men who survived. The lucky ones. Fortunately, they had landed on one of the larger island and were able to make their way to a lighthouse. They stayed with the lighthouse keeper until they were picked up by fishermen and taken to Melbourne.'

'But what of the captain and men who stayed onboard? Could they have got away on another boat perhaps? Drifted to the mainland or another island?'

Sir Percival looked grave. 'It is considered unlikely. Many ships have foundered on those rugged islands and many souls perished. If they had survived we would have heard by now. Unless they landed on an uninhabited island but, even then, their chances of survival would not be good.'

Emma spoke calmly. 'Do you have the names of the men who drowned?'

'No, only this list of the men who survived.'

She read through it three times.

Leonard Thackray – First mate
William Wortley – second Mate
Alfred Burns
Neville Gill
Kenneth Kaye
Jack Mahoney
Mikael Mikelsonn
Leslie Mundy
Harold Pickersgill
Walter Womersley

'I remember them all,' she said softly. 'Mr Burns and Mr Kaye were good men. I am pleased they survived.' She turned the page to see if any names were entered on the other side but it was blank. 'Joshua's name is missing.'

Lady Seaton put her arms around Emma and held her. 'Is there anything we can do, my dear?'

'No, thank you. It was my son's choice to sail and he was fully aware of the perils. I am sure Captain Preston did all he possibly could to safeguard his men and the ship.'

Sir Percival held out his hand towards his wife. 'Come, my dear. I think Emma would like some time to herself.'

When the door closed, Emma walked over to the window. She gazed at the rain streaming down the pane, then her eyes filled with tears and she could see no more.

Chapter 29

A hot wind was blowing from the interior when a rider arrived with the mail. After handing the leather pouch to Sir Percival and attending to his horse, the man was conveyed to the kitchen for some refreshments. Moments later, after briefly perusing the contents of the pouch, Sir Percival strode into the conservatory.

Lady Seaton was sitting with her eyes closed, her needlework resting on her lap. It was too humid to sew. Her hands were clammy and as a result she had used barely six inches of silk the whole afternoon. Emma was sitting by the window reading.

Saying nothing, Lord Percival handed one envelope to Emma, turned and walked out studying the other letter in his hand.

Lady Seaton opened her eyes and frowned. 'Who is it from, Percy?'

But he did not answer.

Emma examined her envelope. It had taken over three months to arrive.

'Is it from Mr Witton?' Lady Seaton enquired.

'No,' said Emma recognizing the writing. 'It is from my sister, Anna in England.'

She wandered over to the window to read it.

Dearest Emma

How good it is to hear you are safe and well. I was delighted to receive your letter telling of your voyage to Australia and your new life in the colony. How exciting that must be. How brave you are to travel to the other side of the globe. I envy you.

I trust both you and Joshua are well. Daniel and the boys are keeping well and wish to be remembered to you.

I should have contacted you several weeks ago but having no forwarding address it was not possible. It is my painful duty to inform you that George Quinlan is dead? The doctor said he had likely died from the drink.

I was contacted because my name and address was found amongst your letters. It appears George had no relatives.

In your absence and with no other monies available, Daniel decided it was best to act on your behalf. He advised the authorities to sell the house in order that George's outstanding debts (and they were quite considerable) were paid.

I know this news will come as a shock to you and I am sorry that this is the main thrust of my letter.

My dear Emma, I know you have suffered in the past. But now you have a new life and all that is far behind you. You mentioned a gentleman you met on the ship. I hope you will find happiness in that direction if that is your wish.

I think of you often and miss you.

Your affectionate sister
Anna

Emma folded the letter and placed it back into the envelope.

'Good news, dear?' Lady Seaton asked inquisitively.

Not knowing what to say, Emma didn't answer. How could she say George's death was good news? That would be terrible. But she remembered how many times in her heart she had wished that to be the case. Now he was dead, she found herself devoid of feeling. She felt neither elation nor bitterness, guilt nor sorrow for the loss of the man to whom she had been married for twelve years. As she stared at the envelope, all she could feel was emptiness.

The arrival of the maid with the afternoon tea-trolley came as a relief.

'Splendid,' Lady Seaton said. 'This heat makes one so dreadfully thirsty. Don't you agree, my dear?'

'It does indeed.'

After setting out the china, the maid disappeared and returned with a plate of cheese and fruitcake. 'Will there be anything else, ma'am?'

'No, thank you.'

Emma was pouring tea when Sir Percival appeared at the door. He was still holding the letter in his hand and appeared preoccupied as he wandered over to his leather chair. His wife observed him quizzically.

'What is it, dear,' she said, pushing her needlework to one side.

'It's Charles's party,' he sighed. 'It appears things did not go well.'

Emma and Lady Seaton were anxious for him to continue.

'This letter is written by a man I do not know. He was with Charles on the scientific expedition. Let me read an excerpt:

We were beset by problems from the very start.

After only a week, the shaft on the wagon broke. A week later one of the horses went lame and had to be shot. The following week two of the horses wandered off which meant discarding some of the equipment. After that we were almost consumed in a scrub fire and then some of the men became sick.

When Henry Machin fell and broke his leg a decision was made to abort the expedition. But Machin could not be moved and Charles Witton volunteered to remain with him until we could return with help.

We left the pair in a small clearing beside a river with two tents and an adequate supply of rations. Charles and Henry were aware it would be at least six weeks before we could get back to them.'

'But they were due back before Christmas, surely they should have been back by now!'

Sir Percival shook his head. His expression was grave. 'It says here the rescue party returned as quickly as they could but it took them seven weeks.' He referred to the letter:

'When we located the place where we had left them, we discovered the river had flooded and with the volume of water and speed of the current we were unable to cross. There was no sign of the men on the other bank and after an unsuccessful search, the rescue was called off.'

'What is he saying, Sir Percival?

'Although not described in so many words, what the writer is implying is that conditions in the area are extremely difficult. The terrain is near impossible to penetrate, the country is inhospitable, the heat unbearable. There are natives and animals in the bushland. Snakes. Deadly spiders. God only knows what lurks there.' He sighed loudly. 'In all truth, if we do not receive word within another week or two, we can only presume that Charles and Henry Machin are dead.'

Emma collapsed into the chair. 'No,' she murmured. 'No.'

For days, Emma could not work. Nor could she sleep.

Whenever a rider appeared on the drive she would rush to the door to enquire if there was any news.

Lady Seaton tried to be of comfort, but nothing helped until one afternoon when the mail arrived. Bustling into Emma's studio waving an envelope around, she cried: 'Emma. A letter from England. This will cheer you up. Maybe it's from your sister.'

Emma smiled and looked at the handwriting. It bore none of the delicate style of her sister's artistic hand. The strokes were thick and uneven. But she recognized the writing. Joshua had written it in England. It was postmarked November of the previous year. Her hands trembled as she opened it, and she was unable to stop the tears running down her cheeks.

'Perhaps it is better if I leave you alone,' Lady Seaton said.

Emma didn't reply. She was reading:

Dearest Mama

I hope you are well and send you my fondest love. By the time this letter reaches you it will be summer in Australia and hopefully I will be at sea.

My friend Samuel also sends his good wishes. I am sure you will remember him. His leg is fully mended, the only sign of the break is a little thickening where you fitted the bones together. He walks and runs with no limp and can climb the rigging as swiftly as any other man. He told me to write and thank you.

The return voyage from Sydney was good. We made good way up the coast of Africa and apart from a few sails blown out and the smell of sulphur (used to kill lice) there were no problems. We docked in London early in November and the Morning Star *was due to sail again for Sydney the following week. But when Sam and I heard that Captain Preston was leaving the ship and that it was to have a new master, we decided to travel to Portsmouth.*

Two days ago, Sam and I signed to sail on a navy ship. I hope you will be happy for me. It is what I want. I do not know if we will sail to the Southern Ocean but hopefully, one day I will be at liberty to visit you in Sydney.

Please give my regards to Mr Witton.

I have not forgotten my promise and I will write to you again.

Your loving son
Joshua

From the doorway Lady Seaton observed Emma's crouched posture, her face buried in her hands.

'What is it dear?' she said, putting her arm around her shoulders. 'Not more bad news?'

'No,' Emma sobbed. 'Wonderful News! Joshua did not sail with the *Morning Star*. He is alive and so is Captain Preston.'

'Praise be!' Lady Seaton shouted. 'Praise the Lord!'

It was early April. The ground was hard, cracked and rutted. On the driveway the horses' hoofs churned up a cloud of dust that floated on the warm air and seemed unwilling to settle. Watching from her window Emma recognized Sir Percival's carriage and returned to her work. Ten minutes later there was a knock on the door.

'Emma, there is someone here to see you,' Lady Seaton called.

'If it is that fellow Winterbourne, who has been begging me to paint his portrait, please tell him I am not available.'

'It is not Winterbourne.' The voice was gentle, Emma recognized it instantly.

'Charles!'

As she rose, he held out his arms.

'Oh, Charles, dear Charles,' she cried, allowing his arms to enclose her. 'We feared you were dead. I thought I would never see you again.'

'My dearest Emma, how long I have wished for this moment. Sometimes I thought it would never happen.'

Lifting her head, she looked into his face. 'But you are so thin! Come, sit down.' She led him to the armchair, which faced the river, and sat beside him on a foot stool. After a few moments silence, Emma asked, 'How did you manage to survive? Sir Percival received some news and told me that you had remained behind to care for another man and that the river flooded and it was thought you had been washed away.'

Charles gazed through the window to the river winding silently through the valley like a silver snake.

'It is a long story.'

Emma smiled kindly, 'If you wish to recall it, I would like to hear it.'

Charles looked tired when he spoke. 'We had been waiting for the rest of our party to return, when a summer storm struck. The rain was torrential and didn't stop. I have never witnessed anything like it. We could see the river level rising by the minute and, when we woke in the night, the water was in the tent lapping at our feet. The current was remarkably strong and was carrying away everything in its path.

'Our only escape was to scramble up the side of the valley but it wasn't easy as Henry couldn't walk. At times I dragged him. Sometimes he crawled on his belly. But there was no path through the thick undergrowth, the only tracks were made by kangaroos and wild pigs. Apart from a bag of biscuits I was able to save, everything in the camp was washed away.'

'Then how did you survive?'

'We were exceedingly lucky. We were found by a group of natives. Old women and children gathering berries. They were very wary of us at first and spoke little English, they but offered us food. After two nights they helped carry my friend to their camping ground. It was not much more than a clearing in the woods with a few shelters made from sticks covered in woven bark. But they shared their meat with us and in their own gruff manner, were kind.'

He paused and inclined his head. 'If only I could sketch the way you do. You would have loved their faces. Their expressions. The stories hidden deep within the blackness of their skin.' He sighed. 'I am sure it spoke of their hardship and told of their history reaching back for many generations.'

'How long did you stay with them?'

'Only a few days. Everything changed when the menfolk returned. There was a commotion in the camp and for a time Henry and I feared for our lives. The following morning the natives moved on without saying a word. But they left some meat in the ashes and I knew which berries I could pick and which grubs and insects we could eat.'

Emma's nose curled as she smiled.

'A strange diet,' he laughed. 'But we survived and stayed in that camp for almost four weeks until Henry's leg had healed sufficiently for him to walk on it. Then we travelled along the ridge keeping the river in sight knowing it would eventually lead us to the coast. When we stumbled across a wagon track we rejoiced. It was on that track we were found – and now we are back. Oh, Emma, how I missed you.'

'And I missed you more than you would know.' Rising to her feet, she offered him her hands and led him to the easel 'I would like to show you something.'

Lifting the cotton cloth from the portrait, she regarded the man standing beside her, his face burnt brown, his cheeks hollow from hunger, but apart from the different hues, it was the same face she had painted. The likeness was remarkable.

'You made room in your heart for me?' he said.

'Yes. More room than you can imagine.'

'Emma, there is so much I want to say, I do not know where to start. Would you walk with me for a while?'

'Yes,' she whispered.

Taking her hand, he led her through the French doors.

On the grassy slope, a flock of pink cockatoos screeched and chattered loudly and when the couple approached, they lifted in the air and, like a rose-coloured cloud, floated to the line of gumtrees at the other side of the river. The cattle wading blissfully amongst the reeds ignored them.

'You once told me you might become a farmer,' Emma said.

'Yes,' he replied.

'And I asked you if you would buy a house cow.'

'And I replied that I would buy a whole herd of cows.'

Emma slid her arm through his. 'I hear there is good land south of Sydney, where the rolling hills are as green as England's and the fields slope gently to the sea. Where the horizon stretches forever and every morning you can watch the sun as it rises from the ocean.'

'A perfect place for a farm, you think?'

Emma smiled. 'Perfect,' she said.

THROUGH GLASS EYES

Book 2 in the Trilogy of Yorkshire Tales

Chapter 1

Heaton Hall, North Yorkshire – 1896

'Oldfield!'

'Yes, Mrs Gresham?'

'Your shoe is still squeaking! Didn't I tell you about that yesterday? And the day before?'

Lucy Oldfield nodded resentfully. 'I tried to fix it, honest I did. I tried whale oil like you said, but it didn't work.'

'Then I suggest you wear another pair.'

'I don't have another pair, ma'am.'

'Then you had better do something about it. I will not have you walking these corridors when every step you take sounds like you are stepping on a mouse. We must have quiet in the house! Do you understand?'

As Lucy's chin dropped, she leaned forward and watched her toes disappear beneath the broad frill of her apron. Why had she listened to her mother and bought the new pair when there was nothing wrong with the old ones? Soft as velvet, they were, and comfortable. And, as she never walked outside in them, except to the pump across the courtyard, it didn't matter that the soles were thin as parchment. If she'd had any sense she'd have had them re-soled. That would have saved her a few pennies which she could have sent to her mother.

Lucy shook her head. The thought of her mother's advice aggravated her at times. Always telling her what to do, insisting she knew best and treating her like she was still a child. Even after six years, her mother's words rang in her head: 'Mind you always wear your own boots and bloomers!' It didn't matter that Heaton Hall supplied its maids with everything from stockings to caps and lengths of cloth to make their own under-garments, Lucy's mother would hear nothing of it. 'Your own boots and bloomers!' she would say. 'No one else's!'

Being reminded of this and a dozen other things every year when she went home for her annual holiday, Lucy had realized it was easier to bow to her mother's wishes than to remonstrate. If she ever did speak out, she was accused of being ungrateful, told in no uncertain terms, how very fortunate she was to have a good job in a fine house – and was made to feel guilty.

But on the subject of shoes, Lucy knew she should have spoken out. The new ones had been uncomfortable when she first tried them on but, as always, mother knew best and had insisted they would soften, wear in, mould to her feet. But they never did! The leather was tough and, despite the grease Lucy had rubbed into them, the right shoe still squeaked and the stitching pinched her toes.

Though she loved her mother, Lucy wished she would listen to reason and realize she was no longer fifteen years of age. She hated the new shoes. And what made matters worse, Mrs Gresham hated them too.

'No point feeling sorry for yourself,' the housekeeper said, 'so take that glum expression off your face. You have a lot to be thankful for, girl. Now get downstairs and fetch some hot water. Nurse is waiting.'

'Yes, ma'am.' Lucy bobbed, turned and tiptoed towards the back stairs which led down to the kitchen. Behind her the sound of Mrs Gresham's heels echoed from the corridor's polished boards, *clack, clack, clack, clack*. When the housekeeper reached the main staircase the sound stopped, her footsteps muffled by the Axminster carpet.

'Damn!' Lucy said, as she flopped down at the table.

'There will be no blaspheming in my kitchen, Lucy Oldfield!'

'Sorry, Cook, I didn't mean that to slip out, but it's Mrs Gresham. She makes me mad complaining all the time about my shoes creaking. I'm sure she thinks I do it on purpose.'

'She's got a lot on her plate at the moment,' said Cook. 'And it's the little things that rattle her.'

'But why pick on me and my shoes? Walk on any of the corridors in this house and the floorboards creak. The stairs creak. The door hinges creak. In fact the whole damned house creaks. I bet if Mrs Gresham leaned over she would creak too. Mrs High and Mighty, she is.'

Cook thumped her fist on the table. 'Have you quite finished with your speech-making?'

Unfastening her right shoe, Lucy kicked it under the table. 'It's her fault if I fall,' she mumbled.

Cook wagged her head and pointed to the kettle. 'You bide your temper, girl and don't forget what you came down for.' Brushing beads of sweat from her forehead, the woman turned to the brace of game sitting head to tail in the baking dish. 'Think about that poor little mite upstairs,' she said. 'God help her! That's what the trouble is. The little lass, being ill, is getting to all of us. Even me, down here in the kitchen.' She glanced across at Lucy. 'You must feel it. You're up and down to the red room more than twenty times a day. And Mrs Gresham spends more time in there than anyone. I tell you, it'd wear a body out trying to behave like there's nothing wrong.'

A blast of hot air hit the woman's face, as she opened the oven door. 'There,' she said, sliding the baking dish onto the top shelf. 'His lordship is partial to a bit of pheasant and if he don't start eating soon, he's in danger of fading away too.'

Lucy trickled the boiling water into a china bowl, added a jug full of cold and tested it on her wrist.

'Best get up there before they start ringing the bell.'

As Lucy climbed the steps, she was conscious of the odd sounds her feet made with only one shoe on. From the kitchen she heard a bell ring. It had a distinctive sound, different from the others – brighter, clearer, and louder. Lucy didn't know if it was because it was the smallest bell on the line or because its brass was shiniest, but she knew it was summoning her and that Nurse would probably scold her for taking too long.

'I'm coming as quick as I can,' she murmured, balancing the bowl carefully so the water didn't slop out.

The nursery was at the far end of the long corridor. Lucy knocked on the door and took a deep breath before entering.

How the room had changed since 1890 when she had first arrived at Heaton Hall. How bright it had been in those days with its broad south-facing window – the vibrant velvet curtains and matching strawberry drapes adorning the four-poster bed. The cords that tied them had silk tassels rolled into tiny balls that hung like bunches of ripe cherries. Everything had glowed with the same succulent shade

– cushions, chairs, even the bell pull. It was no surprise to Lucy it had been called the red room before its role was changed from children's nursery to sick room.

That was how she had known it, its door always open spilling light and sound onto the corridor. Inside, the panelled walls echoed with the high pitched sounds of children's voices, the floor littered with toys and pretty children.

But in the last few weeks, since Miss Beatrice had become ill, everything had changed. Now the door was kept closed. The room was silent. The toys gone. Even the rocking horse had disappeared. The floor was bare to the boards. Even the carpet had been removed. There were no ornaments on the mantelshelf or dresser. No mirrors or pictures on the walls. The heavy velvet curtains were tightly closed to block out any evidence of day. From the table, a single lamp flickered day and night, its wick turned down so low any movement of air threatened to snuff it out. The pale light it cast did not penetrate the confines of the big bed, its four turned posts and heavy canopy reflecting only the sombre darkness of the room's walnut panelling.

'Set it down there,' the nurse whispered brusquely as she twisted the top from a glass jar and sprinkled a generous serving of green crystals into the steaming water.

Although the air hung heavily with the smell of camphor, the pungent odour caught in Lucy's throat. She coughed.

'I hope you are not coming down with a cold,' the housekeeper said disdainfully.

'No, Mrs Gresham, it's just the salts. I shouldn't have breathed them.' Lucy sniffed and waited. 'Is there anything else?'

'Doctor Thornton has been sent for. Make sure Simmonds brings him up as soon as he arrives. And for goodness sake, girl, put both shoes on before you fall and break your neck! I don't need any more problems.'

Lucy nodded and tiptoed from the room.

Outside, the corridor was cold, the air still, but fresher. Lucy breathed deeply and shivered. She hated the smell of camphor, the smell of salts and above all, the smell that always came with sickness in a house.

A feather duster flicked across the small squares of glass in the bay window.

Lord Farnley stood for a moment looking up at the swinging sign:

Terry's Toys for the Discerning Child

And beneath it in small gilt letters:

Proprietor – J G Terry Esq.

It was the first time his lordship had visited the shop.

The bell above the door tinkled, but the diminutive lady wielding the duster didn't turn. 'Mr Terry will be with you in a minute,' she piped.

Lord Farnley gazed around. In his opinion the shop was a veritable Aladdin's cave for any boy or girl, discerning or not. Packed with all manner of playthings, there was barely an inch of spare space for dust to settle on. Even the floor was cluttered. Behind a solid wooden cart filled with alphabet blocks, the battlements of a castle rose two feet from the ground. Its drawbridge was suspended on two lengths of bronze chain. Its mesh portcullis raised. A doll's pram large enough to accommodate an infant stood against the wall while a hobby horse with plaited mane leaned against it. Taking pride of place on the glass-fronted counter was a doll's house, its front wall hinged open to reveal its stately interior. All four floors, from basement to attic, were filled with fine furnishing, each piece, standing no more than an inch in height, was perfectly crafted. At the other end of the counter, a regiment of toy soldiers was assembled in formation, in front of them, a row of archers kneeling, behind them two lines of infantrymen and, at the rear, mounted cavalry, swords drawn, poised for the charge.

After a few moments, the shopkeeper emerged from the back of the shop blowing his nose loudly. On seeing his customer he stuffed the red handkerchief into his pocket. 'How can I be of assistance?'

Lord Farnley stumbled over his words. 'A doll,' he said. 'For my daughter.'

'What sort of doll, sir? Terry's Toys stocks quite a selection.'

The proprietor was not wrong. Dolls were the predominant items displayed on the shelves. There were dolls of every description: rag, wooden, felt and fashion dolls with heads of various compositions. There were Japanese dolls, leather dolls. Dolls with fixed eyes and feathered eyebrows. Sleeping dolls. Talking dolls. Teddy bears.

Golliwogs. Even a doll with a string-pull arm capable of throwing kisses.

Being little more than five feet tall, Mr Terry regarded his customer from over the top of his gold-rimmed spectacles. 'Might I enquire how old the child is?'

'She will be eight on her next birthday.'

'Ah,' the man said, his face broadening in a smile. 'Then this will be a birthday present.'

Lord Farnley ignored the comment. 'I want your very best.'

'The best?'

'The best doll you have.'

'Sir, I can boast a small selection of dolls from the finest workshops in France. Bru, Jumeau, Thuillier and Steiner. But I don't display those particular items on the shelves. Too valuable.' He paused. 'However, if you would excuse me for a moment.' Without waiting for an answer, he shuffled towards the door and after a whispered word with his wife, the pair scurried into the back room.

Lord Farnley admired the metal soldiers while he waited.

Mrs Terry returned first. After hurriedly clearing the counter, she flicked over it with the feathers. Her husband followed carrying a long box.

'What I have here,' he said, as he laid it carefully on the counter, 'is probably one of the finest fashion dolls in the world. A truly exquisite French Bru doll, from the atelier of Paul Girard. It only arrived last week.'

'Then I would like to see it.'

'Certainly, sir.' The shopkeeper stroked the lid affectionately, before lifting it. Inside, the printed label confirmed the toy's French origins. Mr Terry appeared nervous when he carefully peeled back the layers of paper.

Lying on its back, the doll's eyes were tightly closed. The upper lids, framed beneath feathered eyebrows, were shadowed with a hint of blue. Thick dark lashes rested on delicately blushed cheeks. The round bisque face was full, the mouth, as if preparing to smile or speak, slightly open. The rose coloured lips turned upwards softly at the corners. Beneath the hat, trimmed with feathers, dark locks fell in soft waves. The doll's expression was wistful and gentle.

'Real human hair,' the wife said. 'And pearls,' she added, pointing to the tiny ear-rings hanging from the pierced lobes. 'Would like Mr Terry to take it out so you can see it properly.'

'Thank you, I have seen enough. I would like it delivered to Heaton Hall.' Lord Farnley hesitated. 'On second thoughts, I have my carriage outside. I will take it with me.'

Mr Terry glanced at his wife. 'Begging your pardon, sir, but am I serving his lordship himself?'

Lord Farnley nodded.

The man behind the counter appeared flustered and bowed awkwardly. His wife tucked the feather duster into the folds of her serge skirt and dropped several curtsies.

'Is there anything else I can assist you with, your lordship?'

'No, thank you.'

The remainder of the business was transacted with a degree of obvious nervousness on the part of the shopkeeper. His wife assisted him with the packaging, as he was hardly able to tie the ribbon around the box. When he presented the parcel to its purchaser, he appeared both pleased and relieved. Mrs Terry dropped several more curtsies as his lordship was leaving. Outside, the pavement was wet. The driver, who had been sheltering under the wooden awning, took the box from his master and opened the carriage door.

'The Hall,' said Lord Farnley, after climbing in and pulling the tartan rug across his knees.

The servant nodded and laid the box on the seat opposite. It took up almost the full width of the carriage.

The late afternoon sun cast long shadows across the lawns, as the carriage rumbled past the old coach houses and up the driveway of Heaton Hall. The wearied poplars were turning rust and gold. A few had already started to shed. Soon the ground would be littered with leaves and smoke, curling from the gardeners' fires, would drift into the stately house. Lord Farnley never minded the smell of autumn, or the chill of winter, providing there was still some sunshine.

'Shall I take that for you, your lordship?' the butler asked, as his employer stepped down from his carriage.

'No, I shall take it myself.'

'Doctor Thornton is upstairs in the red room. Mrs Gresham is with him.'

'Thank you, Simmonds. I will go straight up.'

'Of course, my lord.'

The square staircase, dating back over 200 years, was decorated with elaborate carvings of twisted vines, fruits and exotic flowers. A huge glass chandelier hung from the ornate ceiling but, as Lord Farnley mounted the stairs, he noticed neither.

The first-floor corridor was shrouded in gloom. It looked longer than usual, dark and uninviting. The narrow windows offered little of the day's dying light and the lamps had not been lit. It was not as Lord Farnley remembered it from his childhood.

'Dr Thornton,' he whispered, as he entered the end room, 'how is she?'

'Resting quietly, I am pleased to say.'

Miss Gresham got up from the chair and excused herself. The two men waited until she had left the room.

'What of the infection?'

Standing beside the bed, the physician looked down at his patient. 'If it were only that then we could be hopeful. But the chest infection is but a complication of the major problem and—' He hesitated.

'Please, say what you must.'

'I have grave fears.'

'Papa.' The voice was hardly audible. 'Papa, is that you?'

Lord Farnley touched his daughter's hand.

'I shall wait downstairs,' the doctor said, closing his bag.

'Thank you.'

Lord Farnley waited until the man had gone before he turned up the wick on the lamp and drew back the curtains. 'That's better,' he said, sitting down on the bed and lifting her limp hand onto his. When he spoke, his voice was tender. 'Now I can see you.'

Beatrice's eyes had sunk deep in their sockets, her hair was lank, her cheeks sallow, her lips slightly blue.

'I have something for you,' he said softly, resting the long box across her legs and guiding his daughter's hand to the ribbon. His eyes smiled sadly as together they unfastened the bow.

'What is it, Papa?'

The paper rustled as he carefully lifted the doll from its nest of wrappings. A pair of luminous blue eyes blinked open and glistened in the light of the lamp. From the silver buckles on the tiny black shoes to the tip of the ostrich feathers decorating the delicately flowered hat, the exquisite French doll stood over twenty-four inches tall. The peacock blue of the cloak, flowing loosely from its shoulders, contrasted strikingly with the room's red furnishings.

Lifting her hand to touch the lace stockings and brush her fingers across the strip of soft ermine which edged the peacock velvet, Beatrice's face beamed with delight.

Her father smiled. He was pleased. The shopkeeper had advised him well.

'Papa, she is beautiful,' Beatrice said, then suddenly her expression changed. 'May I keep her?'

'Of course, why do you ask such a foolish question? The doll is yours.'

'But Mrs Gresham said I couldn't have any dolls because I would make them sick. She said that was why Fred and Bertie had been sent away. She said I would make them sick too.' Her breathing was shallow and fast. 'I hope I will not make you sick, Papa.'

'Hush,' he said, laying the doll on the bed beside her. 'No one will get sick and soon you will be well again. Well enough to play in the garden. To watch the bees and butterflies down by the lake as you always used to, and to have tea parties with the other children. Imagine what fun that will be.'

Winding her frail arm around the doll's waist and drawing it close to her, Beatrice smiled weakly. On the pillow, her cold grey face rested against the doll's blushed cheeks, their brown hair tangled together. Within seconds her eyes were closed.

'Sleep,' Lord Farnley said, as he held her hand in his. 'Sleep, my angel.'

'She warned me, if I didn't keep my hair under my cap she'd cut it off!' Lucy growled.

No one in the kitchen answered.

'Honest she did!' said Lucy. 'I swear Mrs Gresham has something against me. She's always finding fault. First it was the way I spoke, then it was the way I ironed my apron, then it was my shoes squeaking, now she's complaining about my hair. That woman had better not come near me with a pair of scissors.'

'Lucy Oldfield, enough of that!' Cook was angry. The kitchen maids were familiar with the tone.

Lucy held her tongue – though she knew it was true. The housekeeper picked on her more than the others, even though she was always particular about her appearance and neater than most of the other maids. Unlike some of the girls, she liked her uniform and remembered the times she used to stop at the top of the stairs to catch her reflection in the long window. That was until the day one of the under-butlers saw her.

'Don't you know vanity's a sin?' he had said with a glint in his eye.

How embarrassed she'd felt and how she had blushed and run down the stairs so quickly praying he would not follow her into the kitchen. After that, it was a long time before she raised her eyes to her reflection again.

Jennie Porter put down the peeling knife and dragged her stool closer, interrupting Lucy's thoughts. 'Tell me about the young fellow who sent you that letter. Who is he?'

'Just a fellow I met.'

'Well then, tell us where you met him? What does he do? Where does he come from?'

'I don't rightly know what he does. I only met him twice and that was by chance. The first time was at Skipton market about two years ago. The second time was in July when I went home for my week's holiday.'

'And you gave him your address here.'

'Not really.' Lucy's brow furrowed. 'I just told him where I was working.'

'And now he's writing to you. Tell me,' said Jennie, drawing her stool closer, 'what does he say in his letter?'

'That's none of your business, Jennie Porter,' barked Cook.

'Oh, go on. I ain't got no young man writing to me.'

Lucy took off her cap and, not noticing the disapproving look Cook gave her, pulled the ribbon from her hair and flicked her dark curls over her shoulders.

'I've only had the one letter and it was quite respectable. He asked me how I was, if I still had the same job and asked what it's like living at the Hall.'

'Are you going to write back and tell him what you think of Mrs Gresham?'

'Jennie! Get on with those spuds.'

'Yes, Cook,' the scullery maid said, shifting her stool and dragging the pail of potatoes across the stone floor. 'Go on,' she whispered, as she continued peeling. 'Tell me more.'

'He just asked lots of questions like where I came from. He wanted my address. Wanted to know about my mother and if she went out to work. Asked what happened to my Dad and if I had any brothers and sisters living at home. That was all, I think.'

'You'll have lots to tell him,' Jennie said enthusiastically. 'You are going to write to him, aren't you?'

Lucy shrugged, 'Maybe.'

After glancing at Cook to make sure she was not listening, Jennie leaned across the table. 'When are you going to see him again?'

'I don't know that I am,' Lucy said. 'I won't be home again till next July.'

'That is if Mrs Gresham doesn't send you packing before then.'

One of the bells on the wall jangled.

'That's for me,' Lucy said, quickly tying her hair and pushing the loose ends inside her cotton cap. 'Do I look tidy enough?'

No one answered.

'Will someone put another pot on to boil? I expect it's hot water she'll be wanting.' Lucy didn't wait for a response and hurried to the back stairs.

'What's this fella's name?' Jennie called.

Lucy turned, 'His name is Arthur Mellor.'

'You can leave the rest to me, Doctor Thornton. I will take care of things.'

Washing his hands in the china bowl, the doctor thanked Mrs Gresham. 'It's been a long and rather exhausting day and I don't mind getting along. Now with regard to advising his lordship—'

'We don't expect Lord Farnley back until tomorrow but, you can be assured, he will be told as soon as he arrives. Obviously the final funeral arrangements will not be made until he returns.'

The doctor sighed. 'If you ask me, I'd say it's a blessing in disguise. Amazes me she managed to linger as long as she did.' He took out his watch. 'Almost eleven. Time to bid you good night, Mrs Gresham.'

Lucy was about to knock when the nursery door opened. She stepped back and let the doctor pass.

'Blessing in disguise,' he murmured, as he shuffled out.

Lucy hardly dare look towards the bed. 'Has she gone, ma'am?' she asked.

'I'm afraid so.' The housekeeper's voice was softer than usual. 'Peacefully, I'm pleased to say. I'm sure his lordship will be relieved to know that. But he'll be very sorry he wasn't here.'

Tears formed in the corners of Lucy's eyes and the lamp appeared hazy. As she squeezed her lids, a warm trickle ran down her cheek. She didn't see the housekeeper looking at her.

'We must make everything neat and tidy. I know it's late, but we can't leave it the way it is.'

Lucy had wondered why she'd been called from her room at such a late hour. Now she wondered why the housekeeper had picked her to assist her and not one of the other maids. Perhaps it was because she was the only one who was still awake. Most other evening she would have been fast asleep before ten o'clock but, this evening, she had stayed up to write a letter.

The women didn't speak or even exchange glances as they straightened the sheet and pillow under the dead girl. They also straightened her legs and arms and nightdress, and combed her hair. Lucy folded the quilt and placed it in the blanket chest, and finally they straightened the top sheet and pulled it to the head of the bed covering Beatrice's face.

'What do you want me to do with this?' Lucy asked, picking up the French doll which had slid to the floor.

'Burn it!'

'But it's brand new!'

'Are you deaf as well as daft, girl? I said, burn it!'

Lucy hesitated. She knew it was a gift from Lord Farnley.

'Things like that carry disease and we don't want Miss Beatrice's illness passed on to anyone else. Now take it downstairs and burn it! Do you hear me?'

Lucy nodded, tucked the doll under her arm and tiptoed out, closing the door quietly behind her.

Chapter 2

An Ill Wind

The kitchen smelled of meat fat, cabbages and caustic soda, but it was empty. The scullery maids had gone to bed early, as usual, and the milk churn standing by the door indicated Cook had also retired as putting it out for the under-footman to collect was the last job she did each evening. Heat radiated from the great stove and the large kettle standing on the corner of the hob breathed gentle puffs of steam and rattled intermittently. On the pine table, a lace-cloth covered a silver tray. The butler had prepared it in case Lord Farnley returned unannounced during the night.

Lucy was relieved the kitchen was empty. She was tired and in no mood to answer questions. In the morning all the talk would be about the death of Miss Beatrice, but for the moment she preferred to keep her thoughts to herself.

The kitchen at Heaton Hall, though large, was a homely place, warm and comforting. It was the only room the maids could relate to the homes they had come from – most of them from many miles away.

Lucy cast her mind back to the house in Leeds where she had grown up, the back-to-back terrace in Loftholme Street with one room downstairs, one up, and a toilet down the street shared between six families. She thought of the cobbled street and the narrow strip of stone paving where she played as a child. She remembered the warp of washing lines running from one side of the street to the other, and the tall wooden props which held the sheets high enough for the rag man to drive his horse and cart beneath without getting tangled in them.

She pictured her mother down on her hands and knees scrubbing the stone doorstep. Remembered the fear she felt when gypsies were seen in the street. The thrill when she heard the tunes turned on a tingle-airy and was allowed to drop a farthing in the tin cup rattled by the man's pet monkey.

Lucy thought about her mother, living alone but had only scant memories of her father. She was seven when he died. Seven years old – the same age as Miss Beatrice. Instinctively her arms folded around the doll. The porcelain face was cold as marble against her cheek.

From the window, Lucy stared out over the courtyard. The moon was full, the wind blowing from the north bending the trees towards the house. The dark shadows danced impishly around the paving teasing her imagination. She turned from the window wishing she hadn't looked, wishing Mrs Gresham's words would stop ringing through her head – *Burn it*!

But how could she burn something so lovely? It was both exquisite and expensive and would have cost more than she could save in a lifetime.

Burn it! The voice repeated in her head.

How could she burn something she had admired every day for a month when she had seen it resting in the crook of the little girl's wasted arm? It was something she had secretly longed to hold in her own arms? Something she had coveted?

The long case clock in the hall struck twelve. Lucy knew what she was supposed to do. Inclining her head towards the steps, she listened for the clacking of the housekeeper's feet. But the house was silent. Perhaps Mrs Gresham had gone to bed.

Laying the doll on the pine table, Lucy cautiously opened the oven's fire door. The metal handle was still hot. The flames had died but the embers glowed red. The firebox was large and deep, and there was ample room to put the large doll in.

Stacked up neatly beside the cooking stove was almost a week's supply of firewood, including a small pile of sticks and branches that would be used as kindling for the morning's fire. Choosing carefully, Lucy selected an armful of fuel – thick sticks, long branches and short twigs. Breaking them to the size she required, she placed them in a specific fashion on the hot embers. From the drawer in the pine table she took an empty cotton flour bag. It had been washed, ironed and folded neatly. And from the tool drawer – a pair of scissors. Her hands were shaking and the heat from the oven was making her sweat.

Avoiding the stare from the doll's blue eyes, she untied the plaited cord that held the velvet cloak, and let it fall onto the table. Carefully, she removed the feathered hat, sliding the two miniature hatpins from the lustrous hair and weaving them into the hem of her apron. Turning the doll over, she unfastened the buttons running down the back of the gown. The ivory satin reflected the firelight.

Suddenly, the kettle rattled, startling her. She listened hard, but the only other sound was the rustle of fabric in her hands. Hurrying, she removed the layers of petticoats and the doll's delicate chemise. Only the shoes, stockings and pantalets remained.

Then her ears pricked to the sound of footsteps echoing on the first-floor corridor. She stopped, her heart thumping. The footsteps were distinctive. They belonged to Mrs Gresham. She had to hurry.

Grabbing a hank of the doll's hair she sliced through it with the scissors. The dark locks fell onto the table. 'I'm sorry,' she whispered.

The footsteps were getting louder.

With the fire burning brightly, Lucy took the bundle of doll's clothes and fed them, piece by piece, into the flames, carefully draping the garments across the twisted twigs and branches. The dress flared instantly in a burst of white hot flame but the cottons were slower to ignite. The hat's feathers frizzled and the ringlets of human hair smoked and shrivelled before being consumed. Finally the blue cloak, which Lucy draped across the smouldering pile, burned. Then she closed the fire door.

Her hands shook, as she opened the empty flour bag. By now, the footsteps had reached the top of the stairs. Only a dozen more steps and the housekeeper would be in the kitchen. Grabbing the doll by the feet, she shoved it head-first into the flour bag, rolled it into a bundle and dropped it behind the stack of firewood.

Mrs Gresham was at the door.

Looking down, Lucy noticed a fine fuzz of brown on the table. Praying the housekeeper was not watching, she dusted the hair into her palm, then pushed the handful of clippings deep into her apron pocket.

'Oldfield!'

She could hardly hold herself still. 'Yes, Mrs Gresham,' she whispered, not looking at the housekeeper's face.

'Have you done what I said?'

Lucy nodded, unable to answer.

The housekeeper sniffed the air and was satisfied – singed hair has a distinctive smell, then leaning forward towards the firebox she noticed a sliver of peacock blue velvet protruding from the iron door. Opening the door, she inspected the fire. It was burning brightly and within the flames was a distorted, mangled shape covered in the unrecognizable remains of burnt clothing. Satisfied, she flicked the fragment of blue velvet into the blaze and slammed the door.

'What are you looking at me like that for, girl? Go to bed! We have a busy day ahead of us tomorrow!'

Glancing at the pile of firewood, Lucy glimpsed one corner of the canvas flour bag protruding from behind it. Surely Mrs Gresham would notice and if she didn't, the scullery maid who stoked the fire in the morning would find it. What then? The maid would tell Cook, and Cook would report it to the housekeeper. Lucy had been blatantly disobedient and, before long, Mrs Gresham would know her order had been disobeyed. If the deceit was discovered, Lucy would be accused of stealing and instantly dismissed. Imagine the shame. Imagine what her mother would say.

'What are you waiting for, girl?'

Unable to reply, Lucy bobbed a small curtsy. Her hands, wet with sweat, were clasped tightly behind her back with doll's hair stuck to her palms.

That night Lucy did not sleep. At two o'clock she crept down to the kitchen and recovered the flour bag. She was thankful the sky was cloudless and the moon almost full so she didn't need to light a candle. By the time she got back to her attic bedroom, her heart was thrumming in her ears. She was grateful she had a bedroom to herself.

Pulling the doll from the bag, she wrapped it in one of her petticoats and forced it into her wooden suitcase. With its legs and arms bent forwards, it only just fitted. Buckling the leather strap around the case, Lucy slid it under her bed. She could only hope and pray no one would open it.

It was two months since Miss Beatrice had passed away and every day Lucy had looked at her case and wished desperately that she had not taken the doll. As she lay awake at night, she considered how she could dispose of it. She thought of throwing it into the lake, but wasn't certain it would sink. Or burying it in the woods. But if a fox unearthed it or the hounds found it, it might be brought back to the house. What then? One night, after midnight, she got up, dressed herself and prepared to go to the kitchen. She intended to burn the doll in the kitchen fire as she should have done earlier. But just as she was about to step out onto the landing, she heard voices. Had someone guessed what she was about to do? Sitting on her bed, trembling, she waited, but nothing happened. After that, she never attempted to dispose of the doll again.

A few weeks later, rumour spread through the house like wildfire that most of the staff at Heaton Hall was to be dismissed. Like all the other maids, Lucy was shocked – but she was also relieved. At least, when she left, she would be able to take the doll with her.

In a letter from Lord Farnley dated 15 November 1896, the butler announced to the household that Heaton Hall was to be sold. For most of the staff, their employment was to terminate the second week in December.

Though no specific reason was given, Mrs Gresham explained that his lordship had decided the upkeep of the Hall was too expensive and it was his intention to sell the property and move to the south coast. The staff, on the other hand, were of the opinion his lordship's decision was not for financial reasons but because he had lost interest in the house after his daughter's death. Heaton Hall was a fine stately home, built by his predecessors over 200 years earlier. It was a house Lord Farnley had once loved, yet the building itself was only part of the valuable estate. If he had needed extra funds, which seemed unlikely, he could have sold a portion of the estate's 400 arable acres, retained the house with its sculptured lawns and ornamental gardens, or leased out the grazing land and sold his livestock.

Word quickly passed around that Simmonds, the butler, and Mrs Gresham were to stay on, together with two maids, two footmen and the gardeners. But with talk in the village that Heaton Hall might be converted into a boarding school or sanatorium, it was likely those positions would not be secure for very long.

It was drizzling the day the majority of the staff left. The gloomy weather reflected their mood and any sense of excitement or anticipation at the idea of going home for Christmas was dampened by the worry of unemployment. The number of positions coming available in good houses was fewer and fewer every year and, despite the minor irritation Mrs Gresham caused Lucy, the Hall had been a good house to work for. The idea of a job in a factory or noisy woollen mill did not appeal to any of the girls.

Lucy's suitcase was among the pile of trunks and boxes lashed on one of the wagons. Because the doll had taken up much of the space in her case, she had rolled her clothes into a bundle and tied it with piece of string. With the bundle balanced on her lap and a letter of reference, bearing his lordship's signature, in her pocket, Lucy sat between Jennie Porter and one of the other maids in the second carriage. Not a word was spoken as the three coaches and two dray wagons rolled away from Heaton Hall, rumbling down the driveway and out onto the main road which led to York and the railway station.

'Why didn't you let me know, Mum?' Lucy said, when she arrived back home.

'There weren't much point. I mean, what could you do from the other side of Yorkshire? It weren't right for me to bother you with my problems.'

'But I could have helped. I could have come home or asked for some of my wages and sent you some money. Why did you sell all your good stuff and not tell me?'

Mrs Oldfield tapped her daughter's hand. 'Well, what's done is done. Can't cry over spilt milk, can we? Anyhow, I can get around all right now. Me leg's healed a treat and I'm not entirely useless.'

'But how did you manage to pay the rent, and what did you do for food money?'

'I've got good neighbours,' she said. 'When I was in bed, they'd bring me a meal and take it in turns to do me washing. Real good they were. Now I'm right again, I've taken on some mending and if any of me neighbours need anything done, I do it for them for nothing.'

Lucy shook her head, as she regarded her mother resting by the fireplace. 'But how could you manage on a few shillings?'

'I managed and that's that. And now you're home, lass,' she sighed, 'you don't know how glad I am to see you.'

Lucy touched her mother's hand. 'Here, Mum. Use my handkerchief.'

'Ta, lass,' she said, as she blew her nose and sniffed. 'That's enough about me. But just take a look at you. A fine figure of a woman you are now.'

'Well, I was at the Hall six years and we were all well fed.'

'And you talk real proper.'

'I haven't changed, Mum.'

'No luv, I don't suppose you have.' Mrs Oldfield lifted her foot onto the wooden stool. 'But tell me about your young man.'

Lucy was puzzled. 'What young man?'

'The one you've been writing to. Arthur! Arthur Mellor.'

'Arthur Mellor?'

'Such a nice young man. Helped me out no end when I was short of a bob or too. Took some of the things I didn't need and sold them in the market. Always brought money back. I don't know what I'd have done without his help.'

'But I hardly know him! I met his twice and he wrote to me twice, and I wrote back to him once. He's not my young man.'

'Well he makes out like he is. And he says he can hardly wait for you coming home. Sounds to me like he has his mind set on you.' She raised her eyebrows and added, 'you could do a lot worse.'

'Well we'll have to see about that!' Lucy said indignantly. For the present, she had far more important things to concern herself with than finding a husband.

The advertisement in the antique shop window said: *Experience Essential*, but Lucy applied anyway.

With his spectacles perched on the end of his nose, old Mr Camrass scrutinized the reference, signed by Lord Farnley. Young Mr Camrass, whom Lucy considered old enough to be her grandfather, was more interested in her experience handling silverware. He explained that if she was offered the job she would work six days a week despite the shop being closed on Wednesday and Saturday afternoons. Her duties would be mainly cleaning; both the shop, and the house which backed onto the business premises; polishing metal – namely the second-hand silver and brass items which were purchased from deceased estates, and washing the fine china which was bought by the two gentlemen in bulk lots at the auctions. Both father and son made it quite clear that she would perform her duties in the confines of the house kitchen and that on no account should she step into the shop during business hours.

As to the wages, Lucy thought them to be reasonable compared with her pay at the Hall, especially considering the long hours she had worked when in service. But at least at the Hall there had been no deductions for food and lodgings. Now she had rent to pay, and had both herself and her mother to support. It would not be easy, but she would be paid on a weekly basis and she was convinced she would manage.

'They are extremely fussy,' Lucy told her mother later. 'But I'm used to that. And really both gentlemen are very polite and rather nice, especially old Mr Camrass.'

'I am pleased for you,' her mother said.

As Lucy talked about her new job, neither noticed the house door open and a man step onto the doormat.

'Hello! Anyone home?'

'Oh, it's Arthur,' Mrs Oldfield said, her face brimming with a smile. 'Do come in, love, and see who's here.'

Lucy stood up beside her mother's chair and pushed the hair from her face.

'Yes,' Lucy said less enthusiastically. 'Please come in. Mother has been telling me all about you and I'm grateful for what you have done for her.'

'Well, someone had to help her out with you being away and all.'

Lucy turned to the stove. 'Can I get you a cup of tea?'

'Don't mind if I do,' he said then without being invited, he hung his hat on the coat hook, took off his jacket and settled himself opposite Mrs Oldfield in front of the fire. 'Nice and warm in 'ere.'

'Got two bags of coal delivered this week. Our Lucy's got money and she's got a job too. Go on, lass, tell him about your new job.'

'Not now, Mum. Plenty of time to talk about that later.'

'Tell me, Mr Mellor—' Lucy said.

'Arthur to you, love. Call me Arthur or Arty, that's what me friends call me!'

'Tell me Arthur,' said Lucy, 'I seem to be at a bit of a disadvantage. It's a long time since we first met and I don't remember where you came from or what you did for a living?'

'Bad memory, have you?' he said, loosening his tie, 'I work with me father. We've got a place the other side of Skipton. Good land out there. Sheep mainly, but there's plenty of game too.' He leaned over to Mrs Oldfield and whispered in her ear. 'Would you like me to bring you a couple of fat rabbits or a nice red grouse next time I'm out this way?'

'Fancy that, us eating grouse in this place.' The woman looked across at her daughter who was not impressed. 'What's wrong with your face, lass? You're allowed to smile.'

But Lucy was more interested in Arthur's jacket hanging over the back of the chair. She knew the cut of an expensive suit and recognized a nice piece of tweed when she saw one. 'You and your father must be doing very well,' she said.

'Can't complain.'

Lucy handed a cup to her mother. Arthur helped himself.

'So,' he said. 'You've finished at the big house I'm told.'

'That's correct.'

'So, you'll be home here on weekends.'

'I shall be home on Sundays but I take mother to chapel in the morning.'

'Perhaps I should join you, then we can come back here and spend the afternoon together.'

Lucy looked to her mother for support.

'And you and me can take a walk if the weather's nice. Get to know each other a bit better,' he said.

'Excuse me, Arthur, but I have only been home a few weeks and what with Christmas, I haven't caught up on all the jobs that need doing around the place.'

'Then I'll come over and help you.'

'But I want to spend some time with my mother. I've hardly seen her over the last six years. We've a lot of catching up to do.'

'Then I'll sit quiet as a mouse and not say a word.'

Mrs Oldfield looked across at her daughter. 'Oh, lass, you and me's got every night of the week to chin-wag and it would be so nice to see Arthur around the place. Don't be mean.'

There was no discouraging either of them so Lucy just smiled, though her eyes did not show it. 'Whatever pleases you, Mum.'

'Next Sunday then?' Arthur said, grinning. 'It's a date. And let's hope it's not raining.'

'Mother, put your sewing down. We must talk.'

'But I can talk and sew, lass.'

'Leave it, Mother!'

Mrs Oldfield held the yellowed christening gown at arm's length. 'Got it off the ragman for a penny,' she said. 'Told him it'd make a good duster, but I'm fixing this up for that old doll of yours. It'll make a fine dress. You can't have the poor mite sitting around forever with no clothes on. Ain't decent her sitting there in nowt but her britches.'

'Mother! I said leave it!'

Shaking her head, the widow place her sewing on the cushion, folded her arms across her chest and leaned back in the chair.

'You have to stop encouraging Arthur from visiting,' Lucy said.

'But I thought you liked him. He's ever so polite and helpful. And he has done such a lot for us.'

'A lot for you maybe!' she argued. 'There's just something about the man that I don't like. And he comes here every Sunday. Never misses.'

'And isn't it nice that we all go to chapel together? The ladies think he's such a lovely young man, I've heard them saying so.'

'I don't care what the ladies think,' Lucy yelled. 'I don't like it that he comes home after service and sits down like he owns this place and then stays till after dark. Even then it's hard to get rid of him.'

'Lucy luv, you're not being fair.'

'Mum, it's not a case of being fair. I'm twenty-two already and I'm not married, and I would like to find a nice gentleman to walk me out, but I want to choose my own fella and not be rushed into anything.'

'Well, Arthur has been calling round for three months now. I hardly call that rushing things.'

Lucy shook her head. 'I'm wasting my breath, Mum, aren't I?'

'Just settle down, lass. Everything will work out for the best. Now be a good girl and hand me that doll. Let me try fit this dress on her, then you can tell me how you think she looks.'

Lucy flung the doll at her mother and ran upstairs.

'Sorry I'm late,' Arthur shouted, throwing his cap on the sofa. 'I had a bit of extra work to do for me Dad. I'll put the kettle on.'

Lucy looked up from her book. 'Mum's not well.'

'What's the matter?'

'Doctor's not sure. He said she has a big lump in the side of her belly that shouldn't be there. He thinks it could be the cancer.'

'Can he do anything?'

'No,' Lucy said quietly. 'She's too old and besides we can't afford hospitals and doctors.'

Arthur picked up his hat and placed it on the hook behind the door. 'I'll go up and see her then? I might be able to cheer her up.'

'Yes, she'll probably like that.' Lucy dried two cups and saucers.

When Arthur returned Lucy noticed a change in his tone.

'She don't look too good, does she?'

'No, she doesn't.'

'She's a good old lass,' he said hesitantly. 'I suppose I took a liking to her because she reminded me of my old mum. Not that I can remember her much. She died when I was young. But she was a bright spark. Never a bad word for anyone. Just like your mother.'

Lucy sighed and allowed herself to sink back into the sofa.

Arthur sat down beside her. 'I know I ruffle your feathers sometimes, but we could be good friends, you and me, if you know what I mean.'

As Lucy gazed into the fire, he put his hand on hers.

'If there's anything I can do, just let me know.'

She thought about his words. 'Where can I find you if I need you?'

'Don't you worry. I'll come around during the week. If you want I can stay with her in the daytime.'

'But what about work?'

Don't worry about that. I'll fix it with me Dad. It'll be all right.'

'No you mustn't do that. We've got good neighbours who'll give an eye to her. And if she's really sick I'll ask Mr Camrass to let me have some days off.'

'Suit yourself,' he said.

She felt ungrateful. 'I'm sorry, Arthur. I know I sound abrupt sometimes, but it's just my way and I do appreciate what you have done for Mum.'

Leaning forward, he planted a peck on Lucy's cheek. 'There,' he said. 'That wasn't too bad was it?'

Lucy smiled through the tears and let him put his arm around her.

'It's something about a house when someone's sick,' she said. 'You can smell it, can't you?'

Arthur shrugged. 'I wouldn't know about that.'

On Sunday, 13 April, Mrs Oldfield died. The next day Lucy went to work but took the following Wednesday off for the funeral. Arthur stayed for the whole week.

Chapter 3

Arthur Mellor

Lucy felt guilty asking for a day off especially when she had to lie to her employers, telling them she needed the time in connection with her mother's financial affairs. But having spent all his life involved with the antique business, old Mr Camrass was well acquainted with the problems relating to deceased estates. Unfortunately, his sympathetic attitude made Lucy feel even worse. She had not wanted to deceive the two gentlemen, but she could think of no alternative.

It took nearly an hour to walk to the station. It was still dark when she left the house, but by the time she got to the city it was daylight. The platform was cold but the gas fire, burning in the waiting-room, took some of the chill off the air. Sitting on the bench facing the other travellers, she wondered if she was being foolish and behaving like a child. If she had any sense at all, she would turn around and go home and put the silly thoughts out of her head.

However, there were certain things Arthur said that did not ring true and it was those conversations that echoed in her head. There was something about him that nagged her, exasperated her and compelled her to go to Skipton to search for the truth.

Clutching a ticket in her hand and with the engine belching steam across the platform, Lucy climbed into the end compartment. A gentleman got in after her and occupied the seat in the opposite corner, his back was to the engine. As the train pulled away he took a periodical from his coat pocket and did not look up for the rest of the journey.

With her eyes fixed on the view from the window beside her, Lucy absorbed the changing scenery as it flashed by, from the factories backing onto the canal, to the grimy mill buildings, the tall chimneys belching smoke, and the rows of houses, not unlike her mother's, running parallel up the hills like furrows in a field. Then, when the houses disappeared, they were replaced by woods and meadows. She saw sheep and cattle grazing and country scenes, the likes of which she'd not seen since the day she left the Hall. As outings like this did not occur often in Lucy's life, she resolved to enjoy it, no matter what the outcome.

'Skipton! Skipton!' The station-master's voice rang like a tolling bell along the short platform. The train shuddered to a halt.

'Allow me, miss,' the gentleman said, as he opened the door.

Lucy thanked him. He had a kindly face. Fatherly. 'Excuse me,' she said, 'could you tell me the way to the post office?'

'You'll find it on the main road, opposite the police station. I suggest you follow the crowd. Most folk will be going in that direction because it's Wednesday and today is market day.'

Lucy thanked him and stepped down to the platform. As the smoke and steam drifted away, she was able to see how many passengers had got off the train. She was surprised. More than she had expected. But it had stopped at all the small stations along the way.

After joining the queue, Lucy filed past the ticket collector and mingled with the crowd heading for the high street.

It was ten o'clock and the market stalls, which lined both sides of the street, were busy. Some spilled into the side lanes and alleyways. The busiest area was the town's square where the crowds wandered leisurely much to the chagrin of the carters and travellers who were only passing through.

The stalls varied greatly in size and construction, from planks resting on empty barrels to large tables, handcarts and dray wagons each laden with all manner of goods – pots, pans and brushes, knitted socks, felt waistcoats, jars of preserves, fresh garlic, spices, smelling salts, soaps and candles. Each stall had its own distinctive sound and smell.

'Toffee! Bag of toffee, luv?'

'Lavender! Dried lavender!'

'Best price, lady! T'pence a pound!'

'Brand new cure-all! Dr Watts' special formula!'

Lucy walked on, smiling. It was only her second visit to Skipton and she was enjoying the atmosphere. Country markets were always far friendlier than those in the city.

Gazing at the wares made her forget what she was looking for and she had to retrace her steps. The red pillar box outside the post office was almost hidden between two stalls.

'I am looking for a family by the name of Mellor,' Lucy said, to the clerk behind the counter. 'Mr Mellor and his son, Arthur. I understand they have a farm near here.'

'Mellor?' said the clerk, scratching his head. 'Name don't ring a bell.'

'I believe they have some sheep.'

The man laughed. 'There's lots of smallholdings 'round these parts and lots of people got sheep.' He shouted to the back of the shop. 'Ivy, do you know anyone by the name of Mellor?'

'Not 'round these parts!'

'Try the police station. It's over the road,' the clerk said. 'They might know if they've had dealings with them.'

'I hope not,' said Lucy, imagining the worst. 'Thank you anyway.'

The result, at the police station, was the same. No Mellors in this area. As Lucy wandered out she felt confused. Had she misheard Arthur? Perhaps it wasn't Skipton he came from. And if that was the case, she had come on a wild goose chase and it had cost her dearly.

'I'm so sorry!' the gentleman said, as Lucy walked straight into him. He leaned down and picked up her basket.

'No, it was my fault,' she said. 'I wasn't looking where I was going. I'm afraid my mind was on other things.'

'I trust you found what you were searching for?'

Surprised by his comment, Lucy hadn't recognized the quiet passenger who had shared the train journey with her. She smiled politely, unsure of what to say. 'Not exactly, but thank you anyway.'

Doffing his hat, the man bade her good day and continued along the street.

Lucy stood for a moment wondering what to do next. She knew the afternoon train to Leeds was not leaving until half-past three, that meant she had several hours to wait. She hadn't considered idling in the village for the whole day. She had expected to discover where Arthur lived and to visit his farm, even if he wasn't home.

Now she must find something else to occupy her time. A cup of tea appealed to her. It would be nice to be waited on, just for once. There was a little tea shop near the station. She could spend an hour over a pot of tea but, before that, she would waste a little time browsing through the stalls. No one would think it unusual for a young woman to be ambling about Skipton alone on market day.

Lucy would never have ventured down the narrow side street if it had not been for the horse and cart on the high street that was causing problems. It appeared that one of the wagon's shafts had broken, dragging the leather harness down with it. As the horse fought to untangle itself, it became increasingly agitated, forcing its load backwards into a group of stalls. Women screamed. Men shouted. Had she not seen what the commotion was about, she might have feared for her safety. The best thing, she resolved, was to keep herself out of harm's way, so she turned down a narrow alley.

There was only one vendor in this side street. His makeshift stall consisted of a wooden table with two wheels attached at the front. It was cluttered with bric-a-brac and everything looked dowdy. There were vases, glassware, and oddments of china, timepieces, cheap beads and old jewellery. The stall holder – a grubby-looking man – was leaning against the table cleaning his finger nails with the prongs of a tarnished table fork. Behind him, an assortment of men's jackets hung, like washing, on a makeshift line. Drawing closer, Lucy wasn't sure if it was the clothes that smelled or the man himself, nor was she certain which item on the stall caught her eye first, the crockery or the silver locket.

'Excuse me,' she said pointing to a cup and saucer. 'Can you tell me where that came from?'

The man tossed the fork back into the box of cutlery. 'No idea, miss. I get stuff from all over the place. Tell me what you like and I'll give you a good price.'

'May I look?'

'Help yourself,' he said, as he attempted to tidy the display. 'No charge for looking – so long as you don't break anything.'

Lucy picked up the cup and turned it over in her hand. It looked the same, but she could not be sure it had been her mother's. Replacing it on the saucer she reached for the locket. It was heavy. Obviously solid silver, but it had not been polished in a long time. The chain was almost black. As she examined it she remembered the clasp had been hard to open. It needed strong finger-nails.

She prised it open carefully. The lock of her hair was still inside!

'I would like to buy this, Mr—?'

'Entwhistle, 'Arry Entwhistle at your service.'

'How much is it?'

'Well, seeing I've done all right this morning, I'll let you have it for a bargain. Five bob to you lady!'

'Five shillings! I can't afford five shillings.'

'How much have you got then.'

Lucy loosened the string on her purse. There were a few shilling pieces in the bottom and a florin. 'I can give you two shillings,' she said. 'No more.'

'All right,' he said reluctantly. 'Two bob it is.'

'Thank you,' she said, as she slid both purse and locket into her pocket. It had been an expensive day. She had already forfeited a day's earnings. Then there was the cost of the ticket. And now this. She could not afford to spend any more. 'Excuse me, Mr Entwhistle,' she said. 'Do you happen to know a friendly young man from around these parts by the name of Arthur?'

The man grinned like a Cheshire cat. 'You mean, Arty?'

Lucy nodded. 'Yes, that's the name.'

'Aye,' he said. 'Arty's my lad!'

Lucy was shocked. Puzzled. She turned her head and looked around, half expecting Arthur to be standing behind her, watching her. 'Could you tell me where I might find him?'

'You won't find him here, miss. He lives in Leeds. Only visits me once in a blue moon when he wants something. Got his own family, you see.'

'His own family, you say?'

'Aye,' he said proudly. 'A right pretty wife and two bairns already, and another on the way. Shall I tell him you was looking for him next time I see him.'

'No, thank you, Mr Entwhistle, that won't be necessary.'

Lucy sat by the fire cradling the doll in her arms. Rocking backwards and forwards, she was thinking of her mother, of Heaton Hall and Miss Beatrice. How she wished Lord Farnley had not decided to sell the house. How she wished she was still employed there – even with Mrs Gresham to answer to. Not in her wildest thoughts could she have imagined getting herself into the mess she was in now. In a way she was glad her mother had not lived to see it.

Her visit to Skipton during the week was now a blur in her mind. She could hardly remember the journey home. Could only vaguely remember the conversation she had with the gentleman in the train, though she knew she had talked too much. She could not understand why she had agreed to accept a lift with him in a carriage. The only thing she remembered clearly was him leaving her on the doorstep and his concern that she would be all right when he left. She had no idea why he had helped her, did not know his name and could not remember if she had thanked him. Her thoughts were addled. If only she could think clearly.

'Anyone home?' It was Arthur.

Lucy didn't answer.

'Well, what's going on in here? Not much of a welcome for your fella on a Saturday night, is it? No light on. No fire lit. Don't tell me there's no supper ready for me either!'

Lucy gazed into the empty grate.

'Did someone die or something?' he said jokingly.

'No,' she said quietly. 'I went to Skipton.'

'Oh, yes?' he said, sticking his hands in his pockets. 'And what may I ask took you there?'

'I was looking for you.'

'Well,' he said, as he stepped directly in front of her. 'You didn't find me, did you?'

'No, I didn't,' she said, gazing at his boots. 'But I found your father.'

He turned, spread his legs, and leaned his hands on the mantelshelf. 'You went right out to our place, did you?'

'No. He was at the markets.'

'Ah! What a coincidence,' he said cynically. 'You just happened to bump into him at the markets! And I suppose you spoke to him did you?'

'Yes.'

'And what did he say?'

'He said you lived in Leeds and you had a family.'

He laughed forcefully, turned and faced her. 'And you believed him?'

Lucy nodded and tightened her grip around the doll.

'Are you sure it was my father? Mr Mellor, Joshua Mellor?'

'No,' said Lucy hesitantly. 'He said his name was Entwhistle. Harry Entwhistle. But he said you were his son.'

'Huh! There you are, see. You got the wrong bloke!' he said, throwing out his chest and swaying back and forth on his heels. 'What am I going to do with you, girl? You are getting yourself in a real muddle these days. Better not tell any of the neighbours about this, they'll think you're going barmy.'

'But—'

'No buts, come and give us a kiss, I've been out working all week while you've been running around the countryside playing detective.'

He pulled the doll from her hands and tossed it onto the sofa, but, as he pulled her towards him, she turned her face away. His jacket had a musty smell.

'Not in the mood tonight, aren't you, luv?'

She didn't appreciate his tone and ignored his remark.

Neither of them spoke as she put paper and sticks in the grate and lit the fire. She let it burn for a while before adding the coal.

'The kettle won't take long,' she said flatly.

'I know what will warm us up,' he said. 'A nice drop of sherry. Your old mum always used to keep a bottle at the back of the pantry. Wouldn't be any left, would there?'

'Probably. Have a look if you like.' Lucy's voice was expressionless. She picked up the doll, straightened the long christening dress hanging loosely from its narrow shoulders, and rested it in her lap. From the pantry she could hear the sound of jars and bottles being pushed aside.

'Are you staying tonight, Arthur?' she said pointedly.

'Of course I am. Just like every Saturday night!'

'But how will you get home tomorrow?'

'On the train, of course,' he said, as he emptied the remains of the bottle into two small glasses. 'Like I always do.'

'But the ticket collector told me there is no train on a Sunday.'

'No train?' he drawled. 'You must have got it wrong. You're getting yourself confused again. I can see you need looking after.' He handed her a glass. 'I know what women are like. They go a bit funny in the head at certain times of the month.' He lifted the glass.

'Your good health,' he said, before running the contents of the glass into his mouth.

'Arthur,' she said, gazing into the fire. 'Will you marry me?'

A spray of sherry spurted across the room. 'What has come over you woman?'

'I'm serious, Arthur. If I stopped working would you support me?'

'What makes you ask a daft question like that?'

'Because I'm pregnant, Arthur. I'm going to have your baby!'

When Arthur left that night, on the pretext that he was going to the pub to get another bottle of sherry, Lucy never expected him to come back. She wasn't even sorry to part with the few shillings she loaned him. She considered it money well spent.

After that, she never saw Arthur Mellor or Arty Entwhistle again.

A few months later, on a foggy morning early in November, Lucy gave her notice to old Mr Camrass. For the second time she lied to her employer saying that she was going back into service for a while. And for the second time she felt terribly guilty about it.

During her last week at the antique shop, whenever Mr Camrass peered at her over his spectacles, she knew it was not to check her work. It was impossible for her to disguise her rapidly expanding figure.

'You realize that we will have to advertise your position, Miss Oldfield,' he said before she left.

'Yes, of course, Mr Camrass.'

'But you are welcome to call into the shop if you should ever decide to come back to Leeds.'

Lucy thanked him and said she would keep his offer in mind.

James Harrington Oldfield, a healthy six pound baby, was born on the 20 December, 1897. Lucy named him James after her father. Harrington was her mother's maiden name.

The following April, when James was almost four months old, she visited the antique shop. Having left her son with a neighbour, Lucy went alone.

It seemed strange entering the shop from the front entrance. The door-bell was much louder than she had remembered, its ring vibrating along the row of silver cups, through the stacks of polished bowls to the elegant collection of candelabras.

When young Mr Camrass shuffled out from the back room, Lucy felt nervous, not knowing what to say to him. The old gentleman, as always, was extremely polite, enquiring how she was and what she was doing. When she said that she was back in Leeds and looking for suitable employment, he asked her to wait, excused himself and shuffled back into the house. After a while he reappeared followed by his father.

Old Mr Camrass cleared his throat. 'We believe we will be parting with our current employee next week which means the situation that you filled will be vacant again.' He dipped his chin and looked at Lucy over his spectacles. 'Naturally, the hours and pay will be the same as before, but if you are interested, it would save us not only the necessity of advertising the position but of suffering the services of another new employee.'

Young Mr Camrass nodded in agreement. 'So hard to get competent workers these days. Today's young people have no appreciation of fine things.'

Lucy was relieved and delighted. Though it would not be easy for her to work full time, run a house and cope with a baby, having been in service, the prospect of long hours did not daunt her. She found the job at the antique shop easy and knew exactly what was required. Though both Mr Camrasses inspected her work on a regular basis, Lucy never minded that. Nor did she mind being kept busy. With new consignments arriving almost daily from various auctions or deceased estates, the days and weeks passed quickly. And with the regular wage, she could manage to pay the rent, support herself and James, and have a few pennies left over each week, to put away.

Sally Swales, the young mother who lived across the street, was also happy to earn a few shillings each month by looking after Lucy's boy. With six children of her own, one more didn't make much difference.

Chapter 4

November 1905 - The Guy

'Don't you miss not having a man?' Sally said, one evening when Lucy called in to collect James.

'In what way?' Lucy asked.

'You know what I mean?' she said, with a wry smile.

'I can't say I do, but why do you ask?'

Sally shrugged. 'It don't seem natural, good-looking woman like you, working every day and coming home to an empty house. Not to mention an empty bed.'

'You get used to it.'

Sally looked at her quizzically. 'Are you sure you're not kidding me? That you ain't got a man tucked away in the city somewhere? Maybe he calls into that shop you work at.'

'Goodness, Sal! What on earth makes you think that?'

'Well, I hear there was a dapper gentleman came down the street this morning asking after you.'

Lucy was puzzled.

'Knocked on several doors. Said he was looking for, "Miss Lucy Oldfield". He knew your name all right and said he'd been to the house before but he couldn't remember the number.'

Lucy's thoughts immediately jumped to Arthur Mellor. Was he back? Had his wife thrown him out? Was he hoping to take up where he left off? Surely, it couldn't be him. Granted, he usually looked smart, even though his clothes probably came from the market, but she would hardly have called him a gentleman. The idea of him turning up out of the blue made Lucy shudder. No, she thought, even after all these years, Arthur could have found his way to the house with a blindfold on. 'Did the man leave a name?'

'I didn't speak to him. Her at number thirty-eight did. But I gather he said he'd be back. And she said he sounded quite well-to-do.'

Sally peered at Lucy eager for more information. 'That's why I wondered if you'd found yourself a gentleman at last.'

Lucy shook her head. 'Sorry to disappoint you, Sally, but I've no idea who the man is.'

'Penny for the guy?' the cry from a young voice interrupted them. It carried from the top of the street. With the nights already drawing in and no street lights, it was too dark to see who was calling.

'Penny for the guy?' This time it was Sam Swales.

'Penny for the guy?' echoed James.

The two women waited. Listening. They could hear children giggling and the rumble of wooden cart-wheels over cobbles. The voices carried down the row of terraced houses, like sound down a tunnel.

'What are they up to?' Lucy asked.

'It's Guy Fawkes' Day on Sunday. Fifth of November. Didn't James say anything? The lads have been busy these last two weeks collecting stuff to burn. They've built a huge bonfire on the spare ground at the top of the street. You should see it, it's much bigger than last year's. They're very proud of their efforts. I thought James would have told you.'

Lucy shook her head. No, he hadn't told her. Perhaps because he knew she didn't like him playing on the rubble where the old mill used to stand.

The cries were louder as the group of children came into sight.

'Penny for the guy!' yelled James.

Lucy smiled tolerantly. Her son's hands and knees were filthy. He was wearing his cap cocked on the side of his head. The old muffler, wrapped around his neck, was tied under his chin and tucked into the front of his shirt, but he was wearing no jacket. He looked like a waif.

'Aren't you cold?' she asked.

'Not me!' he said, beaming proudly at the group of smaller children circled around him. 'Penny for the guy?' he crowed.

Lucy looked down at the cart and exploded. 'What do you think you are doing with that?'

'With what?'

'With that doll!'

James looked from his mother to the guy perched on the pile of sticks, its head poking from the neck of a child's threadbare overcoat, its legs buried in a pair of short trousers. 'That's Guy Fawkes!' he announced scornfully.

'No, it is not!' Lucy yelled, grabbing the doll in one hand and her son in the other. 'Inside this minute, James Oldfield! That is not yours and you had no right to take it!'

'But, Mum—'

'Inside!' she yelled.

'But it's just an old doll,' he whined. 'Look at it. It's got hardly any hair and it looks like a boy. It makes a great Guy.'

The gentleman standing on the doorstep had a healthy colour in his cheeks. He spoke with a refined accent, was smartly dressed and carried a walking cane with a silver collet.

'You are Miss Lucy Oldfield, are you not?'

'Yes,' she said, cautiously wondering who the man was and the purpose of his call. 'Is there anything wrong?'

'No, on the contrary,' he said smiling. 'But I see you do not recognize me, though I remember you quite clearly.'

'I am sorry but—' As she studied his features she had some recollection of the face. But from where?

'Edward Carrington,' he said, holding out his hand. 'It is several years since we met. You were travelling to Skipton. We shared the same compartment on the train.'

Lucy inclined her head as she tried to gather the scant memories of that day, a day she had often wished to forget.

The man continued, 'You may think this very presumptuous of me. May I come in and speak with you for a moment.'

Lucy glanced up and down the street. A woman standing at the washing-line with a peg poised in her hand, quickly looked away.

'Please do,' she said smiling. 'It will give the neighbours something to talk about.'

After taking Mr Carrington's coat, she cleared a pile of linen from the sofa and invited the gentleman to sit down. Drawing up a straight chair for herself, Lucy asked him if he would care for some tea.

'No, thank you' he said, pausing to clear his throat. 'I find this a little embarrassing as I feel you do not remember what we spoke of on the return journey. Thinking back, it was probably a little unfair of me to speak to you at that time. I recollect you were grieving the loss of your mother.'

Lucy nodded. 'It was not a good day for me. You will have to remind me of our conversation.'

The man spoke quietly, his eyes fixed on Lucy. 'You told me your mother had died and that you were on your own. You mentioned that you were unhappy and wanted to get away from here. You also said you had been in service at an estate in North Yorkshire.'

Lucy felt embarrassed having to admit she could not remember telling him all those things. 'Please continue.'

'Because you were so forthright, I found it easy to talk to you and relate the problems that were confronting me at the time. I explained that I was looking for a suitable companion for my wife, who had suffered an accident and was bedridden.' He leaned back in the chair. 'Although we had only met that very day, I took the liberty of asking you if you would consider the position. Do you remember?'

'I'm sorry, Mr Carrington, but my memory of our conversation is very vague. I had a lot of things on my mind that day. However, I do recall that you brought me home and were concerned for my welfare. But one thing puzzles me,' she said. 'It's eight years since I took that train journey. Why have you waited all this time to contact me?'

He sighed deeply. 'My wife deteriorated rapidly and died a few weeks later. I found myself at a low ebb and decided to return to India where I had spent most of my early life. My father was a colonel in the army, you see.'

Lucy listened with interest as his conversation became more relaxed.

'Having recently returned to England, I again find myself in need of assistance, but this time it is I who need someone to look after me.' He was quick to clarify what he was seeking. 'A housekeeper. Not a companion. I have tried to obtain the services of a suitable woman through the usual channels, but I find most of the applicants are too officious and I do not want to be subjected to a regimented lifestyle in my own home. You, however, appear to have an understanding nature and I don't doubt, with your years in service, you could contend with one quiet English gentleman.'

'Your offer of employment is attractive, sir, but I already have a secure job,' she said, sliding the kettle onto the heat, 'and since we met on the Skipton train my circumstances have changed. I now have a son to care for.'

'Ah, you must pardon me,' he said, standing as if preparing to leave. 'I did not realize you were married. Your title—?'

'No, I'm not married,' she said without embarrassment, 'though some folk address me as missus out of politeness.'

He hesitated for a moment. 'Then please hear what I have to say. You do not have to answer immediately. I own three small cottages in the village of Horsforth just outside Leeds. You may know it.'

Lucy shook her head.

'On the day we met, I was travelling to Skipton to collect the title deeds from my solicitor. But that is not important. Currently I am living in one of the cottages while the other two remain vacant. My proposition is, if you are interested in keeping house for me, cleaning and preparing some meals, I can offer you one of the cottages rent free. And I will pay you a small wage beside.' He appeared embarrassed. 'Though they are quite old, the cottages are pleasant with a small garden at the front and a larger one at the back, where you could grow your own vegetables. And there is a school in the village.'

Lucy thought for a moment before replying. 'Mr Carrington, your offer is indeed appealing, but as a mother with the sole responsibility for my son, I must be practical. Presently I have secure employment – a job which I've had for eight years, a fair wage and, though the housing in this street is not ideal, it suits me and my son. I believe your offer is honest and genuine but I would hate to jeopardise what I already have.'

'Then I shall press you no further and you must excuse me for taking up so much of your valuable time. But if for any reason you should change your mind—' As he got up, he pulled a piece of paper from his waistcoat pocket and handed it to Lucy. 'Here is the address, should you wish to contact me. Now if you will excuse me.'

From the doorstep, Lucy watched as her visitor strolled down the street, his cane tapping on the pavement. Behind her in the kitchen, the kettle was spluttering.

The flames from the bonfire lit up the dark sky and the guy, made from a pillow-case stuffed with straw and rags, burned bravely. When his wooden chair finally toppled, a shower of sparks shot high into the black November night and the children cheered. Lucy watched from a distance, listening to the shrieks, mostly of laughter but occasionally of pain as bubbling sap from a fallen branch burnt a child's finger.

Almost a hundred people were congregated on the site where the old mill had previously stood. There were folks from the rows of houses Lucy had never seen before. Neighbours who emerged on May Day, or New Year's Eve, or occasions like this to mingle and chatter like old friends, but for the rest of the year kept themselves strictly to themselves. Lucy wandered amongst them, exchanging pleasantries, but by eight o'clock was weary.

'Don't be too late,' she said to James who was helping to distribute the hot potatoes, roasted almost black in the bonfire ash. 'Come back with Mrs Swales.'

Walking home alone down the dark street, Lucy thought about Mr Carrington, the man who had visited her that morning. He appeared well mannered, pleasant and polite, but at first Arthur Mellor had seemed to be all those things too. She was conscious of her responsibilities, and though she liked the gentleman's offer, she felt it sounded too good to be true.

Sliding the large key into the door lock Lucy glanced sideways to the windowsill and the wooden box her mother had once grown daffodils in. Now it was warped and empty.

It would be nice to have a garden, she thought.

Chapter 5

Horsforth

It was the burglary at the antique shop that upset Lucy and brought about her change of mind. It wasn't because the shop was broken into or that a constable was sent to the house to question her about her acquaintances, her family and her financial situation. That was disturbing enough, even though the officer assured her it was just a formality. What was far worse was that three weeks after the break-in, old Mr Camrass suffered a heart attack and died. Some said it was due to the stress he had suffered, others blamed January's bitter chill. No one mentioned the fact that he was in his ninety-second year.

After the funeral, it was obvious young Mr Camrass was lost without his father. He found it hard to cope in the shop and it was not long before his own health began to deteriorate. Lucy had not known there was yet another Mr Camrass, Mr Jacob Camrass, a great-nephew of the deceased. He arrived a few weeks later in mid-February to take over the business, supposedly on a temporary basis. Lucy found him knowledgeable about antiques and efficient, but aloof and unapproachable – very different in nature from the two elderly gentlemen who had been her employers for more than eight years. Under the new management, the atmosphere in the shop was entirely different and the work, which Lucy had enjoyed and taken pride in, became a chore. But, despite the change in her feelings and the nature of the proposition Mr Carrington had made, Lucy valued the position she held and was not prepared to give her notice until she had taken a train ride to Horsforth.

It was a fair walk from the small station and uphill most of the way. When Lucy reached the outskirts of the village, the country road was skirted by fields and farms, but the dry-stone walls on either side of the lane blocked Lucy's view. With no sign of any cottages, she wondered if perhaps she was going in the wrong direction. Feeling weary, and on the point of turning back, she heard the *clip-clop* of horse's hoofs and the rumble of a wagon coming up the hill. As the farmer drew closer, he slowed his horse, tipped his cap and enquired where she was heading.

'Mr Carrington's cottages,' he replied. 'They're just around the next bend and up the rise. No more than a hundred yards. You can't miss 'em.'

Relieved, she thanked him. As the horse walked on, with the row of empty milk churns rattling on the back of the wagon, Lucy followed in the same direction.

When she rounded the bend, she caught her first glimpse of Honeysuckle Cottages and felt elated. The three adjoining cottages, set back only a few yards from the lane, had been freshly painted. The plum-coloured doors and windows contrasted warmly with the whitewashed stone walls. The low-pitched shingle roof appeared blue-grey. The building looked very old, but it was quaint and cosy.

The three small front gardens were enclosed behind a low stone wall with tangled branches of climbing roses spilling over into the lane. How lovely they would look in full bloom, Lucy thought. How sweet the scent as it drifted through an open window.

A short pathway of crazy-paving led from each paling gate to the three front doors. The cottages were identical apart from the addition of a porch at the first one. A twisted vine covering it cascaded down in a profusion of new leaves and early flowers. Lucy could smell the honeysuckle from the lane.

At the far end, the third cottage was almost smothered under the outstretched arms of a huge old horse-chestnut tree. Before bursting skywards, a family of crows announced their presence in the uppermost branches. For a while, the large black birds circled noisily, before flying away.

Lucy wasn't sure what she had expected, but the sight of the cottages made her pray that the gentleman's offer was still open. The thought of returning to the row of dowdy smoke-blackened brick terraces made her shudder.

Standing beneath the scented vine at the first cottage, Lucy knocked on the door. There was no answer. She checked the other two cottages, but they appeared empty. Wandering around to the back of the building, she wondered if she would find the gentleman there.

The back gardens were bigger than those facing the lane. Another dry-stone wall enclosed them, separating them from a broad meadow. It was evident someone had been working outside. A fork was angled in a patch of freshly turned soil, a rake resting on a pile of leaves, a pair of Wellington boots standing on a worn mat outside the door.

From the back gate, Lucy gazed across the field to a row of trees and a small copse perched on the rise. The meadow was lush, rich with spring flowers. She could hear bees working busily, birds twittering. Why had she waited so long?

Beneath the twining branches of the honeysuckle, Lucy re-read the letter she had written that morning. Satisfied with its wording, she slipped it back into the envelope, slid it through the letter box and heard it drop in the hallway. If Mr Carrington's offer was still valid, she would give her notice at the antique shop and move to Horsforth, but not before she heard from him.

'I am not going!' the boy said defiantly.

'James! It's all organized.

'I don't care! I'm not going with you!'

'You are being silly and I don't like to hear you talking like that.' Lucy lowered her voice. 'You will like the new house. There is a garden and a meadow.'

'What do I want a garden for? I want to stay here with Sam and the girls. I want to stay at Mill Lane School. You can go to Horsforth if you must and I'll stay here with Mrs Swales.'

'James! You do not live with Mrs Swales.'

'But I spend more time with her than I do with you.'

Lucy bristled, although she knew what he had said was true. 'I've had to go out to work to keep us, but at Horsforth I'll have time to spend with you. Anyway,' she said, 'the arrangements are made and I do not intend to go back on them. I've finished at the antique shop and I start my new job next week. I've paid the last rent on this horrid house, and another family is moving in on Monday. The wagon will be here in the morning to collect our things and I will need your help. What's more, I do not want to hear any more of your foolish talk.'

James did not move.

Lucy picked up the doll from the sofa and fastened the button at the back of the neck. She dusted out the gown and pulled the fraying threads from its hem.

'Take the damn doll if you want someone to go with you,' he yelled 'You think more of that doll than you do of me.'

'That is not true.'

'Stupid doll!' he shouted. 'You are always nursing it. Just like it was a baby. Mrs Swales says you nurse it because you can't have another baby.'

Lucy's face drained. 'James! That is a terrible thing to say. How dare you speak to me like that?'

'Well, it's true, isn't it? I ain't got no brothers and sisters, have I? And I don't have a father either.'

'And what does that have to do with us moving to Horsforth?'

'It's not fair,' he yelled. 'It's not damn fair.'

'James! Stop being daft. It doesn't matter what you think, we're going and that's final. And do not let me hear you swearing in this house again.'

'You won't! I'm leaving and I'm not coming back!'

The ornaments on the dresser rattled, when he slammed the door. Lucy listened, as he set of running past the window and down the street. Anger and frustration were boiling inside her when she turned to go after him, but she stopped herself before reaching the door. She would never catch him, he was too quick, and if she shouted he would probably ignore her. James had never behaved like this before.

Lucy looked at the clock. It was five. Almost tea time. He would come in when he was hungry, she was sure of it. And later when he settled down she would talk to him calmly and make him understand.

Before doing anything else, she stuffed the doll into a bag packed with old linen. Best out of the way, she thought. She had no idea what had caused his sudden outburst. He hadn't objected to the move when she had first mentioned it. So why now? And what had caused his sudden outburst about the old doll? It had been in the house since before he was born. For Lucy, it was something that belonged there, like an ornament or piece of furniture. It was an item she took for granted, but would have missed it if it wasn't there. He had never complained about the doll before. Or had he?

Suddenly her thoughts flashed back to 5 November, the day he had taken it without her permission and paraded it as Guy Fawkes. Had he really wanted to destroy it? To watch it burn on the bonfire? But why? Surely he wasn't jealous of the silly doll. It wasn't even pretty.

Putting the problem to the back of her mind, Lucy tried to think positively about the cottage in Horsforth, about moving, and the packing and cleaning she still had to do. But James's words kept nagging at her. And the fact he had never run off before.

By 7.30 her concern turned to worry. A hurried visit across the street confirmed that he was not at Sally Swales' house. She tried two other neighbours but he wasn't there either. With the tea gone cold on the stove, she sat anxiously at the table listening to the clock ticking. By ten o'clock she was desperate.

James had headed down the street. That was all she knew. Pulling the shawl across her chest, Lucy set off in the same direction. Outside, the night air was cold and damp. Dimmed lamps glowed from behind curtains in upstairs windows. Most kitchens were in darkness. Most folk were in bed. She had to find him, and quickly.

'Have you seen my lad?' she asked the man sitting on his doorstep polishing his boots. 'He's eight years old. He must have run past you. He's not wearing a coat.'

The man shook his head. 'Sorry, lass.'

She hurried to the main road at the bottom of the street.

Circles of yellow light reflected around the bases of the gas lamps. It had been raining. Standing between the tramlines in the centre of the empty street Lucy spun around in all direction. Which way had he gone? What if he had begged a lift? He could be miles away. Behind her were rows of houses, in front, the Leeds and Liverpool canal. Not more than fifty yards to the right was a set of locks. The area looked dark and forbidding.

'Are you all right, luv?'

Lucy jumped. She hadn't noticed the man lying beside the path, propped on one elbow and nursing a bottle in his other hand.

'I'm looking for my son,' she said.

'Mind your step,' he drawled. 'A lot of rubbish gets thrown around here. Don't want to fall in.'

She glanced down at the murky water. It was coal black and still, and smelled foul. It made her stomach churn at the thought of James running along the bank, slipping over and sliding in.

'James!' she shouted, her voice piercing the night's silence. A dog barked, barked again then stopped. Lucy picked her way along the bank, stumbling at times over obstacles she couldn't see, never thinking of her own safety. Then she saw the lock ahead and a dark silhouette sitting astride one of the gates. Her voice faltered. 'James!' she cried.

The boy looked up and raised his hand.

'Thank God!'

Mr Carrington helped James carry Lucy's furniture into the middle cottage. It was not an easy job as the passages were narrow and the heavy beams that ran across the ceiling meant there was little headroom. He had said the cottages were old but Lucy had not realized how old.

Individually, the rooms were smaller than those at Loftholme Street, but each cottage had two separate rooms downstairs and a tiny kitchen. Upstairs there were two bedrooms. The windows were quite small but from the back of the house there was a view across the field to the patch of trees in the distance. From the kitchen door a path of broken slate led through the garden to the old iron gate which opened directly to the meadow.

At Mr Carrington's suggestion, Lucy moved into the middle cottage. He explained that it would be more convenient for her if she had to run between the two on wet days. Furthermore, he said, the old chestnut tree kept the sun off the end cottage and, as a consequence, its back bedroom had a smell of dampness about it and was in need of a good airing.

Despite having the front door wide open while they moved Lucy's possessions in, the new house was warm. Mr Carrington had lit the fire in both rooms early that morning.

As the empty wagon rumbled away, he turned to James. 'Have you ever ridden a horse, lad?'

'No, sir.'

'Then it's about time you learnt.'

James looked across to his mother.

'I like to ride and I enjoy riding with company,' he said. 'The countryside round here is ideal, so I have arranged with Mr Fothergill, a local farmer, to lease the meadow at the back. Now all that remains is to purchase a couple of suitable horses and build a stable. Every boy should be able to ride,' he said. 'I think I learned to ride before I could walk.'

Over the next few years James's education came on by leaps and bounds. Apart from his regular schooling, he learned how to ride and fish. He learned how to trap rabbits, shoot, and cure skins. How to chop wood, dig potatoes and grow beans from seeds. He learned to recognize the song of a willow warbler from a whitethroat and know the difference between a thrush's egg and that of a chaffinch. He learned how to identify a peacock butterfly from a painted lady, and learned the names of all the wild flowers that grew in the meadow. Mr Carrington was a walking encyclopaedia. The stories he told, of life in India and of his travels across the world, mesmerized James.

'When I am old enough I will join the horse-guards and go to India,' James often said, while Lucy would sit back with her knitting and listen to the pair talking late into the evening.

From the day she moved into the cottage, when he first insisted she call him Edward, Mr Carrington was not like an employer. Though she prepared his meals and cleaned his cottage, and received a wage in return, for Lucy it was not like a job. She treated Edward as if he were an older relative who needed a little special care.

The more she came to know him and understand his ways, the harder it was for her to believe he had come from a disciplined army family. He was the most undemanding and patient man she had ever known, and despite their growing companionship he was always the perfect gentleman. He never forced himself on Lucy and James when he felt they did not need his company. Nor did he outstay his welcome when he was invited to share a meal or an evening with them.

James on the other hand was forever running to Edward's cottage, never knocking but bursting through the front door full of excitement, behaving as though the house was his own. Though Lucy reprimanded him, Edward assured her he was no trouble. And one morning when they were alone, he admitted how much he enjoyed having the boy around. He said, for him, James was the son he had never had and from the first day, the pair thrived on each other's company.

A telegram delivered one afternoon upset Edward. It was dated 10 August 1910 and read:

Sorry to advise – Lydia very ill.
Come immediately if possible.
Wainwright – Bombay

Chapter 6

The Accident

'Sit down for a moment, would you?' Edward's tone was serious.

Lucy put down her duster. 'What is it, Edward? Are you worried about your sister?'

'Yes,' he said. 'But not only that.'

Lucy waited for him to speak.

'You have been good to me, Lucy,' he said slowly. 'It is strange how one changes as one gets older.' He paused. 'I love my sister Lydia, but we have lived apart for many years and, though she is my own flesh and blood, over the last five years I have come to regard you and James as my family.' He continued, before she could interrupt him. 'It is my duty to go to India and I will be obliged to stay for however long is necessary. The problem is, I don't want to leave here, or leave you and James.'

'We will be here when you get back. You must not worry.'

'But I do worry. I worry about the journey – it is long and can be hazardous. I worry about the situation in India. The country has changed since I was a boy. I worry about the growing unrest in Europe and the riots in the Home Counties with the suffragette movement. And I worry about leaving you alone.'

'James will care for me,' Lucy said. 'You have taught him so much and he is capable and strong.'

'You are a good woman, Lucy, and a good mother.' He paused. 'I remember the first time I saw you on the Skipton train, how attractive you looked. But you also looked a little lost, which was the way I was also feeling at that time.'

'Edward, you've never told me that before.'

He smiled. 'It is true.' He leaned forward in his chair. 'Before I leave for India, there are things we must speak of.' He took out his pocket book and flipped through his notes. 'Firstly,' he said. 'I will arrange for your wages to be paid into a bank account. Do you have one?'

'No, but I have a little money put away in a tin.'

'Then I suggest you secure it in the bank. If you will accompany me to Leeds next week, I will assist you in opening an account in your name.'

'But I will not be working for you while you are away.'

'No, buts, please. Let me continue. Secondly, I intend to set aside some money to help with James's education. He is progressing well and I hope eventually he will go to the university. He has the brain for it.'

'But that is several years away!' The colour drained from Lucy's cheeks. 'Edward, you are speaking as though you have no intention of coming back.'

He touched her hand. 'I like to be prepared for all eventualities. Don't worry, Lucy, the booking I have is for a return journey even though I can't be certain when I will be returning.'

Lucy was somewhat reassured.

'Now, there is another matter I would ask you to consider. You don't have to answer immediately.' He looked directly at her, when he spoke. 'Would you like to sail to India and visit me when I am there? If the answer is yes, I will arrange tickets for you both. It would be a wonderful experience for the boy.'

'Edward, that is very generous, but it is too much to offer. You are going because you are duty bound and at this time I feel we should stay here. James has school and I have the cottages and gardens to care for.'

He stared down at the book in his hands.

'Perhaps,' she suggested, 'if you go again, then we could accompany you. I would not like to travel alone.'

'Yes, a splendid idea. We will do that.' He folded his pocket book and laid it on the chair arm. 'There is one more thing. How old are you, Lucy?'

It was a strange question.

'I was thirty-five on my last birthday.'

'As I thought. And I will be sixty while I am away. A considerable difference in age, is it not?' he said. 'After caring for me for five years, I think you know me as well as anyone has ever done. But what I ask is that while I am away you consider the idea of becoming my wife.'

'Edward?'

'I will say no more about it and I do not want your answer until I return. Now,' he said. 'I shall need help with my clothes for the tropics. They are packed away and will require airing. Until I get news of the sailing date, I can't be sure when I will be leaving, but I would like to be prepared. Will you see to that for me?'

Lucy squeezed his hand. 'Of course, Edward.'

Less than two weeks later, Lucy and James waved Edward goodbye from Leeds station. As the guard waved his flag, Edward lowered the compartment window and leaned out.

'A safe journey,' Lucy shouted, when the train jerked forward.

James trotted alongside the compartment until he reached the end of the platform. As the engine clattered across the points and the train slowly turned away, the hand waving the white handkerchief disappeared from view.

The station was smoky and cold. Outside in the centre of the city's square the sun glinted on the huge bronze statue of a black-clad knight mounted on a prancing steed.

'The Black Prince,' said Lucy. 'His name was Edward also.'

'Was he a king?'

'No, but he was a great horseman and leader.'

'One day I will be like him' James said.

Lucy did not reply.

It had been pouring for more than three hours. At times the rain, pelting against the kitchen window, sounded like tiny stones. The lane had become a river and a tributary was pouring under the gate into the front garden. A large pool had formed outside the front door and water was beginning to seep into the hallway.

Lucy was worried. James often rode for several hours on Sunday mornings but he was always back well before it was time to sit down for dinner. It was over an hour since she had taken the roast out of the oven and now it was almost cold.

The sound she heard was his boot thumping against the kitchen door. 'Mum! Quick! I need help!'

Alarmed, Lucy opened the door to find James standing in the rain, shivering violently. His hair was stuck to his face and neck, his shirt sopping wet and in his arms, he was cradling a child. She was wrapped in his overcoat.

'Goodness, James. What happened?'

Carrying the young girl into the living-room, he set her down on the sofa. 'Take care of her, Mum. I must get some help.'

'But what happened? Where did you find her?'

'On the moors. A wagon had turned over. Lost its wheel. The driver was killed – crushed underneath it. I didn't see the child at first. She was cowering in the heather, wet through and freezing cold. At first, I couldn't make her understand me. I don't think she is injured but she wouldn't speak.' He turned to the door. 'I must get some help and go back. There may be someone else out there. I'll take Edward's horse.'

'But you're soaked to the skin! At least dry yourself.'

'I'll be all right. But I'll take my coat.'

Lucy slid it gently from around the child whose eyes were open but staring blankly ahead.

'Be careful,' Lucy said, helping him into his wet overcoat.

'I will.'

As soon as he left, Lucy dried the girl's face and hair. But her clothes were soaking wet. After wrapping her in a blanket, she filled the hot-water bottle and laid it carefully between the covers. Pushing the sofa closer to the fire, she added some wood.

With difficulty Lucy coaxed the girl to drink a little of the sweet tea she had brewed. 'What's your name?' she whispered, but the girl did not answer. Her hands were clasped tightly together, the knuckles squeezed hard against her cheeks. Sitting on the edge of the sofa, Lucy stroked her wet hair and hummed the nursery rhymes she used to sing to James. It was not many minutes before the drooping eyes closed and Lucy felt confident to leave her alone, just long enough to search for something suitable to dress her in.

Hurrying up the stairs, she remembered the calico bag in the bottom of the wardrobe. It was full of linen and old clothes, including the nightshirts James had grown out of. One of the smaller ones would fit the child. Reaching in, she found an old cardigan. It had shrunk and no longer fitted her. There were woollen socks too that were also too small.

Humming softly and without waking her, Lucy slipped off the girls' wet clothes and pulled the nightshirt over her head. The cardigan sleeves were far too long so she rolled them over several times. Lucy estimated the girl was the size of one of Sally Swales' daughters – about nine years old.

It was after six when Lucy heard sounds from the lane. From the front door she could see her son and at least four other men with horses. The rain had stopped, but water was still streaming into the garden. James invited one of the men into the living room. 'Mum, this is Sergeant Wilkey.'

The man tipped his hand to his wet hair and leaned over the little girl. 'How is she, missus?'

'She's sleeping,' Lucy whispered. 'She drank a little tea and warm milk, but she won't eat anything.'

'Has she said anything to you? We have to know where she came from.'

'She hasn't spoken.'

He turned to James. 'And you say she didn't speak to you either?'

'Never uttered a sound.'

'Can you keep her here tonight, Missus? Just until we find who she belongs to.'

'Of course.' Lucy turned to James. 'Did you say her father was dead?'

The sergeant answered. 'There was a man's body under the wagon. But we can't be sure it's the little lass's dad. Even if he is, they must have other folk somewhere and before long they will be out looking for them. Until that happens I shall have to notify the authorities and the girl may have to be taken into care.'

'She can stay here,' Lucy said defensively, recalling stories she had heard of the orphans' asylums. 'You can't move her now. I'll look after her.'

The sergeant sounded relieved. 'Right then! We'll leave her where she is until morning. Let her have a good sleep. As for myself, it's been a long day and I've got to get that body down to the mortuary.' As he turned to go, he took James's hand and shook it.

'You did a good job, young fella. If you hadn't come across them when you did, I reckon we'd have had two bodies by the morning.'

Lucy followed them to the door.

'If you have any problems with the lass, your son knows where to find me.'

James watched the men ride away before walking the horse to the back of the cottages and the stable he had helped Edward build. By the time he came in he was tired but had no appetite for food. At Lucy's insistence, he swallowed one slice of meat, ate a cold potato, and drank a cup of cocoa, before going to bed.

The little girl asleep on the sofa looked pale and delicate. Seeing her lying there reminded Lucy of Miss Beatrice, the delicate child in the four-poster bed at Heaton Hall. It reminded her of the expensive French doll that had once rested in the crook of a little girl's arm. The expensive doll she had stolen. The same doll she had forgotten about since she had moved to Horsforth. Although it had been packed away for more than five years, Lucy thought it was about time it was brought out and put to good use.

Chapter 7

Constance

Working by the window in the dim light of early dawn, Lucy busily stitched the pieces of cloth together. She had cut the doll's blouse from a piece of white cotton sheeting she had put aside for patches, and the tunic from an old twill skirt. The cloth was coarse, rusty brown in colour and faded in parts and it was not exactly the material she would have wished to make a doll's school dress from. But it would suffice. After cutting a length of yellow ribbon to serve as a sash, Lucy was satisfied with the result. All that remained was to gather the stitches around the cuffs and sew a hem around the bottom of the skirt. The doll's lace socks and buckled shoes were the ones it had been wearing when she had taken it from the Hall but they were still satisfactory.

When Lucy threaded another length of cotton, she realized the girl had woken and was watching her work. 'Would you mind helping me?' she asked.

Sitting up, the girl nodded and held out her hands. Kneeling down beside her, Lucy placed the doll on her lap. 'There,' she said, carefully slipping the blouse and school dress over its head. Then she slid the sash around the doll's waist and tied a neat bow at the back. Picking up the lengths of cotton around the doll's wrists, she gathered them up tightly and fastened them off securely.

James stopped at the bottom of the steps. 'I see you have a helper.'

'Indeed,' said Lucy. 'We'll be done in a moment.'

The girl watched intently while Lucy ran a line of stitches around the hem. When that was done, the small school tunic was complete.

'Now I'll make some breakfast,' Lucy said.

Crouching down beside the girl, James took hold of the doll's right hand and lifted it. 'And what is your name?' he said, addressing the wistful smile on the porcelain face.

The girl replied in a whisper, 'Constance.'

Glancing across to his mother, James winked. 'I'm pleased to meet you, Constance,' he said, shaking the doll's hand graciously. Then he turned his eyes to the little girl. 'And what is your name?'

'Alice,' she whispered.

'Hello, Alice. My name is James.'

'James,' she repeated.

Lucy smiled, as she laid the breakfast cloth on the table. 'I didn't know you had a way with children.'

'And I didn't know you still had that old doll. I remember it vaguely from Loftholme Street. I seem to recollect you were fond of it.'

'Yes. And you and Sam Swales were going to use it for Guy Fawkes.'

'Was I really going to do that?' James asked.

Still stirring the porridge, Lucy smiled at her son.

'After breakfast I'll ride down to the police station. Sergeant Wilkey may have some news.'

'Good news, I hope.'

Alice wasn't listening. She was busy brushing the tufted patches of brown hair bristling from the doll's crown.

'When I come back, I will find something to fix that,' James said.

The girl looked up at him expectantly, her large brown eyes following his every move. When he donned his coat and hat, she slid off the sofa. 'Can I come with you, James?' she begged, her tone faintly anxious.

'No, you must stay here and look after Constance,' he said. 'I won't be long.'

'Sergeant Wilkey said there have been no reports of missing persons. But he thought, because the accident happened on the moors' road, it's possible the pair were not from around these parts.'

Lucy sighed. 'So what will happen to Alice?'

'The sergeant asked if she could stay with us a little longer. He said we might get a visit from the Welfare Board, but it's just routine and you're not to worry.' James looked at his mother. 'Are you all right?'

'Yes,' Lucy replied. 'Just a little tired. I suppose I am missing Edward. I wish he was here now.'

'Cheer up. Let me show you what I have,' he said, pulling a small animal skin from his pocket. 'It's from a kid goat,' he said.

Lucy turned it over in her hands. The skin had been tanned and was soft and pliable, one surface roughened like suede, the other covered in tight black curls.

'I'll cut a piece to fit the doll's crown,' James said. 'Then I'll glue it on and it will give the doll a fine head of hair.'

When Alice woke the following morning the doll, she had named Constance, was lying beside her. The sight of its new curly wig sent her dashing outside to find James to show him. But James had left for school already.

Though Lucy spent the whole day talking with Alice and playing games, the girl was not content until James returned home. After dinner that evening, Lucy watched from the garden, as James led one of the horses around the meadow with Alice mounted on its back. She was sitting astride the big mare, a hunk of mane grasped in one hand and Constance gripped securely in the other.

It was Thursday afternoon when the knock came at the door. Sergeant Wilkey was on the doorstep with a primly dressed lady of middle age.

'Mrs Oldfield,' the sergeant said. 'This is Alice's great-aunt, Miss Pugh.'

Lucy knew the call was inevitable. As she ushered the visitors into the living room, she tried to smile.

'Miss Pugh is from Ilkley,' Sergeant Wilkey said. 'She is the aunt of Alice's father, the man who died on the moors.'

Lucy expressed her sympathy and listened while the woman explained that she had been caring for Alice's mother who had been heavily pregnant and poorly too.

'Yellow skin and swelled ankles,' said Miss Pugh, the stern expression on her face never faltering when she spoke. 'Not well at all. Doctor recommended bed rest until the baby was born. Least I could do for my nephew was to look after his wife. I knew he couldn't manage to see to her properly, what with work and the little one to mind, and her not being well and all.'

Miss Pugh said her nephew rented a house in Horsforth, not far from Lucy. She also said she knew he'd planned to drive to Ilkley the weekend of the accident, but when he'd failed to arrive, she blamed it on the rain. Knowing he only had the open wagon, she presumed he'd decided to postpone the visit until the following week.

'I never gave it a thought that anything might be wrong,' the woman said.

The sergeant added that when he spoke to Mr Pugh's neighbours, they also hadn't thought anything was amiss. They'd seen him leave in the wagon, but when he never got home that night, they thought he'd decided to stay with his sick wife.

'Don't know what would have become of the little lass if your boy hadn't found her that afternoon,' the sergeant said.

The only good news from the whole wretched affair was that Miss Pugh had helped deliver a baby boy on the previous Tuesday. The infant was small and frail but the doctor thought he would survive. Unfortunately, Pansy, her niece was still far from well and the loss of her husband had been a setback to her recovery. Miss Pugh insisted the young mother and baby stay with her in Ilkley until they were fit enough to return home. But, for now, she was here with Sergeant Wilkey to collect her great-niece and take her back to Ilkley with her.

Saying goodbye was not only difficult for Lucy, it was confusing for Alice. The little girl was fearful of the sergeant who spoke in a gruff voice and was extremely tall, even without his helmet. She was also wary of her great-aunt who carried herself stiffly, never smiled, and had a strange vacant look in her eyes.

Not understanding what was happening or where she was to be taken, Alice clung to Lucy's skirt. Her plaintive pleas upset Lucy who had enjoyed having the little girl in the house but it was obvious that Alice must now return to her mother. 'Take Constance with you,' Lucy said. 'You can look after her now.'

Miss Pugh declined rather abruptly. 'You've done enough already.'

But Alice had the doll firmly secured in her arms and was not going to be parted from it.

'Take it!' Lucy insisted kindly. 'The doll is yours now.' Bobbing down beside Alice, Lucy whispered in her ear. 'When you are back home and your mother is well, I will come and visit you.'

'Can James come too?' Alice asked.

'Of course.'

Sergeant Wilkey helped Miss Pugh into the trap and lifted Alice onto the seat beside her. As the rig rolled away, the little girl looked back and waved. She had the doll seated on her lap and her right arm was tightly clasped firmly around its waist.

The house was quiet when James came home and for two days he said very little. In the evenings he would go riding for two or three hours, not returning until after dark. Though he never said it, Lucy knew he was missing Alice.

She was missing Alice also. And Edward. And now James, too.

Edward's letter was postmarked Bombay, India, 17 July 1911. It had taken two months to arrive. James read it aloud:

My dear Lucy and James

By the time this letter reaches you I hope to be at sea. Wainwright and Lydia have decided to return to England and I will be travelling with them. Currently I am attending to the legal matters regarding the sale of their Bombay house. As I know from experience it is not easy to sell property in India as fewer Britons are investing in substantial houses in this region. However, the house will be sold and as soon as everything is settled we will book our passage.

Although Lydia is slightly improved from when I first arrived, her general condition is poor and I feel her health is continuing to decline. She shakes constantly and is unable to hold her head or hands still and is now finding it difficult to eat.

Wainwright is hoping to find a physician in England who will be able to help her and, although the passage will be a strain, he feels it best to bring her home. Though I have not spoken at great length of my fears, his decision to leave India concerns me. They have lived in the tropics for most of their lives and I fear my brother-in-law has forgotten how cold English winters can be. However, he has taken my advice to live in the south. When we return, I will endeavour to find a house for them in Tunbridge Wells or on the coast. By that means they will be relatively close to the London hospitals and away from the cold of the north of England.

I will contact you again briefly to advise the date of sailing but the next time you will hear from me proper will be when we disembark in Southampton. Do not expect me back in Yorkshire immediately. I feel it is my duty to assist Wainwright and Lydia in purchasing a house and in attending to the legal matters for them. Wainwright was a fine officer, but I am afraid he lacks a business brain. They have been good to me in the past and it is the least I can do.

I miss the cottage and the countryside of England and, of course, I miss you, Lucy and James. I was intrigued to hear about the girl Alice, and the way she entered your lives. I trust a friendship will develop between the two families.

If all goes well, Lydia and Wainwright will be settled by December but in any event, I intend, God willing, to be home in Horsforth to share Christmas with you.

My good wishes to you both
Your dear friend

Edward Carrington

Chapter 8

Pansy

When Lucy first visited Pansy at the house she rented in the village, she was appalled. It was a cold, damp and dingy building backing onto the railway line. Pansy was still far from well and, in Lucy's opinion, she had returned from Ilkley and Miss Pugh's care far too soon.

Pansy was evidently an anaemic-looking woman at the best of times, fine-boned with a sallow complexion and lank mouse-brown hair. She was softly spoken and sensitive and the loss of her husband in the accident had deeply affected her. Apart from being emotionally vulnerable, she was also very gullible, believing whatever stories were told to her. But despite the traumas she had suffered, she was a devoted mother with infinite patience with her two children. The Pughs were not locals and though they had lived in Horsforth for some years, it appeared to Lucy that the young family had few friends.

Lucy visited every day for six weeks, helping with the chores and minding Alice and the baby when Pansy needed to sleep. When Pansy's health eventually improved, Lucy invited her to visit Honeysuckle Cottages, insisting that not only would the fresh air and exercise be good for her, but that the Sunday roast would ensure they all ate a good wholesome meal at least once a week.

After the first visit, the weekend outing became a regular event. Pansy would arrive at ten, exhausted after walking up the hill pushing the baby cart. Ten-year-old, Alice, however, was always full of life, excited to see James and looking forward to being taken for a ride on the horse.

If the sun was out, while the pair was riding in the meadow, Pansy would perch on the back wall and gaze across to the far trees decked in autumn gold, or wander beneath the broad boughs of the chestnut tree to slide her feet through the piles of fallen leaves. Sometimes she would walk to the woods searching for mushrooms and Alice would race up the hill after her. When she caught up to her mother she would take her by the hand and lead her back to the cottage. Sinking exhausted into a chair, Pansy would quickly fall asleep with a contented smile on her face.

James looked forward to the Pughs' weekly visits. By November he didn't ride during the week, because it was too dark by the time he got home from school. But on Sundays he would enjoy leading the horses around the meadow with Alice sitting astride one of them. And when it was time for the family to leave, he would walk beside Pansy, carrying the baby in one arm and leading Goldie, with Alice perched proudly in the saddle. After seeing them safely home, he would ride back up the hill and out to the moors and not return until after the sun had gone down.

Never once did Alice visit the cottages without the doll hooked tightly in the crook of her arm. Pansy said she could never discover why her daughter had called it, Constance, as the family knew no one of that name. By now Alice and the doll were inseparable.

'She won't let it out of her sight,' she said. 'She loved her father very much and used to go everywhere with him, but since the accident she has never mentioned him once. Now it's the doll she clings to.'

It promised to be a real family Christmas. Edward was coming home and Pansy and the two children had accepted the invitation to stay at the cottages until New Year's Day. Getting everything ready for Christmas reminded Lucy of the preparations at Heaton Hall. Decorations to be made, cooking to be done, and everything cleaned and polished until it shone. She remembered the sounds of the carriages, the chatter of house guests, children's parties and sumptuous banquets. Those were the good times before Miss Beatrice became sick.

It was at the Hall that Lucy had learned how to weave holly into wreaths and now every year she collected a bundle of branches to make three wreaths, one for each of the cottage doors. This year had been a good season and the plump ripe berries glowed warmly against the waxy green foliage. The fruits on the mistletoe looked dull in comparison, but Lucy was happy, the sprig fastened over the front door would serve its purpose.

James and Alice spent the Sunday before Christmas sitting on the floor amidst pages of Edward's old newspapers, cutting strips and gluing the pieces into paper chains. With Alice's direction, James strung them around the walls, and hung them from one corner of the room to the other. Lucy picked fresh ivy and laid it in swirls on the mantelshelf. Despite the frosts it bore fresh shoots and green leaves. James potted a small fir tree in a square tin and stood it near the window and Lucy trimmed it with small ornaments and paper decorations.

It was an exciting week. Edward arrived back in Leeds on the Monday and a piano arrived the following day. It was an upright, made in Germany that had belonged to his sister Lydia. As her health had worsened and she had realized she would never play again, she had given it to Edward. It had travelled a long distance, from India to Southampton then on to Tunbridge Wells. From there it went by goods-train to Leeds where Edward met it and transported it home on the wagon he borrowed from Mr Fothergill, the local dairy farmer. When it eventually arrived at Honeysuckle Cottages, Edward announced the piano was to be installed in Lucy's front room. Though she argued against it, he insisted. The piano was soon to become the centre of attraction.

Edward proved he could play a little but his repertoire was limited. But whenever he played, Alice would stand beside him following his fingers. It was Edward's hope that James would take lessons and with that in mind presented him with a box of sheet music which he had bought for sixpence at a market stall in Tunbridge Wells.

It was after he had been playing on Christmas Eve, that Edward asked Alice to address him as Uncle Edward. He also insisted James call him, Edward or Ted, saying he had always hated being called Mr Carrington.

Perhaps, Lucy thought, it made him feel old. When she looked at him closely she could see he had aged visibly in the twelve months he had been away. There were lines on his brow which had not been there before, and though he appeared relaxed and happy, he seemed constantly tired. Occasionally she noticed him looking pensive and attributed it to the worry over his sister's health. She hoped his wearied look would pass when he had been home for a while.

Apart from the joy Edward derived from watching the children, he also enjoyed the company of the two women. He teased them about the latest events happening in London telling them what damage *those wild independent women* were causing. He spoke of speeches and protest rallies and placard-waving suffragettes marching through the streets. Lucy found his conversation exciting but Pansy appeared embarrassed by the actions of bold females, preferring to talk about the seeds she had planted, or the lavender bags she had been making to sell at a local shop. Though she had only earned a few shillings from her enterprise, she was proud of her efforts and said the extra money helped.

Squeezing everyone around the table for Christmas dinner was not easy. Edward carved the turkey and opened a bottle of wine that he had brought with him from the south. After lunch there were presents – a copy of *The Hound of the Baskervilles* for James, and for Lucy, an embossed leather volume with blank pages to use as a diary. There was a teddy bear for little Timothy, a bar of scented soap for Pansy and an Indian doll dressed in a silk sari for Alice. The costume was exquisite – the gold threads running though the cloth glistened. It made the brown tunic, which Lucy had made for Constance, look decidedly dull. Alice was delighted with Edward's gift, but the old doll always retained its pride of place.

After the presents had been passed around, the two families played charades, excusing Edward when he fell asleep. In the evening, they sang carols and no one noticed that the piano was slightly out of tune. It was one of the best Christmases Lucy could remember.

Next morning, Alice asked Edward to play the piano for her and show her a few simple exercises. Her attentiveness surprised him. James, however, was less enthusiastic to learn. He was content to sit and watch. When he eventually became bored, he suggested they give the horses some exercise. Edward agreed it was a splendid idea.

The weather was fine when they left the cottages, even a little weak sunshine filtering between the clouds, but before they returned home an icy wind, peppered with sleet, had blown up. Despite being warmly dressed, Edward suffered from the cold and when they got home he was stiff and sore. That was the last time James and Edward rode together.

Because Pansy and the two children were staying with Lucy, Edward never broached his question about marriage. At times, Lucy wondered if she should say something to him about it, but decided it could wait until later.

A telegram, delivered on the afternoon of New Year's Eve, put a dampener on what would have otherwise been a happy evening. A freak spell of freezing weather had deposited a blanket of snow across the south of England. Edward's brother-in-law, Wainwright, had slipped on the step and broken his hip, and his sister, Lydia, was suffering from regular bouts of severe depression. As a result, they needed his help urgently. Edward tried to hide his concern but Lucy knew he would not refuse their request for assistance. He regarded it as his duty.

'Is there anything I can do?' Lucy asked.

'Nothing.'

'How long will you be gone?'

'I cannot say.'

Edward packed one bag and left on the midweek night-train to London. He said he had business to conduct in the City and intended to travel on to Tunbridge Wells two days later.

Lucy didn't go down to see him off. She bade him farewell from the house. As they stood in the doorway, beneath the sprig of mistletoe, which they had joked about on Christmas Day, she could see the tears welling in his old eyes. He was always happy at Honeysuckle Cottages and it was a wrench for him to leave the friends he had come to love. Lucy feared he was not strong enough to cope with the situation he was going to. When he had left for India she had expected him to return, but this time she wasn't sure.

A few weeks later, Lucy was pleased to receive a letter from Edward. He wrote saying he had bought a small flat close to his sister's house. He had also arranged for a resident housekeeper, and engaged a nurse to visit on a daily basis. By those means the physical and practical needs of both Lydia and Wainwright were largely taken care of, though he still felt the need to be close at hand. Wainwright was improving week by week, with the probability he would eventually walk again, albeit with a pair of sticks, but Lydia's mental condition was unchanged and unlikely to improve.

Being in the flat allowed him time to read and write, or take walks in the nearby park. It also allowed him time to think. He said he had been doing a lot of thinking and that Pansy's situation had been of concern to him. After observing how well both families got on together, he said he had been considering offering Pansy a lease on the end cottage. He thought a peppercorn rental of one shilling a year would be appropriate but he would not go ahead with any agreement without Lucy and James's approval. If a lease was drawn up he assured her, if any problems arose there would be provision to terminate the arrangement immediately.

After reading the letter, James had no second thoughts. He wanted to tell Pansy the good news straight away. Lucy also agreed, and wrote back to Edward advising him to proceed with the arrangements.

The following week, when Pansy opened her door and found Lucy and James standing on the doorstep with serious expressions on their faces, she feared something dreadful had happened, but when they told her of Edward's offer, she almost collapsed into James's arms. She was overjoyed and overcome at the same time. Never again would she have to worry about finding rent money. Alice was thrilled too at the prospect of living next door to James. And Lucy, though she tried to hide her feelings, was delighted about having Pansy, Alice and little Timmy as neighbours.

Because Pansy had been forced to sell off some of her furnishings to support herself and the children, she had few possessions. What furnishings remained in the house were solid but basic. Her husband had been a good craftsman.

When Miss Pugh heard about the move, she made one trip from Ilkley to Horsforth to deliver a suitcase of linens that had belonged to her mother. When they were alone for a moment, the spinster confided in Lucy that she had worried about Pansy's future, with no man to support her. Though Lucy never enquired, Miss Pugh made a special point of explaining her financial situation, stating that she managed adequately on her own because she lived frugally. She confirmed that she owned her house, which had been bequeathed to her, and that she received income from a trust. Unfortunately it was only a small sum and was insufficient for her to provide any financial help to her niece. Miss Pugh said she considered Edward

Carrington's offer to Pansy exceedingly generous, then her mind wandered to unrelated matters and she never spoke of it again.

Edward returned to Horsforth for a short visit in the August of 1912 and again in May of 1913. Lucy felt that since he had slipped back into a bachelor existence, a gap had opened between them and that he was ageing rapidly. His pace had slowed and his back, once straight, curved markedly from the neck. His cheeks, which had glowed with the warmth of India, were now sallow and sunken. The children, too, seemed to sense a change, and though they enjoyed his visits, they quickly became bored with his repetitive conversations.

Alice, however, was always anxious to play something for him.

Apart from providing the piano, Edward had engaged a lady to give James lessons. Every Saturday morning, Alice would sit in the front room and watch as the lesson took place, and when the music teacher left, she would sit at the piano and practice James's lesson repeatedly until she mastered all the notes. While James hardly ever practiced, Alice was determined to learn to play and it was not long before she became quite proficient.

The late spring of 1914 was near perfect. Alice celebrated her fourteenth birthday and, though James didn't seem to notice, she was already blossoming into a woman. Timmy was no longer a baby and, with Lucy minding him three days a week, Pansy was able to earn some money working as a domestic maid.

Lucy enjoyed reading Edward's weekly letters in which he wrote of trips to the seaside or the City, and of the walks he enjoyed in the town's parks and formal gardens. She enjoyed her own garden, cultivating a variety of vegetables or just pottering outdoors in the lengthening daylight hours till it was almost too dark to see. Most evenings, however, she would sit and spin, or sew, while James went for a short ride. Nineteen-fourteen was James' final year at school and his application to attend the University in Leeds had been accepted. He was planning to commence his studies in the September, but on one warm August afternoon when Lucy was enjoying the scents of the garden, she was surprised to see James running up the lane. He was shouting and waving his arms, but until he got closer it was impossible to make out what he was saying.

'War has been declared!' he yelled excitedly. 'The country needs men! I'm going to join the army.'

'But James, you're just a boy.'

'No, I'm not! I'm old enough. I'm going to fight for England. It's my duty!'

Chapter 9

The War Effort

James was infuriated. The first recruitment drive was for men aged eighteen to thirty which meant he would have to wait until his birthday in four months' time. He envied his friends who had already enlisted and were now in training; some had already sailed to Europe. Joining the army was all he wanted to do, and for James, University was no longer an option, so he decided to occupy himself around home until late December – after that he would enlist.

'But why are you so determined to go to war?' Lucy asked. 'You could be maimed or killed.'

'You don't understand, Mum. I have to. And if Edward were younger, he would go too. It's the right thing to do. It's up to every man who is fit to fight for his country. It's his duty, and if he doesn't enlist then he's a coward.'

Nothing Lucy could say would change his mind. She pinned her hope on the rumour that the war would be over by Christmas and the troops would be sent home. Maybe he would not have to go.

Alice gave little thought to the war or the future. She cared only for the present and was pleased to have James home every day. That August holiday, she had more time with him than ever before. They went out walking or riding together. They talked for hours about nothing in particular and in the evenings James listened while Alice played the piano.

After seriously considering that James was using the war as an excuse not to study, Lucy dismissed the idea, but because Edward had provided the money for his on-going education, she felt obliged to write to him. She did not expect him to discourage James from enlisting for she knew his views on doing one's duty, but she felt that her son would listen to Edward's advice.

Two weeks after she had written, a reply came back. It was not addressed to Lucy but to Mr James Oldfield. It bore the Tunbridge

Wells postmark and was dated 15 October, 1914. After reading it James passed it to his mother.

My dear James

Let me offer you my hearty congratulations!
Your mother tells me you intend to enlist on your eighteenth birthday. I admire you, and envy you. I think it will be the best decision you have ever made.
Men who have served in the military are revered and admired. I am thinking here of Wainwright, my brother-in-law, and my father who served in the army in India and South Africa respectively. I know from my upbringing that discipline builds character, and active service builds courage. I am also keenly aware past service is a passport into all walks of life. It is a path I never followed and because of this I shall go to my grave with regrets; regrets that I never made the effort, disappointment in my younger years when I was by-passed for promotion, and regret that I never experienced the thrill and satisfaction of being the victor.
Being in my sixty-second year, I am now too old for active service but I am pleased to say I find myself in demand to serve England in other ways. It is rumoured that if the war is prolonged (I hear talk in the City that the war will not be over as quickly as originally thought), England will suffer from not only a shortage of food, but also a shortage of workers to do the common jobs.
Thousands of men are being sent to fight on the Continent and, as you know, there will soon be another wave of enlistments. These soldiers will not return to England's shores until the war is over and, because of this, there will be a growing demand, on the home front, for those, like me, who are too old to fight in Europe.
Naturally, I have volunteered my services and, because of my previous experiences, I have been offered various positions from munitions factory overseer to correspondence scribe. I declined these because they are in London. I have, however, accepted a job here in Kent, based in Tunbridge Wells. This means I can travel daily from my flat and will never be too far away from my sister and Wainwright.

As I am neither farmer nor teacher, the role I have accepted may sound a little unusual. I am to organize the enlistment of young women to work on the land doing the jobs usually done by the men folk. These young ladies will be taught how to cultivate the soil, plough the fields and plant and harvest crops. If the project is successful and the war continues, this type of activity will become widespread throughout Britain. I will write and tell you how the work progresses.

In the meantime, I gather from your mother's letters that you are currently looking for something to occupy yourself while you bide your time. Perhaps I can suggest a few things. These will not only help Lucy and Pansy but will allow them to contribute to the war effort in a similar manner to my own.

Here is a list:

1) Increase the number of sheep (ewes) you have and buy a ram. Speak with John Fothergill, the farmer who owns the back meadow and leases it to me for the horses.

2) Acquire one or two hand ploughs (again speak with Mr Fothergill) and train both riding horses to work in the shafts. It is essential you take on this chore. It would be too difficult for the ladies.

3) If time permits and the ground is not too hard, plough the back meadow in preparation for spring. Dig up the flower gardens and grow vegetables.

4) Use some of the money set aside for your schooling to stock up on preserves. Fill the pantry, and if you run out of space, store them in the attic – it is dry and clean.

If the conflict in Europe is resolved by the New Year nothing will be lost and you will have a bountiful supply of provisions.

Dear James, you may think these words are the rambling of an old man but do not take them in vain. The coming years may be leaner than we have ever known. Think of your mother and Pansy. How will they manage when you are away?

I suggest you make provision for them now. On that note I will close. Give my fondest love to your mother, and pass my good wishes to Pansy, Alice and Timothy.

Write to me when you are abroad.

Regards as always,

Your dear friend
Edward Carrington

'I'm not strong enough,' Pansy argued, when first confronted with the hand plough. 'It's too heavy! I'll never push it!'

'You don't have to push,' James said. 'Just keep the blade half covered and follow Goldie. The horse will do the work.'

Wearing a pair of James's old boots and with her skirt tucked up at the waist, Pansy was determined not to be beaten. 'If Lucy and Alice can do it, then I will do it too,' she said as each morning she persevered until she mastered the implement. James quickly realized that Pansy's frail appearance was deceptive. She was both fit and strong. Living in the country had done her the world of good.

The Indian summer of 1914 lasted well into October and with the bout of steady rain the soil was soft. As Edward's horse trudged across the field, the simple plough turned a furrow of earth behind it. At first the ruts drew zigzag patterns across the meadow, but slowly, as James showed the women how to work with the plough rather than against it, the lines became straight and parallel. Once Pansy learned to control the horse, the satisfaction she felt was etched in her smile.

Using both horses and two ploughs, it took the women less than three days to turn over the whole of the meadow. James watched from the stable roof where he was working. When Alice lost control of the plough and slid sideways into the dirt, he almost fell off the ladder laughing. The horse stopped, turned and snorted at her lying in the furrow, her hands and face streaked in soil. Alice was sure the horse was laughing at her, too.

James bought timber and netting and erected a new hen house in Pansy's back garden. In the past, the chickens had been allowed to range freely but slowly they had disappeared – victims of local foxes, so he made sure the vermin would not get into the new run.

There was quite a commotion the day he arrived home with two sacks of live pullets. Timothy delighted in running through the hen house, making the birds squawk and sending birds and feathers flying. After being scolded, the three-year-old watched anxiously as James clipped their wing feathers.

'Will it hurt them?' he asked.

'Of course not. They will grow again.'

On those late autumn evenings, with the smell of jam bubbling on the stove, the two families busied themselves preparing for Christmas. There was plenty to do. Fruit for the cakes and puddings to be washed and dried, flour to be sieved as fine as dust, apples to be wrapped and put away in boxes under the bed, jars to be washed, filled and labelled.

Late in the evenings, Alice would play the piano and even though there was no fire in the front room, James would take his paper and sit with her until they were both called for supper.

By late December the pantries in all three cottages were stocked fuller than they had ever been. Apart from the bags of flour, salt and sugar, the shelves were stacked with pots of preserves, jars of sweet chutney and large earthenware pots filled with pickled eggs.

James's eighteenth birthday fell on a Sunday. The following morning he presented himself at the barracks in Leeds. After being declared fit, he swore the oath with a group of six other men, but much to his frustration, he was told he must wait until mid-January to join his regiment.

Lucy and Alice were quietly pleased. Christmas Day would not be the same without him especially as Edward could not join them. Lucy wanted to make sure it was a Christmas they would all remember.

The two families had agreed that this year they would have Christmas dinner in Pansy's cottage. With Timmy's help, Alice made yards of paper chains to decorate her mother's living-room. James found a small fir tree in the woods, which he potted and placed next to the piano and, as usual, Lucy made three holly wreaths, one for each of the cottages' doors.

When Pansy was hammering a nail into her front door to hang the decoration on, a man called to her from the lane, 'That looks right pretty, luv.'

'It does, doesn't it?' Pansy replied, smiling. She didn't know the fellow but with half a dozen dead rabbits hanging from his shoulders, she assumed he was a local.

'What about a nice hare or rabbit for dinner on Boxing Day?' he said.

Pansy thought for a moment. She could make a rabbit stew. She was sure James and Lucy would enjoy it. 'Are they fresh?'

'Fresh this morning. Shot clean through the head. No damage to the flesh. Have a look if you like.'

'How much?'

'A shilling apiece. Three for half-a-crown.'

'Can you wait a minute?'

'I've got all the time in the world for you, luv!'

Pansy didn't notice the sly wink as she hurried inside. She returned with the shilling piece. 'I haven't seen you in the village. Do you come from these parts?'

'I get around,' the man said, unhooking one of his carcasses.

'How long have you lived here?'

'Almost four years,' she said.

'You got kids?'

'Yes, a boy and a girl.'

'Nice family,' the man said, re-adjusting the load on his shoulder. 'I'll be back in a few days to collect the skin. Happy Christmas.'

'Happy Christmas to you!' Pansy echoed.

The man was whistling as he wandered casually down the hill towards the village.

That evening, the smell of mince tarts wafted into Lucy's front room where James and Alice were singing the final verse of 'Good King Wenceslas'. Sitting in the armchair by the kitchen fire, Lucy was dozing, when a noise woke her. It was a strange sound and it was coming from next door. Thinking it might be a chicken squawking with a fox at its tail, she grabbed the broom and ran into the back garden. Only when she was outside did she realize it was Pansy's cry. Her neighbour was screaming and black smoke was billowing from her kitchen door.

'James! Alice!' she yelled. 'Come quick. The house is on fire!'

Chapter 10

Stanley Crowther

Within seconds of the candle toppling, the Chinese lantern ignited in a ball of fire and flames leapt up the decorations. With hardly a sound, tongues of fire ran right and left, consuming the paper chains, link by link, and at the same time scattering burning fragments on the floor and furniture. Pansy had swung at the flames with a towel but her efforts had only succeeded in fanning the blaze. By the time the others arrived, the curtains were well alight.

'Water!' shouted James. 'Quick, grab some buckets, bowls, anything!'

The thick smoke swirling overhead suffocated some of the blaze but when the running flame reached the corner of the room, the fire flared again. The longest chain hanging diagonally across the room seared from the wall and like a fiery dragon's tail curled and twisted before drifting down.

'Alice! Get out of the way!' James screamed. Too late! The length of burning paper settled over her shoulder and slithered down her back. Within seconds her hair was alight and the back of her skirt burning like a torch.

Too shocked to scream, she tried to dash the flames out with her hands.

James pushed her to the ground, grabbed the rag-rug and rolled her in it. Lucy fought the fire as best she could, desperately knocking the other trimmings from the wall before they ignited while Pansy ran back and forth with buckets of water splashing it about in an attempt to dowse the burning woodwork.

Only when the fire was finally out did the three sink to the floor, blackened, coughing and exhausted. For a while no one spoke. They had beaten the blaze before it had really got hold. The acrid smoke, the smell of singed hair and scorched cloth would fade in a few days. The ceiling beams, though charred and steaming, were strong and thick. The damage to the cottage could have been much worse. They had been lucky.

But Alice was not so fortunate. Since James had laid her on the floor she had not moved. Her hands were burned black. One side of her head was bald, her scalp red and raw. Where the fire had burned through her skirt, it had charred the skin from the back of her legs. As she lay on the floor, James knew it was serious.

'I'm going to fetch the doctor!' he said.

After spending three weeks in Leeds Infirmary, Alice hobbled up the path from the taxicab. James had wanted to carry her but she wouldn't let him. Feeling helpless, he tried to chide her playfully for being independent but her forced smile couldn't hide the pain she was suffering. Unable to bend her legs, she swung them stiffly and leaned heavily on his arm.

As she lowered herself down on the bed, he could see tears shining in her dark eyes. At times her face bore the same desolate expression he had seen on that unforgettable day when he had found her on the moors.

'I can't go away and leave you like this,' James said, gently covering her with a cotton sheet.

Her voice was little more than a whisper. 'It's your duty, James. I will be all right.'

He wanted to hold her in his arms. He wanted to touch her hands, but they were swathed in bandages. He wanted to sit beside her on the bed and stroke her hair, but he dare not in case he hurt her.

'I love you, Alice,' he said, realizing for the first time how much she meant to him. 'Damn the army! Damn the war!' he yelled.

Alice smiled. 'You'd better not let your mother hear you swearing like that.'

'Promise you won't tell?'

'I promise.'

When James climbed the stairs to Alice's bedroom the following morning his feet felt heavy. He had come to say goodbye. His waiting time was over. Now he was going to join his regiment. But his burning desire to serve had waned. Now he was angry with himself for being selfish. He regretted his eagerness to enlist more than he had regretted anything else before. It was as if the fire that had burned Alice's hands, legs and hair had consumed his desire to fight. If only he could wait six months until she recovered, then he could leave and not feel guilty.

Though he tried to sound positive, he knew his voice lacked conviction.

Alice listened but had little to say. She realized it was unlikely he would come home again before his company was sent to Europe. James knew it too. He would not see her until he came back from the warfront and neither of them knew when that would be.

Leaning down he kissed her cheek.

'Take care,' she called, as he turned away.

James wasn't able to reply.

Alice heard his footfall on the stairs. Heard the front door creak open. Heard her mother's muffled voice. The words, 'Good luck!' echoed by Timmy's high-pitched cry. She heard the front door close then, lying alone, listening to the silence, Alice knew that James had gone.

On the chair beside the bed, Lucy's old doll sat upright, her luminous blue eyes were fixed on the window across the room. The porcelain face was dirty, streaked with smoke from the fire, the brown tunic smeared with white ash. Alice reached out her bandaged hands. She wanted something to hold onto. But as she touched the doll it wavered and almost fell over.

Pushing her face deep into the pillow, Alice closed her eyes and wept.

Pansy heard the man's cry from the lane: 'Skins. Rabbit and hare!'

'Just a minute,' she replied, collecting the dried skin and taking it to the man at the front gate. When he opened his sack, Pansy dropped it in.

'Have you got any more rabbits,' she asked. 'My daughter likes the stew. She's been sick and it's helping her get better, so I don't mind paying.'

'I'll bring a couple next week. And seeing your daughter's sick, I'll only charge you for one.'

'That's very kind of you, Mr—?'

He winked. 'Stan Crowther's the name, but you can call me Stan.'

She hesitated for a moment. 'Do you do odd jobs, Stan?'

'Depends on what you have in mind?'

'The tree out the back of the cottages lost a big bough in the wind last week. It landed on the garden wall. It needs chopping up, and the wall needs rebuilding otherwise the horses will get out.'

'You got horses, eh?'

'They're my neighbours.'

'Where's your man? Gone to war, has he?'

'I'm a widow,' Pansy said.

'Sorry to hear that. What about the missus next door?'

'She's on her own too. Her lad went off a few weeks ago.'

'So you've got no menfolk around,' he said. 'How do you manage?'

'We're not useless. We manage all right with most stuff. But that limb's too heavy to shift.'

'Heavy, you say?'

'If you can't do it, my neighbour says she'll get someone from the village to do the job.'

Rubbing the stubble on his chin, Stan Crowther stared up at the horse chestnut tree, its long bare branches extending like fingers over the roof. The tree was huge and obviously very old. 'I'll think about it,' he said. 'Perhaps I'll take a look next week.'

Pansy smiled. 'Next week then.'

'What did you say his name was?' Lucy asked.

'Stanley Crowther. He's the man who brings the rabbits. I got two more this morning. Alice likes rabbit stew.'

Lucy stood at Pansy's kitchen window regarding the man working in the meadow just beyond the back wall. While she was watching, he leaned the axe handle against his thigh, arched his back and glanced up at the tree. In the chill of the morning Lucy wasn't sure if it was moist breath or tobacco smoke blowing from his mouth.

'He's not doing enough to warm himself up!' she said cynically. As she spoke, Crowther spat on his palms, grasped the axe handle and swung it above his head bringing it down hard on the bough.

After a dozen strokes he stopped, lifted his cap and wiped his sleeve across his brow.

'And where does this Stanley come from?' Lucy asked.

'The other side of the moors.'

'How does he get here? Surely not on that old bicycle?'

'I don't know,' Pansy said, not lifting her head from her ironing. 'He's doing a good job, don't you think?'

Lucy frowned. 'How much did he say he would charge?'

'He didn't, but he said it wouldn't be much.'

Shaking her head, Lucy wandered out into the back garden. The chickens, expecting some scraps, squawked. On hearing the noise, the sheep, grazing in the meadow, trotted towards the garden gate. Lucy looked at the small flock. Last season's lambs had grown well, they were almost the size of the old ewes.

Stanley Crowther had heard the hens and was looking in Lucy's direction but he didn't acknowledge her. Leaning down he swung the axe again. This time she heard the timber crack.

What was it about this man that irritated her? There was something about him she did not like. It was a feeling she'd experienced before. She shivered. It was cold outside.

The trees on the far hill were bare but in a few weeks it would be spring and their branches would be decked in a haze of fresh green. She thought of James. Wondered if his regiment had reached the Continent. Wondered where he was and if Europe was already warmer and greener than England? She wondered what the countryside of France was like. If the flowers were blooming in the meadows. It was hard to comprehend a war fought on fields bursting with the fragrance of spring.

'Aunt Lucy!' Alice's voice startled her. 'You look worried, Aunty.'

'I was thinking of James.'

'I think of him all the time,' Alice murmured.

Lucy smiled sadly. 'Let's go inside, dear. The wind is cold.'

'Will you help me with my bandages? Ma says you're a good nurse.'

Lucy nodded and followed Alice inside.

Pale morning light fell across the girl's bandaged hands when she rested them on the table. Lucy unwrapped the lengths of linen with care. When the final turn was unwound, Alice held out her hands and screwed her face. 'They look like a pair of hen's feet, don't they?'

Turning them over, Lucy sighed. 'They need fresh air and exercise!'

Alice's laugh was half-hearted.

'I'm serious, girl!' she said, running her fingers across the coils of twisted skin puckering the once soft palms. 'I'm no expert but I think you must leave the bandages off. If you don't start using your fingers soon you'll never use them again.'

Alice looked at her claw-like hands. They were as stiff as dried clay. The yellowish brown scars across her palms that ran right around her wrists, looked as ugly as the one running down her neck. It was only partly covered by her short hair.

'I want to be a nurse,' Alice announced suddenly. 'I want to help the men who've been burned in the war.' She looked into Lucy's eyes. 'I won't be able to do it if I can't use my hands, will I?'

Lucy brushed the hair from the girl's face and smiled sympathetically.

'Will I, Aunty? Tell me honestly.'

'I believe nursing isn't easy.' She paused. 'The girls who do it have strong hands and agile fingers.'

'But it's what I want to do!'

Lucy rolled up the strips of cloth. 'No more bandages! I've some white gloves upstairs, you can wear those. But you must keep away from the rose bushes and out of the hen house. You don't want them to get infected and go bad.'

'But what can I do to make my fingers work again?'

Lucy thought for a moment. 'Stretch your hands and wiggle your fingers, and when they start to work, play the piano for me. I have missed hearing your tunes.'

That evening Lucy sat beside the fire and re-read the first three letters James had written some time ago. All three had been posted in England within a period of six weeks. She smiled as she opened the first one. It was etched with youthful enthusiasm.

James wrote about how proud he was to wear his uniform, despite the coarse cloth of his jacket making his neck itch and his army boots rubbing the skin from his heels and ankles. He was pleased that he had learned to shoot long and straight, and had Edward to thank for that. He said the training was tough, but he was revelling in the company of other boys who, like himself, shared a sense of freedom at being away from home for the first time. Above all, he was counting the days when his regiment would sail for the Continent. It was obvious to Lucy, the thrill of going to war excited him.

The second letter was shorter and though it still bore an air of elation, it was tinged with frustration. He was tired of basic training, PE and more PE, drill and more drill, and a sergeant who seemed to dislike every new recruit, particularly the young lads like himself. But he said he was not alone.

The third letter had been posted in Dover the day before he sailed. Never had a boy sounded more proud to be going to fight for his country.

As Lucy gazed into the fire, she was pleased for him and proud of him too. Every mother should be proud to see her son go off to war – to fight for England. The posters on the streets and in the daily papers reminded her of that fact. But it didn't stop her worrying. Every night she prayed for James. Prayed that he would survive the war and return home safely one day. But she was aware the predicted early end to the conflict had never happened and that the war in Europe was worsening. The army needed more men and rumours were rife that the government was considering conscription. Lucy knew it was every woman's duty to encourage her husband, son or brother to enlist. Enthusiasm for the war was infectious and throughout the country, men were responding in their thousands. The fact that on the battlefields hundreds were dying, and the injured soldiers were being shipped home to fill hospital beds, seemed completely irrelevant.

Every morning and afternoon over the following months, Alice wandered into Lucy's front room, sat down at the piano and attempted to play.

From the kitchen, Lucy could sense her frustration as she reverted to the first few simple exercises Edward had taught her. Despite her previous accomplishment, her efforts were crude and childlike. At times her perseverance gave way to exasperation and she thumped her fists down on the keys or slammed the piano lid shut.

Sometimes from outside the door, Lucy heard Alice sobbing but resisted the temptation to sympathize or interrupt. Then after a short break the notes would ring out again, chords or five finger exercises, repeated over and over again.

'Your girl taking lessons?' said Stan Crowther, standing at the cottage door, one Saturday dinnertime. Pansy listened to the sounds drifting from Lucy's front-room.

'No,' she said.

'What's all the piano playing for then?'

'To make her fingers work again.'

'Good idea,' the man said. 'How old is she? Fourteen? Fifteen?'

Pansy nodded. 'Are you coming in?' she asked.

Crowther kicked off his boots on the front step and followed Pansy into the living-room. 'Can't have her sitting around all day when you're out working. Plenty of jobs for girls in munitions. Time she brought a wage in, isn't it? Helped you with the rent money.'

'She's set her heart on nursing,' Pansy said proudly. 'And besides, I'm fortunate, I don't have to pay any rent.'

'Well, who's the lucky one then?' Crowther said, as his eyes scanned the neat room. 'Nice little place you've got here.'

'Thanks,' she said, a little guiltily. She didn't intend hiding the truth or deceiving the man, but she hardly considered the peppercorn rent of a shilling a year worth mentioning.

'You know they're paying girls two pounds ten shillings a week in the munitions factories, and they're looking for women to work as conductors on the buses because there are no men about to do those jobs. Don't you fancy giving that a try?'

'I've got my job, thank you very much. Four days' work suits me and I don't mind house cleaning. It keeps us in food and I've only got to go as far as the village.'

'Suit yourself. Just thought a bit of extra would be nice to line your pocket.'

Pansy looked at the man sitting opposite her. 'Why don't you get a regular job, if there are so many around?'

'I've got plenty to occupy myself during the week. I don't only come here for odd jobs. There's plenty of work to be had.'

'Tell me something,' Pansy said inquisitively. 'You're a fit fella, why haven't you signed up like the rest of the men folk? I heard the army needed every able-bodied man.'

Crowther laughed. 'Don't be daft, woman! I'm not going to no bloody war to get my block shot off for no one.'

Pansy's eyes narrowed.

He quickly corrected himself. 'But I tried,' he said. 'Failed the eye test. They won't have you if you can't pass the medical.' He sneered. 'I'm classed as unfit.'

From the doorway, Timothy was watching.

'Lad a bit shy is he? Different from his sister, eh?'

Pansy turned to her son. 'Go fetch Alice from next door. Tell her dinner's ready. Then come and wash your hands.'

The boy ran off without saying a word.

'And what about her next door?' Crowther continued. 'I don't think she likes me. How does she manage?'

'What do you mean?'

'With food money and rent and the likes? I ain't never seen her going out to work.'

'That's none of your business, Stanley. She manages all right, thank you very much. Now before I get cross, do you want a plate of stew and dumplings or aren't you stopping?'

'Don't mind if I do,' he said, half-smiling as he unfastened the buttons on his waistcoat. After knocking the ash from his pipe on the inside of the chimney, he slid the empty pipe into his breast pocket, sat down, stretched out his legs and waited to be served.

'Why do you invite him in every time he comes around?' Alice asked. 'I don't like him, Mum. He looks at me kind of funny. Always makes me feel creepy.'

'Well, I quite like him, that's why! And it's a long time since I had a man around the place. And he's handy.'

'Yes, Mum, but he only does the jobs because you pay him while you have to go out to work for your bit of money!'

'Well he works for his and he'll do anything.'

'I'm sure he will,' she said sarcastically, 'given half a chance.'

'Alice! Hold your tongue!'

'But I see the way he looks at you. I wouldn't trust him, if I were you.'

'That's quite enough, girl,' Pansy said. 'Anyway, talking about money, I think it's time you got yourself a job so you can bring some money into the house. All you do is sit around all day fiddling on that damn piano. I reckon if your fingers are strong enough to push them keys, then they're strong enough to work on a production line.'

The words made Alice boil. What her mother was saying was true. She knew she had done almost nothing recently either inside the house or out and it made her feel guilty. But it wasn't her fault. She hadn't burnt her hands on purpose. She didn't set the room on fire. She'd only tried to put it out.

'If that's what you want,' Alice yelled, 'I'll go out and get a job. And I'll save up and go and get a room somewhere else, then you can have your fancy man calling on you every day and I won't have to get out of the house, and you can do what you do with him, whenever you want!' With that, Alice ran from the kitchen, through the cottage and out onto the lane, slamming the door behind her.

From the next cottage Lucy could hear Pansy calling after her, begging her not to go. From the window she saw Timothy running down the hill after his sister, shouting her name.

But Alice didn't look around. She just kept on running, her gait stiff and ungainly as the knurled skin at the back of her legs was stretched to the limit.

Chapter 11

Bad News

It was a long and tedious winter, cold and bleak in more ways than one. Lucy missed the warmth that had previously existed between the two families living next door to each other. With Edward and James away, the atmosphere was not what it used to be, and the widening rift between Lucy and Pansy was pulling the two friends apart.

The month of December 1915 was not an easy month, but for the sake of Alice and little Timmy, Lucy made a special effort. She wrapped presents and made cakes, even helped the children with the decorations. But the sight of the paper chains dangling from the ceiling rekindled memories of the previous Christmas, and when it was time to take the trimmings down Lucy was relieved to pull them from the walls. After screwing the chains into tight balls she pushed them deep into the ashes. The decorations smoked before the flames appeared, but it wasn't the smoke which made Lucy's eyes water.

Alice never once mentioned last year's fire or complained about her burns, even on the days she had to struggle down muddy tracks or through deep snow to get to work. She liked her job at the munitions factory and liked the girls she worked with. Even wearing trousers instead of a skirt was a novelty to her. Wearing the factory uniform made her proud to be contributing to the war effort. Yet her desire to become a nurse never wavered. It was a just matter of waiting until she was old enough to begin her training.

Lucy missed seeing Alice. Missed the times they had spent together and the conversations they had shared as if they were mother and daughter. Because Alice left for work before dawn and was not home until late, Lucy hardly ever saw her.

On the days Pansy worked, Lucy minded Timmy. Though he was only four, he was a bright boy and ready for school, but in size he hardly looked it. He was small, delicate and fine-boned like Pansy, but unlike Alice as a child, he never demanded Lucy's attention and was content to amuse himself.

When she sat alone at night Lucy would think about James and reread all his letters. Though she valued them and anxiously awaited news, she noticed that recently his tone had changed. The youthful enthusiasm of his earlier letters had disappeared and the grim picture he painted was becoming increasingly depressing. Gazing into the fire, with the bundle of letters on her knee, she tried to image the scenes he described, to picture what the battlefields in France were really like. The bullet-riddled houses blackened and pockmarked like lumps of coke, charred piles of rubble where people once lived, villages razed to ash and cinders, the smell – not of wood-smoke and warmth but of bodies rotting in trenches, and the fields so bombed and burned that not even a single blade of grass remained.

Lucy shuddered. It was a horrible war and it was showing no signs of stopping. It didn't end in 1914 as predicted, and 1915 had come and gone and nothing had changed. Now older men were being conscripted to replace the young ones who were being sent home on stretchers, or in boxes, or merely identified as a name on a War Office telegram:

His Majesty regrets…killed in action…deepest sympathy.

How could James possibly live through it? Survive to the end – whenever that might be? If only he could come home. If only he could be injured – not badly but enough for him to be withdrawn from the front-line – not to be sent to the field hospital but returned home to England. But it was said of men brought back home, once they had recovered from their injuries they were sent back to fight on the front-line again. Lucy's heart ached for them. For their mothers. For James.

She couldn't write back. Not immediately. There was nothing positive to write about. She had not heard from Edward and was worried about him also, hoping he was all right. She was worried about the trouble Stan Crowther had stirred up between herself and Pansy, and between Alice and her mother. Since her father's death on the moors, Alice had always been very close to her mother, but now Stanley was demanding all of Pansy's attention creating a rift in their affections.

Maybe her negative thoughts were unfounded, Lucy thought. Perhaps Alice's job in the munitions factory would change her outlook. For the first time she had a little money of her own and she enjoyed mixing with other girls her own age. Occasionally her mother had allowed her to go out dancing and she had met a few nice boys. But they were all very young and none of the boys were interested in courting girls, they were merely biding their time, waiting till they were old enough to go to war.

On the positive side, Lucy was amazed how much movement and strength Alice had regained in her fingers during the past year. Handling ammunition all week had proved good therapy for her fingers. Lucy was only sorry Sunday afternoon was Alice's only chance to play the piano, and because her tunes were always bright, and the music cheered them both, she always looked forward to that.

Alice still limped a little on her right leg, but as the months had passed it had become less noticeable. Her hair had grown sufficiently to cover the keloid scarring running from behind her ear. She was thankful her face was not marked and pitied the poor soldiers burned on the battlefield.

Lucy cut the red cross from a length of satin ribbon. It looked very striking on the tiny bleached apron. The cape she made from a remnant of red velvet and the dress from an old white table cloth. At first, the skirt was too long, falling almost to the doll's feet, but the miniature nurse's veil, with a second red cross sewn in the centre, was perfect. Lucy pinned the veil to the doll's coarse hair so it wouldn't fall off. Heavily starched, it stood out perfectly at the back.

'About time Constance had a change from that old school tunic,' Lucy said, handing the doll to Alice. 'Do you like her nurse's uniform?'

'You're so clever,' Alice said, wrapping her arms around the doll and leaning forward to peck Lucy on the cheek.

'It won't be long before you have your own uniform,' Lucy sighed.

Alice's eyes glowed with excitement. 'Only a few months now.'

'I'm going to miss you,' Lucy said, 'but I know you will make a good nurse.'

'And I will miss you too. Will you write to James and tell him what I am doing? And to Uncle Edward too?'

Lucy nodded.

'And when I'm away, will you take care of Constance for me? After all she was yours in the first place.'

'Of course,' said Lucy, indicating the empty chair near the window. She can sit there, and when you're gone, when I look at her uniform, it will remind me of you.'

Alice smiled. 'And will you look after Mum too? She's not as strong as you and I'm afraid she will get hurt if she's not careful.'

Lucy hugged the girl she loved. 'I promise I will do my best.'

Stanley Crowther visited Pansy every Saturday and Sunday. He always arrived mid-morning and stayed until after tea. He was also on her doorstep early on the mornings she did not work. Occasionally Lucy saw him outside with Timothy but she hardly ever saw him working. It was hard for her to say nothing, but she made a point of never asking Pansy what Stan was doing there. Pansy in turn never mentioned him. Though they lived in adjoining cottages, the two women, who were once close friends, saw little of each other.

Sometimes Lucy wondered if Pansy thought she was jealous. Not of her relationship with Stan, but of her having a man around the house. It was years since Lucy had enjoyed a man's company, and her experiences had been both brief and disastrous. She had never considered her friendship with Edward in that regard. He'd always been kind and considerate. Like a father. Never a lover.

As the months rolled by, Lucy tried to be polite to Stanley, but something about him still rankled her. If they passed on the lane, his tone was brash and cocky, his friendliness put on. Whenever she saw him, he always reminded her of Arthur Mellor. His swagger. The way he turned his head. His false smile. He reminded her how gullible she had been, how vulnerable to Arthur's smooth talking and suave mannerisms. Reminded her how she had been used. She hoped Pansy would not suffer a similar fate.

'Can you lend me a few shillings?' Pansy begged sheepishly. Her eyes were bloodshot, her cheeks streaked where she had rubbed them with smutty fingers.

'Whatever is the matter?' Lucy asked.

'I owe Stan some money and he says he wants it. He's coming back on Saturday and he says if I don't have it he'll find some other way of getting it. Lucy, I know I shouldn't ask but you're the only one that can help me.'

'Come in. Sit down. Now tell me, how much do you owe him?'

'He says I owe him fifteen pounds.'

Lucy's jaw dropped. 'How much!'

'Fifteen pounds,' she said meekly.

'My goodness, Pansy! How on earth can it be so much?'

'I don't know,' she sobbed. 'I thought he visited because he liked me but it seems he's been keeping a tally book. He's written down all the times he's been here, right from the start, and listed all the odd jobs he says he never got paid for. Now he tells me I must have been barmy if I thought he was doing it all for nothing. He says I can well afford to pay him because I ain't got no rent to pay, and 'cause I got my own wages, and the money Alice has been bringing home since she's been working on the munitions.'

'Have you got any money put aside?'

'He's had it all. Every last penny. Always nice-talking me and bringing us rabbits and things. I thought he liked me, Lucy, honest I did.'

Lucy shook her head. 'Pansy, I wish you had listened.'

'I knew you would say that,' she said, screwing her hands together. 'What do I do, Lucy?'

'Well, you don't pay him another penny! And next time he comes, tell him you don't want him stepping over your doorstep ever again.'

'But how can I tell him that. He's always so nice.'

'Don't open the door. Keep it shut!'

'But I can't'

'Well that's up to you, Pansy Pugh, stop right now or he'll be the death of you!'

Lucy trudged slowly back from the village. It was all uphill and her bag of shopping was heavy. As she turned the corner of the lane she saw Crowther's old bicycle leaning on the limestone wall by Pansy's gate. With no sign of the man, it was obvious he had wheedled his way back into the house. Lucy shook her head. There was nothing she could do about it. Pansy had made her bed and now she must lie on it. And, Lucy thought, it was quite likely that Stan Crowther was on it with her at that very moment.

Before she reached the gate she heard the rumble of a motor bike driving up the hill. Apart from the milk wagon, few vehicles ventured up the lane. When the engine rattled to a stop, Lucy turned. The driver was wearing a postal worker's uniform. Lifting his goggles to his forehead, he pulled an envelope from the small leather pouch around his waist.

'Mrs Oldfield?' he enquired.

Lucy's heart almost stopped. She knew it was a telegram and a telegram could only mean bad news.

Chapter 12

The Legacy

Without waiting for a reply, the rider touched his cap, smiled sympathetically and pulled the goggles over his eyes. After kicking the machine back into life, he turned the throttle. The engine revved and backfired blasting black smoke from the exhaust pipe. Driving off in a hurry, the back wheel spun in the dirt sending a shower of grit over Lucy's feet. Within a few seconds, bike and rider had disappeared from view.

Lucy's hands were trembling when she walked inside. She didn't wait to take off her hat and coat before opening the envelope.

The sheet of paper bore only three lines:

Sorry to advise Edward Carrington died Thursday
Funeral Monday
Wainwright

As she caught her breath, Lucy's eyes filled with tears. Fully expecting to read the news that James had been killed, she felt relieved, almost elated, but at the same time she was shocked and confused. Her dearest friend Edward was dead – but how and why? She realized she hadn't heard from him lately, nor had she written. That made her feel guilty. Perhaps he had been ill for some time and she'd not known about it.

She wondered if she should attend the funeral but decided against it. It was too late to organize the journey to Tunbridge Wells and besides she had heard the trains were packed with soldiers. After making a drink, she sat down and wrote a long letter to his brother-in-law, Wainwright, expressing her sympathy, telling him how attached she had been to Edward and how much she would miss him. Though she had never met Captain Wainwright, she felt an empathy with him and concluded the letter by asking after his wife, Lydia. She did not expect to get a reply.

It was not until the following morning Lucy realized the full consequences of Edward's death. Not only had her source of income come to an end, but her rent-free tenancy at Honeysuckle Cottages was over. She hoped she would be allowed to stay on until the cottages were sold and perhaps even continue as a tenant with the new owner, whoever that may be. If that wasn't possible, then both she and Pansy would need to find new accommodation, and she would have to find a job so she could afford to pay rent for a house or rooms elsewhere.

'What!' Stan Crowther yelled. 'When you said you didn't pay rent, I thought you owned this house. You never told me some old bloke from the south let you live here for nowt. I'd like to know what you did for him to get that sort of arrangement.'

Pansy was hurt. 'It's not what you think! Edward Carrington was a dear kind man and he was good to Lucy and me.'

'So he had the pair of you, did he?'

'Get out, Stan! Get out of here!'

'I'll get out if you pay me the money you owe me.'

'I don't have any money and if I did, I'd not give you a farthing of it!'

'Bugger you!' he yelled, before banging the door. 'And bugger you too!' he shouted, directing his abuse towards Lucy's cottage. 'I'll be back!' he yelled, from the gate. 'And I'll get what you owe me, one way or the other. That's a promise!'

'What did you say his name was?' the constable asked.

'Crowther, Stanley Crowther.'

'Not Stanley Green or Stan Blenkinsop? Are you sure it wasn't either of those names?'

Lucy and Pansy both shook their heads.

'Well from your description I'm certain it's the same fellow. Bit of no good, he is. Been known for quite some time. Preys on women who live on their own. And with so many men folk away at the war, right now he's having a birthday.'

'Where does he come from?' Pansy asked.

The old constable shrugged his shoulders. 'Gypsy-type I gather. He has an old caravan somewhere on the moors, though he spends most of his time hanging around the local towns and villages. Once he gets a women's sympathy, he wheedles his way into her life. He sometimes works two or three different houses at the same time. Hangs around one area for a while, usually till he gets found out, then moves on. He's done the rounds in Halifax and Knaresborough and, before he came here, he was over in Ilkley. I reckon his moral values are lower than a snake's belly!'

'Is there anything we can do if he comes back?'

'Apart from kicking him out, I don't know. I can tell you ladies, we'd love to get our hands on him but somehow he manages to keep himself clean. He sweet-talks his way into free food and lodgings, and somehow picks up enough money to pay for his bets and whisky. What we need is something criminal to pin on him, like if he stole something. Then we'd come down on him like a ton of bricks. Trouble is, he's as slippery as an eel. But don't worry, ladies, we'll get him one of these days.'

'What if he lied at his army medical so he wouldn't have to be conscripted? Is that criminal?'

Surprised by her question, Lucy and the constable both looked at Pansy.

'What are you getting at, luv?'

Pansy spoke cautiously, 'Well, he told me he failed the army medical.'

'So?'

'He told the medical board he couldn't see, but I know he can hit a rabbit between the eyes across the meadow. And he's threaded many a needle for me. I'd say Stan Crowther has better eyesight than all of us put together.'

The constable took her words down in his notepad then flipped it shut.

'Leave it with me, ladies. The right words in the right ears can work wonders. Don't hold your breath though. Nothing will happen immediately, but I'll guarantee you this, if the army gets their teeth into him, they won't let go in a hurry!' The constable winked at the two women. 'Mr Crowther, cum Green, cum Blenkinsopp, could be in for a rude awakening.'

The two envelopes in Lucy's hand looked almost identical. The stationery was the same, as was the handwriting. Both were stamped with the Skipton postmark, but while one was addressed to her, the other bore the title, James Harrington Oldfield Esq. Lucy was puzzled as she examined them. The only two people she knew from the Wharfedale town were Arthur Mellor and the man called Harry Entwhistle, whom she had presumed was Arthur's father. Surely after twenty-one years neither of those men would be renewing acquaintance with her, especially as in all those years Arthur had never once enquired after his child.

Taking a deep breath, she sliced the knife blade along the envelope bearing her name. The embossed gold letters printed along the top of the page shone in the light from the window. Proctor and Armitage, Solicitors and Barristers, Main Street, Skipton, West Riding of Yorkshire, it read. She knew it must be important.

Dear Mrs Oldfield,

It is our sad duty to inform you of the death of our client, Mr Edward Carrington of Tunbridge Wells. As executors of his estate we advise that under the terms of his last will and testament you are one of the beneficiaries.

As Representatives of this estate, Proctor and Armitage are under strict obligation to distribute the funds to the correct beneficiaries and require satisfactory evidence of the identity of the persons involved.

As there are certain conditional clauses to address, we feel it would be in your best interests to visit our offices to discuss the matter further.

We look forward to hearing from you in the near future.

*Yours sincerely
J. Cranford Proctor
For Proctor and Armitage*

In James's absence, Lucy opened the letter addressed to him. As she expected, apart from the addressee's name, the content was identical.

Lucy had listened very carefully to all the information as it was presented to her in legal jargon, but she was still confused. 'What does it all mean?' she asked the two rather elderly gentlemen sitting at the opposite side of the heavy walnut desk.

'What it means,' said Mr Armitage said slowly, 'is that under the terms of Mr Carrington's will, two of the cottages, commonly known as Honeysuckle Cottages, have been left to you. The third cottage, the one which our client occupied until he took up residence in the south, has been left to your son, Mr James Oldfield.'

It took a moment for Lucy to catch her breath. 'Can you explain what you mean by the *conditional clauses* you mentioned?'

Mr Proctor answered. 'When the title to the two cottages is transferred into your name, the lease agreement, held over the property currently occupied by Mrs Pansy Pugh, will come to an end. However, when we last spoke to Mr Carrington, which was some two years prior to his death, he made certain requests which he asked us, as his representatives, to outline to you.'

Mr Proctor took off his spectacles and laid them on the desk. 'I may say that Mr Carrington held you in very high regard.'

Lucy acknowledged the compliment with a nervous smile.

'He also had faith in your judgement and felt you would handle the lease of the tenanted cottage in a fair and proper manner. He did, however, express the hope that you would honour the current lease arrangement with Mrs Pugh. But, naturally, as the new owner, you are at liberty to demand a reasonable rent for the cottage and by this means you could provide yourself with a weekly income.' The solicitor paused, allowing Lucy the opportunity to absorb the information.

'Please continue,' she said.

'The other matter our client asked us to convey to you was his wish that you and your son continue living in the cottages rather than selling them. I must again point out that this is not a stipulation, merely a request. Mr Carrington also requested that in the event of your death, the title to your two cottages is passed to your son,

James. Again this is at your discretion. Once the titles are transferred, you are at liberty to dispose of the two cottages bequeathed to you as you see fit.' He leaned forward and rested on his forearms. 'Mr Carrington was aware that you are, if I may say, an eligible woman who may wish to marry. It was our duty to advise him of this at the time he made his will.'

Lucy pondered on what the lawyer was saying 'Perhaps I should make a will right now, Mr Proctor?'

'It may be a little premature as the deeds are not yet in your name.'

'Then if I tell you what I wish, can you have one drawn up for me when everything has been settled?'

'It will be our pleasure.'

'There is just one other matter,' Mr Armitage added. 'The residue of Mr Carrington's estate has not yet been determined, but it is likely both you and your son will be beneficiaries to the terms of several thousand pounds.'

'Goodness,' said Lucy. 'I never knew Edward was such a wealthy man.'

'And an astute man, I would say. We will be in touch when the matter is finalized.'

Once the remainder of the business was concluded, Lucy shook hands with the two solicitors. 'Thank you. Good afternoon.'

Outside on Main Street the air was fresh. Market day was in full swing and it was two hours before the train was due to depart. With memories of Arthur Mellor and his father rekindled in her mind, Lucy had no intention of visiting the stalls. Instead she chose a small teashop where she tried to relax as she considered her situation. It was hard to feel excited about her prospects and she wished James had been home to support her. Above all, she deeply regretted that her new-found fortune was at the expense of Edward's life.

Pansy looked distraught. 'I know you'll say I am stupid, Lucy, but I have told Stan that he can live here.'

'You must be daft in the head, girl! Weren't you listening to what the constable said when we were in the police station? Wasn't it you who said Crowther tricked the army medical board?'

'Yes, but I got it wrong, and now I feel guilty because I said what I did.'

Lucy shook her head in disbelief.

'Stan told me he does have trouble with his eyes but it comes and goes. It was his flat feet that made him fail the medical. And he said the constable had got him mixed up with some other man called Stan, and that it wasn't the first time people had got the two of them confused.'

'But what about the money he wanted from you? Can't you see he's taking advantage of you?'

'He said he was a bit short at the time and it was wrong of him to ask. He told me he was really sorry. He meant it, Lucy, I could tell he did.'

'So what happens now? And what happens the next time he's short?'

'He's promised me faithfully it won't happen again, and when he moves in, he says he'll get a regular job, so I won't have to go out cleaning.'

'And you believe him?'

'Lucy, you don't know him like I do. Stan's good at heart, and he gets on well with Timmy, and I enjoy his company.' She heaved a sigh. 'And he said that although you and he have never really hit it off, he'd like to get better acquainted with you, especially as the property now belongs to you.'

'Huh!' exclaimed Lucy. 'Is that so? Well, all I can say is, I think you're crazy for listening to him. You don't know what you are letting yourself in for.'

Pansy turned away.

'Imagine what Edward would have said. He'd have had Stan locked up by now.'

'Lucy, don't say that. It's all lies. Stan said so. You'll see.'

'Yes I will, won't I?'

Lucy could hear Crowther yelling, but it was the tinkle of falling glass that brought her running into the front room. Through the broken window she saw him standing in the lane. He was facing her cottage.

'I ain't signing no bloody lease!' he screamed. 'And I ain't paying you no two quid a week. You're a thieving greedy bitch, Lucy Oldfield, that's what you are. Got your hands on a bit of property and now you want to squeeze a few lousy bob out of every other poor sod. Well, you won't get a penny out of me. You can stick your lease and your cottage!'

Lucy could hear Pansy's plaintive cry coming from her garden and watched when he turned back to her.

'And you know what you can do, Pansy bloody Pugh! Expect me to work for you so I can pay your bloody rent! Bloody women! You're all the bloody same! Waste of bloody time the lot of you!'

'Don't say that Stan!' Pansy begged. 'I'll work something out with Lucy. I promise.'

'Bloody promises! That's all I get, bloody promises!'

'Stan,' she cried. 'Don't be like that.'

'I got better things to do with me time than get tangled up with your sort. What you got to offer anyway? You think if you feed me a bit of stew occasionally I'm going work my balls off for you. Well you're bloody well wrong!'

Lucy jumped back as the second rock came hurtling through her window showering shards of glass across the carpet. By the time she dared peer out again, Stanley Crowther had gone.

Chapter 13

Night

That night Lucy couldn't sleep. She felt ill at ease. It was pitch black outside. There was no moon and the wind blowing across from the moors was strengthening. The board, nailed across the broken window, rattled as if someone was trying to get in, while the tree branches, rubbing on Pansy's cottage roof, sent an eerie scraping sound along the length of the cottages' eaves. For no apparent reason, the hens squawked – their haunting cries answered by the anxious bleating of the sheep. It was obvious the animals could not sleep either.

Pulling the blanket to her ear, Lucy turned over. She couldn't get Stanley Crowther out of her mind. She hoped and prayed that after tonight's incident she would not see him again. In a way, she felt sorry for Pansy but at the same time she was angry with her for allowing the situation to get out of hand. If James had been home none of this would have happened.

She resolved that in the morning she would speak with Pansy, tell her what she had done and why. Explain that her threat to increase the rent had merely been a ploy to get rid of Crowther and that the peppercorn lease would remain unchanged once the man had gone. The ruse had certainly achieved its desired effect and had worked far quicker than Lucy had expected.

As she drifted to sleep she questioned what Pansy had told her. Had Stan really failed the medical because of his flat feet? Could there possibly be two men with the same name taking advantage of women in the village? In the morning she would speak with the constable again, report what had happened and ask if anything had been done about the man from the moors.

The constable read his notes. 'So, what you are telling me now is that last night one of your sheep went missing and the night before four chickens disappeared?'

'That's right,' said Lucy.

'And you think Stanley Crowther's the culprit?'

Lucy nodded. 'The first night we thought the wind had pushed the hen house door open. That's why I didn't mention it yesterday. But now one of the best ewes has gone, I think someone took it and I'd bet anything it was that man.'

'And you don't think the sheep could have strayed.'

'She was a pet. We raised her on a bottle. She wouldn't have strayed.'

The policeman shook his head. 'Not a lot we can do, I'm afraid. It's hard to prove someone's taken something unless you can catch them with it. Best advice I can give you is to keep a good eye out and make sure you lock everything up, especially your front door.'

'Don't worry I will.' Lucy paused at the gate. 'By the way, Constable, did the army do anything about Crowther's medical?'

'Not to my knowledge. The information was passed on but I reckon they might be too busy with enlistments.'

'What will they do if they catch up with him?'

'If he lied, they'll probably have him sworn in then send him straight to prison. A military prison. Not a civilian one. Once he's served his time – maybe six months, then they'll ship him off to the front-line. That's what I think.'

'Thank you, constable.'

The following morning Lucy noticed Goldie grazing alone in the meadow. Edward's horse had gone.

The constable sounded sympathetic but said there was little hope of getting the animal back. He said he would contact the local knacker's yard with a description. The only chance they had was if the old mare had been sold to a farmer in another district. He said with the war on there was a shortage of horses, especially ones trained to work in the shafts.

It was the bleating of the sheep that awakened Lucy. She hadn't meant to fall asleep but had dozed off in the armchair. Edward's rifle was lying within arm's reach on the table, the box of ammunition was next to it. Lucy slipped the gun under her arm, dropped the box in her pocket and roused Pansy from the sofa.

The pair agreed not to go out through the kitchen. Instead they slipped out of the front door, hurried quietly past Pansy's cottage and stopped by the farm gate which led into the meadow.

They did not have to wait long before the black shadow of a man appeared leading a horse. Crowther's swaggering gait was unmistakable.

'Leave the horse!' Lucy ordered.

The man kept walking towards them.

'Let go of the horse!' she yelled.

The horse whinnied and shook its mane.

'Well, what do we have here? *Owooo!*' he howled. 'A pair of witches out on this fine dark night.'

'If you go any further I will shoot.'

The man stopped. He could see the rifle levelled at him.

'Let go of the horse!'

'You're not going to shoot me. You ain't got it in you.'

Lucy pulled the bolt back, pointed the gun into the air and squeezed the trigger. The rifle cracked. The horse reared. Lucy quickly reloaded.

'Bloody stupid bitch, what did you do that for?'

'That was just a warning. Now let the horse go!'

'I was just going to,' he said, lifting the rope bridle. 'I was only going to borrow it for a couple of hours. I'd have had it back by the morning.'

'Step away from the horse!'

He didn't move.

'So what you going to do now?' Crowther said. It was the same smarmy tone that Lucy hated. 'You ain't going to shoot me, are you?'

'That's far enough!' she said.

He moved towards her.

'That's far enough!' A voice boomed out from behind him.

Surprised, Stan Crowther turned.

Outlined against the meadow were two men. The police helmets were unmistakable.

'Leave it to us now, miss. We don't want you doing anything you'll regret later.'

Lucy's knees suddenly went weak. Her arm dropped and the barrel hit the ground. Her heart was thumping. Behind her she could hear Pansy sobbing. With her hands shaking, she slowly released the bolt, turned the rifle over and let the live cartridge fall into the wet grass.

Would she have fired the second round? She did not know.

*

October 1918

My dear Mum

Thank you for all the news. You do not know how good it is to get your letters.

I am pleased to hear you are well and this season's crop was good. Your description of the ricks of hay made me smile. 'Like Indian tepees' you wrote. I can imagine young Timmy dancing around them. I wonder if the lad will remember me when I get back. What a difference four years make.

I got a letter from Alice saying she had moved to Cookridge Hospital where all the burns victims were being taken. She said she was enjoying her nurse training even though the hours were long and the night work made her very tired. She also said she has moved out of the cottage and was living at the nurses' home. You and Pansy must miss her.

I didn't want to worry you but I got injured and had to spend two weeks in the field hospital.

I was in a trench one night when a mortar bomb came over. It's the size of a rum cask and it seems to roll through the air in slow motion. Everyone just stands and watches to see where it's going to land. If it's close, you cover your ears. The explosion is loud enough to shatter your eardrums.

Well, I saw this one floating in my direction. It was too close for comfort, but when you are stuck in a trench there's nowhere to go. When it went off, I was knocked out. I found out later, I got a dent in my tin helmet. I also got a piece of shrapnel in my shoulder and one in my leg. I would have been all right but they couldn't get one bit out and it turned bad. It laid me up for three weeks. Half the time I didn't know where I was. I remember it was cold in the tent, and every noise seemed so loud, even the flapping canvas sounded like thunder. Anyway I'm better now and apart from a couple of scars, there's no damage. I was lucky.

Though the men in my regiment laugh and joke, we all miss England. Sometimes I wonder if we will ever go home.

It was ironical to learn I am now a wealthy man. Fancy, a cottage of my own and over four thousand pounds in the bank. But that doesn't matter out here. How can I plan for the future when men around me are being killed every day?

On a more positive note, we have heard the fighting is drawing to a close and the war could be over before Christmas.

How I would love to be shovelling snow from the front door instead of shovelling muck from the bottom of this filthy rat hole.

I'm sorry to end on this note, but I can't write it any other way.

All my love to you
Your loving son,
James

*

'He's coming!' Alice yelled. 'He's coming up the lane. Come quick, Aunt Lucy!'

Lucy's eyes filled with tears as she waited by the gate and watched her son striding up the road. Pansy and Alice stood beside her, their arms around each other's waists.

'Go on,' said Pansy to Timmy, encouraging her son to run down the hill to greet him. But the boy was unsure of the slim man in the khaki uniform.

As James got closer, Alice left her mother and ran to meet him, flinging her arms around his neck.

The kit bag dropped from his shoulder as he hugged her. 'My, look at you!' he said. 'I can hardly believe my eyes. And look at you,' he said, ruffling Timothy's hair before sitting the dented helmet on the lad's head.

Alice led him by the hand to the gate and to the two women who were anxiously waiting to greet him. James kissed Pansy on the cheek then took his mother in his arms and held her tightly.

Lucy found it hard to mouth the words: 'Welcome home, son.'

Chapter 14

The Aftermath

'You have to go out and do something, James. You can't just sit around all day.'

'But I like it here. It's quiet.' His voice was weary. 'You don't know how many times I prayed I might sit here and do nothing.'

'I'm sorry,' Lucy said sighing. 'I don't understand what's got into you. I only want what's best for you, but seeing you moping about worries me. You must pull yourself together.'

She waited for James to answer but he seemed preoccupied. She knew he had heard her but he did not reply.

'I'm going to the village,' she said. 'Can I get you anything?'

His eyes, fixed on the empty grate, never shifted. 'No, I'll be all right.'

Lucy closed the door quietly as she left.

James heard the click. Then listened intently to the silence. He was alone and everything was still. He glanced right, then left. His eyes darted around the room. Suddenly everything was closing in – shrinking. There was no space to move – no room to walk – to breathe. The doll sitting on the chair opposite was eyeing him, gazing at him with a glassy stare. He looked away – glanced back. Yes, definitely spying on him. From the framed picture on the mantelshelf, another pair of eyes was on him. A girl. A nurse. He knew the face. From the field hospital perhaps? He wasn't sure.

The fire was out. He was glad. It was always safer in the dark. But it was cold and the night would be bitter. He could see a light shining outside. Was it daylight coming through a hole? A window? No, it was a tunnel through the wall. A way to escape. Looking up at the ceiling, the heavy beams loomed threateningly. What if the house crumbled? What if the roof timbers collapsed? He'd be crushed. Killed. And no one would find him. He must get out. Get away.

When he stepped out onto the lane, he shook his head and gasped. The outside air was clear and fresh. How strange, he thought. How different. The sky was blue, flecked with fine wafts of white. A sparrow landed in the bird bath and splashed its wings. The gravel crunched under his feet. The sound of marching feet was all too familiar.

He had to walk. He felt he had to go somewhere – but where? Just walk. He knew the track well. Knew every fence and dry-stone wall. Knew every hollow tree which hid a squirrel. Knew every patch of earth which stank of garlic. The tangled hedgerows where the blackberries grew. He knew every rut where, after rain, a stream trickled across the path, and knew the contours of the distant hills that offered sanctuary to the setting sun.

Inside the gate of Fothergill's farm, he slowed, his mind battling to remember. The smell. Decay. Deep litter. Dung. Warm steaming hay. The sound of cows. The spring of soft earth beneath his feet. Thick clover wet after rain. Daisies. Cowslips. Dandelions.

He stopped. Looked down. How strange, he thought, to see flowers growing on this ground. He reached out his hand to touch.

Before his eyes the flowers faded – disappeared. The earth grew bare. The mud felt wet and warm, sticky like blood. He stopped, looked up and from the corner of his eye he saw it coming, rolling slowly through the sky straight at him.

'Mortar!' he screamed, as he dropped to the ground, covered his ears and waited for the bang.

The crow landed on the fence and cawed.

Hunched on his hands and knees, James wept.

Lucy rubbed the loose flour from her hands but the dough was still stuck between her fingers when she opened the front door.

Mr Fothergill was on the doorstep with James standing meekly beside him.

'I thought I'd better bring the lad home,' he said.

'What's the matter?'

The farmer shook his head. Moisture was glistening in his eyes. 'Best get the doctor to have a look at him, Mrs Oldfield.'

Lucy was puzzled but took James's arm and led him into the house.

'Let me know if I can be of any help,' the farmer said.
'Thank you,' she said. 'I will.'

The morning of 11 November was misty. But at least it wasn't raining. At eleven o'clock, Lucy thought of the soldiers marching to memorials throughout Britain. Standing in silent remembrance to commemorate the war, but she had no intention of reminding her son what was special about that day.

While she sat reading, James fitted another piece into his jigsaw. She looked up from her book. How many puzzles was that? She had bought at least two dozen in the last few months – every jigsaw the local shop had had in stock. The shopkeeper had ordered more but was still waiting for them to arrive. It didn't matter to James how many pieces each puzzle contained or what the pictures were of – rose gardens, stately homes, boats lolling in quiet Cornish harbours, or waves crashing on angry seas. After completing each one he would mix up a dish of flour and water paste, spread it thinly over the puzzle and leave it to set hard. Then he would start on another.

In the front room, Timothy tootled on the piano hammering out unrelated notes. Lucy hadn't heard the lad come in, but wasn't surprised as he often wandered into the room without saying anything especially when Pansy was at work.

As she turned the page, Lucy noticed James had stopped. Without saying a word, he got up from his puzzle and walked to the front room. Lucy was about to ask if there was anything he wanted, but she stopped herself.

As he stood in the doorway, Timothy looked up at him.

'Can I join you?' James asked.

'Yep,' said Timmy, his fingers still tapping tunelessly, as he slid along the piano stool making room for James to sit beside him.

James hesitated for a moment, looked kindly at the boy, then lifted his hands and rested them on the keys. The ivory was cool.

'Can you play something?' Timothy asked.

'I don't know,' said James.

'Play a Christmas carol and I'll sing the words. We should practise,' the boy said enthusiastically. 'It'll be Christmas soon and you can come round the village with me and Mum.' He looked up, 'Will you come too, Aunt Lucy, when we go carolling?'

From the doorway Lucy smiled at the pair and when James inclined his head and smiled back at her, a tear trickled down her cheek. That single smile told her his battle was over. Her son had finally come home.

Chapter 15

Alice

'Edward had so many interesting things,' Lucy said, as she dusted the ebony elephant and placed it back on the glass shelf in the cabinet.

From the floor, where he was sitting cross-legged stacking his jigsaw pictures, James looked up. 'What am I going to do with these things?' he said. 'They can't be used again.' He laughed. 'I made sure of that, didn't I?'

Lucy grinned. 'Give them to the chapel for the fête or store them in the attic.'

James shrugged, tied them securely and leaned the bundle against a tea chest which bore a faded Bombay shipping mark. 'Is there anything in here you want to keep?'

Lucy shook her head. 'Nothing,' she said. 'I only wish I had a photograph of Edward. Perhaps Wainwright has one.' She sighed. 'Maybe I will write to him and ask.'

'Are you sure you don't mind me moving into Edward's cottage?'

'Of course not! It's what he intended. And it belongs to you.'

James grinned. 'It's not like I'm moving far away, is it?'

'It will be nice for you and Alice when she comes to visit,' Lucy said.

The leather armchair sighed as he sat down on it. 'It's strange,' he said. 'When I was in France, I used to think of Alice a lot. Most of the men had girlfriends, but I didn't, so I suppose I thought of Alice as my girl.' He looked at his mother. 'But she wasn't, was she? While she was growing up, she was like my little sister and we were friends, close friends. I never thought of her as anything more than that. But look at her now,' he said. 'She scares me a little. She's grown into a lovely woman. A nurse. She's independent. And look at me. What can I offer her?'

Lucy scowled. 'James! You have money and the cottage. Compared with most men of twenty three you are very lucky.'

'But is that enough?'

Lucy pushed the key into the clock and wound the spring. 'She'll be here very soon, why don't you ask her?'

After his mother left, James spent half an hour preparing for Alice's visit. He was excited. Nervous. It was an unusual feeling. He had known Alice since she was a little girl, from the day he had found her on the moors, frozen and afraid. From that time they had played together, talked together, confided in each other. Taken long walks and ridden for miles across the moors, always comfortable in each other's company. But since the war, he had only seen her briefly on the afternoons she visited her mother, and his memory, of the twelve months when he had been ill, remained vague.

Now things were different. He was fit and well and moving into Edward's cottage – his cottage – and he was about to entertain her alone. It was a daunting prospect. What would he say to her? What would they do?

For the umpteenth time he went to the door and checked the lane. At last she was there. Walking up the hill, pushing her bicycle.

'So, this is your new home,' she said, as he took her coat and followed her into the front room. She stood for a moment looking around. 'Just as Edward left it.'

James felt guilty. 'Perhaps I should have bought new furniture. I can afford it.'

'No' she protested. 'It's very gentlemanly and hardly worn. And,' she added, 'it suits you.'

Standing by the fireplace, James watched as Alice wandered around looking at the ornaments, admiring some, examining others, asking about particular ones. A group of miniature soldiers assembled in the china cabinet attracted her attention.

'Gurkhas!' he said.

Alice nodded. 'Can I make a cup of tea?'

James apologized. He should have thought of that.

She insisted. 'I'll do it. You sit down.'

After a few minutes, she returned carrying a tray decked with Edward's Royal Worcester teapot and crockery. James watched as she poured the tea. Her hand was steady, but when she sat down, he thought she looked weary. Pulling off her shoes, she leaned back in the chair.

'It's a long ride from the hospital. Are you tired?' James said.

'A little,' she said. 'Tell me what you have been doing.'

James couldn't think. What had he done lately? Nothing really. Just odd jobs around the cottages. Things that needed doing. Propped up the stable roof where it collapsed. Bought six new hens. Went to town. Wrote a few letters to the men he had served with – uncertain if the addresses were correct – uncertain if he would get any replies. Pruned the crab-apple tree. That was about it. 'Not much,' he said.

'Have you thought any more about university?'

'No.'

'Have you been riding?'

'No,' he said quickly, wanting to turn the conversation away from himself. 'Tell me about the hospital.'

Alice leaned back and talked at length about the hospital itself, the building, the wards, corridors, the other nurses and the shift work. She described the nurses' quarters and the strict rules and regulations the girls had to adhere to, but she didn't speak about herself.

'When do you get a holiday?'

'Why do you ask?'

'Because I would like to go away for a holiday and take my mum and your Mum, and little Timmy – and you with me.'

'Where to? And when?'

'Scarborough. By train,' he said. 'Have you ever been there?'

Alice shook her head.

'Neither have I, but I understand there are some nice hotels overlooking the sea. Imagine staying in a hotel and being waited on.'

'It would be terribly expensive.'

'I can afford it,' James said. 'And it's something I'd like to do.'

'Timmy would love it.'

'That means you will come?'

Alice thought for a moment. 'Yes, if I can arrange to get time off.'

'Does Alice Pugh live here?'

'No,' said Lucy wondering who the man standing by the garden gate was. 'Her mother lives next door,' Lucy said. 'But no one's home today. Can I help?'

He looked disappointed. 'Just thought I'd call in. I was in the neighbourhood. First time I've been round these parts.'

'Alice doesn't actually live here,' Lucy explained. 'She lives-in at the hospital. She's a nurse.'

'Yes, I know. I work there as a porter. It's her day off today and she told me she usually goes home when she's got the time. I thought I'd find her here. I wanted to surprise her. Wanted to show her my new transport.' As he spoke, he stepped back allowing Lucy full view of the new motor bike propped up on its stand. 'Never mind. Sorry to trouble you, missus.'

'When I see her, shall I tell her who called?'

'Aye, say Bertie Bottomley was looking for her. On the other hand,' he said, pulling the goggles down to the bridge of his nose. 'Don't worry. I'll catch up with her on the ward tomorrow.'

'You haven't forgotten about Scarborough, have you?' James asked casually.

Alice shook her head, but continued reading the newspaper.

He'd asked the same question every time she'd visited during the past month, but on each occasion her answer had been the same – that it wasn't easy to get time off, but she was still trying.

'Do you have to work?' James asked bluntly.

Alice looked up.

'Wouldn't you prefer to stay at home?'

'But I've got to work! How would I live otherwise? I can't expect Mum to support me at my age.'

'But what if I supported you.' He paused. 'What if you and I were to get married? You wouldn't have to work again.'

Alice didn't answer.

'I can afford it. I've got plenty of money and you can buy whatever you want, clothes, furniture, even a radiogram or a wireless. You must know I would do anything for you, Alice.'

'I know you would. You're very kind, James. But Edward's money – your money – won't last forever and I don't need all those things.'

He turned away, but not quickly enough. He knew she had read the disappointment clouding his face.

'You must give me time to think about it,' she said. 'It's a very good offer.'

When Lucy answered the front door, she was surprised to find John Fothergill standing on the doorstep. It was raining hard.

'Morning,' he said, touching his knuckles to his forehead.

'Mr Fothergill, what can I do for you?'

'If you don't mind, I wanted to have a quick word about that field out the back.'

'Come in out of the rain. I'll make a nice cup of tea.'

The farmer looked down at his Wellington boots caked in farmyard muck. 'If it's no trouble,' he said, kicking his boots off and following Lucy through to the living room. Offering him a seat at the kitchen table, she put the kettle on to boil. When he sat down, the farmer slid his feet under the chair, but not before Lucy had noticed the large holes in his socks.

'I see you've left the field fallow this year,' the farmer said.

'You mean we didn't plant anything.'

'That's right. I took a walk over there yesterday. Some good feed growing.'

Lucy glanced out of the window. The meadow was thick and green, scattered with the tall stems of self-seeded barley. The slender stalks swayed in the still air as a group of birds busily investigated the fresh green ears.

'Is it all right with you if I put a few cows out there? It's nice clean pasture. Shame to waste it.'

Lucy looked puzzled. 'But it's your field, isn't it?'

'That's right, but I'm still obliged by the lease. Mr Carrington paid me five years in advance.'

'But Edward has been dead for over two years.'

'I know. But he was an honest man and generous too and, even though he's dead and buried, I have to honour my side of the bargain. Besides,' he said, 'you and Mrs Pugh did a wonderful job when things were scarce. I take my hat off to you. All that work you did for the war effort. I'd never begrudge you the use of it.'

'Everyone did what they could,' Lucy said.

'I should have done more,' the farmer said, shaking his head. 'But I had enough on me plate at the time.'

As Lucy placed the mug of tea on the table, the farmer glanced at the dirt embedded deep beneath his fingernails. Sliding his hands to his lap he hid them beneath the table cloth. Lucy looked at the man. His face was weathered, his skin leathery, his expression gaunt and drawn, his grey-green eyes half sunken into the sockets. He wasn't a tall man but he was wiry. His hair was wiry too, grey and sparse on top except for his sideburns which were ginger and matched the colour of his overlong moustache. Like his hair, it was in dire need of a trim.

'Well if it's all right with you, Mrs Oldfield, I'll bring a few heifers down tomorrow.'

'Should I get James to move the horse?'

'No, leave it. Cows won't mind a bit of company. They're only interested in what's under their noses.' He sipped the tea and looked around the room.

Lucy watched him, following his gaze. First he glanced at the doll sitting on the straight-backed chair, then at the photo on the mantelpiece. Both the doll and the young woman in the picture wore white uniforms bearing the distinctive red nursing cross.

'Is that young Alice from next door?'

Lucy smiled. 'It is,' she said, taking down the picture and handing it to him.

'Fine girl. Don't see much of her these days.'

'She works away. At Cookridge Hospital.'

'Ah!' he sighed and handed the photograph back to Lucy. 'Do you want a calf?'

Lucy was surprised at the question. 'Pardon?'

'A calf. Only a week old,' he said. 'On the bottle. I'll give you the milk. Much as you need. It's just we can't manage it.'

Lucy wasn't sure.

'If you don't want it, I'll kill it. Just thought I'd ask.'

'I've raised a lamb on a bottle, but never a calf. You say you can't manage. Is it a problem?'

'Calf's no trouble, it's just we can't spare the time messing about with it. There's only me and me daughter, Grace, these days.'

'But I remember Edward telling me you and your wife had two grown boys.'

The farmer rubbed his hand across his thinning hair. 'We lost both boys in Flanders in 1917. Not more than two months apart. That was when my wife took to her bed. Doctor said it was women's troubles but I think it was all tied up with the shock and grief. Same ailment as got to your boy – only worse and she ain't never got over it.'

'I'm sorry,' said Lucy. 'I didn't know.'

'She wouldn't let me tell anyone. Said she didn't want folk knowing her business. Trouble is now at times she can hardly breathe and I think she's proper sick. That's what made me think about a nurse for her.'

'Shall I speak to Alice when I see her? Ask her if she can spare a bit of time.'

'I don't know what my missus will say. She only lets Grace tend to her these days. Doesn't even like me going into her room.'

He wiped the tea from his whiskers. 'It's hard on the lass though, helping me with the milking and trying to look after her mother and the house as well. She's turned twenty years old and says she don't intend to be tied to the farm for the rest of her days. It was all right when she were young but now she grown she says had enough of mucking out sheds. She wants to go to the city to work. What can I do?'

Lucy shook her head.

'Can't really blame her, can you? She's a good lass, but I worry. I don't know what she'll do if she leaves. She's got no learning. We paid for the boys to go to high school, but we couldn't afford it with her. Didn't seem necessary at the time. She left school at twelve to help the missus. Now I wish—'

'I'd be happy to take the calf,' said Lucy.

'That's good. I didn't really want to knock it on the head. Nice little heifer calf. If she grows all right, we'll put her to the bull when she's big enough. You can start your own herd.'

Lucy laughed. She felt sorry for the farmer. He was a nice man.

James asked Alice to marry him three or four times during the summer of 1920. And both Lucy and Pansy tried to encourage her to accept James's proposal.

'You can get a job in the village,' said Pansy. 'Or work as a private nurse in one of them big houses, if you really want to work.'

'Serving cups of tea and bathing some rich old biddy every time she wets herself. No thank you!' Alice was not going to be persuaded.

Even James's new car made no difference.

It was the latest model, a 1920 Morris Tourer – brand spanking new. The metal trim gleamed, even the leather upholstery shone. It seated four or five comfortably and had a concertina top that could be pulled up when it rained. It was one of the few cars in the Horsforth district and certainly the newest one for miles around. Lucy and Pansy felt like royalty when they travelled in the back. Timothy always took pride of place in the front passenger seat.

Much to James's chagrin and disappointment, Alice was indifferent to the motor car, almost averse to it. She complained about the petrol fumes. Said the car was noisy and cold to ride in. And when James suggested he drive her back to the hospital and carry her bike in the back seat, she objected saying she preferred to ride her bike. She argued it was good exercise and asked him what people would think if they saw her being driven to the nurses' home by a toff in a fancy car.

James managed to hide his disappointment.

'I thought of taking Goldie for a walk,' he said casually, after lunch on one of her visits. 'Would you like to join me?'

He was surprised when she accepted, especially as she sounded quite enthusiastic. Perhaps she had spent too much time that morning talking with her mother and Lucy. Perhaps, because it was a fine day, she wanted to get out in the fresh air. James didn't care; he was just pleased she had agreed.

It was a long time since she had been in the saddle and a long time since Goldie had been ridden and at first both seemed a little nervous. Holding the bridle, James led the old horse out of the gate beside Pansy's cottage and into the lane. It was the way he had led her many times when she was a little girl. How could he forget those times? How happy she had been then, full of fun and excitement, chattering non-stop while riding confidently, one hand on the horse's mane, the other wrapped around the waist of Constance, her doll. Walking beside her, James looked up, but Alice was staring straight ahead and did not return his glance.

Skirting around the field on the back lane, he led Goldie along the narrow path and up into the pocket of woodland overlooking the meadow. Mr Fothergill's small herd of cows was camped by the marshy ground at the far end of the field, cudding contentedly. In the distance, the three Honeysuckle Cottages were half-hidden by the old horse chestnut tree.

Alice sighed, as she held out her arms for James to help her dismount. 'Being here reminds me of when I was a girl,' she said, and when she slid from the saddle her body brushed against his, her hands slipping loosely around his neck.

James held her for a moment. 'Shall we sit for a while?'

Alice agreed and with the horse blanket beneath them, they reminisced.

'I remember the thrush's nest' Alice mused. 'I used to lie here and watch you climb, looking for eggs. And we used to catch butterflies and take them to show Edward, and remember, if your mother called, we would pretend we didn't hear her.'

He smiled.

'And sometimes we would fall asleep in the sun,' she said, lying back on the rug.

James laid down beside her and watched as she closed her eyes. The sun, filtering through the branches, flickered across her face. 'And you looked just as you do today – lovely,' he sighed. 'You cannot imagine how many times I have longed for a moment like this.' Closing his eyes, he touched her arm. Her skin was soft and warm. His hands trembled.

A dragonfly hovering over the grass nearby ignored them. Above their heads the new season's acorns decorated the tree's branches like candles on a Christmas tree. A bird flitted between the leaves. The old horse flicked flies with its tail and grazed amongst the wildflowers whose seedpods were firm and full and almost ready to burst and cast their crop on the late summer breeze. Goldie didn't wander far. The cows never stirred. The sun continued flickering and it was almost two hours before Alice decided it was time she should leave.

'Perhaps you'd reconsider what I've been asking,' James said, as he touched her cheek.

'Don't ask me now,' she said. 'Please, not now.'

Chapter 16

Bad Times

Lucy and Alice sat next to each other at the pine table in the farmhouse kitchen. Mr Fothergill, perched on a stool near the fireplace, spoke in a low voice.

'Her mother never made it easy for her,' he said. 'Always picking on the lass.' He sighed deeply. 'The two lads were always her favourites. And I suppose, if I was honest, I'd say Grace was always mine.'

From outside the window, a dog barked. Grace Fothergill kicked off her boots before popping her head around the kitchen door. Plump and freckle-faced, she wore her long ginger hair woven into two plaits. Her impish grin belied her twenty two years. Wearing dungarees, hand-knitted socks and an old jumper, which had obviously belonged to her father, a look of embarrassment flashed across her face when she saw how smartly Alice was dressed, but it quickly disappeared. She smiled. 'Have you been to see Mam yet?'

'No,' said Lucy. 'We waited for you. Did you tell her I was bringing Alice?'

'I told her you might call in just to say hello.' Grace turned to Alice, her expression serious. 'At first she said you were not to bother then she asked if you was a real nurse. When I told her you were, I think she was pleased because she kept asking when you were coming.'

Mr Fothergill fed the fire from the pile of chopped wood heaped beside it. A kitten wandered over to Lucy and rubbed itself against her leg. Grace shooed it out of the door and then beckoned the two women to follow her down the passage which led through the house. The door to the end room was closed. Grace knocked on it gently before ushering the two ladies inside.

As she opened the bedroom door, Lucy was struck by the unsavoury smell. It was always the same – the smell of sickness in a house – only this time it was worse.

Mrs Fothergill was propped up in the bed with a pile of cushions behind her. While draped around her shoulders was a faded blue bed jacket, in her hands she was gripping a towel pulled up under her chin. The once silver hair was dull and matted and she looked much older than her fifty years.

'Hello, Mrs Fothergill, I'm Alice.'

The woman smiled weakly. 'I'd never have recognized you,' she said, fighting for breath with every word. 'Last time I saw you, you were only a girl.' Her words drifted into a bout of wheezing.

'Mam can't talk for long,' Grace said quietly, as she offered Lucy the only chair in the room. 'She gets tired easily.'

Lucy and Alice exchanged glances before Alice sat on the edge of the bed and took Mrs Fothergill's hand. 'How are you?' she said gently, not expecting an answer. It was obviously hard work for the woman to speak so Grace answered most of the questions for her.

'Is there anything you can do for her?' Grace asked.

'I'd like to help,' said Alice, 'but I think your mother needs a doctor.'

'No!' the woman breathed emphatically. She tried to repeat it but her voice was no more than a whisper. 'No. No doctor.'

Alice turned back to Grace.

'How long has she been like this?'

'A few months now,' said Grace, tucking in the sheet at the side of the bed. She whispered to Alice. 'She's got this horrible boil on her chest and it's getting worse. I've tried poultices but they don't help. Trouble is she doesn't like me touching it. Doesn't even like me seeing it.' Leaning forward she said softly, 'Mam, let Alice have a look at your chest'

The invalid murmured something to her daughter but, as she was speaking, Alice put her hand on the towel covering her torso. Instinctively the woman held it to her chin, but Alice pulled it gently from her fingers and peeled the cloth back.

Lucy had never seen anything like it. A purple ulcer had puckered the skin of her right breast. At the top edge a pale cauliflower-like growth was protruding from it. The matter weeping from it, smelled foul.

'That's a bit of a mess, Mrs Fothergill,' Alice said in a kind but pragmatic tone.

'No, doctors, luv,' the woman begged, allowing a tear to slip sideways across her temple.

Alice squeezed her hand, talking quietly as she replaced the piece of towelling. 'Perhaps I can get something from the hospital to help you sleep,' she said.

Mrs Fothergill nodded. Her eyes closed and within seconds her breathing indicated she was sleeping. The visitors left quietly without saying goodbye. Grace closed the door behind them.

The expression on Lucy's face answered the question Mr Fothergill was about to ask.

'Isn't there anything you can do for Mam?' Grace asked.

Alice shook her head. 'You should call the doctor.'

'No point. She'll not let the doctor near her. I'm surprised she let you look.'

'I'm sorry, Mr Fothergill,' said Alice. 'There's nothing I can do. Sleep is probably the best thing for her. A little brandy might help, if she'll take it.'

'Tee-total, all her life. Even before the pledge. Won't allow a drop past her lips. Always been a stubborn woman.'

Lucy needed to get outside into the fresh air. She excused herself by asking Grace if she could look around the garden leaving the girl and her father to speak with Alice. Outside it was cold and damp. A black dog sniffed at her boots before flopping down in a makeshift kennel it was sharing with the family of kittens.

At the side of the farmhouse was an untended vegetable patch overgrown by weeds. The only evidence of recent digging had been done by the hens. She could hear cows and geese but was unable to see them from the side of the house and was relieved when Alice emerged from the kitchen.

As they walked home, Alice was quiet.

'She's not long for this world, is she?'

'No, not long.'

Lucy visited the farm twice a week for the next three weeks but Alice only managed one more visit before Mrs Fothergill passed away. The funeral was a quiet affair. Lucy, Pansy and Alice went. Timothy wasn't feeling well and was allowed to stay home alone. James gave his apologies saying he would wait in the car outside the chapel.

'You must go in for the service!' Lucy said. 'People will think you are rude!'

'I don't care what they think,' he said. 'I'm not going.'

When it was over, Lucy and Pansy chose to walk home, while Alice decided to catch the bus back to the hospital. Having an empty vehicle, James offered the farmer and his daughter a lift back to the farm. Mr Fothergill was grateful. He had found the service exhausting and was grateful to sit in the car and relax.

'Can I get your advice sometime, sir?' James said, as they drove up the hill.

Mr Fothergill was surprised. 'Anytime lad. You know where we live. You're welcome to call in.'

In the back seat, Grace sat bolt upright, her fingers gripping the seat in front. At first, James thought she was nervous then he realized her expression was one of sheer excitement. She took no notice of the men's conversation and, as the car sped up, she soaked up the new sensations – the wind on her face, the sound of the engine, the vibrations thrumming through her body and the movement of the car twisting around the country lanes. For the farmer's daughter, the ride home was the most thrilling experience she had ever had.

'Would you let me take you out again sometime?' James said, opening the car door and offering her his hand. 'If that's all right with you, Mr Fothergill,' he added.

Grace looked at her father, her eyes wide and smiling. 'Can I, Dad?'

'About time you had a bit of fun, lass,' he said. 'And that goes for you too, young man! Go out and enjoy yourself, the pair of you.'

Alice stopped playing, closed the piano lid and turned to James. 'I have something to tell you.'

James glanced up from his book. Through the window he could see it was still raining. He really must finish building the garage for the car.

'I'm going to have a baby.'

James turned around. 'What did you say?'

'Don't worry it's not yours.'

He shook his head. 'Whose then?'

'Someone from work.'

'Bertie Bottomley?'

'How do you know that?'

James shook his head. 'Have you told your mother?'

'No. And I don't want to tell her. Not yet anyway.'

'But what about the hospital? They will know soon enough.'

'I'll have to leave,' she said, wringing her hands. 'I'm stupid, aren't I?'

James looked at her. She was verging on tears. He knew if he put his arms around her she would cry. He wanted to say he was sorry, say he wished it had not happened. He wanted to ask her why on earth she had allowed herself to get into such a situation. Ask her about Bottomley. He wondered how long she had been going out with him and why she hadn't mentioned him before. Wondered what it was that made her love Bottomley and not love him. But James kept the questions to himself. *Yes, you are stupid*, he thought.

'Is Bottomley going to marry you?'

'Yes. We are getting married at the Register Office in three weeks.'

'And where will you live?'

'I don't know, James,' she sobbed. 'I really don't know.'

'Have you time to come in and rest your legs?' Lucy enquired.

The constable took off his helmet. 'Don't mind if I do, Mrs Oldfield. They won't miss me at the station.'

Lucy cleared a chair and invited the policeman to sit down. 'What can I do for you?'

'I don't like to worry you but I thought I'd better bring it to your attention. There's been a bit of funny business going on over the other side of the valley.'

Lucy listened as she offered him a cup of tea.

'Man by the name of Wilkinson, Stanley Wilkinson. He's been bothering one of the spinster ladies in town. I haven't seen him myself but from the description he sounds awfully like that Stan Crowther who was bothering your neighbour, Mrs Pugh.'

'I hope you are wrong, Constable.'

'I hope so too, because this man has a nasty streak. Poor woman had taken quite a beating and was found wandering the streets. She didn't know who she was or where she was. When they brought her into the station, I called the doctor and he took her to the hospital himself. I didn't get the man's description till yesterday.' The policeman sipped his tea. 'I hope I'm wrong but I think Crowther's back. I wanted to warn you and Mrs Pugh to watch out. Will you pass the message on when she comes home?'

'Yes, I will. Thank you.'

Lucy wondered what Pansy would say when she told her. And wondered what would happen if Crowther started coming around again.

That night, though the front door was locked and bolted, Lucy checked it several times before going to bed. Unable to sleep, she was vigilant to the sounds of darkness; mice skittering in the ceiling, tree branches scraping along the eaves and the gate creaking on its rusty hinges. But even by closing her eyes, she could not shut out the image of the man that haunted her. She knew if he returned to seek revenge, it might be more than a rock that would come through the window next time.

Timmy's eyes were itchy, his throat sore. He was hot and felt miserable. Pansy told him not to complain. Said it was only a cold and that it would soon pass. When the red rash appeared on his face and neck she took him to the surgery. She had never seen measles before. The doctor said she must keep him inside and away from school. Though frail-looking, Timmy was a fit lad and the doctor was confident the infection would pass in a week.

But by the end of the week Timothy was confined to bed. The rash had spread all over his body, and the cough, which had developed suddenly, was exhausting him. For three nights neither he nor Pansy slept, then finally, when he was too exhausted to clear his lungs, he drifted into sleep – a deep, deep sleep. Though Pansy begged with him to wake, at times shaking his limp body, he never stirred. He never ate or drank and only twice did his eyes open, but they were glazed and he saw nothing. He never spoke and the few sounds he made were incoherent. Hour after hour, Pansy sat beside him mopping his brow while the fever boiled inside him. She wished Alice were home and prayed for Sunday to arrive as she had promised to come home on her day off. Because she was a nurse, Pansy was convinced Alice would know what to do.

But Timothy Pugh couldn't wait for his sister's visit. He died in his mother's arms on the Saturday morning. He was nine years of age.

Chapter 17

The attic

'Come on, luv, I thought you'd be pleased to know I made it through the war without a scratch,' Crowther crowed. 'And the war changed me. You'll see.'

Pansy felt exasperated. She didn't want Stanley's attention. Or any other man's for that matter. What she wanted was to be left alone. But Crowther was not prepared to listen.

Whenever she went out, he followed her. She would catch glimpses of his reflection in shop windows trailing a few yards behind her. She would see him waiting on corners or standing outside shop doorways, or loitering by the post box. Sometimes he would launch himself at her, questioning her angrily, demanding to know what was in her basket, how much she had spent, how much money she had left. Other times he appealed to her good nature, begging for a few shillings to tide him over.

Even in the evenings, he gave her no respite, constantly tap-tapping on the kitchen window until she succumbed and looked out to see his face pressed against the pane – tongue distorted, lips squashed, eyes staring. Afraid and desperate, Pansy would try to escape his taunts by running upstairs to hide, but he would lob tiny pebbles at the bedroom window, not hard enough to crack the glass but loud enough to remind her he was still there.

'I can't take any more,' she cried, as she stood shaking in Lucy's arms. 'He won't stop.'

'Goodness, Pansy, look at the state of you! Why didn't you tell me what was happening before now?'

'Because last time you said I was encouraging him. Now I'm not. I keep telling him to go away but he takes no notice.' There was real anguish on her face. 'You must do something,' she begged. 'Help me. I'm worn out. I've lost my energy. I feel tired but I can't sleep. I used to like working but now I hate going outside. I avoid people. I don't want to talk. I don't even look forward to Alice's visits. Please help me.'

Lucy waited until the sobbing stopped. 'You remember Miss Pugh, your Aunt who lives in Ilkley?'

Pansy nodded.

'Could you stay with her for a week or two?'

'Probably. But what about my job?'

'Say you are sick or taking a holiday. If they stop you, there are plenty of other houses to clean.

'What will Alice think if I'm not here?'

'I'll talk to Alice. She'll understand. And I'll get James to take you in the car.' Lucy paused. 'As for Stanley Crowther, I'll speak with the constable again.'

Pansy tried to smile.

'I just wish you'd told me sooner, before getting yourself into this terrible state.'

Miss Pugh opened the door apprehensively. She didn't recognize her niece, Pansy, the small slim woman with the suitcase in her hand, or remember James Oldfield who was standing behind her. Jogging the memory took a little time and explanation, but once the jumbled pieces were reassembled she was happy to invite Pansy to stay with her.

Stepping inside the big house, Pansy was both surprised and appalled by the state of the living-room and wondered about the condition of the rest of the three-storey house. Miss Pugh had always been an extremely particular person. Everything was always in its rightful position. Always spick and span. Neat and tidy. Nothing was ever out of place.

But today the living-room was a shambles. A blackened saucepan sat in the armchair by the fire. A pile of dirty clothes was sitting on the coal scuttle. A slice of bread left on top of the writing bureau was curled and dry, and a quarter-inch of dust coated the furniture.

Seeing the worry on Pansy's face, James felt concerned. His instinct was to leave immediately and take Pansy with him. He was afraid that living with the elderly spinster and taking on the responsibility of minding her would drain her even further, and she was not strong enough for that.

'I want to stay,' Pansy said. 'Aunty needs me. Besides, it will give me something worthwhile to do and I want to repay a little of the kindness she showed me when I was ill when Timmy was born.'

Reluctantly James conceded and by the time he was ready to leave, the two relatives were reminiscing happily. Noticing the soft smile, which had returned to Pansy's face, he felt satisfied. That expression had been absent for some time.

As he drove back to Horsforth, James decided Pansy would be fine living with Miss Pugh, just so long as Crowther didn't know where she was. He would never find her there, James thought.

Lucy held the chair steady, while James swung himself up through the hole in the bedroom ceiling and into the attic. The candle, she handed him, flickered from the lack of air in the roof cavity.

'Is there anything up there?' she called.

'Lots of cobwebs! My old jigsaws. Empty boxes. Tea chests.'

From below, she could hear him shifting things about.

'James, be careful.'

For a while there was no answer then his head poked down through the hole. 'Smells like we've got rats in one of these boxes. Can you manage to take it?'

As he lowered the tea chest, a shower of dust floated down and settled on Lucy's hair. She sneezed.

Peering in the box she could see where the rats had built their home. A felt tea-cosy lined with scraps of paper and cloth had made an ideal nest. In the centre, eight pink-skinned babies, no bigger than Lucy's thumb, squirmed like a collection of juicy caterpillars.

After transporting the chest to the back garden, James scattered the contents of the tea-cosy on the ground beside the back wall. Not having the heart to kill the babies himself, he was sure the crows that roosted in the chestnut tree would quickly make a meal of them.

With a small fire of dried leaves and twigs, James burned the nest and its lining. The felted cloth was damp and smoked before igniting, but the stained newspaper, which had been underneath it, burned brightly. As the newsprint curled, James noticed the bold header: *The Bombay Chronicle*, and beneath it in smaller letters, the words: *English language edition*.

Beneath the rat's nest was a stack of similar papers that James fed to the fire. But, on delving under those, he uncovered a cache of unusual items – a long leather glove, its stitches rotted along the seams. A tarnished spur. A crested pendant and a military jacket decorated with gold-braided epaulettes and metal buttons. The uniform had obviously fostered generations of moths. Lifting it out made him sneeze also.

The only item, apparently not affected by the years, was a black wooden box. It was the size of a gentleman's toilet case and was wrapped in a length of canvas. Uncovering it, James realized it was an item of value. It was old and the workmanship was exquisite. The smooth lid was inlaid with shards of mother of pearl depicting an elephant drinking at a waterhole. The box's hinges were metal, blackened, but definitely silver.

James shook it gently. It didn't rattle. As he raised the lid he expected to see a moulded velvet lining housing an assortment of gentleman's toiletries. But the ebony box contained neither partitions nor lining. It was crammed with letters and papers and pieces of folded parchment. Beneath the papers were other items – a ring box, a gold fob watch with chain, a wad of bank notes and two purses. Without opening it, James could feel that the purse made from animal skin contained coins. But the other purse interested him more. It was handmade in black silk with an exotic dancer embroidered on the front in brightly coloured threads. Inside was something hard. Between his fingers, it felt like gravel or small pebbles. Loosening the string, James tipped the contents into his palm.

'Mother!' he yelled.

Sitting across the table from Lucy, James rolled the stones over with his finger. They resembled tiny transparent marbles, glassy but chipped. The colour was a beautiful cornflower blue.

After examining the birth, death and marriage certificates, old school reports and personal letters, Lucy put them to one side. She was busy gazing at the other papers which had almost filled the box. The legal documents confused her. Title deeds. Leases. Stock certificates.

'It appears Edward's father had several holdings and Edward had shares in a sapphire mine in Kashmir.' Lucy looked at the stones on the table. 'Sapphires? Is that what they are?'

James shrugged his shoulders, amazed. 'Is there anything else?'

The coins in the purse included some sovereigns. The fob watch was in a gold case. The wad of banknotes consisted of old notes, both English and foreign. There were cufflinks, a tiepin and an elegant brooch set with a large red gemstone.

'A garnet?' suggested Lucy.

'Or a ruby! This lot could be worth a small fortune! What do we do with it?'

Lucy didn't think twice, 'We pay a visit to Proctor and Armitage and let them sort it out. These things obviously belonged to Edward or his father.'

'But why did he leave them in the attic?' asked James. 'Had he forgotten about them?'

'I wouldn't think so. I'm sure he intended to come back and collect them one day. He didn't expect to die so suddenly.'

'But he lived a very simple life.'

'That was his choice,' said Lucy.

'But if these are his, who do they belong to now?'

'The lawyers will know.'

'But didn't Edward leave the residue of his estate to you.'

Lucy nodded.

'Then they could all be yours!'

The contents of Pansy's letter came as a surprise.

Dear Lucy,

I am writing to let you know I have decided to stay in Ilkley indefinitely. My aunt needs someone to care for her. She is quite forgetful and prone to wandering. I found her on the road the other morning. She was wearing only her nightdress and slippers and it was bitterly cold. As I am her only relative, I feel it is my duty to care for her, but besides that, I like it here in Ilkley. It's peaceful and no one bothers me.

If it is not too much trouble, there are two favours I must ask.

Could James please bring me the rest of my belongings?

The other thing, I beg to ask – can Alice and her husband, Bertie, move into my cottage? Alice says they can afford to pay a small rent. She says they have looked at rooms elsewhere but they are disgusting, and with the baby due in only six weeks, Alice is getting desperate. She told me it would be impossible for them to continue living with Bertie's parents as it is causing too much strife between them.

I hope you will be able to help them out.
Your dear friend,
Pansy

After confirming her thoughts with James, Lucy sat down and wrote two letters. The first was addressed to Mrs Pansy Pugh. In it she told Pansy that she and James would deliver the rest of her personal possessions the following Saturday morning and advised her that they would arrive in Ilkley about eleven.

The second letter was addressed to Mrs and Mrs Albert Bottomley. Wording it carefully, Lucy asked Alice and Bert to visit her at the cottage to discuss a lease to be made out in their names. She suggested a rent of seven shillings and sixpence a week. If that was agreeable, they could move in immediately.

Chapter 18

The Cow and Calf

The sudden clucking of the hens alerted Alice. She knew it was Crowther or a fox, and as it was broad daylight, she settled on the former. Peeping through the lace curtain she saw the man leaning over the hen house. When he walked towards the door she drew back. The handle rattled. Then she heard him shout her mother's name.

'Pansy, Pansy,' he called, his voice was polite at first, but it soon rose in both pitch and urgency. Then the tapping began, first on the door, then on the window. From the room's shadows, Alice watched him as he pressed his face against the pane. Unable to see anyone inside, the man stepped back and looked up towards the bedroom. Picking up a handful of soil, he lobbed it against the window. It showered back into his hair. Alice could see his exasperation festering.

The squawk of the chickens drew Alice back to the window. One of the birds was hanging limply from the man's hand. She didn't see him break its neck but saw the ball of warm red feathers as it disappeared inside his jacket. When he climbed over the wall and headed for the lane, she ran through the house to the front room.

Though Alice had not seen Crowther for many years, she recognized him as the man who hawked rabbits, the man who had wheedled his way into her mother's life, the man Lucy had warned her about. No doubt he had come back looking for Pansy, unaware she had moved to Ilkley. Standing in the hall, Alice watched the brass knob as it turned. She'd locked the door just in time. Outside, Crowther cursed and rattled the knob. Then there was silence. Alice held her breath not knowing what to expect. The gate creaked on its hinges. Venturing into the front room, she watched as Crowther mounted his bicycle and rode off down the hill. Alice was trembling. She felt sure he would be back, but didn't know when.

'Let me explain,' the solicitor said. 'Firstly, we are not certain of the viability of these foreign title deeds. Though they appear authentic and indicate Mr Edward Carrington was the rightful owner, it is possible the properties have been disposed of and new deeds may have been drawn up if these originals were considered lost.' He paused. 'These matters will need investigating. Of course, if the rates and taxes were unpaid for many years, it is possible the properties were sold to offset any accrued debt, which would mean they are worthless.'

Mr Armitage continued, 'With regard to the various property leases, we must assume they all expired some years ago, unless we can find some record of the terms being renewed.' He turned to the next document in the file. 'Of course, with all these investments being located in India, the problem of tracing and verifying them is made doubly difficult.'

'The same applies to the stocks and bonds,' interrupted Proctor. 'I have to warn you, Mrs Oldfield, these documents may not be worth the paper they are written on.' He paused. 'On the other hand—'

'The gemstones,' said Mr Armitage. 'They could be worth a considerable amount because of their number and size. But I am not an expert and we should arrange to have these valued by a professional.'

Lucy nodded, 'Of course.'

'I have no doubt they belonged to Mr Edward Carrington and from the colour would assume they came from Kashmir. I doubt there will be a contest over proof of ownership.'

'Then there are the coins, notes and other curios—' the old gentleman added. 'It may take some time to finalize this matter. Return mail to the Indian sub-continent can take several weeks.'

'Should I notify Captain Wainwright, Edward's brother-in-law of this discovery?' Lucy asked.

'For what purpose?' asked the solicitor.

'Wouldn't he, or his late wife, be a beneficiary if this is part of Edward's estate?'

'Indeed Lydia Carrington-Wainwright was Edward's sister, but because she was married to the captain, Edward saw no reason to make provision for her. On the other hand, our client saw your situation as quite dire and therefore instructed us that the residue of his estate was to pass to you. It will just be a matter of time before we can ascertain the value of the box's contents but as soon as we hear anything, we will let you know.'

'Open the door, Pansy!' The muffled shout came through the letterbox. The tone was intimidating.

'Come on Pansy! Why won't you let me in? I just want a bit of company. Five minutes' chat. Come on, luv. It's dark and cold out here. Don't be mean.'

Getting no response Crowther wandered round to the back of the house and rattled on the kitchen door. It was locked also. A few moments later he began tapping. As expected, his repertoire had not changed. When the stones hit the bedroom window Bertie Bottomley was ready to move.

After shouting abuse at the silent house, Crowther walked back towards the lane where he had left his bicycle.

Slipping quietly out of the kitchen door, Bertie followed him. Hiding at the other side of the lane, James waited in the shadows.

When a light came on in the hallway, Stan Crowther grinned, swaggered up to the front door and waited until he heard the key turn in the lock.

'Now you are seeing sense at last,' he said when Alice let the door swing open. Taking one step forward, she pointed James's rifle at Stan Crowther's stomach.

His chin dropped.

'Get away from here and don't come back!' she yelled.

'Wait a minute, luv,' he said, laughing nervously. 'Put the gun down. I just came to say hello to your mam. We used to be good friends.'

'You have no friends, here!'

'Be fair,' he sneered, his eyes set on her enlarged belly. 'Are you on your own right now?'

Alice didn't answer.

'If you'd like a bit of company, your condition don't bother me.'

But before Alice had time to answer, Bert pounced, grabbing him by the shoulder and spinning him around. Then he landed his fist square on Crowther's chin sending him reeling into the rose bushes.

When he tried to get up, James joined in, swinging at him and landing a punch on his stomach. Crowther rolled over on the ground nursing his gut and groaning.

'Go inside, Alice!' James shouted, when blood started dripping from Crowther's lip.

Alice closed the door and listened. She heard more punches being thrown and then Crowther's whimpering cry.

'Come back again, if you want more of the same!' James challenged, as he watched the man stumble down the lane, bent almost double, his arms wrapped around his belly.

Standing beside the garden gate, James and Bert rubbed their knuckles and then shook hands.

'I think that'll be the last we shall see of him,' James said.

'Certainly hope so,' said Bert. 'Fancy a wee drop to celebrate?'

'Don't mind if I do.'

Alice opened the door. It was the first time she had invited James into her own home. It was a nice feeling.

Though it was broad daylight outside, little light filtered through into the Fothergill's farm shed. From the doorway, James could see Grace struggling to secure the wooden yoke around the cow's neck. He called out to her but his voice was drowned by loud bellowing. When the cow began to thrash about, he felt anxious.

'Be careful,' he shouted.

Grace glanced up at him, rubbed her hand along the animal's rump then stepped from the stall to greet him.

'Can I be of any help?' he asked.

'Yes,' she said, pushing her sleeves high above her elbows and carefully looping a piece of cord around her thumb. Gently she pushed her hand into the cow's rear end. At first the beast didn't move, but when she rolled her arm around, the bellowing grew louder. Closing her eyes, Grace bit her bottom lip and concentrated.

'Got it!' she announced, slowly withdrawing her arm and handing the ends of the cord to James. 'Now, when I tell you, pull slowly but firmly.'

Each time the cow strained, James pulled as instructed, while Grace provided encouragement to them both. Eventually, the calf's head emerged and, after running her fingers through its mouth, she eased it into the world, sliding it gently down onto the bed of hay. As if suddenly petrified, the cow was still and silent, but within minutes of Grace releasing its head from the yoke, it snorted, sniffed at its calf and started licking it.

James glanced at Grace as she wiped her bloodied hands on a piece of rag. She was obviously pleased.

'Would I ever make a farmer?' he asked.

She laughed but did not commit herself to an answer. 'Want a cup of tea? I made some scones this morning.'

'I'd like that but I have to drive to Ilkley.'

'Is anything wrong?'

'No,' he said. 'It was a piece I read in the paper that said a woman had been found wandering near the Cow and Calf Rocks. Mum was concerned it might be Miss Pugh, so I offered to go to Ilkley to make sure everything was all right. Would you like to come for the drive?'

'Of course,' she said, 'if we can just wait a few minutes.'

James agreed and standing side by side, they watched the calf for half an hour. It wobbled and fell over several times but eventually it struggled to its feet determined to take its first drink.

'I was talking to Mum the other day,' James said, trying to sound unconcerned. 'She said you were fed up with the farm and wanted to move to the city.'

Grace laughed. 'What would I do in the city? I love the farm and the animals. I've got no plans to leave.'

Looking across at her, James was unable to prevent a big smile curling on his lips. 'Good,' he said. 'Shall we go?'

Chapter 19

Bertie Bottomley

Six weeks after Rachel Bottomley was born, Alice invited a small group of friends and family to celebrate her daughter's christening. Lucy hosted the party in her cottage.

Unfortunately, Bert got very drunk. His voice was loud and his behaviour, at times, distasteful. Alice was relieved when Grace and James left to take John Fothergill home. The farmer excused himself saying he was anxious to get back to the farm to attend to the milking, but Alice knew he was just being polite.

Pansy never said a great deal to anyone, appearing content to sit beside the fireplace in one room or the other. Lucy tried to entice her outside to take a walk across the meadow or wander in the garden but she insisted she was quite happy indoors. Pansy never admitted that the sound of the tree branches tapping on the window made her feel nervous.

When it was time to leave on Sunday afternoon, she climbed into James's car and it was obvious she was pleased to be returning to Ilkley and her home with Miss Pugh.

Alice had enjoyed seeing her mother and cried a little when she left. She had wanted the visit to be special, had wanted to be able to talk to her mother, intimately, as one woman to another. She had been little more than a girl when she had left home to take up nursing, but now she was married with her own baby and she thought things would be different. She was disappointed she didn't have the opportunity to find out.

From the window, Alice saw James bending over to crank the car's engine. As the motor burst into life, a puff of smoke rose from the exhaust and drifted through the tangled branches of the briar rose. Alice watched as he slid along the front seat beside Grace, and leaned his head towards her and his lips touched her cheek. Their eyes smiled, and as the car rolled away, Grace's arm glided across James's shoulders.

Shaking her head, Alice wandered back into Lucy's living-room. *Why was I so stupid?* she thought to herself.

Lucy was knitting while Rachel slept in the pram. From its seat on the straight-backed chair, the doll's glass eyes appeared to be looking directly at Alice.

'Constance,' Alice said 'I had almost forgotten you.' Picking up the doll, she sat it on her knee and turned towards Lucy. 'Has she been sitting there all the time I've been away?'

Lucy nodded. 'She's part of the furniture. But she's yours to take whenever you want her.'

'May I keep her? For the baby,' Alice asked.

'Of course. I'm sure when Rachel's older she will love her as much as you did.' Resting her knitting on her lap, Lucy looked across at the doll perched on Alice's knee. 'I think it's about time I replaced that old nurse's uniform. It's old-fashioned, too long, and grubby. The haberdasher in Horsforth has some nice remnants. I'll buy some lace and make her a new dress. Modern –1920's style.'

'Aunt Lucy, you were like a mother to me when I was growing up, and here I am back again, twenty-five years old.'

Lucy retrieved the ball of wool which had rolled onto the floor. 'We don't get any younger, lass.'

'Tell me,' Alice asked. 'How did you manage with a baby? You were on your own, weren't you? Was it hard in your day?'

'Probably harder than today. Women who had a baby out of wedlock were thought of as being loose and treated with contempt. But I managed. I had good neighbours. And James seems no worse for it.' Lucy took off her glasses and rubbed her eyes. 'Why do you ask? Are you and Bert having problems?'

Alice sighed. 'Maybe it's just me or my imagination but Bert seems uninterested in me these days. He's working longer hours than before but he never brings home any more money. He says he deserves to keep the extra. That's fine, but he complains all the time that he hasn't enough and has to borrow.'

'And do you give him a few extra bob?'

'Sometimes. He knows exactly what I have in my savings. He even made me draw out money to buy his new motor bike. He said it was necessary to have one with a bigger engine because we live here now and it's further for him to travel. He said it was my fault I got pregnant and had to stop work.' She straightened the red cross on the doll's uniform and seated it back on the chair. 'I had a good wage compared with Bert's but now I can't work again until the baby grows up.'

'Does Bert know how much money you've got left?'

Alice nodded. 'I've seen him looking in my bank book. He said he wanted to buy a sidecar for the bike so he could take me and the baby out, but I spent the money on the pram and cot and told him I couldn't give him any more.' She looked at herself in the mirror. 'Since Rachel was born, I feel flat. It seems there's nothing left between us anymore. He never touches me. Never even kisses me.' She smiled sadly at the picture of herself on the mantelpiece. 'When I see James with Grace, I feel jealous. She's young, and pretty in a way, and they're always laughing and going out, driving or dancing or to a picture show. I wish I could do all those things.' She shook her head. 'How stupid I was! All I ever wanted was to be a nurse. I loved the job and I was good at it. But I made no time in my life for James. And when he wanted me, I never listened. And look where I am now.'

'Give Bert a chance, Alice. A man gets his nose pushed out of joint when a baby arrives. He'll come round. Just give him time.'

'But how long? There's talk about prices going up and men being put out of work. Bert's only a porter and to be quite honest he's not very popular at the hospital. I've even heard people say he's lucky to have a job because he's lazy. What happens to us if he loses his job? What will we do then?'

'You'll manage. Your mam and I managed in the Great War. And don't you worry about the rent if he's out of work.'

'But what about you, Aunt Lucy? How do you cope?'

'I'm fine. Edward left me a bit of money.' Lucy rolled the wool around the ball and pushed the needles through it. 'Come on,' she said cheerily. 'Let's go in the other room. I'd love to hear you play.'

Alice sat down at the piano and lifted the lid. Resting her hands on her knees she thought for a moment. Then, stretching her fingers, she touched the keys lightly and played Beethoven's, *Für Elise*.

'Bert Bottomley! You're drunk again!'

'Too right I'm drunk. And I've spent all my pay on booze. Every penny, there's none left. And no more where that came from either. No more money and no more work. It's all gone!'

'What are you talking about?' said Alice.

'I mean, Mrs Bottomley,' he drawled, 'I am out of work and from this week, unless you have a secret stash of money, we've got nothing.'

'Then you'll have to find another job.'

He laughed as he steadied himself against the sideboard. 'Me, find another job? Easier said than done. You should go down to Leeds and see the queues of men lined up for every job that's going.'

Alice resisted the temptation to ask what he had been doing going to the city. 'Why not try the farms? Maybe you can get some work locally.'

'What! After the hospital. I'm not stomping around in no stinking cow shit.'

'Bertie!'

'Oh, shut up, woman. I'm sick of listening to you. If you want some money, you go out to work.'

'I can't go back yet. I have to feed the baby. Maybe in three or four months, but not now.'

Albert Bottomley had always lacked patience. He sloped around for only two weeks, constantly complaining to Alice about his lot in life. During that time, however, he somehow found enough money to visit the village pub, staggering home drunk every night. Alice wasn't sure if he had money put aside, or if he was getting it from someone else. She didn't think he had resorted to stealing.

When he left there was no final argument or fight. Bert was demanding but never violent. One morning, after eating his breakfast, he said he was off. He put on his leather helmet, goggles and gloves, jumped on his motor bike, kicked it into life, and rode away. Alice never saw him again.

Later, someone told her he had gone to America, but Alice found that hard to believe. How could he have paid the passage? She thought she saw him once when she was on a tram in the city, but it went by too fast. For a while she felt sad. Sorry for herself. At times, lost and a little guilty. But after a while, once Rachel began to smile and coo, life took on a different aspect.

When Lucy agreed to mind the baby three days a week, Alice returned to work. Not at the hospital, but as a nurse in a private nursing home in Headingley. She didn't mind looking after the old gentlemen, but the young men, whose bodies had been broken in the Great War, were her favourites.

'The conservative value of your assets, taking into account the properties, and the sapphires, is around thirty thousand pounds.' The solicitor paused to allow Lucy to digest what he was saying. 'That is a considerable fortune, Mrs Oldfield.'

'Have you given any thought to what you would like to do with the foreign investment properties?' Mr Proctor asked.

Lucy shook her head. 'I cannot imagine what these houses are like. You say they were once quite fashionable. But they are so far away.'

'May I make a suggestion?'

'Please do.'

'You have no commitments that I am aware of?'

'That is correct.'

'And you have never travelled?'

Lucy looked at him quizzically. 'Correct.'

'If I may suggest, in my estimation a voyage to India on one of the modern liners, travelling first-class of course, would be a wonderful experience for you.' Mr Armitage peered over the rim of his glasses. 'If you decide to embark on such a journey, we would arrange for a representative to meet you in Bombay, someone to conduct you around your various holdings. After seeing them, you will be in a better position regarding your decision as to what to do with them.' He cleared his throat before continuing. 'If you will excuse me for being forthright, Mrs Oldfield, but it would be best to embark on this sort of venture before you are too old.'

'But I wouldn't dare to travel alone.'

'Then take your son. Or advertise for a companion. You must remember you are now in the very fortunate situation where money is no object.'

Lucy raised her eyebrows.

'Please give it some thought. From our point of view, if you decide to sell the properties, it would be easier for the business to be conducted in India while you are there. That will facilitate a saving in both time and money. Of course, Mr Proctor and I will attend to all your travel arrangements.' He paused. 'May I suggest winter would be a good time? I gather India gets rather hot in the summer!'

Chapter 20

Captain Wainwright

The first snow of winter had arrived very early causing the temperature to drop to freezing. Blizzards blowing over the Pennines blocked the roads and brought the towns to a halt. On the country lanes, drifting snow was banked to the height of a horse's withers. Lakes became skating rinks, hillsides – slopes for children's sledges. Water pipes froze solid, shops sold out of candles and folk with no stores in the pantry went hungry. For the poor souls without coal or firewood, the only chance to keep warm was to take to their beds. For the farmers, the job of keeping animals fed and watered was near impossible.

Despite his mother's pleas not to venture out, James was concerned about Grace and her father and decided he must go to the farm. Once he stepped outside, the soft snow swallowed his boots. It was deeper than he had thought. Every step he took was an effort. When he eventually rounded the last turn in the lane and saw a wisp of smoke puff from one of the farm's tall chimney-pots, he felt some relief. He was looking forward to spending the afternoon with Grace, then returning home in time for tea.

But when he arrived at the farm, James was surprised to find the fire almost dead and the house empty. Outside, a path had been dug in the snow. It led from the house door and headed towards the cow shed but it stopped half-way. Picking up the shovel, James dug the remainder of the distance. Expecting to find Grace and her father busy inside, he called out.

Two cows turned their heads and looked lazily at him from the stalls. James shouted again. No reply. Swishing their tails, the animals blew steam from their nostrils and returned, unconcerned, to their feed of hay.

Checking outside James found a trail leading away from the barn. The two sets of footprints indicated that Grace and her father had headed towards the far meadow, but there were no tracks to show they had returned.

The far field, which completely crowned the hill, was the largest of Mr Fothergill's paddocks. Every summer it was ablaze with waving wheat and when the sun dropped behind it, it gleamed as if draped in a cloth of gold. Now buried beneath its winter mantle, the field, fences and clustered trees, formed the picture of a perfect Christmas card; vestal white, pure, untouched.

But the wind was biting cold and fine slivers of ice stung James's face like red-hot needles. Screwing his eyes against the sleet, he turned up his collar. 'Grace!' he yelled, following the deep footprints that led towards a wooden stile. Seeing the snow knocked from the slats, he knew the pair had crossed.

'Mr Fothergill!' he yelled. 'Are you out there?'

'Over here!' The voice was faint. It was Grace.

James lumbered awkwardly through the drifts in the direction of the call but could see nothing but snow. 'Where are you?' he shouted.

In the corner of the field, sheltered only by the bare branches of a line of tall poplars, was a group of black and white cows. Completely saddled in snow, they were huddled against the fence line. Not far from the cattle, an arm poked up from the snow and waved. Grace had burrowed a small alcove and was sitting in the snow with her father's head resting on her lap.

'Thank goodness you're here,' she said, as he dropped down beside her. 'I only found him a short while ago. He was worried about the cattle because they'd been here two days with nothing to eat. He said he tried to move them but they got confused and when he fell one trampled his leg. I think it's broken.' She looked up at James. 'I can't move him but we've got to get him out of here otherwise he's going to freeze.'

It took more than an hour to get the farmer back to the house. James supported him all the way, but with the extra weight, his feet sank deep in the drifts, making every step extremely difficult. For Mr Fothergill every jolting step was agony. Unable to do anything to help, Grace went on ahead to build up the fire and warm some water. By the time James reached the farmhouse, he was exhausted.

'We can't get him to the doctor while the weather is like this,' he said. 'And I'd never make it to Horsforth before dark.'

Grace looked to him for an answer. 'What do we do, James?'

'We wait until morning then I'll go down to the village at dawn and get the doctor to come here.' Though he didn't want to leave the farm and didn't want to step back out into the cold, he had promised his mother he would be home. If he didn't return, he knew she would worry. 'Will you be all right if I leave you tonight?'

Thawing out slowly in the warmth of the log fire, Mr Fothergill was apologetic for the trouble he was causing. He had no alternative but to accept James's suggestion and was adamant he would survive until morning.

Wrapping his arms around Grace to say good night, James could feel her body warm against his. 'Take care of your dad,' he said, as he kissed her gently. 'I will see you tomorrow.'

As the time of their departure for India drew closer, James was less and less sure he was doing the right thing, but the arrangements had been made and he knew his mother was not confident to travel without him.

His main concern was Grace. He wondered how she could possibly manage the farm on her own while her father was incapacitated, but when she told him that her father had hired a local man to help out in the dairy until his leg was healed, James felt a little relieved. To a lesser extent, he was also concerned about Alice and baby Rachel being left alone, because Alice was used to being independent. He wondered if she would visit Grace and her father while they were away, but doubted it.

On the morning of their departure, Grace arrived very early, pleased to be able to drive James and Lucy to the station. The morning air was heavy with mist. It was damp but there had been no frost. All the snow of the recent blizzards was gone. They all hoped the worst of winter was over.

Leeds Station was cold and dismal. It was filled with the familiar railway sounds and smells. When she saw the train waiting at the platform, Lucy became anxious. Doors were being slammed and steam was hissing from the engine. After ensuring they had the correct seats, James checked their trunks in the luggage van and after settling the smaller cases on the overhead rack in the compartment, he stepped down to the platform.

There was a host of things he wanted to say to Grace before they left. She must call the doctor if her father's leg didn't improve. She must check on Alice and the baby, if she had time, and make sure the new calf was feeding. Whenever she went to town, she should check the water in the car's radiator and drive carefully. In turn, he told her he would send a card from every port of call on the way, and also from India. He knew, above all, he would miss her, and told her so.

Before Grace had chance to respond, the shrill sound of the guard's whistle echoed along the platform. James closed the door just as the train pulled away, and, as he leaned from the carriage window, he could see tears in Grace's eyes.

'I'll bring you back an Indian elephant,' he shouted. Then a cloud of smoke engulfed her and she disappeared.

The SS *Oceanus* was not due to sail from Southampton until the following Tuesday. This gave Lucy and James time to pay a visit to Edward's brother-in-law in Tunbridge Wells. Despite Captain Wainwright extending an invitation for them to stay with him, they preferred to be independent and booked two rooms at the Grand Palace Hotel. Although Lucy and James had both corresponded with the captain before their journey, neither had ever met him and both were uncertain what to expect. Lucy had presumed Wainwright was older than Edward Carrington – probably around seventy years of age – but that was purely an assumption. She had not known how old Edward's sister, Lydia had been when she died.

The Bower, Wainwright's house in Tunbridge Wells, was a substantial two-storey detached Victorian residence with characteristic tall chimney stacks. The gardens at the front were neat and well-tended and, like every other house in the street, boasted a variety of bare rose bushes. The house's stone walls, once clean and white, now bore the grey shades of advancing age. The tall front door was recessed between two Doric columns, its coloured leadlight glass adorned an otherwise austere façade.

James pulled on the brass bell.

The housekeeper, who introduced herself as Mrs Mac, took their coats and led them into the conservatory where Captain Wainwright was reading.

It was a delightful room, obviously a recent addition to the house, surrounded on three sides by glass walls which reached from floor to ceiling. The conservatory overlooked a lawn where veined leaves and stilled sycamore seeds littered the damp grass. Around the garden an old creeper grew rampant over the eight-foot fence. In the centre of the neatly trimmed lawn was an imitation wishing well, custom built in wrought iron and, tied to the top-most swirl of metal was half a coconut. A family of blue tits was pecking at it hungrily.

Inside the conservatory, the soft furnishings glowed with the warm shades of autumn. Such a different feel to the chill of the north they had left behind. The high-back cane chairs were elaborately decorated with twisted swirls and rosettes and obviously were imported from abroad. A large rug, that reflected the dull sheen of Indian silk, covered the slate floor.

Sitting on the small table, beside Wainwright's chair was a pile of journals and a magnifying glass. The captain had a shawl over his knees, as would an invalid, but he quickly removed it when Lucy and James approached and rose to his feet. He was not as old as Lucy had expected, probably several years younger than Edward. He was also taller than she had imagined, and his back was as straight as a book's spine.

After James had introduced himself and his mother, the housekeeper offered them tea.

Lucy felt a little overawed at first, mainly because of Wainwright's colonial accent and behaviour. He was every inch an English officer and gentleman and obviously a man of means. Some of his mannerisms reminded her of Edward Carrington, but Edward had never displayed the nuances which she associated with money, authority or the affectation of upper class breeding. She soon realized, however, that Captain Wainwright was not trying to create an impression, he was merely being himself.

'Can I get you anything else?' the housekeeper asked.

'Thank you, Mrs Mac,' the captain said. 'I am sure we will manage.'

He waited until his guests were settled before sitting down. 'Now,' he said. 'I am looking forward to hearing more about this trip. I do envy you. The passage is one I would love to repeat. The ports of call: Gibraltar, Port Said, Suez. Fascinating places.'

Lucy relaxed as they spoke of the voyage, and as Wainwright spoke affectionately of his brother-in-law.

'My brother-in-law, Edward was an astute man, honest and loyal. He had intellect, integrity and selflessness and would have made a fine officer. That he did not enter the service was a great disappointment to his father, Colonel Carrington. The colonel could not understand why his son refused to pursue a career in the army. Of course,' Wainwright said, not meaning to sound boastful, 'I was completely accepted into the family. "An appropriate choice for my daughter," I once heard the old colonel say.' He turned to James. 'And you, young man, I understand, served your country proud in France.' He lifted his tea cup. 'I salute you, sir.'

James acknowledged the gesture.

'But to other matters. I have taken the liberty of writing to one of my old colleagues in Bombay advising him and his wife of your intended journey. They live in the town of Nashik, one hundred miles from the coast. Nashik is a cool and pleasant place situated in the hills. You must contact them when you arrive and if time permits, I recommend a visit. You will not only enjoy their company but a visit to them will allow you to see something of the Indian countryside.

Lucy thanked him and promised she would get in touch with them.

Wainwright was exuberant when talking about the country he had lived in for most of his life. He responded eagerly to all James's questions, offering advice on modes of transport, dealing with natives, making purchases, even dress code. He supplied a list of places they should visit and areas to be avoided. He advised James about tipping, about baggage in transit, even how to combat heat, scorpions, crowds and beggars.

By the time the captain had finished speaking, Lucy was a little apprehensive and confused, not sure whether she should forgo the whole venture and request the firm of Proctor and Armitage to settle her affairs by post.

'It is a wonderful country,' Captain Wainwright said, gazing at the glass window as if staring into a crystal ball. 'You will find yourself treated like royalty. It is a shame that apart from my club, the same standards are not maintained here in England. Which reminds me,' he said, taking a card from his waistcoat and passing it to James. 'Introduce yourself to this gentleman and mention my name. If there is anything that requires a little extra persuasion while you are in Bombay, Colonel Winters is the man to see.'

James thanked him. 'I hope that won't be necessary.'

The captain nodded and with a flamboyant flick of his moustache added, 'You are sailing on Tuesday evening, I believe.'

'That is so.'

'Then you must allow me to indulge myself. I intend to hire a car and driver to convey you to the docks and I will accompany you there. When you board, you will invite me to join you as your guest, so I can savour, albeit for only a few hours, the opportunity of stepping inside one of the latest luxury steamers.' He held up his hand to continue. 'And if you will permit, I will order a bottle of the ship's best champagne to drink a toast to your safe journey.'

James and Lucy returned to The Bower the following day to have lunch with Captain Wainwright and to invite him to join them for dinner at the hotel where they were staying.

That evening, Lucy again enjoyed the captain's company, listening intently as he reminisced about his early life in India, about his late wife, Lydia, and about her brother, Edward Carrington. Though he related his adventures in a matter-of-fact manner, Lucy was overawed by his experiences.

James appeared totally relaxed in the captain's company and Lucy was proud of him. Any lack of breeding James suffered was compensated by his personality. Her son exuded charm and wit, traits he had learned from Edward. He dressed and carried himself well, and although lacking in tertiary education, he was well read in both the classics and popular Press and could carry on a conversation on many subjects. His only downfall, Lucy considered, was his accent. Like hers it was not entirely broad Yorkshire, but it was a far cry from that of a cultured English gentleman like Captain Sebastopol Wainwright.

When they waved farewell to Wainwright from the ship's rail, Lucy could see the envy etched in his expression. In a way she wished they had invited him to travel to India with them, but she had business to attend to and was not sure when they would be returning. As the tugs eased the ship from the wharf and the coloured streamers floated down to the oily harbour water, Lucy wondered if she would miss England, and if India would prove as intriguing as the captain had promised.

The SS *Oceanus* was everything Lucy could have dreamed of and more. For the first few days of the voyage she was apprehensive, not used to being treated as if she were an aristocrat.

The service on the ship was impeccable. The ship's décor – sumptuous. The lavish ballroom with its sweeping staircase and chandeliers conjured images from a fairy-tale. The elegant dining room with its highly-polished silverware brought back memories of her days as a maid at Heaton Hall, and when dinner was served, she smiled at the waiter when he lifted the silver cloche. It reminded her of the hundreds of second-hand cloches she had polished for old Mr Camrass, but this was the first time she had eaten from a plate which had been covered by one.

Afternoon tea was also a splendid affair with over twenty different varieties of leaves to choose from. It was served in the finest china cups, with cucumber sandwiches and iced fancies presented on silver platters.

'I don't know why you are nervous,' James said. 'You are as elegant as the rest of the ladies here. And,' he added, admiring the blood-red brooch decorating the lace yoke on her frock, 'you are probably worth more money too!'

She smiled. It was hard to believe.

With the fox-fur draped around her shoulders, Lucy took James's arm as they stepped out onto the first-class promenade deck. The sea was calm. The port side sheltered from the breeze. From the bow they could see the promontory of Gibraltar looming in the distance and the lights of the town reflecting like pin-pricks on the water.

A well-dressed elderly gentleman was leaning against the forward rail gazing towards the land. He was alone.

'Good evening,' James said politely, as they approached.

The man turned. 'Beautiful evening isn't it.'

'It certainly is.'

Both men reached out their hands simultaneously.

'Farnley,' the man said. 'Archibald Farnley.'

Lucy swayed backwards. James steadied her.

'James Oldfield,' he said. 'And may I introduce my mother? Mrs Lucy Oldfield.'

'I am pleased to meet you, madam. Are you travelling through to Bombay?'

Lucy nodded, too taken aback to say more.

'And planning to stay long in India.'

James answered. 'Perhaps a few months. My mother has business dealings to transact.'

The gentleman turned to Lucy, 'Would you excuse me for asking what may appear to be a strange question?'

Lucy nodded nervously wondering if the man had remembered the girl who had once worked in his household as a maid.

'When we were boarding, I thought I recognised someone with you that I used to know.'

Lucy felt a flush of heat colouring her face.

'An old friend of mine. I saw him at the gangway and I have been looking for him, unsuccessfully, ever since. After checking with the purser it appears he is not on the passenger manifest. I am a little puzzled.'

Lucy sighed as she relaxed a little. 'Would you be referring to Captain Wainwright?'

'Yes, that's the man. Sebastopol Wainwright. Polly Wainwright, we used to call him. Captain, eh? Would you happen to know his cabin number?'

'I'm sorry,' Lucy said. 'Captain Wainwright is not on board. He accompanied us to the docks and took afternoon tea with us in the cabin before we sailed.'

Archibald Farnley was obviously disappointed. 'Darn shame. Not seen him in forty years. We were gentlemen cadets together at the Royal Military Academy. Of course he was born to the service as you are probably aware. Unlike me. I soon discovered I was not cut out for the life.' He thought for a moment then added, 'I remember he married the colonel's daughter, Miss Lydia Carrington.'

'That is correct, but I'm afraid Lydia passed away recently.'

'I'm sorry to hear that. She was a fine girl however I am pleased to learn they had many years together. I envy him.'

'And you, sir,' James said. 'May I ask the purpose of your journey?'

'Purely a pleasure cruise,' he said. 'Escape the worst of the English winter. Enjoy the sea air. I will be disembarking at Port Said. Visiting the Pyramids. I am indulging myself for a short while. My son and his family are accompanying me.' He turned to Lucy. 'I have a granddaughter, her name is Felicity. She is two years old and has the face of an angel.'

Lucy smiled.

'You must excuse the ramblings of a doting old man. My daughter-in-law admonishes me every time I use that expression, but believe me, when you see her you will agree. Perhaps you will allow me to introduce her to you tomorrow.'

Lord Farnley smiled. It was the same smile Lucy remembered from Heaton Hall, though the sadness he had carried in his eyes then was now replaced with pride and joy. He was a little plumper than she remembered, and he stooped slightly. His hair had thinned considerably and his upper lip was clean shaven.

She must have changed too, possibly more then she realized. Certainly her wardrobe was now elegant and fashionable, a far cry from the serge dress and frilled pinafore she wore at the Hall. Now, her once dark hair, was seasoned with shades of salt and pepper. Her skin remained healthy, her colour good, but her mouth and eyes were etched with an assortment of lines.

Accepting his invitation, Lucy was careful not to address his lordship by his formal title. She looked forward to meeting his family, especially his son – one of the two boys, who had been sent away when Miss Beatrice became ill. She also wanted to meet the son's wife and the little girl with the face of an angel.

Lucy and James remained on deck, while the ship completed its passage through the Gibraltar Strait. When it entered the Mediterranean, Lucy gazed at the expanse of sea and marvelled at the waves each edged with a sliver of moonlight. From that moment, any reservations she had held about the voyage disappeared.

If only Edward was with her to share the experience. If only she had gone with him to India when he had invited her all those years ago.

Chapter 21

Trouble

Lucy was sorry when Lord Farnley and his family left the ship at Port Said. She had enjoyed their company, particularly that of Felicity, his lordship's granddaughter. With a mop of white blonde curls and pink cherub lips Lucy could hardly disagree with Lord Farnley's affectionate description of her.

James was also going to miss them. He and Freddie Farnley had shared a common interest in motor cars and birds. They often chatted together on deck or in the cigar room, taking the opportunity to escape from the ladies. It was during one of their conversations that James discovered that the family now lived in a modest mansion on the cliff-top near Bexhill-on-Sea, a distance of only twenty miles or so from Tunbridge Wells. As he told his mother later, he felt confident Lord Farnley would be paying Captain Wainwright a visit when he returned to England.

Before the ship sailed from Port Said, Lucy handed the purser three letters for posting, the first addressed to Captain S. Wainwright, the second to Mrs Alice Bottomley at Honeysuckle Cottages, and the third, a letter from James to Miss Grace Fothergill.

Only one week after Lucy and James left for India, Stanley Crowther started making a nuisance of himself again. The first time Alice saw him, she was pushing the pram to the village. Not immediately realizing who he was, she smiled when he tipped his cap and wished her good morning. That was a mistake. She noticed him twice more that day: outside the green-grocer's shop, and at the post office. She wondered if it was just coincidence but when she saw him trailing behind her as she walked home up the hill, she knew that wasn't the case.

After unlocking the door and pushing the pram safely inside, she confronted him. Standing in the lane, arms folded across her chest, she waited until he was within in a few yards of her before she spoke. 'Are you following me?' she demanded.

His mouth dropped open. 'Who me?'

'Yes, you! I know what you're like, but you'll not bother me the way you did my mother. You can sling your hook, Stanley Crowther!'

'Now, that's not a very nice thing to say, is it?'

'Well if you don't go I'll get the police on to you.'

'Whatever for? I am just taking a stroll up a country lane.'

'You're a liar and a con-man and I'm not joking.'

'And what do you think the police are going to do?' He laughed. 'I'll tell them I was out walking when all of sudden you come out from the house, large as life and started shouting abuse at me. Not very lady-like, do you think?'

Alice knew if she argued till doomsday she could not win. Exasperated, she shook her head, turned her back on him and walked into the house. Once inside she slammed the door as hard as she could. The sudden bang startled the baby. Lifting Rachel from the pram, she heard Crowther calling.

'I'll be back tomorrow. You might be in a better mood then!'

The following morning Alice tried to ignore his plaintive cries but they went on and on. When at last she thought he had gone and it was safe to go outside, she wandered into the garden. Intending to scare her, he popped up from behind the wall.

'You're mad!' she shouted. 'Don't you ever give up?'

'Free country! No law says I can't sit out here and watch the birds.'

At first, though his constant visits were annoying, Alice tried to be philosophical. She told herself he was quite harmless. His actions were those of a child – immature and attention-seeking. She thought it a shame he had nothing better to do with his life, and a shame the spell he spent in the army had taught him nothing.

But it was not long before his nocturnal visits started affecting her. Apart from being cold and lonely, the nights were long, and darkness fell early – too early for Alice to go to bed and impossible to sleep with all his taunts and noises. Darkness also brought with it increased abuse. Drunken abuse. Foul language. And threats that would grow to a crescendo culminating in a shower of rocks thrown against the front door, or the clatter of the milk churn kicked around the garden.

Unfortunately, when he had disappeared and the taunts finally subsided, the slightest sound unsettled Alice. Her imagination began to play unkind tricks. The branches moving outside the window became hands, night clouds – faces, the chicken's squawk – a scream, shadows from the fire – ghostly figures creeping around the walls.

Alice knew from what she had been told that Crowther's actions were a repeat performance of the treatment he had given her mother, and every morning she told herself she was being stupid for allowing herself to be affected. But she also knew her defences were being worn down – and Crowther probably sensed it too. How much longer could she hang on? Not much, she thought. Certainly not until Lucy and James got back.

'Take your foot out of the damn door!' Alice screamed.

'Don't be like that. Let me in. I only want a cuppa and a chat.'

'I said get out! Go away! I don't want you here!'

'Strikes me you must be lonely, left all alone!'

Alice wasn't going to let go of the door until it was shut and the bolt shot. She was angry with herself for opening it. Crowther had been cunning and had fooled her. This time he had approached the cottage silently, knocked quietly, like a child, making her think it was someone else. 'Damn you!' she cried.

He laughed and pushed his knee between the door and jamb breaking her grip on the handle. The door banged against the wall.

'It does open after all!' he sneered.

'Get out of my house! You bastard.'

'Such words in front of the baby. Tut-tut!' He put his forefinger to his lips. 'Shh!'

Alice had had enough. After swinging at him with both fists, her knee came up hard and hit him hard in the crotch.

He dropped towards her, his weight pressing on her shoulders. 'You bitch,' he breathed.

'Get out!' she screamed, fighting to free herself and lift her knee again. But this time she couldn't reach.

'Bitch!' he yelled grabbing her neck with one hand and throwing a punch with the other. She could feel the moisture running down her cheek. It was not tears.

'Get out!' she cried, her voice weak and trembling.

As Crowther let her go, she slid down the wall to the floor. She had no energy left.

'Bloody bitch!' he said. 'I'll get you!'

Bombay was a bustling city, far busier than Lucy could ever have imagined. The dusty thoroughfares were crammed with all manner of people and vehicles, all competing in a cacophony of curses, cries and car horns.

The hotel, which the firm of solicitors had booked for Lucy and her son, was just the opposite. It was spotlessly clean, spacious and the atmosphere was relaxing. The only sounds in the reception area were the echo of footsteps across the marble floor and the gentle murmur of quiet conversations.

The letter, handed to Lucy on a silver tray, bore an English stamp. She was thrilled to receive it. In the envelope were two sheets of lightly perfumed writing paper. After reading both pages slowly, she turned back to the first page and started again.

'Did Alice tell you she was planning to go back to nursing while we were away?' she asked.

James shook his head, as he scooped the skin from the top of his coffee.

'She says she is staying with her mother in Ilkley and intends to go back to full-time work at the hospital and to live-in at the nurses' quarters.' Lucy raised her eyebrows. 'It appears Rachel will be living with Pansy and Miss Pugh on a permanent basis.' Lucy looked at James. 'How strange!'

'Did she give a reason?'

'No. Apart from the fact she says she enjoys working.' Lucy finished the letter and handed it to James.

After reading it he frowned. 'She says she's asked Mr Fothergill and Grace to keep an eye on the cottages and feed the animals while we are away. That's odd too, and it means Grace will be kept busy because Mr Fothergill won't be going far on that bad leg of his.' Folding the letter, he handed it back to his mother. Gazing up at the fan rotating slowly above his head, he watched it for a while as it wobbled in its housing. 'What would you say if I returned to England? Would you be all right on your own?'

'Do you think it necessary?'

'Yes,' said James. 'I do.'

The following morning the pair took a taxi to the Bombay shipping offices where James secured a berth on a cargo vessel sailing for London the following week. At the post office, Lucy sent a telegram to Wainwright's friends in Nashik accepting their offer of hospitality.

Three days later, a chauffeur-driven car collected her from the hotel for the drive to Nashik. The journey was long, exhausting and intolerably bumpy and it took most of the day. But, as Wainwright had promised, the cool mountain air was a welcome change from the city. It was also sweetly perfumed with masses of flowers that bloomed in profusion on every hillside. Lucy thought the area delightful and accepted an invitation to stay with the elderly couple for two or three weeks. She hoped when she returned to Bombay, there would be news about the properties that she had offered for sale.

Beneath a yellowed canopy of mosquito netting and with the smell of Indian spices wafting in his nose, James lay naked on the hotel bed, counting the hours until his sailing day. He thought mostly about Grace and about seeing her again. He wondered about Mr Fothergill and the farm and hoped the weather in Yorkshire had improved. He thought about Alice and wondered why she had suddenly decided to leave the cottage and return to work. He wondered if it had anything to do with his growing attraction for Grace Fothergill. No doubt he would find out when he got home.

Six weeks later, James stood in the front room of his cottage staring at the empty shelves in his glass cabinet. All Edward's fine ornaments had gone. The marks in the dust were the only clue as to what had been there. 'Tell me what happened,' he said quietly.

Grace sniffed and wiped her face. 'When I came down to feed the chickens one morning, I noticed the door to Alice's cottage was wide open. I thought maybe she'd come back to get some things, but when

I went in, I found the place in a mess. Pots and pans were scattered on the floor, the cupboard doors were hanging off, every one of the dresser drawers was smashed and the curtains ripped from the rails. I drove straight to the police station and got the constable. We went through the two other cottages together and they were in a similar state though not quite as bad. I couldn't tell the policeman what was missing but I knew you had lots of lovely things and they were all gone. I'm sorry,' she said. 'Dad and I stayed here a couple of nights but after that we had to go back to the farm. Dad said whoever did it got what he wanted and probably wouldn't come back.' She shook her head. 'I'm sorry, James.'

'It's not your fault,' he said. 'I wish Alice had been here then this might never have happened.'

James looked at the list he had made of the items missing from the three cottages but it was not comprehensive. There were probably many more things than he could remember. He was angry with himself. He should have shown more interest in Edward's possessions, but trinkets and ornaments had never been important to him.

Constable Merrifield was sympathetic but could offer little hope the items would be recovered. 'Quite a haul!' he said. 'What surprised me,' he added, 'there was no sign of a forced entry. Looks like the burglar had a key. You don't think it could be anyone you know do you?'

James shook his head.

'Hopefully some of the items will turn up. From what you say, whoever took them knew they were worth a few quid otherwise they'd have been smashed.'

'Is there anything I can do to get them back?' James asked.

'I suggest you scout round the markets. And take a look in the antique shops. You never know, you might strike it lucky.'

Chapter 22

Decisions

'Pull up a chair, lad,' Mr. Fothergill said. 'Try some soup. It's not bad.'

James smiled at Grace. It smelled good.

'You said once you were looking at getting a few acres,' the farmer said. 'Putting a few cows on it. Were you serious?'

'Yes, I was.'

'But your mother said you were going to go to college, become a doctor, or teacher, or some such thing.'

James sighed. 'I thought so too a few years ago and I think Mum still has her hopes. She says I've been wasting my time since I got left the money. Maybe she's right.'

'Well I don't want to know your business, but if you're interested in doing a bit of farming, I've been thinking of putting part of the farm up for sale.'

Grace pushed the stool towards her father and lifted his foot onto it.

'I ain't getting any younger and this damn leg don't work so good since I took that tumble in the snow. Me and the missus hoped the boys would take over when we were too old, but the war put paid to that. So now it's just me and Grace.'

Looking straight at his daughter, the farmer spoke as though she was not in the room. 'She's a good lass but she's been wearing herself out lately minding me and the dairy. I can sit all right and do the milking but she's got to fetch the beasts in and fill the racks with hay. Then there's the horses, the cart, delivering the milk, and the churns to clean. When I asked her about ploughing the paddocks for this year's crop, she was ready to take off. Get a job in the city.'

'I was tired, Dad. That was all. You know I wouldn't leave you.'

'Aye, I know you wouldn't, lass,' he said, turning to James. 'But I got to be honest with myself. It can't go on like this forever.

Different if she was a farmer's wife, but she ain't and it's no life for a girl on her own.' He noticed the look exchanged between Grace and James. 'Now,' he said. 'Don't get me wrong, I'm not suggesting you two get married, but I do have a proposition.'

'Let's hear it,' James said.

'The farm's getting run down because the pair of us is trying to do everything by hand. Now you're pretty good with mechanical stuff, you've even got Grace haring around the countryside like she's some racing driver.'

'Dad!'

'You buy some land off me, lad, and with the money, I'll rebuild the dairy, install some mechanical machines for milking and I'll buy a truck for delivering the cream. Aye, and a tractor, if funds will run to it. What do you think?'

'I like the sound of it but I'll have to give it a bit of thought.'

The farmer beckoned his daughter. 'Come here, lass.'

Grace walked over to her father and rested her hand on his shoulder. Sliding his arm around her waist he looked into her face. 'Me and Grace can make the place run, but we're fighting an uphill battle and not winning. But,' he said, 'with a bit of careful planning, we can make this farm into a good paying concern. I've done me sums. We can run more livestock. Buy a new bull to improve the line. Increase the volume of milk. And our Grace is pretty good at making cheeses, if she's given the time. Think about it serious, lad. But,' he said, as he leaned across the table to James, 'if you decide to do it, you've got to remember this – farming's not for a week or two, or even a season or two, it's for life. But if you give it a go and we work it right, we can both make a decent living. It's up to you.'

'Colonel Winters?'

'Welcome, Mrs Oldfield. I am very pleased to meet you.' The colonel's accent was English southern counties, the sincerity of his greeting, Yorkshire West Riding. He was smartly dressed in a dark pin-striped suit that would have been more appropriate in Bradford than Bombay. He was at least seventy-five years of age, wore gold-rimmed spectacles and carried a walking cane with an ivory handle. Taking Lucy's arm, the retired colonel escorted her up the stone steps into a rather austere sitting-room. Though the entrance to the building had been light and airy, this room was heavy with mahogany and the worn leather bindings of innumerable books. Having invited her to sit down, he settled himself on the settee opposite. A marble-topped coffee table separated them. After barely raising his hand more than a few inches, a waiter appeared and bowed.

'Lemonade for the lady and the usual for me.'

As they waited for the drinks to arrive, Lucy looked around. The fronds of a tall palm tree growing from a huge earthenware pot curled over at the ceiling. Beside the ornamental fireplace were two stools made from the feet of an elephant, the steel-grey skin was coarse and wrinkled, the enormous toenails – highly polished. Above the mantelpiece, a pair of tusks hung like crossed swords. Lucy wondered if they were from the same animal.

'I did not know ladies were allowed into gentlemen's clubs,' she said.

The colonel smiled. 'We maintain our inner sanctum but we like to provide an area for members' guests, most particularly the ladies.' He leaned forward slightly and lowered his voice. 'If truth be told, most of the members would give their right arm to be accompanied by a lovely lady like yourself, though if you asked them outright they would probably argue they are quite content without the company of the fairer sex.'

Lucy sipped her lemonade. It was freshly squeezed and cool.

'But tell me. How is Captain Wainwright? Haven't seen the blackguard in fifteen or twenty years. And that lovely wife of his, Lydia. I heard she was not well.'

'I'm sorry to say that Lydia passed away after a long illness. But Captain Wainwright is very well and sends his regards.'

'Must look him up when I am in England. Must go back to the old Dart sometime. It believe it has changed since 1910.'

Lucy smiled politely.

Colonel Winters clicked his fingers again. This time the servant appeared with a box of cigars. Before selecting one, Colonel Winters turned to Lucy. 'Do you mind if I smoke?'

'Please, go ahead.'

A swarthy hand held the flame steady, while the colonel sucked on his cigar. The blue smoke had the distinctive smell of first-class railway compartments, P&O smoking-rooms and gentlemen's clubs.

'Now,' he said, shuffling in his seat. 'You said when you phoned you had a problem.'

Feeling a little embarrassed, Lucy returned her glass to the table, sat upright and broached the subject. 'I don't know if you can help me, Colonel, but you are the only person I can turn to.'

The gentleman relaxed into the leather chair and listened as Lucy explained her problem which related to the sale of a large Victorian house left to her by Edward Carrington.

'Ah, dear Edward. We were all sorry to learn of his death.'

Lucy smiled and continued. 'The rates and taxes have been paid each year, but the place has been left for a long time without a regular tenant. Unfortunately, the so-called resident staff either died or absconded and the property has been completely overrun by squatters.'

The colonel shook his head sympathetically.

Lucy explained that when the agent had showed her the building she had estimated over 200 people were living in it. 'They have taken over every room, upstairs and downstairs, the attic, the bathroom, the pantries, even the closets. The toilets aren't working; there's no running water; the place is filthy and it's infested with rats and cockroaches. I'm afraid the stench almost made me sick. It was unbelievable.' She took a deep breath. 'And if that is not bad enough, the gardens, which were once sculptured and ornamental, have been replaced by a shamble of shelters made from bits of cardboard and canvas.'

The colonel puffed on his cigar allowing Lucy to continue. She told him she had instructed the agent not to advertise the property until the squatters were evicted and the place cleaned. The company's representative had promised he would attend to the matter personally, but advised that it would incur additional expenses which would need to be paid in advance.

After handing over the fee demanded, and after several letters, frustrating phone calls and two rather perilous excursions to the property, Lucy had come to the conclusion that absolutely no effort was being made to evict the residents. Though she felt sorry for the people who were to be evicted and made homeless, she nevertheless had to conduct her business.

'While the house remains the way it is,' she said, 'no one in his right mind would even consider buying it.'

Colonel Winters laid his cigar in the alabaster ashtray.

'I will require the address of the property and the name of the agent. This business may take a little time and involve some expense.' He looked at Lucy quizzically.

'Cost is no object,' she assured him. 'And even if it were, any expenses would be offset by the sale once it goes through.'

'As I thought. Leave the matter with me.'

'May I ask how you hope to remove all the people and when you do, how you will keep them out?'

'That I cannot answer as I have not yet worked out a strategy. Speaking from experience, I can say dealing with some of the local government bodies is a long and painstaking procedure, and those tactics would get us nowhere in a hurry. In this instance what we need is a more dynamic approach. The first move will be the erection of a high fence around the grounds and the installation of a squad of security guards. If necessary I will call on my friends in the police department.' He paused. 'In fact, I will speak with the recently retired commissioner who is, right this moment, within these walls. Once the vagrants are evicted and the house is empty, I suggest you arrange for it to be refurbished before presenting it on the market.'

Lucy found it hard to thank him enough.

'It is my pleasure, madam. Not only does it give me the opportunity to assist you and return a favour to an old friend, but it gives me something to get my teeth into. One gets bored here with the same routine day in and day out. I have played so many games of chess in the last few years it is a wonder I do not walk diagonally across our checkerboard floor.'

'Thank you, Colonel Winters,' Lucy said, as she shook hands with him.

'My dear lady,' he said holding her hand in his. 'I will enjoy this exercise immensely. And when the house sells, you may treat me to a box of those rather fine imported cigars.'

It was a long time since James had wandered over the moors alone. Sitting on a rock, he gazed across Wharfedale to the grey-green hills in the distance. He had always loved the countryside especially the open moors. It had a peacefulness he found nowhere else. Below, in the valley, the river snaked lazily through verdant fields. Downstream the clusters of smoke-blackened houses blemished the natural landscape. The thought of working in a dirty city was repugnant to him.

But James knew his mother had always wanted him to improve himself and to go to university. So had Edward. He had even left money in trust for that purpose. But Edward was dead, and James now found himself torn between his desire not to disappoint his mentor and his wish to work on the land. He sighed, knowing full well that study and professional qualifications were not what he wanted out of life.

However, time was running out. He had to make a choice. His car was getting older and would not run forever. He was living on the interest from his savings, but that was rapidly diminishing as he was eating into his capital. One day he would likely inherit most of his mother's money, but she was fit and not fifty years of age. Even though James knew she was a wealthy woman, he would never ask her for money. Besides, the trip to India, which she had taken him on, had not been cheap.

But what his mother had said was true, for several years he had had neither job nor income. He had done repairs to the cottages and pottered about with the horses, grown a few crops on the meadow and helped raise a few calves and hens, he had read many books, learned a lot, but earned nothing. He had been thoroughly self-indulgent. And all that time Grace had worked like a navvy, no doubt observing him. What on earth did she think of him?

Here he was, twenty five years of age with no trade, no job and little income, at a time when the queues of men seeking work were growing daily throughout the length and breadth of England.

If Mr Fothergill were to advertise for help, he would have no difficulty finding men eager to work on the farm. Men were becoming desperate. Some would work just for the milk to feed their bairns. Milk was essential and always would be. Being part of a dairy farm was a damn good proposition.

It was a good offer and James knew it. Since he had first mentioned the idea of farming, the price of land had risen and his capital was being depleted. Now, when he really wanted to buy some land, he didn't have enough money. If there was no other way, he could ask his mother for a loan, but he didn't know when she would return to England. It might be weeks or months and Mr Fothergill was waiting for an answer. Summer was round the corner and the fields were still lying fallow.

As he sat pondering his decision a sparrow hawk dropped vertically into the heather. After a few moments it flew up, its prey gripped tightly in its talons.

James knew instantly, he must grab the opportunity while it was available. But he also knew that if he was to accept Mr Fothergill's offer, he would have to find some other way of getting the money.

Chapter 23

Cyril Street

The white-clad waiter was a tall willowy man and his turban made him appear even taller. Lucy took a sandwich from the tray and thanked him.

'You don't mind this heat?' The question came from a man drinking tea at the next table. He flipped the crumbs from his lap and turned to face her.

'No, I don't,' Lucy replied. 'It's the moisture in the air, I hate. Makes everything feel permanently damp.'

'You might like Australia then,' he said.

'Might I?'

'Maybe. Hot there, but not as humid they tell me.'

'You are travelling on, are you, Mr—?'

'Street. Cyril Harley Street.' He laughed. 'Sounds more like an address than a name, don't you think?'

'Lucy Oldfield,' she replied offering her hand. 'Missus,' she said, 'but actually it's, Miss.'

'You are very forthright. I like that.'

'Why not?' she said, inviting him to join her. 'I've become accustomed to that title over the years. I think, because I was single and had a child, people called me, missus, out of politeness. For a long time I was happy to accept it and preferred it, I suppose to being thought of as a loose woman.'

'And were you?' he said, with twinkle in his eye.

Lucy grinned. 'That, I am not telling, Mr Street.'

'Call me Cyril,' he said. 'Care to walk out on the terrace? I think there might be a little breeze outside.'

The hotel's dining room was open on all sides but neither the balmy breeze blowing in from the ocean nor the ceiling fans provided any relief from the sultry atmosphere. The air on the terrace was as moist as it was inside.

'Are you staying in Bombay long?' Cyril asked.

'Not much longer. I'm waiting to conclude some matters that have taken considerably longer than I expected. It's been interesting to see how business is conducted in the colonies.' Lucy dabbed sweat from her brow. 'It's over six months since I left England and it's about time I was heading home.'

'Because you have been in no hurry, might I assume you have enjoyed your stay, and that you have no one back home desperately awaiting your return.'

'You could be correct.'

'In that case, would you care to dine with me this evening?'

'You do not waste any time, do you?'

'At my age, madam, my adage is *waste not, want not*!'

'All right, Mr Street, you have won me over for a meal. But a meal only.'

'Well at least it's a start,' he said. 'Shall we say seven?'

'Seven on the dot. I will look forward to it.'

'For you,' James said, handing Grace a large bunch of pink carnations.

'You shouldn't have,' she said, as she sniffed the flowers and smiled. 'I thought we were here to look at the stalls?'

'We are.'

The Leeds market was crowded with shoppers. Under the glass-domed roof, the still air echoed with the raucous voices of traders competing to sell their wares. The individual shops looked the same as James remembered from his childhood: books, toys, drapery, and shoe shops set amidst the aroma of freshly baked bread and the scent of cut flowers. The city market stocked almost everything from pots and pans, polishes, brooms and buckets, to dusters and dishcloths.

James and Grace ambled through the maze of assorted stalls, to the lane consisting entirely of butchers' shops. Outside each establishment, chalkboards advertised tripe, dripping and kidneys. Inside the shops, butchers smelling of blood and mutton fat, chopped bone and cartilage with sharpened cleavers. A hungry dog sniffed at the doorways, but instead of scraps received cries of abuse.

The fish-market had a very different smell but James didn't notice as they wandered through. He was looking for stalls selling second-hand goods and, whenever he spotted one, he scanned the wares hoping to recognize something familiar – an item that had once belonged to his mother or Edward. Not knowing exactly what had been stolen, Grace wandered along beside him.

'Nothing,' he said, as they left the indoor market and wandered outside to the stalls that mostly sold fruit and vegetables.

'Lovely apples! Granny Smiths! Cox's! Pick your own.'

''Ere 'ave a taste,' a leathery-faced lady yelled, thrusting a segment of orange into Grace's hand. 'Don't come no sweeter than that!'

Grace sucked on the fruit, the juice running between her fingers.

The sun had disappeared and a chill wind had whipped up while they were indoors. Cloth canopies flapped. A tin tray clattered when it blew over and skidded along the ground in front of them. James retrieved it and returned it to the stallholder. It had come from a second-hand stall neither of them had noticed. Amongst the items on display was a teapot. It was a common white pot, stained inside and with a web of clay-coloured cracks running right through it. James remembered seeing a similar pot in Alice's kitchen. He remembered the time she had scalded her wrist when the steam had escaped through a chip in the lid. This pot had a chip in the same place.

'How much for the teapot?' James asked.

'Tanner to you, guv.'

James replaced it and looked around.

''Ave a look,' the man said. 'Come on missus, I got all sorts of stuff.'

Most of the items were damaged or stained. There were odd cups and saucers, bottles, books, tins, biscuit boxes, single serviette rings, certainly nothing of value. James scrutinized every item till he was satisfied that apart from the teapot, there was nothing else he recognized.

'Any idea where this came from?' he said, holding the pot at arm's length.

The man shook his head. 'No idea.'

'Any other things came with it?'

The man shook his head cautiously and turned his back.

'Would a pound jog your memory?'

The man shuffled around. 'Might do.'

'I'm not interested how you got it or who you got it from, I just want to know if there was anything else came with it.'

'Might have been.'

James reached in his pocket and took out a crisp bank note.

The man looked around furtively.

'Well,' said James rubbing the paper between his fingers.

'There was quite a bit of stuff.'

'If it's what I am looking for I'm prepared to buy it off you at a reasonable price. Where is it?'

'Sold it,' the stallholder sniffed. 'Not my sort of stuff. Good stuff, if you know what I mean.'

'Tell me who bought it and the money's yours.'

'No idea, guv. Honest. Sold it to a bloke who came looking. Seen him before. Bit of a toff. Fancy dresser. Only wants quality. Don't think he's a collector. I reckon he's got a shop because he bought the lot.'

'How much?'

'That's my business, guv. I bought it fair and square.'

'Who from?'

The man shrugged. 'Fella comes round at times. Brings me stuff by the sack-load.'

'Is it stolen?'

'I don't ask questions. Just gives him a price.'

'And this other man who came and bought the stuff, the toff – would you know him again?'

'I'd know him if I saw him. Never forget a face.'

James took out a paper and pencil. 'Can you write?'

'Of course I can write. I'm not stupid!'

'Good. This is my address and here's your money. And there's another quid for you if you can get the name of the man who bought the rest of the stuff from you.'

'And what about the fella I got it off in the first place.'

'You get his name and address and I'll give you the same again.'

The man pushed the piece of paper into an inside pocket. 'You'll be hearing from me, governor.'

James nodded and took Grace's arm. They had only gone a few yards when the man shouted after them.

'Hey, guv!' The man was beckoning. 'I got a pile of odds and ends the toff didn't want. He said it was rubbish. That's where the pot came from. Want to have a look?'

James nodded.

Dragging a Hessian sack from under his counter the man unwound the twine tied around the top. Reaching his hand in to the bag, James brought out various items and laid them on the ground.

'You won't find anything of value in there!' the man said.

He was right. The clock's face was broken. The glass vase was badly cracked. The stitched pages of the book had become separated from the binding. There was a pile of old sheet music but some pages were missing or torn. There was a posy of dried flowers and an umbrella with bent spokes. A tortoiseshell hair-brush and a broken picture frame. James looked at the sepia photograph behind the broken glass. It was faded and slightly scratched but he recognized the face of the girl in nurse's uniform. 'Alice,' he murmured.

'Is that some of Lucy's stuff,' Grace whispered.

James nodded.

'You can have the sack for a quid,' the man offered.

'Your customer was right,' James said. 'This lot's worth nothing.'

'All right! Ten bob to you, governor.'

'I'll give you five bob for the lot including the teapot.'

'Done!' said the man.

'And don't forget, those two names. Addresses too if you can get them.'

'Please come in Mr Oldfield and take a seat.'

James thanked the solicitor and sat down opposite the two elderly gentlemen.

'How is your mother?' Mr Armitage asked.

'She is well and enjoying her time in India, despite everything not going quite as she would have wished.'

'Ah! Yes,' he said. 'We received a letter from our contact in Bombay. He said there were some problems. Legal matters have a habit of becoming tedious. I hope the delay will not cause your mother too much inconvenience.'

'On the contrary, I think she welcomed the opportunity to extend her stay, although I don't know how she will cope with the heat of the tropical summer.'

'How right you are,' the elder of the two solicitors said.

'Now, Mr Oldfield, regarding the matter you put to us last week.' Mr Proctor took a file from his desk drawer and leafed through the papers. Selecting one item, he held it at arm's length, read it and passed it to his partner. From the coat of arms embossed on the top of the cream paper, James knew it was from Lord Farnley.

'This is a very commendable character reference you have provided.' He picked out another letter. 'And also this one from Captain Wainwright.' He cleared his throat and leaned forward. 'As trustees of any estate we are obliged to carry out the terms of the will according to the wishes of our clients. But we must consider any request that deviates from these terms very carefully, as our client would have done if he were still alive.'

James nodded.

'In this submission, you are asking that the money, which Mr Carrington set aside for your tertiary education, is paid to you as a lump sum. That you intend to use the money to purchase land.' He turned the page and examined the title deeds of John Fothergill's farm. After re-reading James's proposal, he continued.

'Mr Oldfield, my partner and I have arrived at the following conclusions. Had the money been required for the purchase of a vehicle, or a holiday, or suchlike, we would have declined your request. However, the purchase of land is regarded as a good investment, possibly sounder than leaving the money in the bank which is where it is at the moment. However,' he added, 'once you have invested the money we cannot stop you from selling the asset in a year's time.'

'That is not my intention, sir.'

'We thought not. This brings me back to another point. Mr Carrington's wish was that the money was to be spent on furthering your education. Yet you say you have no desire to pursue a professional career.'

'That is correct.'

'We have noted Captain Wainwright's letter which states that Mr Edward Carrington did not follow the military career his father had intended for him because the army was not his chosen path. Because of this fact, we feel, if our client had been alive today, he would have been sympathetic to your request. He would not have forced you to attend university purely to please him. We also think he would have supported you in whatever path you chose to follow.

'Besides being an astute man, Edward Carrington was a man with a good heart. We believe he would have wanted you to follow your heart.' With that said, the solicitor replaced the papers in the file and closed it. 'We will arrange for the money to be transferred from the trust account and placed into your personal bank account.'

'And may we wish you every success in this new venture,' his partner added.

The letter was from Lucy. It had been written in Bombay.

My dearest James

I hope you and Grace are well. I received your letter and was interested to hear you are spending a lot of time at Mr Fothergill's farm. As you do not mention Alice and the baby, I hope all is well with them too. Have you visited Pansy in Ilkley lately?

As for me, I am very well and still enjoying my time in Bombay. So much so I will not be coming home as planned – at least not for some time.

You may be surprised to learn that I have met a very nice gentleman. His name is Cyril Street. He comes from Kent, though originally he was from the north. He is travelling around the world stopping at the ports which interest him along the way and he has been in Bombay for several months.

Hearing him talk about the places he'll be visiting has made me wish to see a little more of the world. Not wanting to travel alone, I have arranged for a passage on the same vessel as Mr Street. We are booked to sail on the SS Gothenburg *which is leaving Bombay the first week in October. The ship will be calling in at Colombo, Rangoon and Singapore. From there we will take another vessel to Sydney, Australia. My friend, Mr Street wants to purchase some land on the southern continent. He says land is the best investment these days.*

I read in a newspaper recently that poverty and hardship are increasing in England and I know I am indeed fortunate to be in a sound financial position. If there is anything you need, you must write and tell me.

By the time you receive this letter I will be at sea. You can write to me care of the General Post Office in Sydney and I will collect the mail when we get there. At this stage, I don't know when that will be.

Take care of yourself
Your loving Mother

James smiled, folded the letter and slid it back into the envelope. He was relieved to hear all was well and surprised to hear his mother had found a travelling companion and would not be coming home for some time. He hoped she was making a wise decision and, in a way, envied her. He remembered how much he had enjoyed his visit to India, an experience he would never forget. But James preferred to be at home and welcomed the challenge of being a farmer. Above all he wanted to settle down and had been waiting for his mother to return before asking Grace to marry him.

As he put the letter away, he decided he could wait no longer. He would be seeing Grace that evening and would ask her then.

Chapter 24

Marriage

James and Grace were married at the Leeds Register Office.

Grace wore a cotton frock patterned with tiny rosebuds, a pink hat with a net veil, white gloves and white high heeled shoes. Later she regretted she had only bought the shoes the week before the wedding and, as she had no time to wear them in, they made her feet sore. There were no bridesmaids or best man, just the two witnesses, Mr Fothergill and Pansy Pugh.

Pansy caught the 8.30 train from Ilkley and met them in City Square. She brought Rachel with her but apologized that Alice couldn't come as she had to work. It didn't bother either bride or groom that they had few relatives or friends attending the ceremony, though James was disappointed his mother was absent. The only other person he would have wished to be present was the man who had been like a father to him, Edward Carrington.

After the civil service, the wedding group went back to the farmhouse for a meal. Grace had prepared it all beforehand – cold roast lamb, potato and pickles, and apple pie. It didn't take her long to whip up a basin of fresh cream, but by the time they sat down to eat it was almost three o'clock.

It had been several months since James had seen Pansy and he thought she looked well, still thin and pale-cheeked, but content. Rachel was growing quickly, but unlike Alice who had been boisterous and full of adventure, Alice's daughter was shy. Being brought up in the house of the aged Miss Pugh, she had little contact with other children, and as a consequence, her behaviour was that of a child of the Victorian era. Even the dresses Pansy chose for her were rather old-fashioned and too long which added to her delicate appearance.

While James made every effort to encourage Rachel to talk, she insisted on clinging tightly to her grandmother's arm.

'She'll grow out of it quick enough once she gets to school,' Pansy said.

James asked about Alice.

'She's well and still working hard,' Pansy said, dabbing a speck of dirt from Rachel's cheek. 'She's a nursing sister now. Got a ward of her own.' She sounded proud of her daughter's achievements then suddenly her tone changed. 'I wish she had met a nice young doctor instead of getting tied up with that Bertie Bottomley.'

'Does he ever get in touch?'

'No, he's long gone. And good riddance, I say. Alice's better off without him.' Pansy sighed. 'I feel sorry for her at times. She works long hours and only sees Rachel once a week when she visits. Life must be lonely for her.'

'Why doesn't she come back to the cottage?'

'Keeps saying she might one day. I don't think she liked being here on her own when you and Lucy were away. Maybe she'll come back once you and Grace settle down. But,' she said, in a more positive tone, 'I know she loves her job.'

'You must be proud of her,' Grace said.

'I am. But that's enough talk about me; tell me what you're doing at the farm.'

James looked over to the man who was now his father-in-law. 'I bought half the farm,' he said proudly.

'And I'm aiming to make a farmer out of him,' John Fothergill said with a grin.

'Do you think you'll succeed?' Pansy asked.

'He's doing all right so far. We ended up with a good harvest this year, even though some of the seed went in late.'

'And the dairy's improved,' Grace added, tucking her arm inside James's. 'Dad said we're already getting more milk, and with the extra feed we'll have more calves for the market at Christmas.'

John Fothergill put his finger to his mouth. 'Shh! Don't want him to get a swelled head, but I think that calls for a toast.' He got up from the table and hobbled over to the pantry. 'It's only sherry but it'll do the job.'

There was almost half a tumbler each. Ample to drink the health of the newly married couple.

As the afternoon wore on, Rachel fell asleep on the sofa and by five o'clock Pansy was anxious to get back to Ilkley and Miss Pugh.

'We'll be back early in the morning for the milking,' James called to his new father-in-law, as he and Grace prepared to take Pansy home. 'I'm taking this young lady to a hotel for the night,' James announced. 'She says she's never stayed in a hotel before.'

Grace blushed.

There were tears in the farmer's eyes, as he hugged his daughter. 'Now you look after her!' he said to James. 'And don't worry about the morning. I'm not altogether useless. If the cows have to wait a while, it won't kill them.'

Dusk was falling as they waved goodbye. With her head resting on Pansy's lap, Rachel slept all the way to Ilkley. Grace sat close to James, her hand resting on his leg.

With only a fine sliver of new moon on the rise, it was almost black when they reached Miss Pugh's house. Grace declined Pansy's invitation to a come in for a cup of tea, and the newly-weds said goodnight.

As James closed the car door, he leaned across and kissed his wife. 'I'm sure it's past your bed time, Mrs Oldfield.'

Grace grinned 'Do you really think so, Mr Oldfield?'

'I know so!' he said.

It was almost two weeks after the wedding before James, Grace, Mr Fothergill and the cows, were settled in to a regular routine. James took over all the heavy work on the farm and most of the driving, allowing Grace more time in the house for baking.

Within weeks of the change, John Fothergill was loosening the notches on his belt. He was partial to his daughter's curd tarts, but a plate of hot scones and a pat of fresh butter was his favourite. At first his appetite for sweet stuff was treated as a joke but before long the extra weight he gained began placing additional strain on his leg.

Since the accident he had walked with a limp. His leg had healed but the doctor said the hip joint was damaged. It was obvious it gave him a lot of pain. Unable to climb the stairs, he slept downstairs at the farmhouse in the room his wife had died in. He refused to accept a walking stick; instead, when he hobbled to the shed at milking time, he leaned heavily on a staff. As he was unable to do much around the farm, he spent most of each day watching Grace working in the kitchen.

Naturally Grace was concerned about her father. She and James considered moving into the farmhouse with him, but the farmer insisted he was all right on his own and, as James liked his own cottage and the privacy it offered them, Grace agreed she would live at Honeysuckle Cottages. It was very close and only took two minutes by car to drive there.

For more than a week after she moved in, Grace felt confined. The kitchen was tiny, the rooms small, the ceiling low. Quite different to the spacious interior of the farmhouse. Every morning Grace was up before James, anxious to get back to the farm to check on her father.

At first James worried that she was doing too much, helping with the milking, separating the cream, making and tending the cheeses, keeping the farmhouse and cottage tidy and cooking for her father, but Grace argued that her work was physically easier than before he had started working with them.

As James was more active than he had been since his time in the army, by evening he would fall into bed exhausted. But he enjoyed the outdoor work and being with Grace for much of the day. He liked delivering cream and driving in the surrounding district. Being outdoors in all weather didn't bother him.

A week after the wedding the postman delivered a letter for James. The crumpled envelope was daubed with dirty smudges around the stamp and across the back where it had been sealed. James's name and address were scrawled in pencil in a combination of capital and small letters. It was from the man on the market stall. He signed himself, *Tom*, but there was no surname. In the letter, the writer said he would give James some news if he visited him at Leeds market. James waited until Saturday morning to go.

'I got that information you wanted, guv,' Tom said. 'You said it was worth a quid.'

'You give me the information and I'll tell you if it is.'

'I found out where you'll find the toff who bought the stuff you're looking for. He has a shop, like I thought. It's on Pembroke

Way, behind the hotel in Headingley. He didn't want to give me his name.'

'You're not making this up, I hope.'

'Honest, guv!' the man said, holding out his grubby hand. 'Would I do a thing like that?'

James ignored the question as he handed over the pound note. 'No news on the other fellow?'

Tom shook his head. 'Not yet, but he'll be around soon. Not usually this long between visits. Trust me, governor! I'll let you know. Same arrangement as before?' he asked.

'Same arrangement as before,' James added.

There were two antique shops near the Pembroke Hotel, one on either side of the narrow lane. The first was dark and dismal inside. It was crammed with all manner of bric-a-brac but few items appeared to be of any value. While James browsed, the man behind the counter never lifted his head from the newspaper he was reading. With the list of missing items in his mind, James knew exactly what he was searching for. The air in the shop was musty and reminded James of mice. After searching unsuccessfully for over ten minutes, he was pleased to step outside and breathe some fresh air.

When he spied the row of Gurkha soldiers lined up in the window, James knew the second shop was the one he wanted. The bell above the door tinkled as he walked in. The proprietor was smartly dressed in a blue striped suit with a patterned waistcoat. He greeted James and offered his assistance. When James said he was content to browse, the man excused himself and hovered behind the counter watching James's every move.

Like the previous business, this one was equally packed with merchandise, but in this shop most of the antiques were items of value. Seeing the toy soldiers made James sure he would locate more of Edward's possessions. As he scoured the shelves, recognizing various ornaments, James ticked them off his mental list. He was careful not to touch anything in the shop and tried not to show any evidence of interest in his face. But his expression changed to a frown when he realized his inventory had more than a few omissions. He had completely forgotten about the ivory crocodile and the old bugle that had always hung in the hall. And there was the ebony elephant with the loose tusk, the scrimshaw, the cribbage board and the old doll with the black wig that he had cut from a piece of goat skin for Alice when she was a little girl. How did he forget to list all those?

On intuition, James paid another visit to the market the following week. He felt guilty leaving Grace and John at the farm but made up for it by starting work very early and managing to get through his morning's chores before he left.

His visit paid off. The man who had originally brought the sacks to the market had been back with a suitcase full of other goods.

James wasn't surprised that the man's description fitted that of Stanley Crowther, though Tom said his name was Wilkinson. He did not have the man's address and said Wilkinson had got angry when he started asking questions.

After examining the contents of the suitcase, James paid the second-hand dealer thirty shillings, a sum far in excess of what he thought the items were worth. He was also obliged to pay him the pound note they had agreed on.

Armed with the suitcase, a surname and the address of the dealer in Pembroke Way, James paid a visit to the police station.

Three days later, James and Constable Merrifield drove to the antique shop where the toy soldiers were still lined up in the window.

The dealer remembered James but was not pleased when he learned the purpose of the return visit. After presenting the proprietor with a list, the constable informed him that selling stolen property was an offence and that the goods were to be confiscated. The shopkeeper was irate and insisted he had bought them from the market stall in good faith, unaware they'd been stolen.

The only consolation the officer could offer him was that when the matter got to court, the onus would probably fall on the stall holder. He said the police had questioned him the previous day and in his opinion, the man was lying when he said he didn't know the goods were stolen.

After placing all the recovered items into four large boxes, James loaded them onto the back seat of the car while the policeman took down the antique dealer's personal details. Glancing in the car's mirror as they drove away, James could see the man standing in the road shaking his fist and cursing.

With only six items unaccounted for, James felt pleased. He presumed the missing items had been sold and that the probability of tracing them was unlikely. The fact the stolen goods would be held at the station until the case was brought before the magistrate, didn't worry James. He was, however, disappointed the man who called himself Wilkinson had not been apprehended, and the constable had grave doubts the man would ever be caught.

'If he's the same Wilkinson we had around these parts a while ago, he's a slippery customer and if he gets the slightest whiff we're onto him, he'll be off like a flash.'

James felt pleased he had been able to resolve the matter without worrying his mother while she was away. He had not written to tell her about the burglary as she would only worry and could do little from overseas. To his knowledge, nothing of value had been taken from her cottage and, as almost all the goods had been recovered, he doubted he would bother mentioning the burglary at all.

An invitation was extended to all the first-class passengers on board to attend a shipboard party to celebrate Lucy Oldfield's marriage to Cyril Street. From early evening champagne corks popped and the small orchestra in the grand ballroom played non-stop – popular tunes interspersed with leisurely old waltzes. It was an elegant party with garlands of flowers, coloured streamers and balloons though dull when compared with the flash of diamonds and shimmer of sequins that glittered from the ladies' brooches and ball gowns.

It was not until the early hours of the morning that Lucy and Cyril escaped to the cool air of the promenade deck. Around her shoulders Lucy wore a short mink cape, a wedding gift from Cyril.

Standing on the after-deck, gazing across the waters of Bass Strait, they could see the cliffs of the Australian coastline shining in the moonlight.

'They remind me of the white cliffs of Dover,' Cyril said, putting his arm around his new wife. 'Happy?' he asked.

Lucy nodded.

'Homesick?'

'No,' she said. 'Home is where the heart is, isn't that what you say?'

Chapter 25

Home Again

Grace grew increasingly anxious when she heard Alice was planning to move back into Pansy's old cottage, whereas James was delighted at the prospect and mentioned the fact almost every day. Though always busy, he made time to weed Alice's garden, even though their own garden and Lucy's were equally overgrown. He also washed the downstairs windows of the end cottage and replaced the hinges on the gate which Crowther had broken. Though she never said anything, Grace couldn't help feeling slightly jealous. Would James want to spend time with Alice when she came back? And would Crowther reappear and start bothering them?

As each day passed, she found it harder to hide her feelings, and the idea of moving back to the farm became more and more appealing to her. If they stayed in the cottage she knew she would feel vulnerable. Alice was a clever girl, a nursing sister, well educated, and always well dressed. Alice was also intelligent and nicely spoken, however, she was just a farmer's daughter, who had left school at twelve and who could boast no fancy clothes or ways. Alice was not only pretty and slim, but, even in her white satin nurse's shoes, was taller than her. The baggy trousers, Grace wore every day, the broad leather belt and mud laden Wellington boots, made her look even shorter and fatter than she really was and, the fact she was pregnant, didn't help matters.

'Who cares what someone wears. I don't!' said James, pulling his wife to him and hugging her. 'You always look smashing to me. And besides,' he said, 'in a few months' time, when the baby's due, you'll be glad to have Alice around.'

Grace smiled and kissed him. As usual, he was right and she was being foolish, but she found it difficult to talk to him about her feelings. He and Alice had grown up together and were as close as any brother and sister, and, because of that, it appeared to Grace that James's instinct would be to defend Alice whatever happened.

Two things puzzled Grace, though. Why had Alice left Rachel to be brought up by Pansy in Ilkley? And why was she now planning to move back into the cottage on her own, yet not bringing Rachel with her?

'Seems odd to me,' Grace said casually, 'not having the little lass with her. I can promise, when I have the baby, I won't let her out of my sight.'

'And what will you do when you're milking?' James joked.

'She can sit on a stool and watch. Never too soon to learn!'

'It's going to be a girl, is it?'

'Of course,' said Grace, rubbing her hands across her belly.

'Is there anything else of yours in here?' James asked, as Alice rummaged through the four large boxes that he had just collected from the police station.

'The rest of these things came from your mother's place,' Alice said. 'Including this.' As she spoke she pulled the old doll out of the box. The lace trim on the frock had yellowed and the black goat skin pate looked stark against the pale bisque cheeks. Laying it gently on the table, Alice watched as the eyelashes closed across the luminous blue eyes.

'I loved this doll when I was young,' she said. 'When I was afraid of the dark, I would take her to bed with me and talk to her under the covers. I didn't feel scared when she was with me. I suppose I thought she was real.' She turned and smiled at Grace. 'Silly isn't it, the way you think when you're a child.'

Grace nodded and smiled sadly, but her eyes were not on the dilapidated doll, she was looking at the hands holding it, ugly hands – Alice's hands – the skin coiled and scarred from being burnt.

'Why don't you keep it?' James said, closing the box's lid. 'Mum gave it to you, didn't she? And she's no reason to want it now.'

Alice held the doll to her chest and thanked James saying it would be nice to have its company in the empty house. Grace offered to help her unpack her suitcases, but Alice preferred to manage alone.

The rain, which had started soon after she arrived, was getting heavier. Alice ran back to her cottage trying to avoid the puddles and streams forming on the lane. But the water splashed over her shoes and saturated her stockings. As she neared the front door, she was annoyed with herself. She noticed she hadn't closed it properly and the rain was blowing in. The cottage was chilly enough already. It had suffered from being left vacant and always felt cold and damp, and a smell of mould permanently hung in the air.

After rubbing the rain from her hair and drying the doll's head, Alice kicked off her shoes and ran upstairs to find her slippers. As she walked across the bedroom her toes squelched on the bedside rug. It was sopping wet. Looking up she could see water dripping from around the man-hole which led up into the roof.

Why was the ceiling wet? There was no window in the attic. Nowhere the rain could blow in from. As she stood pondering over it, drops of water dripped down to the already saturated rug.

Hurrying to the kitchen, she returned with a stack of pans and bowls and placed them around the floor like stepping stones. In the morning she would tell James and ask him to climb into the roof cavity to investigate the leak. Perhaps when the tree branches moved in the wind, they dislodged one of the slate shingles. Whatever the reason she knew James would fix it, but as she unpacked her clothes and hung them neatly in the wardrobe, she could not escape the constant *plop-plopping* of the water as it dripped into the pans.

It was hard for Alice to get to sleep that night. Rain lashed against the window and water continued to seep in. Across the roof, the branches scraped eerily on the shingles and in the white flashes of the storm, the blot of mottled mould on the ceiling appeared to move and roll like a gathering thundercloud.

As she pulled the doll into bed beside her, its lids slid over the luminescent eyes, but it was well over two hours before Alice's eyes closed.

A few weeks later, James knocked on Alice's door at midnight, and Andrew Oldfield was born two hours after that. His arrival was three weeks earlier than expected and Grace was relieved that Alice had been there to help her.

As the day dawned, James felt guilty knowing Alice was on duty that day at the hospital. But Alice would hear nothing of his concern.

She was used to not getting much sleep and besides that, she was pleased to assist the new baby into the world.

The River Wharfe meandered lazily. Sunlight bursting through the trees flickered on the fresh green leaves and glinted on the water. The woodland path was soft underfoot. To the left, the lush ground was a carpet of blue. Masses of bell-shaped flowers bowed their heads towards the earth shedding tears of morning dew. To the right was the river. A pair of squirrels raced along the path, stopped for a moment, tails erect then scampered across of mesh of twisted roots and up the crumpled bark of an ageing tree. In the silence of the woods the sounds of birds echoed in the still morning air.

Alice loved her weekly visits to Ilkley, especially in spring. Rising before dawn, she would catch the early train so she could share breakfast with her mother and Rachel. But as soon as the meal was cleared away, they would pack a picnic and set off for the day. Miss Pugh's big house was dark, cold and rather depressing and it had a distinct musty smell that reminded her of the hospital. So, unless the weather was really inclement, she always preferred to go out. Alice sympathized with the spinster's mental condition, and admired her mother for looking after her, but was relieved her great-aunt never asked if she could join them.

On the days they spent together, Alice, Rachel and Pansy walked for miles in the countryside around Ilkley. Pansy still appeared thin and frail, but was active and surprised her daughter. Little Rachel could walk well too until she was tired, then the two women would take turns to carry her on their backs.

If the ground was not too slippery, they would take the steep path up the side of Heber's Ghyll, the stream that rose from a spring on the moors and gurgled down through the shaded undergrowth to the river in the valley below. At the top of the Ghyll, where the trees stopped and the moors began, they would stop and drink from the crystal water pouring from a freshwater spring, or ponder the ancient shapes carved on the weathered stones.

When it was fine, they would hike through the heather to the Cow and Calf rocks, always stopping at the bottom of the cliff face, never venturing to climb. Some days they would stroll down to the River Wharfe and wander across the meadows through which the river meandered. Sometimes, when they reached a pebbled beach, Rachel would paddle in the shallow water whilst the two women sat and chatted, gazing contentedly at the river winding lazily by.

'I've decided I'm going to leave the hospital,' Alice said, to her mother, as Rachel danced in the bed of bluebells. 'I'll get a day job, like the one I had in the nursing home. I want Rachel living at home with me before she's too old.'

Pansy squeezed her daughter's hand. 'I'm pleased to hear you say that, dear. I love the little lass, but I know she misses you. It's only right she should be with you.'

'I don't know why I didn't think of it before. Now I'm settled back at the cottage it seems the obvious thing to do.' Alice sighed, as she voiced her thoughts out loud. 'Over the years I've been too involved with work. But, now it doesn't seem important anymore.'

'But you've been a good nurse and your training won't go astray.'

'I know,' said Alice. 'But I wish I hadn't been so blind.'

Rachel presented her grandmother with a bunch of bluebells before running back into the glade to gather more.

'Little Andrew is already walking and Grace is expecting another baby around Christmas time, which means Rachel will have someone to play with at last.'

'I'm pleased, Alice. But I'll miss her.'

'Then you must come to the cottage and stay with us.'

'It's hard for me to leave my aunt long. The old dear is apt to go wandering, if I'm not around.'

Alice looked disappointed.

'But we'll see. You never know what's round the corner.'

As the sun's rays poured between the treetops, Alice and Pansy ambled along the path hand in hand. Knee-deep in blue-bells, Rachel wandered through the woodland, stopping at times to pick another flower. A pair of chaffinches, busy at their nest, attracted her attention. A dragonfly hovered in the air then darted away. She heard a cuckoo and watched as a butterfly settle on the flowers in her hand. Above her head she saw a cloud of tiny flies, and when she heard the bushes rustling she looked around expecting to see a squirrel scampering up a tree.

Engrossed in conversation, the women wandered on, their minds removed from the sights and sounds of the river-bank. They didn't hear the startled screech of a bird or the crack of dead twigs being broken underfoot. They didn't see the man who was following them, loitering in the undergrowth.

Chapter 26

The Car

Lucy's letter bore an American postage stamp. James had read it earlier, but as they sat by the fire in the evening, Grace asked him to read it again.

My dear James and Grace

As I write this letter, the ship is steaming slowly through the Panama Canal. How different the scenery here is from the canal at Suez. Being near the equator, the weather is hot and sticky and Cyril and I are looking forward to being back on the open sea again. We change ships at New York but will not stay there for long as we do not want to be crossing the North Atlantic after the winter storms have blown in. From New York the ship steams via the Azores for Southampton where we will disembark.

But first let me offer my belated congratulation to you both. I was overjoyed to hear that I have a grandson Andrew Edward Oldfield. I am glad Grace and baby are well, and to hear Alice is living back home and was able to share the joy with you. It will be wonderful for us all to be together again at Honeysuckle Cottages. Perhaps one day Pansy will come back too.

I hope it will not come as too much of a shock to you, but Cyril Street and I were married some weeks ago. I mentioned our friendship when I wrote from India. We were attracted to each other when we first met and, as Cyril does not believe in wasting time, we decided to get married straight away. Being practical, as we both are, we agreed it was foolish to pay for two cabins on the ship and two rooms in the hotels, therefore when the ship docked in Fremantle in Western Australia we arranged for a special marriage licence. As our relationship had been a topic of gossip amongst the first-class passengers, it seemed fitting to have a party on board to celebrate. I was hardly the young blushing bride, but it was a memorable day.

I feel sure you will both like Cyril. He is a kind and considerate man with a lively sense of humour. He has the patience and tolerance of Edward, and a considerable amount more energy. Hopefully we will be home within two months.

Give my regards to John Fothergill.
Your loving Mother

'She sounds happy,' said James.

Grace agreed. 'And they will be home before Christmas.'

James smiled. 'Yes,' he said, gazing out of the window. As the wind bent the long grass into waves across the meadow, he tried to picture his mother on the deck of a ship sailing across the North Atlantic. He remembered his voyage to India and wondered if he would ever travel abroad again. 'I'm tired,' he said. 'I think I will go to bed.'

'I will follow in a few minutes.'

James kissed her. For some reason, he felt more weary than usual. The last few weeks had not gone well and there was little for him to feel positive about. The heavy rain had come at the wrong time damaging the crops that were ripening and almost ready for harvest. A month ago the top field had swayed golden in the breeze, waving like the surface of the sea bathed in a glorious sunset. Now the field was spoiled, flattened, the whole crop turning black and mouldy on the ground. A full year's work gone to waste.

Apart from the wheat, the drenching rain had turned the bottom meadows into swamps. The cows, sinking to their bellies in the mire, were coming in for milking with filthy udders. The farm's tracks were gouged with muddy ruts and potholes and James's legs ached constantly from the weight of clay caked around his boots. He was tired of being soaked to the skin, tired of the wind's bitter chill striking through him like a steel blade and tired of everything going wrong. At times he wanted to give up, to ignore the cows and the farm, to stay indoors with Grace.

Lying in bed, he asked himself if he was cut out to be a farmer.

The thirty gallons of milk wasted during the week was due to his own stupidity. No one else was to blame. He had been hurrying. Stubborn. Not listening to Grace when she had advised him to be careful. He had known the roads were bad but had been driving too fast. He remembered the truck rocking from side to side. Remembered his sudden sense of panic expecting it to topple. He had felt the wheels lock, struggled with the steering, but could do nothing. Within seconds the front end had embedded itself in a deep ditch.

Along the road, he had left a trail of spilled milk and littered the verge with dented churns. Fortunately there was no damage to the truck or himself, but it took three hours, and the help of another farmer, to pull the vehicle out of the ditch, and besides that, the missing milk delivery upset several of their regular customers.

John Fothergill had never made a fuss. He had been concerned but seemed philosophical about the accident, and glad that James had not been injured. 'These things happen,' he had said. 'Not a lot you can do about it.' He calculated that the number of cattle they were feeding for the Christmas trade would compensate them for the loss of the season's crop, and if needed, they could buy in extra stock feed. Despite their losses, he seemed quite positive. James, however, wasn't convinced. Market prices fluctuated and though at present the cattle looked good, if the rain continued much longer their condition would start to decline.

As he lay on the bed almost too weary for sleep, he thought about Grace. She was pregnant again and, whether she wanted to or not, soon she must stop working. That was going to mean even more work for him.

What the farm needed was an extra hand. But could they afford it and still support the two households? He must speak seriously with John about taking on some help. Perhaps a young lad to work full-time or a man to work part-time in the dairy and drive the truck.

He didn't know how Grace and her father had managed to run the farm on their own for all those years and wondered why he couldn't manage. What was he doing wrong? As he rolled over, he heard Grace's footsteps on the stairs. They must find time to talk about these things. Yawning, he heard her close the bedroom door but by the time she climbed into bed beside him, he was asleep.

'James! Help!'

James dropped the pails when he heard Grace's cry and ran back towards the farmhouse splashing through pools of mud.

'It's Dad,' she cried, when he was near the house.

John Fothergill was sprawled on the ground outside the back door. He was soaking wet, his face half submerged in muddy water but he was still breathing.

'I thought he was with you!' she yelled. 'I've just found him. I don't know how long he's been here.' Taking her father's arm, she tried to pull him up.

'Let me!' James said

'Is he all right?'

'He's alive, but we've got to get him inside and warm him up, or he'll not be for much longer.'

James grasped his father-in-law under the arms and dragged him into the house. A trail of mud followed them down the hall and into the bedroom. The old man groaned as James hoisted him onto the bed.

'I'll go fetch Alice. She'll know what to do.'

Grace nodded. What would happen now? Her father couldn't stay in the farmhouse alone, at least, not while he was sick and she couldn't stay at the cottage for fear he might have had another fall. There was only one solution – she would have to stay with him.

When more than an hour had elapsed since James had left, Grace started to worry. She was afraid he might have met with an accident; worried that the truck might have gone off the road again, or got bogged in a ditch. She'd wanted to go out searching for him but dare not leave her father. She didn't know that Alice wasn't home and James had gone to the village looking for the doctor or that he had waited in the surgery for almost an hour but the doctor didn't return from his house calls.

But by the time James got back, John Fothergill was beginning to feel better. Grace had removed his wet clothes and managed to get some warmth back into his cold body. While he remained still, the farmer had little pain, but with the slightest attempt to move, the pain was excruciating.

Grace was worried about him, but she was worried about James too. He looked exhausted. He was trying to do everything and it just wasn't possible. If he didn't slow down soon he would make himself sick.

With Mr Fothergill confined to bed, James and Grace slept at the farmhouse for the following week. There was little the doctor could do for the farmer save recommending bed rest and prescribing something to ease the pain in his hip. The old man didn't argue as it was impossible for him to move.

As Grace's pregnancy advanced, James could read the strain in her face. He knew her energies were being stretched to the limit. One afternoon he found her crying over a sheet she had torn in the mangle.

'Leave it, love. It doesn't matter,' he begged.

'It does matter!' she sobbed. 'I shouldn't have let it get stuck.'

He knew she was not coping. They were all under strain.

James didn't want to drive Alice to Ilkley. He wanted to stay at home with Grace and catch up on a few jobs around the cottage. He knew once they got to Ilkley, Alice would be obliged to stop and talk with Pansy and Miss Pugh, which meant they probably wouldn't get back until late in the afternoon.

But he had promised Alice he would take her to collect Rachel and he couldn't let them down. At least it wouldn't happen again. This time Alice was collecting Rachel and bringing her home to stay permanently.

'Why don't you come with us?' James asked Grace 'There's plenty of room in the car. The ride will do you good.'

'I can't leave Dad,' Grace said.

Despite not wanting to leave either his wife or the farm, James enjoyed the half-hour drive. He'd had little opportunity for such luxuries recently.

With the car roof folded back, the wind was exhilarating. Alice, her head wrapped in a silk scarf, seemed more relaxed than she had been for a long time. She was looking forward to having Rachel share the cottage with her.

Speeding past open fields and clusters of houses in the villages, James asked Alice about her new job in Horsforth and how she was enjoying being back at the cottage. She asked him about Mr Fothergill, the farm, Grace, and when the next baby was due.

With the conversation drifting to more trivial matters, James relaxed. Sitting beside Alice reminded him of the times they had spent riding when they were young. Those had been good times, happy times without any stress. He had almost forgotten the fun they had had in each other's company and how much she had meant to him. He looked across at Alice, her eyes watering in the wind, her hair steaming from beneath the scarf. How attractive she was. Mature. Intelligent. Well dressed. The tweed suit she was wearing was well tailored. The silk stockings, smooth and shiny. Her shoes, the latest fashion. Was this really the waif he had found huddled in the heather beside the upturned wagon and her dead father? How much they had both changed since that time.

It was an emotional parting for Pansy and her granddaughter. Pansy had treated Rachel as if she was her own daughter and Rachel regarded Pansy as her mother. Now the little girl was moving back to live with her real mother, Alice – a woman she knew little about. Back to Horsforth and Honeysuckle Cottages – a place she was not familiar with.

The goodbyes were protracted.

Old Miss Pugh was in surprisingly good spirits and appeared to be in full control of her senses. 'You mustn't worry about Pansy,' Miss Pugh said to Alice. 'I'll look after her.' Her tone was confident and convincing. The spinster was certain it was Pansy, rather than herself, who was in need of care. 'We manage well together, don't we dear?'

Pansy smiled. 'Of course we do, Aunty.'

The old woman drew Alice aside and whispered in her ear: 'Don't you worry about her, my dear. She'll be all right. She'll have this place when I'm dead and gone.'

Alice thanked Miss Pugh politely and told her that she and Rachel would be visiting every week.

'But it's such a long way to come,' Pansy argued.

'While the weather's fine and the trains are running, we'll come. You know I love to get out on the moors or walk along the riverbank. I've spent too many years cooped up indoors. Besides, I know Rachel will want to see you.'

Rachel cried, when she hugged her grandmother.

'I will see you next week,' Pansy said. 'The time will fly.'

Rachel had only one small suitcase and a paper carrier bag with a few books and toys which James placed carefully on the front seat. As he drove back to Horsforth, Alice and Rachel talked quietly. James couldn't hear what they were saying and didn't try to join in the conversation.

The following week, Alice and Rachel didn't go to Ilkley as planned, instead, on the Saturday, Pansy came to visit them in Horsforth.

Alice had arranged a party for Rachel. It wasn't her birthday, but as she had never given her daughter a party before, coming home seemed like a good enough reason to celebrate.

Prompted by the party and the fact Mr Fothergill could no longer manage on his own after the fall, Grace decided he should move into the cottage with them. James collected a single bed from the farm and assembled it in the front room of the cottage. During the day the farmer sat in Edward's leather armchair, resting his legs on a stool.

At first Mr Fothergill wasn't sure about living away from the farm. He had grown up in the rambling old house, which his grandfather had built, and this was the first time he had been away. But he knew his incapacity was causing problems and hated being a burden.

'If I was a cow you would shoot me,' he said to James one day. 'Damn nuisance. Rheumatics that's all it is.'

But he never joked to Alice about his leg. 'I wish sometimes the doctor would take it off. I'd manage better without it.'

It was a fun party. Alice made paper hats and toffee apples. They played charades and James amazed them with card tricks he had learned in the army. Later in the afternoon they trooped into Lucy's cottage for a sing-song. If some of the keys were out of tune, no one cared. It was a long time since Alice had played.

When Mr Fothergill started to doze, Grace decided it was time to leave and took him home. Only moments after tucking him up in his bed, he was snoring loudly and quite oblivious to the sound of voices raised around the piano next door.

Glancing from the window, Grace noticed something unusual about the Tourer parked on the lane where James had left it. The roof was still down, but the bonnet was up and the engine was being cranked over. Why had James left the party, she wondered, and where was he going with the car? Perhaps he was planning to take the children for a ride. Or did he have things to do at the farm? It was strange he hadn't said anything before she left.

As she watched, the man leaning down beside the radiator grille stood up. Despite the goggles covering half of his face, Grace knew instantly it wasn't James.

Running out the door, as quickly as she could, she shouted, 'Hey! You! What do you think you're doing?'

The man leaned down and turned the crank-handle again. This time the engine fired and, after quickly closing the bonnet, he jumped into the driver's seat.

Grace reached the lane just as the Tourer started to roll. Jumping onto the running board, she grabbed hold of the passenger door. 'Get out! This isn't your car!' she screamed.

The driver accelerated.

'Stop thief!' she yelled

But the man had no intention of stopping and the car was gathering speed.

Even above the sound of the piano, James heard Grace's screams but, by the time he reached the lane, the car was halfway down the hill and Grace was still hanging onto to the side. He started running but the Tourer was going faster. Twenty miles an hour – twenty-five miles an hour – too fast to take the bend!

The brakes were of little use on the loose gravel and when the driver jammed his foot on them, the narrow tyres skidded towards the verge. When the car hit the soft edge, the chassis bounced and Grace was tossed onto the wet grass which sloped steeply away from the road. Landing on her back she slid to the bottom of the slope like a sledge down a hill of fresh snow.

James watched helplessly. When the car reached the corner, it spun in a complete circle, ran on two wheels, then tottered slowly onto its side before coming to a halt. Though the engine spluttered and died, the front wheel continued spinning in the air, while steam and boiling water spouted from the radiator.

A man was lying on the road at the far side of the car, blood smeared across his face. But James didn't care about him. It was Grace he was worried about. She was lying at the bottom of the slope. After sliding down the grass to where she had come to a halt, he lifted her hand. She didn't move.

'Grace!' he cried.

Chapter 27

The Strid

Grace groaned as she lifted her head. 'I've been kicked by a cow before today, but it never felt quite like this!'

James kneeled down and helped her sit up. 'Promise me you won't ever do anything like that again. You could have been killed!'

'Are you all right, Grace?' cried Alice, sliding down beside the pair.

James jumped up. 'Stay with her! I want to find the bastard who did this!'

Scrambling back up the hill was not as easy as getting down and, although James dug his fingers into the soil, his feet would not grip on the wet slope. After a few unsuccessful attempts, he resorted to the longer route round the bottom of the hill. It brought him out further down the lane. Heading back to his car, up the rise, he wondered what damage had been done. At least the windscreen was still intact and the headlights were in one piece. He was certain the running board would be twisted, because the Tourer was resting on it. He was just thankful Grace was not pinned underneath it.

Walking around to the far side of the vehicle, he expected to find the thief lying on the gravel, but he had disappeared. The only trace of the offender was a few spots of blood.

James was angry. He didn't care about the man's injuries, but he did want to see him punished for what he had done to Grace.

'Coward!' he yelled, scanning the bushes. 'You'll get what's coming to you, one of these days!'

James led the constable upstairs and knocked on the bedroom door.

Having complained of feeling unwell after the accident, Grace was in bed. Alice had insisted she rest, having grave fears she might lose the baby which was due in a few weeks' time.

Grace fastened her bed jacket. 'Come in!'

'Can you describe this man?' the policeman said.

'I'm sorry,' Grace said. 'I couldn't see his face. His cap was pulled low on his forehead and he was wearing a pair of goggles. All I remember was a drooping moustache, brown and straggly, and the look in his eyes as the car speeded up.' A shudder ran through her. 'I think he was laughing at me.'

James looked at the constable, but refrained from speaking.

The policeman closed his notebook. 'Thank you, Mrs Oldfield. If you think of anything else, please let me know.'

'I will.'

Collecting his bike from the front fence, the officer wheeled it out to the lane. 'You said you thought the man was injured.'

'There was blood on the ground, but he took off that quickly, I don't think there was much wrong with him.'

'I hope it's not that fellow, Wilkinson or Crowther, or whatever he now calls himself. I was hoping we'd seen the last of him.'

'Do you think it could be the same man who robbed us?' James asked.

'I'm damned sure it is,' the constable replied, as he wheeled his bike onto the lane. 'Shame the magistrate had to dismiss the case through lack of evidence. This fellow is cunning as a fox, he is. Goes to ground for a while, then when he feels safe, up he pops again. But it's the first time I've heard of him trying to pinch a car.'

'Have you had any other reports in the area?'

'Not here. But I heard of a case last week in Otley. A poor woman who lived on her own was robbed and beaten up. Left her in such a state she could hardly talk. All she could tell the local Bobbies was that the man had a moustache. Hardly enough to go on! But I wouldn't be surprised if it was the same fellow.' He looked James in the eye and spoke quietly. 'That young wife of yours is lucky to be alive. I suggest you keep a good watch around the place.'

Tapping his helmet firmly on his head, the policeman swung his leg over the bike's saddle. 'I'd give my right arm to get my hands on that man! Deserves to be put away for life in my book.'

'We'll watch out,' James said. 'Thanks.'

Though Lucy and Cyril's arrival was expected, the car's engine had hummed so quietly up the hill no one heard it coming. The vehicle was brand new and expensive – the latest model to roll off the production line of the Armstrong Siddeley factory. Even in the greyness of the day, the paint shone and the chromework gleamed.

'They're here,' Grace called excitedly, when she saw them through the window.

James was first outside to hug his mother and shake hands with her new husband.

'It's so good to be home again,' Lucy said.

How well she looked, James thought. And happy too.

'Nothing has changed,' she said, standing at the gate and running her eyes over the three adjoining cottages.

But in James's mind, a lot had changed in the two years since his mother had left to settle Edwards's affairs in India. He and Grace had married. Andrew had been born and another baby was due at Christmas. Mr Fothergill now lived with them permanently as he could only manage to walk a few yards and only with reluctance allowed himself to be pushed around in the Bath chair which James had bought for him. Alice had returned to Honeysuckle Cottages and was settled into her new part-time job at the nursing home. And Rachel had come to live there too, although neither he nor Grace saw much of her. When Alice was working, Rachel was minded by a lady in the village, and every Saturday the Alice took her daughter to Ilkley to spend the day with Pansy and Miss Pugh. James had seen little of Pansy recently, due to the fact her aunt's mental state had deteriorated considerably and she didn't like to leave the old lady alone for very long.

As they chatted around the fire, Grace served tea and Lucy asked about the farm.

'Things are improving,' James said, glancing at his wife. 'We went through a bad spell for a while, didn't we?'

Grace nodded as Andrew crawled onto her lap, his eyelids drooping.

'We've got a labourer and a lad working for us now,' James said. 'Local men. Both good workers. It makes such a difference. Money's a bit tight at times, but we manage.'

'When the baby's born I'll be able to do more,' Grace added. 'I hate being useless.'

John Fothergill shuffled in his chair but said nothing.

'Well I must say you look happy, James. Married life must suit you.'

'And you look happy too, Mum.' James turned to Cyril. 'You must be good for her!'

They all responded to Cyril's broad smile. 'Good for each other,' he said, winking.

While James and Cyril talked about the farm, Mr Fothergill was content to sit and listen. James was filled with enthusiasm. He was eager to show his mother the changes he had made to the dairy, and the modern milking equipment they had had installed. He wanted to take Cyril out to the far meadow to show him the red Angus bull they had bought to cover the black heifers. 'No trouble with the Angus breed at calving time,' he said. He particularly wanted to show them both over the parcel of land he had just managed to lease to run the small beef herd on.

'We'll have a bumper season next year,' James said.

John Fothergill leaned forward in his chair towards Lucy. 'He's got his head screwed on right, that lad of yours. Done far more than I ever did with the place. I could never see further than the end of my nose, but young James here, well, there's no stopping him.'

'Only problem is finance,' said James seriously. 'Can't do anything without capital. That's something I want to talk to you about, Mum, but it can wait until later.' He paused. 'Now tell us about your travels and about yourself, Cyril. My mother has been keeping us in the dark. I want to hear about this man who swept her off her feet.'

'Me!' he said. 'Don't blame me. If anyone was doing the sweeping, it was this mother of yours.'

Lucy smacked his hand playfully. 'You wait till I get you next door!'

He laughed. 'See what I mean!'

The evening sky was changing colour. Across the meadow the hilltops glowed in the dying rays of the sun.

'I want to sell the cottage,' James announced to his mother. 'Grace and I have been talking about it for some time. It would be more sensible for us to live at the farm rather than walking there every day. Besides, Grace misses her big kitchen, and there will be plenty of room for Andrew and for the new baby when it arrives. Apart from that, John will be happy to be back in his own place.'

Lucy thought for a moment before answering. 'But you could lease your cottage and get a decent rent for it.'

'We considered that idea, but right now it's money we need. If we sell, we can put the money back into the farm. It'll pay big dividends in the long run.'

'I know John Fothergill's a good man,' Lucy said, 'but is it wise to put all your money into a farm that's not yours?'

'It is though!' James said. 'He signed over the title to me and Grace some time ago. It's all legal. He said he didn't want problems with it when he was dead. He's a good man, Mother, he really is.'

Lucy agreed, John Fothergill was a generous man.

'Do you and Cyril want to buy my cottage?' James asked, rather uncomfortably. 'You could knock down the adjoining wall and make the two places into one. It would give you much more space, and the cottages are in need of modernising.'

Lucy hadn't considered that idea. 'It's possible,' she said thoughtfully, 'Cyril and I haven't yet decided what we will do in the future. But, somehow, I don't think we will stay in Yorkshire.'

James was not surprised.

'There are places we like overseas. We both enjoy the sunshine. But Cyril likes his home in Kent and I have to admit it's a lovely place. The house is set in a big garden with huge rhododendron bushes around the lawns. I've never seen them in full bloom but he tells me they look beautiful. And Kent is such a nice county.'

As they walked across the back meadow, Lucy's mind drifted. It was a long time since she had felt the field beneath her feet. She smiled: 'I remember struggling across this ground with the hand plough. Me, Pansy and Alice worked this meadow every year while you were away at the war. And I remember the horses too. How patient they were.'

James's smile was wistful as he remembered Goldie, his horse that lived out its years in the paddock and was only put down when it went lame. He thought too of Edward's mare. The horse that was stolen and never recovered.

'You and Edward used to enjoy your rides together,' Lucy said. 'He was such a remarkable man. Without him none of us would be where we are today.'

'We should go inside,' James said. 'You are getting cold.'

'No, just a shiver,' she murmured. 'And a few memories.'

Cyril bought the tree for Christmas. It was the tallest one they had ever had in the house. Its tip touched the ceiling. He also bought the coloured lights which were a change from the tinsel and paper decorations of previous years. This year all the presents were wrapped in fancy paper and the pile was bigger than it had ever been before.

Rachel was so excited, and when it was time for Pansy to arrive from Ilkley, she was constantly rushing outside to look for her grandmother. When the car finally pulled up, she ran down the path, arms outstretched to greet her. In the crisp air their combined breath puffed like steam from an engine. Jumping up and down, Rachel tugged at the shopping bag on Pansy's arm and dragged her grandmother into the house.

'Isn't it wonderful all being together like this?' Lucy said. 'It has been so long.'

Christmas dinner was a feast. Turkey and pork and all the trimmings. The turkey had been raised and fattened on the farm, but James had bought the pig at Otley market.

'We should build some sties,' James said to his father-in-law. 'Get two or three gilts and a boar. We've got plenty of grain and I'd have no trouble selling the piglets.'

Mr Fothergill agreed. The idea was worth thinking about.

Rachel wasn't interested in pigs, apart from the gingerbread ones Lucy had made with currants for eyes and a candied-peel tail. For Rachel it seemed to take forever before the adults were finished at the table and Mr Fothergill's chair pushed through to the other room.

By the time they all sat down, Lucy's front room was crowded. Cyril and Lucy shared the sofa, John Fothergill's Bath chair was squeezed in beside the fireplace, Alice perched on the piano stool with Rachel beside her, while Grace sat opposite her father, bouncing Andrew on her knee. James was content to rest on the chair arm, while Pansy sat on a straight chair by the window.

Once everyone was settled, the presents were opened. Amidst the litter of string and wrapping paper, Rachel and Andrew took pride of place on the rug.

'This is the best Christmas I can remember,' whispered Lucy, as she leaned against her husband and placed a kiss on his cheek.

That evening Alice and James took turns at the piano. They played almost every carol in the book and a few of Cyril's favourite hymns. Even John Fothergill joined in, until he was suddenly overcome by tiredness. When he started snoring, Grace said she would take him back to their cottage. She too was very tired and with the baby due anytime, she had been feeling very weary of late.

Amelia Rose was born at three in the afternoon on New Year's Day – exactly a week later.

That winter was fairly mild. Apart from the water troughs freezing over, and an occasional flurry of snow which didn't settle, James had no problems getting to the farm. The dairyman who worked for them lived nearby and besides being reliable, was an early riser. Every morning he had the cows in the shed before James arrived.

After the birth, Grace was happy for them to remain at the cottage until the baby was a few months old. They decided that they would put off moving back to the farmhouse until spring arrived.

Over the winter, Mr Fothergill also lost the hankering to move back to the farm. The rambling house took a long time to heat through and was bitterly cold without a fire. But the front room of James's cottage, where the farmer had his bed, was always warm. This was the first winter in a long time, he didn't suffer from the cold. He even enjoyed being taken for a drive with the car's heater warming his legs. He enjoyed watching the season as it slowly changed and the criss-cross pattern of winter branches preparing to burst into a canopy of fresh green. John Fothergill always looked forward to spring.

The Sunday after the May Day celebrations, Alice paid her weekly visit to her mother, and because Lucy and Cyril had gone to the seaside for the day and taken Rachel with them, she went alone.

When Alice arrived at the Ilkley house, she was pleased to hear Miss Pugh was well. That meant that she and Pansy could go out for a few hours without worrying about the elderly lady. It was a nice day so they decided to catch a bus to Burley-in-Wharfedale. From there they would amble back to Ilkley along the riverbank. It was a long walk but one they always enjoyed.

Through the valley, the river meandered silently. At its widest point, the crystal water magnified each speckled pebble and darting fish as clearly as if it was in a goldfish bowl. For much of the way, the footpath was soft and flat. But as the river narrowed through the wooded glades, the banks grew steep, the path slippery. Occasionally it was obstructed by a fallen tree or trickling stream. The women didn't mind. They scrambled over and wandered on. They loved the scenery, enjoyed each other's company and chatted avidly. Without Rachel with them, they were able to stride out at their own pace.

When they reached a clearing, they stopped. Ahead, grey boulders, felted with green lichen, almost barricaded the river's course, squeezing the gently flowing stream through a narrow neck and turning it instantly into a gushing torrent. Gurgling loudly, the water rushed through relentlessly, dropping six feet over the edge and disgorging itself into a white, cold, bubbling cauldron of swirling foam. Constantly refilled, the deep pool beneath overflowed, splashing its contents across the rocks before allowing the river to span out again and for the River Wharfe to resume its leisurely journey downstream.

On the left bank, Alice and Pansy found their special seats; two weathered rocks, soft with moss and shaded by overhanging trees. Overhead, the sun was warm. It was a place the women often chose to stop, to sit and talk, and watch the swallows swooping and diving in endless circles across the sparkling water.

Behind them leaves rustled.

The bushes parted.

A man laughed.

'Stanley!' breathed Pansy. Memories flashed back – the face, the expression, the evil grin, masked by the whiskers covering his upper lip.

'So ladies, we meet again! It's been a long time!'

'Ignore him!' Alice cried.

'Two birds with one stone!' he laughed, sliding his hand on Pansy's knee.

As she tried to pull her leg away, Alice stood and swung her handbag at his head but his left arm shot out and sent her toppling back across the rocks.

'Leave us alone,' Pansy screamed.

'There's no one going to help you here,' he leered, forcing her back against the bank and reaching his hand beneath her skirt.

'Leave her alone!' screamed Alice, trying in vain to pull him off her mother.

He swung at her again and hit her full in the face. Then he muffled Pansy's screaming clamping his hand across her mouth.

As if from nowhere, a small dog appeared and snapped at Crowther's feet. He swung his foot at it but missed.

In the distance, Alice heard the sound of someone whistling for the dog.

'Help!' she shouted when she glimpsed three figures heading down the path towards them. She yelled again. This time they heard her and started running.

By the time Crowther saw the men, they were not more than thirty yards away – three fit young men each brandishing a walking cane. Crowther glanced to the bushes and along the track. He could see he'd never escape through the undergrowth or outrun them on the path as they were much younger and fitter than he. If it had been one man alone, he would have taken a chance and stood his ground.

Cursing, he ran across the bed of rocks, leaping from one boulder to another, heading for the point where the river gurgled through the gap. It was only five or six feet across. He'd jumped it once before when he was younger. He only needed speed to clear the distance.

'Come back!' the man cried, as his dog bounded after Crowther snapping at his heels.

'Don't jump!' another yelled.

When the dog jerked on his trouser leg, Crowther hesitated, but he was too close to the gap to change his mind. He leapt, his toes landing on the other side. But the rock was damp with moss and for a second he stood there as if hanging by an invisible thread. Suddenly his arms began to flay the air, turning round and round, faster and faster as he fought to regain his balance. Letting out a choking cry, he knew there was nothing could stop him from falling backwards.

The women watched helplessly when his feet slipped from the rock and he fell back into the rushing water.

Standing close to the edge, the terrier wagged its tail. The man he'd chased had disappeared. It barked and sniffed the air then turned and trotted back to its master.

'Damn fool,' one of the young men cried.

Stepping cautiously, Alice moved towards the water and gazed down. There was no trace of Stanley Crowther. Not even his cap.

'Be careful, lady,' the man said. 'Don't get too close.'

'Is it dangerous?'

'The Strid?' he said. 'It might not look dangerous but no one who's ever fallen in has surfaced at the other end.'

Alice looked at the crystal water flowing downstream from the pool. 'But it's shallow there. Couldn't he swim out?'

'You don't swim out of the Strid, missus. The rocks we're standing on are riddled with caverns underneath. The river swirls into them and carries everything with it. It never gives back what it drags down.'

When Alice stepped back, her legs were shaking.

'One thing's for sure,' the young man said. 'That man will never trouble you again. I can guarantee that!'

Chapter 28

The Storm

It was late, when Alice got back to the cottage and she was relieved when she remembered that Lucy and Cyril had gone out for the day and taken Rachel with them. All she wanted to do was to go inside and close her door on the outside world. Though Crowther was dead, she felt no desire to celebrate.

The following morning, Alice said nothing to Lucy about the incident, and the story she related about her bruises. Saying that she had fallen on the rocks beside the river was not entirely untrue. That day, she didn't go to work, instead she travelled by train to Ilkley and met her mother. At the local police station, the two women gave formal statements about the events that had occurred at the Strid.

'It's unlikely we'll ever find a body,' the constable said, confirming the comments of the young men who had helped them.

'Did you see him fall? Did you see him go under? Did the water pull him down?'

Alice answered as best she could – her mind still visualizing Stanley's face – his eyes wide open, his mouth gaping, gulping for air as the force of water dragged him under.

By the time she travelled home, her mind was blank. She was conscious of nothing but the *clickety-clack* of the train wheels on the railway lines, the carriage swaying side to side and the flash of fields and factories as they flew by. The only thought nagging at her was the fear the police would visit her in Horsforth. She wanted to forget Crowther, get far away from his memory, and forget the face now etched in her mind – the face which would return in the darkness to haunt her!

For Lucy and Cyril, their time in Horsforth was like an extension of the long holiday they had enjoyed together. They went out several evenings each week. Sometimes to a picture house to watch a film, or into Leeds to one of the city's theatres, to a musical recital at the town hall or, on a fine afternoon, to take a stroll across the park at Roundhay or hire a boat and row across the lake.

Lucy enjoyed the evenings when the children would play together on the floor. She would listen when Rachel tapped notes on the piano, and was sorry Alice had never had time to give her lessons. During the day she missed seeing James who was always busy on the farm and away from home from early morning until late in the afternoon.

Grace was a good mother, and the new baby, Amelia Rose was growing quickly. As the days got longer, Lucy knew Grace was becoming anxious to move back to the farmhouse.

Grace rolled over in bed. The noise of the storm was making sleep impossible. It had rumbled around the district for over an hour but now it was directly overhead. The crash of thunder came at the same time as a searing flash of light, rattling the ornaments on the dressing table.

James got up. It was pointless lying in bed. He couldn't sleep either and decided to make a cup of tea and bring it back to bed. But before he reached the door, another flash of white light startled him. A crack, like the sound of a leather horse-whip, accompanied it, then a loud hissing noise and a rumble like the sound of a rock face crumbling.

Grace sat bolt upright. 'What on earth was that?'

In the flashes of light through the window, James could see nothing for the rain beating against the pane. Outside, the wind was howling, then for a moment the rain stopped, and in the darkness light flickered outside. It was coming from the other end of the cottages.

'Something's wrong!' he shouted, pulling his trousers over his pyjamas.

Grace slid from the bed, grabbed her clothes and ran after him.

As soon as he stepped into the front garden, James was shocked. The chestnut tree beside Alice's cottage had been struck by lightning and the huge branches that draped over the roof were alight. At the upstairs window, he could just see Rachel's face. Her mouth was open – screaming – but the wind and storm were swallowing her cries.

'Get the fire brigade,' James shouted, as Lucy and Cyril appeared at their door.

'I'll go,' said Grace, running to the car.

Cyril followed James to the back of the cottages.

The sight that greeted them was horrific.

The old tree had been rent in two and split wide open. Flames were shooting from the centre like the incandescent flame of a huge pressure lamp. The enormous bough, which usually draped its shade over the house, had sheered from the trunk, slicing through the shingled roof and completely demolishing the back bedroom. The burning branches, rubble from the bedroom wall, the wooden rafters and slate shingles were all piled on the heavy beams that formed the kitchen ceiling.

'My God!' Cyril cried.

'The ladder!' James yelled. 'We've got to get them out!'

Clad only in pyjamas and slippers, Cyril ran to get it.

At the front of the cottage, Rachel had opened her bedroom window. Smoke was billowing around her. She was frightened. Coughing.

'We'll get you down!' James shouted as he leaned the ladder against the end cottage wall.

'Mummy!' she yelled. 'Mummy!'

As James grabbed her, he could just see through the smoke that the wall between the two bedrooms was still standing but the doorway to the staircase was filled with smoke.

'Where's your mummy?' he yelled, passing her down to Cyril.

'In bed,' Rachel sobbed. 'In the other room.'

James shook his head. She couldn't be in bed. There was no bed. There was no bedroom. No roof. That part of the cottage had completely gone. All that remained was the pile of burning rubble.

'Don't go in there!' Cyril shouted, as James climbed back up the ladder and in through the bedroom window. A moment later he reappeared, spluttering, and clambered down.

'I've got to get up there!' he cried. 'Alice is in there. I've got to get her out!'

Cyril didn't argue. Hurrying to the back of the cottage, they leaned the ladder against the remains of the back wall. James didn't notice that he was soaking wet, only that the flames were consuming the rotted roof timbers like slivers of dry Christmas paper.

Climbing onto the rubble, he scratched through it with his bare hands, tearing off broken bricks, slivers of slate and lumps of mortar. He knew where the bed had stood, where Alice would have been sleeping. He dug frantically, throwing the stones aside, unaware of the blood oozing from his fingers.

Suddenly he stopped. Sticking out of the rubble was a tiny black shoe, trimmed with a silver buckle. Carefully, he lifted the stones from around it. The doll, he had once wanted to use as Guy Fawkes had not been burnt, nor had the pale hand clasping it. The scars it bore were from another fire.

The clang of the fire engine's bell grew louder as it got closer. Then stopped.

James held Alice's hand until she was finally uncovered and, as they lifted her body down, he cradled the doll in his arms and cried.

Chapter 29

For Sale

'Shall I take it?' asked Lucy.

James looked at her blankly and handed the old doll to his mother.

'I loved Alice,' he said sadly. 'But I never knew how much until now.'

'I know,' she said.

'But why did she have to die like that – alone – afraid – and under all those flames?'

Grace put her arms around him and led him inside. 'There's nothing more you can do here. Come away.'

Early the following morning Lucy and Cyril drove the fifteen miles to Ilkley. Lucy hardly spoke in the car. There were so many things going around in her head. How would she break the news to Pansy of her daughter's death? And what would become of Rachel now she was an orphan?

As soon as she opened the door and saw the expression on Lucy's face, Pansy sensed something was wrong.

'It's Rachel, isn't it? Something terrible has happened to Rachel!'

'No Pansy, it's Alice.'

Pansy took the news quietly and appeared composed as Lucy told her what had happened. While the women talked, Cyril busied himself making tea and was pleased Miss Pugh was in good spirits and able to help him.

Pansy didn't touch her drink but waited until the others had finished before asking them to take her back to Horsforth. She was anxious to see where her daughter had died and the damage the fire had caused to the end cottage she had lived in for many years.

On leaving the house, Pansy instructed her aunt to stay inside, lock the door and not let anyone in.

Old Miss Pugh hugged Pansy and planted a kiss on her cheek. 'This war can't go on forever,' she said. 'Don't worry about me and the house. I'll make sure the door is locked. I'll be all right.'

No one spoke during the journey. In the back seat, Pansy stared blankly out of the window. Her eyes were glazed but her face showed no evidence of tears. Lucy wondered if, because she had lost her husband and young Timothy, she had developed an inner strength and was able to maintain her self-control. But when the car stopped at the cottages and Rachel ran into her arms, Pansy wept out loud.

Lucy and Cyril walked quietly away leaving the pair to grieve together and Lucy felt confident the little girl would be well cared for. She was certain, Rachel would be happy to resume her life with Pansy and the poor demented Miss Pugh.

Less than a week later a telegram arrived from Pansy. It read:
Desperately need your help. Rachel missing.

Lucy and Cyril set off immediately, calling in at the farm on the way. James was out in the truck but Grace said she was sure he would follow them as soon as he got back. Despite Lucy's concern, Grace insisted the farm could manage without him for a while.

When Lucy and Cyril arrived at the tall Victorian house in Ilkley, Pansy was in a state of near collapse. She had neither slept nor eaten since the previous day and had spent the night walking the streets searching for her granddaughter. Her feet were wet and dirty, her clothes damp, but she refused either to change or go to bed.

'She went out to play yesterday morning,' said Pansy, 'to the park. It's only a hundred yards away, so I thought nothing of it. She often went there on her own, but she always came back after an hour.' Pansy raked her fingers through her hair. 'When she wasn't home by dinner-time, I went out to find her. I looked everywhere. By tea-time, I was at my wits' end and went to the police station. The sergeant was on his own and said he couldn't leave, but he told me a constable would call around later.'

Pansy said she was out all that evening but presumed an officer had visited the house, as Miss Pugh told her a soldier had called during the night.

'I sent the telegram first thing this morning. I didn't know what else to do. I've searched everywhere. The only other places I can think to look are the moors and the river-bank, the places we used to go walking with Alice.'

It was some time before Pansy calmed down but when she eventually relaxed a little, her eyes quickly closed. Lucy didn't try to move her from the chair, instead she pulled a blanket over her and left her to sleep by the fire.

Though Miss Pugh appeared quite lucid and was worried about her niece, she was confused. She thought Lucy was her sister and, because so many people had called in to visit, believed it was Christmas Day. Her main concern was that she had made no preparations for the meal and could not remember where she had hidden the presents.

James arrived two hours later. After hearing what had happened, he and Cyril decided they should immediately set off across the moors from Heber's Ghyll to the Cow and Calf rocks. If their search was unsuccessful, the next morning they would take the path that followed the river.

About four o'clock in the afternoon the two men found Rachel. She was huddled amongst a pile of fallen rocks at the base of the Cow rock, asleep. Apart from being cold and hungry and her legs scratched by the heather, she was all right. She couldn't remember walking over the open moors or why she had made her way to the Cow and Calf. She didn't know how long she had been there, but told them she was waiting for her grandmother to collect her.

When they got back to the house, Rachel ran inside to Pansy's arms. As the pair held each other, Lucy could not hide her tears. Cyril excused himself, saying he would drive to the police station and give them the news.

The following day James arranged for a bulldozer to demolish what remained of the end cottage. After the pile of rubble had been cleared, James and Cyril chopped down the burnt-out trunk of the chestnut tree and, after dragging the branches into the meadow, they set them alight.

Because the wood was green and the boughs so thick, the bonfire smouldered for four days. James kept an almost constant watch and was not satisfied until every branch, twig and leaf had disappeared and all that remained of the spreading tree was a pile of ash.

Later that week, James told his mother that he and Grace had decided to leave the cottage and move back into the Fothergill farmhouse.

'Do you want to make the two cottages into one?' he asked his mother.

Lucy shook her head. 'I don't really want to live here anymore,' she said. 'It's never going to be the same.'

That evening Lucy and Cyril agreed. They would move to Cyril's house in Kent. The two remaining cottages could then be put up for sale.

Cyril helped James move his furniture to the farm. After emptying his own cottage, James took some of his mother's things as there was little Lucy wanted to take with her to Kent.

The next morning, Cyril drove Lucy to Skipton where she paid a final visit to Proctor and Armitage, the solicitors who had served her well. Apart from instructing the firm to handle the sale of the Honeysuckle Cottages, she wanted to arrange for the money she would receive to be added to the trust she had set up for Rachel. She wanted to ensure there would be ample funds for Alice's daughter to attend a good girls' school and, if she desired, to take private lessons in ballet or singing. Also, if Rachel proved to be as bright as Alice had been, there would be enough funds to support her through college.

Before returning to Horsforth, the pair stopped at a musical instrument shop and purchased a piano. Lucy arranged for it to be delivered to Miss Pugh's house in Ilkley.

'I hope Rachel's lessons won't drive the old dear crazy,' Lucy said, with a wry smile.

Lucy and Cyril spent their final day with James, Grace and Mr Fothergill at the farmhouse. Before they left, James gave his mother the ebony box, inlaid with mother-of-pearl that had belonged to Edward Carrington – the one he had found in the attic. He also insisted she select some of Edward's fine china and ornaments from the glass cabinet.

'Take Constance too,' he said, handing her the old doll. 'I remember the day Alice gave her that name. We never did discover where it came from, did we?'

Lucy shook her head and looked down at the doll in her hands. The dress was torn and dirty, the strip of goat skin, now almost bald, was peeling from the head. It was nothing like the French doll she had first admired at Heaton Hall.

'Are you sure?' she said.

'She's yours,' he replied.

Lucy took it and wondered.

When the Armstrong Siddeley drove down the lane, the remaining two cottages looked bare. There was no lace at the windows. No smoke curling from the chimneys. No sound of children's laughter echoing from inside. And no tree. The only addition was a wooden sign, planted next to the gate in the front garden. Painted in bold letters across the top were the words: FOR SALE.

Lucy glanced at it for a moment as Cyril drove slowly by, then she wound up the car's window and turned her eyes back to the road.

Chapter 30

The Doll

The letter from Proctor and Armitage arrived only two weeks after Lucy had settled into Cyril's house in Kent. It detailed an offer on her cottage which the solicitors advised she should accept. Lucy replied by return mail. She wanted to close her affairs in Horsforth as soon as possible.

A week later she received a letter from Pansy.

My dear Lucy

I do not know how to thank you for what you have done for me and Rachel. We will be forever in your debt.

What a surprise it was when a lorry arrived with a piano on the back. Rachel was delighted and is keen to start taking lessons.

You will be surprised when I tell you my dear Aunt sat down and tried to play. I think, as a young woman, she may have played the church organ as she knows a few hymns. Her fingers are not agile and do not work in time, but we can recognize the music. Rachel is encouraging her and they are enjoying each other's company.

As for Rachel, she has settled down far quicker than I could have expected. She never talks about the fire or her mother but at times I see her looking at the photograph of Alice on the mantelshelf.

The last few lines of the letter were smudged and hard to read. Lucy suspected her friend had cried a little when writing them.

Despite writing to James three times, Lucy had to wait several weeks before she got a reply from him. He apologized for not writing earlier, saying he had been too busy but adding that the family had quickly settled in at the farmhouse. Mr Fothergill, in particular, was happy to be home.

With the sale of his cottage already going through, James had arranged for some improvements to the farmhouse and the installation of a telephone. He said that on the farm the season was going well and that financially it would be their best year yet.

He finished his letter by saying Andrew and little Amelia Rose were well and added that Grace was expecting again. He sent his love and best wishes to them both. At the bottom of the page Grace added a few words of her own.

Lucy stood at the window watching a summer shower. She knew it wouldn't last long. Already the sun was breaking through forming a perfect rainbow across the sky. She admired the raindrops running down the pane. They were smooth and round like beads of quicksilver. A small bird splashed and fluttered its wings, on the wet grass, bathing itself.

How lovely the summer is in England, Lucy thought.

Though Lucy had travelled across London from one railway station to another, she had never visited any of the famous places. Cyril, however, having spent many years at the Stock Exchange, knew the City well and was pleased to show her the sights.

They watched the boats from Westminster Bridge and wandered slowly through the Abbey. After feeding the birds in St James's Park they strolled down The Mall and by the time they reached Trafalgar Square, Lucy's legs ached. It was a long time since she had walked so far.

'Seen enough?' Cyril asked, as they gazed up at Lord Nelson, the paving around their feet swirling in a sea of grey pigeons.

'Enough for one day,' Lucy said.

Cyril suggested they find a place that served tea and cakes before the long drive home.

Heading down a narrow lane to a small café, Lucy was attracted by a display in a shop window. A tall doll, dressed in a nurse's uniform, was standing beside a miniature bed. Lying on the bed, covered in a sheet, was another doll. The sign suspended above the display was printed in bold red letters. It read: DOLLS' HOSPITAL.

Cyril was happy to wait outside, while Lucy went into the shop and spoke with the proprietor. When she came out, she looked pleased.

'The man said he would be interested to see that old doll of mine. He thinks, from the description I gave, it may be a French Bru and says he doesn't see many of them. He told me they usually only come from private collections. He suggested it could be quite valuable if properly restored.'

As they strolled together, arm in arm, Lucy was silent.

'Are you thinking about that doll?' Cyril asked.

Lucy nodded. 'Next time we are in London, I will bring it with me.'

Not wanting to spend the winter in England, Cyril and Lucy booked a passage on a steamer sailing from Southampton. The ship was calling at Madeira *en route* for the West Indies. Having heard the island offered a pleasant climate, they planned to disembark there and if they liked the place, they would stay until the worst of the English winter was over.

Three weeks prior to sailing, Lucy wrote to Captain Wainwright asking if they could visit him and stay for a few nights in Tunbridge Wells. She explained that she had business to attend to nearby. Wainwright replied by return mail. He said he would be delighted to accommodate them and once again asked to be invited to join them on board, to take afternoon tea with them before the ship sailed.

The first evening with Wainwright was very pleasant. Because Cyril had travelled extensively, he and the captain had much to converse about. They stayed up late talking about ships and foreign ports. Lucy was happy to listen and was pleased the two men got on so well.

The following morning they breakfasted early. Lucy had planned the day's outing well in advance. She and Cyril would drive down to Hastings, have an early lunch in the old town then follow the coast road to Bexhill. If time permitted they would continue on to Eastbourne, arriving back in Tunbridge Wells before dark.

Wainwright declined the invitation to accompany them saying he was looking forward to visiting Southampton docks the following day. Lucy heard him whisper to Cyril about having some shopping to attend to. Something about purchasing a bottle of champagne.

The sprawling house, perched on the cliff-top near Bexhill-on-Sea, looked out across the English Channel. The azure sky reflected on the sea, its surface unbroken except for the white sails of passing yachts which dotted the water like wandering gulls. The breeze blowing from the land was light. It was not cold for the time of year.

From the main gate, guarded by a pair of reclining stone lions, the driveway to the house was bordered on both sides by tall young poplars whose autumn leaves littered the gravel. On the east side of the house was a close-mown croquet lawn and on the grass beyond, a set of swings, a see-saw and a child's wooden play-house. From the top of the cliff, a steep path, with a hand-rail, sloped down to the beach below. In front of the house, the driveway encircled a pond complete with water lilies, goldfish and an ornamental fountain.

As the car tyres crunched to a stop, Lord Farnley came down the steps to meet his guests. He greeted Lucy with a polite kiss on the cheek.

'My husband, Cyril Street,' she said.

After shaking hands, Archibald Farnley invited them inside and accompanied Lucy while Cyril collected a cardboard box from the boot of the car. He carried it under his arm.

Once comfortably settled, the housekeeper served tea then Lord Farnley turned to Lucy. 'I was intrigued by your letter, wondering what it was you were anxious to see me about.'

Lucy took the parcel from her husband. 'This is for you,' she said softly. 'Would you care to open it?'

Lord Farnley looked from her to Cyril before untying the string. Laying the box on the mahogany table, he lifted the lid and pulled back the sheets of tissue paper.

'My goodness!' he said. 'What a handsome doll!'

'Please take it out.'

Gingerly Lord Farnley lifted the doll to an upright position. As he did, the long eyelashes rolled back and a pair of luminous blue eyes gazed out at him.

'It's French,' said Lucy. 'A Bru doll. Made in the 1890s. That's why her face has some fine lines. Like me, she is beginning to show signs of age.'

The doll's cape was folded at the back. Lucy reached out and smoothed it down. The velvet, in a rich shade of burgundy, was as soft as the strip of ermine which edged it. Beneath the cape, the spun-silk dress, trimmed with a yoke of Swiss lace, was decorated with tiny pearls. The pale grey wig shone with the lustre of pure mohair and was set into soft bouncing ringlets which fell to the doll's shoulders. The broad rimmed hat sported three pheasant feathers.

In one lace-gloved hand the doll held a turned wooden walking stick, its handle and ferrule tipped with silver. The kidskin shoes bore silver buckles, polished to a fine mirror finish. A tiny gold brooch decorated the slender neck.

'I thought perhaps your granddaughter might like it,' said Lucy.

Lord Farnley sat down. His face was pale.

'Are you all right?' Lucy asked.

'Yes,' he said, staring at the doll. 'There is something about it which reminds me of a doll I bought many years ago.'

Lucy paused. 'Did it have a velvet cape of peacock blue?'

'Yes,' he said. 'How did you know?'

'This is the same doll,' she said kindly. 'You do not remember me. I was a maid at Heaton Hall. I was with your daughter when she died.'

Lord Farnley shook his head in disbelief.

Lucy continued. 'Your housekeeper, Mrs Gresham, gave the doll to me and told me to burn it. But I couldn't. I burned the clothes but kept the doll.'

'And you've had it all these years?'

'Yes,' said Lucy. 'But it was not right. I should not have taken it. It was never mine to have. Though, over the years, I have loved the doll, I always felt guilty. It was the only thing I ever stole. Now, I want to return it to you, so you may give it to your granddaughter, Felicity.' She smiled. 'I'm sure Miss Beatrice would have wanted her to have it.'

Lord Farnley wiped the tears from his eyes.

'I'm sorry,' Lucy said. 'I didn't mean to upset you.' She glanced anxiously at Cyril, as she waited for Lord Farnley to reply.

'Lucy,' he said, 'this doll means more to me than you can imagine. I never had a single thing to remind me of my daughter. No lock of hair. No pretty dress. No photograph. Everything she had was burned. And when she died, I even lost her image in my mind.

Although I tried long and hard, I could never conjure up her face, except occasionally in a dream, but in the morning she was gone.

'Now,' he explained, 'when I look at this doll, I see the great bed at Heaton Hall, and I see my Beatrice in it.' His face lit up. 'And I can see her face, as clearly as I see yours, smiling a soft smile, serene and beautiful.'

'Lucy,' he said, the tears rolling down his cheeks, 'you have given me more than a doll, you have given me back the memory of my daughter.'

Lucy and Cyril did not wait to be seen out. When they left, Lord Farnley was seated in his chair, but he was not looking at the French doll sitting opposite him, he was gazing at the little girl whom Lucy had returned to him.

*

THE BLACK THREAD

Book 3 in the Trilogy of Yorkshire Tales

Chapter 1

Leeds, 1895
The Homecoming

Whenever she heard her mother sobbing, Amy always remembered the day her father came home.

Though she was almost fifteen, she had never met him before that wet Saturday when he stepped over the doorstep and entered her life. Up to that time, the name Amos Dodd had hardly ever been spoken of.

One thing she did remember was nattering her mother with questions about her father. Why had he gone away? Where had he gone to? When was he coming back?

'You'll find out, one day,' was the most Lisbeth Dodd would say, leaving Amy to draw her own conclusions. All she was told was that he had left home shortly before she was born but, as he had never returned, she thought perhaps he'd gone abroad to seek his fortune. But sometimes, she wasn't sure about that.

Most of the men in their street worked at Fanshaw's Mill and returned home regular as clockwork every night. A few worked away on the railways, and they always came home on Saturday afternoon. One man went away and never came back. She heard he's sailed to Australia in search of gold, but he took his wife and children with him, and everything he owned.

Unlike those men, Amos Dodd had gone away leaving a pregnant wife and, to Amy's knowledge, not once since he'd left had he written. It was possible, she thought, that he could neither read nor write but there were never any messages from him either. No word at all was ever received. Then she wondered why her mother hadn't followed him, perhaps tried to join him wherever he was. And she was puzzled why her mother wouldn't answer questions about him. Didn't Lisbeth know where he was, or didn't she want to say?

Perhaps her mother had learned that he had been successful and felt jealous or inadequate? Whatever the case, she never spoke his name.

Despite not knowing, Amy longed for that day when he would return. She'd convinced herself her father would be rich and she knew exactly how that special event would unfold. It was a scene she'd imagined thousands of times. It would be like the welcome Mr Medley got every night, only a hundred times better.

Since she'd been old enough to climb the cellar steps, Amy had sat on the top one gazing out through the iron railings watching their neighbour as he trudged home from the mill after work. Though his dark hair and whiskers were always speckled with wool-fluff, his eyes would glint when he saw her watching him and he would wave.

'All right, Amy lass?' he'd ask.

'Aye, all right,' she'd reply shyly.

She wasn't the only one to notice. Everyone in the street knew when Moses Medley was heading home. You could hear him whistling from the time he left the mill's gate, and it was always the same merry tune.

As soon as Mrs Medley heard him, she'd open the door and their two youngest lads would scamper down the street to meet their father. When they were within arms' reach, he'd squat down on the cobbles, put his hand in his pockets and pull out a sweetie for each of them. Returning the lads' infectious smiles, he'd ruffle their hair, swing the older boy up and onto his shoulders, and with the little one cupped in the crook of his arm, the gentle giant-of-a-man would continue up the street to deposit the pair at his wife's feet.

'Inside, you two! Wash your hands,' Mrs Medley would say. 'Tea'll be ready in two ticks.'

It was always the same performance. It never changed. As the boys ran inside, Mr Medley would lean forward and peck his wife on the cheek, and she would grin back at him and tap him playfully on the leg. Then he'd wink and follow her inside, closing the door quietly behind him.

With that joyful homecoming fixed in her mind as firm as any gutter-grate, Amy knew that when her father returned, it would be a similar joyful event. He would swagger up the street, bold as brass, dressed in his Sunday best, but he'd not be whistling, he'd be shouting, calling her name at the top of his voice. 'Amy Dodd! Amy Dodd! Where are you?'

Amos Dodd wouldn't worry what people thought, and she wouldn't either. When she heard his voice, she'd run up the steps from the cellar, gaze up at him through the iron railings and reach out to touch the soft curls framing his kindly face against the sky.

In her mind, she was certain he'd be a fine figure of a man and that he'd bend down and kiss her through the bars. Then he'd pull his hand from his pocket, but in place of sweets, there'd be coins – gold coins and lots of them. And in his other hand, he'd have a box wrapped in paper and tied up with fancy ribbon which he'd present to Lisbeth, his wife. Then he'd hug her and invite him in and lead him by his soft warm hands. Then he would announce that his family wasn't going to live in that dingy cellar any longer and that he had come back to take them with him to start a new life in a country far away.

It was a frequently repeated day-dream!

But it was so very wrong.

How stupid she had been!

In all those years, she had never been told that her father was living not more than a mile from the two-roomed cellar which she and her mother called home. Lisbeth never told anyone, not even her daughter that Amos Dodd had spent the last fifteen years staring at the sky through iron bars – the bars of his prison cell in the turreted round tower that dominated the Leeds skyline – Armley Jail.

The thirteenth of April 1895 was a Saturday. And it was wet. The rain hadn't stopped since early morning and, when it poured like that, the water on the street overflowed the gutters, washed over the pavement and cascaded down the cellar steps into their tiny yard. Puddles formed quickly and continued filling until the whole yard was a reservoir several inches deep. With nowhere else to go, it slid over the doorstep, poking its broad wet tongue through the gap under the door. Once inside, it slithered and squirmed until it found the grooves between the slabs, branching into fingers and trickling silently along the narrow channels. As a child, Amy loved watching the water, wondering which stream would win the race to the other side of the kitchen.

Thinking back to the thirteenth of April, she realized her mother must have known her husband was returning. For several days, Amy sensed an unusual awkwardness about her, a distance between them that had never existed before. It was during that week the sunshine disappeared from Lisbeth's eyes and never returned.

From the day Amos Dodd returned, Amy never heard her mother laugh, but she certainly heard her cry.

He never knocked when he arrived, he just flung the door open and stood on the doorstep, dripping wet, allowing the wind and rain to blow down into the room. At the table, Amy glanced at her mother, expecting her to speak, but Lisbeth said nothing. Then she looked at her father and the dream she had held of his homecoming fizzled as quickly as the flame of a snuffed candle.

In appearance, Amos Dodd was far from the father she'd envisioned. He was short – the same height as her mother and perhaps only an inch taller than she was. His coat was wet, smelled wet, and was pitted with holes where the moths had chewed through it. The sleeves were too short and, though he was thin, the buttons hardly met across the chest. He certainly wasn't a rich man.

Needless to say, there was no purse full of coins and no parcel tied with ribbons tucked under his arm. In its place was a sodden bundle of old clothing tied up with twine. The only foreign thing he brought into the house was the stale smell of a smoky alehouse.

'Bloody rain!' he said, dropping the bundle and throwing his wet hat onto the horsehair chair in the corner. Though the fire reflected a glow on his wet face, it didn't disguise the pallor of his skin.

Amy had imagined he would have a mop of yellow hair, like her own, but his hair was short cropped and black as chimney soot. Bristling straight back from his temples, it was divided in half by a cap of crusty skin from which erupted one ugly black cauliflower wart and three single hairs. She stared.

'That's it, is it?' he said bluntly.

For a moment, Amy thought he was looking at something behind her then she realized he was looking at her.

Lisbeth nodded. 'Amy, say hello to your father.'

Was this really her father? she asked herself.

When her mother nudged her, she mumbled the word, 'Hello'.

'Huh!' he said, casting his eyes over the frugal furnishings. Amy held her mother's hand as he moved about the room, sniffing and pawing things like a wild-eyed feral cat. He opened a drawer, shuffled the contents noisily then slammed it shut. He peered into the iron pot, dipped his finger in the stew and sucked on it. Then he reached for the metal vase and rattled its contents before tipping them out on the mantelshelf. Running his fingers through the assortment of pins, buttons, needles and hooks, he ignored the ones that fell off and dropped to the hearth.

With a smirk on his face, he stepped through to the small room where the bed was. As far as Amy could remember, there had never been a door hanging in that gap. Only the remnants of one rotted upright remained fixed to the wall. After rubbing his back across it, her father unfastened his coat and let it drop on the floor.

'Come here,' he demanded.

She felt her mother's hand tighten on hers.

'Come here, woman, I said!'

Amy suddenly felt afraid. To her knowledge, her mother had never been spoken to like that before. Lisbeth Dodd had always been a self-sufficient woman, regarded by others as quietly confident and hardworking. Though she usually kept herself to herself, she was praised on the street for having raised a daughter with no man to support her.

'Can it wait till later, Amos?' she begged quietly. 'How about I get you a nice cup of tea?'

The cutlery jumped on the table as his fist thumped down. 'No, it can't bloody wait. I've waited fifteen bloody years. You get in there right now, or I'll bloody well drag you in!'

Lisbeth didn't move. Her grip tightened. Amy could sense her mother's heart was racing.

'It's either you or the brat! Take your choice. I'm not fussy.'

As he spoke, he slid the braces from his shoulders and began unfastening the buttons on his trousers.

'Go to Mrs Medley's, Amy, tell her—'

'You stay right where you are, girl. You don't move one step outside the door!'

With his pale eyes fixed on her, Amy froze.

He didn't tell Lisbeth again, just grabbed her by the wrist and dragged her through the opening where the door used to be and pushed her towards the bed. She offered no resistance.

Whatever happened after that, Amy didn't see, though she heard the sounds well enough and thought they would never stop – the clatter of the iron bed-head drumming against the wall as it rose to a crescendo. Her mother's pleadings: 'No, Amos. Don't, Amos. Please stop, you're hurting me,' then the muffled, painful cries and her father's breathing, fast and laboured, like a man running from a pack of wild dogs.

Almost as abruptly as the noises started, they stopped; except for the sound of her mother sobbing.

Edging slowly to the entrance of the windowless room, Amy peered at the bed. She could barely see her mother on it. Her face and arms were buried under her cotton petticoat; only her long red hair was visible on the pillow. She was pinned beneath her father who was spread-eagled over her. Amos Dodd lay motionless, eyes closed, his trousers bunched around his boots.

It was the first time she'd seen a man's bare bottom. It was the same colour as her mother's petticoat – greyish-white. The soles of his boots glistened even in that dull light. They were thick with mud and still wet. She was thankful her mother couldn't see her, though she wanted to touch her, hold her, reassure her. After watching and waiting for a moment, she stepped slowly back. The only sound she could hear was her mother sobbing. She was crying in a way she had never heard her cry before.

The fact Amos found no money hidden in the house incensed him, but after turning everything upside-down, he eventually had to accept that the pair had nothing put aside.

'It's time she had a proper job,' he growled, hardly looking at Amy. 'Waste of time doing people's odd jobs and running errands. How much does she make? A farthing here or a bag of scones there. With a proper job, a girl her age could bring home near ten shillings a week.'

He would have sent Lisbeth out to work too, but her mother argued that the jobs she did for the owner of the building was what allowed them to live in the cellar rent free. They couldn't afford to live anywhere else unless he was prepared to go out and work for a living. As for Amy returning to school, Lisbeth wore the brunt of his anger.

'What good is learning to a girl,' he argued. 'They don't need to figure numbers to produce a dozen kids. She should've been working from when she were eleven if not sooner. The younger the better, I say.'

The following day, Lisbeth took her daughter to the main office at Fanshaw's Mill.

The man perched behind the tall desk only spoke to Amy once. 'What's your name, lass?' he asked.

'Amy Dodd,' she answered timidly.

After that he directed all the questions to her mother. He wanted to know how old she was and if she was healthy. He asked if she had bugs in her hair. Did she cough at night? Did her ankles swell? Had she ever run away from home?

'We don't tolerate cheek or misbehaving,' he said.

'My Amy's a good girl.'

He made a note in his book. 'All right,' he said, after checking her hands and the length of her fingers. 'She looks healthy enough. She can start tomorrow. Come here to this office in the morning at six o'clock sharp. Do you understand, lass?'

Having no choice in the matter, Amy nodded.

'And get her a cap, missus. I don't want her hair getting caught up in the machines! A young lass had her scalp ripped off a few months back. Bad for production, it was!'

It was still dark outside when Amy arrived at Fanshaw's Mill the following morning, though the mill windows glowed from the light of hundreds of gas lamps. Climbing the seventy stone steps to the spinning floor made her legs ache, but that was something she would have to get used to. It was the same with the din. She'd never heard so much noise or witnessed so many objects moving so fast. Hundreds of bobbins were turning and filling, while girls, younger than her, moved up and down the gait between the machines removing full bobbins, winding threads onto empty ones, or deftly joining loose ends of broken yarn. Though she tried hard to concentrate on what the manageress was saying, she could hear little for the whirring of spindles and clatter of machinery. She was relieved when a man tapped her on the shoulder and indicated for her to follow him. He said she looked fit and strong and that they needed someone to work at the carding machine. He also said, if she did well, she'd get more money working down there.

By seven o'clock, she'd been shown how to feed greasy wool into the mouth of the machine and had been left to work on her own. One of the few instructions she was given was to make sure her sleeves didn't get caught on the hooks as they tore at the tangle of matted fibres.

The carding machine was the ugliest piece of machinery Amy had ever seen, not that she'd seen much machinery before. It roared with every rotation and resembled a giant rolling pin with dozens of sharp hooks sticking out of it. The looms and bobbins and their webs of dyed wools were pretty by comparison, and the women who worked them didn't look unhappy as they worked. Some even smiled.

During her first few weeks, Amy went home each evening totally exhausted but at night slept poorly on her makeshift bed on the kitchen floor. For several nights, she woke with the same troubled dream. A huge mouth, set with sharp teeth, was threatening to devour her. Lying awake, she'd long to go to her mother, but she knew she couldn't because her father was there.

On the nights when her dreams didn't wake her, it was the sound of the bed frame that did. Or her mother's pleading cries, 'No, Amos, let me be.' Then, as the banging continued, she'd visualize her father, not his face, but his bare white bottom and his trousers bunched up below his knees. And every night when she woke, she'd pray he would go away.

In the mornings, she'd hear her mother get up quietly and tip-toe around, thinking her daughter was still asleep, but Amy would be watching her as she lit the lamp, then set the fire. Lying on the hard floor, she would listen to her mother sighing or sobbing – never humming or singing the songs like she used to do. They'd speak little over breakfast, and only when it was time for Amy to leave for the mill would her mother fold her arms around her. Sometimes it seemed she held her so tightly it was as though she didn't ever want to let her go. Lisbeth never once spoke the word, *goodbye*, and never smiled.

From the day her father came home, Amy never saw her mother smile properly again.

Nothing changed much over the next three years. At first Amos Dodd hardly ever left the cellar, except for a visit to The Hungry Crow. He never got a job, so at times it was hard to know where his money came from, but neither Amy nor her mother dared ask. On a few occasions, he worked for a few days, but he always complained about it. He said he hated the overseers and managers. He hated the navvies. Amos Dodd seemed to hate everyone and everything. He disliked the neighbours, and didn't even like Lisbeth speaking with them. He hated the cellar they lived in. Amy hated it too, though she remembered at one time it had been a cosy home.

Over those three years, she learned never to answer back; in fact she spoke as little as possible. She learned new words from her father, words she didn't know the meaning of but knew they were utterances no God-fearing girl should ever let pass through her lips.

During that time, Amy watched her mother fade from a poor but proud woman to a timid wife who lived in fear of the man she had married. Though Amy never saw him hit her, she often noticed the bruises on her mother's face. Lisbeth always kept the rest of her body covered.

The lifestyle Amy and her mother had enjoyed over those earlier years quickly disappeared, melting like snowflakes on water. From the day her father returned, nothing was ever the same between them. They couldn't talk freely with him around, couldn't share jokes or laugh and they hardly ever hugged.

Amy missed her mother's touch and the physical closeness that had warmed them through the long winter nights in the only bed. How protective her arms had felt, wrapped around her whenever she'd been hurt. How warm the embrace that comforted her when she'd been sick. How secure her mother's lap when she'd laid her head against it and fallen asleep in front of the fire. Now there was neither coal nor money to buy any. Feeling alone and rejected, Amy resented her father for returning and demanding her mother's attention. How she hated the man who had come between them.

The only thing that puzzled her was that her father never tried to have his way with her. She had expected it. Perhaps her mother had threatened him, or perhaps it was because she allowed him to use her whenever he wanted. There were times, however, when his pale stare fixed her in a way that made her shudder.

Because she always woke early, Amy used to light the fire in order to have the kettle boiling before her mother got up. That gave them a little time together. Sharing whispered words, they'd eat porridge and talk about everyday things: work and the weather and the folk on the street. The man sleeping noisily in the other room was never mentioned.

It was when they talked together privately that Amy sensed there were things her mother wanted to say, and there were questions she needed to ask. Yet they never dare chance those conversations in the house. Their only time to talk intimately was on Sundays. Twice a month they would walk to the chapel, arm-in-arm, never hurrying. It didn't matter if the congregation was already singing the first hymn when they arrived, because they never went in. Lisbeth wouldn't step foot inside the place, but she wouldn't say why.

'What is it, Mum?' Amy asked.

'Nothing, luv.'

'But there is something, I know there is. Why won't you tell me?'

'Not now,' Lisbeth said wearily. 'But one day, I promise, I will.'

'Why don't you leave him?' Amy asked. 'Why don't we both leave and run away.'

'I can't.'

'Why not? If we both worked, we could go far away, live somewhere else. We'd be better off without having to provide for him as well as ourselves.'

She sighed heavily. 'You don't know him like I do. He'd follow us and find us. He'd never let me leave him. He'd see me dead first.'

'Did he kill someone? Is that why you are afraid of him? Is that why he was sent to jail?'

Tears welled in her mother's eyes but she stared straight ahead without blinking.

'He swore it was an accident, that he had nothing to do with it.'

'But they sent him to jail.'

'And he still said he didn't do it.'

'Who did he kill?' Amy asked.

Lisbeth paused and put her hand across her mouth muffling her words. 'He killed my sister, Rose. She was five years younger than you are now. At the time, she was only thirteen.'

Chapter 2

1898 – Fanshaw's Mill

Harold Lister's first visit to Fanshaw's Mill was in June, about a month after the accident that claimed young Sally Plunket's life. It was the sleeve of her cardigan that had got caught in the carding machine, and before the power could be turned off, it had dragged her arm and half her chest into its vicious teeth. Word was passed around that the stained wool went right through into the next batch of cloth but Amy knew for a fact that wasn't the case because she and two other girls had the job of stripping the machine and sending the fibre back to be scoured.

It was Mr Fanshaw himself who showed the gentleman through the mill. Though not a word was spoken out loud, the news was quickly mouthed across every floor in the mill that the good-looking young man, who walked with a slight limp, was an engineer; that he was unmarried and that his leg had been broken when he was run over by a coach when he was a boy; that he was working on a new shuttle that would fly faster than the shuttles used in most Yorkshire mills, and that when it was finished he would be taking it to America where his ultimate wish was to build a bridge. It amazed Amy how the women mouthed their messages silently over the thunder of the looms and how fast word travelled through the mill.

When Harold Lister visited Fanshaw's, it wasn't to introduce a new machine but to examine the old ones and find ways to make them safer.

From the look of his clean, soft hands, it was obvious he didn't work hard for a living. His face was soft, too, with a fine fuzz of ginger hair matted loosely along the sides of his jaw, yet the top of his head bore a thick thatch of auburn curls.

Amy was surprised and a little concerned when the over-looker pulled her from her machine and told her she'd to run downstairs and report to the office. Girls off the floor never got called into the office, so when she was told the engineer wanted to ask her about the machines, she was puzzled. What could she tell him about machines?

'It's Amy Dodd, is that correct?' the young gentleman quizzed, putting down his pen.

Glancing across to the table, Amy recognized her name in his journal. The ink was still wet.

'Yes, sir.'

'Tell me, Amy, I hear you used to work on the carding machine.'

'Aye,' she said, 'but that was two or three years ago.'

'Have you been on it recently?'

'Aye, these past four weeks since—'

'Yes,' he said. 'And I gather you are doing well. You're a mender now?'

'I'm a learner. But I'm told I'm doing all right and I'll be a mender before long. I don't miss anything.'

'Then you must have good eyes.' He took out a pocket book and made a note in it in pencil. 'Tell me, Amy, what do you think about when you're feeding the carding machine?'

Amy laughed. 'Don't rightly know,' she said. 'Anything that comes into me head, I suppose.'

'Do you think about the wool or the machine?'

Amy shook her head and while she waited for her comment to be recorded, she glanced through the window. At the other side of the river, the brickworks boasted one of the tallest chimneys around and the pall of smoke spewing from it rose higher than those from the surrounding factories. Bent like stalks of wheat in a wind, the grey columns leaned towards the city, trailing their soot and ash over the rooftops.

'Out with it, lass,' the overlooker said. 'Mr Lister ain't got all day.'

Amy took a deep breath. 'I think about getting away from this place – as far away as possible.'

The overlooker gave her a sour frown. 'You mind your tongue. Girls like you should be grateful to Fanshaw's for giving them a job.'

Mr Lister allowed a smile to curl in the corners of his lips before turning his face away. 'Have you been measured before?' the engineer asked.

'No, sir,' she said, not knowing rightly what he meant but she soon found out when he took a yard-long ruler and laid it along her arms. Then he measured her height against the wall and recorded the figures. After that he asked some strange questions, like what clothes she wore when she worked on the machine in summer, also in winter. Every answer she gave, he marked down in his notebook.

'Thank you, Amy,' he said, closing his book then, before he had chance to add anything further, the overlooker bustled her from the office. Once outside, she was told to get back to work and make sure she made up for the time that had been wasted. The girls on the nearby looms gave her questioning looks. Usually a call to the office meant bad news but as Amy trotted up the stone steps, she felt elated. All she could think about was the young gentleman with the wispy whiskers. Fancy him asking to speak to her! He even called her by her name. And when he touched her accidentally, she had felt a flutter in her tummy. Then she reminded herself he was only talking to her because of what happened to Sally Plunket. There'd be no possibility he'd speak to the likes of her outside the mill.

But she was wrong. Not that he actually spoke, but he almost did. It happened when she was leaving that same evening. She was chatting with a group of women as they came out of the yard. It was always the same at finishing-off time; no one wanted to hang around, but three of the women lived on the same street and were asking after her mother, saying they hadn't seen much of her lately.

As they passed under the stone archway at Fanshaw's main gate, Amy spotted Mr Lister on the pavement by the lamppost. He was speaking with another well-dressed gentleman. Wearing her mother's old coat, which didn't fit properly, and with a scarf tied around her head, she felt dowdy and kept her head down. But she couldn't resist a quick glance as she walked by. She caught his eye and though he never stopped talking, he smiled broadly, his eyes following her as she passed.

It was true, he didn't actually say anything, but she reckoned if he'd been on his own and she'd been on her own, he would have spoken. She was sure he would have said, 'Good evening, Amy,' and doffed his hat. She never mentioned it to the other girls. If she had, they'd have told her she was daft, but she was sure it wasn't her imagination playing tricks.

The next day Mr Lister returned to her floor. He was checking the combs and the drum carder and, because he wasn't wearing a coat and his sleeves were rolled up, he looked like one of the workers. This time he didn't have his pocket book or journal or measuring stick.

'Good morning,' he shouted, as he came up the stairs. 'It's Amy Dodd, isn't it?'

She nodded, gave him a smile and continued what she was doing.

Around her, the machines rumbled and churned. Further along the floor, looms clicked and clacked, belts slapped and a thousand spindles spun endlessly, but Amy was glad of the noise. Silence was always more embarrassing. Sneaking an occasional peep from the corner of her eye, she could see the young gent was watching her every move, but she didn't turn her face his way. It was a funny feeling having his eyes on her. Nice, but it made her nervous and brought the blood to her cheeks.

Just when she'd plucked up courage to smile at him, he grabbed one of the empty bins and pulled it close to where she was working. Without saying a word, he touched her lightly on the arm and indicated for her to stand aside. Stepping into her spot, he started feeding the fibre into the bin, the job she'd been doing.

Then it dawned on her, he hadn't been watching her at all! He'd been watching the roving that was streaming out from the hole in the machine like matter oozing out of a ripe carbuncle.

After filling one bin, he dragged another across and directed the flow of wool into it. When his fourth bin was full, he nodded for her to come back and continue what she had been doing.

Over the sound of the machines, she read the words he mouthed, 'Thank you, Amy', but she couldn't smile or reply. She was angry with herself for thinking stupid thoughts, angry with him too for making her feel the way she did. She envied him for what he was and the things he had when compared with her and her mother, which was virtually nothing. Then she thought of her father, Amos Dodd, who waited outside the main gate every payday to take her hard-earned wage before it even had time to get warm in her hand.

She thought of the publican at The Hungry Crow who reaped the profits from her week's labour. The fact she was destined to a lifetime of hard labour in the confines of the mill made her angrier still.

It was half past six in the evening when she climbed down the stone steps and found her mother asleep, slumped over the kitchen table her head resting on her arms. She wasn't surprised her father wasn't there when she got home that night. When he first came out of jail, he hardly ever went out. Never even poked his nose up the cellar steps. Too used to sitting in a prison cell all day, every day, she thought. But it wasn't long before that habit changed and he was out every Friday and Saturday night then other nights besides. Where he got his money from neither Amy nor her mother knew, but one thing was certain, come Monday morning there was no money left to put bread on the table.

Closing the door quietly, she tried not to make a noise, but accidentally brushed a fork from the table with her sleeve. It bounced three times, clanging on the stone floor with the ring of a tinker's hammer. Though the noise startled Lisbeth and she opened her eyes, she seemed unusually drowsy. Even half an hour later, after drinking a cup of tea, she was still half asleep.

'I'm late with the coal buckets,' she said, thinking it was morning. She sighed. "I hate all those stairs.'

'Mum,' Amy pleaded. 'You're worn out. You've got to stop, and you and I have got to get away from here.'

'Hush!' she whispered, thinking her husband was in the bedroom. 'It'll be all right, you'll see.'

'But it won't be all right. Not now. Not ever. Believe me, nothing will change. It'll get worse. For the present, I'm working all day just to pay for his drink money and you're working yourself to death. And if you can't keep up with the chores, looking after this building, we could lose the cellar.'

Amy thought about what she had said. Perhaps it wouldn't be so bad if they did get thrown out. Then they'd have to find another place to live and, perhaps, her father would find someone else to sponge off.

Taking her mother's hand, Amy gazed deep into her rheumy eyes. *How strange*, she thought, *it's like we've changed places. It's as though I'm the mother and she's the daughter.*

'We've got to make a plan.' Amy begged. 'I've been thinking about it all this week and I have an idea that will work.' The idea has been in Amy's mind for much longer than a week, but she didn't admit to it. 'You've got to sneak a bit away each week and hide it somewhere where he can't find it.'

'I couldn't do that,' Lisbeth said. 'Besides, there ain't enough to go round as it is, let alone any to spare.'

'Listen to me; you must make sure there's a little to put aside. Buy three ounce of lard instead of four,' she said, 'or five pound of spuds instead of six. He won't weigh what's in the bag, and you and I'll manage on a bit less. And if you get a farthing in change, keep it. I'll take a couple of coins from my wage, if he's not waiting for me by the mill gate. And if I can run any errands for anyone or do any jobs after work I will. Then, by next spring, we'll have a few shillings saved between us.'

Lisbeth smiled sadly. 'I know you're trying to help, Amy, luv, but I know I can't do it. I couldn't look him in the eye. He'd see right through me. And if he asked me point blank if I had any money, I'd have to tell. It'd be written all over me face. And if he found out I was trying to trick him, he'd not think twice about taking his belt to me.'

'Don't worry about it then,' Amy said, squeezing her mother's fingers. 'I'll see what I can manage. You don't need to do anything. Only one thing I ask is, when the time comes to leave and I say we're off, you must come with me, because there'll only be one chance.'

Lisbeth Dodd's eyes shone green as wet grass, they fair sparkled, but not for the right reasons. Amy knew her mother was trapped. She wanted to help her and wished she would at least talk about the things that troubled her, or just talk about something – anything to take her mind off the present situation.

'Tell me what it was like before I was born, before you met father. You said you worked in a big house. You said you had a good job. You said, life was good for you then.'

Lisbeth closed her eyes and sucked the air through her nose. 'If only he'd never turned up that day. It was those damn rhododendron bushes.'

'Rhododendrons?'

'It doesn't matter,' she said. 'I'll tell you about it one day.'

How often had she been given that answer? 'Not one day, Mum, tell me now. Tell me about when you were young. Tell me about my granddad and what it was like working in a nice place.' Pulling her chair closer, she took her mother's hands in hers. 'Please, tell me.'

Lisbeth took another deep breath and began, 'When I was about fifteen, I was told I was a bonny lass.'

Amy smiled. 'I'm sure you were.'

'I'd been helping my father until then. There was just him and me and my sister, Rose.' She sighed. 'She was three years younger than me, bless her.'

'What did my granddad do?'

'He was a cobbler. A good one at that. Worked in our kitchen at home,' she smiled. 'It was more like a workshop than a living room. When we ate, there was always a row of lasts lined up along the other side of the kitchen table looking at us. He did all his work sitting on a three-legged stool in front of the fire.'

'What did you do?'

'My job was to deliver the boots and shoes to the customers when he'd fixed them. That was apart from keeping house and looking after Rose when she was little. And once a week I'd go down to the local tannery to pick up bits of left-over leather.' She sniffed the air. 'I always remember the smell of that place. It stunk awful. Enough to make you sick. I'd come back home with a sack full of pieces over my shoulder but sometimes there was that much I had to drag it home. It made father happy. Anyway, one day I delivered a pair of shoes to the Manse. That was the minister's house. He was the same man who used to preach at our chapel.'

'But you never go to chapel.'

'Not now, I don't, but I used to go regular as clockwork. We all did, me, your granddad and Rose, every Sunday morning and I'd take Rose to Sunday school in the afternoon.' She laughed gently. 'Some folk thought dad was a bit gloomy because he always had his head bowed. But he was just checking on people's feet. If he thought their boots needed mending, he'd tell 'em so. Politely, of course.'

Amy smiled.

'I remember that day well, knocking on the back door of the Manse holding a pair of the Reverend's boots in my hands. The cook came to the door, peered at me with a pair of brown beady eyes and asked me what I was up to. Before I had time to explain, Mrs Upton, the Reverend's wife, appeared. As soon as she looked at me I knew she wasn't really bothered about the boots. It was me she was interested in. I found out later, she'd just got rid of her previous maid. She asked me if I wanted the job, there and then.'

'But you hadn't been in service, had you?'

'Never seen a saucer that matched a cup, before I started there.'

'You wouldn't believe how she treated me,' Lisbeth said, her face brightening for a while. 'It was almost like I was her daughter or kid sister, or one of the family. There was no real hard work and I lived-in, and I still got a few bob in wages besides.'

'But what about granddad and Rose?'

'I wasn't worried about them because Rose was twelve and big enough to take over the jobs I'd been doing. And I thought it'd be good for the lass to be occupied till she could get a proper job elsewhere.'

'Tell me about the minister's wife.'

Lisbeth took a moment to think before she answered.

'Mrs Upton was nice, poor dear,' she said, shaking her head. 'About thirty, I suppose. Twenty years younger than him. Educated, but real homely. Not what you'd call pretty and a bit old-fashioned in the way she dressed. But she had a head of thick black hair that she used to drape over one shoulder in a loose plait when he wasn't home. I used to brush it for her. I remember how I could make it shine.'

Amy glanced at the lacklustre look of her mother's red hair.

'Her main failing was that she had no confidence. She was fine at home but hopeless whenever she went out. I think some of the chapel ladies said things to her that upset her. She confided in me. Told me she wanted to have a child but somehow that never happened for her. I think that was why she made such a fuss of me.'

'But you were just a maid.'

'I never felt like a servant. I never wore a uniform all the time I worked there. She bought me three velvet dresses, one brown, one navy and one green and an assortment of lace collars that I changed every day. And she bought me that winter coat you've been wearing for work, and a matching hat. And on Sunday mornings she always insisted I sit alongside her in chapel even though you could hear the murmurs from the congregation. But it didn't bother Mrs Upton, or me for that matter. Sunday mornings. That's what I loved.'

'What was so special about Sunday?'

I used to look forward to Sunday all week, not for going to chapel, or listening to the sermon, or singing the hymns – though I loved to sing in those days. What I treasured most of all was the few minutes after the service had finished, when Mrs Upton would stand at the doorway with her husband chatting with the members of the congregation. That gave me chance to nip out and see Rose and my dad. It was the only time we ever got to talk.'

'What happened to my granddad?' Amy asked.

'He died,' she said, 'while I was at the Manse. I had to sell his tools to pay for his burial.'

'And Rose?'

Pain tightened Lisbeth's eyes.

Amy reworded her question. 'Where did Rose live after granddad died?'

'A neighbour took her in, and I paid her board out of my wages. That was until she got my job at the Manse.'

'And what happened then?'

Lisbeth dropped her head into her hands. 'It never should have happened. I should never have let her go there. I should have kept her away from Amos. It was my fault.'

'Mum, that's a long time ago. You mustn't blame yourself for the things that happened then.'

'But you don't know what went on in that place.'

'Then tell me. Help me to understand.'

'One day I'll tell you. I promise, I'll tell you the whole story,' she said, her voice incredibly weary. 'But not right now, Amy, luv. Not right now.' She lifted her face and pleaded with her daughter. 'You asked me a few minutes ago about running off, saving up and leaving your father. Well, at the moment I don't have the energy to do anything. God only knows what would become of us if we ran off.

'Take it from me, it's not that bad here. At least we've got a roof over our heads, and I know the man who owns this place won't throw us out. He's a kindly gentleman,' she said, 'and he's been good to me and never asked for a penny in rent in eighteen years. We might have to scratch around to make ends meet, but it's better than being in the workhouse, you mark my words.' Lisbeth shook her head. 'It's more than I could stand knowing your father was chasing after me. I'd never dare open the door again, or close my eyes at night. Don't force me out onto the street, Amy. I'm not strong enough for that.'

There was no point saying any more. Lisbeth hated her husband and she was obviously afraid of him, yet despite that, she wasn't prepared to leave him. Then Amy thought about her mother's younger sister, Rose, and wished she knew what had happened to her all those years ago. Had her death really been an accident? Could her father have been telling the truth? She thought not. From what she'd seen and heard of him, he was a mean and cunning man, and all his actions were calculated and deliberate. In her opinion, Amos Dodd never did anything by accident.

Chapter 3

Lisbeth

Amy sensed something was wrong as soon as she opened the door. There was no fire in the grate, no kettle singing on the hob or smell of stew simmering in the pot. The lamp had burned right down. Turning it up, she scraped the wick and re-lit it. On the rug beneath her feet, tiny beads of light reflected like morning sun on dewdrops. She reached down and ran her fingers across the mat, expecting it to be wet, but the scattered specks of lights were the polished faces of tiny mother-of-pearl buttons. The brass jar that had held them was empty and dented. It was lying on the floor under the table where Amy usually put her bed.

Her voice wavered when she called out, hoping that there would be an answer. But there was none. Tiptoeing into the back room, she saw her mother lying on the bed curled up like a sleeping child but, as soon as she touched her arm and tried to lift her, she knew she was dead.

The Medleys were a tower of strength. Without their help Amy wouldn't have known what to do in those circumstances. Mrs Medley sent her eldest boy to fetch the doctor. He arrived very late, examined her mother and asked Amy about the bruises. Were they new? Had she fallen recently? Amy had to tell him she didn't know; tell him her mother bruised easily and always had some. She didn't tell him about her father but she did mention her mother's recent weariness and pains. The doctor shook his head and said it was likely her heart had taken her.

It was midnight by the time Amy and Mrs Medley laid her mother out.

'You can sleep at our place if you don't mind the floor,' the neighbour said, 'at least till after the funeral.'

Amy thanked her. 'I want to stay with Mum while she's here.' The neighbour never asked after Mr Dodd, and Amy didn't mention him either. She didn't care where he was or what happened to him. She hoped he'd never come home again.

Mr Medley took the liberty of speaking to the minister and arranged things as best he could. It was embarrassing for Amy to admit that she had no money.

Lisbeth Dodd was buried in a pauper's grave. That upset Mrs Medley, but to Amy, it made little difference where her mother was laid to rest. Soil was soil whether it was in a graveyard or a garden. Only one thing was for certain – when the coffin lid was nailed down, she was never going to see her mother again.

The evening after the funeral, as Amy sat alone in the cellar; there was a knock on the door. The man standing in the tiny cellar yard looked vaguely familiar. He was reasonably well-dressed, though his clothes looked rather weary. *An undertaker or preacher?* she thought. He was tall and straight, his face gaunt but carrying country colour. His figure appeared slightly undernourished.

'Is your father in, Amy?'

She was surprised he knew her name. 'No, he's not.'

'Do you know when he'll be back?' he said, a concerned expression furrowing his brow.

Amy shook her head and said she didn't know.

'I know you don't know me,' the man said, 'but your mother did. My name is Charles Ogilvy and I'm the owner of this building. It might be best if you invited me in,' he said. There are things I need to talk to you about.'

The name, Ogilvy, was vaguely familiar but the man meant nothing to her. She was sure she had seen him before in the street, and remembered her mother had once pointed to a stranger loitering in the graveyard. It was the same man, though he obviously didn't live in the neighbourhood – he spoke and dressed too well for that.

Following Amy inside, Mr Ogilvy took off his hat and cast his eyes around the room.

'Do you want to sit down?' she asked, looking at the armchair's seat-cushion that had shed its stuffing years ago.

The gentleman didn't answer. 'Before I get down to business, let me offer my condolences. I know what it is like to lose someone close to you.'

'I didn't lose my mother,' Amy said. 'She died.'

'Of course,' he said, breathing deeply. 'Let me explain. When I first met your mother, she was in dire need of somewhere to stay. This place,' he said, glancing around, 'is far from ideal but, at the time, when you were born, she had no one to turn to and nowhere to go. I let her have these rooms and I never charged any rent. However, in return she kept the rest of the building clean and tidy for my other tenants. I'm sure you are aware of that.'

Amy nodded.

'And let me add, I never once begrudged her living here.'

'Ta,' Amy said automatically.

'Unfortunately for your mother, when her husband, Mr Dodd, returned three years ago, I was obliged to review the situation. I told her that with a man in the house it would be usual that there would be another wage coming in.'

'But there was no money. He never worked. He never gave her anything. He even took my wages and, with him here, we had less than before he came!'

'I know. Your mother told me, and that is why I allowed you all to stay, though it went against my better judgement. It was only because of the years I had known Lisbeth that I allowed the previous unpaid arrangement to continue for as long as it did. Now, however,' he sighed, 'circumstances have changed again.

'I'm sorry,' he continued, 'but with your mother dead, my goodwill does not apply to your father. If it were for you alone, Amy, I would be happy for you to stay and continue with the arrangement I had with your mother. However, under the circumstances, I am not inclined to extend the favour to your father.' He hesitated for a moment searching for the right words to say. 'I have no time for a man who has no respect for women, but I shall say no more on that count. I am truly sorry for your situation but I'm afraid that's how it has to be. I understand you have a job at the mill and that you are a good worker. That should provide you with enough funds each week to find yourself a room somewhere. But allow me to offer you a piece of advice. You will be far better on your own, away from the likes of Amos Dodd. As for this place, I have a needy tenant arriving here on Monday. You and your father must be out by Saturday midday or, I'm sorry to say, I'll be forced to call the bailiff.'

Amy looked at him. What could she say?

As he was leaving, Mr Ogilvy apologetically reminded her that the meagre furnishings belonged to the premises. Amy didn't realize that her mother had owned nothing.

'Believe me,' he said, as he climbed the stone steps. 'I am truly sorry this is happening to you. But I'll not harbour Amos Dodd under my roof any longer.'

Amy didn't know how she managed to work for the next two days. She couldn't even remember walking to the mill. After the funeral, Mrs Medley helped her pack her few possessions, and offered to hold them until she and her father found another place. There wasn't much stuff – some threadbare lace-edged linen items, a few pieces of crockery, a pot or two, and little else. Her mother's only personal things were stored in an old shoe box which had been tucked under the bed. She was glad her father hadn't found it, even though it didn't contain anything of value It contained a few old letters, some worthless keepsakes wrapped in a yellowed handkerchief, and a picture which she'd seen her mother looking at occasionally when she thought no one was looking. Two trips up the street were all it took to deliver everything to the safekeeping of her neighbour's house.

'You really must stay with us tonight,' Mrs Medley said. 'And next week, I'll have a word with my sister. She knows someone who might have a room that'll suit you. Don't bank on it, though, lass, but I'll not see you walking the street, do you hear?' Mrs Medley gave her a hug.

'You know where to come if you're desperate,' her husband added.

Amy thanked them both and said she didn't know what she'd have done without their help. Even so, she wanted to go back home while she still had one, wanted to be on her own and to get away from the noise of the Medley children. Somehow their happy laughter didn't seem fitting.

Walking down the street, she thought of the youngest ones, of the fuss their father made of them and of the love he wasn't ashamed to show. Then she compared him with her own father and thought of all those years she'd longed for his return.

Looking down from the pavement to the greyness of the cellar yard, she stood for a moment watching the swirling leaves as they lifted from the ground and danced in a ghostly circle on the cold slabs. It was a mischievous wind which often blew down the stone steps and rattled the door. But it didn't scare her.

Inside the room the air was still. Stagnant. Damp. She was thankful she had lit the lamp earlier. She always hated walking into a dark house.

Though there was no fire, Amy dragged the armchair closer to the hearth and stared into the empty grate. Outside, in the small yard, the leaves skittered and scratched on the slabs. Then from the corner of her eye, she saw something move.

Amy looked up. Amos Dodd was standing in the doorway, the lamplight reflected in the yellow of his eyes.

'It's just thee and me now!' he said.

Chapter 4

The Spider's Web

The front door of The Hungry Crow was closed, yet the unmistakable odour exuding from the building enticed its regulars as surely as a lump of mouldy cheese would attract a pack of starving rats. To the wives whose housekeeping money was exchanged each week for gallons of golden fluid, the rancid smell was a reminder of the futility of their existence. A reminder they were unable to ignore, because it was the smell which drifted from every similar establishment in the north of England. It was ever present and always the same. It was as if the main ingredients – smoke, stale ale, sweat and sour breath – were simmered and stirred in some giant vat and, when ripened to maturity, dished out in ample portions to every alehouse, public house and tavern in the town. The odour was as consistent as the scent of a fine French perfume and might well have been a patented product.

'I'm not going in there!' Amy shouted.

'Are you not?' Amos said, clapping his hand firmly around her wrist. 'We'll soon see about that!'

As they crossed the cobbles, Amy glanced up at the sign swinging above the pub's entrance. Written in large gilt letters was the name: The Hungry Crow. Beneath it, painted in black on white – an evil bird, its beak latched firmly on an unsuspecting worm that it was about to swallow whole. Amy squirmed. She knew she was that worm.

'You're hurting!' she yelled, twisting her arm in an attempt to free it, but her father's grip circled her wrist as tight as a hoop on a barrel.

Amos clouted the door with the steel tip on his boot.

Inside, all heads turned and the burble of voices stilled. After the door closed with a thud, all that was heard was the sound of the six gas mantles hissing from the walls. Nothing was said.

When her eyes became accustomed to the dim light, Amy looked around. The yellowed teeth, bloodshot eyes and threadbare clothes were uniform around the room. There was not a starched collar in sight.

When her shin hit a wooden stool, she squealed, and a cynical laugh broke the silence prompting the rumble of conversation to roll on.

'Sit there and don't move!' Amos ordered.

Amy rubbed her leg, breathing shallowly in an attempt not to inhale too much of the curling blue air. She heard her father shout his order and looked across at him as he waited for his drink. She despised him. How grateful she was he'd been locked away for all her childhood years; at least she had that to be thankful for. But now her mother was gone and each day she hated him more and more. She was desperate to get away, but the thumping he'd given her the previous day, when he had dragged her from the Medleys' house, had taught her to be extra cautious. For the moment, at least, she'd do what he said – within reason.

'If you don't fancy 'im, luv, I'll give you tuppence if you're nice to me.' A stream of saliva ran down the stranger's beard. His words were slurred. After wiping his ample whiskers with the back of his equally hairy forearm, he poked his outstretched fingers towards Amy's hair. Slapping them away before he could touch, Amy slid herself to the far end of the bench.

'Playful little piece,' the man said. The other drinkers showed no interest.

'You!' Amos called, glaring at the drunk. The man, unconcerned, cocked his head and laughed, but his cockeyed smirk disappeared as a steel blade glinted in the gas light.

Amy hadn't seen the knife before. Didn't know her father carried one and was instantly afraid of what he might do.

The room was silent. Amos Dodd had the audience's full attention.

Turning his back, the drunk swayed on his seat, mumbled to himself then buried his face in his pot. On her lap, Amy's hands trembled but she sat upright hoping no one, especially her father, would notice.

'Have a drink!' he ordered, pointing towards his pot with the knife, before slapping it down onto the table.

'I hate beer!'

Picking up his drink, Amos swallowed half its contents without taking a breath.

'I want some water,' she said. 'There's a fountain at the bottom of the street.' She looked at him but he didn't answer. 'I'll wait for you there. I won't go away. I promise.'

'You'd better not!' he threatened. 'Or you know what you'll get!'

Amy nodded and half-smiled, not at him, but at the thought of being able to get out of the place. She was surprised he was letting her go so easily. Sliding cautiously off the bench, she threaded her way out while the other patrons showed little interest. Pulling the door open, she gulped the evening air and set off down the hill before her father changed his mind.

From The Hungry Crow on Mill Street, Bank Lane ran down to the canal. In her eagerness, Amy found herself running along the pavement, her feet falling in step with the plaintive notes of a cornet drifting from one of the houses. It was a simple melody, a few bars being repeated over and over. Amy slowed. She loved the sound of brass, especially the mill's band. Hearing them play and seeing the men in their braided uniforms was always a treat. How the yellow brass shone to a mirror shine on a sunny day. And how the tunes had stirred her mother when they'd listened to the band playing in the park on Sundays. There was a special magic in that music; magic that had been able to make them forget their dismal surroundings albeit for a short time. Magic which at times made them laugh or cry.

But the notes from the upstairs window were not from a seasoned bandsman, more likely from a lad, learning to play; a boy taking lessons from his father. Amy envied him that relationship.

A wire-haired dog, defending a doorstep, growled, baring its teeth. Amy stepped out of its way as it cocked its leg, sending a yellow stream trickling over the paving slabs and into the gutter beside her. She lifted her skirt and stepped onto the cobbles. The dog barked again. A voice shouted from a house. The dog's ears pricked up then it jumped up onto the step and lay down again.

Though it was still reasonably light, the street lamp at the bottom of the hill had already been lit. In a few kitchens, lamps were already burning. Only the houses on Mill Street had gas. Soon it would be dark. Soon the Leeds canal and the River Aire behind it would dissolve into darkness and the area at the bottom of the street would be a place best avoided.

The stone fountain, carved like a giant cockle shell, was set into the wall. Once, when walking with her mother, they had witnessed two girls stripped to the waist, washing themselves in its water. It was then her mother had warned her never to drink from it. 'Fountains is supposed to be for drinking,' Lisbeth had said. 'Don't you ever go drinking there! You might catch something.'

Amy never did though at the time she had wondered what ailed the women and how her mother could tell they carried disease. They were young, not much older than her and they didn't look sick, or sound it, in fact, she remembered hearing them laughing. They sounded fit and happy, but her mother's advice was enough to deter her. Not that it mattered right now; her excuse about wanting a drink was only to get away from her father and out of The Hungry Crow. Besides that, she didn't want to be anywhere near the place when it closed and the men were thrown out onto the street buoyed up on a bellyful of booze. But, even then, she thought it unlikely they would go wandering down to the canal. Most would head for home and bed. Amy thought the fountain seemed a safe place to watch and wait, and hope it wouldn't be long before her father's money ran out.

On the opposite bank of the canal, a group of men were talking. They had gathered around a horse lying on the towing path and even though they spoke in low tones, their conversation carried across the canal.

Fifty yards away to the right, Amy noticed a moored barge. The cabin doors were open and light was streaming from inside. Standing on the deck was a woman. Her hair was plaited and coiled around the back of her head. It was the colour of ripe hay. A pair of gold rings dangled from her ears. Gold was a commodity Amy knew little of. Perhaps the woman was a gypsy, Amy thought. She too was observing the men.

Though the evening was not cold, the boatwoman had a woollen shawl wrapped around her shoulders. There was not a breath of air to ripple the water, no current in the canal to move the barge, nevertheless the woman was rocking rhythmically.

One of the men on the opposite bank lifted his cap and scratched his head. 'I say we leave it here till morning, but best shift it off the path. Too late to do anything else right now.'

The nodding of heads sealed the matter and without speaking the men shuffled around the carcase. Dragging the horse by its legs, the men heaved the ton-weight from the towing path and rolled it over into the ditch alongside.

Amy wasn't sure if the animal was dead or alive, for when they hauled it from the path, its head lolled back, flicking its mane from its dark wet eyes. They glistened brightly and seemed to stare at her across the canal. Even though she closed her own, she couldn't shut out the horse's gaze. If it wasn't already finished, it soon would be.

With a few final words exchanged, the men shook hands and parted company, four of them returning to the line of big barges moored to the left. Two others headed in the opposite direction and, as they passed the woman on the deck of the short-boat, they touched their caps, spoke a few words and then continued on.

Only an old man and boy remained on the bank. The lad knelt beside the horse and stroked its mane.

'These things happen, lad,' the man said. 'Not a lot you can do about it. When your dad's back on his feet, he'll find another horse just as good, you mark my words.'

When the boy looked up, Amy could see tears shining on his cheeks. She felt sorry for him. He had probably known the horse all his life and had walked thousands of miles along the towing path beside it. Now it was dead and from the expression on his face, it might well have been his mother lying on the ground. When Amy heard him sob, she thought of her own mother curled on the bed, and cried too.

'None of that blubbering now!' the old man said, his voice firm but kind, as he touched the boy on the shoulder and coaxed him to his feet. 'Tell your father, I'll pass the message to the knacker's yard to collect it in the morning. Do you understand?'

The boy nodded.

'Now, away with you. Get back to your ma. There's nowt to be gained in crying over a dead nag.'

Though it was obvious the lad didn't want to leave, the man placed a hand on his back and shoved him gently in the direction of the short-boat. When the boy was almost level with it, he turned and looked back. Was he hoping his boat-horse was not dead and that it had risen to its feet?

Amy wiped her eyes.

When he reached the boat, the woman, who'd been watching the events, embraced him briefly then turned, ducked her head and disappeared into the cabin. The boy stood for a moment, took off his cap then followed his mother inside.

In the ditch, the old man squatted for a while beside the mare. He'd lost a few horses of his own over the years, but he always hated to see them go. A good barge-horse was like one of the family. You lived with it and you worked with it, day in and day out. Without it, you couldn't make a living. Gazing down at the massive animal, he could see the muscles in its legs still twitching as if the dead horse was still wanting to walk on into the darkness. Then, after lingering a few moments longer, the man got up, rubbed his face on the back of his sleeve and walked slowly down the path heading to the city.

As she stared into the fading light, Amy's eyes played tricks. The black shape appeared to move, seeming to slither like a giant turtle in the ditch. In front of it, the ribbon of water grew blacker. The towing path was empty and apart from the croaking of several frogs, the canal bank was silent.

'Amy Dodd, where are you?' An unmistakable voice echoed down the street.

For a while, she had forgotten about her father. Swivelling around, she lifted her skirt and dashed back to the fountain. As she reached him, his only greeting was a sharp clip across her head.

'You were supposed to wait 'ere!'

'Sorry,' she muttered. But she wasn't sorry. Under her breath she cursed him with all the dirty words she'd heard in the mill and all the foul names he had called her mother though she didn't know their meaning. She was angry with him for what he was. She blamed him for her mother's death. Blamed him for her Aunt Rose's death. And now she wanted to blame him for the fate that had befallen the horse. Perhaps if he had never come out of jail, none of this would have happened.

'Where are we going?' she asked, as he poked her in the back and directed her back up the hill. 'I'm hungry.'

'Shut your trap!' That was the last they spoke.

The boarding house was the same one they had slept in the previous night. It was in a handy location, only a few doors from The Hungry Crow. Amy didn't know if her father had the money to pay for a room for another night. It wouldn't be long before they'd be sleeping in the open, she thought.

What would happen when his money ran out, when they had no roof over their heads and no food in their bellies? The only reason he wanted her company was for her wages; at least, she hoped that was all. But why couldn't he get a job? She worked, and worked hard. Nine shillings and sixpence for fifty hours of hard toil every week. And most of that went to The Hungry Crow. If he wanted a job, there was work to be had, but it was obvious Amos Dodd had no intention of working for a living.

If it hadn't been for his dislike of her father, Mr Ogilvy would have let her stay in the cellar. She could have taken over the jobs her mother had been doing – emptying slops buckets and carrying up scuttles of coal for the other tenants. That way, she'd have had no rent to pay and, with her money from the mill, she'd have been able to feed herself well and save a little.

Amy was thankful her father hadn't found the box containing her mother's bits and pieces and that he was unaware that she had left things at the Medleys' house. But it upset her that he'd abused Mr Medley for offering to let her stay. Now she worried that her father would return later and harm them. Knowing about the knife made her worry more.

The shadows cast by the candle swayed around the staircase, as Amy lumbered up the four flights of stairs with her father following close behind. Though drunk, he could still find his way to his lodgings in the attic of the Mill Street house.

Amy was thankful for the state he was in. It meant he didn't undress or use the pot. He didn't even stop to loosen his bootlaces; just fell onto the bed fully clothed and within minutes was snorting like an angry sow.

With dead moths floating on the water in the china jug, Amy wondered how long it had been sitting there, but she was so thirsty, she didn't care. Scooping the insects aside, she drank her fill. As she hadn't eaten or drunk anything earlier, she didn't need to use the pot either.

It was obvious she couldn't stay with her father. But where could she go with no money for food or board? She'd heard stories about the workhouse when she was a girl. Her mother had told her that their cellar was far preferable. She wasn't sure if her mother was right, but she didn't want to find out.

Pulling the kapok pillow off the bed, Amy stretched herself on the floor between the wall and the bed. It was like being back home in the cellar only here the floor was wooden.

The sounds from her tummy reminded her of her hunger. She knew in the morning he would take her to the mill to ensure she went to work. But she couldn't work all day on an empty stomach.

Amy wondered what she could do. If she told the girls at Fanshaw's Mill, they'd say they were sorry, but there was nothing they could do either. In fact, many of them were not much better off themselves. If she told the overlooker, he'd likely tell her to go back home rather than turning up for work hungry. He wouldn't want her fainting near any of his machines. That might slow production and that would never do.

Perhaps these were the sorts of problem Mr Lister should investigate. Why girls fainted. Why they stumbled and fell against the machines. He'd get more answers if he asked the right questions rather than all his measuring and book entries. A complete waste of time, in Amy's eyes.

With her head on the lumpy pillow, Amy drew her knees close to her chest and watched a spider shuttling between the bed leg and the wall, weaving its way back and forth across the warp of its web. How fine the thread it spun; far finer than any yarn that flew from Fanshaw's spindles.

Mesmerized by it, she thought about the spider. No doubt it was hungry like her. But it appeared neither angry nor frustrated. It went about its task, patiently and methodically, knowing exactly what it had to do – spin its web, set its trap, then sit back and wait for a meal to fall into it.

Amy tried to relate her situation to that of the spider but she couldn't. There was no one she wanted to trap. She just wanted to get away. Away from her father and away from her life at the mill.

Physically tired, she wanted to sleep but she was conscious of the man stretched out only a yard away. Conscious of his smell. His snores. His horrid habits.

'Please God, don't ever let me grow to be like my father,' she prayed. Then her thoughts drifted to Mr Lister, to his eyes, to his soft downy side-whiskers and to the few words he had spoken in the office. Like the repetitive bars of the cornet she had heard on the street, her own words repeated over and over in her head – *I want to get as far away from here as I can*! She pictured the engineer on the steps, limping slightly on his damaged leg, and forgot about the hard boards beneath her hip. Was his smile real or had she imagined it? She told herself it was real and he had certainly called her by her name.

'Tell me, Amy,' he had said, 'What do you think about when you're feeding the carding machine?'

Maybe she should have answered differently. Told him the truth. Told him what it was like standing for long hours at a machine, legs aching, hunger tightening her belly, tiredness welling through her head. She should have told him what she really thought about while she was standing there – about sleeping each night in a real bed, about drinking from a cup that wasn't cracked, about having a new hat to wear on a Sunday, but most of all about having a father like Mr Medley. A father who would have placed her on his knee when she was little and read stories to her. A man who would have taken her out on Sundays and stood beside her in the park listening to the band or feeding crumbs to the ducks. A father she would have been proud of. A father she would have loved.

Maybe she should have told Mr Lister about her own father. She couldn't help thinking about him; about the way he treated her, about the terrible things he had done to her mother and now the fear he would do the same to her.

But she knew Mr Lister didn't want to hear those sorts of things and a young gentleman like him wouldn't understand anyway. There was no ruler long enough to measure her feelings and no words he could write in his book that would convey exactly how she felt.

But he did say, 'Thank you, Amy', and smiled at her, and it was that smile she kept in her mind.

As she rolled over to face the wall, the bed beside her creaked. She held her breath, praying her father would not wake. Then the lonely silence returned, save for the voices drifting up the stairwell – a late-night argument over money that went on and on and on.

The next sound she heard was the pad of the knocker-up man's pole tapping on the windows below. 'Five o'clock. Time to get up,' he called, his sing-song voice almost drowned by the barking of a dozen dogs. The men who worked on the railway would be up by now.

The grimy window, trimmed with a tattered lace curtain, masked the early dawn. Amy rubbed the grit from her lids and looked across to the leg of the bed. The spider and its web were gone. Had she brushed it away in her sleep or had it decided it was time to leave and try somewhere new? She wondered about it.

Not wanting to stay in the room with her father longer than necessary, she got up as quietly as possible, but the floorboards refused to stay silent. After drinking a handful of water, she splashed a little across her face.

'Where d' you think you're off to?' he growled.

'The mill,' she said, dabbing her face on the hem of her skirt. 'I'll need something to eat.'

Amos grunted, rolled onto his back and scratched at his crotch.

'I can't work with no food in me belly.'

Dipping his hand in his pocket, he pulled out a chunk of dried bread. ''Ere,' he said, tossing it at her. 'That's all I got.' It bounced on the floor and rolled under the washstand settling itself in the fringe of matted hair which skirted the room.

'You get paid today?'

'Yes.'

'Then you'll eat tonight.'

Amy picked up the bread, rubbed the hairs off it and dipped it in the jug of water. She only managed one soggy mouthful but knew she'd have to have something inside her.

'I'll be waiting for thee at the gate when the mill looses. And don't try aught clever 'cause I'll ring thee bloody neck if thee do!'

Amy didn't answer.

The staircase was dark. There were no windows and she had no candle. When she reached the first-floor landing, a door opened. It was the woman who took the money for the rooms. She was wearing a night-shirt with a stained apron over it. Tied around her neck was a moth-eaten woollen muffler. Rags hung from the ends of her grey hair like long rats' tails. 'Where do you think you're off to,' she crowed, 'sneaking out so early?'

'Fanshaw's Mill. I work there.'

The woman looked surprised. 'And what about 'im you're with?'

Amy turned her head up towards the attic. 'My father's still asleep.'

'Your father, you say?' Then she laughed.

As she was about to start down the final flight of steps, Amy thought of her stomach and the cunning spider. 'Can you spare a bite to eat?' she asked as nicely as she could manage.

'This ain't no bleeding almshouse.'

'I get me wages today,' Amy said quietly. 'I can pay whatever you ask.'

'You sure you're coming back 'ere tonight?' The woman's face screwed.

'No choice. We ain't got nowhere else to go.'

The woman worked the sums in her head quicker than the clerk in the mill's office. Surprising how much arithmetic a woman of no learning can pick up on the streets, Amy thought.

'Wait there,' she ordered, closing the door behind her and returning the landing to its habitual darkness.

As Amy waited, her eyelids closed. She was tempted to sit on the steps and sink her head onto her arm but if she did she was certain she would fall asleep.

'Here,' the woman said, reappearing and thrusting a small bundle into Amy's hands. 'You owe me sixpence. And mind you return the cloth.'

'I will,' said Amy, turning quickly and hurrying down the stairs. She felt pleased with herself. *My web has caught its first fly*, she thought.

Chapter 5

Where there's smoke...

It was too early to go to the mill, so Amy took her breakfast bundle down to the canal. The street was empty.

Of the barges which had been moored along the bank the previous night, only the one with the woman and boy onboard remained. Looking across the black water, the dead horse was still in the ditch next to the towing path. Overnight, its belly had filled with gas and its legs were now poking towards the rising sun.

Sitting on a low stone wall, Amy opened her bundle and was surprised by the contents of the rag – a slice of cake, a lump of cheese and a green apple. Though a grub had got under the wrinkled skin, she ate around it and wasted very little.

From her perch, she could see the back of the mill, its brick wall rising five floors perpendicular from the canal's bank. More than a hundred windows overlooked the water. At the bottom of Fanshaw's wall was a narrow path running the full length of the building. To the side of the mill was a lane leading into the receiving yard and loading bays. It was used by the wagons that lumbered in and out laden with bales of wool, or bolts of cloth.

As she watched, a wagon drawn by four draught horses clattered down the cobbled street, slowed at the gate and turned into the yard. It was loaded with coal. Amy could see that Fanshaw's boilers were already alight sending smoke spewing from the mill's chimney.

The sound of a whistle prompted the local dogs to start yapping. In less than half an hour every machine in the building would be operating. From the streets came the regular morning noises, the milk wagon, children's voices, doors banging and the clicking of clogs clattering along the pavements. As the trickle of workers grew into a small army, Amy joined them, heading along Mill Street to Fanshaw's main entrance. But there was little conversation amongst the girls. Their heads were bent, their eyes not fully awake, their gaze following the cracks in the cobbles.

How different to the home-time rush when everyone streamed out together, a mob of girls filling the street, happy to leave the mill's noise and dust-filled air. Looking forward to spending time at home with their families and listening to the sound of voices they could hear.

As Amy joined them, no one spoke. She didn't want to talk anyway. Having slept all night in her working clothes, she felt ashamed. Her apron was dirty and, apart from splashing a little water on her face, she hadn't washed. She thought about the two girls who had bathed in the fountain and envied them.

Nearing the main entrance, she looked up at the words fanned out across the top of the iron gates: FANSHAW'S MILL. The letters stood erect like the stone turrets on the round tower at Armley Jail. Beneath the name was a painted shield depicting a sheep, a goat and a spindle. The sheep was hanging from a hook, its back arched like the contour of the dead horse. Amy's thoughts flashed to her father. Tonight he would be waiting for her outside those gates and if she didn't hand over her wage, she could end in the same situation. She stopped dead in her tracks.

'What's up with thee?' a girl squawked, bumping into her. 'Think you're a blooming statue?'

'Sorry,' said Amy, moving aside, her mind bent on finding some way to escape.

That morning was the longest she could remember. Her head spun like an empty bobbin, with not a single thread of an idea on it. As the throb of the machines counted out every second, she watched the hands of the big clock on the mending room wall. The hands reminded her of the spider's web. Reminded her to be patient. She must wait until six o'clock.

When the machines eventually rattled to a stop, the girls dusted the wool fluff from their hair and ears, grabbed their shawls or coats, and clattered down the stone stairs. There was an air of excitement in the yard. It was always the same on pay day.

The queue at the pay-office window was five deep, disorganized but orderly. Anxious to get home, there were shouts from the women for the clerk to hurry, but he seemed to delight in making the girls wait before he opened his window. Amy made sure she was not far from the front of the queue but she also hid herself behind several taller women. Across the street from the mill's entrance gates, she could see her father waiting. He was leaning against a lamp-post, hands in his pockets, one leg crossed in front of the other.

When the window was eventually opened, there was a high-pitched cheer. By this time, every girl who worked at Fanshaw's was in the main yard and Amy was amongst them, being jostled forward. As, one-by-one, the girls collected their pay, they nattered happily, waited for friends then wandered out through the main gate.

'Amy Dodd,' she replied, to the man in the gold-rimmed glasses. He ticked her name off the list. She wrote her signature, checked the coins on the bench, then stepped aside and waited until several more girls had been paid and a mob of lasses were heading towards the gate.

'Fire! Fire!' she suddenly screamed. Those immediately in front of her turned around, staring at her as though she was daft, but the ones in the queue who couldn't see her became silent. Faces scanned the mill's windows, the loading bay, the engine room, the roofs, looking for smoke. A chill feeling ran through the mob. Most of the workers had experienced the horrors of fire at some time in their lives either at home or at work. A fire in a mill could be devastating.

'Fire!' someone else shouted, then another voice echoed from across the yard. Suddenly, like a bunch of startled rats, the girls took flight, squealing and running helter-skelter for the safety of the street. The pay-office window was slammed shut and an alarm bell started ringing. From the loading bays and mill office, the clerks and labourers came running out, only to be bumped aside by the warehousemen who were anxiously heading for safety.

As the girls ran to the main gate, Amy turned back and wove between them, darted across the yard, around a wagon, towards the mill's side gate. She was running as fast as she could, but rounding the corner, she slipped and fell headlong on the hard ground, the coins bouncing from her hand. As she struggled to get up, a hand reached out and grabbed her arm.

Was it her father? she wondered. If it wasn't him, it was the overlooker and if he knew she was the one who had raised the alarm, she would lose her job.

'Amy Dodd, are you all right?'

She recognized the voice but, as she grabbed for her coins, the only words she could utter were the ones fixed in her head. 'I have to get away, far away,' she cried.

Picking up some of the coins, Mr Lister pushed them into her hand. He could see the fear in her face was far greater than that of an imaginary fire. 'Be careful,' he said sympathetically.

From the side gate, she headed down the street, not daring to look around. It was only a short distance to the canal. She knew what would happen when the panic subsided; it would soon become evident it was a false alarm. The girls who had been paid would wonder what the commotion was about. Those empty-handed would be angry, demanding their pay. There'd be women shouting, men yelling orders, horses rearing, no one listening. General confusion. Only one thing was certain – there was no fire.

With the coins clasped tightly in her hand, Amy reckoned it would take ten or fifteen minutes for the ruckus to die down – ten minutes at the most before her father discovered she was gone, then he would come looking for her. He'd search the yard and the street and then he'd go to the Medleys' house and search there. He might even go back to their old cellar or the junction where the trams were, or perhaps to the railway station. One thing was for sure, he wouldn't be satisfied until he found her. In Amy's mind there was only one place which would be fairly safe – the no-man's land between the canal and the river.

Running helter-skelter down the lane, she almost fell again and, by the time she reached the canal's bank, she was out of breath. Behind her an alarm bell was ringing and the mill's whistle was blowing regular shrill blasts of steam.

Without looking back, Amy turned onto the path that ran along the full length of the building. But it was not really a path at all! Not much more than a ledge the width of three or four bricks, and there was nothing to hold on to. Laying her chest against the wall, her arms outstretched, she slithered along it. At times her feet slipped on the slurry of ooze seeping from between the bricks. Her fingernails broke as she tried to grip them. She knew that if she fell into the water fully clothed, she'd not get out. She couldn't swim, and no one would hear her cries above all the noise.

Now there was a second bell ringing and getting louder. The fire brigade was on its way. Her heart was pounding. Her mouth dry. Time was passing quickly and it was taking much longer than she had thought to get clear of the mill building. Ahead of her was half a mile of open ground – waste land with not a bush or tree growing on it. She had to cross it to reach the bridge. She prayed her father was still searching for her at the mill's gate because if looked along the canal's bank he'd spot her easily.

As she neared the bridge, the bells stopped ringing and the whistle died. Glancing back, she could see people wandering about but no one was hurrying and, thankfully, no one appeared to be following her.

Ahead were the bridges – one for canal, the other for the River Aire. Stone-built topped with steel railings, they joined in the middle to create a single span. At this time of the day they were congested with evening traffic: carts, wagons, horse-drawn trams and workers on foot – hundreds of them, dirty and tired, plodding home from the factories at the end of a long day. Hurrying across the bridge, Amy was confronted by a pack of workmen coming towards her. Leading them was a man Amy instantly recognized – the hairy drunk from The Hungry Crow. Turning her face towards the water, she kept her head down, hoping he wouldn't remember her.

'Well,' he cried, halting in his tracks. 'Look what we have here!' As he spoke, he opened his arms in an attempt to grab her and prevent her from passing. His pals laughed.

Ducking aside, Amy startled a pair of drays as she dashed in front of them. The horses snorted. The driver cursed as he fought to hold them, but Amy kept weaving through the throng. Midway across, she ducked down the iron staircase that led to the tow path.

When she reached the black land between the two waterways, she caught her breath and looked back.

From the bridge's rail the hairy man was leaning over. He smirked, as he shouted, 'I'll tell your pa that I spotted you when I see him at The Crow tonight!'

Chapter 6

The Towing Path

Aware the hairy man had seen her and fearful he might tell her father, Amy hurried back from the tow path, climbed the iron steps to the bridge, and mingled with the throng of workers streaming home from the mills. With the long daily grind behind them, most were impatient to get home and Amy found herself jostled to quicken her pace. The unlucky ones, going in the opposite direction, heading towards twelve hours of night noise and sweat, wore sullen faces. They resisted the urgency to hurry and responded to the elbowing with disgruntled growls.

Moving with the river of bobbing heads, Amy passed the shoddy mill and the new printing shop, the foundry which still echoed with the clang of cold metal, passed the boot makers at the other side of the road and the gates of the tannery whose foul smells often drifted in through Fanshaw's windows.

Glancing back, there was no sign of the hairy man from the pub, or of her father. She was grateful to the crowd for swallowing her up but once the mob reached the rows of houses, the flow began to thin out. Workers peeled off, scurrying up the side streets like scared rabbits running for the warren at the first crack of a rifle. The only sounds on the streets were the clicking of steel toe-caps on cobbles and the clatter of wooden clogs. There was little conversation. Some said a polite, 'Good night,' or 'See you in the morning,' before disappearing into a poorly lit kitchen, but the replies, if any, were merely mumbled echoes of the same phrase, or the greeting was ignored answered only by the slamming of a door.

Amy envied the lucky ones their families and homes; a meal waiting on the stove and the excited cry of children's voices. She felt sorry for the few confronted by the cold comfort of a locked door, the girls left stamping their feet on the stone step, banging on the window, calling out, 'It's me, Mam. For God's sake, open the bloody door!'

As she walked on, Amy reached into her pocket and ran her fingers around the loose coins. Even before spreading them on her palm she knew she was short. There were three florins, a shilling and a sixpence – a total of only seven shillings and sixpence. She checked both pockets. They were empty. Darn it! She must have lost the other florin when she fell in the yard. It was probably still lying where it fell unless some worker had been lucky enough to see the silver glinting in the sun. What sun? she questioned. There hadn't been any that day and probably the coin was still there. That money would have bought her sufficient rations to last her for a few days, but she couldn't go back now. The thought of food reminded her she hadn't eaten since morning. It had been a long day and she was hungry and thirsty too.

The grocer, on the next corner, was busy sweeping the pavement outside his shop. No doubt it was his regular ritual this time of the day, though the steel-grey slabs showed little evidence of his effort. Amy studied him as she approached and found herself staring at his hands. They were pink and clean – so different to the men's in the factories.

'What are you after?' the shopkeeper asked brusquely, leaning the broom against the wall.

Amy blinked. 'Do you have any bread?' she asked, a flush reddening her neck.

'Sorry, luv. All gone. Come back in the morning. I'm closing up right now.'

'Do you have an apple?'

He studied the expression on her face. 'You in trouble, lass?'

She tried to smile. 'Not really. I'm hungry. I can pay. I've got money.'

'Come in 'ere, lass,' he said, rubbing his chubby hands down the front of his apron. 'Let's see what we we've got left over.'

Five minutes later, Amy emerged from the shop, a blot of milk on her chin, a parcel wrapped in newspaper tucked under her arm, and her money only short by the sixpenny piece. She looked satisfied as she stepped out.

'Take care of yoursen,' he said, reaching for the broom. 'An' if you'll take my advice, you'd best not hang around these parts after dark.'

Amy nodded, thanked him and turned back. The bridge she'd come from looked a long way off and the road was almost empty. There were no crowds she could lose herself in, only the stragglers wending their way home; the limp and lame, and the elderly with no youngsters to support them.

An old lady smiled. For her the day had been extra-long, though at her age she was lucky to have a job at all. Perhaps she too should have been grateful for the job at Fanshaw's. But it wasn't just the mill Amy was running away from, though she wasn't sorry to leave.

When she reached the bridge, she felt agitated and angry. She was almost back where she had started from. She was getting nowhere. The thought of her father searching for her made her hurry down the iron steps but as her hand slid along the rusty railing, the flaking metal scratched her palm. She had to take more care.

Below the bridge, the two channels of water lay like a pair of ungainly twins separated only by a cord of lifeless land. On one side, the River Aire flowed purposefully towards the city, leaving only its putrid smell in its wake. Midstream, its current circled constantly, churning the debris carried on its surface. Along the banks, sticks and litter attracted bubbles of brown scum. A dead rat bobbed as if frolicking in the foamy water.

In contrast, on the other side, the canal lay as still as a black shroud, its only trim, the hem of a path tacked along its straight edge. On the twenty-yard strip of land between the two bodies of water, mounds of grey sludge, dredged from the canal's bottom, provided a habitat for weeds and rodents. The dank atmosphere coveted the unhealthy smell. Not a single tree grew in that part of the city.

Judging by the clock in the grocer's shop, Amy guessed it was almost eight, but there was still too much daylight to chance walking beside the canal without being seen. She must wait until it was fully dark before setting off, and pray that there'd be little or no moon that night.

Settling herself on the pile of rubble underneath the bridge, Amy faced the river knowing that it was not used for transport, the barges only travelled along the canal. From the parcel of food she had bought from the grocer, she selected one slice of brawn and the Eccles cake. After breaking the pastry in half, she wrapped the remains of her food in the rag that had held her breakfast. Tying the four corners, she made the package into a small secure bundle.

Gazing along the water, through the tall nettles that flourished in the black silt, Amy could see the mill with its tall chimney poking up from the far end of the building. On most days it gushed with clouds of ash that fell back to the streets for miles around but, for the moment, it was dormant. She looked at the grimy building – five storeys high, but unlike the contours of Armley Jail, Fanshaw's lines were straight, its angles square and it had no turrets running around the top. Yet, considering the fretwork of iron bars barricading its smutty windows, it could well have been a prison. Even the windows on the third and fourth floors were crisscrossed with twisted iron. *Were the mill owners expecting someone to break in or were the bars in place to stop the workers getting out?* She was glad she had left and swore she would never go back.

When her riverside vigil had begun, a cold sickle-shaped moon had emerged from behind the tall chimney. It had looked lifeless and dull at first, but as the evening wore on, it rose slowly while the backcloth of sky darkened and the crescent shone as if honed to a fine polish.

Amy stretched her legs and scrambled from her hiding place. Her bottom was cold, her coat damp at the back. Even though it was July, she sensed the coming night would not be warm. Without clouds, the stars were already pricking patterns in the sky and, as she stood and scoured the heavens searching for the Great Bear, a carriage rumbled over the bridge. She cowered back. After a few seconds it was gone and the bridge was silent again. She waited for a few minutes till she was sure there were no more carriages or wagons, no pedestrians, no voices and no one to see her.

Over the next two hours, she confirmed her decision to follow the canal and get as far away from her father as she could. But which way to go? If she headed towards the city's centre there'd be trains, carriages, barges, even sailing boats that could take her to the coast. But by going that way, she'd encounter more people, more drunks and more danger. She'd heard the ports were rough places, teeming with foreigners who couldn't be trusted, men who might rape her or cut her throat for the cost of a glass of ale.

To the west, beyond the sprawl of the woollen mills, lay the Yorkshire moors. If she went in that direction, there'd be fewer people, fewer roads, little traffic and it was less likely her father would follow her far from the town. She'd been told that Lancashire was over the Pennines. That people there spoke with a different accent and weren't always partial to Yorkshire folk. But she'd also heard there were big towns and lots of cotton mills where good money could be made for an honest day's work. Maybe once she was there, she'd get a job, even if it was in a mill. At least, it couldn't stink as bad as a woollen mill, and cotton must be cleaner and lighter to handle than wet wool. If that was the case, she'd find herself some lodgings, work hard and never return to Leeds. It seemed a good plan.

Following the canal couldn't be difficult. It would be a long way, but it was summer and even if it rained she could easily walk ten miles a day. No different to being on her feet twelve hours in the mill and the earth would be much kinder to her feet than a cold stone floor. She had a tongue in her head and a little money in her pocket. She could ask for shelter in a farmhouse. Farmers' wives were friendly, she'd been told, and she didn't mind working for bread and keep. The thought of begging a lift on one of the barges had crossed her mind, but most of the boatmen looked unfriendly and had no time for strangers.

Wandering the streets alone at night was considered foolhardy. Walking by the canal at night was downright stupid. The towing path was an uninviting place. Amy shivered and hugged the bundle to her chest, treading carefully, conscious of every step, alert to every sound; the whirr of bats' wings round her head, the splash as a rat dropped into the water, the howl of a stray dog in search of a feed, and the yap of a fox. But, despite her fears, she pressed on.

The thread of black water, she had decided to follow, had neither pulse nor current, but tonight its flat surface mirrored the sliver of moon. Along the corridor of darkness only a single speck of light shone faintly in the distance. Though Amy was heading towards it, it hardly grew any closer.

She quickly reached that stretch of the canal opposite the street leading to the mill. A single gas lamp circled the paving slabs in a cold yellow light. On Bank Lane pale illumination filtered from the row of kitchen windows. Higher up the street, on the next corner, was another lamp. Though Amy couldn't see its mountings, she knew it hung from the wall of The Hungry Crow. Not far from there was the boarding house her father had taken her to. She wondered where he was, if he had any money left, wondered if he was already drunk or asleep and snoring on the bed in the dusty attic. She thought about the spider and wondered if it was weaving its web. She thought about the hairy man on the bridge and wondered if he had spoken to her father in the pub. She quickened her pace.

The towing path beside the canal was broad and flat, wide enough for two horses but worn bare in the centre from the regular use of single boat-horses. The grass along the edges was soft, damp with dew, and slippery. Though she felt thirsty, the canal water was far from appetizing and stories of bloated bodies floating in it convinced Amy that her thirst could wait.

Suddenly, the sound of raised voices made her stop. She squatted down. Two men were arguing on the opposite bank. Amy could see them clearly and it was likely they could see her too but she had nowhere to hide.

Suddenly another voice cut like a knife through the night. 'Amy Dodd! Come here, right now!' She knew it well. It was distant but distinctive and coming from Bank Lane.

Throwing herself down on the ground, Amy buried her face into the bundle of food. Had he seen her? Did he know she was there?

'Amy! Amy Dodd!'

The two men near the lamp stopped arguing and wandered off into the night.

With her heart racing, Amy clutched the earth.

'I'll find you, girl,' her father threatened. 'God's oath, I'll find you if it's the last thing I do!'

She shuddered. There was real venom in his tone and he wasn't drunk. Never once, as a child, when she'd dreamed of her father calling her name, had she ever expected anything like this. She waited, hardly daring to breathe. Then the calls continued. Obviously, he had not seen her.

Crawling crab-like, she slid into the ditch beside the path, settling on a layer of slime and sludge scooped up from the canal by the dredgers. As she was directly opposite the lane, she dared not lift her head. If her father walked over to the bank, only a few yards of water would separate them. Desperate to get further away, she tried pushing herself along the ditch, inching her way forward by her toes. But her coat and skirt hindered her legs. Her boots were heavy with caked mud and her fingers sore from clawing the ground. Edging forwards, her head hit something in the ditch. It stunk, worse than The Crow.

Unable to control her stomach, she retched loudly then quickly clasped one muddy hand tightly over her mouth. Had the sound carried? Had her father heard her? She tried to lay still but the fear of him seeing her made her shake uncontrollably. Then, after what seemed like an age of silence, she lifted her head, blinked her eyes, and tried to make sense of the shapes in the darkness. Looming right in front of her was the bloated carcase of the dead horse. Her stomach churned as she dragged herself back from it and stared at it. But the horse no longer returned her gaze. Its eye sockets were now empty, pecked bare by crows. The gaping mouth was lipless – scavenged by a fox, while the yellow teeth smiled at her in a morbid grin. Amy clamped her eyelids tightly shut.

Plop! It was close by and sounded like a stone being tossed into the water.

Plop! Splash!

Then another, and another. Was someone throwing stones at her? She waited, petrified, her heart thumping.

Then a frog croaked. Another answered, and as she lifted her chin only an inch, saw the water ripple when another frog stretched its slippery legs and leapt in. Though there were no stones being directed at her, and there was no one on the bank, her mind would not stop swimming with imaginary images. She was afraid. Afraid of the night. Fearful that the rats or foxes attracted to the carcase might bite her. Afraid she would wake in the morning to find herself covered in ants, or that she'd awake to her father dragging her to the edge to throw her headlong into the murky water. If she sank beneath the surface, who would know or even care? But what could she do? For the moment she had little alternative but to stay put. The cold she could feel was not from the wetness that had soaked through to her skin, but from the deep-seated malignant chill that fear had manufactured so efficiently. With her face pressed into her bundle, her feet stuck deep in the dredged waste, she squeezed her eyes tightly closed. She knew she was trapped.

Chapter 7

Running Away

Harold Lister folded his clothes. He was looking forward to leaving the Leeds mill and returning home. Having brought little more than his nightwear, socks and a shirt for the short visit, his travelling bag was half empty. After placing his notebooks and drafting equipment neatly on top, he sat down in the armchair beside the fireplace. Though, outside, the evening was warm, the empty hearth somehow had a feeling of chill about it.

Thinking back over the past few days, he hadn't achieved as much as he would have liked. Despite Mr Fanshaw being livid at the alarm which had been falsely raised, and even angrier at the report that had appeared in the *Yorkshire Post*, the mill's owner had asked him, only that afternoon, to draw up plans for an external staircase to the main mill building. Designing such a fixture would not be a simple assignment and it would necessitate him spending more time in Leeds – more time in the one-room lodging that the mill provided for him – the room he had grown to hate.

But he had no reason to complain. Mr Fanshaw was a good man to have dealings with, unlike some of the mill owners he had been engaged by. The superintendent of the fire brigade, however, was less amiable, and far less intelligent. Having to consult with him over the evacuation plan irked him. He would have preferred to have drawn up a schedule independent of the brigade's senior officer. However, though the work was not what he would have chosen, it would, no doubt, be a well-paid contract.

Had it not been for the girl's actions, the fire safety standards at Fanshaw's Mill would never have been reviewed and there would have been no necessity for him to return in the following few days.

He smiled to himself when he recollected the event, but his mood changed when he thought of the young woman sprawled out in the mill yard, her hands grazed, grovelling about for the few coins she had lost. How could he forget the look of desperation etched on her face?

How lucky he had been. He had never experienced such feelings in his life. How terrible that a girl could be driven by fear to go to such lengths, especially the fear of her father. How evil could he be? All he'd heard was that the man in question was a nasty piece of work.

Harold shook his head and picked up a copy of *The Times* from the side table. It had been sitting there for over a week. On the front page were details of the Spanish surrender in Santiago de Cuba, but it was the article on page three about Santiago in Chile that interested him. He read it again.

With the export of nitrates and the mining of copper, silver and other minerals, Chile is not only politically stable, but is experiencing an era of national affluence.

Since the opening of the railway tracks across the country, immigrants from many non-Iberian countries are being attracted to this South American country.

Foreign investors and engineers from the United States and Germany are working together to construct bridges, roads and cable railways. Routes to the north and south are being opened and the construction of a rack-railway across the Andes has already been discussed.

With the founding of the Chilean Electric Tramway and Light Company in London recently, German and English investors intend to electrify the tramway system in Santiago, a city with a rapidly growing population.

After reading the advertisement, which appeared beneath it, Harold carefully tore it from the paper, folded the article and placed it in one of the compartments of his desk alongside several similar newspaper cuttings.

It had always been his wish that one day he would sail to America. One of his regrets in life was that, apart from visiting Italy to study its architecture, he had never travelled. The articles he had read recently about some of the engineering projects being undertaken in Chile interested him greatly, as did the geography of the country itself – a narrow strip of land, falling to the sea from the western side of the Andes. In the north was the Atacama Desert – the driest desert on earth, bleached by a burnished sun. In the south were frozen ice fields and glaciers sliding slowly into the sea. It was a country of extremes, and it interested him.

Gazing from his window over the Leeds potted skyline, he considered how very different a place such as Chile would be to the blackened landscape and grime of the industrial north of England.

When Amy next looked about her, the sliver of curved moon was high in the sky. The lamp-lit streets were silent. The two men had disappeared and there was no voice calling her name. For a short while, she had slept.

Chilled to the marrow, she struggled to her knees. The front of her coat, skirt and blouse, even her underwear, was damp. She wasn't sure about her boots as she couldn't feel her feet. She knew she must get up and walk and get the blood moving in her legs.

On rubbing the dirt from her hands, she opened the fine grazes scratched across her palms. They stung as she dabbed the blood on her coat. Then she remembered her money; remembered the coins rolling across the yard. She remembered spending sixpence and hoped the remainder of her wages was safe. The pockets of her mother's coat were deep and had no holes. The coins jangled. But the bundle of food she'd rested her head on was caked in mud. Its contents were damp and probably ruined.

She had to move on, get away from the dead horse, away from the streets opposite, and away from her father.

A faint light still shone directly ahead. Was it a boat? Was it the one with the woman onboard she'd seen previously?

As she drew closer she considered the outline of a barge its thin chimney poking up from the cabin's roof and the brass chains glinting in the moonlight. It was sitting low in the water under the weight of its heavy cargo. Though she'd heard terrible tales about bargees and the types of rogues they were and had often been warned to keep clear of them, she envied this boat's occupants and their freedom. They were dry, safe, warm and, no doubt, well fed. It wasn't until she was almost level that she realized the vessel was moored on the opposite bank. Voices drifted over the water. A man and a woman were talking in comfortable tones with comfortable silences between. Watching the shadowy figures, she observed the woman lift her skirt and squat down on the bank. After a moment she stood up, straightened her skirt and followed the man back on board.

Though Amy knew it was neither the barge nor the woman she'd seen before, she was tempted to call them, ask for help and shelter for the night. But that would mean retracing her steps back to the bridge to cross over the canal. It would mean she would be heading back towards Fanshaw's Mill and that would never do. She must stay on the tow path and continue along the way she was heading.

Unaware if midnight had come or gone, Amy felt tired and struggled to think positively, but there was little to spur her on. Ahead the canal turned slowly and stretched into the darkness. The grey cottages beside the locks looked greyer in the night light. Each bridge she met was different. Each offered shelter, somewhere to hide, but the arches were dark and ominous and when a train rumbled above her head, she felt afraid.

With the fear of stumbling in the dark, she slowed her pace, continuing on the horse path, her eyes glued to the ground. It wasn't long before she stopped. She didn't know where she was. There were no buildings or lights or sounds apart from the croaking of a dozen frogs and the call of the night birds. The ground all around looked marshy. She could smell the damp. A clump of bushes offered shelter. The bundle of spoiled food was her pillow. The coat wrapped round her was her blanket. All she could hope for was that it wouldn't rain.

Sleep came rapidly but with the same disturbing dreams. Her hands and feet were bound. Her hair was caught on the combs of the machine. Her head was being dragged closer to its ugly teeth. She wanted to scream, drag herself clear, call for help, but her mouth wouldn't utter a sound. With her knotted hair being pulled into the mechanical rollers, she woke with a start. A small dog, scratching at the bundle of food beneath her head, was tugging at the tangles in her hair. When she lifted her head, it dropped to the ground and growled. It was broad daylight and she could hear the sound of a man's boots pounding along the path towards her. Was it her father?

'Are you all right, miss?' the man yelled. 'You had me worried. I thought for a minute you was a gonna.'

Amy tried to smile. What a mess she must have looked with her coat-front caked in mud, clay crusted on her hands, her face dirty and her hair dishevelled.

'I tripped,' she said, smoothing her hair. 'I must've knocked my head.'

'So long as there's no real damage. Here, give me your hand.'

The man's help was appreciated. She was stiff and sore. 'Is it Saturday?' she asked.

He looked her up and down and nodded. 'Well, I must get along,' he said.

'Yes,' said Amy. 'I should've been at the mill hours ago. I best get home too, the folks will be wondering what's happened to me.'

'I'm sure they wouldn't want you wandering these parts at night in future. Some odd sorts around at times.'

They exchanged glances.

'I'll remember that,' Amy said. 'Thanks.'

The small dog whined as it scratched at a hole. The man touched his cap, whistled and walked on.

Amy looked around. Everything was green. There were no blackened streets or mills, just trees and reeds, and everything was moist and lush. On a pond nearby, a goosander swam in circles until a kingfisher dived, disturbing it. A family of moorhens ducked in and out of the reeds, the ducklings cheeping unconcerned. But apart from the birdsong, the place was strangely quiet.

In her pocket, the coins rattled. Some consolation at least. There was dampness in the air and she was grateful for her mother's old coat. When the layer of mud dried, she was sure she'd be able to rub it off.

Above, the dark clouds tinged with rusty pink, looked troublesome. It was going to rain. Running away was not working out as well as planned. She should have been further from Fanshaw's by now. Her efforts of the previous night had only carried her a little over a mile and despite her earlier thoughts of travelling in the rain, one spell in a wet ditch had taught her differently. It would be foolish to get soaked right through.

The rain came as expected. Heavy sheeting rain that was impossible to see through let alone walk. Sitting on the towing path, where it curved beneath one of the bridges, she waited. A sparrow kept her company. The time passed very slowly. Then, as quickly as it had started, it cleared and the July sun shone warmly, raising a haze of mist across the meadows. Amy continued, this time at a quicker pace.

By midday she'd passed more locks. She heard the sounds of a forge, and smelt the hops from a brewery. Perched on the hills were houses and churches. Spires and factory chimneys poked up from the distant valleys but she was still too close to the villages that surrounded Leeds to feel free. The woollen coat was cumbersome and heavy, and carrying it made her sweat. She was thankful most of her walking was along a flat path with only short hills to climb beside the locks.

During the morning a couple of coal barges swam quietly by. She stepped off the towing path to let the horses pass but the boatmen ignored her. Considering her appearance, she wasn't surprised. She satisfied her hunger with a piece of cheese salvaged from her rations, washing it down with water from a spring that bubbled out of the bank. Several more barges passed, going in the opposite direction. This part of the canal was busy but, like the railway beside it, she knew it was heading west and taking her away from Leeds.

With no sign of her father, her thoughts turned to food. As she emerged from the marshlands, a field of untended rhubarb offered some relief. Scrambling from the bank, Amy pulled several stalks, broke off the broad leaves and chewed on the sappy stems. Her face screwed when she swallowed but despite the fact it was sour, she collected a handful of stalks and pushed them into her pocket. Five minutes later, pains rolled across her belly and she had to stop.

From behind her came the chugging of a steam barge. Before it rounded the bend, she could see smoke over the cut puffing from its chimney. It wasn't long before it was level with her. At the front was the steam barge. It was towing a dumb-boat. Both barges were loaded with sawn timber. The lead boat was a pretty craft with colourful decorations painted on its flat transom but, in comparison, the barge in tow was dull and unremarkable. Amy lifted her hand to wave but the bargee on the rudder was concentrating on navigating the channel ahead. She watched as the boats swam by, feeling very much alone.

As she walked on, she watched the pair extend their distance till they finally disappeared, but at the next set of locks, she caught up with them. As she walked up the short hill beside the locks, the man on the gate acknowledged her. That was the last she saw of those boats.

In the course of the afternoon, Amy walked several miles through areas she had never visited before. On the surrounding hills, the grey-green fields melded to mauve on the tops. Dry-stone walls criss-crossed the hillsides like cracks in an old plate. The roads and bridle tracks didn't linger beside the canal but crossed on swing bridges barely high enough for a barge to swim underneath. Along the bank, bramble bushes abounded, but it was too early for the blackberries. Then the showers returned.

The next passing boatman was sociable. He knuckled his forehead and wished Amy, 'Afternoon'. Amy smiled and echoed her reply. A young boy, hardly half the height of the horse's withers, strode beside the fine draught horse on the towing path whistling. A small dog poked its head from a painted kennel atop the cabin roof and snapped out a greeting. Had the boat not been heading towards Leeds, she would have asked for a lift but she was confident there would be other barges heading west and hoped one, at least, would stop.

As the afternoon wore on, Amy's stride shortened. Only one more boat floated by that afternoon. It was another steam barge. Resting for a spell, she perched on a stump beside the tow path and gave the boatman a wearied wave. Though she was sure he had seen her, his eyes didn't shift from the waterway ahead. Gliding by, it left barely a ripple in its wake but it was enough to attract a flock of swallows that swooped, skimming the water in search of food. A few feet away a vole crossed the tow path. It stopped for a moment and studied Amy before sliding into the water. On the other bank, a fox appeared, drank from a puddle of water, but when it saw her it turned and slunk stealthily away.

The growing line of dark clouds on the horizon looked ominous. More rain would mean she'd need to shelter somewhere. On the hillside, not fifty yards from the canal, was an old farm cottage. A track ran from the farmyard down to a little-used wharf where boats could moor to load skins, or stock-feed, or unload timber. Amy clinked the coins in her pocket. Perhaps she could purchase a cup of milk and a knob of bread from the farmhouse.

Rubbing the dried mud from her clothes, she raked her fingers through her hair, spat on her hand and tried to wash the dirt from around her mouth and wandered up the track. Cows lowed in the meadow and the smell of the hay-barn reached her before she got to the farm gate. It leaned open, hanging from one hinge with old grass woven through its wooden slats. It was a long time since it had been shut. From the gate, a path, potted with puddles, led to the house. As Amy stepped into the yard a gaggle of geese advanced, necks extended, wings flapping, beaks clacking at her alarmingly.

'We don't want none o' your sort round here!' the farmer cried, as he appeared from the house. 'Be off with you, before I set the dogs on you! We don't want no tramps or beggars around 'ere.'

'I want to buy a pot of milk. I've got money. I can pay,' Amy replied, as defiantly as she dare, but her voice only encouraged the din, and when the two dogs headed towards her, she turned and ran. The black and white pair stopped when they reached the gate, their tails wagging. Amy stopped and looked back. The sheepdogs appeared friendly but the geese were another matter. Returning to the canal path, she heard the farmer's piercing whistle. The dogs responded instantly, turning and haring across the yard, scattering the geese in all directions.

In the doorway of the farmhouse, a robust woman was shaking crumbs from a chequered tablecloth. Within seconds, a scurry of chickens was squawking round her feet, pecking at the morsels.

'What's all the hullabaloo about?' she asked her hubby.

'Bloody gypsies!' the farmer mumbled, patting his dogs. His wife glanced around the yard then disappeared inside.

Feeling drained and tired, the few yards back to the towing path seemed like a mile. Amy knew there was no real shelter, only weeds and rushes, and a hedgerow overgrown with prickly vegetation. If it rained in the night she'd get soaked. Perhaps she should turn back to Leeds after all and shelter under one of the bridges. But she'd no energy or enthusiasm for walking back, and the dark arches were dank and dismal even by day, certainly not the sort of place to loiter under at night. She'd seen enough of Leeds, and the smell of the nearby brewery had reminded her of The Hungry Crow. At the moment, she couldn't go on, but she was determined not to go back either so she'd have to find another alternative.

Chapter 8

Milkwort

Sinking to the grass, Amy pulled a stick of rhubarb from her pocket and bit into it. It wasn't ripe and though she tried to chew it, it was too sour. Remembering what had happened the last time she had eaten a piece, she quickly spat it out.

For quite a while, she'd seen no boats or trains. The air was ominously still – no wind, no birds, only gathering clouds which were rolling down from the moors. Already they had shrouded the sun, and dusk was drawing in all too quickly. Amy hugged her legs and laid her head on her knees. She wanted to sleep, to wake up and find she was somewhere other than on the canal's bank. She knew she had to move on. But where to? Ahead there'd be more bridges to shelter under, she hoped. But how far away were they?

On the far hillside, beyond the trees, smoke was rising from several chimney pots. A row of houses? Another village? Maybe she could ask for shelter there. Then she looked down at her coat. *Who'd take me in looking like this*? she thought. No one. And she didn't want to be turned away again.

As evening changed quickly into night, the wind, streaked with rain, returned. It gusted down the canal, disturbing the stagnant surface. The sliver of moon she'd watched the previous evening did not appear, and there were no stars. The only visible light was from a downstairs room in the farmhouse. She imagined a kitchen and a table set with a gingham cloth. There would be the smell of meat roasting in the oven, cabbage cooking in a pot, a kettle singing on the stove and a cat, with a litter of kittens, in a basket by the hearth. She turned the collar up on her coat and wrapped her arms around her knees keeping the wind on her back.

As she watched, the light in the farmhouse flickered and dimmed. It was as if the lamp's wick was almost spent. Then a moment later, the glow reappeared from the upstairs window shining more brightly. A shadowy figure moved across the room, then within minutes, the light was extinguished leaving the farmhouse as a black silhouette against the sky.

A sheep bleated anxiously from a nearby field. The dogs barked for a while, but the farmer was settled for the night and showed no concern. Soon all was silent on the canal bank, save for the wind rustling through the rushes at the other side.

Using her coat as a blanket, Amy covered her ears to the sound of rain pounding on the slate roof. The pile of hay and manure at the back of the barn exuded warmth and she slept soundly. Sometime during the night, the dogs joined her, though she was unaware of it until morning, when she woke to the drag of a rasping tongue on her cheek. For a moment she thought she was back on the canal path.

In the yard outside, the geese honked and chickens squawked. It was daylight and the rain had stopped. Clambering from the hay, Amy heard the farmer whistle for his dogs. In an instant, they were off, out of the barn, jumping the puddles in the yard to join the farmer as he headed up over the field.

Amy pulled on her coat.

'You should see yourself!' the farmer's wife remarked. 'You look like a blinking scarecrow!'

Amy hadn't noticed the woman leaning over the milking bail. There was no hint of a smile on the ruddy face, but there was a twinkle in her brown eyes.

Rubbing her head, Amy pulled the stalks of hay from her hair, but the ears of wheat were hooked firmly between the thin threads of her woollen coat.

'Come 'ere,' she said. 'Turn your body around.'

Following the instructions, Amy let the woman brush the straw from her.

'Now, tell me what you're up to in our barn. You're no gypsy, that's for sure, and I've seen better-looking tramps.'

Amy couldn't tell a lie. The woman had an honest face. 'I'm heading for Lancashire, and I fell in a ditch, but I've got some money and I just wanted to buy something to eat.' Pushing her hand in her pocket, she retrieved the few remaining coins and held them out. 'I can pay.'

'Running away, I bet! Well, that ain't none of my business. But we got milk to spare, and I've pickled more eggs than I care to mention. If you're quick, I'll feed you up and pack you off before my man comes back.'

Amy was grateful and followed her to the house where she drank two mugs of tea sweetened with honey and a cup of cream, swallowing them as fast as she possibly could. The bread was thick and buttered and the apple pie warm from the oven. By the time she'd cleared her plate, there were six eggs ready to slip into her pockets, they were all hard boiled and still hot.

'How much do I owe you?' Amy asked.

'The dogs and pigs eat what we can't manage. You just get on your way before his nibs comes back.' There was a smile in the woman's eye as she wished Amy good luck. It was like the smile she used to see in her mother's eyes – before her father came home.

Morning mist rose from the canal's bank. The air was dank, the reeds joined by dozens of beaded cobwebs. With the sun reflecting on the dew drops, the rays transformed them into shining gems colouring them with brilliant flashes of blue, red or green. Amy was mesmerized. Then the sun disappeared taking its illusive magic with it.

Aware she was still not far from Leeds, she urged herself to hurry on. She wondered about the canal path stretching out in front of her. Did it ever end or did it wander around England from one corner to the other? She consoled herself with the fact that this morning her hunger had been satisfied and she felt refreshed. She'd been lucky. The farmer's wife had been generous. Others might not be so kind.

During the morning a barge approached. The horse towing it was a black shire, the largest of the draught horses. It was handsomely decorated with bright red terrets and wore a pair of white lace earcaps trimmed with coloured tassels. The polished brasses, hanging from its collar, glinted as they swung. Amy eyed the woman walking alongside it. How strangely she was dressed. Her pleated skirt was wide and short, revealing the tops of her boots. Over her shoulders she wore a brightly coloured crocheted scarf that crossed over her chest and tucked into her skirt. On her head was an ample black bonnet whose flounce fell almost to the woman's waist. In her ears was a pair of gold earrings, on her wrists, bangles that jangled. The woman acknowledged Amy with a nod and walked on, her eyes fixed on the waterway that was her home. At the back of the barge, a boy, resting his arm on the brightly painted tiller, murmured, 'Hello,' but nothing more.

The rain started again mid-morning, the steady drizzle shrouding the hills in mist and making it hard to see far ahead. Not wanting to get any wetter, Amy took shelter in the bushes on the bank and waited for the weather to clear. She ate one of her eggs and threw the shell into the water. A pair of brown ducks squabbled over the broken pieces. A barge carrying coal steamed by heading west, then a short-boat loaded with sheepskins swam east, destined for the tanneries in Leeds. The horse flicked its tail as it walked along, but the boatman didn't seem concerned that his cargo was alive with flies and maggots. Both the flies and the smell of rotting flesh lingered in the air long after barge had gone.

When the rain finally stopped, the sun emerged, and Amy continued on the towing path. Half a mile ahead, it rose steeply beside two sets of locks. A boy working the gates was waiting by the beam. He looked familiar. As she got nearer, Amy heard a woman's voice calling from the bottom of the chamber. 'You can open the paddles.'

Amy smiled at the boy and peered down into the lock and the broad barge that almost filled it. The brick walls dropped much deeper than she had imagined. The boatwoman, whose voice she had heard, stood on the small deck poised with her hand on the tiller. As the boy operated the ground paddles, water began pouring into the chamber and very slowly the level began to rise lifting the heavily laden short-boat with it. Once the water in the lock was level with that of the canal beyond, the boy leaned his back on the beam opening first one gate and then the other. Then he returned to the towing path and started pulling the towrope in order to draw the barge out of the lock. From the deck, the woman pushed against the gate behind her with a pole, but the barge didn't want to move.

'Do you need some help?' Amy asked, tentatively.

The boy didn't answer but handed her the end of the rope which they hauled on together.

Moving very slowly at first, the short-boat slid out of the lock and drifted along the waterway towards the path where Amy was hauling.

'Stop pulling!' the boy shouted. 'Drop the line! Stand aside!'

Amy wondered what she'd done wrong. The barge was moving well. Wasn't that what they wanted? But the boy had stopped hauling and was winding the line around a wooden bollard.

Within minutes, the woman on the tiller steered the barge up against the bank where her son secured the line on a mooring spike. Once the aft line was secure, all that remained was to tidy the lines and close the gates they had just locked through.

'Thanks, for your help,' the woman called. 'Good to get through to the next pound. More chance of getting a tow in the morning.'

Amy looked at her, not knowing what to say. It was raining again, little more than a drizzle, but her hair was plastered to her head and water was running down her neck.

'Are you walking up from Leeds?' the woman asked.

Amy nodded and knocked the drips from her nose.

'We heard you were on the path. News travels fast on the cut. Want to come aboard and dry yourself?'

Amy thanked her and was glad to accept the offer. She hoped the stories she'd heard about barge folk were not true.

'Careful when you jump on. I wouldn't want you to slip.'

Amy bunched her skirt in one hand and took the woman's outstretched hand in the other. Now she understood why the boatwomen's skirts were shorter than usual.

The barge was broad, almost five paces wide, but the strip of deck, where the woman had been standing, was quite narrow. Ahead of the tiller was a cabin, its wooden roof rising little more than four feet above the deck. The cabin's sliding doors, decorated with roses, were open.

'Who's that?' a gruff voice called, from within.

Amy jumped.

'That's Joel, my man. He's laid up. Can't get out of bed. Come in and meet him.' She indicated for Amy to go inside. 'Step down and duck your head, and keep it ducked.'

There were two small steps leading down into the cabin floor but the roof still wasn't high enough for her to stand upright. The woman pushed a stool towards her.

Sitting down, Amy gazed around, wide-eyed. On the right was a bed, broad and solid, running three-quarter the length of the living quarters. Tacked along the edges of it was a fringe of hand-crocheted lace that hid a row of cupboards. At the opposite side of the cabin was a narrow hinged table and bench, and above them a long single shelf also trimmed with white cotton lace. Various ornaments lined the shelves: brass bells and candlesticks, vases and painted plates. On the panelled wall hung at least a dozen horse brasses, all different and all gleaming as if just polished. Narrow lace drapes hung by the side of the two small leaded windows and painted roses, similar to the ones on the sliding doors, were repeated on the panels of the tall cupboard at the far end of the bed. Every piece of woodwork had once been varnished but in parts the old varnish had bubbled and in others it was peeling.

The stove, which backed onto the bulkhead, was open fronted. It had a hob clipped on the top bars and a shiny brass fireguard stood in front of it. The tiny galley was opposite the bed. The brass scuttle, filled with coal, had a thatched cottage and country scene painted on it. A square chimney poked up through the cabin roof and around its neck, it too wore a collar of white lace. The large pot rattling on the hob smelt of mutton stew.

Sitting upright in the bed was a dark-haired swarthy man in his mid-forties, his legs were covered by a brightly dyed felt rug. The colour of his shirt amazed Amy. It was perfectly white – whiter than any she'd seen on any mill worker, even on a Sunday. His waistcoat, made from hand-woven cloth, was trimmed with plaited braid whilst around his neck he wore a bottle-green scarf tied neatly in a knot at the front.

The stories she'd heard of dirty boatmen had always made her wary of them but seeing the appearance of this bargee amazed her.

'How long have you been awake?' his wife asked.

'Not long,' Joel said, as he cast his eyes over Amy. 'Off the cut?'

She didn't understand.

'He wants to know if you work on the canal.'

'No, I don't.'

'Then what's she doing here?'

'She helped Ben pull us out of the Dobson Staircase. She's the lass they've been talking about – walking the cut.'

Joel leaned forward and pressed a cushion behind his back. 'Where you off to, lass? Who you fleeing from?'

The boatman's direct questions surprised her. How did he know she was running away?

'Anything to do with the cut gets passed along from one barge to another. Like the telegraph, but on water.'

His wife interrupted. 'Take your coat off, lass, you're soaked. You can answer his questions later. I've got stew and dumplings on the stove. Want some?'

'Yes, please.'

'What's your name, lass?' the man said.

'Amy Dodd.'

'That's right,' he said knowingly. 'This here is my missus, Helen. My lad's name's Ben – Big Ben they'll call him when he's full grown, like the clock on the River Thames.' He smiled. 'Ten year ago we used to navigate those waters. I worked with my pa for thirty years on the Kennet and Avon, but the railway through to Bath took the trade from the canal and brought ruin to a lot of boatmen. That's when we came here.'

The boat swayed slightly as the boy stepped on deck.

'You got her lashed firm?' Joel called.

'Yes, Pa.'

'Good lad.'

'You all right, Pa?'

'Aye, son.'

As the bargee spoke, he folded back the rug that was covering his legs. From his groin to the sole of his foot, his left leg was cased in slats of wood held together with strips of cloth.

'Doctor said I should get a cast put on it,' he said. 'But we didn't have time for that. I'm not much for hospitals and I told him so. "You're all alike, you boatmen," he said to me, "too independent for your own good." But he was a good doctor and he straightened my leg and boxed it for me. Now I feel like half of me is in a coffin.' He laughed, 'It'll be a long time before you get the rest of me in though,' but when he tried to shift his position, his face screwed with pain. 'Doctor said I shouldn't move it for six weeks, but I told him, "Bugger that! Couple of weeks and it'll be right!"'

Helen smiled sympathetically. 'It was real nasty. The doctor said he'd broken more than one bone, and though he didn't complain much about the pain, he gave me some powder to give him when it's really bad.'

'It works a treat,' Joel said. 'She puts a dose in me cocoa and I sleep like a sunken log.'

His wife tapped him playfully on the wrist. 'Only way to keep you from climbing out of bed.'

Not knowing how to respond, Amy asked, 'How did it happen?'

Joel shook his head. 'Our horse, Bessie, broke down. Just like that,' he said, clicking his finger and thumb together. 'She landed on me breaking my leg. I was just glad it wasn't Helen or Ben walking the path with her that day. A thousand pounds of horse flesh is a fair weight! It couldn't have happened at a worse time. We've got a load of alpaca wool overdue at Saltaire. A right valuable cargo, it is. Come all the way from South America. And here's me laid up and no animal to get us to the mill. And besides that, it's raining.'

'Aye,' Helen said, 'but you must admit, the lads on the cut have been good.' She turned her head to Amy. 'We've had a couple of decent tows from steam barges. But they don't want to wait for us through the rises – the locks, that is. You can't expect 'em to either. That's why we have to pull through on our own. We've been lucky a few times when there's been another boat coming the other way. They've helped us through. Boatmen are good like that when they know you're in strife.' She smiled at her husband. 'If we're lucky tomorrow, we'll get a tow from here right up to Salts Mill. It's not far.'

'If there's no other boats, I can help with the pulling,' said Amy. 'I'm strong.'

'Pulling's for horses,' said Helen, shaking her head, 'but Joel can't get out to go buy another horse till he's back on his feet. I told him our Ben's a good judge of horse flesh but he's choosy when it comes to a boat-horse.'

'And rightly so,' he said. 'A good boat deserves a good horse and *Milkwort*'s a good boat. I should know, I fitted her out myself,' he said, looking proudly around his cabin. 'You'll not see another one like this on the cut.'

'So how will you manage, without a horse?'

'We've worked it out, so we can make the best of a bad thing. When we get this load taken off, we'll live off our docking money and fix the boat up. We can afford not to work for a while.'

'*Milkwort* is ours,' said Helen proudly. 'It doesn't belong to the Leeds and Liverpool Canal Company like most of the barges around here.'

Joel continued. 'We're what's known on the cut as a Number One. We do our own trade. Pick up what we want. Go where we want. No one tells us what to do. Not like the short-boats carrying coal. You'll see lots of them around Leeds. They've got the *L and L* company name on the bow. The men on those barges don't own their craft. They pick up a different boat with every load.' He looked at his wife. 'What we plan, when we get to Saltaire, is to put *Milkwort* in Jentz's Yard. She's well overdue for caulking and a coat of tar on her bottom.'

'Aye, and a splash of paint and varnish in the cabin too.'

'You're not going to Liverpool then?' said Amy.

'Who knows where we'll go?' Joel said. 'When we leave Jentz's Yard, we'll pick up another load and go wherever we have to, maybe back to Leeds then down the Aire and Calder to the coast. But I can tell you, lass, we'll not be going over the Pennines. I can't walk or even stand at the moment, so I certainly couldn't leg it for a mile through the Foulridge Tunnel. And I can't expect Helen or young Ben to leg us through.'

Helen looked at Amy sympathetically. 'I can see by your face you're disappointed we're not going to Lancashire. Is that where you want to go?'

'I don't know what I want,' said Amy pensively. 'I just know I want to get away from Leeds, as far away as possible!'

That night, Amy slept in the small cabin at the opposite end of the barge to the main cabin. Between the two bulkheads was the short-boat's cargo – several tons of imported fibre packed into dozens of bales and covered with tarpaulins.

The forward accommodation was compact. Ben's bunk was built against one wall. It had a curtain around it which could be pulled back when needed, and like the big bed in the main cabin, the area underneath it was made into cupboards. On the opposite wall was a large wooden locker with a flat top. This, with a flock mattress laid along it, was Amy's bed for the night. Against the bulkhead was a fixed cupboard, stretching half the width of the boat. This cabin also had a stove but it was smaller than the one Helen used for cooking. Stacked neatly on the floor was an assortment of items – two sacks of grain, several bags of flour, a barrel of potatoes, containers, buckets, jugs and a wash tub with a sheaf of wheat laying across it. On top was a coil of white cotton rope, and resting against it, a well-worn leather horse-collar and harness.

During the evening, when Amy lay gazing out of the tiny window next to her head, Ben pulled back the curtain and asked, 'Can you read?'

'Yes,' she said. 'Can you?'

'Not yet, but I want to learn, and Pa said, if I learn, he'll buy a newspaper and I can read it to him and the other boat folk on Sundays.'

'What about school?' Amy asked.

'Ain't never been because we never stop long enough in one place. Pa teaches me everything. Says I'll make a good barge man. Says I already know the cut nearly as good as he does.'

'Do you like living on the canal?'

'I wouldn't want to be anywhere else!' With that, Ben let the curtain fall back. 'G'night,' he said.

The flock mattress was not as soft as the deep litter in the barn, but the cabin was cosy, and Amy felt safe. Lying on her back, her mind drifted to the events of the previous week. She thought about her mother's burial, about Fanshaw's Mill, even about Mr Lister and the way he walked, the way he'd smiled at her and the unintentional touches when he measured her which had made her heart flutter.

She thought about the boat people she'd met and of the stories she'd been told of dirty bargees. Then she thought of the painted decorations and all the ornaments that made the cabin look like Aladdin's Cave. How fortunate she'd been to meet up with *Milkwort*. Most of the other boatmen had ignored her, though from what Joel had said, that wasn't the case. He assured her that boatmen didn't miss anything on the cut and word that a girl was wandering the path alone had been passed from one boat to another.

Then her thoughts flashed to her father.

She could still hear his cry echoing in her head: *Amy Dodd! Amy Dodd! Where are you?* No doubt, everyone in the nearby streets had heard him too, and by now they'd all know it was Amy Dodd who had caused the commotion at the mill. And they'd all know that she had run away.

But what if he found out where she was? What if word got back to him that she'd been seen on the canal? Like a flash, he'd be on the tow path after her. She knew that for sure.

In the dim shadows of the Dark Arches beneath the Leeds railway station, Amos Dodd breathed heavily as he thrust himself jerkily into the girl. He couldn't see her face, but he had no desire to. After the final grunt, his knees crumpled. He threw his head back and his whole body shuddered involuntarily.

'That were quick!' the woman said, tugging at her skirt, which was twisted up between the pair. 'Want some more?' she asked, drawing herself away from him.

Dodd didn't answer. He fastened his trouser buttons, sucked in the dank air and tightened the belt around his waist. He was pleased with himself. The bit of news he'd gleaned deserved a treat. The day spent hauling baulks of timber from the barges had paid off in more ways than one. He'd satisfied the yapping of his landlady and he'd heard whispered word of a girl sheltering under one of the Leeds bridges. But that was all he'd heard. Nothing more, and no amount of threats would jog the boatmen's memories. Even so, Dodd was certain it was Amy. It had to be. Now, all he had to do was to find out which way she'd gone. Was she heading east for the Humber and Hull, or west on the Leeds and Liverpool towards Lancashire?

As he'd heard the news near the Basin, he thought it more likely she was on the Aire and Calder. He doubted she'd ever step foot near Fanshaw's again, but he intended to make certain.

'You'll burn in hell when I find you, girl!' he yelled, as a train rumbled overhead.

'What's that you say?' the woman asked. 'Want to find another girl? Aren't I good enough?' she said, sliding her hand up the inside of his leg. 'Good enough for the likes of you, I reckon!'

The punch sent her reeling backwards into one of the stone pillars. With blood oozing between her fingers, she pressed on the tooth that was sticking into her bottom lip.

'Bastard!' she cried.

Amos Dodd ignored her. He had other things on his mind.

Chapter 9

The Rises

The sound of rushing water woke her. She could feel the barge rocking slightly and wondered if they'd turned around and gone to the coast. But the sea was a long way off, and hadn't Helen said the canal was barely broad enough for two barges to pass and there was nowhere up ahead wide enough to turn a short-boat measuring sixty-five feet in length?

After rubbing the sleep from her eyes, Amy looked out of the tiny window. It was dull outside, like daylight veiled by an afternoon storm. Little more than an arm's length away from the barge, she was confronted by a brick wall glistening with blackened slime and it was slowly sinking beneath the boat. Dragging her skirt up over her petticoat, she fastened the buttons of her stained blouse and opened the cabin door. *Milkwort* was rising slowly in the lock. Ahead were the gates which held back the waters of the canal. Above, the sky was dappled blue and grey. The boatwoman with the gold earrings was standing at the stern, her hand on the tiller.

'Stay by the cabin!' Ben shouted when he saw her. 'Don't go near the edge.' Amy glanced down to the water pouring into the lock and bubbling around the bow.

Joel's muffled call could be heard from the main cabin at the other end of the barge. 'Keep clear of the gates!'

Helen didn't answer. She knew the danger of being inside a barge while it was in the lock. She knew that if the rudder caught on the sill, the boat could tip and be inundated by the rising water. It didn't happen often but she'd seen it once on the cut. A barge had flipped in a chamber causing chaos on the canal. It had taken several days for the boat to be righted and the forty tons of limestone bucketed by hand from the bottom of the lock. She'd also seen boats flooded due to carelessness, and she'd heard of a few experienced boat folk who'd died in the locks.

She glanced along the length of the boat judging the distance between the walls and the side of the barge. There was a gap of less than a hand's span, but there was a yard's width from the gate to the bow.

'Can I do anything?' Amy shouted.

'Just stay still. I don't want you slipping over. You'd drown for sure if you fell. That's if you didn't get crushed first.'

Leaning against the cabin door, Amy watched the froth churning, as water poured in from the pound above. Ben was observing from the top of the lock gate.

'Keep clear of the sill!' Joel yelled from the cabin, his frustration, at being unable to control his own boat, was obvious.

'I'm not daft,' Helen mumbled, as she monitored the gap between the rudder and the gates. The chamber filled slowly.

Once the level in the lock was the same as that of the canal ahead, Ben opened the gates and pulled the short-boat out onto the canal allowing it to drift forward for a while. A tree stump made a good bollard to bring it to a stop.

'Give Amy a hand off,' Helen said. 'She can help with the gates.'

From his expression, it was obvious Ben didn't need any help. Nevertheless, he stuck out his hand and helped Amy jump off.

Taking one beam each, the pair pushed the huge lock gates together until the breast posts met sealing off the canal water as tight as a drum.

'Don't forget the paddles!' Joel shouted from the cabin.

Ben shook his head and handed the cotton rope to Amy. 'Go down the path and start pulling when I tell you to.'

Amy looked stunned at his request.

'It's not hard once she starts to move,' he said, smiling. 'You're in luck – we're not carrying a load of slate or stone!'

Amy walked almost fifty yards along the path, dragging the rope through the water, while Ben ran back, quickly closing the paddles and returning to the barge. With his foot, he pushed *Milkwort*'s bow from the bank. 'Pull now!' he shouted.

'Pull!' echoed Helen from the stern, her hand directing the large rudder.

Shaking the wet rope, Amy placed it over her shoulder and pulled. Glancing back, she saw the rope snake up from the canal and splash back onto the surface like a skipping-rope spanking puddles. As she trudged on, the rope stretched, then tightened, and slowly the barge glided forward.

From the deck, Helen steered a course down the centre of the channel. Ben quickly joined Amy on the rope, laid it on his shoulder and leaned onto it. 'Once she's moving, it's easy,' he said.

With the pair of them pulling, *Milkwort* slid along silently at a steady walking pace. Amy had expected them to stop once they were well clear of the locks, but Helen said nothing and Ben kept walking. Though Ben had said it was easy, Amy could feel the sweat running down her legs.

'Is it far to the next lock?' she asked.

'More than three miles to Hirst Lock. That's just past the mill in Saltaire, so we won't be locking through it. Nice clean pound between here and the mill,' he said. 'Not like the Basin in Leeds where all the rubbish gets thrown in. Do you live in the city?' he asked.

'I did.'

'Going back there?'

Amy shook her head, though the boy on the rope in front couldn't see her.

'Do you have to haul the barge by hand very often?' she asked. Then she remembered the dead horse and wished she hadn't spoken. 'You must be strong,' she added.

'That's what folk think, but it's not hard on the cut. Pa says a cart horse can pull two tons on land but a good boat-horse can pull thirty to fifty tons on water.'

'Was she a good horse, the one that died?'

'Aye,' Ben said, 'she sure was.'

Where the River Aire snaked lazily towards Shipley, the canal nudged up alongside it and the Midland Railway shared the course with them. Unlike the city where the narrow strip of land between the two waterways bore barely a blade of grass, here the vegetation was thick and green. Masses of white elderflowers attracted bees, and pink mallow bloomed prolifically from old bushes. The sycamores on the bank provided a canopy of shade, while willows teased the water with graceful sweeps of their slender branches.

Birds flitted through the hedgerows, dragonflies hovered, and the air hummed with the sound of busy insects.

In tiny coves where the canal's bank had collapsed, moorhens and ducks waddled ashore. A pair of haughty swans swam in circles, ignoring the passing boat, but a heron took flight when the short-boat drifted close by.

When another barge passed, Helen spoke to the man on the tiller though Amy couldn't hear what was said. As it chugged by the smoke, puffing from its chimney, settled like a cloud over the damp marsh.

'Will you have one of those one day?' Amy asked, as they watched it pass.

'No. Not me or Pa,' he said. 'We like things just the way they are.'

With Ben hauling, Amy walked beside him listening to him talk about the cut, the canal folk who worked it, and the places they'd visited to pick up or deliver cargo. She'd never heard of most of the towns and wondered where they all were.

Suddenly the *clickety-clack* of a passing train interrupted her thoughts. Suddenly aware of the faces framed in the compartment windows gazing in her direction, she turned her head from the sound. What if her father was on the train? What if he'd spotted her on the barge? What if he was waiting for her in the next town? She hadn't thought about him since she'd woken that morning but now the fear of him finding her returned.

With little over half a mile to the point where the Bradford Canal joined the Leeds and Liverpool, Ben slowed to let three coal barges pass. Though they were all steam powered, they moved little faster than the barge they were hauling by hand.

'I want to stop at The Red Terret,' Joel called. 'We'll moor there for the night. Too late to make it to Saltaire today.'

As they got close to the inn's wharf, Ben stopped hauling and slowed the boat while Helen steered it gently up against the bank.

'Go steady,' Joel shouted, from below.

Helen raised her eyebrows. 'We're already alongside,' she answered, before turning to Amy. 'Poor Joel. He hates being stuck inside.' She pushed her hair under her pleated bonnet, before throwing the aft mooring line to her son. 'Normally he'd never say a word when we moor or lock. He knows darn well that me and Ben can work the boat with our eyes closed, and that goes for climbing the staircases too. But it's eating him up, having to stay below. Still, it'll be better when we're at Jentz's yard. At least, we'll be off the cut then.'

There were several barges moored on that stretch of canal – the three that had passed them earlier, two Hargreaves' boats from Blackburn and three others. Amy remembered what Joel had said about company boats and noted how dull they were in comparison to *Milkwort*. Apart from the names and numbers and a little scrollwork decorating the panels on either side of the stem post, they displayed little or no fancywork, and the mooring ropes and fenders were engrained with coal dust. So different from the white rope fenders that Joel had woven and Helen scrubbed daily.

The Red Terret Inn was located not more than twenty yards from the towing path. Joel knew the bargees from the other boats and he was anxious to talk with them. He desperately needed a boat-horse and wanted to know if there were any for sale along the cut.

'You can come up with me if you like,' Helen said, but Amy declined. She'd had her share of inns and the types of men who frequented them. Thanking her, she said she preferred to stay on the barge. Ben was proud to go with his mother.

While they were away, Joel explained, 'It's not like a city pub, lass,' he said. 'There are stables at the back for the horses. We used to stop here and leave Bessie for a spell occasionally. You can't walk a horse all the time, you know. You got to give it a spell occasionally.'

There was a lot about canal life that Amy had yet to learn.

It wasn't long before Helen returned with three jugs of ale on a tray. Ben strode out behind her, hands in his pockets, talking confidently to two of the boatmen. By the likeness of their gait and faces, Amy guessed the men were father and son. The cut of their clothes and the black dust engrained in the creases of their skin, confirmed they were carrying a cargo of coal.

While it was customary for the bargees to sit on the bank to talk, because of Joel's incapacity, they were invited into the cabin. Ben and Amy sat on the bales of fibre and listened to the conversation as it drifted up from the open door. It was obvious from his voice how pleased Joel was to have some company, and even though the boatmen weren't Number Ones, like himself, he respected their knowledge of the canal. They'd been on this navigation longer than him and they knew every inch of it and everything that happened on it.

Over the next hour, they enjoyed their ale, telling jokes and laughing and exchanging yarns. The company men told of a narrowboat that had sunk in the Trent recently.

'That's a dangerous stretch of water,' one said.

And there was a barge had burnt out at Crown Point.

'Nearly set fire to Timber Island,' the older man said.

'Company boat?'

'Aye.'

Joel asked if they'd heard of any good horses that were for sale.

'There was one,' the father said, 'but I think it's been sold. Belonged to Faraway Farley, the old boatman who never spoke to anyone. His horse was found on the path in Skipton, fifteen miles from where *Faraway* was moored. It must have followed the path on its own. When it was walked back, they found him stone dead in his cabin. Must have been there a week. They said the cabin stunk to high heaven.'

'And that old horse of yours, Bessie, you could smell that too. It were still on the bank when we came through yesterday.'

'The knacker was supposed to take it nearly a week ago,' Joel said angrily.

'He'll not take it now, it's too far gone. It'll end tossed up in the River Aire.'

Joel shook his head.

'Aye, and it'll not be alone. I remember the days when they were pulling fifty animals a day out of that stretch in Leeds. Filthy river, it was.'

The other man laughed. 'Not much better now.'

'Anyone been asking questions about a lass on the cut?' Joel asked.

The younger man drained his pot. 'Aye,' he said. 'At Victoria Wharf, there was a fellow said he was looking for his daughter. Said she'd got herself in trouble and run away. Said he was worried to death about her.'

'I didn't think he looked worried,' the other man said, turning to Joel. 'That's what one of the lads said to him, but this fellow didn't take kindly to the jest and pulled out a knife. Then everyone clamped up.'

From her seat on the top of the cargo, Amy listened.

Later that evening, when the men had returned to their boats, Amy spoke to Helen. 'I should go away,' she said. 'I don't want you or Joel to get into strife because of me.'

'What are you afraid of?'

Amy took a deep breath before speaking. 'The man, with the knife, they were talking about, was my father. And from what Ben has told me, a man on foot can easily beat a barge in a day's travel especially if there are locks along that section of the canal. What if word gets back from the bargees that they've seen me? What if my father catches up to us? What if he knows the name of this boat?'

'Trust me,' said Helen. 'The boatmen out there won't whisper a word that they've seen you and that's the truth. What goes on on the cut stays on the cut.'

'You'll be safe with us,' Joel added. 'See those brasses hanging on the wall over there? Supposed to be magic charms, to keep us safe. The idea was passed to the boatmen from the gypsies.'

Helen smiled.

'As for the name of *Milkwort*, I'll get Ben to take care of that. When we get into Jentz's dock tomorrow, his first job will be to scrape the old paint off. Any boatman can recognize a barge without its name, but anyone, who doesn't use the cut, will never identify it.'

'Why would you do that for me?'

'Well,' he said, looking across at his wife. 'It ain't just out of the goodness of my heart. We've got a cargo to unload tomorrow and a boat to scrub down after it's gone. I'm not much use at the moment and we could use another pair of hands, at least for a couple of days.'

'Where is she?' Dodd demanded, pushing open the front door and forcing Mrs Medley back against the wall.

'Watch what you're doing, you stupid oaf!'

'Where is she?'

'Amy's not here. I told you that the last time you called. And I doubt she'll come back while you're around!'

Amos Dodd sneered at her as he shoved her aside and stepped into the cluttered kitchen. For a moment the two children on the mat froze then the youngest dropped the tin soldier from his hand and ran to his mother, grabbing her tightly around the leg.

'It's all right, kids,' Mrs Medley called reassuringly. 'Now, you get out of my house, mister, before I call a constable!'

'I bet you know where she's hiding.'

'Ain't got a clue and if I did I wouldn't be telling you. Last time I saw young Amy was at Lisbeth's funeral. Strange,' she murmured sarcastically, 'I didn't see you there.'

Dodd didn't answer as he bounded up the stairs.

'Get down here, you! That's private up there!' The sound of his mother's anger set the boy at her leg crying. His brother crawled over to join him just as Dodd's boots thudded down the stairs after finding no sign of his daughter.

'Just as well my hubby ain't here!'

Dodd laughed. 'What would he do? He don't scare me for all his size. Lump of whale blubber, that's all he is.'

'Ten times the man you are, Amos Dodd,' she said, slamming the door hard behind him.

On the street, two women, pegging out washing, looked over to see what the shouting was about. A boy playing with a bottle in the gutter stood up and sidled away.

Fire rose in Dodd's cheeks. With every passing day, the urgency to find his daughter grew, but it was no longer a case of wanting her to bring him money. He'd almost forgotten that. No. Now he wanted to pay her back for tricking him. How dare she run away? Make a fool of him? Now the neighbourhood knew all about him – who he was, what he'd done and where he'd spent the last fifteen years. They laughed at him behind his back. Not that that worried him. Amos Dodd wouldn't think twice about slicing the throat of any man who insulted him to his face. But he wasn't going back inside Armley Jail! He'd promised himself that.

When he'd been searching the streets of Armley and had glanced up at the jail's turreted tower, he'd sworn they'd never drag him in there again. But that didn't mean he wasn't going to find his daughter and when he did, he'd give her what she deserved. But while he was looking, he'd make sure he kept his nose clean.

He didn't see how high the bottle lifted when he kicked it, but he heard the crash as it broke, showering slivers of glass across the pavement at the other side of the street.

'I'll find you,' he yelled, 'if it's the last thing I do!'

Chapter 10

Saltaire

All the company boats left the mooring before sunrise and, by the time Amy got up, the waterway was empty. With the prospect of a long, hard day ahead, Helen prepared a big breakfast for everyone.

As she helped Ben to haul the short-boat through Shipley, Amy's thoughts turned to Leeds. Though the town was surrounded by fields and hills, its wharfs and warehouses encroached on the canal. The tall grey-stone buildings were little different to Fanshaw's Mill or the other factories and foundries which backed onto the waterway in the city.

Once they were through Shipley, the countryside opened up again. The hills were wooded and the distant moors tinged with heather.

At about nine o'clock that morning, *Milkwort* was within sight of the tallest of the chimneys of the Saltaire Mill. As they got closer, the two main buildings came into view but the canal separated them, cutting a path between them.

'Over there!' Helen pointed. 'That's Jentz's Yard.'

Amy looked. On the right, a short stub ran off the canal for a distance of no more than fifty yards. Halfway down it was a pair of lock gates rising little higher from the water than a farm fence. They were old and blackened with rot, and dead weeds that had sprouted between the joints in the damp timbers. Beyond the gates the channel extended for a further boat's length, but it appeared dry.

'The dock's empty!' Helen called, ducking her head into the cabin to tell her husband.

'Good. The sooner we get this load off at the mill, the sooner we'll get her in there.'

As the barge slid past the disused dock, Amy gazed at the buildings ahead. She'd seen lots of mills – Leeds was crammed with them, dismal soot-blackened, ugly structures, crowded together, surrounded by dirty streets exuding the stench of refuse and hardship. But the mill ahead was very different. In the sunlight the carved yellow stonework glowed. And the same colour reflected from every building stretching up the hill and into the village of Saltaire. The mill's main chimney was taller than most and decorated in a manner she'd never seen before.

'It looks new,' Amy said.

'Fifty years old,' Joel said. 'Built by a remarkable man by the name of Titus Salt. You'll see when you look around the town, he didn't just build a mill, he built schools, a hospital and churches for his four thousand workers. And modern houses for them to live in with privies and yards and gardens. He wanted them to be healthy and happy. And because he was a sober man, there's not an inn or pawn shop in Saltaire. It's said that in his lifetime he gave half a million pounds to charity.'

Amy gazed in awe at the impressive structures towering on either side of the canal. On the left, the huge main building rose six storeys high straight up from the canal's edge and, although there was no wharf or horse path, a loaded barge was moored against it. At the opposite side, on the right, the towing path, wide enough for two horses, ran in front of the slightly smaller New Mill building. Half-way along it, the path opened to a broad loading dock. Just beyond the mill buildings, a stone bridge arched over the canal. The road, which led up the hill and into the town, ran across it.

With Helen on the helm, and Ben on the rope, they floated the short-boat up against the loading wharf. Warehousemen spilled from the stores like hungry ants and waited until the boy had moored the barge securely, before scrambling aboard to unfasten the tarpaulins that covered the cargo. Being South American in origin, each bales weighed a thousand pounds and a crane was needed to unload them. Once they were swung clear of the short-boat, they soon disappeared into the mill's underground wool-store.

Chains rattled and clanged and the short-boat rocked as every bale was lifted from it. While Ben sat on the roof of the cabin, watching the cargo being removed from *Milkwort*'s hold, Helen joined Joel in the cabin to discuss their plans for the work to be done over the next few weeks. Wanting to keep well clear of the men and machinery, Amy wandered along the path to the end of the wharf, took off her boots, sat on the edge and dangled her feet in the water.

It was early afternoon by the time the last bale of fibre was lifted from the barge. *Milkwort* looked odd with an empty belly. It smelled of damp hair and rats, though only a few mice and a large hairy spider had made their homes amongst the bales. Once the cargo was off and the quantities checked, Helen and Ben visited the office to collect the balance of payment due to them.

While waiting, Amy watched a new loom being hoisted into the mill building from a barge moored to the opposite bank. A pulley, operating from a landing on the fourth floor, was lifting it slowly. The job looked difficult and the men were having problems securing chains around the machine to ensure it would lift without tipping. It was a slow, laborious procedure and, as the cable was lowered, there was a lot of shouting. Some voices were yelling orders, others advice. There was concern that the load was not fastened adequately and that the cable wouldn't support it. If it crashed down onto the barge, it would sink the boat and crush the men who were on it. From the fourth floor, the men operating the pulley looked down, their faces were grave but they waited patiently and said nothing.

Amy's thoughts again turned to Fanshaw's Mill with its old looms and combs which had been in use since it was built. She thought about Mr Lister and the new loom he was designing and, amidst the noise of the voices, she imagined she heard him call her name. She listened then realized it was Ben who was shouting for her.

'Amy! Get aboard. We're getting towed up to Hirst Lock; there's a winding hole up there where we can turn the boat around.'

Amy looked along the canal, expecting to see a steam barge ready to haul them, but there was none. When she saw a young man parading himself along the wharf like a strongman at the circus, she smiled. Wearing only a singlet and trousers, the broad leather belt pulled tightly around his waist certainly accentuated the dimensions of his chest. With the jeers and whistles from the men on the loading wharf, Jem Carruthers obliged his workmates with a pose to show off his muscles. He was a popular man, soft as butter inside and always happy to lend a hand.

When word had reached him that the bargee was crippled, Carruthers had asked permission to help haul the boat to the old boatyard. It wasn't just out of the kindness of his heart, but being the local heavyweight boxing champion, he enjoyed a little free promotion.

Hirst Wood Lock was no more than half a mile ahead and he was ready for the challenge. Digging his toes into the towing path and with the rope over his shoulder, Jem floated *Milkwort* gently from the wharfside, creating barely a ripple. Once he had the empty barge moving, leading it looked no more arduous, for the athlete, than walking a dog. With an audience of onlookers, the boxer relished the occasion and lengthened his stride. Tiny waves began to curl from *Milkwort*'s bow and a line of rippled wake fanned out on the canal behind. Helen was concerned that the line was too short and he would pull the boat into the bank. On the tiller, Ben was afraid the man was going too fast and wouldn't slow before they reached the lock. Amy stayed in the cabin out of the way.

'We don't have any brakes!' Ben shouted.

Being some distance from the mill and hidden from the view of his fellow workers, Carruthers slowed and followed Ben's instructions.

After stopping and manoeuvring the boat around in the winding hole, the pugilist returned to the path to pull the short-boat back to Jentz's Yard. As soon as felt it moving, he leaned forward and lengthened his stride. The boat responded, slipping smoothly across the still surface. Once he'd passed under the bridge and had the New Mill in sight, the showman increased his pace yet again, and by the time he reached the start of the loading wharf, he was almost running. Helen and Ben were alarmed. *Milkwort* was approaching the barge that was unloading the loom but the canal was little wider than the width of two short-boats.

Jem Carruthers, buoyed by his own bravado, was oblivious to any danger. Cheered on by the workers, he raised one arm, flexed his muscles and kept going. But he was going too fast.

Gripping the tiller with both hands, Helen shouted for Amy to hold tight in case they hit the other craft. Ben watched anxiously, but his mother steered the boat safely. But with less than a foot to spare on either side, *Milkwort*'s wake created another problem. The moored barge was tossed dangerously bringing a barrage of curses from the men on board. Fortunately, by this time, the loom was suspended well clear of the boat which, being light without its load, pitched and rolled but came to no harm.

'What's happening?' Joel yelled, from the cabin, but no one answered.

For Carruthers the self-indulgent event had been a thrill but it was brought to a sudden end by the urgent cries from Ben and Helen.

Releasing the rope, Jem let the boat swim on till it drifted almost to a stop, mid-channel, only fifty yards from the entrance to the dry dock.

'How was I?' Jem asked, flashing a gold tooth, as he grinned broadly.

'Grand,' said Helen sarcastically, while Ben murmured something less complimentary.

'You could have pulled it with one hand,' Ben whispered to Amy as she emerged from the cabin. 'With no cargo in her, the boat is light as a leaf.'

Jem Carruthers chose to be oblivious to the comments, his broad smile not faltering, as he followed Helen's directions and hauled the boat's bow around ninety degrees into the overgrown spur. Being unused for a long time, the rushes had grown up along its length and the bottom had filled with layers of silt washed in by the passing boat traffic. The channel was not only shallow but narrow – just wide enough for one barge.

As Carruthers hauled, his biceps bulged and the forest of reeds bent beneath the bow, brushing the barge's bottom and hindering its forward movement. It was only a short distance to the pair of lock gates but the effort showed in the perspiration glistening on his face. He glanced back to the mill but discovered that his audience had lost interest.

'I doubt this will be here in ten years,' Helen said, looking over the lock gates at the derelict dock. 'If the canal don't fill it in then the company will.'

'Don't they need a dry dock here?'

'Not now. This one was built long before they ever built the mill at Saltaire. There were lots of boatyards in those days up and down this navigation. Now there are new yards in Shipley, but they mainly do repair work and not much boat building. There's not much demand for new boats these days.' He shook his head. 'I shudder to think what'll happen to the canals in twenty years' time.'

Ben jumped onto the bank. It was damp and along the edges, clods of earth crumbled into the dock.

'Careful when you step off,' he called.

Beyond the lock gates was the dry dock, though it contained a small lake, fed by water seeping through the seams in the old gates. The base of the dock was on a slight incline so that at the far end it was much shallower. It stopped at a timber wall with a sluice gate in the bottom corner.

'Make sure the sluice gate's closed before you open the lock gates,' Joel called from the cabin. 'We don't want to empty the canal into the River Aire.'

Ben checked then cranked the rusty paddles on the lock gate allowing the water to flow in from the cut and slowly flood the chamber. Once the level of water in the dock was level with the canal, all that remained was to open the old gates and slide the boat in.

With the amount of silt and weed which had lodged around the gates, that was not an easy task. It took the four of them, including Carruthers, all their strength to push the gates open. Thankfully, once the boat was through, it was easier to close them behind it.

The job of manoeuvring broad timber supports into position under the sides of the boat was even more difficult. Without Jem's help, Ben and the women could never have managed it.

The gap between the boat's side and the dock's bank was narrow and the timbers to be set beneath the hull very heavy. It was imperative that the struts were positioned correctly otherwise the barge wouldn't sit squarely on them once the water had been sluiced out. With Helen's advice, Jem set the stocks beneath the hull – six on each side.

When everyone felt satisfied, Ben opened the small sluice gate allowing the water to gush out of the dock and run down the hill into the River Aire. Helen held her breath. If the supports were not set properly, the barge could slip over tipping Joel out of his bed. And if the water got in he could drown in no time.

The short-boat creaked, as it shifted slightly once the water was no longer supporting it. Finally, it settled on its stumps with only a slight lean to one side.

'We're high and dry,' Helen announced, jumping back on deck and popping her head around the cabin door. 'Thanks to the help of Jem here. We couldn't have managed without him.' She beckoned the young man. 'Come aboard and meet my man.'

Jem's smile was less confident as he bent his back and poked his head into the cabin. 'Jem's the name, boxing's my game,' he announced, stretching out his grubby hand to Joel.

'I'll pay you for your trouble,' Joel said gruffly.

'Don't worry about it. I like to exercise the muscles when I can. Perhaps you'll come and watch me fight one day.'

'I'll do that, and I'll buy you a pot of beer when me leg's fixed.'

'And I'll be pleased to drink it. You'll be around for a while, will you?'

'A few weeks at least,' Joel said. 'But if anyone's enquiring after us, say you ain't seen us, will you?'

'Don't you worry, mister, I can keep my mouth shut.'

Jumping ashore, Jem turned to the two ladies, and bowed, as only a showman could. 'If you need me, you know where to find me,' he said.

Amy smiled.

'Thank you,' Helen shouted after him.

With no money to pay for his lodgings, Amos Dodd laboured for three days at Kilbey's Forge. It was heavy work but Dodd was strong as an ox even though he did little exercise. The job might have lasted a few days longer had he not argued with the overseer and threatened to maim him. Though he was turned off, he collected his pay which gave him enough to pay his dues to his Mill Street landlady and to drink a gallon of ale in The Hungry Crow.

'Did you find her, then?' the man said, wiping the beer from his unkempt whiskers.

'None of your business.'

'Might have seen her the day of the ruckus at the mill.'

'Might you now?' said Amos, taking an interest.

'Might be worth the cost of a jug of ale?'

Before the man had chance to put his glass on the table, Dodd knocked it out of his hands and grabbed him by the throat. His blade drew blood on the man's temple. 'You tell me what you saw or you'll see nowt else, ever again!'

'I'll tell! I'll tell!' the man squawked. 'Let go of me.'

Somewhat reluctantly, Dodd released him.

Rubbing his throat, the man coughed.

'I saw her on Wellington Bridge. 'She were about to take off on the canal path, but when she saw me, she ducked back and hid. She didn't want me to see which way she were heading.'

'And which way was that?'

'She were heading west towards Kirkstall.'

'What then?' Dodd prompted.

'I didn't see her after that, honest, I didn't, but I reckon that's where she'd gone. Kirkstall or maybe Rodley or Horsforth. Plenty of mills along there where a lass can get a job.'

'She might be in Liverpool by now,' someone suggested.

The men laughed but when Dodd spun around, no one volunteered another word.

'What about me beer, then?' the hairy man asked.

Dodd cuffed him with the back of his hand and hurried out. He was aware of all the barges that carted coal to Kirkstall Forge and it was likely his daughter was hiding out on one of those, he thought.

Chapter 11

Jentz's Yard

'I should leave, shouldn't I?' Amy said.

'And where are you going to?' Joel asked, 'and what will you do. You can't keep running all your life.' He shook his head. 'These stories you've told us about your father makes it hard to believe you're the same flesh and blood.'

'I wish to God we weren't,' she sighed. 'But we are and I can't let him find me! He'd kill me.'

'Not while you're on my boat, he won't!' It was the first time Amy had heard venom in the boatman's voice.

'Listen, Amy,' Helen said quietly. 'Me and Joel were talking last night and there is something we want to put to you. Now it's not permanent, mind – it's just for the few weeks till Joel's back on his feet and *Milkwort* is back on the cut.'

'We're asking you to stay here with us,' Joel said. 'There's a lot of work to be done and I'm in no fit state to help. That means Helen and Ben will have to do everything – painting, scraping, varnishing. Not to mention getting underneath the hull and caulking the bottom, if she needs it. Then, of course, Helen's got all her ordinary chores which she's left this past week while I've been stuck down here. What we'd like is for you to stay with us, lend a hand with the jobs and when you find some spare time, you can give our Ben some lessons.'

'Lessons!' said Amy. 'I'm not a teacher.'

'Ben says you know how to read.'

'That's right, I do, but my father took me out of school and sent me to work in the mill.'

'Aye, but you did go to school, and that's more than me and Joel did, and Ben's never stepped inside a school. That's the way it is.'

Through the small leaded window, Amy could see the boy sitting cross-legged on the grass, splicing the end of a rope. Watching him over the past few days, she had seen how he worked the boat and operated the locks like a man. She'd heard he could handle a boat-horse as well as his father. He knew the names of all the weeds and flowers that grew along the bank and he appeared to know every town in Yorkshire. Amy had learned some geography at school but she'd never heard of half the places he spoke about. It was hard to believe he'd had no schooling.

'There's no time for the kids to go to school when you're working the canal,' said Helen. 'It's something you keep putting off, then all of a sudden it's too late and they've grown up and they're off to get a boat of their own.'

'One thing's for sure,' Joel said, 'if a boatman can hold a pen and not just a tiller, then he's better off for it. He'll not get conned with contracts he can't read, or miss what's happening around the country. Not that there's much out there I'm interested in,' he added.

'Things are changing on the canal,' he said with a sigh. 'Good boat-horses are being replaced by steam engines, and barges are being replaced by railway wagons. Before long they won't need boatmen any more. It's too late for me and Helen to change, but it's not too late for the lad.'

'But shouldn't he go to a proper school? Surely this town has got one.'

'Saltaire's got everything. A school and a college to my knowledge. But it's summer now and school's closed. And when they start up again, we'll be off and that'd mean leaving Ben here on his own. He'd have to find lodgings, and that's not easy. Everyone here works for the mill. And besides,' he said, smiling at his wife, 'how can you part with a boy when he's your only one? We're not short of a bob or two, but we can't afford one of them live-in private schools that fancy folk send their youngsters to. Besides, Ben wouldn't fit in – not a lad straight off the cut.'

'Trouble is,' said Helen, 'we don't stay in one spot long enough for him to go to day school. It's the same for all boat folk. Always on the move. Got to go where the jobs are and that can be anywhere on the cut. We never know where we'll end up next – Goole, Rotherham, Nottingham.'

'As for worrying about your father,' said Joel, 'Take my word, you'll be safe here for a while. Forget about him and stop worrying about what might happen until you get there. If you're like me, you'll never look further than the next set of locks.' He smiled wearily at Helen sitting on the edge of the bed, her hand resting on the wooden casing around his leg. 'You give my missus a hand, and give the lad a bit of learning, and you can stay here as long as you like.'

Harold Lister's rooms were adequately furnished and comfortable. They consisted of two spacious rooms on the second floor of one of the larger houses in Saltaire. Albert Road housed most of the company executives, school teachers, and the church minister. That row of through-houses was the best in town.

Harold had used those rooms since his first year at the Science and Art School, and they'd been held for him when he was away at university in Edinburgh. He never had to concern himself about rent payments. Expenses, such as that, came out of a trust fund and the bank took care of all his financial matters.

As he always ate out, he had no need for staff, though a woman serviced his rooms every day. She also took care of his laundry and kept the rooms warmed in winter and aired in summer, if he was working away. For Harold, the place on Albert Road was his home. It was the only one he had known in over ten years.

Slipping a bookmark in between the pages, he closed his book, stretched and walked over to the window. With the mill and town to the rear of the building, his outlook was to the west and the hills and moors of the West Riding. In the distance were the dense groves of Hirst Wood and through the treetops he could see the roof of Hirst Mill. Immediately ahead was a green meadow divided by a railway line. From the window the tracks weren't visible in the cutting, but the signal poking up from the bottom of the embankment indicated there was a train due shortly.

Not far from the line, the canal and river ran parallel and beyond the River Aire the land rose sharply through Trench Wood and Shipley Glen to the open tops of Baildon Moor. Harold considered those places some of his favourite walking tracks.

As he gazed at the scene, a short-boat disappeared behind the gates of Hirst Lock and he thought back to the barge he had seen at the Saltaire wharf that morning. It was a handsome boat and had attracted his attention. Even from the fourth floor of the mill he had admired its faded decorations. Though weathered and worn, they had reminded him of the designs on gypsy caravans which rumbled along the country lanes.

Then he remembered the girl he had met at the mill in Leeds and smiled as he considered that she alone had caused the greatest commotion Fanshaw's had ever seen. The last time he'd seen her, she was sprawled out on the dirt of the mill yard and yet here she was in Saltaire, dipping her feet in the canal. His expression changed as he thought of her hands, scored by the gravel, and the anxious look on her face. What was she doing on the barge on the canal? Didn't she live in the streets near the mill? Then he remembered he'd heard rumours in the mill that her father was searching for her. He heard that she had run away. He couldn't imagine why that would be; nonetheless, he felt relieved to see her safe. And she appeared content in her new environment.

The working class are hard on their womenfolk, he mused, as he dusted a cobweb from the corner of the window pane. Casting his mind back to his own childhood, he thought about his father, a man he hardly knew. Robert Lister was an amiable man, he was told. Generous in proportions, intelligent, but shrewd and uncompromising when it came to business. Harold hoped that his father had been a good husband and that when he had achieved his success he had been kind and generous to his mother. But that was something he would never know.

The last he'd seen of the girl from the mill was when Carruthers pulled the empty barge away from the wharf heading towards Hirst Lock. He presumed by now it would be near Skipton if not heading over the Pennines. In a way he regretted being unable to go down to the wharf to speak to her. He'd remembered her name and, though she'd turned her face and appeared to look up at him when he called, he knew that because of all the noise, she'd neither seen nor heard him. Hoisting the new machine up from the barge and into the mill without causing any damage, or losing the loom in the canal, or injuring any of the men, had been his major concerns.

A train whistle distracted him. He watched as a trail of smoke crawled along the cutting towards the town like a large grey caterpillar. Somewhere beneath the billowing cloud was a railway engine.

In the distance the lock gates slowly closed. The coal barge moved off, disappearing behind the pocket of trees as it continued its journey to Liverpool.

'Good luck, Amy Dodd,' he whispered, as he turned from the window and returned to the chair and his book.

The first morning in the dry dock, Helen rifled the many storage compartments on the boat to see what equipment they had and what was required for the jobs Joel wanted done. While Joel decided what should be bought, Amy listed them on a piece of paper. A little later, Helen and Ben went shopping. They brought back brushes and soda and scrapers. The red-lead, oil-based paints and varnish, linseed and tar were delivered by cart in the afternoon and the following day an unwritten work schedule was put into practice.

If the morning was fine, work started early. Ben did the heavy work, hauling buckets of water from the main canal and carrying them back to the boat. The water that had seeped into the bottom of the dry dock was unsuitable. It was rotten with detritus – dead leaves, branches, rotted timber and small, noisy frogs. It smelt rotten too.

For a week Amy and Ben scraped, scrubbed and caulked the carvel-planked hull. The following week the pair daubed tar on the bottom with a long-handled brush. It was exhausting work. Up top, Helen scraped and sanded but she cooked too, and made preserves. She spent a full day at the wash tub boiling Joel's shirts and the yards of white lace-work that decorated the inside of the boat. Inside the main cabin, Joel worked on anything portable – scraping, sanding or painting, using his leg's wooden casing as a table to rest things on. It took him almost a week to remove all the layers of old paint and varnish from the tiller, before sanding it satin smooth. Then he set to with a camel brush, adding the traditional designs in bright blues, yellows, greens and reds. When the painting was completed it sat in the cabin for another week before the two coats of varnish were added. By the end, he was pleased with his efforts.

In the evenings, while Helen cooked the meal, Amy gave Ben his lesson on the small deck at the bow. Joel supplied them with pencil and paper – blank sheets torn from the notebook in which he recorded his figures. Though Joel couldn't read, he did arithmetic quicker than anyone else Amy had ever known.

For reading practice, the only book on the boat belonged to Helen. It had been given to her years ago but it still smelt as if it was new and Amy could see its pages had never been turned. Helen held it in high regard because it was written by a woman. She had always wanted to be able to read it and now she hoped her son would be able to read it to her one day. Amy was grateful to her for the loan of the book and promised to mind it carefully.

Once Amy discovered that Ben could already recognize some letters of the alphabet, she embarked on her task of teaching him how to write.

The month spent in dry dock was one of continual work for them all. The days began early and finished late. But at least it was summer and the weather was mainly fine.

On days when it rained and showed no signs of clearing, they worked inside. The jobs were the same – scrubbing, scraping, painting, varnishing. Though Helen was skilled in the traditional crafts, and Ben was learning quickly, it was Joel who was most skilled with the brush. He added scrolls, swirls, patterns and sprays of roses to any item that could be carried into the cabin. Happy to be useful again, he painted everything Helen brought him: the scoop, the water jug, even the new chamber pot. Anything plain was transformed into a work of art, and for two or three weeks the cabin reeked with the smell of fresh paint and varnish.

Once the painting was finished, Ben and Joel sat together spending hours twisting and turning old rope into traditional buttons and fenders for use on the barge. There was plenty available as they had to replace the tow-rope every few weeks. It was expensive, but necessary, as it was a danger to the horse to use a rope once it had lost its elasticity.

'We sell these to the boatmen,' Ben announced proudly. 'And Pa lets me keep half of whatever we get.'

Amy enjoyed listening to their chatter as they worked. Joel told stories about life in the southern counties. About the canals he had worked and the previous narrowboat he had owned. About the canal at Devizes with its sixteen straight rises. About the navigation at

Bristol and the tall sailing ships he'd seen. And of the demise of the canals, and the reason they had left the Kennet and Avon.

Helen always had a smile on her face, but said very little. She was content to listen to her husband and son. Amy admired her courage. She was strong in limb and had a heart as big as a ton of wool. Like most wives on the barges, she'd been born on the cut and lived her whole life in the confines of a boat. She'd never slept in a bed that had legs or looked out of a window that was bigger than a handkerchief. She'd never cooked in a real oven yet the food she prepared was as delicious as any from a bake-house kitchen. She never asked for anything. *Milkwort* was her home and she wished for none other.

Though she'd travelled the length and breadth of England, she'd no thoughts about fashion. The most she ever needed were her old-fashioned boat clothes and bonnet, plus a bobbin of cotton thread to make lace. The large gold earrings she wore made her look like a gypsy but Amy doubted she ever considered her appearance. The canal was her bath and her mirror. The reflection it gave satisfied her needs.

In the evenings, when tea had been cleared away from the main cabin, Amy would open the book and read from its pages. Helen listened to every word Amy uttered, watching her lips move as closely as the women working on the looms.

As the novel's story unfolded, Amy knew her friend would never exchange her home on the water for one on land. As she read the passages of *Mary Barton,* she too wondered about a new life in Lancashire. Somehow the idea seemed less appealing than she had previously thought.

Though Joel often appeared to be sleeping, he was listening intently and Ben's eyes were wide open as he followed Amy's finger running along each line of print. The evenings were a time they all enjoyed.

Working hard and long made the weeks pass quickly. Amy's fears, that her father would find her, were slowly subsiding, nevertheless, she never strayed far from the dry dock. It was doubtful, she thought, that her father had got a regular job, but he'd have to do something in order to stay out of jail.

Their only visitors while they were in the dock were a few passing boatmen and Jem Carruthers. The first time he called he arrived carrying two buckets of milk.

'You look like a milkmaid,' Ben dared to say. In a whisper, the pugilist told him he really didn't like ale, but because of his image he was expected to swallow his share. He sparred with the lad and ruffled his hair and said he would give him a boxing lesson whenever they came to Saltaire. Jem returned three times after that, each time with at least a gallon of milk.

Though he couldn't quite walk, Joel removed the long splints from his leg and replaced them with shorter ones, at Helen's insistence. He fashioned a crutch from a tree branch and painted it with geometrical patterns. Though he wasn't tall, hopping about in the cabin wasn't easy, but being able to sit at the table with his family gave him a great deal of pleasure.

When other boatmen visited *Milkwort* after unloading their cargoes, he'd sit out on deck and listen to the gossip. He wanted to know what was happening along the cut. He was told of a horse that had drowned after a tow-rope had snagged on a tree, and of the two boat-horses that had disappeared from the canal after being replaced by boilers and steam. There was also word that a pair of young boatmen was leaving for jobs on the land, and of a fire on a coal barge at Kirkstall Forge. News that the condition of the Kennet and Avon was deteriorating was not good. Trade on the Leeds and Liverpool canal, however, could not have been better.

'It's about time we got a new horse,' Joel said to his wife. 'And time *Milkwort* got its name back.'

Chapter 12

Shipley Glen

A spot of paint splashed from Ben's brush onto Amy's cheek. She scolded him playfully, wiped it with the rag then watched as the name, *Milkwort*, appeared in bold letters on the side of the bow. A fancy scroll beneath it added the finishing touch.

'Come up for a cuppa,' Helen shouted.

Amy didn't wait for a second call. After standing for some time in the mud at the bottom of the dock, she was pleased to climb out. Ben followed her.

'Where are all the people going?' she asked, as she dipped her feet into a bucket of water to wash the dirt off. 'It's too late for church. Is there a rally in town?'

Helen glanced at the stream of folk heading along the tow path towards Saltaire; couples arm in arm, ladies with parasols, families with baby-carts, boys with hoops or dogs. 'They're off to the Glen,' she said.

'What's that?'

'Shipley Glen. You must have heard of it.'

Amy shook her head.

'I thought everyone in Yorkshire knew about Shipley Glen. It's got rides that swing through the air and a switchback railway and all sorts of unimaginable things. Folk come from miles around to visit the Glen. I've heard tell that Bradford's near empty on a Sunday.'

'The Hyde Park of the north, it's been called,' Joel added, from the cabin. 'Ain't you never been?'

'No,' she replied, as she stepped on board. Though she said nothing, her main concern was that there would be people from Leeds who might recognize her.

'Is it far from here?' she asked, as she joined the couple sitting at the table.

'On the other side of the river,' said Joel. 'Do you want to go?'

Amy shrugged. 'I don't think so.'

'I bet Ben wouldn't say no to a ride on the tram.'

'Yes, please!' the boy pitched in, loud and clear, from the far end of the barge.

'What about us finishing the painting?'

'You've been scraping and painting these past four weeks and you've not even taken a stroll into town. It's about time you took a trip out. Besides, it's Sunday and ma says you shouldn't be working.' Joel reached for his leather pouch on the shelf beside his bed. The coins rattled. 'Here, take this.'

Amy shook her head.

'Take it, before I put it away again. Thruppence'll take the pair of you both ways on the tram. It cost a penny up and halfpenny down, if I remember rightly.'

Helen nodded and smiled her approval. 'You best tidy yourself first,' she said. 'Take a look at yourself.'

Even in the reflection of one of the polished brasses, Amy could see her face was streaked with paint. She laughed, then suddenly her smile disappeared. 'What if someone sees me? What if my father's there?'

'Don't be daft!' Joel said. 'There'll be hundreds of people on the Glen, and all out to enjoy themselves. They'll not be interested in you, miss.'

Helen pulled her bonnet from the cupboard. 'Here, take this. No one will see your face under this.'

Amy accepted and thanked her.

'Pa,' Ben said rather timidly, 'can I buy a toffee apple?'

'Away with you, boy!'

'But they only cost a penny.'

'You work that out with Amy. If you buy yourself a treat, then you'll have to walk back. It's a fair way, remember?'

'I'll get him an apple,' Amy said. 'We'll walk back. The exercise will do us both good.'

As they climbed up from the cabin, Ben smiled when Amy sat the voluminous bonnet on her head. The row of tucks at the front radiated from her face like a patterned halo, while at the back the broad frill, from the gathered crown, covered her shoulders and fell almost to her waist.

Half an hour later, the pair was on the towing path heading past the New Mill. Amy looked like a boatwoman with the blue pleated skirt Helen insisted she wear, and the ample hat that hid most of her head.

As they reached the canal bridge, they joined the crowds of people who were pouring from a train that had just arrived. Everyone was heading for the bridge across the River Aire. At first Amy felt anxious. It was a long time since she had been amongst so many people, but she quickly relaxed and followed Ben who was always half a stride ahead of her.

From the bridge they headed along the path towards the wooded hill that rose fairly steeply from the river flats. On the way, Amy stopped and gazed at the men, dressed in white, playing cricket in the park. It was a sight she had never seen before. Halfway across, they joined a long queue which snaked across the green to the bottom of the hill. It seemed odd to Amy so see so many people waiting in a queue. 'What are they waiting for?' she asked.

'For the tram!'

Amy was no wiser, but after waiting twenty minutes, the pair reached the pay booth for the tramway.

'Two, please,' Amy said, placing her threepenny bit on the counter.

'Single or return?' the stationmaster asked.

'Single, Amy replied, and asked, 'Does it go far?'

'Not far at all, just to the top of the hill.'

As the man handed her the tickets and her penny change, Amy looked around. Ahead were two sets of rails like railway lines, but they were on an incline heading through the trees and up the fairly steep incline. She could hear the noise of a pulley wheel turning and within minutes a tram appeared around the bend on the right-hand track. It consisted of two cars, like wagons, each carrying about twelve people. The seats were leather padded and the wooden backs were able to swing to face whichever direction the tram was travelling. The lower end of each car on the line was raised so the floor was horizontal as it went up the hill.

When the tram came to a stop, the folk waiting on the small wooden platform quickly occupied the seats and waited to be conveyed up the hill. There was an air of excitement in the passengers.

No sooner had she and Ben squeezed onto the front seat than a bell clanged and the small carriage juddered and started its quarter-mile journey, pulled by a thick hempen cable. As they neared the halfway point, where the track curved slowly around the hillside, Amy saw the other tram rumbling down the other track. There was only a handful of passengers on board, but they waved as they passed. Above them, the branches of the old trees of Walker Wood reached over and touched each other forming a canopy of shade.

It was a short walk from the ticket office to the green at the top of the Glen. The pathway was crowded with families who had followed the footpath instead of taking the tram. As on any other fine Saturday or Sunday afternoon, Shipley Glen was teeming with visitors. Amy was astounded. It was like May Day but so much better. Ben took her hand and dragged her towards to the huge flat oval. He wanted to show her the Switchback Railway and the gondola on the Aerial Flight which swung high above the edge of the valley. The structures were amazing and unlike anything Amy had ever seen before. For the less adventurous, a convoy of horse-drawn trams offered rides around the green. Both adults and children vied for the open-air seats on the vehicle's top deck, which provided wonderful views across the surrounding countryside. Catering for the tastes of the elderly, the more refined and less adventurous, tea was served in the British Temperance Tea and Coffee House. Alternatively a glass of home-made lemonade could be purchased from a vendor on the green.

Those families who didn't take rides enjoyed the atmosphere with their own games and perhaps a picnic. There were donkey rides, a juggler, Morris dancers, and a Punch and Judy show. Apart from the shrieks from excited children, there were cries from the vendors selling postcards and chestnuts, and from the man with the toffee apples.

'Go buy one,' said Amy, handing Ben the remaining penny.

After offering Amy a bite, the pair wandered through the crowds. Ben compared the Glen with the fairs and shows he'd visited on his travels. He talked of towns and described many different events he'd seen, and Amy realized how much she had missed during the time she had worked in the mill. She remembered an old neighbour in the street, who boasted that she'd never strayed further than two miles of where she was born. Amy was thankful she would never have to say that.

Looking round at the crowd, she examined the faces, wondered where they all came from, and what they did. Some were obviously wealthy. Some were poor. But they all looked happy, as if they didn't have a care in the world. So different from the chalky-cheeked faces she'd seen heading to the mill on a winter's morning.

But the man's eyes, her gaze alighted on, were not those of a stranger. A frisson of fear ran through her.

'Ben!' she yelled, alarming the lad as she grabbed him by the hand and tried to pull him in the opposite direction.

'What's wrong?'

'This way, Ben!' But her efforts were useless. The boy was confused and too big for Amy to drag through the slow-moving crowd.

She felt a hand grasp her arm.

'Amy!' the voice said.

'Let go of me!'

'Amy Dodd!'

'Please let go!'

People looked and a man called to her. 'You all right, miss?'

She stopped, turned and caught her breath.

'What's the matter?' Ben asked, but Amy didn't reply.

She was looking at the man who had startled her. 'Mr Lister, I'm sorry I ran. I was scared.'

'Why would you be afraid of me?'

'Because I didn't want to see anyone from Fanshaw's Mill so seeing you was a shock.'

'Well, I must admit you are the last person I would have expected to see here, though, if I'm not mistaken, the last time we spoke you were running away as though all the hounds in hell were after you. But I can understand your desire not to be recognized,' he smiled, 'you are quite a celebrity at Fanshaw's Mill.'

Amy looked at him quizzically. 'A celebrity? You mean I made a nuisance of myself when I left,' she said, allowing a slight grin to warm her face.

'Too right! And your father caused a worse commotion when he found out that you had duped him – ranting and raving and yelling abuse at everyone.'

'You know about him?'

Harold Lister nodded. 'He searched for you for almost a week. Up and down every street he went, morning and night shouting your name. Drove folks crazy, I heard. Then the children took up the chant and made up a rhyme of their own. Everyone was singing it. I even heard it sung in the mill. You're quite infamous, I'm afraid.'

Amy flushed and enquired, 'What did it say?'

He paused for a moment trying hard not to smile.

'Please,' she said. 'I should know.'

Harold shuffled uncomfortably, smiled and repeated the ditty:

Amy Dodd slung her hook
Set a fire, run amuck
Took off like a butcher's dog
You'll ne'er catch our Amy Dodd

'But I never set a fire!' Amy said indignantly, 'It was only pretend.'

'I know that, but it did take some time to search all the floors to make sure that there wasn't a real one smouldering somewhere. You must have heard how many woollen mills have burnt down in the last ten years. And it happens so quickly too. Then there was the fire brigade. They were none too happy about the false alarm, and a constable came because there was talk that something might have been stolen and the fire used as an excuse to cover the theft.'

'But I never stole anything,' Amy said. 'Oh, dear, was anything else said?'

'I heard tell, you'd run off to meet a young man, but after hearing about your father, I didn't think that was true.'

'Goodness gracious,' Amy said, 'I'll never dare set my foot in the neighbourhood again.'

'Well, apart from Mr Fanshaw, I'd say most folk wouldn't hold it against you. It was the most exciting thing that had happened at the mill in years. Gave the girls something to talk about for a couple of weeks, and I think everyone enjoyed singing your song.'

Amy pondered her question. 'Did you hear anything more of my father – about him looking for me?'

'No, but I heard rumours that he's not a pleasant man.'

'They're not rumours, Mr Lister. It's the truth, and I hate him.'

His eyes met hers, and for a moment they said nothing. Remembering Ben was with her, she felt embarrassed. 'This is Mr Lister, Ben. He's an engineer. He works at one of the mills in Leeds.'

Ben nodded and shook hands in a gentlemanly fashion. 'Can I go watch the Punch and Judy show?'

Amy agreed. On the other side of the oval, the gaily-coloured, red and white striped tent had attracted a large crowd. When they wandered across the green, Amy felt good having a smartly dressed gentleman accompanying her. Sitting on the soft grass, facing the miniature stage, were more than forty children. Ben was amongst them. The taller children and adults formed a semi-circle around the youngsters and all eyes were directed to the tiny stage where the puppets' antics raised cries and jeers from the audience. Amy hadn't seen a Punch and Judy show since she was a girl and she found herself giggling with the others.

'Actually,' Lister said, continuing the earlier conversation, 'I don't work at Fanshaw's, I work at Salt's Mill.'

'Here in Saltaire?'

He nodded. 'This is where I have lived since I was a boy, and I work here most of the time.' He paused, till the sound of cheering died down. 'I knew you were in this area.'

Amy looked puzzled.

'I saw you a few weeks ago,' he said. 'You were with a barge that was unloading its cargo. I saw you sitting on the edge of the canal near the loading wharf dangling your feet in the water. I was high up on the fourth floor supervising a pulley that was hoisting a new loom into the building. I called out, but you didn't hear me.' He breathed heavily. 'That was quite a job. By the time we got it onto the floor and bolted into position, you and the barge were gone. I fully expected that you would have been in Liverpool by now, and never expected to see you here at Shipley Glen. Are you still travelling the canal?'

'Not at the moment. The boat's in an old yard not far from the New Mill. Jentz's Yard.' She caught her breath. 'You won't tell anyone where I am, will you?'

'Of course not' he said turning towards her. 'Would you walk with me across the Glen? I find my leg aches if I stand for any length of time.'

She'd forgotten his limp.

'That'd be nice,' she said, trying to attract Ben's attention, but the lad was engrossed in the puppet show. All the audience was laughing at the cruel, repetitive beatings Mr Punch was administering to his wife and baby. Amy wondered what it was about the performance that made everyone laugh.

'Mr Lister, can I ask why you were at Fanshaw's Mill? And when did you come back here?'

'Please call me Harold or Harry, not Mr Lister,' he said. 'In answer to your questions, I get called on by Fanshaw's and other Leeds mills for special jobs, but I prefer my work at Salt's Mill. As you can see, it's more modern than the others and the work is less taxing, even enjoyable.'

Amy screwed up her nose but Harold didn't notice.

'As to when I arrived, I caught the train from Leeds, the day after the supposed fire! But I've been back to Leeds a couple of times since then.'

'Are you staying in Saltaire now or going away again?'

'I was going to ask you the same question,' he said. 'I have a little more work to take care of here first. Then I must return to Leeds to finish my business with Mr Fanshaw. But I'll only be in the city for a few days.'

'And after that?'

'Back to Saltaire. But what of you? Where will you be going? Will you be staying with the folk on the barge?'

A lost expression settled on Amy's face though the shadow of the bonnet shielded it from Harold. 'I don't know,' she said slowly. 'I'd planned to go to Lancashire. Maybe get a job there in a cotton mill.'

Harold tutted.

'Ben's family are kindly folk but I can't expect them to keep me forever. And I can't go back to Leeds because of my father. I'm afraid he will find me, afraid of what he might do.'

'Shall we sit for a moment?' Harold said, indicating a large, flat boulder worn smooth over the years and now covered in a fine cushion of green moss. It was located at the far side of the oval, perched at the head of the track that zigzagged down to the bottom of the valley. Though the pathway was steep, it attracted a fair number of walkers who trudged down to the beck at the bottom. No one, however, climbed back up the slope. Instead they all chose the easier, but much longer walk back to the town.

'Saltaire is a remarkable place, don't you think?' Harold said, not waiting for an answer. 'Imagine the brain of a man designing a town that would be more fitting in the suburbs of Florence than in the centre of the woollen district of Yorkshire.'

'I've never heard of Florence,' said Amy, wondering why this well-educated young man was taking time to talk to a girl like her. 'This is the first time I've been out of Leeds,' she admitted, 'and coming here on the barge, I saw little more than the horse-path while we were on the cut.'

'The cut?'

'That's what the boatmen call the canal.'

'I guess you were running from your father? You are truly afraid of him, aren't you?'

There was a softness in his voice, the sort of gentleness Amy had only ever heard in her mother's tones. She stood up, resisting the temptation to allow tears to form in her eyes, and gazed blankly at the happy throng milling around the green. 'I caught a glimpse of the church with the fancy tower when we walked here today.'

'Have you stepped inside it?'

She shook her head.

'Then you must allow me to show you both the church and the town, while you are here. Perhaps I could join you and your friends for service next Sunday?'

'You'll not get Joel to step into the churchyard,' Amy said with a laugh, 'let alone in the church itself, but I'm sure Helen will be pleased to have your company.'

'And perhaps afterwards you would like to ride the tramway again. I'm sure Ben would enjoy that. I'd like to tell you more about it and about the man who built it.'

'Titus Salt?'

'No, not Sir Titus. A man by the name of Sam Wilson built this railway only three years ago. And he built all the other rides and entertainments you see around here. He too is a remarkable man.' He turned to Amy, his eyes filled with admiration. 'I was here when the tracks were cleared and the timber rails laid down. I even lent a hand when they installed the cable, and I've worked with Wilson on the problems that they have had with the supply of gas.'

'That is what the bad smell is?'

'I'm afraid so, but Wilson is looking into it and you would not believe the future projects he has in mind. He intends to construct a huge toboggan run completely out of wood. And alongside it he'll build a track for cable cars so that after sliding down the slope, the riders can return to the top of the hill in a tram. He says it will be the longest, wildest and steepest ride ever erected anywhere in the world. The man is a genius,' he said excitedly. 'Today there are hundreds of people at the Glen, but before long there'll be thousands flocking to Saltaire from all over the West Riding of Yorkshire. The wonders of engineering are unbelievable. There is something new every day.'

Amy was surprised at Harold's enthusiasm. It reminded her of Ben's excitement when he talked of the fairs he had seen or had discovered a shilling on the canal path. But never before had she seen such fervour in a grown man. Listening to the young engineer talk, excited her

'If only you could see the funicular lifts in Scarborough. They have huge carriages with glass windows, which travel almost vertically up the side of the cliff on iron rails.' He paused. 'My dearest wish is to visit San Francisco and see the cable cars in that city.'

'Then, I'm sure you will go there one day. But I heard a rumour at the mill that you were going to build bridges.'

Harold looked into Amy's eyes. 'I didn't think you would know that.'

She smiled.

'It's true. But I would like to build a funicular railway also.'

Amy waited for him to continue, but the thoughts of trains and trams and railways were crowding his thinking.

'I think we should find Ben before he gets into any mischief.' Lifting her skirt, Amy allowed Harold to hold her hand, as he guided her between the boulders.

'May I accompany you and the lad down on the tram?'

'We've only got single tickets,' she said. 'The extra penny paid for the toffee apple.'

'Then allow me to pay.'

'Thanks,' Amy said. 'Me and Ben's off down to the bottom of the Glen. I know it's a fair walk but we don't get much exercise on the barge.'

'How long will the boat be in the yard?'

'Joel says for as long as the yard's free and there are no other boats waiting to go in. He's been laid up with a bad leg but he hopes to be up and around in another two weeks.'

'And then they'll be heading on to Liverpool?'

'No. They're off back to Leeds or to the east coast to pick up another load of wool for this mill. It's special wool that comes from South America,' she said knowingly.

'South America. That's a place I would also like to go to.' He thought for a moment. 'Will you go with them?'

'To Leeds? I don't think so.' Amy leaned down and touched Ben on the shoulder, distracting him from the show he was watching. 'Come along, lad, we'd best be going.'

'Then I'll wish you good afternoon,' Harold said, 'and hopefully see you next Sunday morning.'

'Aye, maybe,' Amy said, as she nodded then watched the young gentleman with the limping gait stroll towards the ticket office at the top of the tramway.

After glancing at the children seated in front of the miniature theatre, she and Ben set off down the zigzag track which led to the bottom of the valley. Behind them the laughter from the Punch and Judy show subsided as a chorus of high-pitched voices screamed a warning to Mrs Punch: 'Watch out! He's behind you!' And every time Mr Punch appeared from behind the wings, the same cry went up, and every time it was louder.

Amy stepped carefully on the steep incline leading down into the valley's verdant gloom. Ben was far more sure-footed and ran on ahead, slipping and sliding down the slope and leaving her far behind.

'Don't fall! Wait for me!' Amy called anxiously, but he didn't hear her. The only voices Amy heard were those of the children screaming in chorus:

'*Watch out! He's behind you!*'

Chapter 13

Harold Lister

'Hello.'

Amy recognized the voice instantly. It was Tuesday and she hadn't expected to see Mr Lister until the weekend. Feeling a trifle embarrassed, she looked around to see if anyone else was on the canal bank, but it was empty. It would be a while before Helen and Ben were back from their shopping trip.

'What are you doing here?' she asked.

'I had some time on my hands, so I thought I'd take a walk. Seemed a shame to be indoors on such a fine day.'

Before Amy could respond, Joel's voice bellowed from the cabin. 'Whose that, lass? We don't want no hawkers round here!'

Amy popped her head into the cabin. 'It's the young gent from the mill I told you about.'

'Huh!' said Joel. 'Suppose you'd better bring him in and let me get a look at him.'

It wasn't quite the way she'd have expected Harold to be greeted but she knew what Joel was like. She was also glad to see that her visitor was carrying his coat over his arm and had his sleeves rolled up above the elbows, making him look less like a gentleman.

'This is Harold Lister,' Amy said.

'Huh! Can't get up. Broke me bloody leg.'

'I'm sorry to hear that, sir,' Harold said, sniffing the smell of paint and glancing admiringly at the ornaments and garlands of roses decorating the cabin. Stretching out his hand, he said, 'I'm pleased to meet you.'

'You better sit your body down,' Joel said, pointing to a three-legged stool. 'You'll not stand for long with your back bent over like that.'

Harold thanked him and did as he was bid.

'Do you know anything about boat-horses, lad?'

Taken aback, the engineer replied, 'Afraid not, sir, though I know a little about carriage horses. My father ran a string of coaches on the Leeds to Peterborough run, three times a week, regular as clockwork for nearly twenty years. Did Middlesbrough too and some local routes. I'm told his was the best service of its kind at the time. Unfortunately, he died ten years ago.'

'So that's where your brass came from?'

'You guessed right, Mr—?'

'Call me Joel or Milkwort – that's the handle I'm known by on the cut.'

Harold relaxed. 'My father didn't want me to follow him into the business. He knew the days of horse-drawn coaches were numbered and he wanted me to do something worthwhile. "Build bridges, travel the world, lad," is what he used to say. I'll always remember that. He even suggested I should build more canals.'

'Maybe he was right when you were a lad, but things have changed. Now there's steam barges and soon there'll be no need for a towing path and boats like mine. Before long everything will be carried by rail and they'll not need these navigations any longer.'

'You could be right, Joel.'

'I know I'm damn right. But that's not the point. If you know coach horses, you know drays and shires.'

'I did in my younger days.'

'Never mind your younger days, I'm not interested in them. What I'm interested in is right now. What I need is another boat-horse. Listen to me,' he said, leaning closer to the engineer, 'there's a field at the back of the Gate and Gander Inn in Skipton. The innkeeper there runs the overnight stables for the passing barge horses. We've used that place many times and it's all right.' He paused. 'I've heard word that he's got three horses grazing at the back of the inn. Good horses, I'm told; ones that know the path coast to coast. I gather they're not young and that all three were passed in by bargemen who've gone over to steam.' He sucked in a deep breath. 'I want one of those nags. Trouble is, I can't get out there to look at 'em. My lad, Ben can pick a good animal and he'd got a way with them. Some people seem to be born with it, and I guess your father would have been the same or he'd never have made his living with coaches.'

Harold nodded.

'But I don't want the lad to go alone, not that I don't trust him. What I'm asking you, young man, will you go with Ben and choose me a horse?'

Harold shuffled a little nervously. 'I'd be pleased to do that for you. Would Saturday suit?'

'Fine,' Joel said. 'Now, how about you get out of me cabin and off me boat, and have a talk to the lass outside, as I guess that's what you came calling for.'

Harold couldn't stop himself from grinning broadly, though Joel's fixed expression never wavered.

The following Saturday, as arranged, Harold Lister and Ben left early but at the engineer's suggestion, and expense, they caught the train to Skipton rather than walking both there and back.

Once they had looked at the animals, it didn't take long for them to agree on a horse. Ben recognized the mare, as soon as they walked into the field. She was a handsome part-shire that was once a regular on the towing path. He remembered having spoken to the horse and her owner several times. He even remembered her name – Mallow.

After looking over the two other horses on offer, Harold and Ben settled on the mare, and once the price was agreed on with the landlord, arrangements were made for it to remain stabled there until Joel was on his feet again. Ben wanted to walk Mallow back to Saltaire that afternoon, but Joel had been specific in his instructions and Harold followed the boatman's instructions to the letter.

When the pair arrived back at the boat, Joel was pleased to hear the details of the purchase and the price that had been paid. His only aggravation was that he couldn't collect her right away.

'Mallow,' he said. 'I know her well. She'd be eight or nine years old, at least, and she's got a good temperament. Belonged to old Featherspoon. Fool he was, going over to steam. He won't admit it, but I know he hates it. Still, that's his loss and our gain. Mallow', he pondered. 'She'll serve us proud for a good number of years, you wait and see.'

Next morning, being Sunday, Harold arrived early to take the ladies and Ben to the local church in Saltaire. Amy wondered what the congregation would think of the pair of them in boat clothes, but

Helen wasn't the slightest bit concerned, and Harold didn't seem to notice either. Ben would have preferred to stay with his father but his mother insisted he came along.

'You can try reading the hymns,' she said. 'You know all the words. I heard you singing them.'

After the service, Harold accompanied them back to the barge and was invited on board to share Sunday dinner. When the meal was over and everything cleared away, Harold thanked Helen and turned to Joel. 'Would it be all right if I took Amy for a walk up into the town? She's not seen much of it, I gather.'

'Don't ask me,' Joel said. 'Ask the lass. She can make her own choices.'

Harold looked across to Amy who was squeezed between Helen and Ben on the short bench in the cabin.

'That'd be nice,' she said, easing her way out slowly, not wanting to appear too enthusiastic. Stepping from the cabin, she noticed Joel wink. It was directed at Harold.

'You bring her back safe, young fella. She's a dab hand at polishing brasses.'

Harold took Amy's hand to help her along the gang-plank but released it when she had both feet on the firm ground. They chatted, as they walked on the path in front of the New Mill. He talked about pulleys and cranes and she talked about caulking and tarring the bottom of the barge. Crossing the bridge, they turned towards the town. On the way up the hill, they stopped at the entrance gates to the congregational church they had attended and looked down its pathway to the elegant fretted tower with its cupola and Corinthian columns supporting the portico.

'A wonderful example of Italian architecture,' Harold said.

They passed the works dining room on the right and the huge six-storey main mill building on the left.

From the top of the railway bridge, they could see the well-tended allotment gardens and on the opposite side the three-storey buildings that Harold explained were the boarding houses. Victoria Road was the main shopping street, with shops on one side: the grocer's, butcher's, stationer's, and a post office.

Heading up the main street, a pair of reclining lions guarded the grand Institute building and at the other side of the road the school, with its curved pagoda-like masonry, resembled an oriental temple. The garden in front was planted with roses, sweet briar and honeysuckle.

'It's so beautiful,' said Amy. 'Nothing like the dark mills where I come from.' She laughed. 'And fancy a pair of lions sitting on the side of a mill street. It's not surprising no one ever leaves here.' Seeing all this made her understand why Harold respected the man who had designed the town and why he aspired to be like him.

'It'll be standing hundreds of years from now.'

'Really?' said Amy.

'The Romans built roads and bridges two thousand years ago that are still standing today. Did you know that?'

Amy shook her head. He knew so much and she knew so little. It made her wonder why he had time for her.

'Here we are,' he said, as he stopped outside the corner shop. The fixed sign above the door read: Salt and Pepper Tea Shop. 'Shall we go in?' he asked.

Amy was nervous. Not only had she never walked out with a gentleman before, but she'd never stepped inside a tea shop either.

Sensing her apprehension, he took her by the hand and led her to the round table next to the window. It was set with a lace cloth and in the centre was a small pot containing a bunch of violets. 'Don't be nervous,' he said. Two elderly ladies sitting in the corner exchanged pleasantries. Amy smiled nervously.

'Isn't it pretty?' she whispered, running her hand across the cloth and picking up the flowers to smell them.

'Shall I order?' he said.

'Yes, please.'

The lady who waited on them was rather plump, as if she had eaten a few too many of the shop's delicacies. Her smooth skin belied her age, though the flounce of snow-white curls which framed her rather ruddy face could not deny her sixty-odd years. A pair of dark, beady eyes peered at Amy from over the metal-rimmed spectacles that rested on the end of her rather sharp nose.

'Just visiting Saltaire?' the woman enquired.

'The young lady is,' said Harold.

'Two teas, is it?'

'Yes, and perhaps a piece of cake,' he said looking at Amy.

She nodded and smiled. 'Yes, please.'

'Now,' said Harold, as the woman disappeared into the back room, 'I want you to tell me a little about yourself.'

'Me?' said Amy. 'There's not much to tell. I worked at Fanshaw's for the last three years and I've lived in the shadow of its chimneys since the day I was born. I went to the local school, and I liked that, but that stopped when my father came out of —' she hesitated, and lowered her voice, 'jail.'

Harold touched her hand. 'It's all right, I heard. I think everyone at Fanshaw's knows about Amos Dodd. Just like they now know about Amy Dodd.'

They stopped talking as the woman approached. After sweeping the cloth with a bone-handled brush, she placed a plate of cakes in the centre of the table.

Harold thanked her.

'Why did you talk to me?' Amy said.

'Where?'

'At the Glen, when you saw me. You could have ignored me, but you didn't.'

'I told you, I was surprised when I saw you with the barge. Then when I thought about you afterwards, I was a little concerned. If you remember, the previous time I saw you was in the mill's yard. And with all the talk about your father and him spending time in jail and the rhymes they were repeating about you, I was worried.' He paused. 'You are such a nice girl, Amy, and if you'll excuse me for saying, I find it hard to believe you are related to such a terrible man as Amos Dodd.'

The two china cups and saucers, the sugar basin and milk jug crashed onto the floor beside Amy. The metal tray landed on top of them with a resounding clang. Amy jumped up immediately to help the elderly woman who appeared to be in danger of collapsing. The ladies seated at the other table looked concerned.

Taking the woman's arm, Harold helped her into a chair. 'Is there someone I can call? You look ill, madam.'

'I'm sorry,' she said. 'I'll be all right. My niece is out back, but I don't want her to see this mess. This is her place, you see. I'll be all right, if you just give me a minute. I'm terrible sorry, sir, I think I scared the young lady.'

'Don't worry about me,' Amy said. 'Did you trip or are you sick?'

The woman scooped in a lungful of air. Her cheeks were no longer red. 'No, miss, it were the shock of hearing the name the young gentleman mentioned.' She shuddered. 'Amos Dodd! I knew a man of that name once and, I have to say, I hoped I'd never ever hear that name again.'

'That's my father's name,' Amy said.

The woman put her hand to her heart and sighed. 'Then it can't be the same man. A rogue and a murderer, this fella was, and if you'll excuse me for blaspheming, I hope he's roasting in hell!'

Harold's eyebrows lifted.

'I'm sorry,' said Amy, 'but I think that is my father. He spent fifteen years in Armley Jail, but he's out now.'

At the other table, the two women whispered behind their handkerchiefs.

The woman shook her head. 'God save us all,' she said. 'I've feared this day all my life. If ever I've wished a man harm it were him.'

'But why?'

'I can't talk about it, luv. It would bring too many memories flooding back.'

'But I need to know. There are things I want to find out. How did you know him?'

The woman took a cloth from her apron pocket and dabbed her cheeks. 'You say he's your father? Then I'm sorry for what I said to your face, lass.' Straightening herself in the chair, she continued. 'Years ago, I worked at a place for a minister and his wife. That's where I first came across Amos Dodd. He worked there too. Did the garden and odd jobs about the place.'

'My mother worked for Reverend Upton. She said that was where she met my father.'

'Then your mum was Lisbeth Eccles?'

'That's right.'

'And your aunt was her little sister Rose?'

When Amy nodded, the woman's eyes glazed over, before a stream of tears flowed down her dumpling cheeks. There was nothing Amy or Harold could say to console her.

A sudden shriek announced the shop owner's entrance, when she burst through from the back room. Harold stepped out of the way, as she rushed over, her cries even attracting the attention of passers-by on the street. 'Goodness gracious, Auntie, what have they done to you?'

Despite Harold's pleas to be allowed to explain, and Amy's obvious concern for the elderly waitress, the shopkeeper continued her abuse. Because the woman was visibly distressed and inconsolable, Harold took Amy's arm and pulled her away.

'If we stay we'll only make matters worse. If you must speak with her, I suggest we return another day when she's less upset. Now is not the right time.

Though she didn't want to leave, Amy knew Harold was right and allowed him to take her arm when they left the shop.

As they walked down the hill, they spoke very little. Amy's head was spinning. She wanted to know the truth. What was the woman was concealing? Was it the same thing her mother had promised to tell her before she died? She wanted to know about Rose and what had really happened to her and felt sure this woman could answer some of those questions. Taking Harold's advice, however, she decided to wait a few days and then visit the tea shop again. Hopefully next time the lady would be more willing to talk and would answer her questions.

When they arrived back at the boat, Helen was surprised to see them both in a quiet mood.

'He didn't upset you, did he?' she asked later.

'No, it wasn't Harry, it was some talk I heard about my father.'

'Not him again! Word certainly travels. Trouble is,' Helen said, 'it's always the bad news which travels the furthest. Don't worry, love, you'll be safe in here. Joel won't let anything happen to you.'

Amy was warmed by the boatwoman's hug. They were kind folk and, no doubt Joel, when he was well, was a fit strong man. But from her own experiences, and from what the woman in the tea shop confirmed, Amos Dodd had an ugly reputation and it would take more than a good man to defend her against him.

For the next three days Amy hardly stuck her head out of the boat. She was thankful of the rain because there was less work to do and she found more time to spend with Ben on his writing and reading.

She always felt safe inside the main cabin and, though it was crowded with the four of them around the small stove, she never felt that she wanted to get out. At night, the cabin in the barge's bow seemed a long way from Helen and Joel. And, though she shared it with Ben, she often felt anxious and confused. She feared her father and hated him and wanted nothing more to do with him. Yet she wanted to know the truth about him and her mother. All the things her mother had never told her.

Pacing the bank beside the dry dock, Amy thought about the woman in the tea shop. She knew she must go back and talk with her, but she resolved to go alone and arrive just before the shop shut for the day.

Stamping the rain from her boots before entering, Amy glanced through the window. Three ladies were occupying one of the tables. The rest of the shop was empty. A bell tinkled as she walked in. The patrons looked around and smiled. Amy waited by the door.

Within a minute, the woman who owned the establishment appeared but her cordial expression changed as soon as she recognized Amy.

Speaking in a loud whisper, she attracted the attention of the other customers. 'I didn't think you'd dare come back here again. You can't imagine the state you left my aunt in. It took all afternoon for her to get over it, and even then I think she was just putting on a brave face.'

'I'm sorry,' said Amy. 'I didn't mean to upset her.'

'I don't know what you said to her but she's not set foot in the shop since then.'

'I didn't say anything to her. It was what she was telling me that distressed her.'

'Well, I don't care who was saying what to who, all I know is she's not been back to work since, and I can't manage without her.'

'Perhaps if I talked to her, it'll make her feel better. I need to speak with her ask and ask her some questions. She knew my father, you see.'

'I don't care if she knew Prince Albert, God rest his soul. You leave my auntie alone. You've done enough damage already.'

Amy sighed and turned back to the door. The other customers, looking uncomfortable, reached for their empty teacups.

'I didn't mean no harm,' Amy said. 'If she changes her mind, would you tell her she can find me at Jentz's boatyard. It's on the canal, about half a mile past the New Mill. The boat's name is *Milkwort*.'

About a week later, there was a cry from the bank.

'Hey! I'm looking for Miss Milkywort.' The voice was that of a lad, no more than seven or eight years old. He was sporting a cap that was several sizes too big for him.

Helen stepped out onto the small deck. 'What do you want, lad?'

'I've got to take the girl to see my great aunt. I've to say they met at the Salt and Pepper Tea Shop.'

Amy dropped her sewing and grabbed her coat. She was anxious to meet the old woman and find out what she could tell her about the past. In her eagerness to go she forgot to take Helen's bonnet.

'Will you be all right on your own? Ben can go with you.'

'I'm sure I'll be fine.'

'Take care,' Helen said.

Amy followed the boy along the canal path, finding it hard at times to keep up with him. Though his legs were short, his gait was somewhere between a skip and a trot. They passed the New Mill building and Amy recognized one of the barges she had seen before. It was unloading big bales of cargo similar to the ones Joel had carried. Looking up to the pulley wheel protruding from the fourth floor, she wondered if Harold was up there, but there was no sign of him.

Following the boy, she retraced the route she had taken with him to the tea shop. But when the boy trotted past the doorway and crossed to the other side of the road, Amy felt a tinge of concern. Had he been sent by the woman who worked there or was it a trick her father was playing? Surely he couldn't know about the incident in the shop.

When the boy crossed over from the last of Saltaire's cobbled streets to a narrow dirt track which led up the hill, she stopped.

'Where are you taking me?'

'Up there,' he said, pointing to a small farm cottage. It was much older than the houses of the model village built by Sir Titus Salt. As they approached, Amy recognized the white-haired woman waiting on the doorstep.

'Thank you, Sam,' the woman said, meeting them at the door and handing an apple to the boy. 'Come inside, luv.'

The cottage was cosy. It smelled of jam on the boil. The ceiling beams were so low, Amy's unruly hair brushed across them. Ducking her head, she was led into a small living room. Despite the compact size of the window, the room was bright. There was not a speck of dust anywhere and everything was spick and span. Even the lace mats on the chair arms and back looked freshly ironed. They were bleached as clean as fresh snow.

Amy didn't dare touch anything.

'This is my niece's place,' the woman said. 'Her that owns the tea shop. She lets me have it rent free. In return I do the baking, and help out in the shop. I'm a lucky woman, aren't I?'

'It's very nice,' Amy said shyly.

'Don't worry, I won't bite your head off,' she said, 'or bawl like a baby. Quite a performance I put on in the shop. That's something I've never done in all my life, and I'm sure I won't do it again. It were just the shock of hearing that name again after all them years. Aye, and the surprise at seeing you. Fancy you being Lisbeth Eccles' child. Here, sit down here, luv. The kettle's boiling. I've been waiting for you.'

Amy smiled and thanked her and while the woman busied herself in the kitchen, she tried to think clearly. She'd followed the boy without much thought, and now she was here she didn't know what questions she wanted to ask.

As if recognizing the puzzled expression on Amy's face, the woman poured the tea and said, 'My name is Maisie Jones, I was in service all me life as a cook, and Cook's the name I answer to. So you can take your choice, you can call me Maisie or Miss Jones, or Cook. I'm not fussy.'

'I'll call you Miss Jones, if you don't mind.' Because the woman looked old enough to be her grandmother, the title seemed more respectful.

For a moment neither spoke. Both sipped their tea.

'You want to know about your father, I suppose. What he was like. What he did for a living, that sort of thing.'

'I suppose so,' said Amy cautiously. 'But I also want to know about my Aunt Rose, and what happened to her, and to my mother when my father went to jail. I don't know how she managed on her own when I was born. There were things she never got around to telling me. She died not long ago.'

'I'm sorry,' the cook said, 'I liked your mother. She was a nice girl.'

'But Mum took her secrets with her when she died and, now I've met you, I think you might know the answer to some of my questions.'

'Some things are best left unsaid.'

'I've thought about that too, but I want to know the truth and I won't be satisfied until I do.'

Miss Jones nodded. 'I thought that might be the case,' she said, pausing for a moment. 'Well, I'll tell you what I know, but it's quite a long story. It's twenty years since I was at the Manse and them last few days were the worst days of my life. But I can still remember them like they were only yesterday.'

Amy interrupted. 'Can you start at the beginning and tell me what happened?'

Chapter 14

Cook's Story

Miss Jones kicked off her slippers and stretched her legs out in front of her. 'I knew your mother as Lisbeth Eccles. We worked together at a big house called the Manse for the Reverend Upton and his young wife. An odd couple they were, each in their own way, but I blame him for the way she went. "Suffer little children—" he'd preach on Sundays, especially if there was a christening, but for all that, he didn't want none of his own. Mrs Upton told me that one day, but I'd guessed as much, because they always slept in separate rooms.

'I don't understand,' Amy said, 'what has that to do with my mother?'

'You must let me explain then it'll all make sense. I think it was Mrs Upton's hankering for children that made her fuss over her young maids. She treated them almost like they were her own children. It was weird in a way. But she got rid of them in quick sticks if she caught them talking with any of the local lads.

'Like I said, I remember when your mother first started at the Manse. Only fifteen, she was. Fresh faced and healthy. Or as healthy as any child can be growing up in a city like Leeds. For a time after Lisbeth started, Mrs Upton stopped talking about having a child, then after a spell it started again. She used to natter the Reverend, even while he was at the table. "Wouldn't it be nice to hear the patter of little feet in the house?" she'd say, or, "Imagine how nice it would be to christen your own child." That sort of thing. But she didn't know when to stop and went on and on; morning, noon and evening. Eventually, he had no choice and had to bend to her whim. I think the fact the whispers had spread around his congregation might also have had a bearing.'

Miss Jones continued, gazing straight ahead. 'But it was right odd. It wasn't like he made her that way, if you know what I mean. No, he agreed for her to have a child – but not his! Said she could mind an infant for a spell to see if she could handle it. Then he told her that if all went well, she could keep it.'

'How strange,' Amy said.

'Lisbeth and I decided he must have done that because she couldn't have children of her own. Anyway, one Monday – I remember it was Monday because I was outside hanging the washing – this man arrived at the gate and presented me his calling card and asked to see "the Reverend and his good lady". He was a nice polite gent, but I didn't know his business. What I do know is he spent almost three hours in the house talking with them and when he left, Mrs Upton couldn't contain herself. She announced to Lisbeth and me that she was getting a baby at last.'

Amy smiled sympathetically.

'Well, that put the house in a right stir,' Miss Jones said. 'We had to whitewash the walls and make up baby linens from old sheets. We were sewing from morning till night. Never worked so hard in that house as we did that week.'

'And did the man bring a baby?'

Cook nodded. 'Three weeks later, he was back with an infant in his arms – a right pretty little lad, finest of fine fair hair you ever did see, and a right bonny little face.'

'And the child thrived?'

'No, it didn't. It got sick after a matter of only a couple of weeks. Colic, I think, from over-feeding. Every time it cried, she fed it. Then, when it had a pain it its belly and it cried and wouldn't stop crying. Mrs Upton was beside herself. She couldn't stand the sound of its screaming and used to go out for walks to get away from the noise. She'd leave it for me and your mother to tend to it.' She looked across at Amy. 'Poor little mite, I felt that sorry for it, and I must say your mother was much better than me. I've never had children, but Lisbeth, well, she'd just about brought up her little sister, Rose, so she was pretty good with the young one.'

'So what happened to the child? Did it get better?'

'I don't know.'

Amy looked puzzled.

'It was sent back.'

'Sent back?'

'That's right. Mrs Upton went berserk one day. We all heard her screaming at the child. I was in the kitchen and the Reverend was in his study. I don't know where Lisbeth was, but we all rushed upstairs at the same time, and when we got to the nursery she was shaking the poor mite like it were a piece of carpet. It took the strength of all three of us to get her to stop.

'The very next morning, Lisbeth was given money for fares and sent off with a letter for the man who'd delivered the baby to them. It was a terrible business.'

'Did he take the child back?'

'Aye, he came the next day. Polite and business-like he was. Not a cross word. Never asked what had happened. And Mrs Upton didn't say anything, but I think that was because the doctor had given her some potion to settle her nerves. Anyway, the man left with the little lad in his arms, carrying him just the way he had when he arrived. Cuddling it, he was, like it was his own. I could hear Lisbeth crying when he walked down the street. I don't know how she'd managed to choke the tears till then.'

'Was my father working at the Manse at that time?'

'No,' said Miss Jones, as she filled Amy's cup. 'He didn't arrive until about a year later.'

'And was the Reverend's wife all right by then?'

'To outsiders, she seemed fine, but your mother and me, we knew different. She did odd things, like carrying a rag doll around with her. And she'd talk to it and dress it like it was a real baby. She even got me to fill the tub to bath it in. I didn't like to argue with her, the state she was in. At times she appeared all right for a week or two. And then there were the letters.'

'The letters?'

'Aye, she'd sit down and write long letters and put them in envelopes and give them to your mother and tell her to deliver them to the gentleman who'd brought the child. Lisbeth and I never knew what she wrote in them, but we guessed she were asking for another chance. She wanted another infant to look after.'

Amy shook her head.

'Of course, your mother didn't mind delivering them messages even though it was quite a way off. The address was over in Roundhay, at the other side of Leeds. A nice house, from what your mother said, but it took the best part of a day for her to get there and back, and she was often right weary when she arrived home. But Lisbeth was always happy to go. It was a treat for her to have a day out. Imagine a young lass having her fares paid to take a day out. It gave her plenty of time to stop and look in Leeds markets when she was passing through the city.'

'And after all her letters, did the Reverend's wife get another baby?' Amy asked.

'No, she never did. And she never got pregnant either, poor soul, so that was the end of that.'

Miss Jones closed her eyes, and for a moment Amy thought she was falling asleep.

'Tell me about my father, Amos Dodd. When did he start working at the Manse?'

Leaning forward in the chair, Miss Jones continued. 'He came to the Manse about a year after this terrible baby business. It was early summer and the rhododendrons were in flower. Beautiful, they were. But if it weren't for them dam blooms, he'd have never got a job at the house.' She paused and drained her cup. 'Fred the old gardener was away sick. Well, he was ninety, if he was a day. Too old to work, really, but the Reverend insisted on keeping him on. Anyway Fred didn't come in to work that week, and Mrs Upton got a bee in her bonnet about the rhododendrons. The bushes had grown out over the path and you could hardly see where to walk, so she decided to have them cut down – there and then. That was exactly the time Dodd turned up on the doorstep. His timing couldn't have been better. He was a strong man, said he wanted a job and said he was prepared to do anything. *Anything*,' she repeated cynically before continuing.

'It took him over a week, but he cleared every last rhododendron bush in the garden. And it was a big garden too. Such a shame. Beautiful blooms they were, and had been since spring. Hacked them down to ground level and burnt the lot. Talk about smoke! Anyway, that same week, old Fred sent word he wasn't coming back to the Manse, so Dodd was offered the gardener's job. Walked straight into it. Not only that, he was allowed to have the garden shed to live in, on condition that he tidied it up a bit.

'Mrs Upton seemed quite taken by the new man. It seemed odd to us. She was a well-bred woman, educated and talked proper, whereas he was as common as muck.' She paused for a moment when she realized she was talking about Amy's father. 'I'm sorry, luv,' she said.

'Don't worry,' Amy said. 'He's not changed.'

Miss Jones continued. 'Lisbeth and I couldn't figure out what the attraction was with the new gardener, until he told us. Boasting, he was. "I keep telling her," he said, "If she wants a baby, I'll fix 'er up." Then he'd laugh. "Stupid woman, dumb as a dead dog, she is, believes I'll fetch her one."' She shuddered. 'Then he'd laugh again. Evil it was. I hated that laugh of his. Even now, when I think about it, it sends shivers down my spine.'

'Did anything happen between my father and Mrs Upton?'

'No, I don't think so. He just played with her. Teased her. Lisbeth and I used to watch him, joshing with her in the garden, and her eyes would sparkle – sadly, it was the only time they ever did. I reckon it was cruel the way he made a fool of her.

'But he had a glib tongue, that man, and before long he had your mother's eyes lit up too. He used to invite her to his shed – big one it was – and he furnished it out like a real room; table, chairs and a bed. Don't know where he got them from! Well, I don't have to tell you what happened. One afternoon, when the Uptons were away, he got your mother drunk. She came to me afterwards in a terrible state and I had to sober her up. That was the beginning of the end.'

'So that was how Mum got pregnant. So her and my father weren't married?'

'No, not then. Lisbeth was ashamed of herself when she found she was pregnant but she daren't tell anyone except me. And she made me swear I wouldn't tell because she knew she'd lose her job if the missus found out.'

'So how long was it before she left?'

'She managed to hide her belly till she were about five months gone but then it got to a stage her dresses wouldn't fasten round her middle. So, when Mrs Upton found out about her condition, she sent her packing that same day.'

'And my father, did he lose his job too?'

'No,' said the cook. 'That was all a bit odd. Mrs Upton insisted that Dodd stay on in the garden even though it was February and there was nothing to do. Surprisingly, the Reverend Upton agreed to it. The only condition he made was that Lisbeth and Dodd get married and make it official. Your mother accepted that because of the baby.'

Amy nodded.

'The other thing Mrs Upton insisted was that Lisbeth sent her sister, Rose, along to the Manse to work in her place.'

'So that was why Rose went to work at the Manse?'

'That's right. But it put your mother in a right bind. She didn't know whether to send her sister to Mrs Upton, partly because the girl was not much more than a child herself, also because she knew how odd and highly strung Mrs Upton was at times. And then, of course, there was Amos. On the other hand, it was a job for the little lass, and a good one at that. I think Lisbeth hoped and prayed that when she and Amos married, he'd mend his ways and wouldn't start his games with young Rose. Only thirteen she was – the sweet child.' Miss Jones sighed and shook her head. 'Some men never change, do they?'

'Some men never do.' Amy said, taking a deep breath. 'Tell me what happened at the Manse after my mother left.'

Leaning back in her chair, the woman continued. 'I guess you can imagine. Everything was fine at first. Mrs Upton was in her element with a young girl fussing around her. And she fussed around the lass like a mother hen. Because of the cold, the pair of them was indoors most of the time. As for the Reverend, providing he was left alone, he was happy. As for me, well, I'd got the kitchen and that's where I stayed. And Dodd wasn't allowed in there, I'm pleased to say.'

'But what happened between him and Rose?'

'There was nothing to see for quite a while, then it developed slowly, like mould on a piece of cheese. You tend to ignore it at first then suddenly it's green all over. He was polite at first. But it was put on. Then he started fussing over her. Talking to her every chance he got. Silly talk. Always trying to impress her. But I think your mother had warned her what he was like, because she used to spend all her time indoors. Of course he wasn't allowed in the house and young Rose managed to keep her distance from him for over three months.

'But Dodd was cunning,' she said. 'He never missed a trick. He'd be out there if Rose had errands to run or washing to peg out on the line. He'd lurk about in the garden and stalk her every time she went anywhere. But she was a smart lass and wilful, and she wouldn't give in to him. She told me he'd tried to grab her twice and drag her into his shed but said she'd managed to get away, but that made him downright angry. I told her she should tell the Reverend but she was afraid she might lose her job. As for Dodd, you could see him simmering, ready to boil over. It was obvious what he wanted and he couldn't get it. I tell you, it was a terrible atmosphere to live and work in.'

'How did Rose die, Miss Jones?'

The elderly woman took several deep breaths. 'There was a fire. The garden shed burnt down.' She pulled a handkerchief from her sleeve and screwed it around in her hands. 'Unrecognizable, she was when they brought her out. She was burnt to a crisp. Dodd pretended he was upset. Said she must have been looking for something in his shed and knocked the lamp over but I didn't believe a word of it.'

'What happened to him?'

'Nothing happened right away. The Reverend and I were concerned about Mrs Upton and the effect it had on her. She started behaving stranger than ever. Seeing things and hearing things, she was. It was quite scary. As for Amos Dodd, no one saw him for two weeks. Then the Reverend got word that the police had caught up with him in Wakefield. They brought him back to Leeds and charged him with Rose's murder. Of course he denied it, but at the inquest the doctor, who'd examined her remains, said her wrists had rope fibres burnt into the skin. He also said that she'd burned up more than the rest of the shed. It was like someone had deliberately set her on fire. He must have tied her up and doused her with paraffin!'

'God help us!'

'I warned you, lass, some things are best left unsaid.' After taking a few moments to calm herself, she continued. 'That was the end of the cook's job for me. That was when I came to stay with my niece here in Saltaire. They closed up the Manse when they carted Mrs Upton off to the asylum at Menston. She spent five years there. If I hadn't recognized her dress, I wouldn't have known her when she came out. White like a ghost, she was, both face and hair, and she walked like one of them undead.' She shuddered again. 'She's still alive. She's in a nursing home not far from here. I go and visit her occasionally. Very sad indeed.'

Amy nodded slowly. 'What happened to Reverend Upton?'

'I never saw him again after he asked me to pack his bags and books. After the trial, he went off to Colchester or Winchester or some such place to take up a post at the university. He was teaching theology of all things! I reckon I could teach him a thing or two about godliness!'

'And did you ever see my mother again after that?'

'Aye, just once, at Rose's funeral. There were a lot of people there, but Lisbeth wasn't interested in well-wishers. I felt so sorry for her. Almost full-term, she was, and her clothes hardly fitted. She looked terrible. I spoke to her when the service was over and offered to help if I could. But she was in such a state, what with losing her little sister, Rose, and with the baby due any tick of the clock, there was nothing I could say or do that would help. She told me then that she hated Amos and the last thing she wanted was to have his baby. She told me what she was going to do, but made me promise I'd pass it on to nobody. In all these years, I never broke my promise, but as your mother's dead and gone, I suppose I can tell you now.'

'Please,' Amy said.

'She told me she was going to see the man who had delivered that little blond-haired infant to Mrs Upton.'

Amy looked puzzled. 'Do you think she was going to ask him to take her baby?'

'I don't know what she had in mind. And I didn't ask.'

'Do you know where I can find this man?'

'I don't. All I know was that he lived in Roundhay. Lisbeth told me it was somewhere near the park. She'd been there several times delivering those letters.'

'I don't suppose you know his name.'

'Oh, yes,' she said. 'I remember that. It was written on the card he handed me the first time he called. His name was Ogilvy, Mr Charles Ogilvy.'

Chapter 15

Charles Ogilvy

For two days, Amy considered the cook's words and, though she knew Helen sensed something was troubling her, she never mentioned the conversation. Nor did she mention it to Harold when he called that day after work.

Though she still wanted to get away from her father, unravelling the mystery lurking in the past now seemed more pressing. It was a chance to find out what secrets her mother had taken with her to that six-foot plot of unconsecrated ground.

Maybe Mr Ogilvy could fill in the missing jigsaw pieces – no matter how dark they were. Nothing could be worse than the conversation she'd had with Miss Jones so now she was prepared for anything.

During the previous weeks while she'd been busy working on the barge, thoughts of her father had slowly been pushed to the back of her mind and her feeling of fear had ebbed. She'd heard no word of him in almost a month and thought it unlikely she would bump into him in Leeds but that was a chance she must take. There was no choice. She had to go back to the city. It was the only way to get to the truth.

'Are you sure about this, lass?' Joel asked, after Amy finished telling him and Helen the cook's story. 'Seems daft going back into the lion's den when you're safe and sound with us here. Why not wait and speak to Harold. He'll be here in the morning to go fetch the horse with Ben. Talk with him. He'll listen and he'll know what's best to do. And if it means going back to the city then maybe he'll go with you.'

'I can't wait,' said Amy anxiously. 'I've been thinking about it since I talked to Miss Jones and I know I have to go even though I don't know what I'll discover.'

Joel shook his head. 'Well, it's your life, Amy lass, but I think you're foolish. And I reckon Harold would agree with me on this score.'

'How do you plan to get to Leeds?' Helen said.

'I'll walk there – along the towing path.'

'Now that's the daftest thing I've heard yet. You're planning to walk the way you came, when round every corner, under every bridge and behind every bush you'll be thinking your father's waiting to grab you. You'll scare yourself silly!'

Amy looked at Helen for support. 'I have to go.'

'Don't try to stop her, Joel,' Helen said. 'It's best she finds out what she needs to know. Only then can she put it to rest. Tell me, luv, when you've seen this man, Mr Ogilvy, where will you stay in Leeds? You'll not get your business over and done with in time to get back to Saltaire the same day.'

'I'll stay with the Medleys. They were neighbours on the street near Fanshaw's Mill. Mrs Medley will let me stay with them for a night or two.'

'All right,' said Helen. 'When you go you'll wear my bonnet and skirt so you look like a boatwoman and not a mill lass. And you'll take money for your fare,' she said, handing Joel his purse. 'You've earned a few shillings with the work you've done on the boat.'

'When are you taking this trip?' Joel asked glumly.

'Tomorrow morning. I'll catch the early train.'

'And when will we expect you back?'

'I'll be back on Monday, I promise.'

The journey to Leeds didn't take long. Gazing at the canal from the train window, Amy thought back to her trek to Saltaire and the state she was in when she met the family on *Milkwort*. How lucky she had been.

From Leeds the journey to Roundhay, though much shorter, took longer than she had anticipated. Having reached the area, she then had to find where her mother's old landlord lived. She was fairly confident that with a tongue in her head, the local shopkeepers or the postmaster would be able to direct her to his house. Unfortunately, not being familiar with that part of Leeds, Amy hadn't taken into account the types of residences in the area. Many of the houses in

Roundhay were big and fancy. Many stood in their own grounds surrounded by well-kept gardens and stone walls. Iron gates, reminiscent of those at Fanshaw's Mill, blocked some entrances. The streets of slightly less opulent houses seemed to stretch for miles, and shops were few and far between. On finding a grocer's shop, she enquired if the shopkeeper knew where Mr Ogilvy lived. The man seemed suspicious of the strangely dressed girl asking after the premises of a gentleman and said he didn't know. She got the same response from the next two shops she tried.

It was the coalman just finishing his rounds, who stopped his cart and gave Amy directions. He remembered Mr Ogilvy well. He was the gentleman who gave him a couple of shillings each Christmas.

A small kindly lady answered the door at the Roundhay residence. She smiled sympathetically when she saw Amy. 'You'd be looking for Mr Ogilvy, I presume?'

'Yes.'

'Does he know you are coming?'

'No, I don't expect so.'

'Don't worry, I'll tell him you're here. What's your name, young lady?'

'Amy Dodd.'

'I'll be back in two shakes.'

The porch was remarkably warm with the sun shining directly through the glass, in fact it was more of a small conservatory than a porch with two cane chairs and a table on one side. In the centre of the table was a large, round glass bowl with two orange fish swimming in circles. Amy had seen plenty of fish at the markets hung up by the gills, and dead ones floating on the surface of the canal, but she'd never seen live ones swimming in a bowl on a table. She wondered why they were there. They were too small to eat.

'Amy, please come through into my study,' Charles Ogilvy called.

The housekeeper stood back, and smiled again, as Amy followed the elderly man down the hall.

'Two teas, Mrs Smith, please.'

The room, at the back of the house, was austere and colourless. The curtains were chocolate velvet and the armchairs a dark-walnut shade of leather. Scores of books vied for places on the two tall bookcases and more were hidden behind the swirling green glass doors of the chiffonier. Apart from the portrait of a young woman above the fireplace, there were no ornaments to brighten the room, no sprays of roses painted on the walls, not even a pattern on the wallpaper. Though it was summer and the porch had been very warm, the sun hardly ever reached to this side of the house and the air was cold.

Mr Ogilvy's manner, however, compensated for the chill. 'Please sit down,' he said, showing Amy to a chair. 'You look well, Amy. But tell me, what brings you here?'

'Are you my father, Mr Ogilvy?'

The man was startled by the question. 'Goodness! No, girl. Whatever gave you that idea?'

Amy suddenly felt deflated; foolish and embarrassed. Since she had spoken with the old cook, the silly notion had been festering in her head. A notion that something had transpired between her mother and the man to whom she had delivered Mrs Upton's letters. For Amy, the idea seemed quite feasible. He had provided a home for her mother and her for almost eighteen years. And the thought that Amos Dodd was not her father appealed to her. And it wasn't just the conversations or wishful thinking that had led her to consider the idea. After all, she looked nothing like her father in build, or face, or eyes, or the colour of her hair.

'I'm sorry,' she said, wiping the tears on the cuff of her blouse. 'I've been told some terrible truths recently about my father and the horrible way Rose, my mother's sister, died. I was told that before I was born that my mother had nowhere to go and you were the only person she asked to see. I thought perhaps you were my father and not Amos Dodd. I wished you were, because I hate my real father.'

Mr Ogilvy handed Amy a handkerchief and waited until her sobbing stopped.

'I'm sorry that you feel like that. Are you living with your father?'

'Not for more than a month. He made me work and took all my money so I ran away from him. I think you know what sort of man he is.'

Mr Ogilvy nodded. 'Where are you staying now, Amy?'

'In Saltaire. On a barge on the canal with a family of canal folk.'

'Then I am pleased you are free of him.'

'I don't know if I am free. I heard he was searching for me, trying to find me.'

'Then why have you come back to Leeds?'

Amy looked into his eyes. 'I came to see you. I spoke to a lady who told me that you helped my mother. I know that was the case after I was born, because you provided her with the cellar to live in. But I want to know what happened when she came to you after Rose had been buried and Amos Dodd had been locked away in Armley Jail. She had no one to turn to, but she came to you. Did she want you to take her baby? Did she have me in the workhouse?'

'Who suggested you speak to me? Surely it wasn't Mrs Upton? I gather she is not a well woman?'

'No, it was their cook. She was at the Manse when—'

'When those tragic events happened.'

Amy nodded, just when the housekeeper interrupted them with a tray of tea and sandwiches. Amy didn't realize how hungry she was until she saw the food on the plate.

'Cold pork,' the housekeeper announced.

'Please help yourself, Amy. Mrs Smith knows I don't eat a great deal, yet she is forever bringing me extra morsels.' He stood up and faced the window, his fingers intertwined behind his back. Outside a passing breeze fluttered the leaves on the beech tree but the branches remained motionless. There was no sound save the ticking of the clock in the hall.

'Did my mother come to see you after my father went to jail?'

'She did.'

'Did she want you to take her baby and find it another home?'

'She did,' he said, turning to face her.

Amy caught her breath. 'She didn't want me, then?'

'Amy,' he said, drawing up a straight chair. 'Believe me when I say, it's not as simple as that. I have witnessed instances like that dozens of times. Your mother was distraught. Her sister had suffered a horrible death. Her husband had been convicted of the heinous crime of murder and sent to jail for life. Her past employer had been certified insane. She was only seventeen years of age with no family or obvious means of support. On top of that she was due to have a child within days. When Lisbeth Dodd came to me she was at her wits' end. She didn't know what she wanted but I could see she needed help. Taking a child from her as soon as it was born would only have added to her despair.'

'But you were able to help her, though?'

'In a small way,' he said, leaning back. 'I arranged for her to see a midwife and directed her to a place where she could have the baby.'

'Was it the workhouse?'

'No, it was a home for unmarried mothers.'

'Are you a doctor or something?'

Charles Ogilvy smiled sadly. 'Unfortunately, no. My roles over the years have been several, but have included a seat on the Board of Governors of various charitable organizations, one being a home for unmarried mothers – for girls who, for one reason or another, had become pregnant. It was from this very establishment that a child was procured for the Reverend and Mrs Upton at the Manse, which you mentioned. Unfortunately that particular arrangement did not work out well.'

'So, you arranged for a midwife for my mother, and for her to have the cellar room to live in after I was born.'

Mr Ogilvy pondered over his answer. 'Yes, I did.'

'And that is all that there is to know?'

'Did you expect something different?'

Amy sighed. 'I wanted it to be different. I wanted you to be my father. I want anyone to be my father other than Amos Dodd.'

With his warm eyes on her, she could feel his sympathy, but she also felt lost and disillusioned. Mr Ogilvy had been her only hope of learning the truth but he could tell her nothing.

Sensing her disappointment, Mr Ogilvy excused himself, walked over to the desk and took out a sheet of paper. After writing something on it, he placed it in Amy's hand.

'The home for unmarried mothers, which I mentioned, was closed several years ago due to lack of financial support. I believe the building still stands, but it has fallen into disrepair. Such a shame,' he said, shaking his head. 'What I have written here is the address of the midwife who attended your mother. Her name is Mrs Sneddon. If you decide to visit her, I don't know what condition you will find her in. Let me warn you, she is now an old woman. She is also a drunkard. If you choose to speak to her, I suggest you call around noon. And if she asks you for money, you would do her a favour by not giving her any. She will only waste it on drink. A gift of food would be better.'

Amy looked puzzled. 'But what can she tell me that you haven't said already?'

'I cannot say. My advice is, speak to her. She was there when you were born. There may be things about your birth that you should know.'

'What things? You must tell me! Did my mother have twins? Do I have a brother or a sister somewhere? Tell me, please, I must know!'

He paused, choosing his words carefully, 'All I will say is this, Lisbeth Dodd was a good woman, and a good mother, and for all the years I knew her, I know she loved you dearly.'

'And I loved her more than words can tell. She was the only family I had.'

'She was indeed.'

'What are you saying?' Amy asked.

Mr Ogilvy hesitated a moment. 'I believe Amos Dodd was not your father.'

Amy was lost for words. It was the best news she had ever heard. She didn't care who her father was. He could be anyone. But he wasn't Amos Dodd.

'But,' he added, before she had chance to respond, 'there is more.' He paused again and took a deep breath. 'I have reason to believe that Lisbeth Dodd was not your mother.'

As a swirl of light-headedness smothered her thoughts, Amy swayed on the chair. She could feel her cheeks tighten as the blood flowed from them. She couldn't comprehend what he was saying. Lisbeth Dodd was not her mother? Then a torrent of memories started tumbling into her head: conversations, hugs, Christmases, bath times in front of the fire, songs her mother had sung to her, arguments they had had over silly things.

'What are you saying?' she cried. 'I came here longing to hear the news that Dodd was not my father, but this – I didn't come to hear this!'

'I'm sorry, Amy, it is something which, if you hadn't come here, I would have never revealed.' He repeated his words gently. 'I believe Lisbeth Dodd is not your mother, but, let me add, I am not sure. The only person who knows the truth is Mrs Sneddon. She was with your mother when she gave birth – the day you were born.'

Chapter 16

No One's Child

If Amos Dodd was not her father and Lisbeth Eccles not her mother, then she belonged to no one.

What had happened the day she was born? Where did her mother go to have her? If she wasn't her mother's child, then whose child was she? Did Mr Ogilvy really know the truth and was he purposely withholding that information? Had he something to hide? Had money changed hands?

So many questions were bombarding her brain when she left Charles Ogilvy's house. She had no recollections of saying goodbye, of fainting in the sun-porch due to the heat, or of the hug the housekeeper gave her when she helped her with her coat.

She didn't remember how she found her way into Roundhay Park or notice the hours slip by as she sat gazing into the lake. She was, however, conscious of the still water, black and inviting, just like the canal. Like a dark winter blanket, she could easily slide under it; hide from her past and block out the words she didn't want to hear.

Sitting, alone on the grass, she remembered there were things her mother had always promised to tell her, but never did. Why did she wait so long? Amy wondered. Was she afraid I would have loved her any less? Surely not? Lisbeth Dodd was everything to her. Then she thought about Amos Dodd. Was she afraid that if I knew the truth, I would tell him that he was not my father?

So whose child did her mother carry? Was it his? Or was she pregnant to another man? She hardly dared imagine what would have happened if that had been the case.

A family of ducks swam towards her, her fanning the dark surface with tiny ripples. The adults quacked, demanding attention. When they received nothing, they swam further along the bank, the ducklings paddling desperately behind in an effort to keep up.

Had Charles Ogilvy told her the truth when he said he wasn't her father? And if he wasn't, why had he allowed her mother to live rent free for almost eighteen years? Would a man do that if he was not in some way responsible? Surely no man was so charitable to forgo income for so many years? Yet, from the little she had seen of him, Mr Ogilvy was just that – kind-hearted and charitable, a man of principle. Though he lived in a large house, he did not live to excess and the trappings in his room were not those of a spendthrift. The same questions kept emerging. Was Charles Ogilvy hiding something? Did he really know the full story? Was his honest appearance merely a deceitful ploy? She had heard he'd arrived at the Manse alone on the day he delivered the infant to Mrs Upton. Strange, she thought, for a man to bring the child. Even stranger, the fact he called back and took it away. Strange there was no nurse or nanny to accompany him. Were his dealings with orphan infants legal? Was he in the business of buying and selling babies?

A thousand and one thoughts whirled through Amy's head, but one cold fact always emerged – Amos Dodd was not her father! And if he was not her father, then he had no right to claim her, chastise her or make her work for him. If she could prove that fact then she would be free of him. But proving it would not be easy. Speaking with the midwife was the first step and from what Mr Ogilvy said, Mrs Sneddon may hold the key to the truth.

The sound of tram's wheels screeching along metal lines and the *ding-ding* of a bell brought Amy to her senses. In front of her were the steps to the Corn Exchange building and from its splendid dome, a mob of pigeons fluttered down to the pavement, settling around the feet of a shabbily dressed woman broadcasting crumbs from an old cane basket. A group of men standing near the entrance to a private club talked, while smoke from their cigars swirled around their top hats like smoke from a chimney stack. They ignored the boy who held out his cap hoping for a spare coin. Across the road, the old lady selling posies smiled. Standing in her regular spot, she waited patiently for trade to come to her. Most folk were in high spirits. It was the weekend.

Instinct had brought Amy safely back to the city. But where should she go from here? Her plan had been to stay the night with the Medleys, but for a moment she considered trying to find Mrs Sneddon. Then she remembered what Mr Ogilvy had told her. It would be futile to visit the old midwife in the evening. Accepting his advice, she decided to wait till the following day and go at noon. She would stick to her original plan and go to the Medley's house.

Walking back along the road beside the mill brought mixed memories. Fanshaw's iron gates of were still open though work had finished earlier that afternoon. Amy shook her head. It was Saturday – the day that the cost of a week's labour was exchanged for a jug of misery and heartache. It was a ritual played out in most alehouses in the mill towns of Yorkshire, and The Hungry Crow was no exception. With the smell of the public bar already in her nostrils, she pulled Helen's bonnet forwards over her eyes and kept her head bowed. She had no alternative but to pass directly in front of the Crow on the way to the Medleys' house'.

A cat meowed, from a window-sill, but Amy never looked up. A small girl sitting on a doorstep smiled shyly. A couple walked by arm-in-arm, talking quietly.

How nice it will be to see the Medleys, she thought, visualizing their compact kitchen, crowded with children, and the smell of fresh tarts straight from the oven oozing with lemon curd. She would ask Mrs Medley if she could stay for two nights and on Monday morning she'd catch the early train back to Saltaire. She knew Helen would worry, if she didn't arrive back as promised.

'Well, look what we have here! If it isn't Amy Dodd!' The voice, like a breath from the grave, sent a chill through Amy's spine. He was on the pavement not more than five yards ahead of her – legs apart, hands on hips – waiting. A half-smile twisted his lips, as he spoke. 'Decided to come back to your father, did you?'

'You are not my father!' she yelled at the top of her voice. 'And you can't make me work for you.'

'Huh!' he scoffed.

'Do you understand? I'm not your daughter and I'll prove it!' She wanted to sound triumphant, but when she announced her news, her voice fell flat and emotionless. 'Did you hear what I said?'

Amos Dodd's answer was to latch his hand around her wrist and almost pull her off her feet. 'You dare cross me, you little bitch!' he said, swinging his other hand across her face. 'I'll teach you to run away from me.'

Amy grabbed her bonnet. 'You can't make me work for you,' she cried. 'You're not my father!'

'What do I care whose brat you are?' he said, dragging her along the pavement.

'Let her alone!' a woman shouted from her doorway.

'You mind your own bloody business, else I'll give you a dose of what she's going to get. Tried to run off from her father, she did. Ungrateful little hussy!' He sounded convincing.

'He's not my father!' Amy yelled.

The sting of his hand across her cheek sent her reeling, but he pulled her back to her feet and towed her behind him. Across the street, a young couple with a pram stopped and looked. The woman whispered to her husband then they hurried on not wanting to get involved.

It was pointless to shout on a Saturday night. House doors remained shut to a woman's wails. If a man chose to chastise his own daughter then it was likely she'd been misbehaving, in which case she deserved it. Most folk stayed indoors and minded their own business.

Amy knew he was taking her back to the room they had shared after her mother died. If only Mr Ogilvy had let her stay in the cellar and her father had been forced to go elsewhere. If only her mother had not died. If only Amos Dodd had died in jail. Or even better, if only he'd been hung for his crime.

The cat squealed, as he kicked it from the doorway. Three boys, playing in the street, stopped and watched.

'Out of the way!' he bellowed, to the landlady.

'In a bit of a hurry are you? Not even so much as a beg-your-pardon or by-your-leave.'

'Bugger off, you old bat. Keep out of my way. I've paid for my lodgings.'

Amy's feet hardly touched the steps as he dragged her along behind him up the three flights to the attic. As the door banged behind them, he turned her around.

She never felt the punch that knocked her out.

When she awoke, she found it hard to breathe. A rag was tied tightly across her mouth. Her tongue was swollen and the taste of blood filtered through her nose. She couldn't move her hands because her wrists were tied to the bed's head posts. She felt helpless, but was relieved that there was no sign of Amos Dodd. No doubt, he would have found the money Joel had given her and headed off to the Crow. Was the return train ticket still safe in her pocket? She wondered.

Sharp at eight o'clock on Saturday, Harold strolled along the canal path towards Jentz's old dock. It was a lovely morning and the good weather promised to attract hundreds of visitors to the Glen that afternoon.

He was looking forward to the day's outing with young Ben to collect Mallow. It was several miles to Skipton, and even though he knew it would take most of the day, he intended for them to walk the distance there and back. A jaunt along the river bank would make a change from his usual hikes across Baildon Moor.

Walking the horse back along the towing path would be a new experience for him and it would provide Ben an opportunity to acquaint himself with his new animal before harnessing it to the barge. From his childhood, Harold had always loved horses, so what a treat it would be walking back along the canal, beside the boy and the boat-horse.

Striding out, he considered the letter in his pocket and was pleased at the thought he had some interesting news to share with Amy. Hopefully, when he and Ben got back, there would be time to take her for a ride on the tram.

The still water of the canal glinted in the sun, reflecting the buildings like images on a photograph. Bees buzzed busily on the wild flowers colouring the banks. On the waterway a pair of richly coloured mallards swam apart, while an empty barge chugged slowly by, leaving a stream of smoke to dissolve into the otherwise clear sky.

Harold was looking forward to seeing Amy and considered asking if she would like to accompany them for the day. He hoped she would agree.

'Good morning,' he called, when he caught sight of Ben sitting on the deck, but when he waved, the boy got up and disappeared into the cabin. A moment later, Helen appeared.

'What's wrong?' Harold asked.

'Amy's gone to Leeds.'

'What?'

'She left this morning – only an hour ago.'

'What on earth for?'

'She was talking to the lady from the tea shop during the week. It seems there's more to Amos Dodd than meets the eye. And there's a man in Leeds who knows more about him. He also knew Amy's mother. She'd gone to find him.'

'And you let her go alone?'

Helen looked guilty. 'She promised she'd be back on Monday.'

Joel appeared from the cabin, dragging his foot along the deck. He straightened as he slipped the crutch under his arm and leaned up against the cabin roof. 'She's got a mind of her own, that girl, and so she should have. There's a dark side to that man Dodd, and Amy wants to know the truth, especially if there's a chance he's not her father. If she can get him out of her life, she'll rest easier in bed at night. But it don't make it no less of a worry, her going off on her own.' He rubbed his leg. 'I couldn't go with her and besides I think she wanted to go alone.'

'Did she have money with her – for fares, I mean?'

'Aye, she did,' said Helen. 'I made sure of that. And she'll be safe. She's going to stay with a family by the name of Medley. They were neighbours in the street near the mill.'

'That's good,' said Harold. 'I know Moses Medley. He's a gentle-giant of a fellow. Good-hearted bloke who works in the warehouse at Fanshaw's. I'm glad Amy will be staying with them.'

After a cup of strong tea and piece of warm teacake running with honey, Harold and Ben set off for the Gate and Gander Inn at Skipton. Since hearing of Amy's decision to go to Leeds, Harold's enthusiasm for the trip had waned. Now he wished he was not committed to collecting the horse, but he knew Joel didn't want Ben to go on his own. He had offered his services in good faith and wouldn't go back on his word. But now he wanted to get to Skipton and get back as quickly as possible so that he could catch a train to Leeds that afternoon. The pair of them would still have to walk the horse back along the canal, but if they caught the train to the market town instead of walking there, it would save them at least three hours. Ben didn't object to the chance of travelling on a train.

Having started the day feeling elated, Harold now felt angry. If only Amy had told him and waited. He had been planning to go to Leeds on Monday and if Amy hadn't left, they could have travelled together and he could have made sure she arrived safely.

The big part-shire was as meek as a kitten and didn't object to being bridled and blinkered. In fact, Mallow appreciated the attention. The enforced rest had improved her condition and her black coat shone in the sun. She was rested and ready to work again.

'Wait till we get her home,' Ben said. 'I'll plait up her mane and comb her feathers. And when I dress her in her collar and brasses, and add the swingers and terrets, she'll look a real picture.'

Harold could understand how pleased Ben was.

On the way back, they stopped briefly at the Five Rise in Bingley and Harold chatted to a boatman locking through the gates while Ben gave the lock-keeper a hand. The man obviously knew the boy well.

As they strode at a steady pace, Ben talked about locks, their names and numbers, the ones that leaked or jammed and the mishaps that had occurred on the cut. His knowledge of the navigations from one coast to the other amazed Harold. But Ben had been born on a short-boat, he'd ridden a boat-horse before he could walk, and walked on the towing path since the time he could toddle. The canal and its banks were his home.

He told Harold how Amy was teaching him to read. That he planned to read to his mother one day.

In turn, Harold told him about the letter he had written applying for a job with the Chilean government.

'What sort of job?' Ben asked.

'Building tramways.'

'Like the one at Shipley Glen?'

'Much grander than that,' he said.

'Is that place far from here?'

'Chile,' Harold said. 'It's at the other side of the globe almost.'

'Is it like Yorkshire with canals and coal mines and factories and farms?'

Harold smiled. 'Quite different, I think. It's got mines, but they dig for silver and gold, and emeralds, and it has got rivers that thunder down from great snow-capped mountains that reach high into the clouds. But it's got good farmland too on the hillsides. A wonderful place to grow grapes, I would say.'

'How will you get to Chile?' Ben asked.

'On a sailing ship. Or maybe a steamer,' Harold replied. 'It's a bit like the canals. Things are changing very fast these days. Soon there'll be no sailing ships crossing the ocean.'

'I saw some big ships down at Grimsby. We took the barge down the river once, but when the sea waves came in with the tide, they rolled over the deck and I was afraid the sea might sink us, but Pa got us through. I bet the waves in the ocean are really big.'

'I imagine they are,' said Harold.

Mallow snorted.

On the opposite bank a tree had fallen gouging a large chunk out of the canal's wall. Over time, it had become lined with silt, and reeds had grown from the mud, creating a tiny beach. A swan, who had adopted it for her nest, was busy tending five grey cygnets.

Ben rested the horse for a while and they watched for a few moments, but no sooner had they set off again than the swan's squawking made them turn. With wings flapping and head outstretched, the swan was heading over the field after a fox, which had one of her cygnets in its jaw.

'Cunning,' Harold said. 'He waited until we passed before pouncing.' But how cunning was Amos Dodd? That man had a black streak running through his heart. He was equally as cunning and dangerous too, just like a fox.

Chapter 17

Amy's back

In the attic, Amy struggled to loosen the ropes binding her hands to the bed but they cut deep into her wrists. Her fingers felt hard and swollen. As she tried to turn, her stomach hurt from the punches he'd thrown at her. As she leaned back against the bed head, exhausted, the image of the man she hated flashed through her brain – his twisted smile, his pale eyes and the tarry black wart stuck on the top of his bald head. She thought about her mother, Lisbeth Dodd, the only mother she had known and was thankful, at least, that she was not the child of that horrible man.

How alone it made her feel. She had despised him when she thought he was her father. Now she hated him even more. But she also feared him. Having learned the extent of his evil, she could only imagine what lengths he would go to to get rid of her.

She didn't know what the time was, or how long she had been there. The day was still bright outside so perhaps only an hour, she thought. Her mouth was dry and she wanted a drink. Surely he didn't intend to leave her there and not come back? Or did he?

The cloth across her mouth prevented her from screaming and her jaw ached from the pressure on it. Tears no longer flowed but the dread of what would happen when he returned was foremost in her mind.

As she began rocking, the iron frame bounced rhythmically against the wall. If she made sufficient noise, she thought someone might hear. Swaying backwards and forwards as far as her bindings would allow, Amy continued relentlessly. *Bang. Bang. Bang.* But no one came. Could no one in the building hear her? Her head hit the bed head every time she threw it back, and though the exercise was tiring her, she kept going.

'What the hell is going on up here!' It was a woman's voice. 'Can't you give it a rest for a spell?'

Amy listened as footsteps pounded up the stairs. She heard a key rattle in the lock and welcomed the sound of the hinges rasping as the door was pushed open.

'What the—!' The words trailed away, when she saw Amy tied to the bed. 'The lout!' she said. 'All the same, they are. Bastards every one of them!'

Amy recognized the woman but doubted she'd remembered her face or the rations she'd sold her for sixpence over a month ago. Likely a lot of lasses passed through her premises hiring rooms by the hour both by night and by day.

'How long has he had you trussed up like this?' she said, as she slowly unfastened the rag. 'I'll need a knife to cut these.'

Even with the gag removed from her mouth, Amy couldn't speak. Her jaw was stiff. Her throat raw. She needed a drink. 'Hurry,' she tried to call, as the woman trundled down the stairs, but her cry was no more than a whisper. Fearing Dodd could return anytime, she continued desperately pulling at the ropes, the bed head banging against the wall.

'Hold your horses – I'm coming as quick as I can!' the landlady mumbled, puffing on the stairs. Wielding a large pair of scissors, which seemed hardly sharp enough to cut the rind off a slice of bacon, she worried the blade into the knots and cut through the twisted hessian. Amy's arms and shoulders hurt when she tried to fold them across her chest. Her hands were swollen and red and when she stood, her legs were weak. The water on the dresser was tempting but the moths' wings put her off. She cupped her hands and swilled it across her face then sucked a mouthful into the back of her throat, gargled with it and spat it out onto the floor.

'Hey, watch what you're doing!' the woman yelled.

Amy didn't reply, as she grabbed Helen's bonnet and rushed through the door.

'There's gratitude for you!' the voice called from the attic.

Amy hobbled down the stairs as fast as she could. There was no time to stop and say thank you.

The late afternoon train leaving Saltaire was packed. Even most of the first class seats were taken. The majority of the passengers were weary, but happy, after spending a day at the Glen. Only the small children were silent but they were soon fast asleep on their mothers' laps or on the floor of the compartment.

Harold Lister was pleased to have a seat, but his mood was sombre. The more he thought about Amy, the angrier he felt. He was angry with Joel for letting her go to Leeds alone, though he knew the boatman would've had little chance of stopping her. He was angry with himself also for not offering her more help. And why hadn't she spoken to him first? Why didn't she wait just one more day? They could have travelled to Leeds together. He could have arranged for her to have a room in the small hotel where he lodged. She'd have been safe there as it was a pleasant place where only respectable people stayed. She'd have had time to do all the things she wanted, and he wouldn't have bothered her. He knew he would have been busy at Fanshaw's, but at least he'd have been close by in case she needed his help.

The most he could do now was find her and make sure she was settled at the Medleys' house and in no immediate danger.

From the street, the sound of voices drifted into the kitchen.

> *Amy Dodd, slung her hook*
> *Set a fire, run amuck*
> *Took off like a butcher's dog*
> *You'll ne'er catch our Amy Dodd!*

Mrs Medley jumped up from her knees and raised her fist to the three boys in the street. 'Didn't I tell you lads to stop singing that song? Amy Dodd's not here no more, and you'll not be calling people behind their backs, especially when what you're saying ain't true.'

'Aye, missus,' the biggest boy said boldly, 'but she *is* back. We saw her, not far from here, early this afternoon.'

'What did you say?' Mrs Medley asked, the holystone she'd been rubbing the step with clasped in her hand.

The three lads stood their ground as she hurried across the cobbles towards them. Their expressions looked somewhat sheepish. 'We weren't giving you no cheek, missus. Honest!'

'And I'm not accusing you of it, lad. I want to know exactly where you saw Amy. Are you sure it was her?'

'Sure we're sure! She lived on this street, didn't she?'

'Anyway,' the little one added, 'them words ain't right. Rhyme says they'll never catch her.'

Mrs Medley looked at him quizzically. 'What do you mean?'

'Well, they did. We saw the man who caught her and dragged her off.'

'What man, for God's sake?'

The boy shrugged his shoulders and looked at his companions for help.

'Dunno,' one of them replied. 'Didn't take much notice of him. Must have been someone from t'mill, because he weren't a bobby.'

Mrs Medley spun her head around. Her son was standing in the doorway. 'Jimmy! Go get your da. Tell him it's urgent. Tell him it's about young Amy. And you three,' she said, turning back to the boys, 'Don't you dare move. Stay right where you are and when Mr Medley comes out, you take him to where you saw this fella with Amy. Do you hear me?'

Seeing the stone gripped tightly in her fist, the boys stood rooted to the spot. They hardly even blinked.

A few minutes later, the three boys were trooping along the street with Mr Medley following close on their heels. A short distance from The Hungry Crow the boys stopped.

'That's the house with the moggie on the doorstep!'

'You sure, lad?'

'Certain. The fella kicked it out of the road when he dragged Amy inside.'

Mr Medley reached into his coat pocket. 'Here, lads,' he said, pulling three sweets from the inside pocket, 'take this for your trouble. Now, get on your way and say nothing to no one.' With that, he glanced at the building, turned and hurried back towards home. He had to get help.

As he walked towards Fanshaw's Mill from the station, Harold consciously tried to improve his mood. He wanted to see Amy and, though he was concerned, he didn't want her to see his frustrations.

On the streets, the children peered at the smartly dressed stranger, wondering why he was visiting that area. Well-dressed men were often bailiffs or lawyers or rent men and were best to be avoided. Few of them ever brought good news to that neighbourhood.

It was not hard to discover which house the Medleys lived at. Everyone around Fanshaw's knew them.

Mrs Medley was very cautious when Harold knocked on the door and introduced himself.

'I'm a friend of Amy Dodd,' he said. 'And I've come to pay a visit. Wanted to make sure she was all right.'

'Then I hope you haven't come too late,' Mrs Medley said anxiously, peering down the street, before ushering him into the living room. 'Outside, you kids,' she ordered.

'Where's Amy?' Harold asked.

'Well, she's not here, as you can see.'

'But she's supposed to be staying with you. She came down on the train from Saltaire early this morning and left word she'd come to you and ask for a bed for two nights. She's supposed to be back in Saltaire on Monday.'

'Is that where you've come from?'

'Yes, Amy and I are friends. Has something happened to her?'

'I'm not sure. We'd not seen hide nor hair of her this past month then, about an hour ago, I heard the kids singing their silly rhymes and discovered they'd seen Amy being dragged off by some fella. Moses, my husband, reckons it must have been her father, Amos Dodd, and that he's got her locked up in a boarding house near the mill.'

'Where?' Harold shouted, as he jumped up. 'Tell me, where?'

'It's on the same street as The Hungry Crow. My Moses should be there right now. He went to get a crowbar and a couple of strong lads to help him. They'll find her and get her out, trust me, even if they have to break the door down.' Mrs Medley shook her head. 'It worries me, though. My husband is a big fellow but he wouldn't harm a flea. Amos Dodd ain't big but he's a strong bugger and nasty too. I'd not like to see him when he's angry.'

Harold thanked Mrs Medley but didn't wait for any more instructions. He knew where the public house was. If Dodd had dragged Amy away, what did he intend to do with her? He couldn't send her back to Fanshaw's to work for him. She'd never get a job there. His main concern was the way Dodd had treated Amy and he wouldn't put anything past him. The man had not spent fifteen years behind bars for nothing.

The three men, talking in the street, touched their caps to Harold when he ran up. They'd spent all their working lives in the yard at Fanshaw's and knew the engineer by sight, though they'd never had occasion to speak to him before. After a brief introduction, Moses Medley thanked his mates and they turned and walked off up the street.

'Where's Amy?' Harold asked.

'She's not here, but she was earlier. That father of hers had her trussed up in the attic like a prize turkey, I'm told. God only knows how long for. But she got away from him, thank goodness, and the woman who runs this place said she's been gone about an hour. She said the man went berserk when he found she'd run. I reckon he's on the prowl again to get her back.'

Harold couldn't hide his desperation. Amos Dodd could have killed her up in that boarding house or done things to her too terrible to consider. Dodd was an evil man who respected no one, not even himself.

But where was Amy now? He'd just come from the Medleys' house, and she wasn't there. Last time she'd run away she'd gone to the canal, even slept under one of the bridges. She may do that again, he thought. She may have begged a lift on a barge or set off walking on the towing path. Then he remembered that she had some money and considered that she may have caught a train back to Saltaire. There were crowds of people at the station earlier and he'd never thought of looking for her. Now he was annoyed with himself for not being more observant.

'I was surprised to see you, Mr Lister,' Medley said, as they walked back to his house. 'Did the mill send you to look for the girl?'

'No,' he said. 'Amy and I became friends in Saltaire. Good friends. But I'll tell you about that later.'

After a drink and a bite to eat with the Medleys, they resumed their search for Amy. Moses volunteered to scour the local streets.

He said he'd search the mill yard if the gates were open. He'd check the schoolyard too and go as far as the main road. Mrs Medley said she'd search near the mill, and the children would help by keeping their eyes and ears open.

Heading down the hill to the canal, Harold checked all the alleys and house yards, fearing the worst. He thought of shouting Amy's name, but was worried she may think it was her father calling. Besides, he didn't want Dodd to know someone else was looking for her.

The canal bank was empty, the water as dark and motionless as ever. Beyond the canal, only a narrow strip of lifeless land separated it from the River Aire which slithered through Leeds like a great grey slug. Gazing at the water, Harold imagined Amy's body floating to the surface. He shuddered at the thought. Please don't let me find her here, he prayed.

It was dusk already and in an hour it would be pitch black. After walking to the city and back, he felt satisfied she wasn't hiding there. He'd checked under all the bridges and seen few signs of life, only a handful of drunks, curled up in the darkness, amongst the litter and rubbish under the bridges.

Wandering wearily back to the Medleys', he hoped there would be better news awaiting him, but he doubted it. If so, he would go back to his room in the hotel, sleep for a while, if he could, and resume his search in the morning. If he didn't find her soon, he feared he may never find her.

Chapter 18

Mrs Sneddon

When Amy ran down the boarding house steps and out into the street, she had no idea where she was heading. All she knew was that she was free. She didn't know what time it was save for the fact it was daylight and there was a smell of cooking in the air.

As she hesitated for a moment to get her bearings, a voice called out; 'I'm looking for a bit of fun. What do you say?'

Ignoring the man, Amy picked up her skirt and looked both ways. Her neighbour's house offered a safe haven and it was only a short distance away, but to get there she must pass the open doors of The Hungry Crow. The fact that her pocket was empty suggested that her father was probably drinking there at that very moment. Amy turned in the opposite direction. She would wind her way through the streets and go down to the canal. She'd been safe there once before and since she'd lived on the barge, the area didn't scare her any more. Besides that, in her present confused state, it was the only place she could think of.

Conscious of her boots clacking on the paving, Amy ran. She was conscious too of kitchen doors wide open to the light and warmth of a summer's long afternoon –conscious of faces peering out, of men sitting out on the doorsteps reading or smoking a pipe. As she ran by they looked up and watched her pass.

'You'll cop it when you get home!' one shouted.

The words hit hard. She had no home. No family. Nowhere to go. And now it seemed nowhere to hide. She knew he'd look for her at the Medleys', and if he asked for her along the street, a dozen eyes couldn't deny they'd seen her hurrying by.

The bridges were the only safe places she knew. The only places she felt certain he wouldn't look.

Pushing her hand into her pocket, she fingered the lining. She already knew the money was gone but she'd forgotten about the ticket. That was missing too. Searching the other pocket, her fingers touched on the piece of paper Mr Ogilvy had given her. She wondered if her father had read the address that was written on it. Would he go there and get to Mrs Sneddon before she did? But he would have no knowledge of the midwife, as Lisbeth had only visited her after he had gone to jail. She remembered her mother had said he couldn't read, and she'd always believed her. Now she wasn't sure. Maybe, during his fifteen years in jail, he'd learned something.

She thought back to the conversation she had had with Mr Ogilvy. He'd advised her to visit Mrs Sneddon around noon. But that meant she'd be walking the streets in broad daylight when everyone would be able to see her. And now her father knew what she was wearing, he would easily recognize her. Perhaps she should go this evening. The night would hide her. But she had no knowledge of the streets or suburb where the woman lived and the only places she could seek help would be at the inns and brothels. Without instructions, she could easily find herself walking around in circles. The streets were no place for a lass at night. And besides, by evening, Mrs Sneddon would be in no fit state for talking. The bridge was her only choice.

Climbing down the metal steps, she stumbled in the shadows. At her feet, a huddled figure, cuddling an empty spirit bottle like it was some cold dead infant, moaned and rolled over. Amy squeezed her nose. The woman's rancid smell turned her stomach.

'You won't mind if I share your accommodation for the night,' Amy said, not expecting an answer. If Mrs Sneddon was in a similar condition then she had made the right decision not to visit her that night.

Close beside the woman was a pile of large posters – adverts for a music hall show that was long gone. They'd obviously been pushed or dropped from the bridge but the wind hadn't had time to lift them into the river. Selecting the cleanest ones, Amy climbed up to the darkest part of the bridge, beneath the arch where there was little more than two feet headroom. After moving the stones from the ground, she spread some of the posters on the dirt and crawled onto them. Then she pulled the other ones over her. Being completely hidden from view, she was sure no one would find her.

The sun had come up very early – too early for Amy's liking and she had no choice but to stay where she was until later. Overnight, she had only slept intermittently, but she felt rested. Now, ravenously hungry, she tried to concentrate her thoughts on positive things. She thought about Harold and the tramway and the day they had met at Shipley Glen; about foreign places and him building bridges and canals and funicular railways. How clever he was. How polite he was. How nicely he spoke and dressed. She envied his upbringing and questioned his reasons for liking her, but felt sure he did.

She thought about Helen and Joel, too, and young Ben. And the Medleys. How good they had been to her. And she thought of her mother – Lisbeth Dodd. He had killed her too – she was certain of that. Life had been fine for them while he'd been in Armley Jail. Life had been hard at times but they'd enjoyed it together. That had all changed on that wet Saturday when he had walked through the door.

'She used to smile then,' she said out load to the river.

Fingering the piece of paper in her pocket, her thoughts turned to the midwife. Finding Mrs Sneddon was not something she was looking forward to. She was afraid of what she might learn. Yet she had to find out and was entitled to know. After all, hadn't her mother promised she would tell her everything one day?

In her heart, Amy knew Lisbeth wanted her to know the truth. She'd just been too afraid to tell her.

'I'll always love you, Mum,' she said sadly.

It was mid-morning when Amy climbed from under the bridge. The drunk had moved to a different spot but was still asleep, or dead. She couldn't tell. She'd already decided not to climb back onto the bridge but to follow the canal into the city, go under the Dark Arches, and find her way into Hunslet from there.

The woman lived in a dingy part of town which Amy was unfamiliar with.

Looking longingly at fresh loaves and ham, that she couldn't afford, she asked a shopkeeper for direction to the address on the paper.

Number thirty-seven Holroyd Close appeared vacant. Pieces of wood, nailed across empty frames, swung gently in the breeze. The windows upstairs, which had retained their glass, wore layers of dirt and grease, turning them dusty brown. Four steps led up to the front door with a spiked railing on either side. Amy knocked and waited but there was no response. She turned the knob but the door was locked. From the pavement, another set of stone steps led to a cellar, not unlike the one she had grown up in. She climbed down. The door wasn't closed but she knocked on it anyway. It squeaked when she pushed it open. Inside, all was dark. There was not a sound. After waiting a moment, she called out and ventured in.

Apart from a table and a wooden box beside it, which served as a chair, there was no other furniture. There was a gaping hole in the wall where a fireplace had once stood. Now it contained only dislodged bricks covered in a fall of soot. It had been a long time since a fire had graced that hearth. There was no fender, and no rug, and where the drifting soot had blown across the room, black footprints had trampled it hard into the remaining warp threads that had once been a carpet. The hum of a fly trying to escape from a bottle broke the silence while other flies sat silently around the rim of a night-soil bucket behind the door.

The only window to the room had been boarded up. The only light came from the chute where the coal was once deposited. Fifty years ago, this building would have been a fine home.

Amy wasn't sure if Mrs Sneddon was alive or dead. She was curled up on the floor, like the woman under the bridge, and her odour was just as revolting.

Touching the woman's arm, she remembered how stiff her mother was when she found her on the bed.

But Mrs Sneddon was still alive. She grunted. 'What's up? What do you want?'

'I want to talk to you,' Amy said.

'Bugger off. I don't want to talk to no one,' she said, rolling herself over to face the wall.

'I'll make you some tea?' Amy said, before realizing there were no pans or kettle, no tap and nowhere to heat the water. 'Mrs Sneddon,' she said loudly, 'I've been talking with Mr Ogilvy.'

Like a puppet on a string, the woman sat upright, swayed a little then focused her eyes on Amy. 'What did you say?'

'Mr Ogilvy sent me to see you.'

'Are you about to have a baby?'

'No, I'm not. He said you can tell me about my mother.'

As if the string holding her up had snapped, the woman collapsed backwards, her head banging on the stone floor.

'Mrs Sneddon, wake up. I must talk to you.'

'Go away. Leave me alone. I got nothing to say.'

'If you tell me some things, I'll give you some money.'

The woman hauled herself up again. 'How much money you got? Let's see it.'

Amy had nothing. Her father had stolen it all. 'I'll get you the money when you tell me what I want to hear.'

'Huh! Expect me to believe that.'

'I will, or I'll bring you some food. I promise. You have to help me. Mr Ogilvy said you would.'

'Now there's a gentleman if ever there was one. Salt of the earth,' she drawled. 'Do anything for anyone that man would.'

'Mr Ogilvy sent my mother to see you when she was pregnant. You helped her deliver the baby.'

'I bet you don't know how many babies I've helped into this world.' She pondered on her own question. 'Lots,' she said, slurring her words. 'Seen 'em born and seen 'em die, I have. Aye, there's lots of 'em die. They don't all find nice homes to be raised in, though Mr Ogilvy tried hard to place 'em all. God bless his soul,' she said. 'He were the only one of all them governors who ever visited the place. A real gentleman he was.' She paused. 'You're wanting a child, are you?'

'No. I want to know what happened to my mother when she came to you.'

'How should I know? They stayed a while till they'd had their bairn, then once it were fed for a day or two, it were put to the bottle and were taken off 'em and given to someone who wanted it. The girls who came to me went back to their fancy homes as though nothing had happened. Or back to the street, or back to wherever they came from. Didn't even give their real names, most of them. Too ashamed they were.'

'My mother's name was Lisbeth.'

'Beth, Lisbeth, Elizabeth – what's the difference? Known hundreds of girls by that name.'

'She was married to a man called Amos Dodd. He murdered her sister.'

A strange smile cracked across the woman's lips as fleeting memories broke through her addled brain.

'Now it's coming back,' she said. 'Splashed all over the newspaper it was at the time, and Mr Ogilvy told me I shouldn't mention it to anyone. Aye, I remember he came to visit the mother, after it were born and there was a bit of a to-do.' She scratched at her hair and frowned.

'What do you mean?'

'Don't rush me. Give me a minute.'

Afraid to interrupt the woman's trickle of thoughts, Amy sat silently, hardly daring to move.

'It were dead.'

'What!'

'The baby – a boy, if I remember rightly. Bright red hair. Born dead. It had the cord around its neck, tight like a noose it was. And I remember the poor lass. That confused and upset, she was. She wanted it, but she didn't want it, if you know what I mean. She said it died the way her husband should have done – on the gallows with a noose tight round his neck. I remember her saying that.' She shivered. 'I've never heard a woman say that of her new-born infant before.'

'Was that the only child Lisbeth had? Did she give birth to two?'

'Now you're confusing me. Let me think.' She scratched at her parchment breasts under the shawl. 'I remember. That was the time Mr Ogilvy turned a blind eye – the only time he ever did. Always so particular about interviews and paperwork and such-like, he was. It was the only time.'

'I don't understand. Tell me what you remember?'

The woman lifted her wrinkled hands and smoothed them over her matted hair, as delicately as a young girl would if admiring herself in a mirror. 'There was a young lass brought in the same day Lisbeth arrived. More dead than alive she was. Been knocked down in the street and trampled under the horse's hoofs right outside the place. I reckon, when it happened, she was making her way across the road to come here as she was just about ready to drop. There was little I could do for her, besides pulling the baby out when it started to come. I was on my own and it was Bedlam. There was Lisbeth, the wife of that convicted murderer, on the next bed, moaning about her dead infant, while this young lass, quiet as the grave, was bleeding to death with her newborn infant draped across her chest screaming its head off for a feed.

'Then, to make matters worse, another woman started yelling that hers was coming. I tell you, I didn't even have time to wipe me hands between them. And the noise was near driving me batty. "Here," I said to Lisbeth, "do something with this one. If you can't feed your own, you might as well quieten this one down."'

'And did she take it?'

'Oh, aye,' the old midwife said. 'No trouble.'

'And was it a girl?'

'Boy. Girl. What did it matter? It worked a treat. Too well in fact. It were later that afternoon when Mr Ogilvy called in to check on Lisbeth. When he saw her, she was sitting up in bed with the infant in her arms, feeding it like it were her own, while the young lass, it rightfully belonged to, was cold as stone on the next bed. She were covered in a sheet with Lisbeth's dead infant, not even cleaned, lying next to her.

'I could see Mr Ogilvy was pleased Lisbeth had survived the delivery and he was happy the child was healthy. I weren't going to spoil it and say anything about the swap, but I think she must have said something to him because I saw him lift the sheet on the other lass, and look at the dead infant beside her. Red hair, it had, exactly the same colour as Lisbeth's. As alike as two boiled carrots. Then he looked at me, and I reckon he knew, but to this day, he never said no more about the matter. If he knew about the swap, he turned a blind eye. And if Lisbeth didn't tell him then I think he worked it out himself.'

Amy sank back on the floor. It was not what she had expected to hear. 'So it would seem that Lisbeth was not my real mother – but who was the girl who died? What was her name? Where did she come from?'

'It were never discovered, who she was. She was nicely dressed, though a bit grubby. I think she'd been wearing the same clothes for some time. I remember, I got a few bob for her clothes.' Mrs Sneddon sighed. 'I could do with a bit of that money right now.'

'Did she have a purse with her?'

'Not when they brought her in,' she said, turning her head and rolling her eyes towards the wall. 'Must have lost it when the coach ran her down.'

'Then there was nothing of hers that was kept?'

'No,' she said, then she remembered. 'Aye, there was one thing.'

'What was it?'

'An old handkerchief. She had it gripped in her hand when she died. It took quite an effort to prize it from her fingers, but I managed. I reckoned it was no good to her dead and I could have sold it for a half-penny, but with Lisbeth bawling her head off, I handed it over. Aye,' she said, 'I gave the handkerchief to Lisbeth to wipe her tears with.'

Chapter 19

The Handkerchief

The churchyard was almost empty. Most of the morning congregation had already dispersed. Parents with children, dressed in their best clothes, old and young couples had all hurried home looking forward to their mid-day roast meal. Only a few lonely souls lingered by the gate carrying on seemingly inconsequential conversations. For them, there was no meal waiting for them at home and therefore no reason to hurry away.

As was his habit, whatever town or hamlet he visited, Mr Ogilvy dawdled in the churchyard, not to spend time over idle gossip, but to read the inscriptions on the tombs chiselled decades, sometimes centuries earlier by long-forgotten stone masons. They were skilled men, for sure. While most gravestones stood upright facing the test of time, others leaned forward, adopting the stance of old age and attracting the moss and lichen of the passing years.

Pausing at a strip of vacant earth between two monuments, Charles Ogilvy recognized an unmarked grave. Neglected. How sad, he thought, as he wandered on, reading each epitaph carefully.

The inscribed ages interested him – young men, old women, wives, sons, daughters. He read the verses, rhymes, religious texts and followed the lines of a family that spread over a century or more like branches of a tree. He read of the family's patriarch, his wife and sons, and their sons' sons, and so on. Sometimes, five lifetimes were summed up in a score of words. The brevity was remarkable. He shook his head and moved along.

The smaller stones attracted his attention. The infants' graves. Perhaps they held what he was searching for.

He thought about his wife, so beautiful, so warm, and the two wonderful years they'd shared. But that was forty years ago. He remembered how much she'd longed to have their child and how cruelly fate had turned against them. So tragic that her wish, once granted, brought about her end. But how were they to know? They were young and very much in love.

He closed his eyes and visualized her face. Her pain. Those images would never ever fade. But death brought peace. Serene, but cold and empty. And once her soul had gone, he laid her in the ground to rest in peace.

As to their unborn child, he never saw its face. Never knew if he was to be blessed with a son or a daughter. Never gave it a name.

Yet he had felt it move within her belly. It had lived a brief life within her womb and made them both feel proud.

But it chose to die, as many did, and it chose to take her with it on its final journey.

He buried her in the shade of a lilac tree and instructed the mason what words to carve upon the stone:

FAITH OGILVY
BORN 1835   DIED 1857
AGED 22 YEARS
IN GOD'S LOVING CARE

That was all. Nothing more. There was only one name on the tomb. Her name. The child was never mentioned. Only one casket had been lowered into the grave. She had carried the child within her and never a word was inscribed to its memory.

He asked himself the same question he'd asked a thousand times – what words were possible? It had no name. It had never been born so it had no date of birth. And it had no date of death as neither of them had known the day on which it had decided to die.

But, for Charles, the words **IN GOD'S LOVING CARE** had never been enough. Even after forty years, he thought, there should be more. He ambled on. Perhaps one day he'd read words that told a story similar to his own. A father and husband stripped of all he loved. A grief more profound than any other.

From the trees, a goldfinch flew down and bathed its wings in an ornamental urn. The sun twinkled through the canopy of trees as the breeze rippled over a thousand leaves creating a chorus of gentle chatter.

Charles Ogilvy moved on to the next inscription. It was a pleasant Sunday and he was in no hurry.

When Mrs Smith opened the front door to the Roundhay house, she almost fell over the girl asleep on the floor.

'Goodness me, girl!' she said. 'How long have you been there?'

Amy didn't know. She couldn't remember anything of the long walk. She did recollect her talk with Mrs Sneddon and of walking across Leeds Bridge. She remembered gazing down at the barges moored along the bank and of longing to be back in Saltaire. She remembered she had no money and no ticket. She knew Mrs Medley would loan her the fare, but she dare not go anywhere near Fanshaw's Mill again for fear of meeting that man – Amos Dodd.

It had taken every ounce of her energy to walk the last mile to Mr Ogilvy's house and when finally she arrived she succumbed to her tiredness. Sleep was one of the things she wanted and it came very easily in the warmth of the porch with the afternoon sun streaming through the glass.

'Here, let me help you up.'

Amy gazed up at the woman. She was motherly, middle-aged with a caring but worried expression etched on her face. She didn't question where Amy had come from or what she'd been doing, or even why she was slumped on the porch floor.

'I'm afraid Mr Ogilvy's not home,' she said. 'He had business to attend to and left yesterday afternoon not long after you'd gone. But he did say that if you were to come back, I was to take right good care of you. He's a very good man, you know?'

Amy hardly had the energy to walk inside and allowed herself to be helped into the kitchen. Mrs Smith kneeled down and loosened the laces on her boots.

'First of all, a drink and then a bath for you, young lady, and then something clean to wear.'

'But—'

'No, buts. I'm used to young ladies turning up at all hours that God sends. It used to get the neighbours' chins wagging, but I think they are used to it now. And some girls would arrive in a far worse state than you. Now tell me, have you eaten today?'

Amy shook her head. 'I don't think so.'

'I thought not. Then it's a bath first. You get yourself cleaned up and then you can eat, and after that there's a room upstairs you can lay down for half an hour, till you're feeling a bit better.'

'You're very kind, but I need to talk to Mr Ogilvy.'

'He's not here. He's gone down south on business and won't be back for three or four days.'

'Then I should get going. I promised I'd be back in Saltaire by Monday.'

'Well, as it's only Sunday today so there's no rush, is there?'

Lacking the energy to argue, Amy sat at the table her hands clasped around a large cup of tea laced with honey, watching the woman fill various-sized pans with water and putting them on the stove to boil.

'Now, upstairs,' she said. 'And get your things off, while I bring up the hot water.'

Following Amy up the carpeted staircase, she directed her into a bedroom. Against the far wall stood a four-poster bed furnished with pretty patterned drapes. The bedspread matched, and the pillowslips, though yellowed, were lace-edged. Catching sight of herself in the dressing-table mirror, Amy hesitated. She felt ashamed of her appearance but the woman didn't seem to notice.

'Drop your dirty clothes outside the bathroom and I'll pick them up later.'

Amy had never been in a bathroom before, not one with a real bath and a brass tap that discharged water straight into it. Carting the hot from the kitchen, Mrs Smith emptied the pans into the bath one by one then added some green crystals that slowly melted on the bottom and made the whole room smell sweet.

'There's soap and a scrubbing brush, and I'll fetch you a towel. Now mind you don't fall asleep. And when you are all washed, you sort yourself out some clean clothes. You'll find underwear in the drawers and dresses in the wardrobe.'

'But—'

'I said no buts. They're all clean and they've all come from folk who have more money than sense, or poor souls who have no need for them anymore. We get more things dropped off than we know what to do with. You have a good look. I'm sure you'll find something that fits.' With that Mrs Smith closed the bathroom door and left Amy to her toilet.

Amy had never sat in a deep bath before. It was long too. At home, in the tin bath, she had rested her chin on her knees but in this one, her legs were stretched almost full length. The water wasn't hot but it was comfortably warm and changed colour quickly when she slid the soap over her skin. How dirty she was.

All three drawers in the dressing table contained clothes: camisoles, petticoats, stockings, bloomers and nightshirts. Every item was folded neatly and carried a hint of lavender. Tiny bags of the dried flowers were tucked in the corners of each drawer.

The wardrobe smelled of camphor. It was packed so tight with dresses, blouses, skirts and coats, it was near impossible for Amy to prize her hand between them. Sitting in the bottom was a box containing belts, scarves and fancy collars, and on top a stack of hat boxes of various sizes. A line of shoes and boots stood in a file along one wall. Some looked as though they had hardly ever been worn.

'Now don't you look a picture,' Mrs Smith said, as Amy stood in the doorway to the kitchen. Though her hair was still wet, it fell into waves on her shoulders. 'The blue gingham suits your blonde hair,' she said.

'I took a pair of boots,' Amy said guiltily. 'The soles were peeling from mine.'

'Mr Ogilvy will be pleased when I tell him. Now, let's get some food into you.'

As Amy ate, she tried to concentrate on what the housekeeper was saying, but her mind was drifting about as though she was dreaming. When her hand dropped onto the edge of her plate and sent her fork bouncing onto the floor, Amy shook her head with a jerk.

'You're falling asleep, girl. Upstairs right now. Get yourself into bed and rest for a while. I can see you need it.'

The sound of knocking was part of her dream. It was a strange dream. She could see herself in a narrow stairwell. It was the one in the boarding house where Amos Dodd had taken her. The door at the top of the stairs was closed. Then suddenly the scene changed. Now the door was on the top floor of Salt's Mill – five floors above the ground. How could someone be knocking on that door from the outside when there was a sheer drop straight down to the canal below? In her dream, the knocking continued, then the door hinges squeaked just as they had in the boarding house, and a woman's voice called her name.

'Amy!' the voice called. 'Amy, there's a man here to see you.'

Mrs Smith's voice was soft as a whisper, as she tapped her on the shoulder. 'He says he's been looking for you everywhere.'

'My father!' she cried, sitting upright, her hand cupped across her mouth.

'No, no, dear. It's not your father. It's a very nice young gentleman by the name of Mr Lister. We've been having a bit of a chat. He's been very worried about you and was so relieved to find you were here.'

'Harold?'

'Get yourself dressed and come down and have some breakfast.'

'Breakfast?'

'Well, it's only an hour to noon, but I saved it for you. You slept for more than fifteen hours. I don't think you knew how tired you were.'

How pleased she was to see Harold and how relieved he was to see her too. When he held out his arms to her, she allowed him to hold her. How good he felt. How long it had been since she'd felt the warmth of someone's arms around her.

'Oh, Harold,' she said, 'I'm so glad to see you. I've so much to tell you. The things I've found out about my father – no, about Amos Dodd. He's not my father after all. Can you believe that?'

'Amy, dear Amy, I was so worried about you when I heard he'd caught you and locked you away.'

'But I got away,' she said, shaking her head. 'I was so afraid of him, Harold. He's a terrible man. But how did you know?'

'Joel told me you had come to Leeds and that you would be lodging with the Medleys near the mill.'

'That's right.'

'Well, I followed you from Saltaire late on Saturday. Mr Medley told me your father had taken you to that boarding house but when he got there, you'd disappeared and so had Amos Dodd. Mr Medley didn't know where you'd gone and I think he was pleased when I turned up. Oh, Amy,' he said, taking her hand. 'I was afraid something dreadful had happened to you. You should never have come back to Leeds. I don't know why Joel allowed you to leave the barge.'

'I had to come and Joel couldn't have stopped me. There were things I had to find out.'

'And now you have discovered those things, can I take you back to Saltaire?'

Amy nodded. 'There's just one thing I must get before I leave. There's a small box of my mother's possessions at the Medleys'. I wanted to collect it yesterday but I dare not go alone in case he caught me again.'

'Then as soon as you are ready, we'll take a cab to the Medleys' house. I'll stay with you while you collect the items you want, then we'll drive to the station and I'll see you safely on the train for Saltaire.'

'But I don't have any money.'

'Here,' Mrs Smith interrupted before Harold could continue. 'Mr Ogilvy left this to give to her if she came back.'

'Five shillings!' Amy said. 'That's more than half a week's pay!'

'Let me take care of her,' Harold said.

'No,' she said. 'Mr Ogilvy would have insisted. He'll be pleased to hear Amy is safe, and in good company. And if you are able to write, I suggest you send him a letter. That would be thanks enough.'

With Helen's skirt and her dirty undergarments packed in a small leather suitcase, Amy thanked Mrs Smith. Carrying Helen's bonnet in her other hand, Amy boarded a cab with Harold for the journey back to the street in Leeds where she had lived for almost eighteen years.

Mrs Medley hugged Amy. She even hugged Mr Lister for bringing her back safely. But she gave the children strict instructions not to go shouting about it on the street.

Of the oddments which Amy had taken to the Medleys' for safe-keeping after her mother died, only one of them concerned her. It was her mother's shoe box, which had been hidden under the bed for as long as she could remember.

'There's something in here I must show you,' she said, lifting the lid carefully.

It wasn't the wooden shoemaker's last or the bundle of old accounts that interested her. She could look at those later. Nor was it the sketch of two little girls standing hand in hand in a garden. What intrigued her was the piece of yellowed cloth that was tied around a handful of assorted objects.

As she scattered them on the table, her friends gathered around, looking inquisitively at the contents: a military button, the crushed remains of a dried flower, a cheap brooch with most of its coloured glass missing, a pair of brand new leather bootlaces and a crumpled concertina cut-out of a string of paper dolls holding hands. There was certainly nothing of value.

It was the old cotton handkerchief Amy was examining. She straightened it and smoothed it gently on the table. It was yellow with age and so thin you could see the weave of threads in the centre. The strip of tatting around the edges had rotted away in parts but the decorative satin stitches were still intact. In one corner, the letters AMY stood out in gold thread, while in the opposite corner, a rearing horse was cleverly worked in blue embroidery silk.

Harold examined it closely. 'A solid-looking steed, indeed.'

'A carousel pony,' Mrs Medley suggested. 'How old were you when you made that, Amy?'

'It isn't mine,' she said, examining it more closely.

Mrs Medley looked puzzled.

'I think it was my mother's.'

'I wonder why Lisbeth put a horse on a hanky.'

'Lisbeth wasn't my mother.'

'What?'

'It's a long story,' Amy said. 'But I think this handkerchief is the only thing which belonged to my real mother. I believe her name was Amy, and that Lisbeth Dodd who raised me, named me after her.'

Leaning against the carriage door, Harold spoke quietly, as there were other people seated in the compartment. He was apprehensive about letting Amy travel alone, but didn't want to show his concern. While they waited for the clock to tick over, he mentioned the horse on the handkerchief. He talked about Ben and Mallow, and told her about the two dozen horses his father worked when he was a boy. He didn't mention Amos Dodd.

'When will you be returning to Saltaire?' Amy asked.

'In a couple of days, maybe even tomorrow. I don't have much work to attend to here, but if I don't get it finished, I'll leave it. I can come back to Fanshaw's later.' Glancing up the platform, he saw the guard check his watch and return it to his waistcoat pocket. The red flag was poised in his hand, the whistle clenched between his teeth.

'Be careful,' he said, squeezing her hand. 'Stay on the barge and don't venture out on your own.'

'Don't worry about me. I'll be all right.'

'And don't come back to Leeds,' he said teasingly.

Amy smiled. 'I don't have reason to.'

The sound of the whistle echoed around the station's roof. Steam hissed and the engine's wheels slipped on the rails before making purchase and jolting the train into motion.

'I'll miss you,' Harold shouted. As the train moved slowly along the platform, Amy's hand slipped from his. He stepped back and waved. Amy returned his gesture then pulled up the leather strap, lifting the window, and stepped back into her seat.

Satisfied at seeing her heading safely back to her friends, Harold's thoughts turned to Fanshaw's Mill and the job he had to finish. The sooner he got back to the mill, the sooner it would be done. Once that was attended to he could return to Saltaire.

In his hurry to get away from the station, he didn't notice the man who strode purposefully across the platform. The peak of his cloth cap was pulled low on his brow, but it failed to hide the evil smirk on his face. Swinging the door of the last carriage open, the man hoisted himself into the moving train and grinned.

Chapter 20

The Man on the Train

'Good riddance!' Joel cried, tossing the old splints over the side of the barge and into the empty pit beneath. The short ones, bandaged to his upper and lower leg, had allowed movement in the knee and served well. Now, he was able to drag himself out of the cabin and onto the barge's small deck. 'I'll have these off in a week,' he said, to his wife, 'and in a couple of days I'll go down to the mill office and enquire if they have any loads for Leeds or the east coast. Then we'll be on our way.'

Helen didn't say anything. They'd spoken little that morning. It was Monday and Amy was due back, but Harold's concern on Saturday had worried them both. Though they were glad he had followed her to Leeds, Helen could sense an air of foreboding on the boat. It was a feeling she'd experienced before with Joel, and in the past he'd laughed at her and put it down to the Romany blood in her veins. But it was the first her son had shared her feelings.

Sitting on the roof of his cabin weaving a piece of rush matting, Ben appeared busy, but watching him she noticed how many times he stopped, stood up and squinted down the canal to the town.

'She'll be coming on the train,' Helen called. 'She's money enough for a ticket. Why don't you go along to the station and enquire what times the Leeds trains are due? I'm sure she'll be pleased if you're there to meet her.'

Ben didn't wait for confirmation from his father. He was off like a shot.

'I hope she's all right,' Helen said. 'There's not much of her and from what she says that father of hers is a brute of a man.'

'I was thinking the same,' Joel said. 'I'm glad Ben's gone. I'd not like to see her walking back here on her own.'

When the last afternoon train steamed under the bridge into Saltaire station, Ben was engulfed in a cloud of smoke. When it cleared, he leaned over the iron railing watching each compartment door as it opened, checking every passenger as they stepped down. Unlike the weekend traffic, there were few people on the train at that time of the day on a Monday.

Amy was one of the first off, though initially Ben didn't recognize the blonde-haired girl in the blue gingham dress carrying a shiny leather suitcase. Then he noticed she was holding a large cotton bonnet in her other hand. It was his mother's and it was unmistakable.

Though he called from the road bridge, the sound of the engine muffled his cries and Amy didn't hear him. He watched her as she stopped for a moment, donned her hat then followed the other passengers up and over the pedestrian footbridge and down the other side to join the queue handing their tickets to the collector. For a moment he lost sight of her.

On the platform the engine whistle sounded and the train began pulling slowly away. As it did, the door of the last compartment opened and a man jumped out. Ben watched, as he hared up the steps two at a time. After hesitating for a moment on the bridge, he proceeded more slowly down the other side lingering beside the pillar at the door to the waiting room. Ben watched, as the man reached into his waistcoat pocket, retrieved his ticket and sidled slowly towards the gate.

As she climbed the stone steps from the station, Amy was delighted to see Ben waiting for her at the top.

'Come with me, Amy, and don't argue!' he said, grabbing the suitcase from her hand and heading up towards the town.

Amy's smile quickly disappeared. 'What's wrong? Why aren't we going to the boat? Where are you taking me?'

'Just walk with me, Amy. I don't know what your father looks like, but a man got off the train and I watched him. I just got a funny feeling about him and I want to make sure he's not after you.'

Trusting the boy's intuition, Amy quickened her step. She didn't dare look around. She didn't want to see the man she feared. 'He mustn't catch us,' she said.

'Walk quickly, Amy. We'll be all right.'

Hand in hand, the pair hurried up Victoria Road, past the shops and the school and the stone lions guarding the Institute.

'Is he still following?' Amy asked anxiously.

'Hard to tell,' said Ben, scanning the stream of workers walking home from the mill. 'I think everyone who got off the train is coming this way.'

Unable to resist the urge, Amy glanced down the street. It was milling with folk all heading home in their direction, but there was no sign of a man resembling Amos Dodd.'

A card in the window of the Salt and Pepper Tea Shop said CLOSED, but inside the owner was still tidying the tables. Banging on the glass, Amy attracted her attention. Though disgruntled, the shopkeeper agreed, under the circumstances, to let them go through her premises to the back entrance.

'You go,' Ben said. 'I'll stand outside and wait.'

'But what if it *is* him and he comes after you?'

'Why should he? He doesn't know me, and besides, I can look after myself. I'll head off up the hill and lose him. Don't worry, he'll never catch me.'

With little time to think or thank the woman, Amy hurried through her shop and out to the narrow cobbled laneway at the back. Workers wandering in that direction looked at her strangely, wondering what was wrong. Amy didn't care. Running around the back of the school and down George Street brought her to the railway embankment. If she ran along Albert Terrace and over the station bridge it would bring her to the canal, and on the other side was the towing path.

By the time she reached the path, she was panting, and when she ran past the workers unloading a barge, they stopped what they were doing and stared at her. It reminded her of the time she ran from Fanshaw's Mill. Amos Dodd didn't catch her then and he wasn't going to catch her now.

From *Milkwort*'s deck, Joel saw her coming. 'Get me the mallet, woman,' he said to his wife. 'I think someone's chasing Amy.'

Helen pulled a heavy wooden hammer from one of the boat's cupboards. 'But where's Ben?' she said.

'Don't worry about the lad,' Joel said. 'He can take care of himself. Just get Amy on board and leave the rest to me.'

When she reached the dry dock, her legs were like jelly and she struggled to cross the plank. Frightened and exhausted, she collapsed into Helen's arms, tears rolling down her cheeks, her words of explanation almost incoherent. The events of the weekend had suddenly hit her like a slap in the face.

'Where is he?' Helen called.

'There's no one on the path,' Joel called. 'Unless he's hiding somewhere.'

'Dodd doesn't hide,' Amy stammered.

'I wish I could get my hands on him!'

'I hope you never get the chance.'

Though she feared for herself, Amy now feared for her friends. If Amos Dodd was on her trail, there was no way they could escape his malicious anger. Yet Joel was not fit enough to defend his family. With the short splints on his leg, he could barely walk. As for getting away, that was impossible as the dock was dry, and even if it was full, a man on the path could walk faster than the horse could tow a barge. Thinking of the family she had only known for a matter of weeks, Amy asked herself how she could have done this to the people she loved.

Joel stood guard on the deck for more than half an hour, the wooden mallet resting on the cabin roof. But apart from a boy with a dog, no one suspicious ventured along the canal bank. Helen paced anxiously, her eyes set on the path leading from the front of the mill.

Surprising them all, Ben came trotting up the towing path from the other direction, swinging Amy's suitcase in his hand.

'I took a detour,' he said. 'Went up to the next set of locks and crossed the canal there. No one followed me,' he announced proudly.

'Where's this man who was on the train?' Joel asked.

'No idea,' said Ben. 'He got lost in the crowd in Saltaire. He never came as far as the tea shop. I guess I was mistaken. He must have lived in the town.'

Amy wasn't convinced. 'Did he have a bald head with a wart on the top?'

'I wouldn't know,' Ben said. 'He was wearing a cap. I'm sorry I scared you. It was just a strange feeling I had.'

Joel looked at his wife.

'I don't like those feelings,' Helen said.

None of them slept well that night. Dogs howled. Owls hooted and the frogs that resided on the damp ground beneath the barge croaked throughout the night. Amy was glad it was summer and the hours of darkness were few, but having slept for so long at Mr Ogilvy's, she had trouble sleeping at all. At the other side of the cabin, Ben seemed to be sleeping peacefully, but the bunk creaked noisily every time he rolled over. When finally she dozed, her dreams were troubled.

Breakfast, next morning, was a quiet affair.
'When Harold gets back from Leeds, we'll move on,' Joel said. 'There's no money to be made while there's no water underneath us.'
Amy wanted to thank him but didn't know where to start. She told them what she had discovered; about the talk she'd had with Mrs Sneddon, and about the day her mother had given birth. She also showed them the handkerchief with her name embroidered in the corner.
'I loved Lisbeth Dodd dearly,' Amy said, 'and she'll always be my mother. I don't expect I'll ever know who my real father was, but at least I'm not the child of a murderer.' Strong words, she thought, but the truth. 'You've both been kind to me and I don't want to leave you, but I must get away, far away, and make a new start. I know Mr Ogilvy will lend me a few shillings. It's not charity I'm asking for, because I'll pay him back one day. But I can't stay in the West Riding. There are too many people here who know my name.'
As the words slipped out, Amy pondered on what she'd said. Amy Dodd was the only name she'd ever known, the name her mother had given her. She thought of her real mother, the girl who had died holding the handkerchief, and wondered if she would ever discover who she was.

Though Joel was unable to move far, he was convinced he could stand on the deck and handle the tiller. He was anxious to get back to work again. The following morning, he supervised as Amy, Ben and Helen prepared the barge so it would be ready to be refloated the next day. After clearing most items from the bottom of the dock, Ben tied lengths of old tow-rope to the wooden stocks supporting the hull, in readiness for when the water poured in.

'When we flood the dock,' Ben said, 'the barge should float off on its own. But if it jams on the baulks of timber, we can drag them out from under the boat.'

'Always a worry,' added Joel. 'There's always a chance the boat might slip, and you wouldn't want to be under it if it does. I'll warn you now. Keep clear of the barge when we flood the dry dock and the water rushes in.'

Amy handed a bucket up to Helen, and when the boat woman glanced towards Salt's Mill, she immediately recognized the gait of the man on the path.

'We've got a visitor,' Helen whispered.

'It's Harold back from Leeds!' Ben shouted.

A broad smile stretched across Amy's face, as she collected the remaining cans and brushes from the bottom of the dock. 'There's not much left down here,' she called.

'Come on up,' Helen said, washing her hands.

'You'll stop for a cuppa, won't you?' Helen called to the engineer, before disappearing into the cabin. Harold didn't hear. He and Ben were talking to the horse that was grazing not more than thirty yards from the barge.

'She looks good,' said Harold. 'Has she settled?'

'Sure has,' said the boy. 'She'll be a grand horse, just like old Bessie.'

'Mallow,' said Harold. 'An unusual name.' The horse pricked its ears and snorted, tossing its mane. As they turned to the dry dock, the draught horse continued to feed contentedly.

Leaning down, Harold held out his hand and helped Amy climb up from the bottom of the dock. She was still smiling, as together they dragged the ladder onto the canal's bank.

'I'm filthy,' she said, swilling her hands in the bucket.

'It'll not be the first time I've got my hands dirty,' Harold said. 'But with me it's usually grease and that doesn't wash off so easily.'

He watched her closely as she dabbed the mud from her skirt and scraped her boots. 'So where's that pretty girl I met in Leeds yesterday?'

Amy blushed and they laughed.

'I'm glad you're all right.' His tone was serious.

'Joel's moving the boat from here tomorrow. He's decided it's time to go.'

'What will you do? Where will you go?' he asked. 'Had you thought about staying in Saltaire? There are nice boarding houses on William Henry Street, just near the station. I could arrange to rent a room for you there, if you'd allow me.'

'I don't know just yet,' said Amy. 'I'd still rather get away.'

'Are you leaving tomorrow?' Harold called to Joel.

'We'll float her out in the morning and leave Saltaire the day after that.'

'I'll watch for you moving from the mill and come down and lend a hand if you'll let me. Do you know which way you will be heading?'

'Depends what we can get. If there's no cargo available we'll slip back into Leeds. Always plenty of work there. But I'd rather cart cloth than a cargo of stone, especially since the boat's been spruced up and is looking so good.'

Amy admired the barge, which had been transformed over the previous six weeks. The name, *Milkwort*, painted on the bow stood out in white letters on a blue background edged with gold, and a flourish of fancy scrollwork decorating at each end. On the cabin roof the five-gallon water barrel was circled with hoops of green, yellow and red, each broad ring bearing scrolls or geometric patterns of different shapes and sizes. On the barrel ends Joel had painted a house with a garden and trees, and on the horse's proven box a landscape of meadows and rolling hills and sky.

From the red-leaded deck at the stern, the painted bands twisting around the tiller resembled a maypole ready to twirl and the rudder itself was a patchwork of pictures and patterns. Helen said the designs were the best Joel had ever painted and they made *Milkwort* quite different to any other short-boat on the Leeds and Liverpool canal. As he'd learned his craft on the Kennet and Avon, those were the images he knew and enjoyed recreating. With the new white buttons and fenders, which Ben had woven, the short-boat was a sight which would make any Number One proud.

'Come with me to the Glen,' Harold said. 'It'll be our last chance. There are things I want to talk to you about. I have so much to say. I don't want you to go and I know I'm going to miss you. I have plans for the future – a long way from here and I must tell you about them. Amy, please say you will come?'

'When, Harold?' she said.

'Now, if you can. Ben can come too.'

'Take the lass on your own,' Joel said, from the barge. 'I trust you.'

Harold smiled. 'I want to show her the tramway. Explain how it works, show her the winding mechanism. There'll be no one there right now. But we must go quickly because it'll be closing time soon.'

Helen winked at her husband. 'Away with you,' she said. 'Just bring her back safely.'

'I will.'

Harold talked all the way along the towing path about tramways and trains and industrial engines. Only the appearance of Jem Carruthers silenced him for a moment. After exchanging brief greetings, Harold and Amy walked on, crossing the river and the field by the park that led up to the Glen. Once they reached the tramway, Harold took delight in showing Amy the cables and surge wheel that tensioned the rope. His enthusiasm was infectious, like a child with a new toy. Amy enjoyed listening though she couldn't understand all he was saying.

'Last tram up!' the man in the pay booth said. 'Penny a piece. Tuppence for two.'

'Two to the top,' Harold said. 'We intend to take the long way back.'

They were the only passengers on the tram. The twin carriages, which passed them on its way down, carried only three.

The green at the top of the Glen was almost empty. A boy ran, chasing a rabbit that quickly disappeared into the bushes. A young couple with an infant ambled back towards Saltaire with a long-legged hound lolloping behind them. On the green, Sam Wells' Aerial Flight and the Switchback were strangely silent. The pair crossed the oval to the far side.

'It's so peaceful,' said Amy, as they stood together, looking down into the verdant valley. On the slopes, shaded beneath oak and birch, bluebells, goldenrod and honeysuckle grew between the outcrops of rocks, and near the beck, weeping willows veiled its course.

'Can you manage the hill?' Harold said. 'It's very steep.'

'Better than you can,' Amy said, challenging him and setting off at a run down the stony slope. Three-quarters of the way to the bottom, the path zigzagged back and forth. When she could hear the burbling of the Loadpit Beck, she stopped. Breathless yet giggling, she turned and looked back up the slope.

But Harold wasn't there! In his place, standing near the top of the path, was the man she hated. His stance was unmistakable. It was Amos Dodd.

Chapter 21

Amos Dodd

Amy ran helter-skelter down to the stream in the bottom of the valley. She could hear the sound of his boots slipping on the gravel not far behind her. Suddenly it stopped and Dodd let out a muffled cry. Unable to keep his footing on the incline, he fell, tumbling head over heels down the path. For a few seconds, Amy watched him rolling and sliding down the steep hillside before losing sight of him completely.

For a while there was no sound in the Glen, save a single bird's cry and the sound of water trickling over the stones.

Amy dived for the reeds. They were tall and thick and rustled loudly. Sinking into the silt, she waited. Any moment she expected his hand to reach in and grab her. Her heart was pounding and she hardly dared breathe.

Then she heard him again, calling her name: 'Amy Dodd! Amy Dodd!' Peering through the tall reeds, reminded her of the bars at the top of the cellar steps where she had sat for hours looking to the road and longing for her father to come home.

'I'm not Amy Dodd,' she murmured to herself.

He was up and running again. He had a cut on his face. It was bleeding. But he was unaware she had stopped. Leaping over the beck, he ran past the clump of reeds where she was hiding and headed up the path leading out of the valley at the other side. He thought he was following her back to the canal on the longer but easier pathway. Amy was relieved she had waited as he would have easily out-run her before she reached Saltaire.

Climbing over the rocks and pulling herself up on the roots of trees, she struggled up the steepest part of the glen's side. Her feet and skirt were caked in mud and dripping wet but she didn't care.

'Amy Dodd!' she heard him cry. 'I'll get you this time. And it'll be the last time you ever cross me!'

Heading in the opposite direction to the voice, she thought about Harold. He'd disappeared and she didn't know where to look for him. As she ran across the green, she knew she had to get back to the barge as quickly as possible.

Above the ticket-office window with its painted sign, *Halfpenny Down*, hung a board which read *Closed for the Day*.

A pair of empty carriages was sitting at the platform but the ticket collector had already left. Not knowing where to find the footpath which led to the bottom, Amy chose to run down the hill between the two sets of tramlines.

Harold shook his head and stood up unsteadily. He felt dizzy but was aware something hard had hit him on the back of the head and it was bleeding. Not knowing how long he had been laying beside the path, he pulled himself onto one of the boulders and looked around. There was no sign of Amy or Amos Dodd at the bottom of the Glen but, from his vantage point, he could see a head bobbing at the other side of the valley. It was Dodd running. He was taking the long way round to the river and canal. Harold knew he must find Amy before Dodd caught her and felt sure she would have headed back to the barge.

Holding his head, Harold made his way across the green to the footpath which wound down through Walker Wood close to the tramway. When he arrived at the bottom near the pay booth, he saw Amy running down between the lines.

'You're all right!' he cried, gathering her into his arms.

'Yes,' she breathed. 'What about you?'

'I'm fine,' he said. 'But we must get back to the barge and warn the others.'

Helen heard them calling as they neared *Milkwort*. 'Goodness gracious, what happened?'

'I was hit from behind,' Harold said, unaware of the blood on his shirt collar. 'When I woke Amy was gone and Dodd was at the other side of the Glen. I imagine he's on his way here right now.'

'Then we'll be ready for him,' said Joel, grabbing the mallet.

They waited.

Half an hour passed. Then an hour. But there was no sign of Dodd.

'He doesn't know where I am,' said Amy, trying to smile. 'If he did, he would have been here by now.'

Helen and Joel tried to relax and went into the cabin. Amy and Harold sat on the upturned buckets on the bank. Ben kept watch from the roof.

'It couldn't have taken him so long to get back here,' said Harold. 'He must have gone into Saltaire.'

'He's coming!' Ben yelled.

Jumping up, they all knew who the man on the towing path was, and when he saw the large can he was carrying, Harold knew why he had gone into the town.

'It's him, my fa—' Amy murmured, half under her breath.

'On the boat, all of you!' Joel cried.

'No!' Harold yelled. He could almost smell the fuel from that distance.

'On the boat!' Joel called again.

'You're not going to burn my dad's boat!' Ben screamed, as he leapt from the cabin roof and ran headlong at the man, but one swing from Dodd's fist caught the boy's head, sending him reeling across the grass.

Joel slid his hand around the cabin door and reached for the mallet, but as Amos saw the movement of the cripple, he opened the can and tossed it into the bottom of the dock. Picking up a boat-hook, he swung it at Joel's head.

Though the bargee's balance was limited, he grabbed the end of the pole and hung on.

'Leave them!' Amy cried. 'I'll come with you.'

'No, you won't!' Harold replied, launching himself towards the man's legs. 'You'll not take her!'

'The paddles, Ben!' Helen shouted, throwing him the handle. 'Open the paddles!'

Ben scrambled to his feet and headed to the lock gates. As he opened the paddles, water started flowing into the dry dock. By the time they were fully open, water from the main canal was gushing in, spilling across the dock's muddy bottom and surging around the struts holding up the barge. The water bubbled from the gates and slowly swirled to the far end. The paraffin can turned in the current splashing iridescent colours on the moving surface.

'Grab the mallet!' Joel yelled to his wife, while grappling the man for control of the boat-hook.

'Get ready to open the gate,' Helen yelled to Ben.

Amy knew what was about to happen and ran to the other lock gate ready to lean her weight against the beam.

'I heard there was a fight!' The cocky voice belonged to Jem Carruthers. No one had noticed him running along the path from the mill. Grabbing Dodd by the shoulder, he turned him around and landed a resounding blow on the side of his jaw.

With Harold hanging onto Dodd's legs, the man reeled back dropping the pole. At the other end, Joel lost his balance and fell heavily to the deck.

Amos Dodd was quickly back on his feet. He kicked out at Harold and turned to face the pugilist. But his jail-yard tactics were no equal to those of a prize ring fighter. His boot came up, hitting Carruthers squarely in the groin.

As Dodd caught his breath, Harold threw himself at him again.

'No, Harry, don't!' Amy cried. 'He'll kill you!'

Just as Dodd opened his mouth to speak, a barrage of punches from the boxer forced him back towards the bank.

On deck, Joel could feel that the barge had floated free from its supports and knew there was only a matter of inches difference between the level of water in the dock and the canal outside. 'Now!' he ordered. 'Open the gates!'

With one on each side, Amy and Ben leaned against the lock gates, but the water pressure was still too great. 'Push harder!' Joel yelled.

The opened paddles continued feeding water into the chamber and the level crept up slowly while Ben and Amy continued pushing the beams with all their strength. Suddenly, the gates opened and a torrent rushed through the gap like water from a break in a dam wall.

As *Milkwort* was buffeted by the flow, Dodd caught his foot on the ladder, stumbled and found that his other foot was entangled in the ropes tied to the stocks under the barge. Twisting and slithering like a barrel of snakes, the ropes were sliding into the water, following the baulks of timber to which they were tied.

Turning his head to look behind, Dodd realized he was too close to the edge. As he did, the soft bank gave way beneath his feet. At the same time, a rush of water washed under the boat, carrying the heavy timbers to the head of the chamber. Dragged by the rope around his ankle, Amos Dodd slid between the barge and the dockside and disappeared beneath the murky water.

Milkwort bobbed like a cork, bouncing several times from one side of the dock to the other. But the bank was soft and the boat suffered no damage. Joel rode his barge, clinging to the cabin roof.

Exhausted, Harold hauled himself up on the bank while Amy stood by the open lock gates, waiting for the water to settle and the man she hated to swim to the surface.

But Amos Dodd didn't come up. The ropes wound tightly round his ankle had followed the baulks of timber under the barge. They had settled in the mud at the bottom of the pit and secured him as surely as if he was anchored to the seabed.

Amy waited with Harold until the local constable arrived, but it wasn't until they had sluiced out the muddy water that the body of Amos Dodd was recovered. Once she had identified the corpse, she was allowed to go back to the boat. Harold walked with her.

By that time, Jem Carruthers had hauled *Milkwort* to the far side of Saltaire's New Mill and secured it to a mooring near Hirst Wood Lock. On this occasion, his pace had been slower, knowing Joel was at the tiller watching his every move. Ben had followed on the towing path, leading the horse. The following day they planned to harness her but until then, she could graze freely on the strip of meadow between the River Aire and the canal.

At midday the following day, Harold returned.

'It's strange,' said Amy, gazing down the canal. 'I hated him and I knew he was evil, but in a way I feel empty now he's dead.'

Harold looked puzzled.

'I know he wasn't my father, but he was the only person I thought I was related to. Now I realize I have no one and I feel very much alone.'

'You have me,' Harold said.

'Do you mean that?'

'Of course,' he said, taking her arm. 'Would you care to walk for a while?'

'I'd like that.'

'There are things I wanted to say earlier, but I never got the chance.'

As they crossed the bridge over the River Aire, Amy waited for him to continue. There was an anxious look on his face.

'If you sail away with the barge, I may never see you again.'

'Yes, you will, I'll make sure of it. Besides, I can't stay with the boat forever. I will have to make my own life soon. Maybe I will go back to Leeds and get a job.'

'Not at Fanshaw's, I don't think,' he laughed.

'Perhaps I could work here in Saltaire. It's a mill after all with the same sorts of looms and combs, and jobs for menders and burlers.' She hesitated. 'You mentioned boarding houses and rooms.'

'I didn't mention engineers doing jobs that they were growing to hate.'

Amy was surprised. 'I thought you enjoyed your job.'

'I do to an extent.'

'But you would rather be building bridges.'

'Come,' he said, taking her hand. 'Can you run?'

'Of course. I've done plenty of running. But what are we running for?'

'Because I just feel like running. And because the tram is coming down the side of the Glen.'

Amy wasn't sure about Shipley Glen, but Amos Dodd was dead and could never bother her again, and Harold had things he wanted to show her. Taking his hand, she ran beside him. He hobbled across the grass at a reasonable pace.

'One way or return?' the man in the ticket office asked.

'One way,' said Harold. 'If that's all right with you? I thought we might walk down the Glen to the beck and follow the track around the fields back to Hirst Lock.' Releasing her hand, he reached in his pocket for the pennies to pay the fare, but as they stepped into the open carriage, he took hold of it again and rested it between his.

'I had a letter, Amy,' he said. 'It's about a job.'

'That's nice,' she said, as the bell rang and the cable started pulling the carriage up the hill.

'I sent an enquiry almost six months ago but only received a reply late last week. I've been offered a position with an engineering company to build a funicular railway.'

'A what?'

'A railway that runs up a hill and works on the same principle as this,' he said, pointing to the other carriage coming down. 'They are balanced together. It's gravity that carries them.'

Amy listened.

'There's a place where they are building elevators that run almost vertically up the side of steep cliffs, but they are far bigger and grander than the Shipley Glen Tramway.'

'Where?' she enquired.

'A long way from here, I'm afraid.'

'Where no one knows the name of Amy Dodd?'

He smiled. The carriage stopped and they alighted. 'This way,' he said.

There was not a soul about at the top of the Glen. Apart from a pair of rabbits, they had the green to themselves. Skirting the open ground, they headed for the path that zigzagged down to Loadpit Beck at the bottom.

The trees were filled with the sound of birds, though it was impossible to see any of them. Their boots crunched on the loose stones disturbing a squirrel, which skittered away and bounded up a tree, running so high it was lost in the branches. Harold held Amy's hand to prevent her from falling.

In the valley bottom, the beck gurgled over the rocks, spilling out over the soft earth to feed the wild mint and meadowsweet which was growing in abundance.

The trickling song of the water was magnified in the silence of the valley.

On the other side of the beck, the rise from Shipley Glen was gradual and they helped each other. At the top, their path was blocked by a swinging gate.

'I've never seen a gate like this before,' Amy said innocently.

After passing through it, Harold stopped at the other side. 'If I told you it was a kissing gate, would you believe me?'

'I suppose.'

'And if I said you were supposed to kiss the person waiting for you at the other side, would you believe that also?'

Amy laughed. 'So this is why you brought me here?'

'But of course,' he said, swinging the gate wide enough for her to step through. Leading her by the hand, he pulled her gently towards him and slid his arms around her waist. 'May I?'

'Please.'

The thrill of that first kiss ran right through her. He kissed her again. She didn't want him to let her go. 'Oh, Harold,' she said. 'I've never felt like this before.'

'Amy, I want you to come with me. I want to take you away from Leeds and the mills. Away from Yorkshire and England.'

'And where do you want to take me?'

'To Chile.'

'Where?'

'South America.'

'When, Harold?' Amy smiled.

'As soon as a passage can be arranged.'

Amy had no idea where Chile was but she didn't care. At times she had to pinch herself and ask herself if she was only dreaming. But it was true. Harold explained he had no family. No ties. There was nothing to hold him and he was tired of living his life in rented rooms. How he had longed for a new life and a wife to share it with.

It was hard for the pair to part for a spell, but Harold had work to finish at Fanshaw's and Joel had heard that there was a cargo waiting in Bradford to go to Leeds.

Amy didn't see Harold when *Milkwort* stopped in Leeds, but while the cargo was being unloaded on a wharf near Leeds Bridge, she went shopping and bought bread and preserves and fresh milk and delivered them to the cellar Mrs Sneddon lived in. The place was empty, but she left them anyway. It was the least she could do.

Amy stayed with the barge for a month and by the time they sailed back into Saltaire, Harold had completed his contract with Fanshaw's and was prepared to close up his rooms in Albert Road.

When he offered the premises to Joel, for Ben to live in rent free while he attended the elementary school, the lad jumped at the idea. Joel wasn't too happy, but when Miss Jones, the old cook from the tea shop, said she'd keep an eye on him, he agreed. Helen was delighted and Harold said he would speak with the headmaster personally.

Joel decided that once his boy started school, he would only take cargoes that kept them near Saltaire, so that, at the weekends, the lad would be able visit his mother.

Helen admitted she was going to miss Amy and she was sorry to learn that Harold and Amy were planning to leave England and that she would never see them again.

'We'll be back in a few years for a holiday,' Harold said. 'Who knows, I may be building bridges in Yorkshire.'

It was October when Amy and Harold were married.

A dozen gaily painted barges lined the towpath that afternoon, but *Milkwort* looked the prettiest with garlands of flowers gathered from the river bank adorning the cabin roof. Ben led Mallow, its terrets plumed in vermillion and blue, and its polished brasses swinging freely, flashing with the gold of the sun.

Joel sat proudly astride the mare, holding Amy in front of him, her legs resting to one side while Helen walked proudly beside her son.

The bride's gown and shoes were gifts from Mr Ogilvy's store and no one guessed they were not brand new. In one hand Amy held a bunch of pink mallow flowers, in the other the old handkerchief which had belonged to her mother.

As the horse clip-clopped up the pathway to the elegant church, Harold waited on the stone steps to lift his bride down.

It was a lovely ceremony and afterwards, on the canal bank, the passing boatmen joined in the celebrations. It was a happy affair, with music from banjos, fiddles and accordions. Some sang, others danced, while others were content to sit and watch, clapping their hands and tapping their feet to the rhythm. Miss Jones, the old cook attended and Mr and Mrs Medleys came on the train from Leeds with four of their children.

Jem Carruthers was dressed like a showman, complete with his championship belt and the lucky young lady who accompanied him hardly left his side.

Mr Ogilvy sat quietly enjoying the atmosphere, but excused himself after a couple of hours. 'I would like to take a walk around this remarkable mill town and take another look in the church and its interesting yard. But first, a gift for your wedding,' he said. 'When your ship sails away, you can gaze through this glass and look forward to your new life in a land far away. And when you arrive, you can stand on the shore and gaze back towards England and remember those loved ones you have left behind.'

Amy kissed him and thanked him for everything he had done for her and for the woman she would always regard as her mother – Lisbeth Dodd.

That night in the quiet of Harold's rooms, they watched a train from the window. It was heading to Leeds.

'I'll have to learn to talk nicely like you, or everyone will know I come from the streets.'

'I think you'll find in Chile, accents don't matter a jot. There are people settling there from all over the world. Besides,' he said, 'I love the way you speak and when we get there, we can both learn to speak Spanish and no one will guess where we come from.'

'And tell me again what it is you will build.'

'A funicular railway that will slide up the side of a steep cliff.'

'And what else,' she asked, smiling.

'I will build us a house on the top of a cliff that will look out over the blue Pacific Ocean.' Harold folded her in his arms.

'I don't think I'll miss this town, or the mills or the memories. Perhaps a few of the memories I'll take with me, but only a few.'

'In a few years we will come back for a holiday and we'll search the canal for *Milkwort* and you can wear Helen's hat and be the barge girl that I fell in love with. I promise.'

'Are there canals in Valparaiso?' she said, gazing into his eyes.

'I don't think so. But there are in America. And maybe one day we will go there also, and I will build my bridge.'

'I hope so,' Amy said.

Chapter 22

A M Y

Charles Ogilvy sauntered along the canal bank near Hettersley. It was a fine afternoon for a walk, and after the exhausting journey from Leeds on the previous day, he wanted to relax before embarking on the business that had brought him south. He always enjoyed taking a walk on Sundays, particularly if he was visiting places he'd never been to before. He believed the fresh air was beneficial to his lungs and the exercise good for his stiffening joints. The canal banks were ideal to wander along. The scenery was pleasant, the air was clear and the terrain was flat.

From the hull of a barge in a dry dock, the sound of hammering echoed across the navigation. The smell of tar and paint drifted across the water and he thought of the stories Amy had told him of Joel's boat when it was in Saltaire. It hardly seemed like three years since Amy and Harold had been married. How quickly time had marched along since then.

As a narrowboat steamed by, he raised his hat to the boatman. The man's head twitched imperceptibly, but Charles knew his greeting had been acknowledged. Nearing the village, he could see a church spire poking up from the woodland surrounding it. On first glance, it appeared slightly crooked and he decided to investigate.

A footpath, between two giant privet hedges, led to a lych-gate decked with a climbing rose. He ducked his head as he swung the gate. It opened wearily and led into the graveyard.

He estimated, the church had been built in Norman times, but the spire must have suffered damage later in its history and had been rebuilt at a later date. The use of a lighter coloured stone was the reason for its twisted appearance. An optical illusion. He smiled and sauntered on.

In the yard, many of the old gravestones leaned at precarious angles. Some had fallen. Those that formed part of the pathway had been worn smooth beneath countless Sunday feet scurrying across without even stopping to consider what they were. Such a shame, he thought.

Of the carved inscriptions, many had fallen victim to wind and weather, their eroded words masked under clumps of moss in mottled shades of rose and yellow.

At the far side of the church, shaded by boughs of knurled trees, four large stone tombs graced the silence. As he passed, he stopped and read the epitaphs. The last monument stood four feet high and eight feet long. A family tomb, he thought. He stopped and read:

Andrew Madeley Yellering
Born 1801 Died 17 December 1866

Alice Margaret Yellering
Born 1842 Died 1867

Alphonso Maurice Yellering
Born January 1829 - Died October 1885
Aged 56 years
Rest in Peace

Sophia Grace
Beloved wife of Andrew Madeley Yellering
Born 1805
Followed him from this life on 16th March 1887
Aged 82 years.

Algernon Michael Yellering
Born 18th May 1827 Died July 4th 1894
Aged 67 years

The inscription told him nothing of the lives of those departed, however, the size of the grave indicated the family had money. Skirting around it, he glanced down at the far end and was immediately attracted to a carving. His eyes widened. It was not a religious symbol such as a cross, or shield, or angel as he would have expected. Instead, there was a stallion rearing up on its hind legs, its hoofs pawing the air. How odd, he thought. Looking closer, he read the inscription chiselled beneath it.

AMY
El Caballero
Rest in peace

'Amy!' he said out loud, remembering the handkerchief she'd shown him on her wedding day.

Turning back, he quickly scanned the names carved on the tomb and noticed that every member of the Yellering family, except the wife, bore the same familiar initials – AMY. He was intrigued and wanted to learn more.

The village of Hettersley backed onto the canal. It was small but scattered with outlying farmhouses dotted between fields of rye and barley. It wasn't hard for Charles to locate members of the Yellering family; the village consisted mostly of them. After speaking to one of the young Yellering wives who worked in the local shop, Mr Ogilvy was directed to speak to the family's matriarch who lived close by.

Mrs Phoebe Yellering's house was a substantial two-storey eighteenth century cottage. It stood at the end of a lane lined with lime trees. Vines graced the south-facing slope and the garden was dotted with lemon and orange trees. The glass-house windows were speckled red and green with ripening tomatoes and on the loamy ground outside, yellow pumpkin flowers bloomed on the same stems as mature prize-sized vegetables. In the orchard, green-leaved almond trees lacked evidence of fruit but the branches of the apple trees were already bent under the weight of the season's crop.

Mrs Yellering, a nimble seventy-year-old with faded blonde hair, welcomed the stranger and invited him to sit in the parlour while she prepared some tea.

On entering the room, Mr Ogilvy gazed around in amazement. Above the mantelshelf a pair of glass eyes gazed coldly at his from the head of a huge black bull. Much of the hair had shed from its leathery skin but tufts still sprouted at the base of its curling horns. On the wall a pair of barbed banderillas hung beneath a feathered fan fashioned in ivory and trimmed with black lace. Foreign trinkets decked each piece of furniture – postcards from distant ports, plates and vases decorated with exotic scenes. But the item which interested him most was the statue of a horse carved from a solid piece of cherry wood. Standing almost two feet high, it was perfect in every detail. Rearing up, the stallion's powerful hoofs flailed the air, its thick tail trailed on the ground and its nostrils flared.

'May I?' he said, brushing his hand across its mane.

'Of course,' she said. 'His name was Fernando. He was Andrew Yellering's prized Andalusian.'

'A magnificent animal,' he said, resuming his seat. 'Would you care to tell me a little about it?'

Mrs Yellering poured tea into two fine china cups. 'My husband's father was Andrew Yellering. You may have heard of him in your younger days. He was known as the great El Caballero,' she said. 'He had a troupe of magnificent Andalusian horses, the best outside Spain. His wife, Sophia and all the Yellering family were involved in the performance. They toured the length and breadth of England, a little like a circus.' She laughed lightly. 'Most people thought he was a Spaniard, but he was born right here in Hettersley.' Her old eyes sparkled as she continued. 'The items you see in this room are things he collected on his trips to Spain almost eighty years ago. They were passed to me when his wife died.'

He smiled. 'Andrew Yellering is dead now, I presume?'

'He died in 1866 and sadly the troupe died with him. His eldest son tried to keep the show alive, but he was not nearly the showman El Caballero was. I remember the day the horses were sold. I hate to think what happened to them.'

'And the rest of the family returned to Hettersley?'

'Yes,' she said. 'Sophia Yellering, Andrew's wife, lived another twenty years. This was her house. I cared for her until her death, only three years ago. She was eighty-two.' She paused and looked quizzically at her visitor. 'Are you involved with horses, Mr Ogilvy?' she asked. 'Is that why you are interested in my family?'

'No,' he said. 'You must excuse me for not explaining the reason for my visit, but I enjoyed listening to your reminiscences.' He looked across at the stallion standing on the table. 'It is the horse engraved on the family tomb which brought me here.'

She smiled. 'That symbol was the emblem of the troupe. The family has retained it to this day, though the show's been gone for more than thirty years.'

'It interests me,' he said, 'because I have seen it once before – stitched on a handkerchief.'

'Ah,' she said. 'Then you would have seen one which I made. I've embroidered so many over my lifetime, I've lost count.'

'Do you sell them?'

'Oh no, Mr Ogilvy. I make one for every child born a Yellering – the children, grandchildren and great grandchildren of El Caballero. I have been stitching them since I was a young mother myself and now it is a family tradition that I maintain.'

'Are they always the same?'

'I have no pattern but I know the work by heart, so, yes, they are all identical. Let me show you.' Taking a tapestry bag from the dresser, she placed it on her lap. Inside were several white cloths. Taking one out, she opened it and showed it to her visitor. In the corner was the outline of a horse.

'And here,' she said, 'are Andrew's initials – AMY.'

It was identical to the one Amy had shown him on her wedding day.

'Mrs Yellering, I would like to ask you a question which may be painful.'

She touched his arm. 'I've seen much in my life, and like you, sir, I'm growing old. But I feel I'm strong enough to face most things. Please, ask me your question.'

Charles Ogilvy spoke tenderly. 'Did you have a grown daughter who you lost about twenty years ago?'

The woman caught her breath. 'I did,' she said. 'Her name was Angela.'

'Will you tell me a little about her?'

Mrs Yellering folded the handkerchief and rested it in the palm of her hand. 'She was the second oldest of my seven children. Five of them are still living here in Hettersley with grown families of their own. My Angela was a quiet girl and because of that I think she got the least attention. By the time she reached twenty-one she had seen two of her sisters marry. Then without us knowing, she took up with a young fellow we didn't know. He wasn't from this village and, as we'd only seen him here at harvest time, my husband thought he was an itinerant. The first I knew of their affection was when she told me she was in trouble.

'Unfortunately, when her father discovered what had happened, he sought out the young fellow and took to him with a horse-whip. It was no wonder he went away. We didn't see him again for almost a year. As for Angela, her father hardly spoke to her again. He said he'd not have a loose woman living under his roof.

'Those were the worst days of my life,' Mrs Yellering said. 'No matter how much I begged and pleaded, he'd not listen to me. Stubborn as a mule he was. Said she should leave home rather than bring shame on the name of Yellering.'

'Her father drove her off?'

She nodded. 'It broke my heart when she left. I never forgave him and he knew it, but he was too proud to go back on his word. Angela loved her father and, though he wouldn't admit it, I think he loved her more than the others.'

'What happened to your daughter, Mrs Yellering?'

'She went away. She said she loved the man and wanted to have his child. She told me she'd go up north to find where he was working. She said she knew he'd marry her.' The woman heaved a heavy sigh. 'I remember the day she left this house as if it were yesterday. She looked so bonny. She was wearing the green dress I'd trimmed with ribbon, the matching bonnet too. I watched her walk down the road, a suitcase packed with her clothes in one hand, a purse with money in the other. I made sure of that.'

'Did you ever see your daughter again?'

'No. That was the last time.'

'And what of the young man?'

Mrs Yellering sipped her tea. 'He came back a year later looking for Angela. He was a nice young fellow. He'd been busy working up north and had built himself a small carting business and was doing well. He wasn't a vagrant after all, but even so, I was surprised my husband didn't take to him with the pitchfork. But by that time the fight had gone from him. Seeing the young man again dashed our hopes. We'd prayed she'd gone to live with him, but when he turned up, we knew our worst fears had been realized.'

'You considered something untoward had happened?'

'What other could we think? Deep down, I knew she wasn't coming home.'

'And the young man?'

'He didn't know she'd headed off in search of him. He looked for her for years, travelling round Yorkshire, hoping he might bump into her somewhere. Eventually he stopped looking, sold his business and bought himself a small house in the next village. Angela never did return and we could only guess what fate had befallen her.'

The old woman looked into Charles Ogilvy's damp eyes. 'Do you bring news of my daughter?'

'I do,' he said. 'Your daughter died twenty-one years ago in Leeds. She was run down by a coach on the road.'

The woman sniffed, as her head nodded. 'I always thought it, but I never gave up hope that one day she'd walk through that door. Alphonso, my husband, God rest his soul, went to his grave a few years later. He rued the day he'd sent her off and I'm sure it was a broken heart that took him.'

'Mrs Yellering, I spoke of a handkerchief. Did your daughter have one with her when she left here?'

'She did indeed; in fact she had two. She carried her own in her pocket. It was something she always had with her, though she never used it. That handkerchief was a keepsake she would never part with. It was already twenty years old by then.'

'And the second one?'

'Brand new. I had made it for her unborn child. I remember giving it to her and watching her fold it neatly. It was the last thing she laid in her case before she closed it.'

'Dear lady,' Charles Ogilvy said, placing his hand on hers, 'That child was born. It survived the accident.' He smiled. 'You have a granddaughter. Her name is Amy and she is living in South America.'

The tears that flowed had been held for over twenty years. Mr Ogilvy sat patiently beside the woman and waited.

'May I ask what happened to the young man who was the infant's father?'

'His name is David Bliss and like his name, he is a gentle, quiet man. He lives in the next village only a few miles from here. Seven years ago he married a local girl and now they have three daughters.'

'But please,' she begged, 'tell me about Amy. I want to hear her story.'

Chapter 23

Valparaiso, Chile – 1901

From the house, perched on the edge of the cliff, Amy stood at the window gazing out across the blue Pacific Ocean. She'd watched the sky change slowly from pink to mauve, and seen the rays of burning orange fan the horizon as the ball of sun slipped into the sea. The Chilean coast certainly boasted the most magnificent sunsets she'd ever seen.

Alongside their residence on the cliff top, other elegant tall houses vied for the best views over the extensive panorama. Standing like candles decorating a cake, each building was different, reflecting the builders' origins – French, German, English and Swiss, providing a kaleidoscope of colour, design and style.

Below, on the narrow strip of coastal land, the busy port of Valparaiso bustled with the trade of foreign ships whose crews were thankful to make port after battling the Horn. On arrival, captains were anxious to make repairs while the seamen were eager to challenge their land legs in the taverns before embarking on the voyage north. New immigrants arrived tired but excited to be stepping foot on their chosen land. For ships heading south, the storms of the Southern Ocean awaited them, but once safely through the Magellan Strait they would be turning north and heading home to Europe and England.

Glancing left, Amy's eyes were attracted to the graceful movement of the great funicular as it began its descent down the cliff face. Sliding as smoothly as a giant sled, it dropped from the cliff top down to the city streets where waving palms and historic Spanish buildings were testament to Chile's Iberian background. The ascensor, *Cerro Artillería*, was the longest in Valparaiso. Other funiculars were steeper.

'I will never tire of this view,' Amy said, when Harold joined her in the sitting room. 'I love to watch the sailing ships drifting over the ocean.' She sighed. 'Sadly we are seeing less and less of them. Now it's the belching smoke trailing from dirty funnels of passing steam ships. It reminds me of the soot and ash that poured from the mill chimneys in the West Riding. How things are changing.'

'And, if the canal they are planning in Panama is ever cut, this port will suffer. But what a feat of engineering it will be. Imagine a canal broad enough to carry the huge steam ships that you mention.'

Amy thought back to the canal at Saltaire.

'Things are changing,' he said. 'But for the better, and these are exciting times we live in.'

'They are indeed,' she said, turning her face from the window. 'Why are you smiling like that, Harry, dear?'

'We have a letter,' he said. 'You will excuse me for opening it but it was addressed to both of us.'

'From England? Is it from Ben?'

'No,' he said, handing the larger of two envelopes to her. 'It's from Charles.'

She smiled. 'I think every ship that sails from England must carry at least one letter from Mr Ogilvy. How is he?'

'He is well and his fundraising for the orphanage is keeping him busy. But it is a long letter and you must read it all.'

Amy sat down at the rosewood table, slid the pages from the envelope and began:

My dearest friends

Sincere congratulations on the birth of your second child. I am delighted to hear that young Joel is doing well. It seems like no more than a few months ago that I was with you in Saltaire celebrating your marriage.

How quickly the years fly by!

I read with interest that you are considering travelling to the United States and wish you well. I wonder if we will ever see you back in Leeds again.

When you left England three years ago, Amy said she would miss the friends she had left here, but, as neither of you had family in this country, it was unlikely you would return to these shores.

Before I go on, let me divulge a pastime of mine which may sound a little strange. For many years, I have taken an interest, nay, delight, in wandering around graveyards reading the epitaphs on tombstones and it was on one of my recent expeditions that I made a startling discovery.

Last week when I was in Berkshire on business, I happened to visit the tiny village of Hettersley. It was here I discovered a family by the name of Yellering.

Enclosed is a letter from a dear lady I met there...

Without finishing the letter, Amy reached for the envelope. It was empty.

'I was saving it,' Harold said, revealing the other letter he had concealed behind his back. After handing it to her, he placed his hand gently on her shoulder, leaned forward and kissed her hair.

Amy smiled at her husband and squeezed the envelope gently between her fingers. It was soft and fairly thick. Opening it, she took out a sheet of writing paper in which a small package was enclosed. It was wrapped in plain brown paper.

'You must read the letter before you open it,' Harold said.

She looked puzzled and read:

My dearest Amy

My name is Phoebe Yellering and I am your grandmother.

Over forty years ago, I gave birth to a daughter. Her name was Angela and when she was almost twenty-two, she left home. I have never heard from her since that time, but recently I learned of her death and that she had a child. I understand that child is you, Amy.

To hear this news, after so long, has been the most wonderful gift any woman could receive. I will never be able to thank Charles Ogilvy enough.

He also told me you are married and have two young children – my great-grandchildren. I am enclosing with this letter a small traditional gift for each of them that I send with my fondest affection.

Without reading any further, Amy laid the letter on the table and reached for the soft package. Within the wrappings were two cotton handkerchiefs, each edged with lace and folded neatly. She opened one and laid it on the table.

Embroidered in one corner, in gold thread, three capital letters spelled out her name: AMY. On the opposite corner, sewn in blue silks, was the figure of an Andalusian stallion.

Harold slid his arm around her as tears glazed her eyes.

'I don't understand,' she said. 'It's the same as my mother's old handkerchief. How is that possible?'

'You will understand when you have finished Charles's letter,' he said. 'But let me read the rest of your grandmother's message to you first.'

She handed it to him and listened.

Amy, dear, you cannot believe how excited the family was to hear of your existence. I wept, when I learned of the dreadful times you have been through, but am pleased to hear your life has changed now that you are married.

Though you are not aware of it, you have aunts and uncles, cousins, and three half-sisters all living here in Hettersley. And David Bliss, your dear father, is longing, with all his heart, to see you.

I hope one day, you and your good husband will come home to England so all the family can meet you.

Pray God I will live long enough to see that happen.

Your loving grandmother
Phoebe Yellering

Amy held the handkerchief to her heart. She was afraid of wetting it with her tears.

'Perhaps one day we can go back to England and visit them.'

'I will make enquiries about a passage in the morning.'

'Oh, Harold,' she said, resting her head against him. 'After all these years, I will be meeting my father. It is something I always longed for. What a wonderful thing to look forward to.'

Harold stroked her hair, 'Wonderful indeed.'

* * *